Readers love ARIEL TACHNA

Home and Away

"*Home and Away* is a sweet sports romance…. This was a light read and would be a great weekend book."

—Paranormal Romance Guild

No Limits

"If you're looking for something sexy, steamy, and kinky, *No Limits* is a must read!… I truly fell in love with this trio and love their story."

—Amy's MM Romance Reviews

Rebuild My Heart

"With an interesting and well-drawn plot, loads of lovely characters and a delicious romance, I feel this is a great story that has pretty much everything I need from a good read."

—Long and Short Reviews

"I really enjoyed this story and thought it was a good addition to the series. If you haven't read this series, I would definitely recommend it!"

—Bayou Book Junkie

Published by DREAMSPINNER PRESS
www.dreamspinnerpress.com

THE GUARDIAN OF MACHU LLAQTA

ARIEL TACHNA

Published by

DREAMSPINNER PRESS

5032 Capital Circle SW, Suite 2, PMB# 279, Tallahassee, FL 32305-7886 USA
www.dreamspinnerpress.com

The Guardian of Machu Llaqta
© 2022 Ariel Tachna

Cover Art
© 2022 Kris Norris
https://krisnorris.com
coverrequest@krisnorris.com
Cover content is for illustrative purposes only and any person depicted on the cover is a model.

Trade Paperback ISBN: 978-1-64405-983-8
Digital ISBN: 978-1-64405-982-1
Trade Paperback published January 2022
v. 1.0

Printed in the United States of America
∞
This paper meets the requirements of
ANSI/NISO Z39.48-1992 (Permanence of Paper).

ACKNOWLEDGMENTS

THIS BOOK would not be what it is without the tireless efforts of my editing team, particularly my sensitivity reader, who made sure my respect and admiration for the descendants of the Inca people showed on the page. Gin, I've never rewritten a book four times before. Anne, thank you for being my tireless sounding board. Susan, thank you for fixing the academic and military references and timeline.

DEEP IN the rainforest, in a land time passed by, dwelled a forgotten people known only as the Lost Ones, if they were known at all. They lived as they always had, simply and in harmony with the land. From time to time, one of them would wander the wider world to see what had been learned in their absence and, if the wanderer deemed it worthy of the goddess, bring it back to aid the Lost Ones. In time the goddess blessed them for their faithfulness, bestowing on them Chapaqpuma, a guardian who would ensure no harm came to them from outside, for everyone knew outsiders meant trouble—disease, famine, war, and death followed wherever they trod.

The role and gifts of Chapaqpuma passed down from generation to generation, parent to child to grandchild and beyond, for the need of the goddess's protection never waned. The gifts of the goddess were bountiful, but the price was high, and Chapaqpuma could not walk that path alone. Instinct pushed Chapaqpuma to find a mate, a partner in whom to balance the senses so that the guardian could always return to the valley in proper form, yet few were they who could meet all of a guardian's needs. Thus it became the way of the Lost Ones for Chapaqpuma to take not one but two mates, a balance to each other as much as to the guardian, so that when calamity came, Chapaqpuma had the strength to ward it off and the humanity to return home after.

Thus was the way of the Lost Ones.

Thus is our way now.

CHAPTER 1

DR. VICTOR Itoua stopped outside the anthropology department chair's door, glanced down at the grant recipient notice in his hand for courage, and rapped sharply on the thick wood.

"Come," Dr. Fowler called from inside.

Victor opened the door and walked in. "Do you have a minute, sir?"

"One, maybe. What do you need?" Victor might be accustomed to Fowler's curt tone and short, blunt ripostes, but they never failed to leave him on edge. At least Fowler spoke to everyone that way.

"I've come to submit notice for a sabbatical for the summer and fall semesters. The grant I was hoping for came through, and I'll need at least six months in the field to do it justice." Victor handed the dossier to Fowler and braced himself for the response.

"Really, Itoua?" Fowler frowned. "I thought we'd agreed you would stop this nonsense with the Philli-philli. Next you're going to tell me you're going to search for Sasquatch."

Victor suppressed a sigh with the same blank stare he'd learned to maintain in the face of any criticism. They looked at him askance because he was foreign, because he was Black, because he approached things differently from most in the establishment. He didn't let it stop him, but some days it got old. "If you look closely, sir, the grant is to research the origin and evolution of the Philli-philli legend among the Indigenous peoples of the Andes and upper Amazon, not to prove or disprove the existence of such a creature. The *legend* exists and is a valid subject of study regardless of its veracity."

"Fine." Fowler tossed the dossier on his desk. "But you better get the best damned paper in the world out of this—and not one hint of any of your crazy ideas about whether there's such a thing as a half man, half beast running around South America—or you'll be looking for another job."

"Understood, sir." Victor gathered his papers and turned to leave.

"And take Harris with you," Fowler ordered. "He's the only one crazy enough to put up with your theories for that long."

"Yes, sir."

Victor had already planned on asking Jordan Harris, the department's best—in Victor's opinion—research and teaching assistant, if he would be interested in the project. Every time Harris had gone into the field with him, his help had been invaluable, as Victor had known it would be from the first time they met, on a joint field expedition he'd done in the Yucatan with Harris's supervising professor during his undergraduate years. He would still ask, not demand, but now he'd have Dr. Fowler's prior approval to add to the discussion.

And if it meant he had six months or more to spend with the object of his unrequited, unethical, and impossible crush, *eh bien*, he'd survived worse.

He glanced at his watch. At this time of day, Harris would be finishing up his last section of Intro to Anthropology. Victor could catch him outside his class, suggest a cup of coffee in his office, and talk to him in private.

Harris was finishing his lecture when Victor arrived at the classroom, giving Victor a moment to just look at him. It was unprofessional, not to mention unethical given Victor's role as supervisor to the department's teaching assistants, a position Victor had fortunately not held when Harris was hired. If he had, he would never have been able to suggest Harris apply to the department's combined master's/doctoral program when he realized Harris would be finishing his gap year internship in a matter of months and was looking for an advanced degree program and a job to go with it. Victor would never act on it, of course. If he thought he had a shadow of a chance, he might feel differently, might look harder for a way around the issues, but Victor wasn't blind. He'd seen the kind of men Harris went out with. Young, beautiful, flashy. All the things Victor wasn't. No, he knew where he fit in Harris's life—as a mentor, maybe a friend, but it would never go beyond that. Harris could have anyone he wanted. Why should he settle for Victor?

Even knowing all that, though, he couldn't seem to stop himself from looking. Harris wasn't what Victor would call classically handsome, even with his blue-gray eyes and sandy blond hair. His nose had been broken at least once, possibly more, but paired with his crooked smile, it gave him a seductive air more than a dangerous one. The same went for the scar on his jawline, barely visible unless he started letting his beard grow out. Then the lack of stubble drew the eye like a magnet. And that didn't even take into account the calluses on his hands. Victor had never asked him where he worked out or what kind of martial arts he did, but Harris had to be maintaining his skills somewhere. Victor might not have kept up with all the skills he'd learned during his mandatory military service in France, but being a decent shot had come in handy more than once on field expeditions too, for hunting and for defending himself from anything—human or animal—that might think any of his team would make easy prey.

Harris hid his rough edges well enough to pass muster at the university, but Victor was a past master at seeing beyond the obvious. He had to be if he was going to make it as an anthropologist. Harris always wore a sports jacket and dress shirt when he was teaching, but Victor had seen him switch them out for a T-shirt—usually one with a punny Lord of the Rings quote on it—as soon as his classes were over, topped by a beat-up leather bomber jacket when the weather was cool enough to justify it.

Harris dismissed class, Victor's cue to step inside.

"Do you have a few minutes, Mr. Harris?" Victor asked as the students filed out.

"For you, sir? Sure."

Victor tamped down his instinctive desire to preen at Harris's reply. He was never impolite to any of the professors, but his response to Victor was always a touch warmer than his interactions with anyone else. Victor told himself it was the camaraderie of time spent together on field expeditions, nothing more, which did absolutely nothing to stop the feeling. No other reason for Harris to be nicer to his graying, fortysomething supervisor.

"Good. I'll put on a pot of coffee."

Harris's smile widened. "If you're offering coffee, I might even have more than a few minutes."

Which was exactly why Victor made sure to have a fresh pot brewed whenever he had a meeting with Harris.

He didn't let that show, though, rolling his eyes instead. "Meet me in my office."

"Sir, yes, sir." Harris threw him a half-assed salute.

Victor turned away so Harris wouldn't see the smile he couldn't quite hide, although knowing how good Harris's observational skills were, he probably saw it anyway. The man had been a Marine sniper, the best of the best to hear him tell it. Then again, Victor had seen him shoot in the field. He'd never seen Harris miss, so maybe his tales weren't all tall.

Victor went back to his office and started the coffee brewing by rote, his mind racing as he went over plans for the upcoming trip. Most of his research was at his apartment rather than in his office, but he'd spent enough hours staring at it that he didn't need the maps in front of him now to start thinking about where they would need to visit. Rumored sightings of Philli-philli ranged from Quito, Ecuador, all the way down the coast to Santiago, Chile, far too great a distance for even a mythical creature to cover, but the majority of the sightings were in Peru between Lake Titicaca and the ruins of Huánuco Pampa. He flipped his atlas open to Peru and started marking places on the map: Cusco, Pisac, Urubamba, Ollantaytambo, of course, but anything they heard there would be tainted by modern influences. They'd still start there, if only to see if there had been any new sightings or rumors, but ultimately they'd have to head into the mountains and possibly the Amazon headwaters to get closer to the original legends. Victor might hope they would find more than just legends, but he'd keep that to himself.

He looked up when Harris rapped on his open door. He'd unbuttoned his dress shirt, revealing a Mordor Fun Run T-shirt. He had his leather jacket hooked over his shoulder and looked good enough to eat. Not that Victor was looking.

"Hey, boss. Is that coffee ready?"

Victor inhaled the rich, dark aroma of brewing coffee and glanced at the nearly full carafe. "It should be. Pour yourself a cup and have a seat."

Harris froze on his way to the coffee pot. "Is this a good seat or a bad seat?"

"I suppose that depends on whether you're interested in going in the field with me again." Victor kept his tone even by force of will. He'd learned as far back as the first joint expedition that Harris had a whole host of abandonment and authority issues and that the best way to address them was to be as honest and steady as he could be.

Harris spun to look at him. "You got the grant?"

"Coffee first. Then we'll talk," Victor said with a chuckle.

Harris shot him a disgruntled look but poured two cups of coffee and doctored them both with cream and sugar. When Victor took a sip of the mug Harris handed him, the coffee was exactly the way he would have made it for himself.

Another sign of just how observant Harris was. Another sign of just how gone Victor was on him. *Get it together. No lusting after your subordinates.*

"Okay, I have coffee. Now spill. Did you get the grant?"

Victor allowed himself one moment of internal glee before pulling his professional façade back into place. "I got the grant."

Harris's eyes, always sharp and focused, brightened, and he leaned forward. "When do we leave?"

Any other time, the slight breathlessness in Harris's voice would have set Victor's imagination racing, but he was too excited about the grant for it to register as more than shared enthusiasm. That said, it was one thing to gamble with his own career. Gambling with Harris's was something else entirely. "Harris... Jordan, have you thought about this? You know as well as I do how the academic community views Philli-philli. You'll get about as much respect for whatever we accomplish in Peru as you would for chasing Sasquatch or Nessie."

Harris's expression didn't change a bit. "I know, sir. I've listened to people talk smack about you for it since I got here, but that's their problem. I'm never gonna be in the big leagues. Eventually I'd like to be an assistant teaching professor instead of just a TA, but that's really a matter of getting off my ass, finishing my thesis, and applying somewhere as opposed to needing publications or shit like that. And honestly, the only reason I want that is for the salary. I like what I'm doing here. I like the teaching, I like the students, and I like the opportunities to do research with you. And anyone else who has ongoing projects."

A shiver of delight ran up Victor's spine at the notion that the last sentence was tacked on as an afterthought, but believing that would be self-delusion. He wouldn't allow himself to imagine such a thing with Harris sitting across the desk from him. He wasn't anything special, just a boring associate professor whose obsession meant most of his colleagues kept him at arm's length.

"If you're sure, then we leave as soon as the semester is over. Dr. Fowler has approved a sabbatical through the end of fall semester. That gives us seven months to see what we can find. Of course we can petition to extend if we need it, but it's a good chunk of time to start."

"Good thing my passport is up-to-date. A month isn't a whole lot of time to prepare," Harris replied.

"Do you need help getting things set?" Victor asked before he could stop the words from escaping. "Subletting your apartment or anything like that?"

"Nah, I got it covered. I usually go on field expeditions in the summer anyway, or travel if I can't find one, so I have someone lined up for the first three months already, and I'll figure something out for the fall. Or ask my neighbors to keep an eye on things if I have to. It wouldn't be the first time."

Harris's predilection for joining every possible expedition had made him invaluable as a research assistant, but it had slowed down his doctoral program. Of course that meant more time for Victor to spend with him, both in the field and at the university, so he wasn't going to complain.

"In that case, here's what I was thinking...."

JORDAN HARRIS let himself into his crappy studio apartment, tossed his jacket on the back of his pullout couch, and flopped onto the lumpy cushions.

Peru. Incan ruins. Legends of Philli-philli. And Dr. Victor Itoua. Months and months of close proximity to Dr. Itoua, watching him be all sophisticated and shit as he asked people all the subtle questions that drew out information they didn't even know they had with a finesse that no one else, in Jordan's experience, could match. He'd probably be all casual too, instead of in his usual suits, meaning Jordan would have to suffer through glimpses of strong forearms and broad shoulders not hidden beneath tailored suit coats. Oh, and no tie. That was practically naked by Dr. Itoua's standards, which would leave Jordan perpetually horny. And he'd have to do it all without giving away how hot he thought his boss was. Even if they weren't at the university, it was university-approved field research, and while Dr. Itoua might unbend enough to lose the formal attire, he'd never unbend enough to forget who they were or why they were there. And even if he did (he wouldn't, but even if he did), he took his role as Jordan's supervisor too seriously to abuse his power. Never mind that it wouldn't be an abuse of power at all since Jordan had been head over ass for the guy since they first met. Since Dr. Itoua had looked at him and seen someone worth working with rather than someone with good aim and a bad attitude, a kid with a GED and nothing going for him but enough time in the Marines for the GI Bill to pay for his education. No, Dr. Itoua was too goddamned honorable to take what Jordan would give him willingly.

Not that Jordan blamed him. He knew his own worth all too well, and while he made a decent teaching assistant, the rest of his life was pretty much the definition of *fuckup*. Witness the crappy apartment, secondhand couch, and lumpy cushions. He could take notes, catalog information, and teach classes, but he'd never have Dr. Itoua's ability to slip in and out of whatever culture they were studying or find the connection between random facts that everyone else missed. Dr. Itoua would say he had his grandparents and the summers he'd spent with them in the Republic of Congo to thank for that, but Jordan had always thought it was more than that.

Jordan himself, on the other hand, was too brash, the veneer of civilized society sitting on him like an ill-fitting jacket, something he had to force into place when he was dealing with the faculty bigwigs, rather than something that came to him naturally. At this point he only even asked for details ahead of time out of sheer stubborn fuckery— and the desire to impress Dr. Itoua with his interest. He definitely didn't want to lose out on a chance to work with the guy because he thought Jordan didn't care about his projects. Even his longstanding obsession with Philli-philli.

Jordan grabbed his cell and texted his best friend, Nandini Rakkar, who he'd met in the Marines and who'd gotten a job with Interpol straight out of the service. With Nan, he didn't have to pretend. She was as foulmouthed and cocky as he was. More now since she was still in an environment where she could get away with it and he had to keep it under wraps around anyone except her. And sometimes Dr. Itoua.

I'm so fucked.

The phone buzzed back almost immediately.

When aren't you?

Fuck you too. Seven months of field research, just me and Dr. Itoua, in the Andes. Kill me now.

Nandini didn't reply for so long Jordan thought she'd given up on him (or was coming to actually kill him—he never knew with her) when the phone buzzed again.

The Philli-philli? Watch your back.

WTF, Nan? Not you too.

Watch Itoua's back if you won't watch your own. His back, Harris, not his ass.

Jordan's cheeks burned at the jab. He'd watch Dr. Itoua's ass all day any day if he could get away with it, but still…. *I know my job, Rakkar.*

Then do it, because there've been reports of renewed criminal activity in the Amazon basin. Too soon to tell what kind exactly, but enough to be taken seriously.

Jordan tossed his phone into his bag and stalked out of the room. Damn sneaky Interpol agents, always thinking they knew everything and only sharing it in cryptic little dribbles designed to drive him fucking crazy.

Fine.

He'd go to Peru and do his job, both as research assistant and as bodyguard—he had no illusions that his military background and ability to shoot everything from a bow and arrow to a sniper rifle added to his value in the field, both for hunting and for protection—and he'd help Dr. Itoua prove once and for fucking all that the Philli-philli legend was a worthy topic of academic pursuit, if only for its prevalence among the Indigenous tribes of the Andes.

VICTOR SET his briefcase by the credenza in the entry to his condo, pulled off his tie, and slipped off his shoes. He'd spent the drive home thinking about the weather in Peru and what he would need to take with him, not the fact that he'd be spending the next seven months with Harris. Arriving in June, they wouldn't have to worry about the rainy season for the first few months, but they would have to take the varying weather into consideration, what with the altitude in some places counteracting the subtropical latitude. If they stayed in the alpine desert and cloud forests, they'd be looking at weather from near freezing to midsixties, but if they ended up in the upper Amazon basin around Manu or farther north, they'd have warmer weather, more humidity, and the rainy season starting in September.

Who was he kidding? He could pack for this kind of fieldwork in his sleep, especially in Peru.

He poured himself two fingers of cognac and slumped into his favorite chair, all pretense gone. Only here in the privacy of his own space could he truly let down his guard, which was what worried him most. He trusted Harris with his field notes, his "crazy" obsession with Philli-philli, and his life, but not with his sanity, and having Harris with him on this research trip was guaranteed to test that. He sighed deeply. He'd dealt with his Harris-inspired obsession for years. It hadn't killed him yet. The next few months wouldn't be any different, even if this would be the first time they would be alone together in the field.

He just needed to grow a pair and deal with it. Yes, he'd probably be sharing lodgings with Harris while in Peru, at least some of the time, but while they were in the outlying villages, they could find a house, cabin, hut, something with separate bedrooms, and if they were out in the rainforest, they could sleep in separate tents. Even if he had to carry his own damn tent. It would take weeks, if not months, to win enough trust to move past simplified stories and get to deeper truths, and even if they managed to get a lead sooner than that, he had no illusions they'd find what they were looking for right away. The Andes were immense, and the rumors had Philli-philli showing up at locations impossible distances apart, even for a supernatural creature of legend.

He'd just have to pull his professionalism around himself so tightly that nothing could get through, not even the sight of Harris's arms in the tight T-shirts he preferred. Or his ass in the cargo pants or jeans he wore most of the time, even when he was teaching. And if they ended up in the rainforest, Harris would replace them with cargo shorts, and then he'd have to deal with Harris's legs instead.

Just the thought was enough to make his cock stir. He banged his head against the headrest of his recliner. He was so fucked.

CHAPTER 2

JORDAN SET his towel down on one of the benches surrounding the swimming pools in the hot springs in Aguas Calientes and stepped into the water. After four days of hiking the Inca Trail and sleeping rough, his whole body ached, and that wasn't counting the effects of the altitude. He was in damn good shape, but the altitude fucked with his breathing. He'd drunk so much coca tea to counteract the symptoms of altitude sickness since they'd arrived in Peru that he'd fail even the most basic drug test at the moment. Good thing he wasn't in the Marines anymore.

Speaking of coca tea....

"Here, they had it in the bar, so I got a cup for you too."

"Thanks." Jordan took a sip of the slightly bitter tea and pointedly didn't stare at Victor's—he was supposed to call Dr. Itoua Victor now, and wasn't that a mindfuck—bare chest. His bare, so-smooth-it-looked-like-silk chest.

"You're welcome. After we've unwound a bit, you can return the favor and get us both pisco sours." Itoua slid into the water next to Jordan and leaned back against the lip of the pool.

Jordan gulped a sip of tea and winced as the hot liquid burned its way down his throat. Desperate for something else to focus on—no, really, if he kept staring at all that bare skin, he'd end up embarrassing himself—he looked up at the mountains on either side of the Urubamba river that bisected the town.

"The weather here is crazy." *The weather, Harris? You couldn't come up with something more original? You could've at least compared it to the heat in Mexico when we were working in the observatory at Monte Albán the summer we met.*

"It's the altitude. Machu Picchu is over a thousand feet higher than we are here. It really does make a difference in both temperature and humidity. And wait until we get down into the jungle. You'll be wishing for the weather here."

"What's this, if not jungle?" Jordan asked facetiously, looking at the thickly wooded landscape surrounding the baths.

"Cloud forest." Itoua bent forward and stretched his legs out in front of him as he massaged his quads. Nope, not looking. Not noticing Itoua's thighs were nearly as thick as Jordan's and covered in a light dusting of dark hair without any of the silver that had started to appear at his temples, making him that much more attractive in Jordan's eyes. Nope, no way, no how. Looking somewhere else. Anywhere else. Jordan took another drink of his tea and focused on the mist floating along the river and the acrid smell of sulfur from the water. "Still tropical, just at a higher altitude," Itoua continued, oblivious to Jordan's distress. *Thank fuck.*

"Whatever you say, boss," Jordan replied. "Still looks like jungle to me."

Itoua chuckled and straightened. "Don't play dumb, Harris. I know you better than that."

At least Jordan wasn't the only one having trouble remembering to leave formality behind them. Then again, hearing Itoua call him Jordan fucked him up every time, so maybe it was better this way.

"And what did I say about calling me Victor since Dr. Fowler isn't around to insist on 'appropriate professional address'?"

Jordan snorted at Itoua's hilariously accurate imitation of Fowler's snooty upper-class accent. The hint of Itoua's own French accent that slipped through only made it better. "You just called me Harris, so you aren't doing any better than I am. And after nearly eight years, it's a hard habit to break, doc—Victor." He set his empty cup aside and sank deeper into the water. "Can we just stay here for the next six months? I don't want to move."

"Maybe not six months, but definitely for the next six hours," Itoua replied. "I arranged rooms for us in town for tonight and tomorrow night, so we don't have to move from here until they close, and we can come back tomorrow. The day after, we catch the train to Ollantaytambo to stock up on supplies for our trek into the rainforest. We'll head for the Camino a Willoq toward Quellouno from there, stopping when and as we find interesting villages. And from Quellouno, we'll head north into the Parque Nacional del Manu."

"Way to harsh my buzz," Jordan grumbled, but it was all for show. Once they were on their own, they could decide how far to travel each day or even if they *wanted* to travel on any given day, rather than having to stick to the rigid schedule for the Inca Trail. He appreciated Itoua arranging it for them since he'd never visited any of the Inca sites before—Mayan and Aztec, sure, but he hadn't made it this far south—but he was ready now to get started on their fieldwork. As soon as he finished soaking.

"Don't pretend, Harris. I know you're as eager to get started as I am."

And that right there? That was half the reason he'd gone and fallen in love with the guy. Nandini was the only other person who'd taken the time to get to know him that well, and while he loved her like a sister, the thought of anything else… ew, just no. He liked his balls right where they were, thank you very much.

VICTOR BIT back a laugh when he saw Harris's choice of T-shirt when they met for dinner that evening: Gollum's Sushi Bar. That was a new one. At least, he'd never seen it before, and it looked crisp, if wrinkled from being in Harris's backpack. He never thought he'd see the day when he'd be *grateful* for Harris's hilariously irreverent Lord of the Rings T-shirts and baggy cargo shorts, but after spending six hours next to him in nothing but the tiniest bathing suit known to man, it was a relief to only have to deal with his forearms and calves. And if he didn't change that line of thought right now, he'd be in trouble… again. "Classy, Harris."

"We're in Peru, land of ceviche. I thought it was appropriate."

"We're on the wrong side of the mountains for ceviche. Rainbow trout, though…." Victor licked his lips, remembering the fish dinner the porters had made their first night on the Inca Trail.

"You think they have the same dish we ate on the trail?"

Great minds. "We can look," Victor replied as they left the hotel.

They walked along the river toward the local market until they reached the Pachacútec statue. "The condor, the puma, and the snake," Victor said reverently. "The Inca trilogy—the heavens, the earth, and the underworld, the beginning of a new life." He cast a quick glance up the mountain toward Machu Picchu, abandoned for hundreds of years after the Spanish arrived. Their guide had said the Inca people abandoned Cusco, cutting the paths behind them so their sacred places were never discovered. History as written by the victors claimed they had been beaten into submission, retreating into villages in the highlands or dying from diseases to which they had no immunity. Colonial records showed the many atrocities the Spanish committed, enslaving or outright killing anyone who rose against them. Victor knew all the theories, even the debunked ones, but none of them sat right with him. Summers spent with his grandparents in the Republic of Congo had driven home how different history looked to the colonized than to the colonizer and how the old ways flourished even under brutal regimes determined to snuff them out. An empire with the breadth and scope of the Incas didn't just disappear. Not that he had any proof of the continuation of an organized Incan nation, and arguing for it in academic circles as a Black immigrant would get him nowhere, but in his bones, he knew there was more to the story. He held little hope of finding anything on this expedition to support that, but any time he came to Peru, there was always the chance he might stumble on something someone else had missed.

"The hunter or messenger, the guardian, and the shaman," Jordan replied with a smile.

"A recurring trio of characters," Victor said. "While we don't have condors in the Plateaux, we do have the messenger between the world of the living and the world of the dead. And of course we have the hunter and the shaman in everyday life and in our great tales, and the majority of our fables include talking animals. It has always fascinated me how cultures with no contact developed such similar beliefs." He could lecture for hours—and had—on Joseph Campbell and Carl Jung, the masks of god and the collective unconscious. Harris had heard it all before, though, and didn't need yet another lesson on the concept.

They continued through the market and beyond to a small restaurant tucked away in one of the alleys.

"The restaurant is supposed to serve Peruvian specialties. Although I suspect that's all we'll be eating once we get out into the rainforest."

"You know me, I'll eat anything you put in front of me as long as I don't have to cook it," Harris said with a shrug.

"I know better than to try to make you cook." Victor didn't comment on the rest. He had learned bits and pieces about Harris's younger days over the years, enough to know that he'd experienced hunger more often than any child should, and not the *oh, I'm hungry, I want dinner now* kind of hunger, but the kind of hunger that led to malnutrition and unhealthy attitudes toward food. He'd never seen Harris actively hoarding food, but he always seemed to have a snack in his pocket or backpack if anyone happened to mention being hungry. It had never interfered with their fieldwork, but they'd always gone into a specific location and set up camp. They'd never had to live off the land and the generosity of the people they were studying. Victor had enough experience with the terrain not to worry about them going hungry, but he worried how Harr—Jordan would deal with it. "I still haven't recovered from the last time you tried to feed me."

"Hey, it's not my fault. You were sick. I had to do something!"

"Tell that to the poor lady whose house you almost burned down," Victor retorted. He missed this when they were at the university. Jordan never bantered with him this way when others were around to hear, and as much as Victor enjoyed it, he could only arrange so many opportunities for them to talk privately without opening himself up to accusations of favoritism or worse. The last professor in charge of the TAs had gotten fired for getting involved with one of her TAs. Victor couldn't take the chance of anyone reading more into his relationship with Jordan than would be appropriate for two professionals, one in a supervisory capacity over the other. If he lost his job, he would lose his visa and his career. There was much less interest in studying Peruvian subcultures in Europe.

JORDAN LEANED back against his pack, having finally found a spot where the wind didn't carry smoke into his face, and watched as Victor—it was getting easier to think of him that way with just the two of them in the middle of nowhere—fried up the fish Jordan had caught. In the six days since they'd started the trek toward Quellouno, Jordan had seen a side of Victor he'd never seen before. They'd been in the field together in the past, but it had always been as part of a larger group, local porters and guides, if not other researchers, even during the year he worked as Victor's intern. Now it was just the two of them, and Jordan never wanted to go back.

Okay, he might not complain about a little more variety in their diet. Even if the fish wasn't always the same type, they were eating it more meals than not. Victor still had quinoa for their breakfasts, and he'd found wild potatoes—purple no less, and not just the skins—to add to their dinners, but they hadn't seen anything Jordan could hunt since they left Ollantaytambo. Alpacas were considered domesticated whether they had any markings to indicate ownership or not, and vicuñas were protected from hunting, and while Jordan could imagine a point at which he'd hunt the various rodents that populated the Andes, he wasn't there yet. At least they hadn't come across any sign of the criminal activity Nandini had warned him about, and Jordan had been looking. Of course they were still in relatively populated areas, which might explain it. Either way, Jordan wasn't planning on letting down his guard.

Victor hadn't run out of spices, though, and trout wasn't the same as paiche which wasn't the same as catfish, so that provided a little variety. What Jordan wouldn't give, though, for a thick steak, seared just so, all but black on the outside and mouthwateringly pink on the inside.

He pushed the thought aside until they were somewhere they could have alpaca without poaching from some poor farmer's livelihood. He'd make do with fish. He knew what it felt like to be hungry. He wouldn't wish it on his worst enemy, much less on some Peruvian farmer just trying to keep his family afloat.

"I have a little of the boiled water left from this morning if you want some while tonight's water cools down," Victor offered, breaking Jordan out of his thoughts.

"I'm good." Jordan held up his backup canteen. He'd expected water purification tablets like they'd done so often before, but Victor assured him that in the Andes, boiling was sufficient. Once they got down into the Amazon basin, they'd have to be more careful, but for now they had crisp, clean spring water to boil for cooking and drinking, and if they didn't mind the cold, for bathing.

"You should drink more water," Victor fussed.

"I'm good, doc. I've got the big CamelBak in my backpack. This is just extra, in case we have to hike longer than expected to find a good campsite," Jordan assured him. "While we're waiting for the fish to finish cooking, tell me about your first trip to Peru."

"You don't want to hear about that, Jordan," Victor scoffed, or tried to, but his tone was the slightest bit off. Most people wouldn't have noticed, but Jordan wasn't most people. He could write a thesis on the subtleties of Dr. Victor Itoua's expressions and tones of voice, not that Dr. Fowler would accept it. The quirk of his eyebrow, which was as good as a jaw drop from anyone else. The twitch at the corner of his mouth meant more to Jordan than a full-out belly laugh from anyone else. Straightening his tie would have been downright nervous fidgeting in anyone else, and when he shot his cuffs, heaven help the person he was heading to deal with. Jordan especially liked that one, as long as it wasn't him. Victor might put on a bland façade, but not even Jordan's drill sergeant in the Marines could deliver a dressing-down like Victor, except he did it without ever raising his voice.

"No, doc, really, I do," Jordan said. "It's either that or tell me what got you obsessed with the Philli-philli legends."

"It's the same story," Victor muttered.

"See, now I really gotta hear this," Jordan said. "Come on, we're in Peru looking for it. The least you can do is tell me why it means so much to you."

"Him," Victor corrected. "Or at least it was him when I saw him. The legends I've studied don't give a gender, and some sightings have suggested Philli-philli is female in form."

"Wait." Jordan leaned forward so he could see the expression on Victor's downturned face. "Did you say you *saw* him?"

"It was probably just my imagination," Victor demurred.

"Oh, hell no," Jordan said. "You don't get to drop that bombshell and then pretend like it's nothing."

"And make you think I'm as crazy as everyone else thinks I am?" The bitterness in Victor's voice surprised Jordan. He knew Victor had taken some hits in the academic community for his interest in Philli-philli, but Jordan had never seen him show more than mild annoyance at it. This was *way* more than mild annoyance.

"Hey, I'm sitting right here in the middle of nowhere on the side of the Andes, headed even deeper into the middle of nowhere because I trust you. You say you saw him? Great, I believe you. I just want to know when and how so I know what to expect when we find him again," Jordan said.

Victor glared at him across the campfire, but Jordan waited him out. Victor might not believe Jordan's words now, but they had time for Jordan to prove himself. Eventually Victor took a deep breath and began, "When I was sixteen, I got accepted to a summer program that sent kids to archaeological digs to give them some experience. I'd planned to spend the summer in the Republic of Congo with my grandparents again, but my grandfather insisted I apply for the internship, specifically in Peru. I asked him why, but all he would say was that it was important. My parents weren't thrilled with the idea, but when my grandfather said something was important, everyone listened. I ended up in Vitcos."

Which explained where Victor's fascination with the Inca came from.

"It was in the early '90s when the Shining Path was at the height of their activity. We'd been assured we were well out of their reach but, *bof*, they might have been overly optimistic. We'd been in Vitcos for almost a month, and it was amazing, so much more than I had expected it to be. I was learning so much about the Inca Empire, about the culture, the history, the fact that the word Inca actually refers to the king, not the people or the empire, all the different ideas about how Vitcos fit into Inca history, and speculation about who might have been there before them, since some of the structures are too old to date from that time period."

Victor's eyes danced with excitement in the firelight as he spoke, making Jordan's heart thump harder in his chest.

"One night, not long before the internship was over, I was restless, so I got up to take a walk. I didn't go far—we were staying right outside the ruins—but the next thing I knew, I was surrounded by people with guns speaking rapid-fire Spanish. I just froze. I didn't know what to do, and my Spanish wasn't all that good in those days, especially since most of my exposure was to Castilian Spanish."

"You must have been terrified." The father in one of Jordan's many foster placements had been a gun nut and a drunk. Mostly Jordan had managed to hide when the man got crazy, but one night he hadn't been fast enough, and the man had cornered him, brandishing the gun in Jordan's face and threatening all sorts of shit. A teacher overheard him telling a classmate about it the next day, and he'd been pulled from that placement and sent back to a group home until a new one could be found. The memory had stayed with him, though.

"Completely," Victor said. "I was sure I was going to die there or be kidnapped or something."

Jordan didn't find the situation the least bit funny, but Victor laughed.

"Yes, I was a bit melodramatic as a teenager."

"What happened? I mean, you obviously got away alive." For which Jordan was insanely grateful.

"Philli-philli happened," Victor replied. "I know how that sounds, but I heard a feline scream, and there was suddenly a... figure between me and them, more erect than a cougar, but still moving mostly on four legs. Much shouting ensued, and a whirlwind fight. When it was all over and the guerilla fighters had fled or were dead, the figure turned to me. It was dark, but the moon was almost full so I had enough light to see more than just the outline. He straightened to stand on his hind legs, and I swear, he had fangs and claws like a cat but his eyes were human. 'Go back where it is safe,' he said in English. I didn't have to be told twice. When we went up to the ruins the next morning, the bodies were gone, and I couldn't see any sign of the fight. Not that I really knew what I was looking for, but there should have been some trace."

"And you've spent all the years since trying to figure out what happened," Jordan finished.

"Not what happened," Victor said. "I know what happened. I've been trying to find him to say thank you." He pulled the frying pan out of the fire. "And that's enough memories for one night. The fish is ready. Eat while it's hot."

Jordan accepted the subject change, even though he had a thousand questions. They could wait until later, when he could ask them as academic curiosity rather than a burning desire to know more about teenaged Victor. He couldn't afford to give himself away.

CHAPTER 3

VICTOR ZIPPED the tent door closed, stretched out on his sleeping bag, and stared at the nylon roof. What in the world had possessed him to tell Jordan that story? He'd never told *anyone* about his encounter with Philli-philli. When it first happened, he hadn't wanted to be sent home early, not even the few days left in the summer program. He hadn't told his parents because his mother would never have let him out of her sight again. He'd thought about telling his grandfather, but when he returned home, it was to the news that *Nkóko* had died peacefully in his sleep while Victor was on the plane back to France. (He could imagine how that conversation would have gone. *Trust your heart, Mayangi. It is always more reliable than your head.* But without Nkóko there to say the words, he had never quite managed to believe them.) And he'd known the kind of derision and scorn he'd be met with if he said anything to anyone else.

It was worse once he went into anthropology. Even now, while he'd love the professional vindication of having a paper about Philli-philli published, albeit one on the origins and cultural impact of the legend on Indigenous people in the Amazon headwaters, he'd told Jordan the truth. The most important piece of it to him was being able to say thank you.

Except Jordan hadn't reacted like most people did when the subject of Philli-philli came up. To be fair, he'd never reacted disparagingly when their colleagues had made comments, though he'd always seemed amused at Victor's passion for the topic. No, Jordan wanted to know "what to expect when we find him again."

What was Victor supposed to do with that? No one should trust him like that. No, really, just take him completely at his word before he even started the story and not question it in the least when he actually told it. Jordan's only reaction had been sympathy for the terror he'd felt at the time.

And people at the university wondered why Victor "put up" with Jordan. Given the chance, he'd do a whole lot more than just put up with him. He couldn't ask Jordan to give up his dreams of a career in anthropology so they could be together, and there weren't any positions available or even on the horizon that would let Jordan advance out of Victor's line of supervision so they could be together without one of them having to find a job at a different university.

Victor rolled onto his side and tried to get comfortable. At least they'd found a grassy area for their tents instead of bare ground. He needed to stop obsessing over Jordan. Of course, he'd been telling himself that for years, and it hadn't made a whit of difference. Not when he went and did things like he'd done tonight.

Victor had made an art out of studying Jordan without seeming to, but tonight he hadn't bothered trying to hide how closely he was watching for Jordan's reactions. His face had been open and earnest the whole time, an expression Victor saw all too rarely at the university. And he understood that. His colleagues could be… hidebound, and they often overlooked the value of Jordan's nontraditional education. Of course most of them didn't see or value Victor's past either. They didn't see the grandson of an influential Mbochi shaman when they looked at him. They saw another untenured professor—and an immigrant at that—in his conservative suits and sensible shoes. Even the ones who had worked with him in the field never looked past his academic competence. They relied on the local guides and porters to manage the daily pieces of an expedition rather than take care of those things themselves, and Victor let them because that's why those people were hired, but when Victor was in charge, he hired fewer locals and relied more on his own skills. When Victor had shot and killed a snake as it was trying to strike one of the others, everyone had gaped at him. Everyone except Jordan, that is. Jordan had nodded like it was perfectly normal. *Nobody* saw Victor that way unless they had it shoved in their faces, but Jordan had seen it straight off. Victor had started falling for Jordan right then, and it had only gotten worse with each subsequent time Jordan saw him for who he really was.

Growing up straddling multiple cultures and ways of life had turned Victor into a chameleon, but Jordan always saw beyond the façade. It made Victor feel… valued.

Bon, d'accord, Victor had also noticed how the firelight cast intriguing shadows across Jordan's rugged features and highlighted the muscles in his arms. Jordan hadn't had occasion to hunt yet, using the bow strapped to his pack since Peruvian law prohibited bringing any kind of guns with them, but Victor could admit to hoping he'd be able to soon, if only so he could watch Jordan as he drew the bow. He always looked good, no matter what he was doing, but every time Victor had seen him shoot his bow, he'd worn such a peaceful, contented look that Victor wanted to tell the world to go to hell and set Jordan up at an archery range so he always looked like that.

He'd never asked where Jordan had learned archery or why it made him smile that way for fear of making him self-conscious. Maybe now that it was just the two of them, he could find a way to bring it up. Jordan was a better shot than Victor, what with having been a sniper, so it made sense he'd do the hunting when they reached an area where they could hunt, and conversation about it would be the next logical step.

Bon Dieu, he was pathetic. He was a grown man. He could just ask instead of obsessing about it like a wet-behind-the-ears teenager. There was no one out here to see his interest and use it against him. Jordan hated standing on ceremony. He wouldn't care if Victor asked.

Except Victor already had enough trouble keeping the boundaries in place. If he let them go now, they'd be impossible to resurrect when they returned to the university and had to go back to being Mr. Harris and Dr. Itoua. Even just asking Jordan to call him by his first name and taking the same liberty in return would be a step too far in Dr. Fowler's eyes.

And if Dr. Fowler knew the rest of what Victor was thinking, he'd be out of a job faster than he could blink.

At least he'd never done anything about his feelings. Some lines simply didn't need to be crossed. With a frustrated huff, he punched his pillow into shape and closed his eyes. Sleep. He needed to sleep because the sun would rise around five and they'd be up and on their way again. It was hard enough keeping his thoughts under control when he was rested. If he was tired, he ran the risk of letting something slip, and he couldn't do that to either of them.

THE MINUTE Jordan got to his tent, he stuck his hand down his pants to adjust his aching hard-on. Fuck, what did it say about him that listening to Victor all earnest and open had him as wound-up as seeing him in swim trunks had done when they were in the hot springs?

That he was stupid in love with his boss, that's what.

And it sucked, because if Jordan knew one thing about Dr. Victor Itoua, it's that he would never look twice at someone who worked for him. He was too damn honorable. Okay, he got it. It was an ethics violation that could cost Victor his job, and Victor had no reason to take that risk for someone like Jordan. Not that Jordan could stop himself from lusting over him, even knowing it would never go anywhere.

He couldn't fucking help it. Victor was everything Jordan wanted (and wanted to be) and could never have. Parents who were still around and would have cared if Victor had told them about his encounter with the Shining Path. And maybe they wouldn't have believed him about Philli-philli, but that was a separate issue entirely—Jordan was pretty sure no one but him had ever believed Victor on that score, if anyone had even heard the story. And then there was the fact that Victor was the kind of man who was still looking to say thank-you to a possibly mythical creature all these years later.

All without counting the fact that Victor listened to him and respected him and even seemed to *like* him. Nobody liked him. Before the Marines, he'd been bounced from foster home to foster home too frequently to make friends. Once he enlisted, he had comrades, but he'd already learned not to trust easily. They thought he was useful, maybe. Thought he could do his job, most of the time. Found him amusing, sure. But actually liked him? Some days he thought Nandini liked him, but other days he wasn't so sure. He had no doubt she loved him, would do anything in her power to help him when he asked, and would have his back no matter what, but that wasn't the same as liking him. But Victor did all of those things and more.

So of course Jordan had gone and fallen head over ass in love with him. And no matter how many times he told himself it was hopeless, that he'd get his head on straight (*Ha! Straight. Yeah, right.*) and get over it, he never did. He still found himself jerking off to a fantasy of Victor actually loving him, not just fucking him, although he'd take fucking. God, would he take fucking!

And this time wouldn't be any different. He'd go through the usual song and dance with himself when he was done, but it wouldn't stop him from doing it now, and it wouldn't stop him next time. For once in his life, he'd found a good man, and he couldn't let that go.

He stripped down and stretched out on his bedroll, then took a minute to listen to the night sounds. He'd perfected the art of jerking off silently in the Marines, but he'd still rather wait until Victor had settled so he wouldn't be interrupted. Coitus interruptus was no fun, whether he had a partner or his trusty left hand.

When he heard nothing except the rustle of the breeze and the calls of the night birds, he closed his eyes and let his imagination take over.

He ran his hands down his chest, stopping to play with his nipples. When he was alone and didn't have to worry about being overheard, that was enough to wring the first moan out of him. In his mind's eye, he let the sound escape, loud enough to alert Victor. Being the man he was, Victor would come to investigate, to make sure Jordan was okay, and Jordan would grow a pair and let Victor see him lying there on his bedroll, naked as a jaybird and his hand on his dick.

Fantasy Victor never had the same hang-ups as real-life Victor, so instead of apologizing and leaving, he'd stay, his gaze sharp and hungry as he watched Jordan stroke himself. Jordan bit his lip as he imagined Victor's face, the way he'd study Jordan to catalog exactly what he liked. That big analytical brain that never stopped connecting actions to meaning would see that Jordan didn't just want to get off. He wanted to savor the moment, to share it, even.

He ran his hand over the head of his cock and smothered a gasp. That would be what broke the stalemate between him and Victor.

Victor leaned closer, almost without meaning to.

See something you like? Jordan asked.

You know I do. Victor's voice was deep and husky, but so, so tender, and it called to something deep inside Jordan, that hidden place where he tucked away his deepest hopes. Because Victor might be frantic or rough or needy, but he would never be callous or cruel. No, he'd always be good to his partner.

Then do something about it, Jordan urged, and that was all it took.

Victor nudged Jordan's hand aside and replaced it with his own. His hand was firm and hot in the cool night air when he closed it around Jordan's shaft, dragging another moan out of him. He worked Jordan slowly, drawing it out until he was bucking into Victor's hand, trying to get him to go faster. Not that he gave in to Jordan's silent plea.

Do you want me to beg?

Never, Victor replied. *I just want to be good to you. Lie back and let me take care of you.*

Jordan had to stuff his fist in his mouth to stop the noise that tried to tear from his throat at that thought. He'd never admit aloud how much he wanted someone who would put his needs above their own, even just sometimes. He wasn't selfish. He'd be happy to take turns and put Victor's needs first half the time. He'd even be happy with his needs being second most of the time as long as they were met.

He sped up his strokes as he imagined Victor leaning down to kiss him, to gentle him into the caress so he could take his time with Jordan, giving him all the tenderness that had been missing from his life.

He squeezed his eyes shut and bit the heel of his hand hard as his climax broadsided him and splattered across his abs and chest.

God, he was pathetic, coming like that from the thought of a loving kiss and gentle caress.

He wiped up the mess with his dirty T-shirt and tossed it aside before curling up on his side as if he could protect his tender underbelly. He needed to get the fuck over himself already. He couldn't do much about it in the jungle, but when this was over, he was going to find the first available, interested guy and fuck him silly. Anything to get the image of Victor loving him out of his mind.

CHAPTER 4

JORDAN LACED up his boots and shouldered his pack. They'd left the Andean highlands behind for the headwaters of the Amazon over the past two weeks, and Jordan could feel it with every swampy breath he took. Even without daily rain, it was humid and warmer—not warm, probably only in the upper 60s—than it had been in Machu Picchu, enough to make him dread the start of the rainy season as the heat and humidity increased, especially if they still hadn't found a place to settle by then.

They'd come across a few isolated settlements already, but they hadn't lingered more than a couple of days in each. Victor worked his magic each time and charmed the elders. Jordan had always suspected Victor's upbringing had more to do with that than his training as an anthropologist, but even with his charm and gift for drawing people out by making connections between their stories and beliefs and the ones he had grown up hearing, any mention of Philli-philli was met with blank stares and either incomprehension or a repeat of the pop culture legends, neither of which got them anywhere. The only new information they'd gotten, which hadn't led anywhere so far, was a reference to a temple that was supposedly where Philli-philli lived when he wasn't saving people.

If it were Jordan, he'd be getting frustrated by now, but Victor—except he was back to calling Jordan Harris for some reason, so Jordan was going to have to call him Dr. Itoua again—didn't seem bothered by the lack of progress. He thanked the elders for their time, traded meat Jordan had hunted for supplies for the next leg of their trip, and moved on.

That was the one good thing about having moved into the Amazon region. He could get his bow out and actually hunt. He'd even gotten some appreciative gestures from the other hunters in the settlements when he went out with them. Jordan sent a silent prayer of gratitude winging toward Scott, the one good foster father he'd had, who had taken Jordan bow hunting with him before his cancer got too bad to go hiking. Jordan hadn't been able to stay with the family after Scott died, but he'd kept in sporadic contact with them and always made sure to mention that he'd kept up with his archery. It made Pam, his foster mother, smile sadly, but at least she was smiling, something she still didn't do often enough to suit him or her other kids.

He wouldn't need to hunt today, though. They had enough meat left from yesterday to hold them at least until tomorrow evening, and by then they might have found another village. He could hope, anyway. He had good boots, but even with them, he'd kill for more than a couple days' rest before they set out again.

"What d'you suppose the chances are of finding another settlement today, doc?" Jordan asked as he had each morning when they broke camp. He really wasn't nagging. He liked hearing the answer. It gave him so much insight into the way Victor's mind worked. Jordan didn't know if he'd ever lead his own field research, but if he did, he'd have Victor's example as a guide.

"I haven't seen any signs of regular use," Victor replied. "It's always possible hunters come this way occasionally, but if they were here regularly, we'd see some indication—a slight trail, broken branches, something."

Jordan nodded as he scanned the area around him. He might have good eyesight and fantastic aim, but Victor had the experience. The Marines had always stuck Jordan up high somewhere and told him when and what to shoot. He'd learned some tracking tips with Scott and his kids as well as in the Reserves, but Victor was still better at it.

They hiked at a deliberate pace mostly in silence, not rushing, but also not lingering longer than it took Victor to determine which direction to go next. Jordan hadn't been part of that bit of planning, but all other feelings aside, he trusted Victor to have a purpose in his decisions.

They stopped for lunch when the sun was directly overhead. Jordan pulled the granola bars from his pack—he didn't know what else to call the pressed grain and fruit mixture the people in the last settlement had made and given them before they left. Regardless of what he called them, they made a perfect lunch—filling, nonperishable, and requiring no cooking. He handed one to Victor before taking one for himself. He propped his pack against a tree and leaned against it, feet out in front of him. He'd gotten so used to the smell of damp, decaying leaves that he barely noticed it now, another background awareness instead of a constant, cloying annoyance. Victor mimicked his pose, even going so far as the tip his head back and close his eyes.

"You okay there, doc?" Jordan asked.

Victor hummed affirmatively but didn't open his eyes or say anything else, so Jordan let the silence fall again. They'd spent enough time together not to need to fill it with meaningless words, and it gave Jordan a chance to soak in the marvel that was Victor Itoua in field gear.

He'd overheard undergrads talking about the professors and which ones they liked, which ones were hot, and any number of other criteria more than once over the years. Victor always figured on the list of the ones they liked, but the students never seemed to see past the façade of unassuming academic to the man underneath. As far as Jordan was concerned, they were all blind, because seriously, could they not see how Victor filled out a suit? And now, without that protective camouflage—yes, Victor thought of it that way too. He'd admitted as much to Jordan one time when he asked why Victor always wore a suit, even when other professors dressed more casually—the lean, rangy body that Jordan spent way too much time fantasizing about was right there on display with nothing to hide it.

Fucking hell. Sweat beaded on his upper lip despite the temperature as he stared. He'd told himself he wasn't going to keep doing this to himself, but he couldn't seem to help it.

Determined to focus on something else for the rest of their break, he studied the small clearing where they sat. It wasn't all that different from any of the others they'd passed since they reached the headwaters and the edge of the rainforest, but the more Jordan looked, the more something niggled at his brain. With a frown, he rose and stalked the perimeter, trying to put his finger on the cause.

"Harris?"

Of course his movement roused Victor out of his relaxation.

"Not sure, doc." He continued his circuit. It was probably nothing, just different vegetation as they continued to descend from the highlands, but he had to be sure.

About halfway around his circuit, he stopped and studied the ground and the flora. He felt Victor come up beside him, but he didn't look up.

"Something came crashing through here not long ago," Victor said.

"Any idea what?" Jordan took a few steps in the direction of the disturbed branches and fallen leaves.

"No, but whatever it was, it was in a hurry," Victor replied. "Good catch. Get your gear and let's see if the trail leads us anywhere interesting."

Jordan stuffed the last of his lunch in his mouth and grabbed his pack again. He gestured for Victor to take the lead, but he shook his head. "It was your find. You take point this time. I'll tell you if I see anything you miss."

Great. Just what he needed. With his luck, he'd lead them right into the lion's den, or whatever the Peruvian equivalent was. The puma's lair? Did pumas even have lairs? He rolled his eyes at his wandering thoughts and focused on the matter at hand. He had a trail to follow in the hope of finding something that would help them, not kill them.

Or get them thrown in jail. Peru had strict laws about uncontacted tribes, and they were skirting the areas that were prohibited, even for researchers like them. He'd just have to hope Victor stopped them before they crossed into forbidden territory.

The subtle signs he'd started tracking gave way to more obvious signs of passage—human passage. "Do we keep going, sir?"

"It's a gray area," Victor admitted. "We aren't in the Kugapakori, Nahua, Nati Territorial Reserve yet. Let's keep going. If we haven't found people or a settlement by nightfall, we'll turn back tomorrow so we don't cross that line."

Jordan nodded and turned back to the trail, and it was a trail now, not just signs of passage he happened to be following. The detritus on the forest floor was worn away, leaving bare dirt. They walked for another hour, if Jordan's internal clock was right, before the forest gave way to a cleared field planted with crops. That was a start. Most of the uncontacted tribes were hunter-gatherers, not farmers. Still, it wouldn't pay to be overly confident.

"¡Hola!" Jordan called as they stepped out of the shelter of the trees. He didn't see anyone right away, but better to play it safe and announce their presence. Less likely to be taken as a threat if they didn't sneak in.

No one answered, but he caught movement in the undergrowth on the far side of the field. Victor saw it too, because he held his hands out, palms up, and repeated the greeting in Quechua. Jordan just hoped they were still dealing with people who spoke Quechua and not one of the other Indigenous languages. His Quechua was sketchy at best, but it was still more than he knew of Aymara or any of the forty-plus other languages still spoken in Peru.

A child peeked out at them before disappearing again.

"Let's hope they bring back an adult who's interested in talking, not shooting," Jordan muttered.

"Have a little faith?" Victor replied.

Jordan snorted. Life had never given him any reason to up 'til now, but he'd try since Victor asked. Even so, he missed the comforting weight of a handgun on his hip or a sniper rifle on his back. He'd checked, but he couldn't find a legal way to bring a gun with him to Peru nor to acquire one after he arrived, and since he could hunt with his bow, he hadn't had a justification for acquiring one illegally. Not that Victor would have agreed to that anyway. Victor always expected the best from everyone, but Jordan was a realist. He drew an arrow out of the quiver but didn't set it on the string. He could have it nocked and ready to fire in a matter of seconds if necessary. He'd go for a warning shot rather than a kill shot—he didn't actually want to hurt anyone—but he wasn't just going to stand there and let them get killed either.

A few minutes later a man stepped warily into the field from almost the same place the child had been. Victor repeated the Quechua greeting, followed by the one sentence they both had mastered—*I don't speak much Quechua. Do you speak Spanish?*

Jordan studied him surreptitiously. He was short and wiry, typical of the people they'd met in the area so far, lean from limited resources with rangy muscles from the hard life they lived, but Westernized enough to be wearing boots and cargo shorts rather than the sandals or bare feet more typical of the uncontacted tribes. And in this case, a white T-shirt with a red diagonal stripe across the front and the Peruvian national soccer team logo emblazoned on it. *Okay, good.* That meant they hadn't strayed into forbidden territory and that they'd have some chance of finding someone who spoke enough Spanish to answer their questions.

"A little," the man answered in Spanish.

Bingo. It might not be much, but they had one person they could communicate with.

Victor launched into his explanation that they were researchers interested in local customs and lore. The man looked bemused, but he heard Victor out and beckoned for them to follow.

Victor shot Jordan a knowing grin.

Jordan rolled his eyes but left it at that as they followed the man away from the field. It took almost no time to reach the main settlement—yes, he was making assumptions, but that was his job, thank you very much, and out here, anything more than two or three structures clumped together was almost always communal space—and he cataloged a dozen or so buildings, everything from a wooden cabin that probably had several interior rooms to huts made from the fronds of some kind of large-leafed tree. Their guide led them to the wood cabin and an elderly man sitting on the steps.

He said something to the man in rapid Quechua, too fast for Jordan to follow and possibly not in the same dialect he'd started to pick up more of from the porters on the Inca Trail. When he was done, the elder nodded and turned to Jordan and Victor.

"Welcome to our village," he said in halting Spanish. "I am Paucar."

"It is an honor," Victor replied with a bow. "My friend and I are looking for a place to rest. We would gladly help in the village in any way we can in exchange for shelter and some conversation. My friend is a very accomplished hunter."

Jordan smiled on cue and marveled once again at how Victor always knew exactly what to say to charm people into accepting them.

"Sami says you wish to hear our stories," Paucar said.

"That's right," Victor replied. "Too many stories have been lost because people didn't listen to them. We don't want that to happen again."

"I do not know that our stories are any different from other stories, but you may stay as long as you contribute to the village," Paucar said after a moment of silent deliberation.

Jordan reached for his bow with a grin. He'd let Victor figure out the rest of the arrangements. He had better things to do. "I'll be back with something for dinner."

CHAPTER 5

THREE WEEKS later, they were still in Paucar's village. It was the longest they'd stayed in any one place since arriving in Peru, but hey, people kept telling them interesting stories, the kind that led to really good anthropological studies. They hadn't made much headway into the Philli-philli legends or the even more elusive temple that was allegedly his home, but Jordan had a solid feel for the rhythm of life in the village. And he'd gotten the always-welcome reminder that he was better at this than he thought. His sniper skills were good for more than lining up shots. The details and patterns he noticed and cataloged out of habit were exactly the kind of thing they needed in fieldwork.

Which made the sudden current of excitement running through the village noteworthy. The closest thing he'd seen had been their arrival, but that had an undercurrent of uncertainty. This was no such thing. He kept silent tabs on the pulse of the village as he wandered in search of Victor. He had no obvious reason to seek him out, so he kept his gait easy and his movements aimless so as not to draw attention to himself, but if anything, the charade only heightened the sharpness of his vision as he absorbed every detail.

Of course that's when Victor had to step out of his hut, looking as cool and collected in his light trousers and loose shirt as he'd ever looked in any of his suits, except that seeing his skin—several shades darker than normal after all the time they'd been spending outdoors— taunted Jordan, leaving him perpetually horny. But even jerking off in the relative privacy of his hut wasn't enough to stop his gut from clenching every time he saw his boss. The hardest part wasn't ignoring how damn sexy he looked just the slightest bit undone. No, the hardest part was seeing the new side of him Jordan had gotten peeks of since the night he'd shared his reasons for trying to find Philli-philli. Sure, Victor was one of the best, so it wasn't any surprise that they'd been accepted into the village easily, except this wasn't just his training kicking in. He was finally getting to indulge a side of himself he rarely let out, the curious, interested, fascinated-with-Philli-philli side. The

Victor side. And that? That was even more smoking hot than his bare forearms or the patch of smooth skin at the open neck of his shirts or the glimpse of strong ankles between the hem of his pants and his sturdy sandals. Fuck, he was turning into a Regency romance novel, but he couldn't seem to stop.

He tucked all that turmoil away and sidled up to Victor. "Any idea what's going on, doc?" he said, low enough not to be overheard by the few villagers who spoke bits of English. Most people spoke Quechua among themselves and Spanish with Jordan and Victor, but a few had shown an interest in practicing what little English they'd picked up.

"No," Victor replied just as quietly. "Even the ones who usually translate for me are only speaking Quechua."

Jordan frowned. The crowd seemed cheerful in their anticipation, but he'd spent enough time observing people to know that moods could change on a dime. Then one of the older children burst out of the jungle, shouting in Quechua, "He's coming! He's coming!"

Jordan knew a lot more Spanish than Quechua, but he understood that particular phrase and tensed, ready for whoever this "he" was, feeling Victor do the same beside him. The crowd, though, cheered at the announcement, and seconds later, an unknown man arrived from the same direction the child had come from.

Jordan bit back the gasp that wanted to escape his throat as possibly the most beautiful man he had ever seen scanned the gathered villagers with the sharp eyes of a hunter. He was taller than most of the villagers, his back straight and his gait confident. He smiled indulgently at the children dancing around his legs, brushing over heads with long fingers that looked like they could kill or caress with equal dexterity. His black hair was cropped close to his head, the cut looking recent despite the state of the rest of his clothes. The trousers he wore, covered in dust and stains, had tattered up to midcalf, giving Jordan a glimpse of muscular bronzed legs to match the muscular arms and smooth chest visible beneath the loose, open vest he wore. His gaze met Jordan's over the head of the villagers, lingered for a moment, and moved on to Victor. Jordan's hackles rose as the man's gaze lingered even longer on Victor. And sure, Victor was worth looking at, but who did this guy think he was, acting like Victor was ripe for the picking? *Well, fuck that.*

"Relax, Harris," Victor ordered before Jordan could take a step forward.

He stopped out of habit, so used to obeying orders that he didn't even process it before he acted, but he didn't lower his guard. He was here as hired muscle as much as research assistant, and he didn't care if that motherfucker knew it.

VICTOR SIGHED internally at Jordan's—he couldn't go back to calling him Harris in his head even if he forced himself to use it aloud—belligerence. The man hated anything and anyone who might knock him off his perch as the strongest, fastest, sexiest, any other -est. Most of the time he worried for nothing, his time in the military having honed his body to a finely tuned fighting machine that doubled as the epitome of masculine perfection. The man currently conversing with the village elders looked like he might actually give Jordan a run for his money. Not for his aim. Nobody beat Jordan's accuracy with any kind of ranged weapon, a fact that had endeared him to the hunters in the village when he went out with them the first time and every time since, but the man was certainly a fine specimen in every other regard, just the type to push all of Victor's buttons, except for one pesky fact. All of his buttons were reserved for the irritating idiot currently puffing up like a bird of paradise in a mating dance. Victor didn't know who Jordan thought he needed to impress, or maybe the display was automatic.

Finished with the elders, the man approached where he and Jordan still stood. "I am T'ukri," he said in accented but easily understandable English.

"Dr. Victor Itoua." Victor offered his hand. "And my research assistant, Jordan Harris."

"The elders speak highly of you and your interest in them." T'ukri's grip was firm but not crushing, his hand callused from use. "They say you wish to explore the rainforest."

"Academic interest," Victor explained. "I've discovered in my studies that what locals consider legend or folklore often has a basis in the forgotten past. Places like Machu Picchu, for example, passed out of history into myth before they were rediscovered by the outside world while often being known in local cultures."

"And you think to find something like this here?" T'ukri asked.

"Probably not on that scale," Victor admitted, no matter how much he wanted to believe another such city existed—had continued to exist after the arrival of the Spanish, "but any traces of abandoned, forgotten, or undiscovered cultures can only lead to a more complete understanding of ones that continue to exist today, not to mention allowing us to preserve those cultures for the future. We're looking into the origins of the Philli-philli legends. The real legends, not the ones passed around in popular circles today."

T'ukri's eyes narrowed, but he nodded sharply. "Today I rest and bathe. Tonight we feast. Tomorrow we discuss my requirements for those I guide into the jungle."

"I'll look forward to it," Victor said easily.

"Me too," Jordan added, elbowing his way into the conversation with all the grace of a rampaging bear.

"Until tomorrow." T'ukri gave a slight bow.

"With me," Victor growled once T'ukri was out of earshot. Jordan knew how much was riding on the success of this expedition, but he'd barged into the conversation anyway. Victor could only hope T'ukri had missed the byplay between them or would discount it, because he could not lose this chance.

Jordan fell into step beside him as Victor did his best to amble rather than stalk back to the hut the villagers had offered him, more grateful than ever that they'd found a separate hut for Jordan. Once they were inside, safe from prying eyes if not ears, he rounded on Jordan. "What the hell was that?"

"What was what, sir?" A flicker of surprise crossed Jordan's face, but Victor was too angry to keep his professional façade in place. If that meant Jordan saw him as a little more human at the end of their conversation, so be it.

"Don't play dumb, Harris. I know you too well. We just found possibly the perfect guide to take us into the rainforest and you got into a pissing contest with him. I was waiting for you to whip out your dick so you could see whose was bigger."

Jordan's eyes went wide at that, but Victor didn't back down.

"He was looking at you like you were the entrée for tonight's feast," Jordan grumbled.

Victor bit back a snort. Jordan's eyes had failed him if he thought T'ukri would be attracted to Victor, even if the assertion raised his hopes about Jordan's interest.

"And that is your concern because?" Victor knew what he wanted the answer to be, but he was also willing to acknowledge his own delusions.

"Because I'm supposed to watch your back, doc," Jordan replied. *Delusions one, Victor nothing.*

"I'm nothing more than a curiosity, an unknown face in an unlikely place," Victor said. "Now that he knows who we are, he won't give me another glance."

Jordan snorted. "Whatever you say. I'll keep watching your back anyway. Something about him doesn't sit right with me, and I'm going to find out what."

Victor refrained from rolling his eyes. "Just don't run him off. We need him if we're going to make any progress beyond what we've already learned here." The villagers might be willing to tell them stories, but none had shown any interest in taking them deeper into the rainforest in search of Philli-philli or the temple. No one had refused point-blank. They just ignored or sidestepped the question.

"Yeah, yeah, make nice with your secret admirer so he'll lead us to our deaths in the jungle."

"Enough, Harris," Victor said, at the end of his patience. Only Jordan could even make him break a sweat, and Jordan cut through his defenses like a hot knife through butter.

Jordan tossed him a mocking half salute and left the hut whistling like he didn't have a care in the world. Then the tune to "I Want Your Sex" penetrated, and Victor gritted his teeth to keep from storming after Jordan and kicking his ass. Jordan was a sarcastic shit at the best of times, but Victor had never before known him to be cruel.

He might have to revise that assessment.

T'UKRI ACCEPTED the mug of *chicha* from Paucar and reclined easily on one of the woven mats scattered across the open area at the center of the village. With the sun sinking toward the horizon, the temperatures would drop quickly, and the large fire would be welcome. He had bathed and rested, and now he was looking forward to the feast. From the smells wafting about the village, the women had made *cuy*, a treat he rarely got unless he was here or at home.

Movement along the outskirts of the crowd caught his attention, and he looked over, not rising from his supine position, but ready to pounce if necessary. The two foreigners he had met earlier were there, not imposing, but present. He studied them discreetly as they drifted along the edges of the gathered throng. Dr. Itoua and Mr. Harris. Victor and Jordan. Outsiders interested in ancient lore and hidden ruins. That could make them many things. Academics as they claimed or treasure hunters were the two most obvious, but either could be a cover for other things as well, more nefarious things.

Poachers, human traffickers, bounty hunters, drug runners… he had seen them all and more, although the shady ones usually gave themselves away quickly enough, and he sensed none of that from these two. If only he could put his finger on what he did sense.

"Come, eat, T'ukri," Kichka, Paucar's wife, urged. "You must be tired from your travels."

"Thank you, honored mother," T'ukri replied with a deep bow of his head. "Your welcome is as generous as ever." And had been since T'ukri saved one of the village children from a puma attack when he first started visiting ten years earlier.

He rose from his seat and helped himself to the cuy and *olluquito con charqui* before returning to his place. Around him the village children laughed and played tag, tumbling over and around each other like so many puma kittens while the adults looked on indulgently. No one seemed at all bothered by the outsiders, but T'ukri did not drop his guard completely. The village was so remote they had little contact with anyone outside the neighboring villages, and even then, only rarely.

The two men stood together, clearly comfortable in each other's space, and a blind man could have seen Harris's reaction to T'ukri's presence. A bear marking its territory had more subtlety than the blond man with his broad shoulders and thick chest. Itoua had named him research assistant, but T'ukri knew a fighter when he saw one. Harris would make sure Itoua went home safely. T'ukri could respect that in a man, especially in the jungle, but it did not make him trustworthy, only shockingly attractive. He could hear Ch'aska laughing at him now. His sister always said his interest in outsiders would be his downfall one day. He had never wanted her to be more wrong than in the moment when she appeared most right.

Transferring his attention away from Harris—the man had the eyes of a condor and no doubt claws to match, and T'ukri had no desire to be caught staring—he focused on Itoua instead. Where Harris was all outward brawn despite the keen intelligence in his eyes, Itoua was his foil: smooth, unassuming, with a kind face and kinder eyes. More than that, T'ukri recognized the touch of otherworldliness that characterized a shaman. Itoua might be an anthropologist, but he was not as harmless as he wished to appear. No shaman ever was. If Harris was a condor—*malku*—swift and precise, Itoua was a forest boa, alert, intelligent, and able to pass largely unseen. T'ukri had learned respect for both at an early age, and condors mated for life.

The children demanded his attention then, bringing a smile to his face as he forced his thoughts away from the outsiders and back to more important matters. Like the peals of laughter when he caught one of the children and swung her over his head.

"My turn, my turn," they all shouted, clamoring around him. He laughed with them and swung them each in turn.

VICTOR SUPPRESSED the sigh that wanted to escape. He still didn't know what had possessed Jordan earlier, but his assumption had been further off the mark than Victor had ever known him to be. T'ukri might have given Victor a passing once-over when they met, but it was Jordan who caught his eye during dinner.

He still didn't know who T'ukri was to merit the celebration currently going on in the village, and all his attempts at asking had resulted in the same incomprehension and a repetition of T'ukri's name, as if not knowing him was impossible.

That alone made Victor suspicious, but he might have let his concerns slide with the understanding that things were different here if it weren't for the way T'ukri kept staring at Jordan. Victor knew that hungry look all too well. He saw it on the faces of men and women at the university every day, always directed at Jordan right before they made a move on him. He imagined his own face would look much the same if he let his control slip for even an instant.

He could imagine it all too easily. He'd seen Jordan shirtless too many times to count, and given the lack of privacy in the field, he'd seen him naked a time or two as well. T'ukri had traded his torn pants for a loose wrap similar to the loincloths the village hunters wore. The vest he'd been wearing earlier was nowhere in sight, leaving his torso completely bare. His biceps and shoulders couldn't rival Jordan's—it would take a god to do that—but the firelight reflected off his skin and limned his muscles in gold. Victor wouldn't blame Jordan one bit if he took T'ukri up on the offer in his dark eyes, and what a sight it would be! Two alpha men in their prime, vying for the upper hand.

Victor had to avert his eyes and think of the half-eaten carcass they had stumbled upon the last time they went out with the hunters to stop his traitorous cock from giving away the direction of his thoughts, but *bon sang*, what he would give to be a fly on the wall if they did end up fucking.

Not that he had a shadow of a chance of that. Neither of them had any reason to give him a second glance when they could be wrapped up in each other instead.

"Agradiseyki," he said automatically when one of the children offered him food. He consoled himself with the thought that their sabbatical would end, and when it did, Harris would return to the university with him. T'ukri might get him for a night or a season, but in the end, his life outside the rainforest would win.

JORDAN FINISHED his olluquito con charqui, amazed once again at the variety of dishes the villagers managed to create with the limited ingredients they had on hand, and faded into the shadows cast by the flickering light of the bonfire. Something about T'ukri didn't sit right with him, and not just the way he was still looking at Victor like he was the best thing he'd ever seen. (Okay, so Jordan looked at him the same way. Sue him. Victor *was* the best thing Jordan had ever seen—and the little slips in his façade he had started allowing now that they were alone in the field only made him hotter—but T'ukri didn't know him well enough to realize it.)

He couldn't put his finger on exactly what was bothering him, though, so he settled with his back against one of the trees along the outskirts of the village and simply watched, letting the details filter through his vision until he could find the pattern. The villagers clearly knew T'ukri well, given the way the normally shy children clambered all over him, demanding his attention. It had taken days before they would even meet Jordan's eyes, much less approach him. Then Kichka came to check on him—for the third time—and *that* was the clincher. People checked on Kichka, not the other way around. She was the headman's wife, the most important woman in the village. The only person she waited on, and then only rarely, was her husband.

Jordan's gaze sharpened and focused in on T'ukri's bearing and mannerisms: the confident way he swung the children around, no hesitation in his gestures, just the complete surety that his body would do what he wanted it to; the way he reclined on the mat when the children left him alone, outwardly as carefree and relaxed as he could be, but with the harnessed power of someone who could spring into action at a moment's notice; the regal nod of his head when anyone brought him anything, as if he was as used to being served as he was to fending for himself.

He acted like a lion surrounded by his pride.

Son of a bitch.

He needed to talk to Victor, and he needed to talk to him now, but he'd been an asshole earlier in the day and Victor had been avoiding him ever since.

He'd fucked that up and good. But they were supposed to talk to T'ukri tomorrow about guiding them into the jungle. He needed to talk to Victor before that so they could decide what to do. He'd wait until people started turning in so it would be less obvious what he was doing. And in the meantime, he'd show that fucking cat not to mess with him.

CHAPTER 6

T'UKRI STOOD in the door to the hut he used when he came to the village, cloaked in shadow. He had retired early, claiming fatigue from his journey, but sleep eluded him. For as long as he could remember, he had known where his future would take him, but he had never expected that when it brought him here, it would offer him everything he longed for only to show him he could never have it.

Tradition dictated he would find not one but two people to share his life, to support and balance him, for only once in all their history had one elevated to Chapaqpuma found everything they needed in only one mate. T'ukri had accepted that as he had accepted that the mantle of his father's leadership would one day pass to him. That it would happen so soon, not at his *papānin's* death but at his *tayta's*, had been less expected. He had not imagined that loss would have a double cost: not only the absence of a beloved family member, his second father, but also the loss of stability Yuri's support had given his mother and Huallpa all these years.

Today when he shook Itoua's hand, his whole body had lit up in primal recognition. He had not shaken Harris's hand, but he had not needed to. The look of pure challenge in his eyes had been enough to set T'ukri alight. He had thought to court them properly, but how to do it now that he knew they were lovers? Bad enough that they were foreigners, unfamiliar with his people's customs. Bad enough as well that he would take two male lovers with no way to produce an heir. But to approach these two men, already together, on top of everything else—it seemed impossible.

He rolled his neck and stepped deeper into the shadows so Harris would not notice him as the other man slipped silently into Itoua's hut. No matter. T'ukri had always thrived on challenges. He would find a way to win them over not only to him but to his people and their ways. They wanted a guide into the rainforest to see things no outsider had ever seen. T'ukri could give them that.

If they proved themselves worthy of his trust.

No sounds filtered through the humid night air to feed his imagination, but he did not need them to know exactly what was happening inside the hut not far away. He could see it as easily as if he were in the hut with them—Harris tearing at his clothes in his impatience to get naked, Itoua slowing him down with gentle hands and whispered admonishments not to rip the fabric in his haste. Harris would slow down—T'ukri had already realized Harris would listen to Itoua even when he listened to no one else. Their skin would gleam in the moonlight filtering through the trees, splashes of light and dark, as they kissed.

T'ukri groaned at the image and pulled loose the knot holding the fabric around his waist. Naked now, he stretched out on his sleeping mat and ran his hand over his chest, imagining them touching each other the same way. He had seen a glimpse of smooth skin at the collar of Itoua's shirt, and he could imagine Harris gliding his fingers across it. Would Itoua's skin be sensitive beneath the protection of his clothes? He liked to think so. Harris would take advantage of it if it was. Like the condor, he would exploit any advantage he could find, but Itoua would enjoy being captured. Who would not enjoy being cradled in Harris's strong arms, protected from anything that might try to tear them apart?

T'ukri slid his hands lower, circling his erection and moving down to cup his sac. They would be naked by now, wrapped up in each other, rocking together as they sought completion. It would be easy to imagine Harris on top, but T'ukri found even more appeal in the reverse, in Harris's strength yielding to Itoua's, offering up his body as the feast it was for Itoua to gorge himself.

He gripped tighter, pushing himself toward completion as the image of Itoua thrusting slowly, leisurely into Harris's willing body floated before his eyes. If he were there, he would find the spot where they joined and lavish attention on both of them with all the reverence he could summon. The joining of bodies and of lives was sacred to his people, and he would show it with every touch, every kiss, until nothing remained but the final pinnacle and then bliss.

With a sigh, he climaxed, ropes of white spattering across his belly. He slumped back against the sleep mat and stared blindly toward the ceiling.

Ch'aska was right. They would be his downfall for sure.

VICTOR HAD just shed his shirt and was about to step out of his pants when he heard a telltale rustle behind him. He spun around and glared at Jordan, who stood there in the inconstant light of the guttering oil lamp.

"Harris. I didn't expect to see you again tonight."

"You know me, doc. Always turning up where I'm least expected," Jordan replied jauntily, but the tension in his shoulders belied his jovial tone.

"Did you need something, or were you just testing whether you could sneak up on me?"

"I don't care what he says, T'ukri isn't just a jungle guide," Jordan said.

"We've been over this—"

"No, doc, just listen," Jordan interrupted. That in itself was unusual enough to catch Victor's attention, but the look on Jordan's face cemented it. Despite Jordan's reputation for stating the obvious, Victor had learned to listen when he said it was important.

"I'm listening."

"On the surface, it all adds up. He comes into the village wearing beat-up clothes from days or weeks in the jungle, but he's clearly not some random wanderer. I mean, there was the excitement of him being here in the first place, which is odd in a village that doesn't seem to have much traffic in or out. He's not from here, but he's clearly welcome. They have a hut set aside for him, for Christ's sake. They throw a feast in honor of him showing up, and okay, maybe they just wanted an excuse to have a party, but then, and this is what really got me, Kichka herself kept checking on him. I don't know who he is, but he isn't just some jungle guide."

"Theories?" Jordan raised some valid points.

"I'd say someone of rank from another settlement, maybe even another tribe, but then why would he pretend to be a guide?" Jordan replied. "Why not admit who he is?"

"Because he doesn't know us? Or because it's not an official visit?" Victor suggested, playing devil's advocate as he always did when they tossed ideas around. The return to something akin to normal soothed the restlessness that had overtaken him at noticing how closely T'ukri had been watching Jordan and vice versa. At least now he knew Jordan's attention stemmed from suspicion, not interest.

Not the time, he scolded himself.

"Then why come at all?" Jordan shot back. "He was too interested in you to have a girlfriend in the village."

Victor ignored the repeated assertion of T'ukri's interest. He hadn't won the argument earlier. He wouldn't win it now either. "Even village elders have to earn their living somehow, and out here, there aren't a lot of options. Being a guide would be a good way to earn some money and have an excuse to drop in on other villages. He could learn all kinds of things without anyone thinking twice about it."

"Like a jungle spy?" Jordan asked, clearing pondering the idea. "I suppose that's possible, although he'd have to be damn good not to make anyone here suspicious. They obviously know he's not one of their own, but they welcome him with open arms. It just doesn't add up. I mean, if they thought he was a spy or there was any chance of him being one, they wouldn't be so excited to see him. Paucar *smiled* at him. I didn't think he could smile at anyone except his grandchildren."

Victor laughed despite himself. "You might be right about that one. He'd give Dr. Fowler a run for his money in the dour and intimidating department. But I didn't mean spy in any official or covert fashion, rather as one who gathers information. Plus if he's guiding people into the area around his own tribe, he can control who goes near them. Out this far, there aren't a lot of tourists. If they're here, they're either adventure seekers or they're bad news. Your friend Nandini mentioned increasing criminal activity."

"Yeah. Or they're researchers like us. Regardless, he moves like he's trained to deal with bad news," Jordan said. "Did you see the way he constantly scanned the edges of the village? He looked all relaxed and half drunk on the chicha, but if you looked close, he was all bunched up, like a cat ready to pounce. All he needed was a reason."

"Looking closely, were you?" Victor asked archly.

"Looking at things is my job," Jordan retorted. "Well, and shooting things used to be, but you don't let me do that."

"Only our dinner," Victor replied. "So T'ukri's a guide and a warrior. And maybe something more. Does any of that change our decision to ask him to guide us into the rainforest?"

"I guess not," Jordan said. "I'd feel better if I thought we could trust him, but I'll just have to sleep with one eye open."

"You do that anyway." In all the time they'd worked together, Victor had never known Jordan to sleep deeply unless he was sick.

"All we can do is keep our wits about us and see what comes of it. Unless there's something else, I'd like to get some sleep."

Jordan's gaze raked over him from head to toe, making him feel much more naked than he should while still wearing pants. "Maybe I should stay here and keep watch."

"Now you're being ridiculous. Save the hyperawareness for when we're in the rainforest."

Jordan opened his mouth, probably to protest again, but Victor'd had all he could take. He imbued his voice with as much finality as he could. "Good night, Harris."

"Sir."

Victor turned his back. Jordan would leave or not, but he was going to sleep. He waited until he heard the slight rustle that presaged his exit before unbuttoning his pants and climbing into his bedroll in just his briefs. He'd deal with everything else tomorrow.

BACK IN his hut, Jordan fanned cool air across his face and tried to calm his body down. Victor had stripped off his T-shirt and was about to take off his pants. Damn, why couldn't he have gotten there fifteen seconds later? Just long enough for him to have stepped out of them so Jordan could get a good look at him in his briefs. His hands itched to touch as it was. He wasn't sure he'd have been able to stop himself from touching if he'd found Victor undressed that far, but fuck it all, maybe that's what he needed to do. Maybe he just needed to go for it. Yeah, Victor could do better, but he hadn't. It had been a good two years since he'd dated anyone, as far as Jordan knew, and that relationship hadn't lasted more than a couple of months.

He could sympathize. Finding anyone outside of their field for more than a quick fuck was a challenge with the possibility of being out of the country for months at a time when grants came through, and Jordan'd had enough of sleeping with his fellow students only to have gossip do the rounds *again* about how someone was tapping his ass.

He missed sex, but more than that, he missed the closeness that came with it, the companionship of being with someone for more than just the time it took to get off. That had been fine when he was twenty, but he was thirty-three now, well past the stage of wanting nothing but meaningless sex.

Victor was the kind of man who would give Jordan everything he needed if he was interested, but Jordan couldn't figure out how to find out without jeopardizing their friendship and their working relationship. As much as he wanted more, he couldn't lose what he had with Victor now. He just couldn't.

He took a deep breath and settled onto his bedroll. God, he'd been in the field so long he even missed the crappy mattress on his pullout couch. He was getting too old for this shit.

CHAPTER 7

AFTER BREAKFAST the next morning, when normally Jordan would go out with the hunters and Victor would sit with the elders and ask questions that would help in their quest to find out more about Philli-philli, Victor summoned Jordan to his side with a sharp nod of his head and approached T'ukri.

"Good morning." Victor offered T'ukri a cup of the instant coffee he had hoarded carefully since their arrival, limiting himself to one cup a week.

"Good morning." T'ukri took the cup and inhaled deeply before taking a sip. "Even instant coffee is a treat in the rainforest."

Victor didn't need to turn his head to feel the satisfaction radiating off Jordan. He'd been right. T'ukri had traveled far enough afield to have come across instant coffee. Chances were, the rest of Jordan's observations would be just as accurate. "I hope it's a welcome treat."

"Most welcome. Paucar speaks well of you. You ask interesting questions and are respectful of their answers. Tell me what you seek to see, and I will do my best to guide you there."

Victor shot Harris a quelling look before he could blurt out more than they wanted to reveal. They had earned Paucar's respect, which seemed to have earned T'ukri's as well. They didn't want to lose it by rushing things now. "We have heard tales of an abandoned temple where a lost tribe once worshipped the ancient gods and goddesses, the Earth Mother or perhaps the great cats." Victor kept a sharp eye on T'ukri's expression. "The tales place it in a dozen or more different places in the foothills of the Andes, but most of those locations have either been explored already to no avail or are in areas protected by law from anyone who isn't part of a local tribe. A guide like you, though, might know of something others don't, or at least know of people who might tell us more of those tales."

T'ukri's expression didn't change, but Victor saw suddenly what Jordan had meant when he talked about the readiness that invested

T'ukri's body. "The puma are revered by many tribes, back to the Inca and before."

"If the stories are to be believed, this went beyond simple reverence to the belief that the gods and goddesses had blessed the tribe with a guardian, human in form but imbued with the strength and speed of the puma."

"Such a belief could offer much comfort to people struggling to eke out a life in the rainforest," T'ukri replied.

"Indeed, that's the function of all such beliefs. What do you think? Could such a temple exist?" Victor pressed.

T'ukri shrugged. "Many things could exist, Dr. Itoua. Whether they do is another question entirely."

"Are you going to help us or not?" Jordan broke in, clearly losing patience with the delicate diplomatic dance. Victor didn't roll his eyes. A little good cop/bad cop never hurt. He'd maintain that role for as long as it was useful.

"As long as you understand any search runs the risk of failure, I will guide you into the rainforest."

"Good enough for me," Jordan said.

"We'll need today to prepare supplies, but we could leave as early as tomorrow," Victor proposed.

"We leave in three days," T'ukri replied. "I have business to attend to before we go."

"Three days, then."

Victor excused himself, expecting Jordan to follow him so they could discuss tasks, gear, and more, but he stayed where he was, gaze locked with T'ukri's. Victor turned back to the two men. "Harris, we need to decide who's packing what and if we're leaving anything behind."

Jordan waited a moment longer before turning on his heel and stalking toward Victor, who continued on to his hut and waited for Jordan to join him inside.

"Well?" Victor asked when they were alone.

"He definitely knows more than he's letting on," Jordan said. "We need to know what 'business' he has to take care of."

"Don't let him catch you," Victor cautioned.

Jordan scoffed. "Like he could. Even people who are worried about being followed only look to the side and behind them. Nobody ever thinks to look up."

"We aren't in the US anymore," Victor reminded him. "There are plenty of dangers lurking in the trees. People here *do* look up."

"Even if he does, he'll never see me," Jordan repeated.

"All right, but be careful."

"I know the drill, doc. And I'm always careful."

He tossed a sketchy salute and stepped back outside. Within moments he'd faded into the bush, and even knowing where he'd gone, Victor couldn't track him. He shook his head and turned back to his own gear to sort everything out before he packed.

T'UKRI STAYED where he was until Itoua and Harris were out of sight. They had played their hand subtly, but they had shown enough. It remained to be seen whether they knew more than they had already said and whether they had ulterior motives in seeking the temple where the guardian lived. They had not used either name for the guardian—not Chapaqpuma as he was properly known nor the colloquial Philli-philli from the cat ears that manifested along with the fangs, claws, thicker muscles, strength, and flexibility of the puma. Nor had they called the goddess by name or even given away that they knew it was a goddess who had blessed T'ukri's people—and indeed, it was not the cat goddess but Pachamama, the goddess of the Earth, to whom they owed their allegiance—but they had heard enough to ask some of the right questions.

He would watch them as they traveled, and only then would he decide what they might stumble across in the jungle. He could take them to any of a dozen places in varying states of decay, places his people had once inhabited and had abandoned for safer ground. They would see a culture lost to the mists of time, its guardian passed into legend. Or if they proved untrustworthy, they would see nothing at all, returning to this village safe but empty-handed. And if he found they had more nefarious purposes—he had heard rumors of terrorists, drug runners, and illegal miners in the area—well, the jungle had ways of protecting itself. T'ukri would not even have to raise a hand to ensure they did not return.

But if they proved themselves—*oh goddess, let them prove themselves*—they might find more than they had ever imagined.

And so might he.

Do not get ahead of yourself. Time will tell, and rushing now will change nothing in the end.

He had his own preparations to make if he intended to take them home. With a lightness to his step, he returned to his hut to prepare.

When he left the hut an hour later and headed back into the rainforest, the usual watchfulness settled around him, a heightened awareness of his surroundings that came from all his years living with the rainforest's vagaries and dangers. He was not surprised to feel the weight of a gaze on him. The woods were full of watchful creatures, but this one was different.

He smiled softly as he continued toward the spring-fed pool a few miles away from the river. He had succeeded in catching the malku's attention, it seemed. Good. Let him follow and watch and learn. It could only aid T'ukri's cause.

JORDAN CURSED silently as he followed T'ukri deeper into the rainforest. The man moved too damn fast. As good as Jordan was, T'ukri could lose him if he tried. Fortunately he didn't seem to have noticed Jordan's presence, making it easy enough for Jordan to follow.

He recognized the first part of T'ukri's path, having gone that way with the hunters more than once, but when he reached the stream that cut through the undergrowth as it gurgled down toward the river, T'ukri turned upstream instead of downstream. Taking extra care to note landmarks as he passed them in case T'ukri escaped him and Jordan had to make his way back alone, he followed where T'ukri led until they reached the source of the stream. Jordan found a stable perch at the fork of two branches where the foliage hid him but was sparse enough to give him a decent view of what T'ukri was doing.

He nearly fell from his seat when T'ukri loosened the rope holding his pants up and dropped them to the ground, giving Jordan the perfect view of a fucking perfect ass. *Holy shit.* He'd known T'ukri was attractive—he had eyes, thank you very much—but he hadn't expected that ass beneath the loose pants or wrap T'ukri wore in the village. Now he wondered what else the man was hiding.

And thank fucking Jesus, he was going to find out. T'ukri chose that moment to turn sideways just enough to show Jordan his profile. His long, naked, perfect profile with his thick, half-erect cock sticking straight out from his body.

Mouth dry, Jordan worked his tongue to try to draw up some saliva, wishing as he did that he was sucking something else instead. T'ukri stepped forward into the water, and even at a distance, Jordan could see the goose bumps puckering his skin, but the cold water didn't do a thing to his erection.

What must he be thinking of not to soften at all? Jordan would put money on him thinking about Victor. That always got Jordan hot and bothered, and nothing short of bleeding out could kill his hard-on then. Fucking cat, dragging him all the way out into the fucking jungle to do nothing more than fucking bathe. Jordan was totally getting him back for this. He didn't know how yet, but he'd find a way.

To add insult to injury, T'ukri dove gracefully into the water without a care in the world, when Jordan had done well to have a sponge bath since arriving because everyone from Victor to the village children warned him not to go in any body of water deeper than a puddle for fear of what might be lurking beneath the surface. It'd serve T'ukri right if he got eaten by an anaconda. Or a black caiman. Or something equally big and deadly. Except that would make Victor sad. With a sigh, Jordan nocked an arrow, ready to shoot if anything threatened T'ukri's safety.

For the moment, though, the only thing disturbing the pool was T'ukri himself, his body cutting cleanly through the water as he surfaced and then dove once more, giving Jordan another view of his ass as it cleared the water only to disappear again beneath the surface.

The fucker was taunting him. Never mind that he didn't know Jordan was there. It was the only explanation. He was determined to kill Jordan with the world's worst case of blue balls so he could have Victor all to himself. *Well, fuck that.* Jordan had withstood far worse torture than watching a gorgeous man swim without cracking. He still had the burn scars from his father's cigarettes to prove it. He'd survive this too.

After playing in the water a bit longer, T'ukri waded to the shallows and sat down on a rock near the edge of the pool. He pulled some sort of plant Jordan didn't recognize from the pocket of his pants and began scrubbing at his skin with it, humming tunelessly as he did.

Jordan's gaze tracked the motion of T'ukri's hands as he paid attention to every inch of his skin, from the tips of his ears down to the tips of his toes. He set the crushed leaves aside and retrieved fresh ones—different ones? Jordan's couldn't tell for sure—from his pocket. Jordan nearly gave himself away when T'ukri shredded the leaves between his hands and then carefully rubbed them over his cock and balls. He didn't seem interested in getting off, though he took his time before he moved on… to roll onto his knees, ass toward Jordan, spread his cheeks, and rub over *and then into* his hole with the stuff. The fucking fucker was fingering himself open right in Jordan's line of sight!

Oh, the bastard was in for it. And he didn't even stop at one finger. No, he worked all the way up to three. Jordan didn't know what was in that plant, but from the sounds T'ukri was making, he was feeling no pain. Finally satisfied—okay, not satisfied, his cock was as hard as ever, but finished—T'ukri pulled his fingers free and waded back into the water until he was waist deep. He splashed water over his face and chest, washing away any bits of the plant that remained, then returned to his rock and sat down facing Jordan. He shifted a few times to get comfortable, rested his hands on his thighs, and closed his eyes.

He was either the ballsiest fucker on the continent or he was too stupid to live. Or both. No, definitely both. Anything could come out of the jungle. Jordan would bet a year's salary all the local wildlife used this as a watering hole. With his luck, there was a cougar just out of sight, waiting for an easy snack, and there T'ukri was, serving himself up on a silver platter. Or worse, some of the criminals Nandini had warned him about. And Jordan was going to have to be the one to rush in and save him, blowing his cover. *Fuck that.* Victor would just have to come up with an explanation. Jordan was so over it he couldn't even see it behind him anymore, whatever it was to begin with.

He was demanding hazard pay for this.

CHAPTER 8

BY THE time Jordan made it back to the village that evening, he was hot, hungry, and horny. And the only thing he could do anything about was to eat. Even if he went back to his hut, he'd run out of lube a week ago and couldn't justify the trek back to civilization for more. He'd known the expedition would be long, but he hadn't expected the constant provocation. Victor cocked an eyebrow at him when he slipped into camp a few minutes behind T'ukri, but Jordan just shook his head. He'd tell Victor what he'd seen later, but if he had to do it now, he'd come in his pants, and that was more humiliation than he could deal with at the moment.

T'ukri had said three days. If this was only day one, he didn't even want to think about the next two days. If he had to watch a repeat of today two more times, he'd explode for sure.

He made it through dinner and the evening festivities— apparently having T'ukri there merited more than one night of dancing and drinking—without cracking, but he couldn't meet T'ukri's eyes either. Not when all he could see each time he looked at the man was him on his knees with three fingers in his ass.

When the village quieted for the night, Jordan left his hut for Victor's again, not sure if he hoped Victor would be fully dressed, down to his underwear, or somewhere in between. He didn't know how much more he could take without losing it.

Fortunately for his sanity, Victor was still dressed when Jordan slipped beneath the cloth that covered the entrance and provided him with some privacy.

"Well?" Victor said.

"He went out to a pond north of here, spent a while swimming, then meditated until it started to get dark."

"That's… anticlimactic," Victor said.

Jordan groaned at the unintentional pun.

"Harris?"

"Trust me. You don't want to know."

"Just tell me, Harris."

Jordan huffed and crossed his arms defensively over his chest. "When he was finished swimming, he used some kind of a plant to... well, if it'd been soap, I'd say he took a bath. A very thorough, very personal bath."

Victor blinked slowly, his face so carefully blank that Jordan knew he was trying not to laugh. "Harris."

"Fine. I sat in that fucking tree and watched him jerk it for a bit, then work himself open with three fingers. I gotta say, sir. He's got a damn fine ass."

"Your opinion is noted, Harris."

"Don't give me that, Itoua. You're the one who pressed for details."

Victor pursed his lips slightly. "And then he spent the rest of the day meditating, you said?"

"Yeah, the only thing missing was the chanting. Seriously, doc, cross-legged on a rock, hands on his thighs, eyes closed, didn't move for the rest of the day. And stark naked the whole time. Whatever he was thinking about made him pretty damn happy too. He stayed at least half hard the entire time. Never known a guy who could have even a partial stiffy for that long without getting off, but when it started to get dark, he just stood up and got dressed like he didn't even notice and came back here like he didn't have a care in the world."

"Are you suggesting you couldn't have ignored an inconvenient erection when you were in the Marines?" Victor asked.

"If I'm focused on a target, I'm not thinking about anything likely to give me an erection," Jordan retorted.

"Not even when your target is a stunningly attractive man pleasuring himself in front of you?" Victor challenged.

"Fuck you. That was uncalled for."

"Somehow I don't think I'm the one you want to be fucking," Victor replied.

Jordan flushed and looked away, though he hoped Victor wouldn't notice the sudden heat on his cheeks in the flickering light of the oil lamp. Victor didn't talk that way. No, it was all *attractive man pleasuring himself*, never *fuck* or anything that coarse. He never blinked at Jordan's language, but he also never changed his own word choices. Jordan had always assumed it was a second-language issue.

He was more careful when speaking a language he didn't know well than when speaking English, not that anything but a slight accent remained in Victor's speech most of the time. Hearing him talk that way now shouldn't have left Jordan hard and aching in his pants, but damn if he could stop the reaction. "Like you'd lower yourself to fuck trailer trash like me anyway."

VICTOR FROZE, not even the mixed emotions of having admitted his desires enough to distract from that last retort. Jordan couldn't have just said what Victor thought he said. "First of all, you aren't trailer trash. We've had this conversation, and you know how I feel about you putting yourself down. Secondly, why would you presume to know the first thing about my taste in bed partners?"

He could feel Jordan's glare like a tangible thing even in the dim light. "Because I know you, *Victor*. You wear suits that cost more than I make in a month. You're a classy guy who could have anyone."

Victor swallowed hard. This was an opening he never thought he'd have in a conversation he'd never believed would happen. Now that it had, he couldn't let it pass. All the reasons to hold his tongue meant nothing in the face of Jordan's self-doubt. "And if I told you I wanted you?"

"I'd ask who you were and what you'd done with Dr. Itoua."

Victor's heart broke for the abused boy who couldn't believe anyone would want him. He shouldn't do this. They'd both be out of a job, and Victor, at least, would have a mark on his record that would keep him from ever working in a university again, which would mean losing his visa and having to return to France and accept that his parents had been right when they told him he was wasting his time on a dead-end career. But he could hear the defiant hurt in Jordan's voice, even if he couldn't see it in his eyes in the low light. He'd seen it before in other contexts, situations he couldn't control. This one, he could. Squaring his shoulders, he took a step forward until he was toe-to-toe with Jordan, so close they were breathing the same air.

"Then you don't know me nearly as well as you think you do." Before he could second-guess himself more, he leaned forward and brushed his lips over Jordan's. They were rough, chapped from a day in the rainforest with too much sun and not enough water, but nothing had ever felt so good.

Jordan gasped against his mouth, the puff of air all the more erotic for being real, not some fevered imagining.

"Victor?" Jordan's voice broke on the word.

"Yes, it's me," Victor whispered, not moving back. He'd started this. He wouldn't push any harder, but he wouldn't be the one to move away. If Jordan wanted this to stop, he could step back. Victor refused to be yet another man to let him down.

Jordan grabbed Victor's hips and pulled him closer, initiating another kiss, which Victor returned gladly. They might have stood there all night, making out, if it weren't for the sudden scream of one of the pumas that hunted in the jungle around the village. They startled apart, staring at each other with wide eyes.

"Don't say this was a mistake," Jordan begged, the vulnerability on his face and in his voice making Victor want to find everyone who had ever hurt him and kill them with great prejudice. He didn't consider himself a violent man, but some provocations deserved that strong a response.

"It's not a mistake." Victor took Jordan's hand and drew him toward the two stools by the little table that held the lamp. "But we do need to talk about this."

"Aw, Victor," Jordan whined. "I suck at talking."

"I know, but this is important." Jordan still looked grumpy as a cat in water, but he sat down, never letting go of Victor's hand.

"Talk, then."

"Have you thought about this?" Victor asked. "I mean, thought about what it will mean. I'm your supervisor. Fowler would have no choice but to fire us if he found out."

Jordan shrugged. "And? My life is full of screwups already. One more won't change anything."

"Jordan," Victor chided. "At least pretend you're taking this seriously. If I lose my job without another one lined up, I could lose my visa and have to leave the US."

"I am," Jordan said. Victor's face must have betrayed his disbelief, because Jordan leaned forward and squeezed Victor's hand more tightly in his. "No, really, doc, I am. Look, we all know I'm dispensable. You're the one with the PhD and the grants and all the rest. If Fowler starts to suspect, I'll just resign. You won't have to leave."

"That's hardly fair to you," Victor protested. "What about your career? Your degree? Your dreams?"

"Are you telling me we can't do this?" Jordan asked. "Because if you are, then why'd you kiss me in the first place?"

"I'm telling you we have to be careful," Victor corrected. "We can't just rush into this without thinking it through."

"You say that like I haven't thought about this a thousand times," Jordan replied. "And okay, we weren't usually in the jungle in my fantasies, but that doesn't change the important part."

"I wasn't talking about fantasies." Although he'd be most interested in discussing them later, because a thousand times.... Not even in his wildest imaginings had he considered that Jordan might be somewhere thinking the same about him. "I was talking about our lives. About how to do this in a way that's fair to both of us."

Jordan groaned. "I'd much rather talk about sex."

Victor huffed a sharp laugh. "Talking is all we could do. I didn't exactly plan this, so I don't have supplies. And even if I did, you deserve more than a hard bedroll in a hut in the middle of the Amazon. You deserve a soft mattress and softer sheets—"

"Yeah, stop right there," Jordan said. "I've never had those things in my life. I don't care if I have them now."

"All the more reason for you to get them," Victor insisted. "But we're in the middle of an expedition. We can't afford to be distracted right now. When we get back from the trip into the rainforest with T'ukri, we'll go into town for a few days and do this right."

"I'm not gonna be able to wait that long to kiss you again," Jordan said.

Victor smiled. "I didn't say anything about kissing. As long as we're discreet, I don't see that being a problem. It's not like the people here are going to tell Fowler about us."

"Does that mean I can stay here tonight? Just to sleep," Jordan said. "I can get up early and go back to my own hut so no one suspects anything. Please?"

Jordan so rarely asked for anything that Victor could only nod. "Just to sleep."

Jordan grinned at him brightly, toed off his boots, and flopped down on Victor's bedroll.

"Are you really going to sleep fully dressed?" Victor dropped his hand to the button of his pants. "I'm going to feel underdressed."

Jordan stripped down to his boxer briefs—no T-shirt—so fast Victor almost missed it. They were revisiting that too, when they had time and leisure. All that golden skin—and the dark ink of the Marine Corps tattoo on his left shoulder—in front of him deserved to be appreciated inch by smooth inch as Victor unveiled it to his sight and touch.

Sleep now, he reminded himself. *Sex later.*

That was going to be easier said than done, but the moment he lay down, Jordan settled in on his shoulder like he'd always slept there, slung one arm around Victor's middle, and dropped off.

Jordan had always dozed off quickly, a soldier's ability to rest anytime, anywhere, but it had always been dozing, not deep, restful sleep. Yet here, in Victor's arms, he appeared to be soundly asleep. Even when Victor shifted and pressed a kiss to the top of Jordan's head, he did nothing more than mumble a little and pull Victor closer. The trust inherent in that gesture left Victor boggling and swearing to always be worthy of it.

CHAPTER 9

JORDAN WOKE the next morning in the best mood he'd been in...
maybe ever. He hadn't slept that deeply since they left the US, which
was a nice change in and of itself, but *holy fuck*, he'd slept with Victor.
Okay, fine, only in the literal sense, but he'd *slept with Victor fucking
Itoua*! Nothing could bring him down this morning, not even if he had
to spend another day watching T'ukri play with himself in the jungle.
He had something so much better than that stupid cat to come home
to that he wouldn't even have to think before saying no if T'ukri saw
him and invited him to join in. No matter how sweet his ass looked, it
would never be worth as much as a single smile from Victor.

Victor blinked awake and smiled at Jordan.

Nope, not worth more than this.

Then Victor pulled him down into a kiss, and all thoughts of
T'ukri and his magnificent ass evaporated like mist.

"I wasn't dreaming," Jordan said when they separated.

"Only if I was too," Victor replied, still smiling. Jordan probably
should've been freaked out at the smile, but they weren't at the
university, even if they were on a university-approved sabbatical, and
there was no one around to see Victor with his guard down. Jordan
could get used to that smile. Even better, he could get used to knowing
he was the only one who got to see it.

Jordan dropped another kiss on Victor's lips and settled back
with his head on Victor's shoulder. "I suppose we should get up before
we get caught," he said against Victor's neck.

"Or before T'ukri leaves on whatever business he has today,"
Victor replied.

Jordan groaned. "Maybe we'll get lucky and his business today
will be in the village. I really don't want to spend another day stuck in
a tree while he sits there doing next to nothing."

Victor chuckled. "It didn't sound like nothing to me."

"Yeah, well, the bath/playing with himself portion took about an
hour. The rest of the time, he sat there doing nothing." Except being

naked and half-hard and incredibly distracting, but that was yesterday, when Jordan still thought he had a snowball's chance in hell of catching Victor's eye. Now that he knew otherwise, he didn't want to move farther than arm's length from Victor's side.

Except Jordan was a professional, and while he might not *want* to move, it wouldn't stop him from doing his job.

"It does make me wonder what the point of it was," Victor said. "If he didn't know you were there, then he wasn't trying to seduce or distract you, so why put on a show like that? Unless it wasn't a show but a ritual of some kind?"

"How the hell should I know? You're the one with all the background on Andean subcultures, not me," Jordan replied.

"You're the one who was there," Victor countered. "Think about it today if you can. Beyond the obvious, did he do anything that might give you a clue as to his reasoning?"

Jordan tried to think back, but all he could see was T'ukri working himself open. "I'll think about it, doc, but nothing's coming to mind right now."

"Maybe today will give you some new ideas, especially if you're watching him with that in mind. I'll bring up the subject with the elders if I can find a way to do it, but since no one knows you followed T'ukri—and might consider it an affront if they did—I'm not sure how far I'll get with questions along that path."

Jordan groaned. "I really hope it's not a repeat of yesterday. I've got better things to do than stare at his ass."

"Like what?" Victor asked in his "really, Harris?" voice.

Jordan couldn't stop his grin. Victor had walked right into that one. "Like stare at yours."

Victor patted him on the hip. "Get moving, Harris. You aren't going to learn anything staring at my ass. You can do that during your off hours."

Jordan groped Victor's ass in retaliation. "I'm going to hold you to that."

He pushed up to sitting and turned right, then left, stretching his back. When he rolled onto his knees to stand, Victor groped him back. "I'd rather you hold me to this."

The image of himself on his knees, much as T'ukri had been the day before, with Victor behind him flashed through him, making his elbows tremble. "Fuck. Are you sure we have to wait? I swear all my bloodwork is negative, and you can take me with just spit. I don't need much prep. Just slick yourself up and go slow."

"*Ma foi*, you'd tempt a saint." Victor slipped his hand between Jordan's legs and fondled his balls. "But we can't. We don't know what business T'ukri has today, and we can't let him slip through our fingers. He's our only lead."

Jordan moaned and sank down to his elbows as he spread his legs wider to leave more space for Victor's big hand. "Your mouth is saying *no*, but your hands are saying *yes*. You aren't taking advantage when I'm begging. Even if you won't fuck me, have some mercy and get me off."

"If we lose track of T'ukri today because of this…."

Jordan nearly broke, ready to hump the bedroll to get some relief when he realized Victor was rolling to his knees as well.

"I'll track him, I swear," Jordan promised. "Just do it already."

Victor grabbed Jordan's hips and shoved him over onto his back. "I'm not fucking you with just spit, but neither of us can concentrate like this." He snugged one thigh between Jordan's, right up against his balls, and lowered his weight so their cocks rubbed together through their clothes.

Victor felt huge and heavy and so fucking good against him. Jordan bucked his hips in time with Victor's movements. He wanted to strip his boxers off and do the same with Victor's briefs, but he'd already pushed. He didn't want to push so far that Victor backed off. Instead he worked his hand under the back of Victor's undershirt. As good as the skin-to-skin contact felt along their legs, he wanted more. He wanted it all, if Victor would give it to him, but for now, he'd take what he could get—Victor's weight pressing him into the ground, Victor's thigh giving him something to grind against, Victor's strong back beneath his hands, and Victor's mouth sucking on his like he needed it to breathe.

His whole body throbbed with the need to come, but he didn't want it to be over yet. Even knowing they'd have a next time, that this hardly even counted as a first time, he wanted it to last. His body, primed by weeks of proximity, all of yesterday's provocation, and a night of sleeping in Victor's arms, had other ideas, though. His balls drew up hard and he was coming between one breath and the next, his shout lost in Victor's mouth.

"Oh *merde*," Victor groaned, his breath hot against Jordan's lips. "I knew it'd be good with you, but I never thought—" He broke off as he jerked hard against Jordan, his face contorting with passion as he climaxed.

The sight was nearly enough to get Jordan hard again.

Victor lay there panting for several minutes before he levered himself up and rolled to the side. He reached for Jordan's hand as he did, keeping it in a tight grip.

"At least we finally convinced Kichka we didn't need the village women to do our laundry," Jordan quipped.

"I'm sure they've seen semen stains before," Victor observed dryly.

"I thought you didn't want anyone knowing about us." Jordan rolled to his side so he could see Victor's expression. His eyes were closed and his face smooth of any tension.

"Who are they going to tell? And it's not a question of what I want, Jordan." Victor opened his eyes and turned his head so their gazes met directly. "If I had my way, I would tell anyone and everyone that we're together. I'm not ashamed of you, so get that thought out of your head right now. The *only* reason I'm worried about people finding out is because of our jobs, but if it's a choice between you and my career, you'd win, hands down. If we can find a way to have both, that would be my preference, because I believe in the value of what we're studying, but I've earned something for myself too."

Jordan swallowed hard at Victor's blunt declaration. That sounded like a lot more than just fucking. Sure, Victor had talked about a soft mattress, about Jordan having what he deserved, but it had all been about sex, not about more. This, though… if he let himself think, it sounded a lot more like weekends spent together snuggling on the couch with takeout pizza and cheap beer, like a real relationship—not that Jordan knew what that looked like outside of TV shows and books. Still, he knew Victor's situation, knew that his job at the university meant more than just a paycheck. It meant staying in the US and continuing his research as opposed to facing potential deportation.

"Would Fowler agree?" Jordan asked.

"Fowler has been looking for a reason to fire me for years," Victor said. "According to him, my Philli-philli obsession is an embarrassment to the university. He'd love nothing more than for me to come back from this sabbatical and tender my resignation. I'd prefer not to give him that satisfaction, but I will if I have to."

"I'll leave that up to you," Jordan said. "Just warn me before you say anything to him so I can be prepared."

"Of course I will," Victor exclaimed. "We're in this together, whatever happens, okay? I'll do my best not to spring anything on you."

And that right there was the best thing Jordan had ever heard. "Deal."

T'UKRI WOKE well before dawn on the second day of his ritual preparations. If he were at home, he would have left as soon as he could, but here in Paucar's village, the laws of hospitality overrode the demands of the ritual. The goddess and the ancestors would understand.

Still, he could not sit idly in his hut, waiting for the sun to rise above the horizon and the villagers to stir. Today he would hunt, but his weapons were prepared, the traditional spear sharp, so they needed no attention. Restless, he left his hut to pace along the edge of the village, stretching his senses to full awareness. Perhaps he would catch a trace of likely game. He would settle for a capybara if that was all he could find, but he hoped for a mountain tapir or even a deer. The larger the game, the greater the proof of his hunting prowess and his worthiness as a mate.

As he patrolled the perimeter, he heard the stirring of small forest creatures, mice and insects, hedgehogs and hummingbirds, but nothing to lead him toward larger game. He continued his circuit, light enough on his feet not to leave more than the slightest rustle of leaves behind him. He was no longer the guide or the prince; he was a predator, already on the hunt even before he left the confines of the village.

Then a different scent reached his nose, one that drew him even more strongly than the scent of prey. He stalked closer to Itoua's hut, following the tantalizing musk that emanated from it. On edge as he was, he forced himself to stop a discreet distance away. Without mates to pull him back, he could not afford to lose the thread of his humanity, but he gorged himself on the mingled scent of the two he desired.

Harris would follow him again today, he was sure of it, and he would prove his abilities. Itoua would not see it, but Harris would tell him about it. Whatever their motivation for going into the rainforest, they were partners, and T'ukri did not see them keeping secrets from one another.

He lingered as long and as close as he dared, until he was glutted with their scent and the village had begun to stir. Only then did he slip away to join Paucar for the morning meal.

Harris wandered up when he was about halfway done, looking in a better mood than T'ukri had seen him since he arrived. He would remember that if they agreed to his suit—sex was a good way to soothe his mate. When Itoua joined them, the closeness between them was nearly tangible. They had always stood easily near each other, but something had changed overnight. T'ukri would have given much to know what, but he would bide his time. He had to finish his ritual preparations before he could act on his desires, and then he would have days or even weeks in the rainforest with them to discover everything he needed to know.

He took his time finishing his breakfast until he saw that Harris had finished his as well. Harris would not realize it, but T'ukri could show himself considerate as well as capable of providing for a family. When he bowed to Paucar and excused himself for a hunt, he caught the hint of a smile on the old man's face.

"Shall I send warriors to accompany you?" he asked in Runasimi.

T'ukri glanced toward Itoua and Harris, but they did not appear to be listening. "They understand little of our language—Quechua as they call it," Paucar continued. "Not enough to understand our discussion."

"Thank you for your offer, honored father, but this is a hunt I must undertake alone," T'ukri replied in the same language.

"Are you sure?" Paucar asked. "They are not of your tribe, not even of our people."

"And yet they call to me as no others have ever done," T'ukri said. "I will not rush into anything, but if they show themselves worthy, then they are my choice."

"They are good men, as far as we have seen," Paucar told him. "Harris is always ready to help with the hunting, and Itoua spends his time with the elders, listening to our stories and learning from them. It is only that they do not know our ways."

"If they wish, they can learn, and if they do not wish, then all will be as it has always been," T'ukri replied with a shrug. "The ways of the goddess are many and the paths visible to few."

"May she bless you on your hunt," Paucar intoned.

T'ukri bowed in thanks before gathering his spear and knife from his hut. He did not bother changing into the clothes he usually wore in the rainforest. When he was out of sight of the village, he would strip and complete this hunt as the goddess intended.

He took his time as he walked toward the pool where he had completed the ritual cleansing yesterday, senses attuned to the jungle as he listened for any sign of Harris following him. His malku was good, he would give him that. If T'ukri had been anyone else, he would not have known he was there. When he reached the pool, he stripped and folded his loincloth, keeping only a thin leather strap with the sheath for his knife. He would hunt with the spear, but he could not complete the final step in the ritual without a knife.

Stepping into the pool, he poured a handful of water over his head, a quick evocation of the purification ritual he had completed the day before, cleansing himself inside and out, physically and mentally, so that he would come to the rest of the goddess's rituals—and eventually his bonding bed—free from doubt and regret. He shook the droplets from his hair and eyes, took up his spear, and studied the bank of the stream for signs of prey.

On bare feet he followed the tributary until he found the distinctive hoofprints that marked the presence of deer. After fading into the underbrush, he crouched down and waited. Time stretched as he held position, and his senses narrowed to the wind in the trees around him, the smell of rain in the air, and the stark awareness of a pair of eyes on his back. He did not preen beneath the gaze, though he wanted to. Instead he focused on his appointed task—to prove his prowess as a hunter so that his desired mates might deem him worthy of their attention.

Eventually his patience was rewarded when a large stag came warily to the stream. T'ukri readied his spear but waited until the animal relaxed enough to lower its head to drink. He launched the spear with all the force he could muster, grunting with the effort. The deer started to lift its head, but the spear caught it right in the eye.

T'ukri leaped forward as it fell to drag the carcass to the bank. Giving silent thanks to the animal for its sacrifice, he pulled the knife from his belt and slit its throat. He would roast the heart over the fire tonight, but first he had to complete the ritual. He dipped his fingers into the pool of blood and painted down the bridge of his nose, an acknowledgment of the enhanced sense of smell that aided him in the hunt. He added another line beneath each of his ears, in thanks for the acute hearing of the great jungle cats. A circle around each of his eyes was testament to the sharpness of his vision that allowed him to notice the smallest shift in the leaves that might signify danger. He dipped his hand fully in the pool of blood and placed it over his heart, signifying his desire for a mate. Finally he drew lines down the cuts of muscle along his hips, arrowing inward toward his groin, a request for stamina and virility when the time came for him to claim his mates.

He bowed his head once more in gratitude for all the goddess's blessings. Then he grasped the legs of his kill and heaved it onto his shoulders. His legs trembled beneath the weight until he locked his knees and steadied himself. This was as much of a test as the kill itself. Had he been with a hunting party, they would have strung the beast from a pole and carried it over the shoulders of four or five men, rotating among the party so no one suffered undue strain, but T'ukri was alone and preparing himself for his mates. He would bring the deer back through sheer force of will or not at all. He took one graceless step, caught his balance, and took another, drawing on the reserves of strength and stamina he rarely touched. He was T'ukri, son of Huallpa, Yuri, and Llipya, chosen by the goddess to take his father's place as Chapaqpuma and eventually as their king. The weight of a deer was nothing next to the weight of those responsibilities. If he wished to be worthy of his name, he would do this. Failure was not an option.

"Pachamama, lend me your strength," he breathed as he made his way back toward the village. Later he would return for his clothes, but until his prey was delivered to the village—to his mates, though they would not see it as such—he would remain as he was, marked only by the blood of a successful hunt and the signs of the goddess. Itoua and Harris would not understand, but the rest of the village would know and bear witness in the absence of members of his own tribe.

He strode into the village center to the excited shouts of the children and the cheers of the older boys who had started imagining their own coming-of-age ceremonies. He hefted the deer off his shoulders and let it fall to the ground. "The hunt was successful. The goddess grants her blessing," he said in Runasimi.

"Seen and witnessed," Paucar and Kichka intoned.

CHAPTER 10

VICTOR HAD seen many wondrous and unbelievable things in his career. It was to be expected from a life spent studying other cultures. He might have even gone so far as to consider himself immune to them now, but that was before he watched T'ukri stride back into the village completely naked but for a leather belt, carrying a deer that had to weigh more than twice what T'ukri did.

His analytical mind cataloged the shape and location of the bloody marks on T'ukri's skin, too neat to be from injuries and too precise to be accidental, while the more mortal side of his attention fixated on T'ukri in all his naked glory. The way the villagers crowded around him and the reaction of the village elders when T'ukri dropped the deer clearly indicated actions of significance, but Victor hadn't seen anything like it from the other villagers since their arrival.

Then T'ukri looked in Victor's direction, meeting his gaze boldly, before nodding and turning toward his hut, giving Victor an equally unfettered view of his backside. Jordan had told Victor T'ukri had an ass on him. He hadn't doubted Jordan's assessment, but seeing it for himself… Jordan might have understated the situation.

Victor might have been embarrassed to be caught staring, but T'ukri's brazen manner had invited his gaze, sought it out almost. Jordan's insistence that T'ukri was interested in him floated through his memory, but that couldn't be right. What about him could possibly interest T'ukri? He'd be leaving eventually, yet everything about the display suggested the hunt today was a courting ritual. He shook his head and went to find Jordan. Maybe he'd seen something that would shed more light on whatever that had been just now.

"See something you like?" Jordan asked the moment Victor stepped into his hut.

Victor didn't startle. He'd trained that reflex out of himself years ago, but his heartrate picked up a little at the sudden spike of adrenaline.

"It was a little hard not to notice," Victor replied dryly.

"Now you see what I had to deal with all day yesterday and today." Jordan reeled Victor in for a kiss, which Victor gave gladly. Yes, T'ukri was nice to look at, but that was all it was. An attractive body wrapped up in an anthropological mystery. Jordan was just as attractive and with so much more to offer as well.

"What happened today?" Victor asked when they separated.

"He went hunting," Jordan replied.

"I figured that much out on my own. Details, Jordan."

Jordan settled on one of the stools and rubbed his hand through his hair. It was starting to get long. Any time now, Jordan would take a razor to it, if past experience was any indication, which was too bad in Victor's opinion. He liked Jordan's hair a little on the long side.

"He left camp with a spear and a bowie knife, although I'm sure that's not what he'd call it, and went out to the same pool as yesterday," Jordan narrated. "He poured water over himself, but didn't bathe per se, and then he took the spear and the knife and headed out, completely naked. I know I told you I could track him if he left before I was ready, but now I'm not sure I could have. He doesn't move through the forest so much as he becomes the forest."

"How so?" The description intrigued Victor. He'd have to watch once they began their trek with T'ukri to see if he noticed the same thing.

"Even with the hunters from the village, there's some sign we've passed. A broken twig, a footprint in mud, a string caught on a stray twig, something. But with T'ukri, there wasn't any of that. And okay, sure, no string from his clothes since he wasn't wearing any, but he moved so lightly, so fluidly that he didn't leave any indication he'd been through there. If I'd lost him even for a second, I doubt I'd have been able to find him again," Jordan said.

Victor thought back to his military service and the tricks they'd been taught to pass unseen, but Jordan was right. The training was all about erasing the signs of their passage, because leaving some sign in the first place was inevitable.

"So he went hunting," Victor prompted.

"Yeah, he finally found a likely spot—I could see animal tracks, decent sized by the depth of them in the mud—and settled down to wait. He'd make a damn good sniper." Coming from Jordan, that was high praise indeed. "Once he found his spot, he didn't move until the deer showed up, and when he finally made his move, he threw that spear straight into its eye. Killed it instantly. I could've done the same with the bow in my sleep, but to throw a spear that hard at that distance takes some muscle as well as skill."

"Could you have done it with the spear?" Victor asked, not because he doubted Jordan's skills but because if Jordan said no and T'ukri had managed it, then Victor wanted to know how.

"I could've hit the target. I honestly don't know if I could've gotten the spear that deep, though," Jordan replied. "It was several inches in, and I got the feeling it didn't go deeper because it hit the other side of the animal's skull."

T'ukri didn't look like he could match Jordan for pure physical strength, but looks could be deceiving. "Go on."

"So he kills the thing, drags it out of the water, and slits its throat. He said something I didn't understand, and I don't think it was in the same variant of Quechua they speak in the village either, and then he started painting blood on himself."

"In what order?"

Jordan frowned. "He started with the nose for sure, then I think it was the ears before the eyes. The handprint on his chest was after he was done with his face, and then those damn lines pointing straight at his dick. When that was done, he picked the carcass up like it didn't weigh much of anything and carried it all the way back here draped over his shoulders. That motherfucker had to weigh three hundred pounds, and yeah, I can squat that or even carry it a short distance, but that wasn't a short distance. And then he strode into the village, cool as you please, and dropped it at Paucar's feet like a tribute."

"I saw that part," Victor said. "I also heard what he said."

"Did you understand it?" Jordan asked, sounding surprised.

"No, I haven't suddenly learned that much Quechua overnight, but the way he spoke and the elders replied suggests they're aware of what he's doing and why, and that it has some kind of significance. Markings like he put on his face and body aren't random. And to do it in blood from a deer he hunted alone suggests a ritual hunt. The question is why. What purpose did the ritual serve? And does it tie into the bathing and meditation yesterday? And why would he need to do any of it before taking us into the rainforest?"

"Fuck, you're hot when you go all college professor on me," Jordan said.

Victor felt heat rising up his neck at the compliment, but he brazened it out. "Focus, Harris. We need to figure this out."

Jordan snorted. "I spent the day watching a super hot guy do super hot things completely naked, and now I'm here with an even hotter guy who's doing even hotter things, and you expect me to concentrate?"

"Don't patronize me," Victor ground out. He had no trouble imagining Jordan's reaction to T'ukri hunting—he'd had his own reaction to watching the man return with his kill—but that was no reason for Jordan to make fun of him. Once Victor might have been able to squat something as heavy as the deer, but he hadn't kept it up, not at that level of fitness. Not to mention the graying hair.

Jordan was suddenly up in his face, pulling Victor's hips to slot against his own. "I know what I find attractive in a man," he informed Victor, "and while T'ukri's pretty damn sexy, it takes more than animal magnetism to draw me in. And before you say it, who got me off without even getting me naked this morning, hmm? It wasn't him, believe me. I am right where I want to be with exactly who I want to be with. I find you incredibly attractive, and I always have. And you don't get to tell me I don't."

"I still don't know what you're doing with an old man like me," Victor muttered.

"Last I checked, I was trying to have a relationship with you," Jordan said. "One that will hopefully involve lots of smoking-hot sex and plenty of nights spent curled up around each other too. And meals and teasing and watching TV and drinking beer and whatever else either of us decides to do when we have time off. I want that, Victor. T'ukri's hot. I'm not going to deny that, and if you weren't in the picture, I might take him up on what he's waving around, but you *are* in the picture. I don't want a casual fuck with a stranger when I have a chance at a relationship with you."

Victor couldn't help himself. He had to follow that declaration with another kiss. Jordan could have anyone he wanted, and yet he wanted Victor. He kept his hands on Jordan's shoulders—his fucking amazing shoulders—and stopped Jordan's hands when they would have wandered. "We still have to figure this out."

Jordan sighed. "So you think the marks have meaning beyond just showing he made a kill."

"Yes. They're too deliberately placed to just be splashing blood on himself," Victor said.

"Well, sight, smell, hearing, those are the senses most animals rely on when hunting, so it could be an acknowledgment of that," Jordan mused. "But that doesn't explain the handprint on his chest or the arrows on his hips."

"Obviously hunting is about eating, but this wasn't just a hunt. T'ukri went alone, and he brought back a huge animal, far more than one person could consume," Victor mused. "Probably more than the village could consume at once."

"So he has an ego problem," Jordan said.

"Or he was thanking the village for its hospitality, but if that was it, why go alone? He could join a troop of hunters like you've been doing. Unless he has something to prove?" Victor replied.

"Like what?" Jordan asked. "Nobody seemed surprised when he lugged that thing in here, so it's not like they doubted his abilities."

"No, but we might have if we hadn't seen it for ourselves," Victor said. "We're asking him to take us out into the rainforest. Maybe this is his way of proving to us that he's capable of doing the job."

"Not buying it," Jordan said with a shake of his head. "This is personal. The way he cleaned himself out and stretched himself yesterday, the way he painted himself with the blood. Whatever his reasons, they're deeper than that. They have to be. Why else would he go to all the trouble? We were ready to leave right away. He's the one who asked for the delay."

"Something personal, then," Victor mused. "Some sort of vision quest, maybe? Although that tends to be more associated with North American First Peoples than with South American tribes, unless the person is a shaman."

"We could try just asking him," Jordan suggested. "I mean, not telling him we've been spying on him, but just a casual observation about that being a big animal for one hunter and was there any reason he'd gone alone, or something like that."

"You think he'll tell us?"

"I don't know. It can't hurt to try. We've gotten answers to a lot of our questions since we've arrived."

"You're right. I saw T'ukri return, so I can ask the elders about it tomorrow. While we haven't seen any of the warriors here perform a similar ritual, Paucar and Kichka clearly knew what T'ukri was doing, so they're familiar with it. And we've only been here a few weeks. It might simply mean no one has needed to perform it yet. You could try asking T'ukri tonight if you get an opening as well. Casually."

"I can do casual, doc," Jordan said with a mock-hurt look on his face.

"As casual as a bull in a china shop," Victor muttered.

Jordan laughed, which had been Victor's goal. "I'm going to clean up and change before dinner tonight. I reek of the forest."

Victor was tempted to offer his help, but they couldn't afford to slip now, not when they finally had their first lead.

WHEN JORDAN came out of his own hut fifteen minutes later, in clean clothes and having wiped off the worst of the sweat, T'ukri had already reappeared. He'd tied a cloth around his hips again, but hanging much lower than usual so that the lines he'd drawn in his iliac creases were still visible.

Damn if that wasn't worse than him being naked. Now, with the cloth in the way, the lines hinted at the hidden power beneath the garment without revealing anything. Jordan shook his head at himself. He'd seen the guy naked multiple times now. There wasn't any mystery left. Or there shouldn't have been. And yet he struggled not to stare. He'd jokingly called it animal magnetism when he and Victor were talking about it earlier, but now he wondered if he should have made it a joke. T'ukri *oozed* sex, which made no sense. Jordan had seen him practically jerking himself off and fucking himself open with his fingers. If any moment should have left Jordan feeling stalked, it should have been that one, not T'ukri looking at him across the village grounds now.

Except T'ukri hadn't known Jordan was there then. Now he knew and was watching Jordan as pointedly as Jordan was watching him.

With a shrug, Jordan pulled up a piece of log next to where T'ukri fucking lounged, indolent and on display for anyone who bothered to look. Jordan shouldn't look. He should turn away and go back into the hut with Victor. He loved Victor, and he wanted Victor. This morning had proven that beyond any doubt. Yet here he was, fighting the urge to adjust himself in his pants because of T'ukri. Motherfucking, overweening cat. Preening like he owned the place and everyone had to bow down to his majesty. He had a thing or two to learn if he thought sex appeal alone was enough to distract Jordan. He had a job, and that was all that mattered. "That was a bigass buck you dragged in here. You hungry or something?"

T'ukri looked at him with an amused smile dancing around the corners of his mouth. "Or something. It seemed an appropriate offering to thank Paucar for his hospitality."

"Then what's with the blood?" Jordan asked. He meant to look at the marks on T'ukri's face. Really, he did. Except that those stupid fucking arrows on his abdomen were practically flashing at him. *Look at us*, they shouted. *Look at the tentpole he's not even trying to hide under the loincloth he's wearing.* He dragged his gaze back to T'ukri's face. "I've gone hunting with Paucar's warriors plenty of times, and I've never seen them do that before."

T'ukri's eyes flashed with something Jordan couldn't identify and would have missed if he hadn't been watching so closely. "I am not one of Paucar's warriors."

"You got me there." Jordan certainly hadn't had this kind of reaction to any of *them*. "Is it typical of your tribe?"

"Under certain circumstances," T'ukri said. "And before you ask, yes, this is one of those circumstances, Mr. Harris."

That didn't answer Jordan's question at all, but T'ukri's tone made it clear the subject was closed. With a shrug, Jordan leaned back on his elbows, hoping his own stiffy wasn't as obvious beneath the heavier fabric of his shorts. "We're about to spend who knows how long in the rainforest together. Think you could call me Jordan?"

T'ukri rose from his seat and turned the hunk of meat suspended over the flames. "If you wish, Jordan. Is Dr. Itoua not joining us?"

Jordan swallowed down the surge of jealousy, only half sure it was because he didn't want to share Victor with T'ukri. T'ukri had agreed to guide them both into the rainforest. Of course he'd want to know where Victor was. And even if that wasn't his reason, Victor had made his feelings for Jordan perfectly clear. Jordan didn't need to be jealous.

"I'm sure he'll come out when the food's ready, if not before," Jordan replied with forced casualness. T'ukri didn't seem to notice the off note in his voice.

See, Victor? I can do casual.

T'ukri checked on the meat again, bending to turn it and giving Jordan a perfect view of his ass. The wrap he wore might cover it, but it did nothing to hide the shape. The image of T'ukri with his fingers up his ass flashed through Jordan's mind again. God, he bet T'ukri was an eager bottom.

Fuck. He had to think about something else. Cooking. That was it. T'ukri was cooking. In fact, it was the first time he'd seen T'ukri— or any of the men—cooking. Great. Another thing to wonder about. Their list of questions kept getting longer without satisfactory answers to any of them. He kept track of T'ukri in his peripheral vision, all too aware of the firelight reflecting off his smooth skin as twilight fell and the jungle drifted into night. He bet it tasted salty after being in the jungle all day.

What the fuck is wrong with me? If Jordan weren't such a dyed-in-the-wool cynic, he'd swear it was some kind of magic. He looked around for a distraction, only to find none. Usually the village children flocked around T'ukri like bees to honey, but tonight they all seemed occupied elsewhere. Even Paucar and the warriors all seemed to be eating with their own families, something that hadn't happened since T'ukri's arrival. Yeah, something fishy was going on.

"Dr. Itoua, please, join us."

Jordan looked up as Victor approached, stool in hand, and took a seat next to Jordan. They didn't touch, but Jordan looked his way and smiled. Victor returned it with a quirk of his lips.

"Was it a good hunt today?" Victor asked.

"A very successful one." T'ukri turned his potent gaze in Victor's direction.

Oh fuck no. He wasn't getting Victor, no matter how hot he thought he was. After a moment T'ukri turned back to the fire again, flashing his ass in Victor's direction. Apparently satisfied with the way the meat was cooked, he pulled it from the fire and drew the knife from its sheath. He cut the meat into three pieces and offered one to Victor. Victor took it with a surprised "thank you." Jordan started to bristle, but before he could say anything—or before Victor could nudge him—T'ukri offered the second piece to Jordan.

"Thank you," Jordan said automatically. "Is this from your kill today?"

"The best piece," T'ukri replied with a pointed look. He cut a bite-sized piece from the chunk still in his hand and put it into his mouth, his gaze fixed on Jordan and Victor as he ate.

Beside him, Victor went stiff. Too stiff. Something had occurred to him that Jordan had missed. Whatever it was, it didn't stop him from taking a bite of the meat in his hand, so Jordan did the same. The iron-soaked flavor of organ meat burst across his tongue as he chewed. What was he missing? The villagers shared food among themselves all the time, and more than once, Jordan was sure they'd given him or Victor the choicest offerings as a way to impress them.

To impress them…. Oh shit. T'ukri was trying to impress them, but that didn't make any sense. They'd already asked him to be their guide. Besides the fact that Jordan and Victor could take care of themselves just fine, T'ukri didn't need to win them over.

Unless it wasn't about being their guide at all, but what else could it be? That was the only connection between them. Except T'ukri had watched Victor like he was the best thing on the menu since he'd walked into the village, and he'd been preening all evening. Had he gone hunting for Victor's benefit? For Jordan's? But that didn't make sense either. The villagers made sure Jordan and Victor had plenty to eat. T'ukri didn't need to go hunting for them.

Yesterday T'ukri had spent the day doing what Victor said was probably a purification ritual, one that included cleaning himself out. Then today he'd gone hunting alone and smeared blood over his heart and groin. *Fuck.* He was coming on to Victor. The meat that had tasted so good a moment ago turned to dust in his mouth.

But he'd given the meat to both of them. Victor first, but he'd deliberately cut the meat into three pieces and served Jordan before he ate. Holy fuck, how had he missed this? Unless he had lost all touch with human nature out here in the boonies, T'ukri was propositioning *them*. Not Victor. Not him. Both of them. *Fuck, fuck, fuck.* What were they supposed to do with that?

And okay, the guy had been in the wild alone for who knows how long, so Jordan got that he was horny, but both of them? Jordan was all for whatever floated a person's boat as long as it was consensual, but T'ukri was out of luck. Jordan wasn't interested, and he was pretty sure Victor wouldn't take him up on it either.

A week ago Jordan might have been tempted, but things had changed. He had Victor now, and the thought of having sex with someone else held no appeal. He just couldn't see a single thing to justify accepting T'ukri's interest, not even his own admitted attraction to the man. He'd meant it when he told Victor he wanted more than just sex. He had a chance at something real and lasting with Victor, and no matter how sexy T'ukri was, it wasn't worth throwing away that chance for what would amount to a fling. At the end of the day—week, month, whatever—he was going home to the university. He was going home with Victor.

Now he just had to figure out how to turn T'ukri down without losing their guide. At least so far, it had all been relatively innocent. A shared meal didn't *have* to be a prelude to seduction. Even if T'ukri insisted that it was, Jordan could claim cultural differences to cover up accepting by mistake. He'd talk to Victor when he could get him alone, and they'd figure out a plan.

Victor always had a plan.

Fuck, he hoped Victor had a plan.

CHAPTER 11

T'UKRI STRUTTED back to his hut when Jordan—he had been invited to call him by his first name—and Itoua finished the offering he had given them. He had made his first tribute and been accepted. Tomorrow when he faced the ancestors, he would have that much going for him. Nothing else, perhaps, given that his desired mates were outsiders, but that much. And he would cling to that for all it was worth.

They *had* watched him. Itoua had been there when he came back with the deer. T'ukri had felt his gaze following him as he delivered his prize and had it witnessed, as he returned to his hut for a covering, as he finished preparations for his offering, and as they ate. And Jordan— Jordan could not keep his eyes off T'ukri from the moment he joined him by the fire. He had preened and postured invitingly, and Jordan had reacted. His clothes were not as revealing as T'ukri's own, but T'ukri had not imagined the erection hiding beneath the thicker cloth. It was far less than what he wanted, but it was a workable start. If they saw him as desirable on a physical level, he could hold their interest long enough to prove his worth as a mate on an emotional and spiritual level as well.

And in two days, he would guide them into the rainforest, into his territory where he could control their interactions. He would have them at his side all day and near to hand at night, close enough to show them how things could be.

Then it would remain only to see if they could accept all that he was. If they could, he would have all his heart desired.

He lay down on the sleeping mat with a smile on his face.

Yuri's beloved voice drifted through his mind, ever the teacher of lore and legend. It had fallen to him to teach T'ukri all he needed to know to one day take Huallpa's place. *"Few were they who could meet all of a guardian's needs. Thus it became our way for Chapaqpuma to take not one, but two mates, a balance to each other as much as to the guardian, so that when calamity came, Chapaqpuma had the strength to ward it off and the humanity to return home after."*

The strength to sustain him and the compassion to draw him back to himself. His mother provided the strength and Yuri the compassion for Huallpa. If T'ukri had read them right, Jordan would be his strength and Itoua his compassion. Already Jordan had proven himself capable, following T'ukri through the jungle even when he was hunting and doing his best to move unseen. T'ukri had heard tales as well of Jordan hunting with Paucar's warriors. They spoke of his prowess with a bow, his aim unparalleled by anything they had ever seen. Whispers of him never missing had begun to circulate with the same reverence as the villagers spoke of Chapaqpuma. If Jordan stayed long enough, he would become their guardian in the villagers' minds, much as T'ukri already was in his own people's minds. And T'ukri had no doubt he could—and would—defend them if it came to that. He was not blind to the darkness that shadowed Jordan's aura, but T'ukri had seen enough already to know Jordan would allow no harm to come to those he took under his wing.

If Jordan accepted his suit, he would stand beside T'ukri against any threat, lending his strength and his aim and his cunning to any fight just as T'ukri would bring his. They would be a wall between Machu Llaqta and the world. And when the fight was over and they came home weary and burdened, Itoua—dare he think of him as Victor?—would be there with the gentleness that shone from his very soul to remind them of why they fought. Perhaps Victor would fight beside them as well. He had the look of one who could take care of himself if pushed into it, but he did not have a warrior's soul. His truest calling would always be to bring them home.

Now he had only to convince the ancestors of his logic and win their approval. Yes, they were outsiders, but who better to help protect against the outside world?

"ARE YOU as freaked out right now as I am?" Jordan asked as he followed Victor into his hut. Victor didn't need the question to know how unsettled T'ukri's overture had left Jordan. Otherwise he wouldn't have followed Victor so openly.

"Yes." Victor set down the stool he'd carried back in with him and took a seat. "That was quite a show T'ukri put on for us tonight."

"I told you he was interested in you." Jordan sat down on the other stool, only to bounce right back up and pace the length of the hut.

"You did, and I told you he was interested in you, and it appears we were both right," Victor replied. "But that was more than just interest."

Jordan stopped his pacing and turned to face Victor with a frown. "Not following you there, doc."

"Offering food he killed and cooked himself, and not just any piece, but the best piece. And then you add in the purification ritual yesterday. Don't you see, Jordan? He's courting us. He's not looking for a roll in the hay. He's looking for a spouse." He paused, then added, "Or two."

"Like together? All three of us?" Jordan asked. "But that's...."

Victor smirked at Jordan. "Hot as hell?"

Jordan swallowed hard. "I wouldn't kick him out of our bed if you were good with him being there too, but you said courting, and I'm not seeing that."

"What's not to see?" Victor ran his hand through his hair. "He cleans himself, inside and out—but doesn't get off—and spends the rest of the day meditating. It's not just about cleanliness, and it's definitely not about self-pleasure or he wouldn't have stopped. Which begs the question of why. Because he's anticipating a not-distant future where he won't have to take care of those needs himself. And with two male lovers, he doesn't know how the roles are going to shake out, so he cleans himself inside as well and opens himself a bit so he's ready for us, no matter our preferences."

"Okay, maybe," Jordan allowed, returning to the seat, "although I think that's stretching it."

"Rituals, Jordan. We're talking about a tribe—or tribes, since T'ukri isn't from Paucar's tribe—steeped in who knows how many generations of rituals. Everything has layers of meaning beyond the surface."

"Uh-huh. Go on." Jordan still sounded skeptical, but he hadn't stopped listening, and Victor was just getting going.

"Bon, d'accord, so he cleans himself, physically and symbolically, ready for a new stage in his life," Victor said. "What's next? He has to prove his worth. He's a warrior, a hunter, so how does he do that? By showing he can provide for a family."

"And the blood?" Jordan asked.

"Again, symbols. The handprint on his chest is obviously for his heart, and the lines on his abdomen for sex, both parts of courting and marriage. And you already pegged the others as the senses he uses to be successful as a hunter. Then he doesn't just bring the meat back to show he's a capable hunter. He picks the best piece and prepares it himself before offering it to his chosen one, or ones, all the while bearing the marks from the hunt to show he's willing to put the needs of his potential partners above his own."

"And we took it and ate it and thanked him," Jordan said. "We just accepted him without meaning to, didn't we?"

"We probably said we were open to the courtship," Victor admitted. "That doesn't mean we'll accept him when all's said and done."

"Yeah, no," Jordan said. "Not unless he's a lot less attached to his tribe than I think he is. When this expedition is over, we're heading back to the university. Kind of hard to keep a relationship going in those circumstances."

"He may think he has enough to offer to tempt us to give up institutional academia. For all he knows, we'd love an excuse to spend the rest of our lives learning about him and his people, whether they're the source of the legend of Philli-philli or not. And if we really do find the temple and all the rest, he might even be right, which means we have a decision to make. We need him because right now he's our only lead on the deeper stories and the temple. Sure, we could just head into the rainforest ourselves, but we have no clue where to start searching, and wandering aimlessly hasn't gotten us anywhere, not to mention having to win the trust of whoever we might find. If we have any hope of tracking down the truth behind the tales in the time we have left, it's through him."

"And that means being around him for who knows how long," Jordan said.

"And staying in his good graces because we don't want him to change his mind if we upset him," Victor said glumly.

"And since we're polite, he ends up thinking we might be interested in return. That feels really fucking dishonest," Jordan said.

"I agree. Do you have a better suggestion?" Victor asked.

"Maybe see if we can get it across that we're together and happy with each other?" Jordan suggested.

"I'm certainly not opposed to the idea, but if I've read this right and he's truly courting both of us, that may not be a deterrent. He only has to win us over to the idea of him, not to the idea of each other as well." Victor really wished he thought that would work. Like Jordan, he wouldn't kick T'ukri out of bed if the opportunity came up, but not at the risk of this new, fragile thing he was building with Jordan. He liked sex as much as the next man, but his relationship with Jordan—a real relationship that would last beyond the bedroom and enrich his life as a whole—was worth far more than a bit of fun in the sack. Or a paper. Even this paper. All that without considering that T'ukri appeared to be far more invested in this than a bit of fun.

"Fuck."

That summed it up as far as Victor was concerned, but it didn't help them. He had a goal, one that would determine the future of his career—or indeed whether he had a future career—but was the goal so critical if the only way to complete it was to lead T'ukri on indefinitely?

JORDAN WOKE slowly the next morning, lulled by the warmth of Victor's body. They'd talked more last night before falling asleep and had decided Jordan would move his things into Victor's hut so that there would be no question as to whether they were together.

Fuck, they were *together*. He didn't think he'd ever get used to that idea.

"You're thinking too loud," Victor murmured next to him, eyes still closed.

"About that," Jordan said. "Now that we know what T'ukri's doing, is there any reason for me to follow him today? I feel bad enough spying on him as it is."

Victor sighed and opened his eyes. "We think we know what he's doing, but that doesn't mean we're right, and it doesn't mean we can afford to let him out of our sight. He's still our only lead."

"Victor," Jordan whined.

"I know. But if we don't know what's going on, we can't be prepared for what comes next." Victor rolled onto his side and kissed Jordan.

Jordan grumbled a little but made to sit up. Victor's arms tightened around him, holding him in place. "This is the last day,"

Victor reminded him. "Tomorrow we head into the rainforest and we won't have to sneak around anymore. He'll be our guide and we'll have the perfect excuse to keep him in sight."

"You don't seriously think he's out to get us, do you?" Jordan couldn't put his finger on when it had happened, but T'ukri had moved firmly into the "good guy" category in Jordan's brain. Didn't mean Jordan trusted him all the way, but nothing about him made Jordan worry he would do anything to deliberately hurt them.

"No," Victor replied. "But he's—"

"Still our only lead," Jordan finished with Victor. He sat up, and this time Victor let him. "Fine. I'll follow him, but if I have to spend another day watching him prance around naked, I get a blowjob tonight to make up for it. I've been perpetually horny since he walked into the village."

"Such a hardship," Victor quipped. "I'll spend the day working myself up to it."

Sneaky motherfucker. Jordan had intended his comment as a joke on Victor, but Victor had turned it right back around, and now Jordan would spend the day wondering what Victor was doing to "work himself up to it."

"Bastard," he grumbled.

"I'm quite sure my parents were married at the time of my conception," Victor replied, cool as ice. "But you're welcome to ask them if you doubt my word."

Jordan snorted a laugh despite himself. "I'm never going to win one with you, am I?"

Victor smiled from his spot on the bedroll. "It depends on what you consider winning. Now, go on before he leaves without you. I'll be here when you get back to give you your reward."

Jordan followed T'ukri out of the village again, not at all surprised when he went to the pool and stripped down. He poured water over his head like he'd done the day before and spent a minute scrubbing off the bits of leftover blood, but he didn't hang out in the water. Instead he settled back down on the rock where he'd meditated the first day.

Great. Another day watching him do nothing.

T'ukri grabbed a pouch from his belt and shook some kind of yellow powder onto the rock in front of him. He dribbled water into it and stirred until he had a thick paste, which he proceeded to smear on his face. Ten stripes: two on each cheek, three on his forehead, one on each temple, and one on his chin, all painted inward toward his nose. Next were twelve stripes on his chest, circling his heart. Finally he ran stripes up his thighs and down his abdomen, pointing toward his groin. With Victor's lecture about rituals and symbols and the idea of courting in mind, Jordan tried to guess what they might mean today.

Unlike the marks the day before, these all pointed outward—or inward. T'ukri had painted them from outside to inside, so Jordan went with that. So the focus was inward. Mind, heart, body? It seemed too simple, but nothing else jumped out at him.

T'ukri pulled a second pouch off his belt and got out some kind of herb. He closed his eyes and chewed on it for a few minutes. Then he grew still, so still that Jordan had to focus to see his chest rise and fall with his breaths. His very slow, barely there breaths. That wasn't worrying or anything. And Jordan had no clue what he'd taken, so he didn't know how to bring him out of it if he stopped breathing entirely.

He nocked an arrow and prepared to defend T'ukri against anything that might think he was easy prey—or already dead. Fuck, he hoped T'ukri didn't die on him. How would he explain *that* to Victor?

AS THE ayahuasca took effect and he slipped into a meditative state, T'ukri conjured an image of his grandfather's face. Only once before had he sought audience with the ancestors, after the goddess's gift first manifested, but then he had Huallpa and his mother and a shaman to guide him. This time he had to find them alone. That would be the first test. Could he even come before them to state his case?

The air shimmered around him as he slipped deeper into the trance. He was usually safe in the rainforest, his gifts tricking other predators into believing he truly was the puma from whom he had taken his name, but today he had Jordan watching him too. He would not have been safer in the heart of the temple of Pachamama herself.

With a smile on his face at the thought of Jordan's strong arms protecting him, he fell the rest of the way into his mind, letting all connection with the world outside his skin disappear. His awareness narrowed to the *thump-thump* of his heartbeat, the slow in and out of his breathing, and the gentle throb in his groin. Heart, body, soul, all centered on one goal: winning his mates.

"You risk much coming to us so far from home."

The voice startled T'ukri into opening his eyes, but it was not the pool and rainforest where he sat that met his gaze. Rather it was the temple of Pachamama, ghostly in its lines but recognizable nonetheless. "I risk nothing, honored grandfather," he replied with a bow of his head to Inti, whom he remembered from his early childhood, though the man before him bore more resemblance to Huallpa than to the old man T'ukri remembered. "I am as safe in the rainforest as I am in the temple."

"Safe from the creatures who dwell there, perhaps, but what of other men?"

"I am not alone. My mate—one I would call my mate—stands watch. Whether he accepts my suit or not, he will not let any harm befall me."

"And if he is the threat? Who will protect you from him?"

T'ukri bristled at the implication that Jordan would somehow hurt him. "A warrior he may be, but he would not harm me for no reason. He is a good man."

"Now, perhaps," another voice said.

T'ukri turned to see a woman he did not know, but he bowed to her nonetheless. "Honored grandmother, I would take the man he is now as my mate. His past formed him, but it does not define him."

"And his present?" she asked. "Does it define him?"

"Insomuch as it defines us all," T'ukri replied, not sure where she was going with her questions.

"He is not all that he appears," she said. "Or perhaps he is more than he appears."

"And I am not?" T'ukri asked. "I have time to learn all his secrets and he mine before we bond. I ask only your blessing to continue."

"You truly believe outsiders—the very men you were empowered to defend against—are your best choices as mates? Are there no worthy warriors among your peers?" a third voice asked.

T'ukri bowed to the newcomer, another man he did not recognize. "There are many worthy warriors among my tribe, and even more among the wider diaspora who keep to the old ways but do not claim Machu Llaqta as home, but while they would stand at my side, they do not stir my heart or my body. My mates must ground me as much as strengthen me. To do that, they must touch my heart. These two outsiders as you call them have done that. I look at them and I see my future. I see them at my side in a fight. I see Jordan's gifts supporting and enhancing mine. And I see the strength and wisdom of a shaman in Victor to outshine any doubt that may try to take me. No matter what comes, we will face it, and we will triumph, for how can such goodness fail?"

"All too easily, my son," Inti replied. "It takes only a knife in the dark or a spear gone astray. They are not of our world. Will they stay with you?"

"If they will not, then they are not the mates for me," T'ukri said, "but I could find a way to share them with their old lives if they were willing to share my life too."

"Are you so sure? Could the memory of them alone draw you back?" the woman asked.

T'ukri gave the question the consideration it deserved. Chapaqpuma had two mates so they could do what the guardian could not and ground him in his humanity when he had given in to the animal nature of his gifts. T'ukri had seen Huallpa struggle without Yuri. It was one of the reasons T'ukri had ascended into the role of Chapaqpuma while Huallpa still lived. Huallpa remained king, but he could not remain Chapaqpuma. If T'ukri shared Jordan and Victor with their old lives, if they spent part of their time away from him, he would face the risk of having to fight without them. He had done it before, but it had been a struggle, and that was before he had met his mates. If he bonded with them and they left, would he be able to draw himself back? And if he could not, would he pose an even bigger risk than the ones he fought? He looked deep within himself, to the core of his humanity, and entwined with it the gifts from the goddess. He felt along the seam between them, but they were so enmeshed that he could not separate them. He was T'ukri and he was Chapaqpuma, and one did not preclude the other. Then he conjured the image of Jordan's and Victor's faces as they had looked the night before, skin gilded gold in the firelight. His soul leapt toward the image, in perfect harmony with itself.

"Yes," he replied.

"Then prove it. Change now, without their presence to ground you," she challenged.

The demand shocked T'ukri, but if the only way to win her blessing was to do this, then he would do as she demanded.

"Palta, no," Inti said. "This is not something you have the right to ask."

"Why not?" she said. "He asks our blessing. Why should he not prove his claim?"

"What if he fails?"

"If he fails, then we will not bless his union," she said with a shrug.

"And he will be trapped between his two selves," Inti said. "You were Chapaqpuma's mate, but you were never Chapaqpuma. You do not know what you ask of him."

"Grandfather," T'ukri interrupted, "I can do it. And if I am wrong, I will break off the courtship and return home. Mama and Ch'aska helped draw me back the last time. They will be able to help me again. But it will not come to that."

"I pray to Pachamama that you are right," Inti said with a shake of his head.

Once again, T'ukri reached for his inner being, the mix of human and preternatural that made him who he was. He coaxed his gifts to the surface, feeling his fingers elongate, his teeth sharpen, his muscles thicken, and his senses heighten. Having seen his father's transformation, he knew the shape of his face had changed, that his limbs had stretched and curved, ready for a puma's pounce rather than a human jump. He reveled briefly in the flush of power that came with allowing his extra senses free rein, but the challenge he faced was not to free his gifts, but to come back to himself after.

He focused his inner eye on Jordan's and Victor's faces, on the strength in their auras, on the shadows and light that made them who they were. No, he did not know all their secrets—Palta was right about that—but he knew the core of them. He shook himself all over, a cat shaking water from its fur, and returned to himself, fully human once more.

"Are you satisfied, honored grandmother?" T'ukri asked, unable to keep the edge of smugness out of his voice.

"They are and will always be outsiders," she said coldly. "I cannot bless this folly, but I will not oppose it. It will be on your head if it all falls to dust." She disappeared before he could reply.

"Grandfather?" T'ukri asked, trying not to despair.

"You have my blessing, T'ukri. If the thought of them alone prior to your bonding gives you that much control already, I look forward to seeing what your bond will do," Inti said.

"Honored grandfather?" T'ukri asked the other man, whose name he still did not know.

"As one Chapaqpuma to another, I give you my blessing," he said. "May your mates be your strength and your comfort for many long years."

T'ukri bowed deeply to them both. "I am honored by your blessings."

When he straightened, only Inti remained. "Not everyone will see it as Guaman and I do," he warned. "Many will share Palta's fears."

"Do you think she is right?" T'ukri asked.

"I do not *believe* that she is right," Inti responded, "but I do not *know* that she is wrong. Our gifts in death differ much as they did in life. Palta has been said to have the Sight, but she is not unbiased. She lost her mate and her son to defending our people against the colonizers. It is possible her bias has swayed her interpretation of what she has seen. It is also possible that the events she has seen will not come to pass. For all her wisdom, she is still only human, and the choices of each determine the paths that open before them. If you choose this path, you will spend your life defending your choices, especially if they are not always by your side. Do not let that discourage you. Your faith in your mates will make you stronger than others' doubts."

"Thank you, Grandfather," T'ukri said.

"Now go. Your mate grows anxious."

T'ukri grinned at his grandfather. "Then I should return to him."

"I expect not to see you again for many years."

T'ukri bowed once more and opened his eyes to the rainforest. He took stock of his body, but he felt none of the ache he associated with the aftereffects of his transformation. It must have occurred only on the ancestral plane, then. Good. He would not have wanted Jordan to find out this way. He would share his gifts when the time came, but not before.

Feeling lighter than he could ever remember, he dove into the pool and removed the ochre from his skin. Unlike the blood marks, these had served their purpose now that he had the ancestors' blessing.

He glanced toward the tree where Jordan sat motionless and considered calling him down, but it would not be right to take the next step in their courtship with only Jordan. They would have time once the three of them were alone in the rainforest. While he had no fear for his own safety and he believed in their strength, he would take no chances now that he had the ancestors' blessings. Once they bonded, his gifts would protect them too. Until then, he would not let either of them out of his sight if he could help it.

CHAPTER 12

JORDAN RETURNED to the village ahead of T'ukri, feeling deeply pensive. Watching T'ukri today had felt far more intrusive than it had the previous days, which was ridiculous since all T'ukri did was sit and meditate, even if he was naked the whole time. After three days of it, it was hardly worth mentioning. All the rational arguments in the world didn't change the way he felt, though.

"Are you all right?" Victor asked as soon as Jordan walked into their hut.

"Not sure." Jordan moved into Victor's space, wrapped his arms around him, and rested against his chest. "It was a... strange day."

"What happened?" Jordan didn't have to look up to know Victor was frowning. Funny how he knew the different tones of his voice so well.

"Nothing, really. He went back to the pool, painted some lines on his face, chest, and groin with pigment, took some kind of drug, and didn't move. And I mean didn't move. It looked like he was barely even breathing. Then, hours later, he opened his eyes, washed the pigment off, and got dressed like nothing had happened, like I hadn't just spent hours hoping he wasn't going to die on me."

He pulled away to look up at Victor. "I was really afraid he was going to die on me, and I wouldn't have the first idea of what to do about it. Did you get a chance to ask Paucar and the elders about the hunt today?"

"I did, although I had to keep the questions to what I saw when he returned yesterday."

"And?"

"And Paucar shrugged and said that T'ukri's ways were not the ways of his village and that all would be revealed in time."

"That's helpful." Jordan rolled his eyes. "It would be nice to get a straight answer for once."

"This is getting to you too, isn't it?" Victor asked.

"Too?" Jordan parroted instead of answering. He was more interested in what was bothering Victor.

"It's like we talked about yesterday. He has this image of us that's based on incomplete information, and if we're right, he's courting us based on that. Bon Dieu, Jordan, how am I supposed to feel? I'm damn tempted to call it all off and just go home," Victor said.

"You'd do that?" Jordan asked.

"If I thought for a moment it would make things right, yes," Victor replied, "but we've set something in motion, and I'm not sure even leaving would be enough to stop it now. I don't know how else to explain it, but this feels bigger… more important than I can put into words. Your reaction just now proves my point. You've started to care about him, not just as a lead in our research, but as a person."

"He's a decent man," Jordan said. "Cocky as hell, but decent."

"Like you have room to talk about someone being cocky," Victor said in that deadpan Jordan so loved. "It's more than that, though, isn't it?"

Jordan shrugged. How was he supposed to answer that question without making it sound like Victor wasn't enough for him or like he was questioning his commitment to their relationship already? "It isn't, but it could be," he said finally. "Right now he's a decent man with just enough mystery surrounding him to be fascinating. If we left today or tomorrow, that's all he'd be, and that would be the end of it. And I'd be fine with that. If we stay, we're going to get to know him better, and that edge of mystery will probably be solved, one way or another."

"And which way it will be solved is something neither of us can predict," Victor added. "You realize it's been less than a week, right?"

Jordan shrugged, feeling defensive, but he forged ahead. He'd started this conversation. He wasn't going to chicken out now. "Yeah, so? I've spent the past three days watching things I suspect no outsider has ever seen."

"And that creates a sense of intimacy between the two of you, at least on your side," Victor continued. "It's logical. The question is what happens now. A part of me says we should call it off and let it go, for our sanity, for our relationship, for his sanity, and probably his safety. And yet I can't quite seem to make the decision."

"You always have hated what-ifs. So what do we do, doc?" Jordan asked.

"I don't know," Victor admitted. "Thoughts?"

Jordan took a deep breath and rolled the dice. "Yeah, I have a few, although I don't know if you're going to like them." He moved away to pace the confines of the hut, resisting the urge to wrap his arms around his waist as he did.

"I'm listening," Victor prompted. "Talk to me, Jordan."

I'm listening. Those words and all they implied—that Victor was open to listening to and *hearing* Jordan when so few people in his life had bothered—had always been his kryptonite. He was helpless to hold anything back, so he took a deep breath and let it all come spilling out.

"If we do this, if we keep going and walk into the jungle with him tomorrow, we see it all the way through to the end. The courtship, the mystery, Philli-philli, all of it. We commit to it fully, knowing we might not come back from it. We know what he wants. At least we think we do. If we go into the jungle with him, we're accepting his right to try to convince us. Maybe it works out, maybe it doesn't, but I can't sit back and let him court us, knowing we're just using him for information."

Victor breathed a sigh so deep and heartfelt Jordan feared for a minute he'd fucked everything up for good. "*Mon Dieu*, I love you."

Jordan froze, trying to reconcile Victor's declaration with everything Jordan had just said.

"You don't see it, do you?" Victor asked when Jordan turned to look at him. "You make all these comments about your twisted past and terrible upbringing like they're all there is to you, and you don't see what a pure soul you have."

Jordan shook his head, too overwhelmed by Victor's image of him to focus on anything else. "After all the shit I've pulled, all the people I've killed? And don't tell me about it being in the service of my country. I still killed them, no matter who ordered it. You're out of your mind if you think there's anything pure left in me, but for what it's worth, I love you too. That doesn't solve the problem of what to do about T'ukri or the grant or anything else."

VICTOR COULDN'T decide if he wanted to jump for joy at the knowledge that Jordan loved him back or if he wanted to rage—or cry—at Jordan's poor opinion of himself. He'd never let himself imagine Jordan would feel the same way, not even over the past few days. Yes,

Jordan had said he wanted a relationship, but hearing the words made it real in a way nothing else could. Having that reassurance gave him the courage to consider the rest of what Jordan was suggesting. Actually letting T'ukri court them, giving that courtship true consideration, possibly not coming back.... They were big, scary thoughts when he'd devoted so much time and effort to his degrees and his career. Not just establishing his career but defending it, doing quality research that would stand up even to the extra scrutiny that came from people who wanted to discredit him because he believed Philli-philli was more than just a legend, because he was Black, because he wasn't American. If he walked away now, they'd all proclaim he'd gone off the deep end and use that to invalidate all the papers he'd published, all the work he'd done on preserving the cultures of endangered peoples. He wouldn't be there to hear it, but if his work was no longer considered valuable, what would happen to the people he'd sought to protect? Would they also be no longer valuable? Could he take that chance?

Going with T'ukri under Jordan's conditions wouldn't have to mean saying yes to his courtship and leaving everything behind, but it would mean being open to that possibility. He ought to refuse. He'd gotten enough from Paucar and his tribe to write a paper if they left now or even if they stayed but learned nothing more. Not the paper he wanted and believed he could write if they found the temple, and not the chance to say thank you that had driven him since his teens, but enough to keep his job and his visa and the life he'd built at the university, maybe even get tenure.

A life of hiding his relationship with Jordan for fear of being fired if Fowler found out about them.

The instincts his grandfather had tried so hard to awaken in him rebelled at the thought. At all the thoughts. Of not getting the best paper possible. Of not saying thank you. Of not having Jordan by his side.

He'd said it earlier, though he doubted Jordan had truly understood. Something was at work here. Something bigger than them, and he felt compelled to see it through.

"Could you really do it?" Victor asked Jordan. "Could you leave everything behind if T'ukri convinced us to accept him?"

"Honestly?" Jordan said. Victor nodded, hoping he wasn't setting himself up for heartbreak. "I could leave the university in a heartbeat. We don't have to be associated with a university to do the same work. And I don't believe staying here has to mean leaving everything behind completely. I mean, we'd be *living* the culture we were studying in a way no one else ever has. Think of all the papers we could get out of that. And the only person I'd really be leaving behind would be Nandini, but I doubt I really could leave her behind. When I told her we were coming to Peru, her first question was to ask if we were looking for Philli-philli, and her second text was an order to be careful. Hell, for all I know, she's sitting in Cusco laughing at us right now, waiting for me to tell her we've found him and we're staying here because we also fell in love. Nothing surprises her."

Victor couldn't argue with that. He had only met Nandini a few times, but she had left quite an impression on him. He also noticed that Jordan consistently said *we* and *us*, not *I* or *me*. He'd already decided whatever they did, they'd be doing it together. That gave Victor the courage to reply, "Then let's do it. Let's take the chance and see what comes."

"Really?" Jordan asked like he was surprised Victor had agreed. "I mean, it's easy for me to walk away, but you've invested a lot more in the university and your career than I have."

"And what has it gotten me?" Victor replied. "A boss who's looking for an excuse to fire me? Colleagues who don't want their names on papers with mine so my 'obsession' doesn't taint them? Don't get me wrong. I love what I do. I love the research and the teaching and the knowledge, but I don't love all the trappings that go along with it. I just understand that they're necessary to get me to the part I do love. And yes, a part of me would love nothing more than to find the deeper legends, maybe even prove Philli-philli is real, and write a paper that silences all the naysayers, but even with T'ukri's help, I don't know how realistic that is. And I've definitely hit the publish-or-perish wall. If I don't come up with a solid paper out of this grant, I'm probably finished as anything other than an instructor, assuming I don't lose my job and visa and have to start over somewhere else, so it's not like I'd be giving up all that much unless we find something stellar."

"I didn't realize it was that bad," Jordan said. "I'm sorry no one else sees what a brilliant man you are."

It wasn't that they didn't see. It was that they discounted it, but Victor knew what he'd seen, and he wasn't going to back down. Jordan knew all that, though, so Victor simply said, "Thanks."

"What do we tell him?" Jordan asked.

"I don't know that we have to tell him anything," Victor replied. "We don't know if he's familiar with the American university system, so an explanation might not mean anything to him, and I don't want him to think we're considering his courtship as a way to get him to reveal secrets to us."

"And if he finds out?"

"Then we'll explain and hope he believes us," Victor replied. "We can play it by ear, give it a few days, even a few weeks, depending on how long it takes us to go wherever he's taking us. And then we see how we feel and how he does. It could be as he gets to know us better, he'll change his mind and it'll be a moot point. Or we could decide we're not interested in what he's offering. And if he doesn't change his mind and we haven't changed ours, we'll tell him when the time seems right. I don't know what else we can do. Or it could be we're reading this entirely wrong, and he really is just offering to guide us into the rainforest to look for Incan ruins." He didn't believe that last assertion, but he wasn't infallible, no matter what Jordan thought, and he had been wrong before.

"You mean you don't have a plan B?" Jordan joked.

"I don't have a plan A," Victor said. "Not for this. For the expedition, sure, but this became personal the moment we started considering his courtship. Emotions aren't predictable the way actions are."

"No, I don't suppose they are," Jordan agreed.

Noise outside drew Victor's attention. He wanted to ignore it—this conversation with Jordan was too important to rush—but if it was T'ukri returning, that could be just as important. He and Jordan would have other chances to talk about this and anything else but only this one chance to see whatever piece of ritual T'ukri might perform next.

"We should go see what's going on," Victor said. "We can continue this later."

"Lead the way, doc," Jordan said, but he leaned up for a kiss before Victor could move.

Victor gave it to him willingly. He suspected they'd both need all the comfort they could get as they navigated the minefield they'd just created for themselves. He just hoped they wouldn't step on one.

CHAPTER 13

T'UKRI WALKED back into the village in harmony with himself and the universe. He had won the ancestors' blessing. Nothing short of his mates refusing him could bring him down. He ducked into his hut to leave his pouches, then returned to the fire pit in the center of the village. He took what had become his seat and waited. Jordan had returned before he did, so he would be in the hut with Vic—Itoua. He had to go back to calling the good doctor by his last name until he was given permission. He might think of them as his mates already, but they had only consented to hearing his suit—if indeed he had interpreted their reactions correctly. Surely they understood that accepting his offering showed their openness to his courtship, but that was far from winning their acceptance. Taking liberties they had not allowed would not help him.

His presence at the fire acted as honey to flies for the village children, who flocked around him. He smiled and welcomed them, though his attention remained fixed on the dark opening to Itoua's hut. Before long, Jordan and Itoua both emerged. Jordan looked at him across the open space, nodded, and smiled. Itoua's expression remained reserved but not cold. It made sense. He had not spent the past three days observing T'ukri at his rituals. T'ukri would have to see if he could nurture that connection tonight and over the upcoming days. He did not want to lose his mates because he paid too much attention to one and not enough to the other.

"Tell us a story, T'ukri," the village children begged, drawing T'ukri's attention to them.

T'ukri knew many stories, the lore of his people learned at Yuri's knee, the legends and stories of the children's tribe, and stories from much of the Andes and the Amazon basin, for he had traveled far, a wanderer even before he became Chapaqpuma. He could easily pick one and keep them entertained for any number of hours, but while he was sure Itoua would appreciate them all, one tale in particular begged to be told. Did he dare, now, while he had not yet won his mates? Could he reveal even a little of his secret?

But they already knew enough of the legend to ask vague, if leading, questions. Recounting the legend itself would tell them only that he had heard it, not that he lived it. With a decisive nod, he turned to the children. "What story shall I tell you?"

The children settled around him, calling out suggestions, but the most frequent request was for the tale of the guardian. It was always their first request if he let them pick the story. He settled more comfortably in his spot and tipped his head to his mates in silent invitation to listen. He would have to tell the story in Spanish for them to understand, which would be hard for the younger children, but the older ones would translate, and they all knew the story. It was more important for his mates to hear it in his words than through someone else's translation.

"Many seasons ago, when the land was fresh and new and the waters teemed with abundant life, the people worshipped many gods and goddesses, for life was precarious, and they needed all the protection they could gain. Some chose to worship the great bear with his strong arms and mighty voice, peaceful until angered, but merciless when defending his territory. Others chose the condor, great ruler of the skies, who traveled here and there at will but always returned to his nest. Still others chose the caiman with his thick skin and sharp fangs. And others chose the great snakes, cunning in their hunt and deadly in their bite. And to each people, the gods granted their blessings. One people, though, chose differently, preferring the stealth and sleek power of the great cat. Pachamama looked with favor on their offerings and granted them her protection.

"Ages came and went, each of the peoples learning to live in harmony with the others, for balance is necessary in all things, but then the outsiders came."

Jordan flinched at that. Good, he had understood that much of the tale. T'ukri did not blame all white men for the deeds of the past and indeed Chapaqpuma predated the Spanish colonization, for outsiders came in many guises. He feared not all of his people would be as open-minded, as Palta had reminded him all too clearly in his vision today. The better T'ukri's mates understood the prejudices they might encounter, the more prepared they would be to counter them.

"Chaos followed in their wake," T'ukri continued. "The children of the tribes began to disappear, taken as slaves or felled by diseases against which they had no defense. The people turned to their gods for help. What the bear or the condor, the caiman or the serpent bestowed on their followers, I cannot say, but Pachamama in her wisdom and grace granted to her people a guardian as protection from all who would wish them ill."

Itoua sat up a little straighter at that. Good, he too understood at least something of the tale. T'ukri had not changed physical form today under Jordan's watchful gaze, but over the past three days, especially during the hunt, he had let glimmers of his gifts shine through. "The guardian took his task—or hers, for the goddess does not discriminate—seriously, warding off all who came with evil intent. And when the guardian grew old and ill, a new guardian rose among the people to take on the role of protector, so that in each generation, one person bore the gifts of the goddess and Pachamama's people remained safe."

He could end the story there, for the origin of Chapaqpuma was complete, but the lore went on. He glanced at Jordan and Itoua, trying to decide what else to say, when all around the village, mothers began calling their children to come eat.

"But the rest," the children protested.

"Another time," T'ukri said. "Go, your mothers are calling."

They went with mutinous expressions, leaving T'ukri alone with Jordan and Itoua. "Join me?" he asked.

Jordan moved first, but Itoua followed so quickly T'ukri might not have noticed the delay if he had not been watching. "Your story sounds a lot like the one we're trying to chase down," Itoua said.

"I thought you might enjoy it, Dr. Itoua," T'ukri said.

Itoua smiled. "Please, we're going to spend who knows how long together. The least you can do is call me Victor."

"I would be honored," T'ukri said with a formal nod.

"Tell us more about the guardian," Jordan said. "Is it just legend, do you think?"

No, T'ukri wanted to shout, but this was neither the time nor the place to reveal such information. "I have traveled many places and met many people. Beliefs vary from tribe to tribe, but many take comfort in the idea of someone to protect and watch over those who cannot defend against unknown dangers."

"Then it isn't a legend of just one tribe?" Victor asked. "Interesting. How similar are the beliefs you've encountered in different places?"

"Victor, this isn't an interrogation," Jordan teased. "Give the man a chance to breathe."

Victor flushed ever so slightly, bringing a smile to T'ukri's face. "It is fine, Jordan. I admire passion in all its forms, academic as well as physical."

The flush deepened, and was that not interesting? Was this the way to win Victor's interest? It would make sense that a man who had dedicated his life to intellectual pursuits would be flattered by a different kind of attention.

"That doesn't excuse me getting carried away," Victor said. "We should eat something. Would you like to join us?"

Did Victor realize what his casual invitation meant? He was a student of human interaction, so surely he had some idea. If he did, it was one more reason to hope they were open to his courtship. "I would be delighted."

"It's nothing as special as yesterday's dinner," Victor warned. "Just a bit of rabbit stew. I put out some traps today. Jordan and I try to add to the village stores every few days. We wouldn't want our presence to leave anyone else hungry."

The explanation was mundane and logical, but T'ukri could not stop the thrill at knowing Victor had made the meal with food he had caught himself, much as T'ukri had done the day before.

He had to stop reading meaning into every little gesture. Out on the trail, they would only have each other to rely on, so of course they would feed each other with food they had gathered or killed. It would be a matter of survival, not courtship. Plus, as Palta had reminded him today, they were outsiders who did not know the traditions of the Runa.

"Don't let him lie to you," Jordan said. "Everything he makes tastes better than I think it should. Don't ask me to cook for you, on the other hand. I'll hunt all you want, but I can't cook to save my life."

"Believe me, he's tried," Victor quipped.

T'ukri laughed. "Then Jordan can hunt, and you and I will cook when we are in the rainforest," T'ukri told Victor. "As long as each of us contributes to the partnership, how we each do so is less important."

The fire pit behind Victor's hut was small, clearly intended for a single family rather than for a large crowd like the one in the center of the village where T'ukri had prepared his courtship offering the night before, but T'ukri preferred the simple intimacy of it. Yes, his offering had to be publicly made and received, and he had followed the laws and traditions to the letter, even if no one from his tribe had been there to witness it, but Victor and Jordan were not bound the same way, both because they were the ones being courted and because, as outsiders, they did not know the law. If—when—the time came to formalize their courtship into a bond, they would have to do so in the prescribed manner, but this moment was between the three of them, not in front of his people, gathered to watch Chapaqpuma—their guardian, prince, and future king—bond with his mates.

Victor ladled a thick stew into three bowls. He offered Jordan one first, as was proper given their relationship. He should always serve his lover before one he was only considering. It spoke highly of his regard for Jordan. Then he gave one to T'ukri. T'ukri accepted it with a short bow and genuine thanks. When Victor had his own bowl in hand, T'ukri took a taste of the stew.

Jordan was right. The stew seemed simple, chunks of meat in a thick broth along with some potatoes and vegetables, but the flavor was rich, supplemented by a spice T'ukri did not recognize. Perhaps something Victor had carried with him in his travels. The thought warmed T'ukri as much as the stew did. Victor had cooked for them and used not only meat he had hunted but something from his own stores to make it more flavorful. Even if he did not intend it as a courtship gesture, it spoke well of him.

"This is delicious. What did you put in it?" T'ukri asked. "If sharing would not give away any secrets, of course."

Victor laughed, a warm, gentle sound that brought a smile to Jordan's face. *He should smile more often.* "No secret," Victor said. "It's cardamom. It goes well with almost any meat, so I use it to add extra flavor to stews when I don't have any other spices."

"I am sure someone would have shared some spices with you," T'ukri replied.

"I'm sure they would have, but after weeks of eating food prepared by the villagers, I wanted a different flavor. If you'd prefer something more traditional, I can ask." Victor started to stand, but T'ukri grabbed his hand to stop him. Victor and Jordan both tensed minutely at the gesture, only relaxing when T'ukri released him. Interesting indeed that Victor had some warrior instincts when T'ukri had viewed him as a shaman. He would have to remember that.

"There is no need. As I said, this is delicious. I love encountering different tastes as well as different tales when I travel."

"You should see what he can do with a fully stocked kitchen rather than a rations travel pack," Jordan said.

"How long have you been together?" T'ukri hoped Jordan's comment was a simple statement, not a way of pointing out something T'ukri would never share with them.

"We've been coworkers and friends for eight years," Victor said. "The rest is… newer."

It was and was not an answer. Certainly eight years of friendship and working together would lead to a depth of familiarity it would take T'ukri a long time to match, but T'ukri had not thought their romance was new. Perhaps the ease of a long friendship added to the depth of their intimacy on other levels?

"You are fortunate to have such a strong foundation to build on," T'ukri said rather than pressing for more details. No matter how much he wanted to know, it was best if they shared their secrets in their own time.

The two exchanged fond looks, an expression T'ukri desperately wanted directed at him.

"That's one word for it," Jordan said after a moment. "We'll have to tell you that story sometime. But not tonight. Tonight we should discuss the trip into the jungle. Anything special we should know?"

T'ukri almost asked for the story anyway, but Jordan was right. With the journey looming, they needed to be prepared.

"You have gone hunting with Paucar's warriors, so you know much of what you need. The most important thing is never to go off on your own. Here near the village, the worst the rainforest has to offer is kept at bay by the smell of fire and the noise of the village. As we travel into wilder parts, that will not be true. Danger lurks in every corner, and not all of it is obvious," T'ukri replied. Part of his reason for wandering was to keep an eye on the increasing number of people in the headwaters. It would not do for the valley to be caught unaware. "I know you are experienced, but do not let that make you overconfident. I would not lose either of you if I can help it."

"We'd rather not be lost," Victor replied so dryly T'ukri could not decide if he was joking. "We'll stay together. We'd planned to take a tent so we could sleep at night with relative confidence that we were safe. We have a second one if you want it."

T'ukri pondered why they would have two tents when they only needed one. Was their romance truly so new they had not planned on sharing a tent? If so, perhaps he was not as late as he had feared. "Thank you, but no. I am used to sleeping beneath the canopy. I will be fine."

They exchanged looks at that as well, though their expressions were more calculating this time. He was tempted to tell them now, to lay it all out in the open, but while his heart had made its decision, his mind wavered. He silently cursed Palta and her accusations. *There is no rush*, he reminded himself. They were accompanying him into the rainforest. He had time to set his mind at ease before he gave in to the demands of his heart. Besides, his mother would never forgive him if he arrived home bonded before she had a chance to meet his mates.

CHAPTER 14

EVENTUALLY DARKNESS fell, and T'ukri excused himself, leaving Jordan and Victor alone at their hut. "Ready for bed?"

Jordan wiggled his eyebrows, making Victor laugh. "Come on, Harris."

Jordan threw a flirtatious look over his shoulder as he walked into the hut, and Victor remembered the joking promise he'd made that morning. Jordan hadn't actually said whether T'ukri had spent the day naked, but given the mentioned lines on his groin, Victor imagined he had. The lightheartedness of the joke had gotten lost in the seriousness of their conversation when Jordan returned, but Victor wasn't one to break a promise.

"Are you coming, Victor?" Jordan called softly.

"Not yet," Victor replied without thinking. The choked laugh he got in return was worth the lapse in his usual persona. Jordan had never fallen for it anyway.

Jordan had lit the oil lamp in their hut and stripped off his outer layers, leaving only his boxer briefs in place. Form-fitting as they were, they left little to the imagination.

"See something you like?" Jordan drawled.

"More than one thing." Victor winked. Jordan's smile morphed into a cocky grin as he sat down on the bedroll and reached for his shorts.

"No, let me." Victor couldn't put his finger on why it felt so important for him to take care of Jordan tonight, but he had already decided to follow his gut feeling on much weightier matters. Following it now was an easy decision. He quickly stripped his own outer layers off and stretched out next to Jordan. Propped up on one elbow, he took in the full length of Jordan's body in the low light.

"How did I get so lucky?" He kissed Jordan before he could reply. Jordan would counter by saying he was the one who didn't deserve Victor, and that would lead to an argument they didn't need to revisit tonight. He'd work on Jordan's self-esteem another time.

Jordan opened his mouth beneath Victor's, letting him explore to his heart's content. Victor took his time. They'd kissed before, quick pecks as they said hello or goodbye, and deeper kisses during the frantic make-out session yesterday morning, but they'd always been rushed. Victor fully intended to hit the desperation stage before the night was over, but they didn't have to rush this time. Night had fallen, and T'ukri was safely tucked away in his hut. They didn't have anywhere to be before first light tomorrow, and Victor intended to take full advantage of it.

Jordan tried to roll toward Victor, but Victor caught his hip, keeping him flat on the mat. If they started rubbing against each other, they'd end up racing toward climax, and that was the opposite of what he wanted. He wanted—no, he *needed* Jordan to understand how much Victor loved him, how much Victor wanted him. They could get off after he'd burned that realization into Jordan's skin.

Jordan whined deep in his throat when Victor pushed him back down flat, a soft, entreating sound that Victor could get addicted to. He caressed Jordan's side tenderly to settle him. "Relax," he murmured against Jordan's lips. "We'll get there. Let me savor you first."

"You're killing me here, Victor."

"La petite mort?" Victor joked.

"Not fast enough," Jordan muttered.

Victor laughed and kissed Jordan again. Jordan retaliated by wrapping his arms around Victor's shoulders and pulling him down on top of himself.

"Behave." Victor poked Jordan's side to punctuate the demand.

"You know I don't do well with orders." Jordan rocked his hips beneath Victor's.

"If you don't behave, I won't blow you. How's that for incentive?" Victor asked.

Jordan groaned. "Fuck, Victor. Just hearing you say it out loud is almost enough to make me come."

"Then it'll really blow your mind when we get to the real thing." Victor bent enough to press sucking kisses along the tendon in Jordan's neck, down to his collarbone and across the broad, muscled shoulders that had caught his attention the first time they'd met. Since then Victor had come to see Jordan as more than an attractive package or even a talented marksman, but his fascination with Jordan's shoulders and arms had never waned.

"You planning on leaving marks, boss?" Jordan asked.

Victor nipped a little harder. "Don't call me boss when we're in bed."

"What about sir?"

"Not that either." Victor sucked hard on the curve of Jordan's shoulder. If he wore a regular T-shirt, it wouldn't be visible, but if he wore one of the sleeveless ones, T'ukri would be able to see the mark.

Jordan gasped, then quipped, "Possessive? I like that in a guy."

"I'll show you possessive." He was playing right into Jordan's hands, but that was beside the point. They'd passed the time for teasing. He grabbed Jordan's underwear and pushed it down to his knees. He settled his weight over Jordan's legs so they were trapped between his own. Jordan might have hurried him along, but Victor was still the one in charge.

"Fuck, please," Jordan begged.

"Did you want something?" Victor was so close he could feel the heat radiating from Jordan's skin, but he didn't touch his cock yet. He was a greedy bastard. He wanted more of that begging first.

"Fuck you, Itoua." Jordan squirmed, trying to lift his hips enough to initiate contact, but Victor hovered just of reach.

"Not tonight," Victor replied. "No condoms, remember?"

They didn't need them, probably. They'd both had extensive bloodwork done before they left on the expedition, but Victor had a plan and he was sticking to it.

Jordan groaned. "Do something. Anything. Just touch me, for fuck's sake!"

Victor had mercy on him and licked a single stripe up his cock from root to tip. Jordan stuffed his fist in his mouth to muffle his shout. Victor wanted so badly to reach up and pull Jordan's hand away so he could hear him scream, but while they'd said they were done hiding, Victor didn't want to share Jordan's sex noises with the whole village.

He scooted down a little more and nuzzled the base of Jordan's cock, taking the time to savor the musky scent and the feel of wiry hair against his skin. Another time, when this wasn't still so new, he'd rub his face all over Jordan's groin and just revel in it, but neither of them had the patience for that tonight. He mouthed his way up Jordan's cock, careful to keep his teeth behind his lips, until he reached the head. He licked across it and played the tip of his tongue into the slit, reveling in the bitter taste. He drew back the foreskin and sucked gently on the sensitive head. Jordan's hips bucked again, and this time Victor didn't stop him. With Victor's weight on top of him, the movement wasn't enough to choke Victor.

He sucked a little harder, savoring the spurt of fluid that coated his tongue. He shifted a little so he could get his hand on Jordan's balls and rolled them in his palm. They were full and heavy. He'd be getting a mouthful before the night was over.

"Victor." The desperation in Jordan's voice urged Victor to hurry. As much as he wanted to draw it out between them, to show Jordan how much he cherished Jordan's trust and his love, Victor was starting to feel the effects himself. He rutted against Jordan's legs as he took more of the shaft in his mouth.

JORDAN GASPED and tried to curl double, but Victor's weight on his legs held him in place.

Holy fucking hell! Victor "never a hair out of place" Itoua was going down on him like a goddamn pro. He should've known Victor would be as good at blowjobs as he was at everything else, but he'd spent so long convinced it wouldn't ever happen that he couldn't quite make his brain accept it was happening now. Victor worked him thoroughly but oh so fucking tenderly that Jordan didn't know if he wanted to beg him to hurry or for him to never ever stop. God, he'd been blown before. He wasn't some motherfucking virgin, but this wasn't just a blowjob. He didn't know what it was besides the best thing he'd ever felt.

"Shit, Victor," he begged, unable to put his desires into words.

This was comfort and tenderness and safety and love and lust and desire and everything all rolled up in his cock sliding between Victor's lips, in Victor's tongue along the shaft, in his throat swallowing around the head. *Shit, fuck, holy hell*, Victor was deepthroating him. What had started as a joke because Jordan had spent the day watching T'ukri naked again had become something far beyond a simple reward for a job done well.

After everything they'd said to each other, after all the things they'd discussed, this was affirmation. This was him and Victor united in the face of whatever the future held. Good or bad, they'd deal with it together.

He clutched at Victor's shoulder with one hand, not wanting to grab his head. He didn't want Victor to feel trapped or forced. Jordan knew what that felt like, and he'd never put another person in that situation. The other hand he kept pressed against his mouth to stifle any sounds. Victor shifted, freeing his legs, and Jordan drew his knees up so they framed Victor's ribs, an approximation of a hug.

He bit the base of his thumb to stifle his scream. When he could catch his breath, he gasped, "Fuck, Victor, close." He struggled to get the words out past the haze of lust in his head. Victor tapped his hip to show he'd heard him and didn't let up in the slightest.

Oh fuck! Victor was going to swallow. That realization pushed him over the edge. His balls drew up tight as he came… and came… and came. And Victor worked him all the way through it until he collapsed back on the mat, panting for breath, so sensitive that the whisper of Victor's breath over his cock was exquisite torture.

"You gotta let me." He reached for Victor's underwear.

Victor arched so Jordan could finish stripping him, but before Jordan could even get his mouth on Victor's dick, he was climaxing, his come exploding all over Jordan's face.

"Merde, sorry," Victor gasped. "I didn't realize I was that close."

"'S okay," Jordan said. "I like that I can get you that worked up."

"The noises you were making and the way you just gave yourself to me. Of course I got worked up. I'm not made of stone."

No, Victor was all flesh and blood. Hot, naked flesh Jordan still wasn't well enough acquainted with. "Tomorrow night, I get to blow you."

"Okay."

Jordan looked at Victor in surprise.

"What? Did you expect me to say no?"

"I expected you to point out that we'd be in the jungle and that T'ukri would be sleeping a few feet away," Jordan said.

"We're in the jungle now, and T'ukri's sleeping a few feet away," Victor replied. "And yes, tomorrow night we'll be in a tent, not a hut, and T'ukri may be sleeping closer than he is now, but that doesn't change anything. I can't let the fact that we decided to let his potential courtship proceed change the way I treat you now. You're my partner and my lover. He's someone who might someday get added to that. Or not."

Jordan nodded and reached for his discarded boxers to clean off his face. When that was done, he snuggled close to Victor. "I feel the same way. If his courting us gets in the way of us, we stop it right then. But you have to tell me if you feel that way. I'm shit when it comes to relationships. I don't want to fuck this up because I missed some sign that should have been obvious but that I didn't know how to read. I didn't exactly have any good role models growing up."

"I'll tell you," Victor promised, "as long as you talk to me too. Relationships go both ways. Deal?"

Jordan kissed the side of Victor's neck and snuggled closer. "Deal."

CHAPTER 15

T'UKRI ROSE well before the sun the following day. He had completed the required rituals, but he had made no preparations for the trip itself. While he was confident in his ability to travel lightly and swiftly through the rainforest and to live off its bounty as he did so, he would not be alone on this trip, nor could he move at his usual speed. His malku had proven better than T'ukri had expected in the rainforest, but T'ukri had not traveled far, and he had yet to see how Victor would fare outside of the village. Neither had seemed worried when discussing the trek, and they had made it as far as the village alone over some difficult terrain, but that guaranteed nothing. Over the distance they had to cover—and allowing time for him to be confident in his decision to take them home—they would need provisions.

He checked the pouches on his leather belt and the pockets of the pants he wore as a guide, making sure he had matches as well as flint and steel so they would always have a fire at night. From another pouch he withdrew his snares and checked each one over for wear. He could not set snares as they traveled, but they would not travel every day. At times they would stop to rest for a day or two, to replenish their supply of meat, to gather what greens and tubers they could find, to bathe and rest and clean their clothes and gear. They were not soldiers on a forced march. Their trek had no timeline beyond T'ukri's courtship. If they arrived in a week or a year, it mattered not, as long as when they arrived, he could present them as his desired mates with confidence.

Palta's words that they were not all and also more than they appeared lingered in his mind, but he pushed that aside. The jungle had its ways of bringing out the heart of a person, and that was what mattered in the final reckoning.

He examined his spear next. The hunt two days prior had been a simple one, though even the simplest throw could damage the point, making it that much harder to bring down his prey the next time, but the point was as sharp and the edge as lethal as ever. He would have no trouble feeding his mates while on their trek.

He dressed not in the comfortable wraps he had been wearing in the village but in his more Western attire, and went in search of breakfast.

Kichka welcomed him to her fire with a knowing smile. "I will prepare the deer hide and save it for your next visit. It would make a fine piece for a bonding bed."

Heat rose in T'ukri's cheeks as he bowed his head to Kichka. "I would be honored to present the work of your hands to my mates."

Kichka smiled impishly, giving T'ukri a glimpse of the girl she had once been, before age and responsibility matured her. "They are good men. They may be outsiders, but they have never once hesitated to join us in our traditions. You have chosen well."

That required more than a simple bow of his head. He rose and bowed to her formally. "Thank you for your blessing, honored mother."

"Eat. They will be out soon, and you should be ready for them."

T'ukri hurriedly consumed the quinoa porridge she offered him. As he thanked her once more for her hospitality, he heard the rustle of movement behind him and turned to see Victor walk out of his hut. He had spent days studying his mates, yet still Victor surprised him. Gone were Victor's light pants, shirts, and sandals, replaced by an outfit similar to what Jordan usually wore: camouflage pants, dark T-shirt, and heavy black boots. T'ukri had seen the competence beneath Victor's kind exterior, but he had not looked deeper. Looking at him now, T'ukri could imagine Victor dealing with situations he had previously assumed would fall to Jordan. Then Jordan stepped up beside Victor, and T'ukri wondered if he had truly seen them at all. Jordan wore a similar pack to Victor's, but lighter, and clipped to it were a bow and quiver. Here, finally, was the hunter Paucar's warriors had praised, the warrior T'ukri had sensed beneath the surface. T'ukri would pity anyone in the path of Jordan's arrows except that he already knew those arrows would only seek those who deserved to die.

Yes, these were indeed worthy of being his mates.

"Have you eaten?" he asked when they approached.

"We finished the stew from last night," Victor said easily. "It wouldn't still be good when we returned anyway."

If T'ukri had his way, they would not be returning at all, or only with him to gather any items they left behind now when he came to collect the deer hide. "Then shall we go?"

Before they could reply, a commotion at the edge of the village drew their attention. Five men in mismatched camouflage with heavy rifles strode into the clearing. T'ukri tensed. Soldiers would have been in proper uniforms, so whoever these men were, they were trouble.

Jordan and Victor had reached the same conclusion, if their expressions were any indication. Jordan pulled his bow from its hook, although he held it loosely at his side rather than drawn and threatening. Yet.

Good. T'ukri would prefer the upcoming conversation to end peacefully and without him having to reveal his true nature, but if it did not, he would have assistance.

T'ukri moved smoothly to Paucar's side, to act as translator if necessary and to be better able to defend him if it came to a fight. Around the village, the warriors gathered, as tense and battle-ready as T'ukri.

"Who are you and what do you want?" Paucar asked the men.

"We're just introducing ourselves," the man in the lead said with a toothy grin that raised T'ukri's hackles. "It's always a good idea to know who the players are when we're new to an area."

"There are no players here," Paucar said. "Only a village living a peaceful life."

"Good to know." The man patted his rifle. "Then we won't have any trouble."

T'ukri frowned and took a step closer to Paucar. He could not let the guardian inside him loose, as much as he wanted to, but he let some of the anger he was feeling seep into his aura. There might be no "players" in Paucar's village, but if these men were looking for trouble, T'ukri had no issue with making sure they found it.

Paucar caught his eye and shook his head. T'ukri subsided but kept a watchful eye on the men as they looked around the village one more time before leaving.

"That was unpleasant," Victor said when they were gone.

"Nandini said there were reports of criminal activity in the area," Jordan added. "It looks like she was right."

"If you prefer to change our plans, I will understand," T'ukri offered. He could court them as well in the village as in the rainforest.

"We'd probably be in more danger here than we would in the jungle," Jordan said. "It's a lot harder to find three people on the move than a village in a fixed location. But it feels wrong to leave them at the mercy of those men."

"Your feelings do you credit, but we would not keep you from your research. My hunters may not have your aim, but we have fended for ourselves for many years," Paucar interrupted. "We will be fine."

"You're right," Jordan said. "I didn't mean to imply otherwise. I just spent so long in the military always thinking about protecting civilians that I have trouble getting out of that mindset."

"As I said, your feelings do you credit, but we have nothing those men want. They know that now. I doubt they will be back."

T'ukri would be making sure of it before they left the area for good.

Paucar turned and gestured to one of the women, who approached, a large burlap sack in hand. "Provisions for your journey. In appreciation of all your contributions during your time with us."

"No thanks are necessary," Victor replied as he took the bag. "You have done so much for us already."

Jordan unshouldered his pack and added the sack to it. T'ukri could not guess how much weight the supplies would add, but Jordan gave no sign of feeling it.

"Thank you," he said to Paucar when everything was settled again. "Hopefully we'll see you again on our way home."

Paucar nodded and shook their hands, but the smile he offered T'ukri spoke volumes about when and why Paucar expected to see them again. He might not know T'ukri was Chapaqpuma, but he knew T'ukri was courting them, with all that entailed.

"Are you ready?" T'ukri asked them.

Jordan grinned at T'ukri as he nudged Victor. "Into the wild."

"Geek," Victor muttered, his voice full of affection.

"Like you're one to talk," Jordan shot back, an open smile on his face. "How many Star Wars dolls do you own again?"

Victor didn't reply to the rhetorical question, although he would be getting revenge for the *dolls* comment. Right now, though, he was too entranced by Jordan's expression to think up a witty reply. How many people ever got to see this side of Jordan? He had a reputation around the university as a *rousing* good time, but Victor had seen him after those nights, looking loose physically but somehow even tenser than before, nothing like the easy, laughing man in front of him now. Did those one-night stands realize what they'd missed out on? Or had they been so focused on being able to brag they'd bagged Harris that they'd missed everything that made him Jordan?

Never again, Victor swore. From now on, Jordan would have all the affection he could stand to go along with the sex. He would know what it meant to be loved, not just fucked.

T'ukri's open, curious expression caught Victor's attention, and he kept a scowl off his face by force of will alone. Victor might have agreed to see what T'ukri's intentions were, but if he thought for one moment that Victor would let him toy with Jordan in any way... well, Victor might not have Jordan's level of military experience, but he had his own ways of dealing with things.

"It's a movie reference," Jordan explained as he gestured for T'ukri to lead them out. "From my favorite movie series, which is based on my favorite book. I'm not completely obsessed like Mr. Star Wars back there, but sometimes I just can't resist a good line."

"Not completely obsessed?" Victor repeated. "Then what's with the T-shirts?" Today's had an image of Sauron using the One Ring to do the hula.

Jordan smirked. "I told you. I can't resist a good line."

Victor rolled his eyes. It was so much more than that, but he let Jordan have his delusions.

"Movies are not a luxury we have this deep in the rainforest, but books are a valued treasure," T'ukri replied. "Perhaps you will share yours with me in the future."

Victor relaxed marginally as they left the village behind. The offer seemed genuine, and that allayed some of his worry that T'ukri only saw Jordan for his looks. He forced his gaze off Jordan's ass and onto his surroundings. Even with T'ukri guiding them, danger could come from any direction, as the odd encounter that morning had proven, and Victor meant to watch Jordan's back, not his backside.

"I don't have it with me, but I bet I could find a copy in Cusco," Jordan said. "We'll have to head that direction at some point to check in with the university and pick up more supplies, so I could look for one then."

T'ukri's flinch was so minute Victor thought for a moment he was imagining things until Jordan glanced his way with a raised eyebrow. Whatever had caused the reaction, Jordan had seen it too. They'd discuss it later, if they could find a moment alone. For now they would both keep their eyes open for any other oddities.

"Do you have a thought to where we might find more information on Philli-philli?" Victor asked.

Another flinch, though T'ukri's expression was serene when he turned to look at Victor.

"A few, but such places are not easy to find, even for me," T'ukri said. "We will explore and we will see what we can find. Sometimes the goddess is willing. Sometimes she is not."

The villagers had referenced a whole pantheon of gods and goddesses over the weeks they'd spent there, and T'ukri's story of the guardian had included more than a few as well, but as Victor tried to remember exactly what he'd said, he thought Pachamama, the Earth goddess, was the only one identified by name. He had no way of knowing if she was the goddess T'ukri referred to now.

"Makes it hard to believe in them, doesn't it?" Jordan drawled from T'ukri's other side.

"Only sometimes," T'ukri replied. "Other times it makes it quite easy."

Jordan spluttered a little. "Okay, you got me there."

T'ukri smiled at him before turning to include Victor in the warm expression. Yes, Victor could see why Jordan would find T'ukri attractive, and not just on the physical level. Even in a language not his own, he managed to banter with them. Victor returned the smile, and they fell into comfortable silence as they continued deeper into the rainforest. The undergrowth thinned out as they entered a section of tall canopy, the huge trees enough to block direct light to the forest floor. Even the sound of their footsteps seemed hushed. With greater sightlines, T'ukri scouted ahead of them some, giving Victor an opportunity to see what Jordan had meant when he talked about T'ukri becoming the forest rather than moving through it. Even keeping his gaze fixed on their guide, he nearly lost sight of him among the tree trunks and gently swaying vines.

But only nearly. T'ukri never strayed so far that he disappeared from sight entirely, which reassured Victor after the confrontation in the village. He wouldn't want any of them going off alone now that he'd seen the truth of Nandini's warning.

When the sun had started its descent, T'ukri called a halt for the day near the bank of a small creek with crystal clear water running over a bed of stones. "We can make camp here. I will set snares and see what I can find for us eat for dinner."

"We have the provisions from Paucar. We can use some of those," Jordan said.

"Better to save those for times when I am unsuccessful in my search," T'ukri replied.

"Do you want one of us to go with you?" Victor offered. "I'm not sure it's safe to wander alone."

T'ukri smiled. "But if one of you went with me, the other would be here alone. I have seen no sign of those men today as we traveled, but if they are in the area, it will be easier for me to avoid them if I am alone. And you will be safer here together."

Victor glanced at Jordan, who nodded. "Very well. We'll get the camp set up and a fire going to prepare whatever you find."

"I should return within an hour, two at the most," T'ukri said.

It would still be light, although barely, then. Victor might not like it, but he had no reason to argue. He would focus on pitching the tent and starting a fire, and then he would have the remaining time with Jordan—always a good thing in his estimation.

T'UKRI KEPT his gait easy and normal until he was well out of sight and hearing of their campsite. He could not transform into Chapaqpuma in the mortal world without a bond, but he could avail himself of some of the guardian's gifts.

He had not lied to Jordan and Victor. He had not seen any sign of the mercenaries as they hiked, but he had been aware of their location all the same. The jungle's secrets were no secret from him. He took a deep breath until he caught a whiff of their tobacco and sprang off in that direction. Even traveling at speed, it would take him thirty minutes or more to reach them and that much time to return. That left him an hour to deal with them and to find something for dinner. With his senses on high alert, finding a few rabbits or the like should not be difficult as long as dealing with the mercenaries did not scare off all the game in the area.

He slowed when he neared the camp and took stock of the situation. Only three of the five men from that morning lazed around a campfire, their guns nowhere in sight. If anything proved how unprepared they were for the terrain, it was that. T'ukri might be by far the most dangerous thing in the area, but he was by no means the only potential threat.

Keeping to the brush and using the shadows to his advantage, he ghosted around the edges of the camp until he located their weapons, all stacked together near one of the tents. *Stupid outsiders.*

Grimacing with disgust, he removed the magazines from the rifles. He would destroy them later if he could, but this would do for now.

That done, he hefted his spear and strode into their camp. "You are trespassing on tribal land. Leave or face the consequences."

The leader snorted. "You're that jungle guide from the village this morning. Do you really think you can scare us off?"

He gave a dismissive wave of his hand and his goons lunged at T'ukri.

T'ukri took the first one down with a kick to the groin. The other one circled him warily, looking for an opening T'ukri did not intend to give him. Using the shaft of his spear as a club, he swung in a circle, connecting with his man's knees.

"Enough," the leader roared, grabbing one of the rifles T'ukri had disarmed. He pulled the trigger, but nothing happened. He tossed it aside with a growl, drew a knife, and rushed at T'ukri.

T'ukri took a step to the side, grabbed his own knife, and slit the man's throat.

Blood spurted everywhere, coating his hands, his knife, and soaking into the ground at his feet. Later, he would feel sorrow for the man's death, but now he was the jungle predator, protecting his territory without remorse.

"Well?" he said to the other two.

The one he had kicked in the groin started to back away, but the other drew a pistol that T'ukri had not seen from beneath his vest. Cursing under his breath, he dove to the side as he threw his spear, aiming for the man's shoulder. When he dodged, though, the point caught him between his ribs. The pistol clattered to the ground. T'ukri rolled to his feet and faced the remaining man. When he still did not move, T'ukri smothered a curse and pounced, wringing the final man's neck.

He went to check the man he had speared, but he was clearly dying. "Who sent you and why?"

The man coughed, blood speckling his lips, but did not reply.

"Tell me." T'ukri grabbed the haft of the spear. He did not want to cause the man more pain, but if it was the only way to learn what he needed to know, he would do it.

The threat appeared to be enough, though, because the man gasped out a name. "Ramos. He wants to mine...." His eyes rolled back in his head and he lay still.

T'ukri muffled another curse, but at least he had a name now, even if he had little else to go on. Alluvial gold mining might be illegal, but this far up into the Amazon basin, where people were few and far between and law enforcement even scarcer, stopping such mining was a challenge.

T'ukri retrieved his spear and cleaned the point and his knife on the dead men's clothes. His own had escaped the worst of the spray, although he would have to find a place to wash his hands and arms. A few dead rabbits or a capybara could not explain the mess, and Jordan and Victor were too smart to fall for such a lie.

He could only hope the two missing men found their dead compatriots and carried word back to this Ramos that the rainforest was not unprotected.

JORDAN LOOKED around the clearing they were using as a campsite, but they'd done everything they could to prepare for the night until T'ukri returned with meat.

"It's taking a long time," Jordan said when he joined Victor next to the fire.

"Hunting is an art, not a science," Victor replied with a shrug. "He will return when he returns."

"I'm just saying it never took me two hours to find game when I went hunting with Paucar's men. Maybe to find something big enough for the whole village, but not a couple of rabbits or something for the three of us."

"Are you worried he abandoned us or that something happened to him?" Victor asked.

"Maybe a little of both," Jordan admitted. "I mean, if he abandoned us, we just go back to Paucar's tomorrow and keep learning what we can from them, so it's not the end of the world." And in a lot of ways, it would be simpler. "And I saw him hunting that deer. He wouldn't be easy prey for anything—or anyone—who tried to take him out, but that's no defense against bullets, and those men this morning were well armed."

"But we haven't seen any sign of them or their passage all day, and we left in a different direction than they went," Victor pointed out. "So unless they doubled back and followed us, I doubt they're close enough to be a problem."

Great. Just what Jordan needed. Another reason to watch his back. Although, as Nan was fond of saying, it wasn't paranoia if someone was really after them, and he and Victor had been wearing their packs that morning. If the men were at all observant, they would have noticed, and they might have decided to follow, since Jordan especially stood out pretty obviously next to the bronzed skin of the tribesmen. Victor was darker than any of them, but they might have missed that at a glance. There was no way they could have missed the presence of a white man.

"It might be worth standing watch tonight, just to be safe," Jordan said.

Victor started to reply, but a noise in the jungle caught both their attention. Jordan set an arrow to his bowstring, ready to defend them if necessary. He only relaxed when T'ukri appeared, a smile on his face and a good-sized capybara in his hand. "It is no deer, but it will make a good dinner for us tonight, roasted over a fire."

"I've never had capybara before," Victor said. "You'll have to show me the best way to prepare it."

Jordan would leave that task to the two of them, although with little else to occupy him—he'd already gathered plenty of firewood and the tent was ready—he stayed where he was as T'ukri joined them and began to skin and gut their dinner.

"If we were at home, I would season it, wrap it in banana leaves, and bury it in coals to roast for hours, and it would be so tender the meat would fall off the bone, but we do not have time for that tonight."

"Maybe one day we can make camp early—or not travel at all—so you can prepare it for us," Victor replied. "It sounds delicious."

"Perhaps," T'ukri said. "When we have been traveling a while and need a day to rest."

"You were gone a long time," Jordan said. "Everything okay?"

"It took me some time to find what I was looking for," T'ukri replied. "Having strangers in the rainforest has left game scarce and skittish."

Jordan looked at him sharply, but his face was serene. Did T'ukri mean the men from that morning or Jordan and Victor? After weeks of living in the village and hunting with Paucar's warriors, Jordan was hardly a stranger in this part of the jungle, and while Victor might not have gone out with them very often, he wasn't inexperienced. Their passage today shouldn't have caused more than a momentary disruption for the local fauna. "Did you see any sign of the mercenaries while you were hunting?"

"Nothing to suggest they will be a problem," T'ukri said.

"That's good, but I think we should set a watch tonight. I'll take the middle shift. I never sleep through the night anyway."

T'ukri looked like he wanted to ask about that, but Victor caught his attention before he could. "Shall I fashion a spit for the meat? Or did you have another way to prepare it?"

Jordan shot Victor a grateful smile, although he was sure T'ukri would remember and ask about it later. And really, if they were doing this courtship thing, T'ukri would find out eventually because Jordan wasn't exaggerating. The couple of nights he'd slept next to Victor were definitely the exception to his usual sleep pattern, and while he'd love to pretend he was done with nightmares, he was too much of a realist (no, Nan, he was not a pessimist, thank you very fucking much) to expect to get that lucky.

Victor put together a makeshift spit and T'ukri set the carcass over the fire, leaving Jordan alone with his thoughts.

"I do not think a watch is necessary," T'ukri said when everything was settled again, "but I will take the first shift if you are set on having one."

"At least for a few nights," Jordan replied. "Until we're sure they aren't following us. It never hurts to be careful."

"Indeed."

They fell into a comfortable silence after that, as T'ukri turned the meat over the flames and Victor used some of the supplies from Paucar to whip up a vegetable dish of some kind.

Once everything was settled, Victor went to his pack and came back with a map of the area. "By my calculations, Paucar's village is here," he said, pointing to the mark he had added when they found the village, "which would put us about here now. Where are we heading?"

T'ukri examined the map for a moment before shaking his head. "Somewhere in this area." T'ukri circled a wide, empty area with his finger. "The landmarks I use to find my way are not the kind that appear on the maps of outsiders."

Which was fair, Jordan supposed, even if he didn't like the answer. He hadn't seen T'ukri use so much as a compass, much less any of the more sophisticated GPS equipment some of their guides and porters had used on past expeditions. T'ukri's comment underscored the distance between them, though, courtship or no courtship. They'd lost their minds, thinking this could work, no matter how much he wanted it to.

"What kind of landmarks?"

"The kind locals depend on," T'ukri replied. "A tree with a twisted trunk, an exposed rock face, a bend in a stream or a waterfall. Nothing that would appear on a map, except perhaps the stream, but there are so many in this area that they would not all fit on a map that size."

It wasn't a satisfactory answer by any means, but Jordan couldn't think of a way to ask for a better one without sounding rude or suspicious. He might be suspicious, but that was his default state, and he didn't want to be rude. He'd ask Victor about it later. They could always bring it back up again, and unlike T'ukri, they did have compasses along with the skill to track their location on a map. Once they reached their destination, they could pinpoint it then.

"The meat should be done," T'ukri said. "Shall we eat?"

Jordan grabbed his and Victor's mess kits from their packs as T'ukri began carving the meat. They ate in the silence of hungry men, too focused on the food to bother with conversation, and by the time they were done, the sun had sunk below the horizon and their campfire was the only light to be had.

"If we're sleeping in shifts, we should go to bed," Victor said. "We don't want to be tired tomorrow."

T'ukri fetched his spear and rested it across his thighs. "Sleep well. I will wake you later."

Jordan followed Victor to their tent and inside. Once he'd zipped the flap shut, he stripped off his pants so he was wearing only his T-shirt and boxers. "Well?" he asked Victor softly.

"Well what?"

"Something isn't sitting right with me, but I can't put my finger on what. I mean, he was gone longer than I thought he should've been, but he had an explanation. I would've liked a better answer to your question about our destination, but it's not like the map we have is particularly detailed."

"So we do what we always do on expeditions," Victor replied. "We trust our guide until we have reason not to, but we watch each other's backs regardless."

"Except this isn't a regular expedition, is it?" Jordan asked. "I mean, just the fact that we're sharing a tent is already a huge change."

"In some ways," Victor agreed. "But not in as many as you think. If anything, I can worry about you less since you're right here with me, so I know you're safe."

There was that. "I'm probably worrying for nothing."

"There's nothing wrong with being cautious. We've only known T'ukri a few days, no matter how strong a connection you feel to him after observing his rituals."

And that was the problem, wasn't it? Jordan *wanted* T'ukri to be the man he had built up in his head from watching the rituals. He *wanted* the relationship they seemed to foreshadow. There was already so much riding on this expedition, between the paper and Victor's job and visa status, not to mention Nandini's warning, which had become a lot more relevant after the confrontation that morning. The potential of starting a relationship with T'ukri added even more weight to it, and Jordan wasn't sure it wouldn't crumble like a house of cards at the slightest provocation.

They'd lost their fucking minds. No two ways about it.

"Try to get some sleep," Victor said. "We aren't going to solve this tonight and probably not any time soon. The only way to get answers is to see it through."

Jordan nodded and pulled Victor down next to him. His shoulder was the best pillow Jordan had ever had.

THE NIGHT passed quietly, only T'ukri waking Jordan and then later Jordan waking Victor disturbing the peace. When the stars started to fade into morning, Victor built the fire back up and put water on for tea. He was almost out of coffee, but Paucar had included a packet of coca leaves in the supplies he'd given them. They might be away from the highest altitudes, but it was still cool in the mornings, and a hot drink was welcome.

T'ukri stirred first. Victor gave him as much privacy as he could, keeping his back to where T'ukri had slept beneath the stars until he heard T'ukri up and moving around. "Tea?"

"Yes, please," T'ukri replied. "And I will start some quinoa. We can eat it with the last of the vegetables and meat from last night."

"I'll wake Jordan while you get that started," Victor said.

"If he is still asleep, do not disturb him. It will be a few minutes before the quinoa is ready. We can wake him when it is time to eat."

Victor glanced toward the tent, but Jordan had taken the middle shift, and he had said himself the day before that he slept badly more nights than not. If he was still asleep now, they could afford to let him stay that way. Plus, it would give Victor a chance to spend some time with T'ukri.

"How long have you been a guide?"

"For a little over ten years," T'ukri said, "although I often go home between treks for weeks or months at a time. I miss my family too much when I am gone to stay away for long."

"You are fortunate to have a home to go back to," Victor said, thinking of his tense relationship with his parents and what he knew of Jordan's life bouncing from group home to foster home and back again.

"You do not have one?" T'ukri asked, his eyebrows lifting in surprise.

"Of course we have places to live," Victor said, thinking of his condo, "but a place to live is not the same as a home. My grandparents lived in the Republic of Congo until their deaths, and my parents live in France. I speak with them on birthdays and holidays, but it has been many years since I considered their house my home."

Jordan could tell his own story when, or if, he was ready.

"I cannot imagine what life would be like without my home to ground me," T'ukri said with a shake of his head.

No, Victor did not imagine he could, and he hoped T'ukri would never have to.

The sound of the tent zipper drew their attention as Jordan stumbled out, all his usual coordination gone as he blinked at them with bleary eyes. "Fuck. It's morning."

"It does usually follow night, yes," Victor said dryly. "There's coca tea if you want some."

"I would kill for real coffee," Jordan muttered, but he took the mug of tea Victor held out to him.

"We grow coffee in my village, but I do not take the beans with me when I travel," T'ukri said. "Another reason to go home often."

"Bastard," Jordan grumbled. "Taunting me that way."

Victor laughed and finished his tea. "Drink up. We need to break camp. We're wasting daylight."

Jordan grumbled a little more, but he drank his tea and set the cup aside, looking more awake. "I'll pack up and get the tent down while you finish making breakfast. I'm not hiking all day without something to eat."

"The quinoa will be ready soon," T'ukri said.

Victor followed Jordan back to the tent to pack his own gear and help dismantle the tent. It was designed so a single person could set it up or take it down, but it still went faster with two.

By the time they were finished, T'ukri had the quinoa done, so they ate and headed out. Much like the day before, T'ukri scouted ahead periodically, drifting in and out of sight. Then late in the afternoon, he disappeared completely. Victor glanced at Jordan to find him unclipping his bow and drawing an arrow as he scoured their surroundings. A moment later they heard the sharp cry of an unknown animal, followed by a silence so deep and thick it seemed the world had stopped spinning. Then a monkey chittered overhead, and everything returned to normal. Jordan dropped his guard and eventually returned the arrow to his quiver, though he could draw again in a second.

And then T'ukri reappeared carrying a couple of dead rabbits.

"If you'd told me you were going hunting, I'd've gone with you." Jordan gestured to his bow.

"For such a small target, your arrows were more than we needed," T'ukri said. "A well-placed stone to the head left the meat intact for us to enjoy."

"You haven't seen me shoot," Jordan replied, not quite belligerent, although Victor had spent enough time with Jordan to know that could turn on a dime.

"I have not," T'ukri said, either ignoring or not seeing Jordan's reaction, "but I look forward to the time when I do. Paucar spoke highly of your skills. And your kindness in sharing them with his village."

When he'd seen Jordan shoot, he wouldn't question whether he could bring down something the size of the rabbit without damaging the meat, but Victor wouldn't save T'ukri from that pitfall. He would have to learn that one on his own.

Thunder rumbled in the distance, drawing their attention toward the sky, but the canopy was too thick to let them see the approaching storm. "If you would?" T'ukri held the rabbits out toward Victor. "I will check the skies."

Victor took the rabbit skeptically, not sure how T'ukri intended to check on anything through the leaves overhead, but T'ukri simply scaled the nearest tree like a ladder until he disappeared into the greenery above.

"How did he do that?" Jordan asked softly.

Before Victor could answer, T'ukri dropped back down beside them. "We have an hour, perhaps two, before the storm is upon us. I know a spot not far ahead where we can take shelter until it passes or for the night."

"Let's go," Victor said. He'd hiked in worse than a rainforest thundershower, but that didn't mean he liked doing it. If they could stay dry, he'd take it.

JORDAN WOULDN'T admit to being curious about the shelter T'ukri claimed to know of. He'd only been this far into the jungle while hunting with Paucar's warriors once, when game had eluded all of them, but he hadn't seen anything more substantial than the forest canopy to provide protection from the weather. Then again, it hadn't rained while they were out, so maybe it was in some out-of-the-way corner they'd skipped.

"Not far ahead" turned out to be a forty-five-minute hike slightly east of the direction they had initially been heading, but not so far east as to be a complete change of direction. By the time T'ukri slowed, the rolls of thunder were nearly constant, and the dappled patches of sunlight from early in the day had given way to a uniform gloom that seemed more like dusk than midafternoon. Jordan looked around, seeking the shelter T'ukri had promised, but he still couldn't see anything more interesting than a particularly large deadfall of branches.

The deadfall that T'ukri was walking purposefully toward.

Well, shit. Did he expect them to burrow under a pile of brush like snakes? They'd probably find snakes under there if they started digging, and Jordan really didn't want to deal with a snakebite on top of the rain. He had a multipurpose antivenin, but given the variety of snakes in the area, it wouldn't necessarily be more than partially effective.

"Give me one moment," T'ukri said. "It has been some time since I last used this shelter. I should make sure nothing dangerous has taken up residence in my absence."

Jordan frowned as T'ukri reached for the pile of brush. He glanced at Victor, who met his gaze with a pinched expression of his own. That made him feel a little better. If Victor's experience in the jungle hadn't given him a better feeling about this, then they were on the same page. *As always*, Jordan thought. Worst case, they had their tent and could pitch it in a matter of a minute. It only slept two, but they could squeeze T'ukri in until the storm passed.

"We should have brought the second tent," Jordan murmured to Victor as T'ukri pulled away a section of brush to reveal an empty space beneath it.

"Or maybe we shouldn't have underestimated him," Victor murmured back. T'ukri ducked into the open space and disappeared completely.

A moment later T'ukri popped back out. "It will be snug with all three of us, but it is safe. Come, the rain will start any second now."

And fuck if T'ukri wasn't right. Jordan felt the first drop of rain hit his arm as they crossed to the entrance of the shelter. Victor shrugged off his pack and handed it to Jordan before ducking into the small arch. He reached back out for his pack, then took Jordan's and his bow so Jordan could follow him in. T'ukri came in last, pulling the brush back into place behind him. With that source of light gone, the interior of the shelter was almost pitch black.

"Just a minute." Victor was digging in his pack from the rustling Jordan could hear. After a few seconds he switched on a flashlight, pointed carefully behind him so it wouldn't blind anyone. "There. Now we have a bit of light to see by."

Jordan looked up from where he sat, squished between Victor and T'ukri, to examine the roof. What had, from the outside, appeared to be a random pile of brush now resolved into a carefully woven net of branches and leaves, crisscrossed so tightly the rain didn't penetrate.

"Fucking brilliant," Jordan said to T'ukri. "Did you build this?"

"No, though I always check on it when I am in the area. There are shelters like these scattered throughout the region, if one knows how to look. Local guides and hunters share their locations, a trade secret of sorts. Knowing where to seek shelter can mean the difference between life and death in the right circumstances."

"Truth," Jordan replied.

"The construction is ingenious." Victor ran his hand along the inside. "I've built my share of makeshift shelters, but nothing like this."

T'ukri beamed beneath the praise.

The patter of rain on the branches above them increased, signaling the beginning of a downpour. T'ukri rapped his fist against the frame that supported the entryway. "The first rain of the season. At home the children will dance to celebrate, and their mothers will despair of ever getting all the mud off them."

"That would be something to see," Victor said with a soft smile.

"There are no children here to lead the celebration for us, but it is still the first rain of the season, and it must be marked. Will you dance with me instead?" T'ukri asked.

"I thought the point of finding shelter was to stay dry," Jordan joked.

"Skin dries faster than cloth," T'ukri replied with a challenging arch of his eyebrow. "With you or without, I will dance."

Jordan swallowed hard as he exchanged glances with Victor. When he looked back at T'ukri, he had already pulled off the vest and belt he was wearing and was unbuttoning his cutoffs. Feeling like all the air had been sucked out of the small space, Jordan watched as T'ukri shimmied out of his clothes and turned to move the brush out of the way, his ass practically in Jordan's face. T'ukri stood into the rain with the same grace that had marked everything Jordan had watched him do, took two steps away from the shelter, lifted his arms and his face to the sky, and began to dance.

"Fuck," Jordan breathed.

"He probably would if you asked him," Victor said next to him, his tone so flat Jordan tore his attention from the spectacle of T'ukri dancing in the rain to look at Victor instead.

"Hey, whatever you're thinking, stop." Jordan nudged Victor's shoulder with his own. "You know I didn't mean it literally."

"I know." Victor tore his own gaze away from T'ukri. "He's just so...." He waved his hand toward T'ukri.

"Yeah, that exactly," Jordan said. "We could join him. Make him as crazy as he's making us."

THE IMAGE of Jordan and T'ukri dancing together in the rain flashed through Victor with all the power of the lightning flashing overhead. He could see it clear as day, and what an image it was. Jordan wouldn't say anything more, but Victor could see the way he was vibrating with excitement. T'ukri had talked about the children of the village being the ones who danced in the rain, but Jordan had never had the chance to be a child, not really. All the mud puddles Victor had played in as a boy, all the splashing and laughter and joy, had been denied Jordan.

"Go on," he said. "I know you want to."

"I want *us* to," Jordan insisted.

Victor knew that too. "Not exactly my style, Harris."

"Fuck that. We're in the middle of the rainforest with no one around to see but you, me, and T'ukri. And T'ukri and I don't care."

No, Victor didn't imagine they did, but then they were both a good deal younger than he was. Younger and more fit and less inhibited. "Go on. Make him regret teasing us."

Jordan got a mulish expression, but Victor kept his unflappable mask in place. Jordan could glare all he wanted. Victor had developed a resistance to everything but his puppy-dog eyes years ago, and Jordan wasn't deploying those. "Fine, but don't blame me when you miss out on all the fun."

Jordan pulled his T-shirt over his head, revealing his strong back and his tattoo, but before he could strip his pants off, Victor pulled him in for a quick kiss. "Who says I won't be having all the fun I need, watching you run around in the rain like a forest spirit come to life just for my enjoyment?"

"I think you've got me mixed up with T'ukri. He's the forest spirit if ever there was one."

Victor looked outside to where T'ukri swayed and leaped beneath the falling rain. Jordan had told him how in tune T'ukri was with the rainforest, but seeing it for himself took his breath away.

"Go on. Before you miss your chance," Victor urged.

Jordan finished stripping and stepped outside, his lightly tanned skin the afterimage contrast of T'ukri's darker complexion. "Is there a trick to this? Or do we just jump around like madmen?"

T'ukri threw his head back and laughed, the sound so full of joy that Victor almost joined them despite his reservations. "The only 'trick,' as you say, is to enjoy the rain, but if you wish to learn one of our dances, I will teach you."

Jordan glanced back at Victor, but Victor shook his head and waved for Jordan to go on. Jordan shrugged and turned back to T'ukri. "Sure, but I should warn you, dancing has never been my strength."

"Then it is good that our dances are less formal than most." T'ukri brushed past Jordan, close enough their shoulders touched, and circled behind him. "Turn to face me."

Jordan turned as directed so he was looking straight at T'ukri. Victor couldn't see T'ukri's expression, but he recognized the mischief in Jordan's. He had seen it far too often, usually right before Jordan did something ill-advised and sometimes dangerous but always exhilarating—for him, anyway. It was usually hell on the people watching. Maybe he *should* join them, if only to keep Jordan in check.

Jordan circled T'ukri as T'ukri had circled him, but he didn't stop at brushing shoulders, instead bumping his hip against T'ukri's as he passed. Every muscle in T'ukri's back went rigid, and when he turned to follow Jordan, his expression had changed from joyful to lustful. Victor's gut tightened in protest, but he pushed the concerns aside. They had agreed to let T'ukri court them both. If T'ukri's focus was on Jordan now, that was because Victor had chosen to stay in the shelter. He had no reason to worry, and certainly no reason to be jealous. If he went out there, T'ukri would include him too.

Probably.

They circled each other again, two predators looking for weaknesses; then T'ukri laughed again, breaking the tension as he used Jordan's shoulders for a base to jump into the air, higher than Victor thought he should be able to, except that when Jordan did the same, he jumped almost as high.

Maybe.

When T'ukri approached the next time, Jordan braced himself and tossed at the same moment T'ukri jumped, propelling him even higher than before.

He hoped.

T'ukri whooped and cupped his hands so Jordan's next leap started with a boost from T'ukri.

Or not.

Victor turned away, trying to block out the image of them together. They were playing more than flirting, enjoying each other's athleticism for the pure pleasure of it, not with any ulterior motive. They'd tire eventually and come back inside, wet and laughing, but they'd come back inside. They weren't going to suddenly fall to the ground out there and go at it. Even if T'ukri were willing, Jordan wouldn't do that. He'd made it clear they were in this together and that if T'ukri didn't want both of them, he couldn't have either of them.

That was so much easier to believe when Jordan was curled up around him, not outside frolicking naked in the rain with T'ukri.

CHAPTER 16

HIGH ON the exhilaration of dancing in the first rain and the undercurrent of desire that ran through him at seeing Jordan naked, T'ukri grabbed Jordan's biceps—how had he developed such incredible muscles?—and twirled him around one last time. "It grows dark, and we have left Victor alone. Perhaps we should return to the shelter and prepare something for dinner?"

"Lighting a fire in that small a space with us all in there won't be easy." Jordan moved effortlessly with the twirl, grasping T'ukri's arms in return. "But if anyone can manage it, it'll be Victor."

"You have so much faith in him," T'ukri observed.

"He's the one person who's never let me down," Jordan replied. "Everyone else... well, it hasn't always been pretty, but Victor says what he means and does what he says he'll do. It makes it easy to believe in him."

"You are fortunate to have each other," T'ukri said.

"Believe me, I know." Jordan released T'ukri's arms and turned back toward the shelter. T'ukri followed leisurely, enjoying the view. Jordan's back was as muscled as his arms, every inch of him chiseled granite, and that continued down over his buttocks to his legs. Whatever hardships had shaped this man, they had left him in perfect physical condition, apart from the scars that marked his skin at random intervals, everything from the pucker of a bullet hole to the slash of a knife wound and perhaps even the bite of some kind of belt—and the smear of black ink across his shoulder, a practice T'ukri had heard of but that his own people did not engage in. No, Jordan's life had not been easy, to judge by those marks, but he had retained the ability to laugh and to play. He bore scars, but he had overcome. T'ukri wondered if he would find similar marks on Victor's body when he was finally allowed to see.

Jordan bent to enter the shelter, eliciting a flush of heat that spread from T'ukri's groin across his skin. Jordan's skin would taste cool and sweet from the rain, he was sure, but he did not make a move to find out. One day soon, he would have the right to reach out and touch or taste when presented with Jordan's naked backside. For now, he would settle for drinking in the sight.

When Jordan had time to get settled, T'ukri ducked in after him. Jordan had scooted as close to Victor as he could get, a peaceful look on his face, but Victor's face was not so calm. T'ukri tensed, looking for what had upset him. Finding nothing immediately, he pulled his cutoffs back on. At home or if they were already his mates, he would have stayed undressed, letting the freshly washed air caress his skin, but Victor already looked uncomfortable, and T'ukri did not want to add to it.

"Shall I start a fire so we can roast the rabbits?" he asked when he was partially dressed.

"Is it safe to have one inside?" Victor eyed the low ceiling dubiously.

"No, but the rain has eased off enough that I should be able to start one right outside. The cover for the entrance is built at an angle to keep a small section of ground outside the walls dry as well," T'ukri explained. "And the beauty of the shelter is that it provides all the dry wood we need for a fire. We will simply add a few more branches to the top before we leave in the morning."

"Ingenious," Victor said. "I prepared the rabbits while you were... dancing."

"You did not have to do that," T'ukri said.

"I know, but you hunted, so I'll cook. And tomorrow it'll be Annie's turn to make sure we eat."

"Aw, man, that stupid name again. Did you have to go there?" Jordan said with a scowl.

"Annie?" T'ukri asked. Victor obviously meant Jordan, but this was the first T'ukri had heard that name. "Is that not historically a female name?"

"Yes, damn it," Jordan replied, still glaring at Victor.

"Unless you're a Star Wars fan," Victor replied. T'ukri did not understand that reference either, but Victor's answer did nothing to mollify Jordan.

Jordan folded in on himself a little, but he met T'ukri's gaze as he replied, "Annie Oakley was a sharpshooter in the American West during the mid-to-late 1800s. When I was in the Marines, I worked as a sniper. The guys in my squad started calling me Annie Oakley because of my aim. Then they shortened it to Annie. Victor found out when he met my best friend, who I sometimes hate. She still calls me that when she wants to annoy me."

"I think that is not a nickname I will grow accustomed to," T'ukri said. "Even were it one you liked, I have started to think of you as a condor, malku, in my language."

"A condor," Jordan said slowly, clearly considering the idea. "I could get used to that. Fast, powerful"—he paused to glare at Victor— "and not female."

"No, definitely not female." Not that T'ukri had doubted that before today, but he had all the proof he needed after watching Jordan dance in the rain.

"And Victor?" Jordan asked. "Have you started to think of him a particular way?"

T'ukri turned to where Victor was hunched over a small pile of wood, starting the fire. "Yes. A boa, sleek and deadly, always alert, able to pass unseen, only striking when absolutely necessary, but that is not all there is to you. You are also the one who organizes everything and who makes sure things go as planned or who fixes them when they do not. I have not found an animal yet for that side of you. Perhaps there is not one. Perhaps that is simply Victor."

Victor flushed visibly even in the low light, but when T'ukri glanced to Jordan for reassurance, Jordan had a smile on his face. "That's a perfect description of him. Both the boa and the rest."

Victor shot Jordan a look T'ukri could not read, but some of the tension that had filled the small space dissipated, so he had done something right. Now he had only to keep doing it.

One thing was clear: he could not court Victor the same way he courted Jordan. Jordan responded to the open physicality he had so far employed, but while he did not think Victor was immune to it, he would not win him that way.

JORDAN LET out a shuddering breath when Victor's shoulders dropped a bit at T'ukri's description. Jordan couldn't list all the ways T'ukri had nailed it without overstepping his bounds, but Victor had noticed too, and that was what mattered right now. He'd known when he went outside with T'ukri that leaving Victor alone in the shelter was a bad idea, but he hadn't been able to resist the lure of playing in the rain. T'ukri might have called it dancing, but for Jordan, it had been pure, acrobatic fun.

Right up until he'd come inside and seen Victor's face. He still had a shit-ton to learn about relationships, obviously. And they were considering adding a third. Yeah, he'd lost his ever-loving mind.

Okay, first things first. Make sure Victor felt loved and appreciated and see if he could get rid of any lingering doubts.

His skin had dried enough despite the humidity in the air that he could pull his boxers back on, which would hopefully help a little now that he wasn't giving T'ukri a free show. That done, he scooted around until he could peer over Victor's shoulder at the fire he'd started. When Victor turned his head questioningly, Jordan smiled and dropped a kiss on his nose.

Victor snorted and shook his head, but he was smiling as he added more wood to the growing flames.

Jordan one, Victor's issues zero.

"Sorry about calling you Annie," Victor murmured.

Jordan nuzzled Victor's neck instead of replying out loud. No, he didn't like the name, and it wasn't easy to talk about his past, but at least it was his time in the Marines, not his time in foster and group homes, and T'ukri had taken the revelation in stride instead of asking all kinds of questions. They'd said they were going to give this a shot, and if he couldn't even share his military career, he'd never be able to share the rest.

He could feel T'ukri's gaze on them, but he remained as much of a respectful distance away as the small space allowed. Good, he accepted that Victor and Jordan needed time for themselves too.

"Get the rabbits for me?" Victor said.

Jordan turned back toward the interior of the shelter, only to have T'ukri hand him the carcasses. Victor skewered them on a stick and held them over the flames, turning it slowly so they would cook on all sides.

"Now we wait," Victor said with a rueful smile.

"What is that tool you used to start the fire?" T'ukri asked, looking at the flint-and-steel combo Victor always carried with him.

"I carry flint and steel, but I strike them manually. I have never seen a frame like that."

"It's a trick he picked up on one of his first expeditions," Jordan said. "Matches can get wet and not light. Flint and steel are impervious, and having them in that metal frame holds them at the perfect angle to spark every time."

"Ingenious," T'ukri said, sounding impressed.

"See? I'm not the only one who sees through that bland façade you wear," Jordan said.

Victor shot him a look, but he sat a little taller all the same. Jordan still didn't know how people missed it when it was as clear as a neon sign to him, but for as long as Jordan had known him, Victor had hidden his competency beneath a façade of unassuming professor unless it was absolutely necessary, and people at the university bought into it.

Jordan shifted to lean against the wall of the shelter. "Tell us a story while we wait," Jordan asked T'ukri. "Something about you, since I told you about the Marines."

"Is that the significance of the drawing on your shoulder?" T'ukri asked.

"My tattoo?" Jordan turned his head as if to look at the mark. "Yeah, it's the Marine Corps emblem. Nandini and I got them together when we finished basic training."

"It is an odd practice, to me, marking your skin with such images. My people believe our bodies are a gift from the gods and that we should keep them as perfect as possible, without any permanent mark or scar. Scars happen when someone is injured, but we do not choose to create them ourselves."

"It's one of the few things in my life I can really be proud of," Jordan replied.

"And it is part of your culture to commemorate such things," T'ukri finished. "I did not mean to imply judgment. Only to explain my own culture, as you have expressed an interest in it."

"Indeed we have," Victor said. "You were going to tell us a story?"

"Yes, a story about me," T'ukri said. "But nothing about me is all that interesting."

"That's because it's your own story," Victor said. "To us, it's new… and interesting."

"Very well," T'ukri said. "When I was very small, I decided I was old enough to be a warrior like Papãnin and my cousin, Micay. Even then I was aware enough to realize they would not agree with me, so I snuck out when my mother was working and Tayta—Yuri—was with another shaman. Papãnin had left that morning on a hunt, and I imagined I could catch up with them."

Jordan wondered who Yuri was, besides a shaman, but he didn't interrupt to ask. He could ask when the story was over.

"I gathered my spear and my chest plate—children's toys, of course—and started off in the direction I had seen the warriors go that morning. I marched along, a brave little man, until I realized I did not know where I was. I plopped down right where I was and started screaming for my tayta. Someone must have seen me leave, or perhaps it was simply a mother's intuition, but one way or another, my mother had followed me. But she wanted me to learn a lesson, not just come home safely, so cunning woman that she is, she hid in the brush and rattled branches. I jumped up, sure I was about to be eaten by a puma or something worse. I tried to run, only to trip and land right in Tayta's arms. I was so scared I burst out crying. Tayta calmed me down, as he always did, and then my mother stepped out of the undergrowth, as stern and regal as ever, and I lost it all over again. I was more scared of her anger than being eaten by a puma. She just shook her head at me and told me if I was that determined to be a warrior, she would start training me with the older children. It was the happiest day of my life until I discovered the next day just how much work it would be. Then I decided I had been a fool."

Victor chuckled. "Your mother sounds like a formidable woman."

T'ukri smiled in the low light. "You have no idea. Though if I can persuade you to come home with me, you will have the chance to meet her and my papãnin, Huallpa. Unfortunately Yuri now walks with the ancestors."

Jordan bit back a surprised gasp. They'd extrapolated T'ukri's intent, but prior to T'ukri's backhanded invitation, they hadn't had confirmation. Even now, the invitation was to meet his mother, not to spend the rest of their lives together, but they were finally getting somewhere. A glance at Victor revealed an equally stunned reaction, and something they would need to talk about when they were alone, but for now, it was enough to know they hadn't been completely off base.

"Was Yuri your brother?" Jordan asked.

T'ukri shook his head. "My papãnin's other mate, and a second father to me. His death gutted our family."

"Is that common?" No one else would have heard the tension in Victor's voice, but Jordan knew him too well not to notice it.

"In my tribe, yes, though few of the surrounding tribes still hold to the old ways," T'ukri replied. "While it is not a requirement, we seem to do… better with two mates at our side rather than one."

"Do you have any brothers or sisters?" Jordan asked as he digested the information that their relationship would be easily accepted by T'ukri's people—at least in theory. He hadn't let himself dwell on it, figuring T'ukri wouldn't have started such an open and obvious courtship if their relationship broke any deep-rooted taboos, but this was a step further. This was open acceptance built into their culture.

"I have a younger sister," T'ukri said. "She is alternately my best friend and the bane of my existence. What of you?"

"I'm the oldest of three," Victor said, giving Jordan a moment to gather his composure and decide how he wanted to answer. "My family all lives in France. My parents are retired and have an apartment in Marseille. My sister is a doctor in Lyon, and my brother is a teacher in Strasbourg. We aren't close."

Jordan grimaced a little. Victor rarely talked about his family. All Jordan knew was that things had been tense since Victor came out to them shortly after finishing his military service. "I don't have any siblings, and my parents died in a car accident when I was a child," Jordan said in a monotone.

Victor reached over and squeezed Jordan's hand. T'ukri bowed his head and raised his left arm across his chest solemnly. "My comfort for your loss."

Jordan nodded in return, unsure how to answer since it hadn't been all that great a loss in his opinion. Even the one story was enough to show him how very different T'ukri's relationship with his family had been to Jordan's own.

"The rabbit's ready," Victor said, breaking the moment.

The somber mood lingered as they ate quickly. The rabbits were perfectly cooked, crispy from the flames on the outside, juicy and not too done on the inside, but Jordan barely paid it any attention, caught up in his racing thoughts. In the space of a few minutes, he'd learned more about T'ukri than he could completely digest.

T'ukri had a close-knit family. His tribe accepted polyamory and had no apparent issues with same-gender relationships. T'ukri was observant enough to see through Victor's façade, something only a few people had done. T'ukri was not too proud to share stories that put him in a less than perfect light.

Any one of those revelations would have been a lot to process. All of them together…. If he hadn't already been in love with Victor, T'ukri would have won him pretty much completely with that story. As it was, he'd have to check in with Victor when they had a bit of privacy, but the sense of family alone was even more seductive than T'ukri's smoking-hot body.

They finished eating, and Victor buried the fire, making sure no coals lingered that might set fire to their nest overnight. Jordan pulled out their bedrolls and looked at the space. It was going to be one hell of an interesting night, all three of them squeezed in there together. He shrugged and stretched out in the middle, on one edge of the sleeping mat. He could spoon around Victor, leaving the remaining space behind him for T'ukri.

T'ukri turned his back to Jordan, giving them that much privacy as Victor came in and pulled the covering over the entrance. Victor eyed the spot Jordan had left for him and grimaced again. He'd been doing a lot of that today. Jordan really should have suggested they set up their tent for the night once the rain stopped so he could reassure Victor in private, but it was too late for that. He'd have to settle for sleeping curled around Victor and hope that got his point across.

Victor started to stretch out still fully dressed.

"Come on, Victor. You aren't going to make me sleep next to you with those heavy pants on, are you?"

Victor rolled his eyes at Jordan's wheedling. "Hand me the flashlight."

When Jordan passed it to him, he promptly switched it off. Jordan thought about making a snarky comment, but he'd already pushed Victor enough today. Instead he listened patiently to the rustling of clothes as Victor stripped off his pants. He lay down in front of Jordan, fumbled in the dark for his wrist, and wrapped it around his own chest. Jordan scooted closer until they were pressed together from shoulder to knee, to give T'ukri a little more space, but mostly to offer Victor silent reassurance.

Once they were settled, T'ukri lay down as well. They weren't touching, but Jordan could feel the heat from his body. He had just started to drift off, listening to the quiet sounds of their breathing, when T'ukri shifted and hit Jordan in the back with his elbow.

"Sorry," T'ukri whispered as he settled down again.

"It's fine," Jordan replied.

Ten minutes later it happened again. When it happened a third time, Jordan sat up. "Okay, this isn't going to work." Keeping Victor's hand in his, he shifted until he was facing T'ukri's back and Victor was snug against his back. He kept his arm and Victor's between his body and T'ukri's, mirroring T'ukri's position so they had a little more space.

Not much. And feeling T'ukri's body heat through his boxers against his cock wasn't particularly helpful for his peace of mind, but it was still better than an elbow in the ribs.

Yeah, they were definitely setting up their tent from now on, even if it was pouring down rain.

CHAPTER 17

JORDAN WOKE slowly the next morning, warm and comfortable. He could hear the calls of the forest birds, so it had to be getting light outside, but in their little shelter, it was still dark and quiet.

He started to stretch, only to realize that during the night, he and Victor had shifted enough that not only was he feeling Victor's morning wood pressed against his ass, but he also had T'ukri's ass pressed against his own morning wood. *Well, fuck.* Was this heaven or hell? He didn't lift his head, but as he took stock of the rest of his body, he realized both he and Victor had their arms draped over T'ukri. Victor's hand was only on his arm, but it was more contact than he'd had up until now. Jordan's hand was right over T'ukri's heart. *Fucking hell*, talk about skipping a step or twenty. He'd never lost track of his surroundings like that, not even when he was a kid. He wasn't sure what that said about T'ukri and their eventual relationship, but he had some thinking to do on top of the conversation he needed to have with Victor.

T'ukri stirred and then sat up as if waking up with Victor and Jordan spooning him was the most normal thing in the world and didn't even deserve a comment. He pushed open the shelter door and stepped outside, letting in fresh air along with the morning light.

Damn, Jordan would say they stunk up the place except that the mixed scents of the three of them smelled good. Too good. He'd be addicted before he knew it. And all they'd done was sleep. If they ever got around to fucking…. He pushed the thought aside. He was horny enough as it was, with no way to do anything about it. He didn't know where T'ukri had gone, but he wouldn't be gone long enough for what Jordan had in mind.

Behind him Victor shifted. Jordan rolled over to face him. "You okay?" he asked when he saw the disgruntled look on Victor's face.

"Yeah. I keep telling myself we need to be rational about this, and then I wake up with my hand on him, not just on you."

"You're not responsible for where your hand ended up while you were asleep." Jordan refused to let Victor feel guilty about that, no matter what else he might be feeling.

"That doesn't hold water, and you know it. You slept last night, and that shouldn't have happened with him so close."

Jordan couldn't even argue when he'd had the same thought. Before the past few days, he'd never slept well in the field unless he knew Nandini was nearby, keeping watch, and even out of the field, he rarely slept through a full night undisturbed. He hadn't been surprised when he slept well next to Victor, but T'ukri was still a stranger in many ways. Not that his subconscious gave a damn.

"I know. Are you okay otherwise?"

Victor shrugged. "I don't know yet."

Before Jordan could press for an explanation, T'ukri stuck his head back in. "There is quinoa for breakfast if you are hungry, and then we should be on our way. Now that the rains have started, we should plan to do most of our travel early in the day so we can set up camp before the heat brings them on."

"We'll be right out." Victor sat up and reached for his pants, so Jordan did the same.

T'ukri nodded and stepped back out.

"We aren't done with this conversation," Jordan said as he pulled his clothes on.

"I'm not avoiding it," Victor promised, "but now isn't the time."

Victor was right, so Jordan pulled him into a quick kiss before sticking his feet in his boots and crawling out of the shelter.

The humidity had dropped overnight, leaving the air fresh and clean. Jordan stretched a little, reaching up as high as he could, then bending double to work out the kinks from sleeping on the ground.

He could feel both Victor's and T'ukri's eyes on him as he straightened and arched into a backbend, but neither said anything. He figured Victor didn't say anything because T'ukri was there. He wasn't sure what held T'ukri back, but feeling his admiring gaze was enough for now. While Jordan wasn't above using his flexibility to catch a lover's attention, that wasn't his goal at the moment. He did a few lunges to loosen up his legs before the day's hike, then smiled at T'ukri. "I'll take that quinoa now before Victor makes me go pack up our gear."

"Like I'd trust you anywhere near my gear," Victor retorted.

"You don't trust me? I'm hurt." Jordan winked at Victor as he mimed being shot in the heart.

"Smartass."

Jordan turned and grinned at T'ukri. "Don't you love his brand of pillow talk?"

"He does have a way with words," T'ukri said with a deadpan perfect enough to rival Victor's.

"One of you is bad enough. How am I supposed to deal with two?" Victor muttered.

Jordan just whistled innocently as he took the quinoa from T'ukri, but his heart rate picked up at Victor's words. Victor's comment might have been off the cuff, but he'd talked about dealing with two, both Jordan *and* T'ukri, not just Jordan. Despite whatever misgivings he was still feeling, he had to be coming around to the idea, or he wouldn't have said it. Jordan was tempted to ask T'ukri to take a short walk so he could talk to Victor now, but he didn't want to be that obvious. He could wait a few more hours. At worst, they'd sleep in their tent tonight, and he could talk to Victor before they fell asleep.

T'UKRI FROWNED when they reached his usual ford on one of the hundreds of streams that crisscrossed the jungle, their water levels rising and falling with the rains. He had not expected it to be so high. He looked upstream and down, but the path it took was too twisting to see a more likely spot to cross.

He glanced skyward, taking in the clouds that had started to form. "Normally I would suggest we cross and push on to a clearing another kilometer or so ahead, but the water is swift and high, and I do not like the look of those clouds. We should make camp now so we have time to cook before it storms," he told Jordan and Victor.

"You two make camp. I'll get us some fish." Jordan unhooked the bow from his pack and strapped the quiver to his hip.

Victor unlashed the tent as if Jordan's suggestion were perfectly normal, but T'ukri trailed along behind him as Jordan found a perch above the water. After listening to Paucar's warriors' tales of hunting with Jordan, T'ukri wanted to see for himself.

For several long minutes Jordan simply sat in his perch, an arrow resting on the string of his bow but not pulled back to shoot. Behind him T'ukri heard Victor setting up the tent. When he was done and it was silent again, T'ukri turned to look at Victor, who had come up beside him. "Can he truly catch a fish with a bow?"

Victor chuckled. "Yes."

Victor gave no explanation, no reassurance, just that one word, but his tone conveyed everything he did not say. His faith in Jordan's abilities was boundless. "The water will throw off the arrow and his aim."

"No, it really won't," Victor replied.

T'ukri's eyes widened, but he left it at that. Jordan would make the shot or he would not. All they could do was wait.

Almost faster than T'ukri could track, Jordan drew and loosed the arrow on the bowstring. It pierced the water, a thin wirelike fishing line trailing behind it. When Jordan pulled the arrow back to him a moment later, a large fish dangled from the barbed tip. It had gone straight into the fish's eye.

Victor's smug smile said *I told you so* far louder than any words.

"A very impressive shot," T'ukri called up to Jordan.

"It wasn't bad," Jordan replied. "Two more that size? Or do you think we need three?"

"Two should be plenty," Victor said as he caught the fish Jordan tossed down to them. "I'll start gutting this one. You can give the other two to T'ukri."

Again Victor's faith resonated through his words. Jordan had said he would catch two more, and Victor accepted it as fact. T'ukri shook his head, not in disbelief, but at how much he still had to learn about his mates. Above him Jordan returned to watchful stillness, so motionless T'ukri could not even see him breathing. Then the same flurry of movement and Jordan tossed a second fish down to T'ukri, even bigger than the first. "I can bring the third one when I come down if you want to get started on that one," Jordan called.

"Does it bother you if I stay to watch?" T'ukri asked.

"No," Jordan said.

T'ukri caught an odd undercurrent in Jordan's voice, but now was not the time to ask. Just as T'ukri was not ready to lay out every detail of his past and present, Jordan and Victor were entitled to the secrets of their pasts. A time would come, he hoped, when those secrets could all safely come to light, but he would not press.

Jordan repeated the feat of marksmanship and speed a third time and hopped down from his perch with all the lightness of a bird alighting on a branch. His malku was aptly named indeed.

Not his *malku*, he reminded himself. *Not yet. Soon, please Pachamama, let it be soon, but not yet.*

"I see now why Paucar's warriors admired your skills as a hunter," T'ukri said as they walked back toward the tent. He kept back his comment about how quickly and efficiently Victor had gutted the fish and started the fire. Silent, deadly, and as whip fast as a boa. Instead he took out his own knife and began preparing the fish Jordan had tossed him.

"I enjoyed hunting with them as well," Jordan replied as he prepared the third fish. "They taught me a lot about the area and the native plants. What's safe, what to watch out for, that sort of thing."

"Is this your first time in Peru?" T'ukri asked.

"Yes. Not my first time in the field, but it's usually been in Mexico or elsewhere along the Caribbean," Jordan replied. "I'm enjoying learning about a new place."

"If you have those fish ready, we can put them on the fire," Victor interrupted.

"You got it, doc," Jordan replied.

T'ukri had nearly forgotten that in the outside world, they were more than lovers. He had not thought a relationship such as theirs between a supervisor and a subordinate would be accepted, but perhaps escaping those constraints was part of the lure of the rainforest. If so, he could use that to his advantage.

When they had the fish grilling over the fire in a cleverly constructed web of green branches, Jordan sat down with his back against Victor's bent knees. "Tell us another story?" he asked.

"I keep telling you my life is not as interesting as you think it is," T'ukri demurred.

"We would still like to hear it," Victor replied quietly. "If you don't mind."

That made all the difference. T'ukri might resist one of them asking, but both of them asking for the same thing? He would never deny them if it was in his power to do so. "What would you like to know?"

"You mentioned training with the warriors after you convinced your mother to let you," Victor said. "I'm sure you have some stories from that. I certainly have plenty from my military service in France."

"Get him to tell you about the time he—" Jordan didn't get a chance to finish his sentence because Victor had clapped his hand over Jordan's mouth.

"We want to hear T'ukri's story," Victor said. "I don't care if that's your favorite. You know it already."

"But I do not," T'ukri said.

"Another time," Victor replied. "Please."

"As you will." T'ukri settled himself more comfortably and tried to decide which story to tell. Victor was right that he had plenty. One stood out, though. "I told you the first day came as a shock to me. I was young to start training, but my mother had allowed it, and no one would dare gainsay her. I came limping home from the first day, every muscle aching from how hard I had worked trying to keep up with the older, stronger boys and girls. Cusi, the brother I never had, was waiting for me right outside my family's house, arms crossed and as mad as I had ever seen him. 'It is not fair,' he shouted at me. 'You get to be a warrior, and I do not.' I could hardly tell him I regretted my insistence, so I puffed my chest out as big as it would go and told him how amazing it was, determined to make him jealous. Thank the goddess my mother did not hear me. She would have given me such a lecture for that. And that was before she decided on a punishment. Cusi was having none of it. 'You have to teach me,' he insisted. So instead of going inside and begging Tayta for something to ease the strain of overworked muscles, I found myself going through a *second* round of training with Cusi. He had no more skill than I did, but that did nothing to lessen how hard the exercises were. By the time we had finished and his grandmother had called him home for dinner, I could barely stand. I do not remember ever sleeping as soundly as I did that night."

Until last night, but he did not think Victor was ready to hear that.

Jordan laughed outright, and Victor chuckled softly in that understated way he had. "That's a good one. Did you ever tell Cusi the truth?" Jordan asked.

"No, but he begged to go with me until his grandmother relented. When we got home after his first day of training, he looked at me and said, 'How did you do it, when I made you teach me in the evenings?' I just smiled at him."

"And I bet that drove him batshit," Jordan said as he started to reach for the fish.

"Don't touch," Victor ordered. "You hunt. I cook."

"Yeah, yeah. I'm not as bad as that."

"Cancún," Victor replied. Jordan pulled his hand back and let Victor check the fish.

"What happened in Cancún?" T'ukri asked. "A story for a story?" Jordan buried his head in his hands.

"Don't look at me," Victor said, though Jordan hadn't moved. "You're the one who tried to cook just now."

"Fine," Jordan huffed. "We were in Cancún for a few days on our way home from a dig near Chichen Itza. Victor had caught some kind of stomach flu or something. Whatever it was, it wasn't pretty. Things were a little tense in Mexico at the time, so I was trying to keep a low profile, so I didn't want to go to a restaurant to get food. I begged the lady who owned the house where we were staying to let me use her kitchen, figuring I could at least make Victor some tea and toast, something easy to settle his stomach."

"It's a miracle he didn't burn the house down," Victor interjected. "We had to pay for the landlady to renovate the entire first floor to get the smoke stains out."

"I see." T'ukri smothered a laugh with effort. "I will make sure not to let him cook. I doubt my family's house would survive."

Victor and Jordan exchanged pointed glances. It took T'ukri a moment to realize what he had said. "That is, if you are willing to come home with me."

"You might persuade us," Victor said after a long moment.

T'ukri exulted silently at his acceptance and took the fish Victor handed him on a banana leaf. The fish was light and flaky with just the hint of smoke to season it. "My mother would love you for your cooking alone. Now that Tayta is gone, making sure we are fed has fallen to her. We do not starve, but cooking is not her strength. Cusi took pity on me and invited me to eat with his family frequently before I left. His mother is a wonder with food, and he has picked up many of her secrets."

"I know Jordan keeps me around for my cooking," Victor said, his expression fond as he looked at Jordan.

"Not just for your cooking," Jordan squawked. The way he turned to face Victor as he continued spoke of his need to convince Victor of his words. T'ukri would have to watch that as well, then.

Victor came across as confident to the core, in the subtle, restrained way of a shaman who *could* command the elements but knows he does not need to, but Jordan seemed to think otherwise.

"You do know that, right?" The words were soft, so soft an ordinary human might not have heard them.

"I know," Victor replied, his voice and expression tender.

For a moment T'ukri felt like an outsider, but then Jordan turned back and grinned at him. "It's a pretty damn good reason, though, isn't it?"

"A good reason indeed, although I am sure I can find better. His ability to anticipate and fulfill the needs of those around him before they even realize what those needs are, perhaps?"

Jordan beamed. *A much better reason, then.* He would remember to tell Victor that regularly.

The sun started to set, and although thunder still rumbled in the distance, the sky overhead had cleared, allowing a few of the brighter stars to shine through. "It appears the rains missed us today. We can hope the stream will go down enough overnight for us to cross safely in the morning."

"We can cross even if it hasn't," Jordan said. "It won't hurt us to get wet."

T'ukri did not answer. He could not. Not when all he could see was Yuri's beloved face, slack and bloated from the water they had found him floating in. He could not stay still. If he did, he would see Huallpa's destroyed expression when it hit him that Yuri was gone. He had gone into seclusion, seeing no one but Llipya for weeks. It had taken only three days for T'ukri's gifts to manifest, a clear sign that Huallpa would never again be Chapaqpuma. "We will check in the morning. I wish you both a good night. I am going to scout a bit to make sure all is safe for the night. I will see you in the morning."

He had seen no signs of the mercenaries returning, but he almost wished they would, if only so he could provoke a fight with them to burn off this tension.

"WHAT DID I say wrong?" Jordan asked when T'ukri was out of sight.

Victor had been asking himself the same thing since the moment T'ukri tensed up. "I don't know. Do you want to wait for him to come back?"

Jordan thought for a bit. "No, I don't think so. He can take care of himself, and if he sees us waiting up for him, he might not come back as soon. He needs to sleep too. We can ask him about it tomorrow if we can find a good time to bring it up."

"Yes. Would you stow our gear and spread out the bedrolls while I take care of the fire?"

"Sure thing, boss." Jordan had called him that earlier in the day too.

"Think you could drop calling me 'boss'?" Victor asked. "Outside of the university, I'm not your boss anymore. I'm your partner."

Jordan grinned. "I like the sound of that."

Victor liked the sound of it too, and the more he thought about having to hide their new relationship when they went back, the more he hated it. As he smothered the fire with dirt, he stewed over their options. Even if he turned over responsibility for the TAs to someone else, Fowler disapproved of relationships within the department. Victor might be able to convince him to ignore it, but it would still skirt the ethical line because even if Jordan was a TA, he was also still a student. No, if they went back, they would have to hide.

If they went back.

He shook his head at himself. It had only been two days since he and Jordan had agreed to consider T'ukri's silent offer. Forty-eight hours shouldn't have been enough for him to reconsider his plan for the rest of his life, but here he was, thinking *if they went back*.

He shouldn't be so easy to sway, but he'd always had one weak spot, and T'ukri had found it without even trying. Victor had carefully cultivated his everyman image, finding it especially useful in winning the trust of tribal leaders. No one special here, nothing to look at, just a professor doing his job, perfectly forgettable. Only Jordan and Nandini had seen through him—and she didn't count since he'd long since stopped hiding around Jordan. And now T'ukri.

He'd fallen for Jordan the first time they'd worked together. It had been a routine field expedition, not even one Victor was leading, so it wasn't like he'd done some heroic stunt in the field. No, Jordan had just taken one look at him and known he was more than he let on.

T'ukri shouldn't have seen more than a mild-mannered professor, competent enough, but nothing more. No one special, nothing to look at, just a guy doing his job. Instead T'ukri had seen more to him than anyone had seen since his grandfather died.

What was Victor supposed to do with that?

Apparently, rewrite his plan for the rest of his life.

"Is everything okay?" Jordan asked. "You've been standing there staring at the ground for a while now."

"Just thinking," Victor said.

"Well, come think in the tent where we can get naked and snuggle up together." Jordan grabbed Victor's hand and tugged. Victor quirked his lips as he followed. Snuggling up to Jordan, naked or otherwise, sounded perfect.

Inside the tent with the flap zipped closed, Victor finally relaxed. He stripped down and went into Jordan's outstretched arms.

"Wanna tell me what you were thinking about?" Jordan asked.

"Us, the university, T'ukri, the future. It's all a jumble in my head," Victor said.

"It's been a couple of crazy days," Jordan agreed. "A little more detail would be useful."

Victor sighed and tried to put his thoughts in order. "If you'd asked me a week ago what could persuade me to leave academia, I'd have told you 'nothing.' And I would have meant it too. To suddenly find myself wondering if I want to go back has left me feeling like I just jumped out of a plane only to discover I forgot my parachute."

"Good thing we jumped together, then," Jordan said. "Between us I'm sure we can find a parachute somewhere, even in free fall."

Victor laughed. "I don't know what I did to deserve you, but I'm so glad I did it."

"Do you want a list? Because I could go on all night."

"You really mean that, don't you?"

"Yes. If anyone should be asking what he did, it's me," Jordan replied. "But since I know what you'll say to that, I won't bring it up. You should stop wondering too, though. It doesn't matter what we did to deserve each other. We're here together now, and that's what matters."

"When did you get to be so wise?" Victor asked.

"It must be all those times Nandini kicked my ass trying to knock some sense into me."

"What do we do now?" Victor hated to put the burden of an answer on Jordan, but he was floundering.

"What do you want to do?" Jordan asked. "Not what you think we should do. Not what you think is possible. What do you want?"

"In an ideal world?"

"Yes."

Victor rested his head against Jordan's shoulder and set aside all his reservations. "In an ideal world we'd find some way to do it all. Find Philli-philli so I can say thank you, write my paper, complete my grant, restore my professional reputation, get tenure at the university and secure my immigration status, accept T'ukri's courtship, proclaim it to the world, or at least all relevant parties, and keep doing research to show the world, at least the academic world, how much value there is in the underresearched tribes in the Amazon. But some of those things are mutually exclusive."

Jordan nodded but didn't say anything. Victor stayed where he was and let possibilities roll around in his mind. "I don't know what it is about him," Victor said after a while.

"I do," Jordan said. "He's the real thing, and he doesn't care who knows it. And because he is, he sees other people more clearly too. And he wants to take us home and introduce us to his mother. You never talk about them, but I know you miss your family. Accepting T'ukri means accepting his family too."

"You are all the family I need," Victor insisted.

"And nothing will ever change that, but you could have a mother again, or a mother-in-law. You could be a son and brother again. That's got to be seductive."

Victor thought about the stilted texts and phone calls he exchanged with his parents and siblings on their birthdays and anniversaries, about all the things he didn't say about work or his personal life. He didn't date much, but he'd had a few relationships over the years. He hadn't told his family about any of them.

"What about you? You'd have a real family for the first time," Victor said.

"No, I had a real family for the first time with Nan, and eventually with you, but yes, the idea of being part of a network of family is appealing. I'm not gonna lie."

"You really want to do this."

"I really want *us* to do this," Jordan clarified. "If you aren't on board with it, then I'm out too. But yeah, I want it all. Crazy or not, this just feels right."

Victor took a deep breath and let the familiar scent of Jordan's body soothe him. Jordan was right about how crazy it was, but Victor couldn't get past the seductive offer of a family, of a lover—or two—and the open acceptance T'ukri offered. Enough to consider rewriting his plans for the rest of his life. "No more searching for Philli-philli, then?"

It was half statement, half question, but he didn't worry Jordan would misunderstand.

"I know how much it means to you to say thank you, so maybe no searching without T'ukri," Jordan proposed. "And if things don't work out with him, we'll deal with it, but the more I learn about him, the more I like him. Not everyone would share the kinds of stories he's shared with us. They'd pick stories that made them look good. His first successful hunt or his first battle, or a time he really impressed someone. Instead he told us about going alone into the woods and getting scared and about how his best friend conned him into doing twice the training everyone else was doing."

"We owe him a story or two in return," Victor said.

"You made me tell him about Cancún. I'm pretty sure that counts as a story in return," Jordan protested. "If anyone owes him a story, it's you. I even told him about that damned nickname."

"I'll have to come up with a good one, and no, I'm not telling him the story about the time I pranked my CO in basic training," Victor said.

Jordan snorted, but the humor didn't last.

"If we're doing this, if he's really courting us, I have to tell him what happened after my parents died, and you have to tell him about your family's reaction to you coming out," Jordan said morosely.

"Yes, but that doesn't have to be now. We both have other easier stories we can share until we're sure of his intentions." Victor kissed Jordan's collarbone.

"Yeah."

Victor heard rustling outside. They both froze, listening for any threat, but the sounds resolved into T'ukri's footsteps. Victor angled his head up so he could kiss Jordan good night. Jordan returned the kiss with a flick of his tongue, but Victor wasn't willing to take it beyond a kiss with T'ukri right outside. Not when they were seriously thinking about including him, possibly soon.

"Love you," Jordan whispered against his lips.

"Love you too… malku." Victor fell asleep to the feeling of Jordan's smile.

CHAPTER 18

As THEY settled around the fire the next night with a duck roasting for dinner, Victor took a deep breath and started the story he'd decided to tell.

"I got my first job when I was fifteen, stocking shelves and doing odd jobs at a hobby shop close enough to home that I could walk there."

Jordan perked up immediately, a sly grin on his face like he knew exactly where this was going. Scratch that, he did know exactly where it was going. Victor hadn't told him the story in these exact words, but he'd talked often enough about his collectibles for Jordan to make the connection.

T'ukri turned his way as well, giving Victor the same look of concentrated attention he'd given Jordan when they were dancing in the rain. Victor took another deep breath. He could do this.

"I already knew the owner pretty well. I'd been buying used items from him since the first time my parents gave me an allowance. Star Wars was always my favorite."

"Dork," Jordan said in an affectionate stage whisper.

Victor ignored him. "But those weren't the only things I collected. I loved comic books. I read them all and had quite a collection of Astérix and of Tintin. My parents indulged me with toys when I was younger, but as far as they were concerned, I should've outgrown my fascination with Star Wars by the time I started working there. They weren't about to spend good money on some useless Star Wars figurine or the like, no matter how much I insisted they were collector's items."

His mother had wanted him to try out for the debate team, insisting his attention to detail and fascination with history made him a strong candidate. His father kept trying to persuade him to pick a sport. He didn't care which one, just something to get him out of his room for more than a few minutes at a time. Victor had tried track, because the one thing he'd always enjoyed was running, but he'd enjoyed it for the freedom it offered. Track practice was the exact opposite of freedom.

"My parents set certain requirements about the money I earned, to teach me about budgets and savings and financial responsibility, they said. First, I had to put half of everything I earned in a savings account. Second, of the remaining money, I had to put half toward buying things I needed. Not the big stuff. They still bought my clothes, food, that sort of thing, but if I needed anything for school, I had to pay for that. And once I started driving a couple years later, I had to pay for my insurance and gas. But the remaining money was for me to use as I wanted. And what I wanted was the original Luke Skywalker figure Mr. Jacquet had on display in the shop window. I worked and saved for months, and I know he gave me a discounted price, although he denied it until the day he died. When I finally got the money I needed, I walked into the store feeling lighter than air. I was going to make my first real purchase with my own money, a true collector's item that would be the start of a collection worthy of the films I loved."

He could feel Jordan holding in the comments he wanted to make. He almost told him to go ahead, but Jordan beat him to it.

"Victor has the best collection of Star Wars memorabilia of anyone I know," Jordan said, obviously done waiting. "You should see it. It's amazing."

"Perhaps someday I will," T'ukri said, "but we should let Victor finish his story."

Victor smiled. "There's not much left to tell. I did buy the figure, and since then I've amassed quite a collection of other items as well. It's one of those things I can do between projects, when I'm stuck in the office. One day I'll have a place worthy of displaying it. For now most of it is in the spare bedroom of my condo."

"And your parents' reaction when you showed them your first purchase?" T'ukri asked.

Victor didn't flinch at the prompting, although his parents' disappointment had been clear as day. "They told me if that's how I wanted to spend my money, that was up to me. They've never understood, and I doubt they ever will, but I always point out that their lesson about budgeting stuck with me."

They'd never understood much of anything Victor had done from that point on. Not his degrees in history and then anthropology, not his decision to immigrate to the United States or to "settle" for an academic career, and certainly not his decision to come out, but he'd learned to live with that too.

"Dork," Jordan repeated, making Victor laugh and shake his head.

"I should see if the duck is ready. It can get stringy if it's overcooked." He pushed to standing and walked the few steps to the fire. Out of the corner of his eye, he saw T'ukri lean over to Jordan.

"What is Star Wars?"

Victor shook his head at himself as Jordan started to explain.

AFTER JORDAN and Victor went into their tent, T'ukri lay awake for a long time, mulling over Victor's story. His tone had stayed lighthearted throughout, but T'ukri had heard the shadows that lingered beneath Victor's words, of parents who had not understood their child, who had tried their best—T'ukri chose to believe that because the thought of a parent deliberately neglecting their child rankled too much to contemplate—but who had lost that connection too early. Where T'ukri had talked of his friends along with his training, Victor had spoken only of his parents' opinion of his purchase, not of showing it to his friends.

It seemed a bleak life, though perhaps there were pieces T'ukri was missing, as he had missed the significance of Star Wars. More than ever, he wanted to take his mates home, to introduce them into the life of his family and of the tribe, where everyone knew everyone else and they worked as a community to see to everyone's needs. He wanted the sad memories replaced by new ones. T'ukri's mother could never replace their mothers, but she could offer them the same love and affection she showered on her own children. Huallpa was a shadow of the man he had once been, but even in the depth of his grief, he had always made time for T'ukri and Ch'aska, sharing their grief as they, too, struggled to accept Yuri's loss.

And Jordan had lost his parents as a child, he had said. He had mentioned the death of his parents, but not finding a new family, only his time in the Marines. T'ukri knew what he would gain from a bond with Victor and Jordan, but he had worried what he had to offer them. Now he knew. Beyond his own affection, he could offer them a place in a family they had too little of. It would be up to them to accept it, but T'ukri would make the offer all the same.

"I GUESS it's my turn for a story," Jordan said at dinner the following night. "Although mine isn't a very happy one."

"Jordan," Victor said with a worried glance.

Jordan shook his head. "It's okay, Victor. It's time."

T'ukri frowned. Jordan had not even started his story, and he could already tell he was not going to like it. "Not all stories have to have happy endings. The sad ones have lessons to teach and value of their own."

Jordan forced a smile. T'ukri might have been pleased at being able to read him so well already, but it tore at him to see Jordan upset. Victor obviously felt the same because he moved to sit behind him, bracketing Jordan with his knees as if he could shield Jordan from the memories.

"I told you my parents died in a car accident," Jordan said. "I didn't tell you the rest."

"If the telling is too painful, you need not do it," T'ukri said.

"No, I need to. If we're doing this"—he waved his hand back and forth between the three of them—"thing, you need to understand."

T'ukri nodded, wishing he could join Victor and complete the circle of protection, but Jordan's admission of "this thing" between them was not an invitation, however encouraging it might be.

"After my parents died, I got sent to an orphanage. If my parents had family, they'd either lost touch or they didn't want me. By the time I was old enough to go looking, I'd stopped wanting to know. Either way, I ended up in a group home. I was only six and about as scrawny as they came, so the bullies went for me right away. I tried to stand up to them, but that just gained me a reputation for being a fighter, which made it even harder to find a foster family willing to take me in. My only friends were a group of Spanish-speaking kids who didn't care if I didn't speak their language. They just taught me all the bad words and slang they knew. I did end up in a few foster families eventually. One family tried to use me as a servant. Another wanted the money but didn't buy things for me with it like they were supposed to."

T'ukri fought the rage growing inside him. If he let it get the better of him, he would change without his conscious volition, and with no bonded mates to draw him back, he could lose himself in the guardian. The last time that had happened, several generations before he was born, half the tribe had been wiped out.

Victor had his face tucked against Jordan's hair and his hands clenched tightly on Jordan's arms. He knew what was coming and was already bracing for it.

"I got lucky after that one. I got sent to the one awesome foster family I ever had. Scott and Pam had a couple of kids of their own, but they were mostly grown and gone, and I think they had empty-nest syndrome. Anyway, they didn't care that I was a scrawny eleven-year-old with a bad attitude. They loved me anyway. Scott's the one who taught me to shoot a bow. We'd go hunting every weekend during the hunting season and to an archery range off-season. It was the best two years of my childhood. Then Scott got cancer and died. Pam fought to keep me, but the adoption hadn't been finalized, and the change in circumstances was enough for child services to pull me."

T'ukri could no longer restrain himself. He rose from his seat and moved close enough that he could reach out to Jordan. He did not touch, as much as he wanted to, but he hoped Jordan would take his outstretched hand. His relief when Jordan took the offering and clung was palpable.

"I ran away from the group home a couple of times after that, trying to get back to Pam, which got me labeled a flight risk, so I was in almost complete lockdown except for school. They did find one other family to take me for a short time, but I broke the father's nose when he tried to rape me, and that was the end of that."

"How could anyone do that to a child?" T'ukri asked, horrified.

Jordan shrugged. "There are a lot of bad people in the world."

"Did he face justice?" It would do nothing to change what had happened, but it would give T'ukri the peace of mind of knowing his mate had been avenged.

"I never told anyone what happened, not then. The punch was enough to get me pulled from that placement and sent back to the group home. They didn't try to place me again after that. As soon as I turned eighteen, I left the group home, figuring even life on the streets had to be better than that. That didn't go as well as I'd hoped, but eventually I enlisted in the Marines. I figured war couldn't be any worse than what I'd already been through."

T'ukri suspected he had not heard the whole story or even the worst of it—life on the streets of America could not be that much different than life on the streets of Cusco, and he knew how people survived there—but he was not going to ask tonight, not when Jordan looked so small. In that moment T'ukri could easily see the scared, hurt child he must have been.

"It is late," T'ukri said. "We should sleep. Go. I will take care of the fire tonight."

Jordan nodded and let Victor lead him toward the tent. That alone worried T'ukri more than anything else he had seen or heard. Jordan had never been docile, but now he seemed broken, as if anything more than putting one foot in front of the other required more effort than he could summon.

Their flashlight flickered on for a moment as they got settled, then flicked off again. T'ukri stretched out on his own sleeping mat and braced himself for a restless night.

VICTOR BUNDLED Jordan into their tent. Past experience with him and the kind of story he'd told tonight suggested Jordan would need as much physical contact and comfort as Victor could provide to stave off nightmares. He doubted he'd be able to keep them all away, but he'd do his best.

Jordan smiled wanly at him as he pulled Jordan's clothes off. Victor stripped as well and lay down next to him, touching him everywhere he could reach. Jordan burrowed into his arms and clung with a neediness he rarely showed.

Damn everyone who'd ever hurt or betrayed Jordan to hell and back. Jordan didn't deserve this.

Usually Jordan was a restless sleeper, even when he slept well—not that Victor expected that to happen tonight—but Jordan didn't move as they lay there, as if by being still he could hide from all the demons chasing him. He'd been that way the whole time Victor had known him. Cocky as hell on the outside, but any time he thought no one was watching, he got small and still, like he could pass unnoticed if he didn't move. Victor had studied enough psychology to recognize the signs of past abuse, even if he didn't learn the whole story until much later. As Jordan grew more secure in his place at the university, he'd relaxed and those signs had disappeared.

They were back tonight with a vengeance.

Victor had no better idea how to help now than he'd had when he first noticed, but he had options now that hadn't existed then. He cupped one hand around the back of Jordan's head, offering him a sense of security. With his other hand, he stroked Jordan's back, showering him with the tenderness he'd never received as a child. What Jordan had shared with T'ukri was bad enough, but he'd left out the worst parts—the beatings when he acted out, the constant fear of being denied food, the things he'd resorted to on the streets to have enough money to buy food or pay for shelter. Victor had done a little digging, after Jordan first admitted how bad things had truly been, but the worst offenders were no longer foster parents in Jordan's hometown, and he'd had to settle for that.

Victor pushed those thoughts away and focused on providing Jordan what comfort he could. A rumble of thunder sounded overhead, and the first drops of rain pattered on the roof of their tent.

Just what they needed. A storm. And T'ukri was outside with no shelter.

It wouldn't have mattered who was out in the rain—Victor wouldn't leave them there—but he'd heard what Jordan said a few days ago when they'd talked. *I want it all.* And he'd chosen tonight to talk about his parents' death and his time in foster care, all the pain and misery of his childhood tied up in a bow and handed to T'ukri, a gift of trust so deep and so powerful that Victor couldn't miss the significance of it. And T'ukri had grown righteously angry on Jordan's behalf. He'd offered his hand for Jordan to hold, and Jordan had clung to it as he'd finished his tale. Jordan would never do anything to make Victor think he wasn't enough—he was too kind for that—but Victor was man enough to accept that Jordan had made his decision. He wanted T'ukri there with them. Victor might be less certain of his own stance, but that was a problem for a different night. Right now Jordan was hurting, and T'ukri could help. All Victor had to do was invite him in and make that known.

He heaved a sigh, kissed Jordan, and rolled to his knees so he could reach the zipper on the tent flap.

"Come inside before you get soaked," he called to T'ukri.

"Are you sure? I would not want to intrude."

Lightning crackled overhead and the rain started falling more steadily. Victor reminded himself again of the way Jordan had held

T'ukri's hand as he talked, the barely contained fury on T'ukri's face that matched the rage burning in Victor's chest. "I'm sure. You can help me comfort him. He gets nightmares when he talks about his past."

T'ukri crossed the space in three large strides. He startled visibly when he saw both Jordan and Victor were naked, but aside from the first glance, he kept his gaze fixed on Victor's face as he climbed into the tent. "How can I help?"

"Get undressed and lie down behind him. Physical contact helps keep him grounded in the present," Victor explained as he zipped the tent back up, shutting out the building storm.

T'ukri had not moved when Victor turned around.

"I wouldn't have suggested it if I didn't mean it," Victor said softly. "But if it makes you uncomfortable, leave your clothes on. Either way, I want your help, and Jordan needs it."

T'ukri nodded sharply and pulled his clothes off with an economy of movement Victor might have admired in other circumstances. T'ukri lay down behind Jordan as Victor had instructed. Victor nudged Jordan until he was spooned into the curve of T'ukri's body. Then Victor returned to his own spot with Jordan's head on his shoulder.

Jordan let out a shuddering breath, but Victor could feel the tension draining out of him. His skin still felt cooler than Victor thought it should, but with the three of them crammed into a two-man tent, the air inside was already growing warm from their body heat. Victor reached over him to squeeze T'ukri's arm in silent thanks. T'ukri grabbed his hand and twined their fingers together. Victor almost pulled back out of habit. He had invited T'ukri inside to help Jordan, not because *he* needed anything. But the feeling of T'ukri's hand in his as they cradled Jordan between them stirred something inside him, adding to the ever-growing feeling that had started when they met T'ukri. He had always kept himself a step removed from the TAs he worked with, even Jordan, not wanting to cross a line without an express invitation. His personal life hadn't been much better after he'd come out to his family. They hadn't quite rejected him outright, but it had put a strain on their relationship that left even the simplest of interactions stilted. He'd convinced himself he could be satisfied with his almost-friendship with Jordan and the professional respect of his students. Finding out Jordan loved him too was more than he'd ever dreamed he'd have, but even in that, he'd seen himself as alone in taking care of Jordan when he needed it.

The hand in his now reminded him he didn't have to be alone. He could ask for and receive support even as he supported Jordan. And when the time came that he needed support, he could find it from more than one source if he had the courage to reach out and take what was on offer.

The thought was too big to digest with Jordan still shivering slightly between them. Victor needed to focus on soothing him, but tomorrow when sunlight drove away the rain and the somber thoughts of the night, Victor had some serious thinking to do. He'd considered accepting T'ukri's courtship because Jordan wanted it and Victor hadn't seen any reason against it, but he was beginning to want it for himself as well.

With a smile, Victor moved their joined hands to rest on Jordan's hip. Maybe this would work out after all.

CHAPTER 19

HANDS GRABBED at him, pinning him down. He tried to scream, but his face was pressed into the mattress, and all he got was a mouthful of fabric. He fought as hard as he could as his assailant pawed at his clothes, but he couldn't find the strength to get away.

He was better than this. He knew how to fight, but his body didn't cooperate. Fear choked him as something hard and blunt nudged his dry hole. It'd rip him open and tear him to shreds. He didn't want it, not like this.

He thrashed in the other man's hold. He had to get away. He had to get back to Victor.

No, that wasn't right. Victor wasn't in the foster system. Victor was at the university. Nobody at the university tried to hurt him. But someone was holding him down.

A scream escaped, and hands shook him. Not to silence him. To wake him?

Jordan gasped and sat up, searching the darkness for any clues to his whereabouts as he tried not to puke his guts out.

"Jordan, stop."

Jordan flinched and shied away, his flight instinct warring with the familiarity of the voice. "Victor?" he croaked, his voice broken. Was he with Victor? He would be safe with Victor. He rubbed his sweaty palms against his thighs, but that only moved the mess around. He swallowed hard as his dinner tried to make a reappearance, but he couldn't resist the urge to curl in on himself protectively.

"Relax, Jordan. We have you," Victor ordered.

Even in the total darkness, Jordan trusted that voice. He took a deep breath the way Nan had taught him, willing his racing heart to steady.

"You are safe, my malku," a second voice said, startling Jordan and undoing what little work he'd managed on his pulse and breathing. Only then did he register the twin lines of heat, one in front of him, one behind.

"Wha—?" His voice cracked. He swallowed around the lump in his throat and tried again. "What happened?"

"You had a nightmare," Victor said. "I was hoping having both T'ukri and me here would keep them away, but apparently that didn't work."

T'ukri. The second line of heat was T'ukri. He blinked a couple of times to clear the fog of the nightmare from his brain. It did nothing to improve his vision in the darkness, but it did help him wake up a bit. They were in Peru, on an expedition. Except they'd put the expedition aside because of T'ukri.

T'ukri who was in the tent with them, curled protectively around Jordan. Curled nakedly around him, if Jordan's senses weren't playing tricks on him.

Fuck, he hated it when the past reared up and bit him in the ass. It was fifteen years ago and more, but when it grabbed him in his dreams, it may as well have been the present.

"I don't... I can't...." He shook his head again.

"You are safe, Jordan," T'ukri said in a voice so sure, so compelling that Jordan had no choice but to trust it the way he trusted Victor's.

"The last thing I remember is coming back to the tent after dinner," he said, racking his memories for details that simply weren't there. Fuck his stupid brain anyway.

"You were pretty out of it," Victor replied. "We got settled for the night, but then it started raining."

Jordan listened carefully. Yes, that was the sound of rain pelting the tent.

"I couldn't leave T'ukri outside in the rain, and you were still so out of it. I thought having him here might help you," Victor continued.

"I would help in any way I can," T'ukri added. "You have only to tell me what I must do."

If Jordan knew the answer to that, he'd have sent these nightmares back to the hell they came from years ago. "Keep me focused on the present," he said, feeling the weight of T'ukri's expectation in the silence. "It was a long time ago. I just have to remember that."

"You're safe," Victor said in the voice that Jordan had dreamed about more nights than he could count. "We're right here, and nothing can get past us to hurt you."

"And if something happened Victor could not stop, I would," T'ukri added. "No one will hurt you while we stand watch."

Jordan clung to that thought amid the terror still making him want to hurl. *They* were standing watch. Not Victor. Not T'ukri. Both of them. Victor had asked T'ukri inside, had put him behind Jordan to watch his back.

Victor hadn't said it that way, but he didn't need to. Now that the confusion had started to fade, Jordan could think clearly enough to know their current positions were Victor's doing. Jordan's face was buried in Victor's neck, the familiar, beloved scent of his skin surrounding Jordan, the first thing he smelled when he took a breath. The first thing he would've seen if there was enough light to see by.

Usually it was Nandini, if it was anyone, holding him and whispering reassurances in his ear, but she wasn't here. Instead Victor took on that role, leaving T'ukri to guard Jordan's back.

It should've bothered him, but it didn't. T'ukri would have his back, no matter what. He'd said it, sure, but Jordan had known it before tonight and the nightmares and the sinking sense of loss and violation and desperation that always hit him after a trip down memory fucking lane.

He reached blindly for Victor. When he found his arm, he clung so tightly it had to hurt, but Victor didn't say anything. He just moved closer, if that was possible, and let Jordan hang on for dear life. With his other hand, Jordan reached behind him for T'ukri.

T'ukri caught his hand and held it, his tight grip a comfort Jordan hadn't known he needed.

"Relax now," T'ukri said. "Even if you cannot sleep, rest safe in the knowledge we are here and will allow nothing to harm you. Not tonight. Not ever again."

For a moment Jordan let himself believe it. He kept a tight grip on both of them as he forced his breathing to match Victor's. In, out, in, out, slow and steady, not fast and frantic like it had been when he woke up.

To keep himself in the present, he concentrated on physical sensations. On Victor's breath ruffling his hair. On the heat of Victor's chest against his nose. On the weight of Victor's thigh between his own. On the sweet scent of woodsmoke and duck fat that hung in the air, so different than the miasma of alcohol-soaked breath and vanilla cigar that never left his would-be rapist.

On T'ukri's breath against the back of his neck, where it should have tickled but didn't. On the tangle of feet, too many just to be Victor's. On the softness of T'ukri's limp dick snugged right up against his ass.

The comfortable intimacy of it stole his breath. This was Victor's doing too. He'd put money on it. T'ukri would have come in out of the rain at Victor's invitation no matter what else was going on between them, but he wouldn't have chucked his clothes off and snuggled up against Jordan's ass without Victor's permission. He wasn't a fuckwad like the one foster father or the johns who'd paid him for sex so Jordan could eat something he hadn't dug out of a dumpster. He was a decent, honorable guy who would've respected whatever boundaries Victor put up. Except Victor hadn't put any up. If he had, T'ukri wouldn't be wrapped around Jordan like a vine, holding him as tightly as Victor was, keeping him safe and centered and *here*.

If he could just get rid of the hungover feeling he always had after his nightmares, he'd make something of that—something important—but he couldn't quite pull it all into focus.

Tomorrow, he told himself. Tomorrow when it was light and he'd slept, he'd figure it out. Until then he'd take what he could get and drown himself in Victor and T'ukri. Everything else could wait until dawn.

CHAPTER 20

T'UKRI ROSE with the sun in the morning, leaving Jordan and Victor to wake together without him there to make things awkward. He had not slept after Jordan's nightmare, too caught up in the whirl of emotions the experience had brought to life in him. Jordan's story had been heartbreaking from beginning to end, but the bleakness had gone even deeper than his words explained. He was such a powerful, energetic man, his presence as bright as the noonday sun. To see that dampened, covered in the storm clouds of the past, shook T'ukri to his core. T'ukri would have said nothing could clip Jordan's wings, that he had the strength to soar above the fray and keep himself safe and whole, but last night had proven that even his malku—his majestic malku—had a weakness. His past held specters he kept at bay through force of will alone, and sometimes that was not enough.

T'ukri wanted these foster parents in front of him, subjugated beneath his claws, begging for mercy as Jordan had surely begged over the years of his childhood. T'ukri would show them as much mercy as they had shown Jordan if the goddess should bring them to cross his path. Then again, Victor had known the story, so perhaps justice had already been served upon them.

He could accept that. If anyone could bring justice to bear for one of his mates, it was the other. Once they bonded—and he knew now that he would ask them to be his mates—they would be as one life, one spirit, one will. Any action by one would be seen as an action by all three. Their word would carry the same weight as his within the tribe, and they would answer to all for his actions just as he would answer for theirs.

The sound of the zipper on the tent opening drew his attention. Victor stepped out, dressed for the day in the now familiar pants and T-shirt.

It had been a week since they left Paucar's village, and last night had been hard for all of them. T'ukri knew a place a half day's walk away where they could set up camp and spend a night and a day resting, bathing, cleansing their clothes, and recovering from the physical and emotional toll of their trek. The time to simply exist together would be good for all of them. He would suggest it when Jordan joined them.

First, though, he needed to speak with Victor.

T'ukri had sensed from early on that Jordan was more open to his courtship than Victor. Perhaps it was his upbringing, or perhaps it was simply his personality. Either way, winning them had clearly meant winning Victor because he would not separate them, regardless of their choice. Last night Victor had offered T'ukri not just shelter from a storm he could have easily weathered, but also a chance to comfort Jordan at Victor's side. He had invited T'ukri into more than just their tent. He had invited T'ukri into their lives, and that deserved recognition.

When Victor set a pot of water over the fire he had already started and sat back to wait for it to boil, T'ukri joined him, sitting so he faced Victor rather than the fire. He waited for Victor to look up. When he did, T'ukri cupped Victor's cheek in his palm. "Thank you for last night."

"I couldn't exactly leave you out in the rain," Victor demurred, though he leaned into the touch.

"That was not what I refer to. Even bringing me out of the rain, you did not have to let me help you with Jordan. You did not have to let me see you both unclothed. You shared an intimate moment between you with me, and for that I say again, thank you."

Victor met his gaze, his eyes bright in the filtered light of dawn. "You're welcome. Thank you for being willing to help."

"Anything in my power to do for you, you may consider it done."

VICTOR FROZE at T'ukri's words. The thanks had already caught him off guard with T'ukri's perceptiveness of the whole situation, but that last... it was quite a vow, one more suited to a formal ceremony than to sitting around a campfire waiting for the water to boil. Realizing T'ukri was waiting for a response, Victor bowed his head in acknowledgment. That seemed to satisfy T'ukri. He stood and moved away to gather the gear he hadn't brought into the tent during the night.

Victor stayed where he was, mulling over the puzzle T'ukri had presented him with. Ever since Jordan first brought it up, Victor had been trying to imagine how a triad could work between them. Jordan and Victor were both so fiercely independent. Trying to add a third unknown personality to that mix had to be a recipe for disaster.

He'd softened that stance a little over the week of their hike as T'ukri moved with and around them in everyday tasks like hunting and making camp. Jordan, usually so protective of his place, easily shared hunting duties with T'ukri, something he had always complained about if they had to rely on local guides in the past. T'ukri cleared a spot for the fire each night while Victor gathered wood but stepped back when Victor was ready to cook. That ease had surprised Victor, but T'ukri was an experienced guide, and he'd credited it to that. Then Jordan had pushed the envelope by telling T'ukri about his childhood. It never got easier, hearing Jordan talk about that time of his life. This was only the second time Jordan had ever laid it out that clearly in Victor's hearing.

Victor had been prepared for a night of sleep broken by Jordan's nightmares. He hadn't been prepared for how right it had felt to have T'ukri there too when Jordan woke up screaming. Then T'ukri had to go and say exactly the right things at the right times. He couldn't have done better if Victor had fed him the lines.

That had been enough to make Victor accept that T'ukri had already carved out a place in their lives. And to top it all off, T'ukri had thanked him this morning for including him. Not for the shelter, which Victor could have brushed off as common decency. No, T'ukri had thanked Victor for including him in caring for Jordan, like he knew what a huge step that had been for Victor. Bon sang, maybe he had known. He'd certainly surprised Victor in other ways. Why should this time be any different?

With those two gestures, T'ukri had secured his place in their lives. Now Victor just had to find a way to show him.

JORDAN TRUDGED through the jungle, every nerve on high alert. There wasn't any more danger than there'd been for the past week, but damn if he could get his body to believe it.

Hyperawareness, the shrinks called it, and Jordan had identified exactly two triggers for it—too many hours sitting in a sniper's nest and nightmares about his final foster father. Stupid fucking brain. Always fucking him over.

He'd known when he started talking about his childhood that this would happen. It was why he never talked about it. He'd never told anyone but Victor and Nandini before yesterday, and if he had his way, he wasn't telling anyone else ever again. He still had nightmares sometimes even if he didn't talk about it, but these days they were usually about other things. Or not as bad or as detailed as the one last night.

Everything after he finished telling T'ukri about joining the Marines was a blur. He'd woken up with Victor, both of them naked, in the tent this morning. Victor had kissed him, made sure he was awake and aware, gotten dressed, and left him to pull himself together in private. He appreciated the gesture, but he kind of would've preferred Victor stay to answer a few questions. Like why Jordan had vague memories of T'ukri comforting him too when he woke up screaming. Or why he had the oddest sensation of being sandwiched between the two of them. And especially why that sensation was coupled with the feeling of bare skin, and nothing but bare skin.

Had Victor really brought T'ukri into their tent to help comfort him? And let—or told—him to get naked in the process? It would explain the blur of memories, but it didn't quite fit with where he thought things were. They'd discussed going ahead with the courtship, but that was a world away from sleeping naked together in the tight confines of the tent. It could've been wishful thinking, but he didn't usually hallucinate after his nightmares. Sure, he couldn't remember all the details, but what he did remember had usually happened. And if that held true this time, then T'ukri had been in their tent last night.

Fucking hell. He needed to talk to Victor.

He could drop back to walk beside Victor easily enough, but T'ukri wasn't scouting ahead like he usually did. No, he was right there too, keeping both Jordan and Victor within his line of sight at all times. Jordan couldn't decide if he felt protected or smothered. He could feel Victor's gaze on his back too. Like they were both keeping an eye on him to make sure he didn't snap. *Well, fuck that.* He'd been dealing with his own shit for years. He wasn't going to lose it because of one stupid fucking nightmare, even if it had been the worst one.

But damn if it didn't make him feel cherished to have them so concerned.

Victor's concern made sense, but the more he thought about it, the surer he was T'ukri had been there too. Unless he'd heard Jordan scream from outside, he wouldn't have any reason to be worried, and that meant Victor *had* brought him inside and let him help comfort Jordan after the nightmare.

Maybe they were making progress after all.

ABOUT HALFWAY through the afternoon, earlier than they usually stopped, T'ukri called a halt. "We will make camp here for the night. The stream should be safe if we wish to bathe or see to our clothes. We could use a rest."

Victor glanced over to Jordan to make sure he didn't decide T'ukri meant him instead of them, but Jordan's expression didn't change. A little grumpy, maybe, but that was his resting face half the time.

"Clean clothes do sound nice," Victor said. "And a bath sounds even better."

"Let me make sure nothing has changed since my last visit here, and then we can enjoy the water," T'ukri replied.

We can enjoy the water, he'd said. Victor tensed automatically, but he'd made his decision that morning. He wasn't going to balk at the first hurdle. Better for T'ukri to decide now rather than later if he didn't find Victor attractive enough to continue, when Victor had fallen even harder for him.

He watched T'ukri out of the corner of his eye as he walked along the bank of the stream.

"You okay with this?" Jordan said softly at Victor's side.

Victor turned to face him, smiling. "Yes. I'm okay with all of it."

Jordan looked surprised, but a smile grew as he took in what Victor had said. "Do I remember T'ukri in the tent with us last night?"

"Yes. I thought having us both there might make you feel safer."

"Fuck, I love you," Jordan said.

Victor smiled even wider. "I love you too. Are you feeling okay now?"

Jordan shrugged. "Getting there. But you don't have to hover, okay? If I need you, I'll let you know."

"Maybe I like being close to you."

"I like having you close, but I can feel you worrying from a mile away, much less a few feet." He leaned in and kissed Victor softly. "I'll be okay. I've been dealing with this shit for years."

And didn't that just break Victor's heart. "I know, but you don't have to deal with it alone anymore. Even before we got together, you didn't have to deal with it alone, but definitely not now. And I know T'ukri would say the same thing if you asked him."

"If you asked me what?" T'ukri said. If Victor hadn't trained himself out of his startle reflex years ago, he would have jumped sky-high. How did T'ukri move so quietly?

"If Jordan has to deal with his nightmares alone," Victor said. "I told him he didn't and that you'd agree with me."

T'ukri stepped close, well into their personal space, but Victor didn't step back. This was where he wanted T'ukri, inside their circle of intimacy. "You are right. I would have your burdens be mine to share."

Though the words were directed at Jordan, T'ukri never took his gaze off Victor as he spoke, making it clear he intended it for both of them.

"The stream is safe. Nothing lurks to bother us in the deeper sections."

Victor grabbed the hem of his T-shirt and pulled it over his head. "What are we waiting for?"

T'ukri grinned as he ran an appraising gaze over Victor's chest. Victor made himself stand still and let T'ukri look. Jordan hovered at his shoulder like he was ready to defend Victor if T'ukri said anything negative, which Victor appreciated, but he didn't think it would be necessary. Not if the heat in T'ukri's eyes was any indication.

That gave him the courage to walk to the edge of the stream, untie his boots, and strip the rest of the way off. He didn't look back at them as he walked into the cool water. When he reached the deepest part, it swirled around the tops of his thighs, lapping occasionally at his balls. He bent over to splash water on his face, well aware of the show he was giving Jordan and T'ukri, but then, that was the point.

Behind him Jordan whooped. Victor turned to watch him tear his clothes off and take a running jump into the stream, splashing water all over Victor. The chill felt incredible on his sweaty skin. T'ukri followed more slowly, but he never once looked away from Victor, and if anything, the heat in his eyes grew more intense.

If it hadn't been for the cold water, Victor would've been getting hard. As it was, he let himself watch with open appreciation as T'ukri undressed and strode into the water like he owned the place. Then again, this was his territory, so maybe that wasn't so unreasonable.

"If you wish, my people use this plant for washing. I do not know the name in Spanish, but we call it *saqta*. It smells sweet and works well against both sweat and dirt." T'ukri offered a handful of crumpled leaves.

Victor took a few, wondering if this was the same plant Jordan had seen T'ukri use in his purification ritual. If so, it seemed it could be used as lube as well. Maybe he'd wait to bring that up until they'd had a chance to talk about things a little more. He hadn't wanted to rush with Jordan. He wasn't going to rush with T'ukri either. "Thank you."

JORDAN WATCHED T'ukri carefully, ready to jump to Victor's defense if he did anything to trigger Victor's self-esteem issues, but T'ukri's gaze was as appreciative as it was assessing. Even so, Jordan ran a hand down Victor's back to the swell of his ass. It wasn't like he'd had that many opportunities to see and touch either. And if it made Victor glance at him with a warm smile, well, he was allowed to be greedy, wasn't he? Especially this early in a new relationship. Not that he expected it to change any time soon. Or ever. Never sounded pretty fucking perfect, now that he thought about it. An entire lifetime spent being greedy for Victor's smiles. Hell yeah, he could live with that.

"I should have known your keen eyes would pick out only the best of men, Malku." T'ukri's words might have been addressed to Jordan, but he kept his focus on Victor.

Good, let Victor see T'ukri was interested in him too. Jordan had tried telling him that from the day T'ukri showed up, but Victor hadn't been listening. T'ukri's open appraisal and obvious approval would be a little harder to ignore.

"I definitely won the jackpot," Jordan agreed.

T'ukri tilted his head like he didn't quite understand the expression, but he nodded all the same. Victor squirmed a bit under Jordan's hand and T'ukri's gaze, but Jordan didn't let him pull away. After a moment T'ukri turned his attention to Jordan. "And you, Malku? You saw how effective the saqta is. Will you use some as well?"

Jordan flushed as Victor turned toward him with an amused twitch on his lips. "Well, Malku?"

"You knew I was there?"

"You did not give yourself away, if that is your fear, but yes, I knew you were there. Few are the creatures who can hide from me in the rainforest."

"And you still...?"

"The goddess's rituals are set, no matter who might be watching." T'ukri's expression turned mischievous. "But she will forgive me for being more... thorough than required."

"I knew it!" Jordan took a step closer to T'ukri. "And what were you thinking about?"

T'ukri put on an expression of complete innocence. "Of how I wanted to be worthy of the goddess's blessing on my future endeavors."

"What 'endeavors' might those be?" Victor asked suddenly.

Jordan blinked, torn out of the sensual battle of wills and words with T'ukri. *Victor* was playing along. Sure, he'd known they were making progress, but between Victor being the first to get naked and now the open flirting, they'd left progress behind and were arriving at the destination. T'ukri looked as surprised as Jordan felt.

"Why, winning the approval of the ancestors, of course." T'ukri's little smirk matched the one Victor had worn earlier. "What other reason would there be?"

As far as Jordan was concerned, Victor had never looked so good as he did right then, fully naked, head up, shoulders back as he stepped boldly into T'ukri's space. "Courting us."

Oh, hell yeah!

THE BREATH rushed from T'ukri's lungs at Victor's blunt words. They had been circling this moment from the first time T'ukri had laid eyes on them, but now that it was here, he barely dared to believe it was happening. He had dreamed of his mates since he was old enough to understand the term, had played out every scenario his imagination could create. And then nothing. His fellow warriors had not roused his interest beyond casual dalliances, before or after he became Chapaqpuma, and so he had wandered. Until he wandered into Paucar's village. They were everything and nothing like he had imagined, and they were exactly what he needed, but even then he had held back, needing to be sure they could feel the same. Now, though….

If they were in Machu Llaqta, he would drag them to the temple this very moment and complete the bond, but they were not, and so he held the guardian in check. Only a few days more and they would reach the valley. He could wait that long. No longer, but that long.

"And to do that, I had to win the approval of the ancestors." T'ukri held Victor's gaze as Jordan moved to stand beside them.

"Did you?" Victor asked.

"I did. My grandfather gave his blessing. All that remains is to introduce you to my family. My mother would never forgive me if I bonded before she met my mates." He pushed aside Palta's concerns.

"Good." Victor took the final step closer to cross the distance between them and kissed him. T'ukri gasped into the kiss, the warm, dry touch of Victor's lips against his own. His body stirred in response, the guardian purring at the attention. He had told the ancestors these were the mates for him. He had been right.

"My turn," Jordan said. Victor stepped to the side and urged T'ukri into Jordan's arms. Where Victor's kiss had been warmth and safety, Jordan's was fire and strength. And where Victor had kept the contact chaste even when T'ukri gasped, Jordan kissed him deeply, claiming T'ukri's mouth with his tongue.

Yes, this was what he needed, what he had always hoped to find when he selected mates of his own. Just as his mother's fire had been balanced by Yuri's gentle patience, Victor would balance Jordan, and together they would make him whole as he hoped he would make them whole.

He arched against Jordan without thought, finding strength to match his own. It would be so easy to give in to that strength and beg Jordan to bear him down and claim him, to beg Victor to ground him through it. The hardness against his thigh assured him Jordan was more than willing. He broke the kiss and rested his forehead on Jordan's shoulder, panting harshly. "I cannot," he forced out between his clenched teeth as he fought his desires and the guardian's instincts to continue. "We must not do this yet."

He took a step back, pitting his will against every fiber of his being, which longed for the passion he would find when he finally claimed and was claimed by his mates.

"Why not?" Jordan asked.

T'ukri started to reply, but Victor sent Jordan a quelling look.

"That's the wrong question," Victor told him. "Tell us what is and isn't allowed, and we'll abide by it."

Jordan grumbled a little, but he nodded his agreement anyway.

"Some would say we have done too much already, being naked in the stream together, but that is not a bond." T'ukri pushed away the images that flashed through his mind of their bodies wrapped around one another, limbs entangled. He had vague memories of crawling into bed with his parents—all of three of them—as a child and being swallowed up by their embrace. Thinking back, it was the safest he had ever felt. Being similarly surrounded by his mates would be even better. "A bond will only occur when we find satiation together."

"So we can mess around all we want as long as we stop short of coming," Jordan summarized. "I can live with blue balls for a few more days if it means doing this right."

"You are already bonded," T'ukri said. "You do not have to abstain for me."

"Yeah, no," Jordan said. "That was before. Now that we're in this together, we'll be doing it right. If you don't get to come, we don't either. Right, Victor?"

"Of course," Victor said. "You're our guide in this just like you are in the rainforest. We don't want to make things complicated for you with your people."

They would bring complications simply for being outsiders, but T'ukri would worry about that when the time came. First he had to introduce them to his mother and Huallpa, and then he had to explain to them about the guardian. If neither of those things sent them screaming into the jungle, they could worry about how to consummate their bond.

"What is your expression? We will cross that road when we come to it?"

"We'll cross that *bridge* when we come to it," Jordan corrected.

"And we will," Victor added, "but I meant what I said. Tell us what we need to do so your people will accept our relationship."

"For now it will be enough that the ancestors gave their approval and that we have waited to bond until they can meet you. The rest will come as they get to know you as I have," T'ukri replied. "I will bathe separately to avoid temptation. I will prepare my shelter for the night and bathe when I am done."

"Don't do that." Victor caught T'ukri's hand. "You've told us where the line is. We won't cross it until you tell us it's time. You don't need to run from us."

"As tempting as you are," Jordan said with a leer that conveyed exactly how attractive he found T'ukri, "I sat in that tree and watched you fuck yourself with your fingers. If I can do that and hold my perch, I can take a bath in a stream with you and not jump you."

"And if I cannot resist you?" T'ukri asked.

"Then we'll help you explain to your mother what happened," Victor said with a shrug. "But I don't think that will be necessary." He crumpled the saqta in his hand and began to rub the cleansing liquid over his arms.

T'ukri watched for a moment as Victor unselfconsciously scrubbed his chest and under his arms. Jordan started to do the same, although he winked at T'ukri when he worked his way down his chest to the nest of light curls at his groin. T'ukri tore his gaze away. Jordan might have been able to keep his perch while T'ukri completed the purification ritual, but T'ukri knew himself too well for that. Now that the guardian had his mates' acceptance of his courtship, any delay was too long. Especially having held Jordan in his arms and cradled his body as he slept. He had touched Jordan's skin, felt the rock-hard muscle beneath as he had helped Victor comfort him from the nightmare. Now, though, with no memory-fueled terror to color the scene, T'ukri knew better than to allow himself to touch and taste any of the bounty spread out before him. His mates were a feast for his senses, and he wanted nothing more than to gorge himself on them.

Soon, he promised the restless guardian.

He forced himself to look away, to keep them on the edge of his peripheral vision rather than stare at them directly. He finished his own ablutions quickly and stepped onto the bank to retrieve his clothes. Dressed, he began gathering branches to make a shelter for himself so that if it rained during the night, they would not feel obliged to invite him inside. Now that they had accepted him, sleeping in such tight quarters with them would be torture.

He lost himself in thoughts of what he would say to his mother and Huallpa to convince them to accept Victor and Jordan. He would start by telling them of Inti's approval and of Palta's challenge. Huallpa especially would see the import of that. Then he would explain how Jordan had kept watch over him through the preparation rituals. He could hear Huallpa's chuckle at that, but Jordan did not know his guard had been unnecessary. He would follow with Paucar's and Kichka's approval. Though they were from a different tribe, their approval would still carry weight in Machu Llaqta, for they kept to many of the old ways. Then he would share Victor's respectful demeanor with the elders, the careful consideration he had for everyone around him, and how that resulted in such a deep caring that T'ukri knew Victor would be able to draw him back to himself when he let the guardian loose. Finally he would tell them of the yearning he sensed in both men for a true home and a true family, something T'ukri could provide.

The sound of branches landing on his pile startled him out of his thoughts.

"That wasn't enough to make a shelter for all three of us. We can leave our shirts and shorts on, but we aren't sleeping alone in our tent with you out here," Victor said. "And the tent is a little small for all three of us, especially if we're trying to be good."

T'ukri did not see how sleeping together regardless of how dressed or undressed they were would help with being good, but he simply nodded and added more woven branches to the roof he had constructed between two trees.

CHAPTER 21

VICTOR KICKED dirt over the embers so they wouldn't spark during the night and cause a fire. Jordan had already spread their bedrolls under the shelter T'ukri had built and was sitting cross-legged on them wearing nothing but his boxers. Victor would see how T'ukri reacted to that. He might have to make Jordan put a shirt back on, no matter how much he groused. If a shirt made the difference between T'ukri sleeping with them or sleeping elsewhere, Victor would insist.

"Ready for bed, T'ukri?" Jordan called.

"In a moment," T'ukri called back. "I must do my final check for the night."

Victor joined Jordan under the shelter but left a little space between them. He started to warn Jordan not to push but stopped himself. Jordan might play at being the jokester, but he knew when to take things seriously.

T'ukri appeared in front of them and glanced back and forth between them.

"Where would you be most comfortable sleeping?" Victor asked.

Jordan patted the space Victor had left. "Right here would be a good spot."

"That is not a good idea," T'ukri said.

"Would you be more comfortable like we were last night?" Victor asked.

"It is not a question of comfort but of control. If I were to sleep between you as Jordan suggested, I would not be able to restrain myself. It would be too much like my dreams come to life for me to resist."

Jordan groaned. "You really shouldn't say things like that. I'm trying to be good, but you'd tempt a saint."

Victor ignored him, even if he was right. "Then what would give you the most control?"

"If I lay behind one of you, I could move away if it got to be too much," T'ukri said.

Jordan reached up for T'ukri's hand. When he squatted down, Jordan looked him dead in the eye. Victor had experienced that piercing, demanding gaze more than once and knew how hard it was to look away. "We may joke and tease and flirt, but we will never ignore the word *no*, and we will never pressure you into anything. You can always move away or ask us to move away or do anything you need to so you feel comfortable with us. If you want us to pitch the tent and sleep in it, tonight or any other night, tell us. Yeah, I'll probably pout and complain a bit, but that's more out of habit than anything."

Victor heard the echo of Jordan's foster experiences and life on the streets in the promise never to pressure T'ukri and wanted to beat Jordan's foster father bloody, but he kept his expression clear. "Jordan's right."

T'ukri shook his head. "I know that. I am acting like an unblooded boy who has never known a lover's touch rather than an experienced warrior, but you are my mates, and that changes everything."

"Tell us a story," Jordan suggested. "We can lie here together, however you're most comfortable, and you can tell us another story until we fall asleep. That will keep our minds off messing around."

T'ukri sat down on Victor's other side and stretched out. Victor settled next to him, close enough to feel the heat from his body but not quite touching. Jordan snugged up behind Victor, fitting their bodies together tightly.

"I told the children in Paucar's village part of the legend of Chapaqpuma because they asked. Would you hear the rest?"

Victor tensed and felt Jordan do the same, but he kept his voice steady. "If you like. We definitely enjoyed the first half."

"I may have embellished a little for them," T'ukri admitted. "Tayta would scold me if he were still alive."

"I'm sure they didn't mind," Victor said with a smile. "Tell it to us however you want."

T'ukri took a deep breath, rolled onto his back, and stared at the ceiling above them. "*Deep in the rainforest, in a land time passed by, dwelled a forgotten people known only as the Lost Ones, if they were known at all. They lived as they always had, simply and in harmony with the land. From time to time, one of them would wander the wider world to see what had been learned in their absence and, if the wanderer deemed it worthy of the goddess, bring it back to aid the Lost*

Ones. In time the goddess blessed them for their faithfulness, bestowing on them a guardian who would ensure no harm came to them from outside, for everyone knew outsiders meant trouble—disease, famine, war, and death followed wherever they trod."

Victor recognized the cadence of a beloved story repeated over and over again. Nkóko had told stories like this when he was still alive, stories of Nzambi Mpungu who made the world and all who inhabit it, and of the *amazimu*, man-eating monsters. Unlike when T'ukri told his story to the children, this telling had weight about it, like the words themselves carried lessons to be learned and rules to be followed.

"The role and gifts of Chapaqpuma passed down from generation to generation, parent to child to grandchild and beyond, for the need of the goddess's protection never waned. The gifts of the goddess were bountiful, but the price was high, and the guardian could not walk that path alone. Instinct pushed Chapaqpuma to find a mate, a partner in whom to balance the senses so that the guardian could always return to the valley in proper form, yet few were they who could meet all of a guardian's needs. Thus it became the way of the Lost Ones for Chapaqpuma to take not one but two mates, a balance to each other as much as to the guardian, so that when calamity came, Chapaqpuma had the strength to ward it off and the humanity to return home after."

And that was the explanation that had been missing for the custom among T'ukri's people of taking more than one spouse. Whether Chapaqpuma was real or a legend, the story promoted a triad relationship as a positive one. It also made the stories of Philli-philli sound like children's tales in comparison. Whether this was the deeper legend Victor was searching for or something unique, it was exactly the kind of story that made his anthropologist heart sing.

"Have you ever met one of the wanderers?" Jordan asked. Victor was tempted to kick him, but at least he hadn't asked if T'ukri had ever met Chapaqpuma.

"I meet wanderers regularly," T'ukri said. "Take yourselves, for example. Are you not wanderers, coming to the Amazon to see what can be learned to take back to your people? That is the beauty of legends. Whatever they meant to the people who first created them, they have relevance for us all."

Wasn't that an interesting answer? "By that argument, you could be a wanderer for your people as well."

"I am indeed a wanderer for my people," T'ukri agreed easily. "And knowing my sister, she will take her turn when she is old enough."

"Is she a lot younger than you?" Jordan asked.

T'ukri rolled to his side so he was facing them. "She will be sixteen this year. When she is eighteen, Urpi will take her into the world outside our village to help her find her way."

"Who's Urpi?" Jordan asked.

"My other best friend," T'ukri replied. "Many in the village expected me to take Urpi and Cusi as my mates because we were always together as children, but Cusi is like a brother to me, and while I love Urpi, I do not desire her. My inclinations have always run toward men."

"Lucky for us." Jordan reached across Victor to grab T'ukri's hand and tug him closer.

"Definitely lucky for us," Victor agreed as T'ukri moved where Jordan wanted him. Where he wanted him was apparently almost as tightly pressed against Victor as Jordan was.

Not that Victor was complaining.

"Lucky for me as well," T'ukri said. "While they would make suitable mates easily accepted by my family and tribe, they would not satisfy the longing for adventure inside me. I can tell already that being with you will be a grand adventure worthy of many tales to pass down to future generations."

Victor laughed softly. "I'm looking forward to those adventures, whatever they turn out to be."

Jordan pushed up on one elbow to lean across Victor and run a hand down T'ukri's arm until he could clasp their fingers together.

"Jordan?" T'ukri asked.

"You're all snuggled up to Victor, but I want to touch you too."

T'ukri pushed up until his position matched Jordan's and kissed him above Victor. Bon Dieu, but that was a beautiful sight. Without the cold water from earlier to keep him under control, he felt his body stir. He rolled flat between them so he had both hands free. He slipped one hand beneath Jordan and wrapped it around his hip, right where the waistband of his boxer briefs gave way to skin. His other hand he ran along T'ukri's jaw and down the curve of his neck to rest on his shoulder. He knew where the lines were with Jordan, but they had promised not to push for more than T'ukri could give without violating his people's traditions.

T'ukri broke the kiss with Jordan to look down at Victor. Even in the deepening twilight, Victor could see the intensity in his eyes, and he shivered beneath it.

"Cold, my own?" T'ukri asked. "Or is it something else that makes you tremble?"

"Like you have to ask," Victor replied tartly. "I'm lying here watching two of the most beautiful men I've ever seen kiss over me. I'm definitely not cold."

T'ukri slid back to the ground and rested his head on Victor's shoulder. On his other side, Jordan mimicked the position, which put their clasped hands on his abdomen, right below his navel. "We could make you warmer," Jordan purred before turning his head to nip at Victor's collarbone.

"I'm sure you could, but you aren't going to. We promised T'ukri we wouldn't push," Victor retorted.

"You are not pushing if I am offering." T'ukri flattened his hand on Victor's belly and dragged it slowly upward. "I admit to great curiosity at how you will feel in my arms. I have held Jordan, but so far you have eluded me."

What was Victor supposed to say to that? He wasn't fool enough to say no except that saying yes was a risk they'd decided not to take. Then again, T'ukri was an adult. He could make his own decisions. Instead of answering, he turned his head so he could kiss T'ukri for the second time.

Unlike that afternoon in the stream, there was no hesitation between them now, only heat. Jordan urged him onto his side and spooned up behind him, only to start rutting against him when he was settled. He rocked back against Jordan as the kiss with T'ukri continued, gentle brushes turning into nips, turning into the wet hot slide of tongues. Unable to stop himself, Victor reached for T'ukri's hip and pulled him closer so he could rock back and forth between his two lovers. He wanted to strip away their remaining clothes and let them drive him wild, but that would cross all the lines. Instead he gripped T'ukri's side firmly and kissed him back with all the skill and passion he could muster. When T'ukri moaned into his mouth and then rolled onto his back, panting, Victor couldn't stop the smugness in his chest. He might be graying and on the wrong side of forty, but he'd still managed to reduce this gorgeous man to a moaning, panting mess.

Jordan nipped along his shoulder like he knew what Victor was thinking, but Victor couldn't bring himself to care. After years of resigning himself to being alone for the rest of his life, he had not one but two men who wanted him. He was a lucky bastard, and he didn't care who knew it. He was going to be selfish for once in his life and hold on to this gift with both hands.

CHAPTER 22

"WHAT MADE you decide to study anthropology?" T'ukri asked Victor as they made camp a few nights later. It was a question he had wanted to ask from the beginning but one that had seemed too personal until now.

"My grandfather," Victor replied. He did not say more until they had their shelter prepared for the night and started the fire to cook the quail Jordan had shot earlier. T'ukri waited patiently for the rest of the story. He had learned the rhythm of storytelling at Tayta's feet and knew that questions of importance required serious consideration in the answering.

When they were settled around the fire and the quail was roasting, Victor rested his hands on his knees and began. "I told you my grandparents lived in the Republic of Congo but that my parents immigrated to France before I was born. They both worked full-time, and in the summers they sent my siblings and me back to the Plateaux to stay with my grandparents. My brother and sister hated it—the heat, the dust, the absence of their friends and most modern conveniences— but I loved it. Nkóko, my grandfather, was the village shaman and the wisest person I have ever known. He was greatly revered in the village, but to me he was just Nkóko, the one person who always had time for me."

T'ukri sympathized with that. He felt much the same way about Tayta.

"My parents were always busy with work, and at school I was one of a classroom full of children. No one had the patience for all my questions, especially since my questions tended toward the philosophical at a very young age. But Nkóko never ran out of time or patience for my endless questions." Victor's smile bore a hint of grief, but it spoke far more of remembered joy than of sadness. T'ukri hoped a time would come when his own smile when speaking of Yuri would look the same.

"When we grew older, our parents gave us the choice of staying in France, but while my siblings jumped at the chance, I continued to spend the summers with my grandfather up until I turned sixteen. I had planned to spend that summer with him as well, but Nkóko wrote to me telling me not to come, to apply instead for the summer program in Peru that had caught my eye. To this day, I don't know if my parents told him about it or if this was more of his shamanic ability. I had never mentioned the program, but I did as he said and applied. I fell in love with Peru and with the Inca that summer."

T'ukri sent a silent prayer of thanksgiving to Victor's grandfather, for surely the ancestral plane welcomed all ancestors, not only those of his own people. A shaman like Victor described would be a force in any plane. He would sense T'ukri's gratitude wherever he now dwelled.

"As I continued to study, I realized I didn't just want to study history. As fascinated as I was—and am—by the ruins and what the Inca people created, I didn't want to spend my life in libraries, surrounded by dusty old books and historical accounts written by the conquerors. I want to be out in the field, meeting the descendants of those people, learning the lore and legends they live by now. That led me away from history or archaeology and into anthropology."

"What did your grandfather think of your choices?"

"He never knew," Victor replied. "He died while I was in Peru that summer. But I like to think he would have approved. He was a shaman, after all, who believed in the power of lore and belief and who taught me that no knowledge is ever wasted, even when we do not understand its purpose at the time we learn it."

"He sounds like a very wise man."

"The wisest," Victor replied.

T'ukri burned to know more, but Victor's expression had shuttered. T'ukri turned to Jordan. "What of you, Malku?"

"Nothing nearly as exciting as Victor, I'm afraid," Jordan said with a self-conscious laugh that T'ukri was coming to hate. Jordan should not question his own worth.

"That does not make me less interested in hearing about it."

Jordan rubbed the back of his neck and poked at the fire. "I didn't have the most conventional childhood, but you knew that already. With all the bouncing around from foster placement to group home and back out again, I never stayed in the same school for very long, and my life was always chaotic, so my grades weren't great. I enlisted in the Marines as much because I didn't see another path forward as for any other reason. In some respects it was the best choice I could have made. It gave me a purpose and a structure I'd never had before, but suddenly having structure after eighteen years of chaos was a big adjustment. I… made it work, but I was always a bit of a square peg in a round hole. Nandini helped with that, smoothing my rough edges when she could, but by the time my tour was up, it was pretty obvious that if I didn't leave on my own, I'd end up leaving with a dishonorable discharge on my record, and I didn't want that."

"I didn't know that," Victor said. "What could you possibly have done to end up in that much trouble?"

"Got too friendly with the locals," Jordan replied. "My CO was of the opinion that anyone who wasn't American was in league with the enemy, which was fucking ridiculous. He didn't appreciate me pointing out the errors in his logic."

That sounded like the man T'ukri had fallen in love with—putting his own career, if not his life, on the line to protect the innocent.

"So anyway, when the time came to reup, I didn't. Of course that left me with the problem of what to do with the rest of my life. I'd racked up enough credit with the GI Bill to pay for college, and I figured why the hell not? I'd served my country. The least they could do was pay for my education. Even if I went to school for four years and didn't get a degree, at least I'd have learned something."

"You obviously learned something," T'ukri said with a smile.

"You could say that." Jordan laughed again, a real laugh this time. "There I was, a freshman in college and a military veteran with war zone experience. I didn't exactly fit in with most of my classmates, but I was determined to do my best anyway. I'd half-assed my way through high school, but I wasn't going to make the same mistakes in college. I was going to use all those organizational skills the Marines had pounded into my head and draw up a plan, so I sat down with a course catalog and the list of graduation requirements and started charting out the next four years of my life. One of the requirements was three classes in the social sciences. I'd had more than enough of politics in the military, so that was out. Economics looked like it might have more math than I really wanted to deal with, which left anthropology, psychology, and sociology. Anthropology fit best into my schedule for my first semester, and I figured what the hell, I'd really enjoyed getting to know the local people when we were deployed in the Marines, and it seemed like that might translate into anthropology."

"I take it you were right," T'ukri said.

"Damn straight. It was the last class in my rotation, and by the time I got there for the first session, I was completely overwhelmed and starting to wonder if I'd made a mistake. I was older than all my classmates and didn't have jack shit in common with them. The professors were all old men in stuffy suits who looked like they hadn't seen the world outside of their offices in a decade at least. And while I appreciate a good book as much as the next person, I never really understood literary analysis, so my English class was my own personal hell. And then Dr. Jones walked in wearing jeans and a T-shirt. I just about fell out of my seat right there. And when he started talking to us about what we'd be learning in the class, I had an epiphany. Everything he was saying made sense to me when he talked about how understanding another culture meant understanding not just economic and political systems but also language, gender, race, ethnicity, kinship, family, religion, and more. I stayed after class to talk to him that day and pretty much every day after that. By the time the semester ended, he'd convinced me to sign up for a seminar with him the following semester. I went on a research project with him in Central America as soon as I was eligible, and before that was over, I knew I'd found my calling. He's the one who introduced me to Victor."

"And the rest is fate," Victor finished.

Or the mysterious hand of the goddess. Whichever it was, T'ukri would be eternally grateful.

"WE SHOULD reach the village in two days," T'ukri said as they made camp a little over a week later.

"About fucking time," Jordan muttered.

T'ukri laughed. He could not help himself. Jordan's grumpiness made T'ukri want to wrap him up in the softest wool and protect him from anything that would upset him. And if he tried, Jordan would pitch a fit and fight his way out. After watching him in the days since they left Paucar's village, T'ukri had no doubt he could do it too.

"What do we need to know when we get there?" Victor asked. "Are there rules we need to follow or traditions to observe?"

T'ukri's stomach churned as he thought of all he had not told them, yet the very fact that Victor had posed the question proved once again how justified his choice was. Not everyone would have thought to ask. "A few. We will meet the sentries first, for even with the goddess's protection, we guard our borders carefully. One of them will run ahead to announce our arrival. My parents will meet us along with the elders of the tribe."

"Does everyone get that kind of welcome?" Jordan asked.

"No," T'ukri said slowly. "My parents sit on the council of elders. Papãnin...." He took a deep breath and reminded himself he had to tell them. He could not let them walk into the situation unaware and at risk of offending someone in their ignorance. "I suppose you would call him the chieftain of our tribe."

"Your tribe?" Victor asked. "Not just the village but all your people?"

"We are not scattered the way some tribes are, although even villages like Paucar's are mostly independent, but yes, all our people," T'ukri replied.

"You're a prince." Jordan sat down hard as if his legs could no longer support him. "Victor, we went and fell for a fucking prince."

"Don't tell me you're surprised," Victor replied. "You're usually more observant than that."

"You knew?" Jordan accused.

"Suspected." Victor turned to T'ukri. "Too many things didn't add up. You were obviously more important than you claimed to be."

T'ukri should have known better than to think he could fool them. Paucar's tribe had refrained from using his title at his request, but that had not stopped them from treating him with deference. Victor had obviously picked up on that. "I did not set out to deceive you, but it is safer for me if outsiders see me only as a guide."

"A fucking prince," Jordan repeated with a shake of his head. "You sure you want to take up with me? I'm not exactly princess material."

Victor nudged Jordan's back with his knee before T'ukri could reply. Jordan glared up at Victor's unrepentant face. "No putting yourself down."

"My people do not judge merit the same way yours do," T'ukri said, drawing their attention back to him. "You are a skilled hunter, as you have proven more than once since we left Paucar's village behind. That is more than enough to qualify you as my mate."

"And me?" Victor asked, though he sounded more confident than Jordan had.

"You are a match for Jordan's strength in all ways, but it is not a warrior I see when I look at you. No, you are the shaman. I see the same wisdom in your eyes that I saw in Tayta's eyes before he died. If it comes to that, I know you will both stand beside me in a fight, and when it is over, *you* will bring us home and remind us what we fight to protect. Many warriors lose sight of that when the battle fever takes them, but you will not let us fall prey to that madness."

"He's got you pegged, Victor," Jordan said quietly.

"It will be my honor to stand beside you and to guide you home," Victor said formally.

T'ukri bit his lip at the surge of emotion Victor's vow evoked. The words were so close to the ones he would say when they completed their bond in front of his people.

Jordan pushed to his feet, offering T'ukri a nod of his own. "I swore a long time ago that I'd protect anyone who needed it. That's especially true for people I care about. If my marksmanship or anything else the Marines pounded into my head can aid your people, as a hunter or as a warrior, it's yours."

T'ukri reached for them both. He needed the contact to steady himself. The guardian whined inside him, wanting them with a desperation that bordered on madness. He only hoped he could convince his parents quickly. The longer he had to wait, the harder it would be to remain the master of his emotions.

He had spent enough time with Cusi to know all his grandmother's stories, the most common being the tale of the guardian who took an unsuitable mate and lost himself when she could not bring him back. He had killed his mate and Cusi's grandmother's family along with many others before disappearing into the woods. T'ukri could not let that happen to him, not so soon after Yuri's death. His people would not deal well with losing a second Chapaqpuma so soon. He owed Jordan and Victor those two stories as well, especially Yuri's, so they would understand the cloud that hung over his remaining parents.

Their embrace gave him the strength to silence the guardian inside him, but it did nothing to settle the jittery nerves. Neither he nor Jordan had brought down any game that day, which gave him an excuse to run for a time. "Will you finish setting up camp while I find us something for dinner?"

"We can do that," Victor replied. "Are you sure you're okay to go alone?"

"We are not far from where I grew up. I know these woods nearly as well as the land of my birth," T'ukri said. "I will be well."

"See you when you get back, then."

T'ukri gave each of them a quick kiss and turned to sprint into the underbrush. He would run until his nerves settled, and then he would find something to bring back for dinner.

T'UKRI RETURNED to camp just as the sun was setting. "The goddess was generous tonight. If we roast the tapir, we should not have to hunt again before we reach my home."

"The fire's ready." Victor took the tapir and spitted it. "You never did tell us how to go about greeting your parents."

T'ukri settled next to where Jordan was checking his gear and tried to decide what to say. They so rarely had visitors from outside the tribe that formalities were reserved for times of ritual. T'ukri could not ever remember a true outsider coming far enough into their territory to have a chance to greet the royal family. If protocols existed, he did not know them, but he could not leave his mates with nothing to guide them.

"They will be wary," T'ukri said finally. "It is not often outsiders visit our home. We prefer the protection our remote location offers us and rarely invite others in. Within the tribe we observe formalities only on special occasions, when a ritual requires ceremonial roles."

"But we *are* outsiders," Victor said, "and not just from another village or tribe. You don't have any suggestions?"

"How did you first greet Paucar?" T'ukri asked, at a loss for what else to say.

"With a respectful bow and a request for shelter within his village," Victor said.

"Then offer my parents the same," T'ukri said. "They will understand the intention and the respect. The rest will come in time."

Jordan humphed next to him, but he said nothing else.

"Do they speak a language we know?" Victor asked.

"We decided some generations ago that all within my family as well as all those who would choose to wander should learn Spanish as well as our native Runasimi. These days, many wanderers learn basic English as well. You will be able to greet them," T'ukri replied.

"Good. It wouldn't be a great start to our visit if we couldn't even speak to them."

T'ukri would have to teach them Runasimi after they bonded. He doubted anyone would agree before that. Still, they spoke multiple languages already. One more should not be that hard when they were surrounded by it every day.

"Is there a spot where we can clean up a bit before we meet them?" Jordan asked. "I'm back to being a sweaty, disgusting mess. Not the best first impression."

T'ukri understood the desire, although he doubted that would be the reason for his parents' disapproval. And T'ukri had rather come to enjoy the scratch of whiskers on Jordan's and Victor's jaws. They had been clean-shaven in Paucar's village, though, and Victor in particular had shaved every chance he got, but the opportunity had not always been available. In the valley, though, he would be able to return to his usual habits.

"There is a spring where we can bathe and change before we meet them," T'ukri said, "although I will have only our traditional attire to offer you."

"Is that kosher?" Jordan asked.

"Kosher?"

"Allowed," Victor replied. "Will it bother anyone if we're wearing your tribe's traditional clothes when we aren't part of the tribe?"

Again T'ukri had no answer, but the image of Jordan and Victor in the brightly colored tunics and loose pants his people wore filled him with the desire to push on through the night so they could reach home that much more quickly. If he had been alone, he might have considered it, but he would not risk his mates in the darkness. He could wait two more days, especially since they would not have to hunt or cook tomorrow. They could make camp late and eat as night fell so they would reach the border by midday the day after. And that night they would sleep under his roof, even if his mother would not allow them in his bed.

"You are my mates," T'ukri said finally. "You may wear them if you wish."

And if anyone disagreed, T'ukri would make his position clear as forcefully as necessary.

CHAPTER 23

JORDAN STUDIED the scenery as they left camp the last morning in the jungle. From everything T'ukri had said, he expected some kind of hidden entrance to the village, a pass or tunnel it would be easy to miss if someone didn't know it was there. Jordan wanted to recognize the landmarks in case he left the village without T'ukri and someone decided it would be funny to leave him behind. Maybe T'ukri's people were kinder than that, but in Jordan's experience, bullies existed everywhere. He wouldn't be surprised if the warriors put him through some kind of hazing. Victor would probably escape it, being older and more dignified, not to mention more of a shaman than a warrior, but Jordan just knew some young buck was going to try to take a piece of him. Jordan wouldn't go on the offensive, but he'd be damned if he let someone make a fool out of him.

As they walked, he looked for a path or any kind of sign that others had passed this way recently. T'ukri's people didn't let outsiders in, but T'ukri was proof that they went out, which meant there had to be a path, however faint.

He couldn't find a single fucking trace.

The more they walked, the more the landscape seemed to run together until he would have sworn they'd passed that rock formation before. "Are we going in circles?" he asked Victor softly.

"It feels that way, doesn't it? At least T'ukri hasn't blindfolded us to keep their secret safe. Just keep watching. There will be some kind of sign eventually."

When they passed the same rock formation for the third time, T'ukri stopped and walked up to it. "Here," he said, gesturing for Victor and Jordan to come closer. "This is the key."

He brushed away a bit of moss to reveal a groove in the rock. It looked like any of the dozens of other cracks and chips until T'ukri brushed more of the moss back. "You know you are home when you find the goddess's symbol."

Jordan looked at it more closely until the fissures resolved into the head of a large cat. "Did someone carve that in the rock?"

T'ukri smiled. "Only the goddess. Come, we are close now. We will meet the sentries soon and they will take us to the stream so we can bathe before we go into the village."

T'ukri stepped around the rock. Jordan and Victor followed. As they passed it, a chill ran over Jordan's skin, raising the hairs on his arm with an almost electric charge. He frowned and looked at Victor for confirmation. Victor nodded silently.

Jordan rested his hand on his bow. He didn't reach for an arrow, but he could have one nocked and aimed in the blink of an eye if necessary.

They hadn't gone far, maybe five hundred feet, when a voice called out a challenge. Jordan might not understand much Quechua, or Runasimi, or whatever T'ukri called it—and this didn't sound quite like any of the variants they'd encountered so far—but he knew a demand when he heard one. T'ukri called back, his voice light. A moment later another man appeared, a spear in hand and a bow on his back. He was a little shorter and stockier than T'ukri, but he carried himself with the same confidence, like the jungle was his playground and nothing there could hurt him.

"Cusi, I had hoped you would be here," T'ukri said in Spanish. "Come, I have people for you to meet."

Cusi said something else in Runasimi, but T'ukri just laughed. "Do not be rude. Victor, Jordan, this is the brother of my heart. Cusi, be the first to welcome my mates to Machu Llaqta."

Victor nodded respectfully, not quite a bow, but definitely an acknowledgment of the introduction. Jordan made himself do the same, although the gesture felt awkward. He really wasn't cut out for this formality bullshit.

Cusi's expression lost none of its distrust, but he acknowledged the nod before turning his back on them and talking to T'ukri in their language. Jordan glared. Yeah, he wasn't much to look at, sweaty and gross after a week since they'd last had a chance to clean up, but that didn't mean Cusi had to be rude about it. He opened his mouth to say something, but Victor squeezed his arm gently and shook his head.

Jordan grumbled under his breath and resolved to show Cusi just what he was made of at the first possible moment. It would be in bad form to shoot the spear out of his hand, wouldn't it?

"Relax," Victor ordered under his breath.

Jordan shook his hands and arms out, trying to release the battle-ready tension that had grown since they'd passed the rock with the cat head on it. He didn't know what was going on here, but he damn sure didn't like it. Nothing added up. Not the absence of any kind of path. Not the mark on the rock. Not the clearly organized sentries, far more like an actual military than anything they'd encountered in the other villages they'd visited. And definitely not the name. Machu Llaqta. Jordan didn't know what *llaqta* meant, but he knew *machu*, and that was *old*—and not just in modern Quechua either. That went all the way back to the Inca people and the "old mountain" of Machu Picchu. If they were dealing with Inca shit, they'd walked into even more of an unknown situation than he'd expected.

Finally T'ukri argued Cusi down and looked back at Jordan and Victor with a smile. "We can go to the stream to clean up. Cusi will send word ahead that we have arrived, and someone will bring us clean clothes. He cannot accompany us until a replacement arrives to take his post, but I am sure Mama will send someone as soon as she hears. She knows what it would mean to me to have Cusi with me as I bring my mates before the elders."

Jordan could have done without that reminder and without Cusi's sour expression, but he'd dealt with worse. As long as he kept it to nasty looks, it wouldn't even make Jordan's list of unpleasant things in his life. He focused on T'ukri's smile instead. He could deal with pretty much anything if it meant T'ukri would keep smiling at him that way.

Once they left Cusi, they followed a clear path down the hill into a narrow valley. Jordan would've said they were far enough into the Amazon basin to have left that kind of topography behind, but he couldn't deny what was in front of him. At the base of the hill, T'ukri veered off the main path onto a smaller one. "The stream is just ahead."

They rounded a bend, and Jordan stopped in his tracks. He'd seen his share of amazing things in his life, both natural and man-made, but they hadn't prepared him for this. The stream T'ukri referred to tumbled down the cliff face in misty sheets to pool at the base before burbling deeper into the valley.

T'ukri walked to the water's edge and undressed quickly. Jordan let himself look because he didn't know when he'd get his next chance. Probably not until after they'd bonded, if T'ukri was right. He'd curled up behind T'ukri and rubbed against him. He'd stretched out between Victor and T'ukri and grabbed those perfect curves as they made out. He'd kept his hands outside T'ukri's clothes, but that hadn't stopped him from memorizing the feel. His palms itched to reach out and touch now, but he didn't know how long it would take someone to arrive from the village, and he didn't want to fuck things up before he'd even met the elders. He didn't think they'd look kindly on Jordan feeling up their prince before they were bonded or married or whatever the hell they called it.

Besides, if he got his hands on all that bare skin, he might not stop, and then T'ukri's mother would kill them all.

T'ukri looked back over his shoulder and winked at Jordan before diving into the pool.

And just like that, his dick perked up and stood at attention. *Fuck.* How was he supposed to get naked with a stiffie? If it were just the three of them, he wouldn't care, but T'ukri had said someone would bring them clothes.

Maybe the water would be cold and that would help him settle down. He pulled off his clothes quickly and jumped into the water.

And of course it was warm. No help there. At least it would make shaving easier.

Victor joined them at a more sedate pace. Jordan was tempted to tackle him just to ruffle his perfect exterior a bit, but he refrained. He didn't care all that much about his own image, but T'ukri would have a hard enough time selling the elders on them without Jordan making things worse.

T'ukri swam to the far side of the pool and plucked leaves off one of the plants. "Here," he called. "Help yourself to all you need."

Jordan was halfway across the pool when he heard rustling in the undergrowth. He glanced toward his gear, but he'd never reach it in time.

"Cusi said you brought outsiders home," a woman's voice called in Spanish, "but he left out a few details. I will speak to him about what constitutes relevant information."

T'ukri spun around at the sound of the voice coming from the cliffs above them, adding to Jordan's tension. A minute shiver ran over his skin, a cat shaking water from its fur, and then he relaxed. "Quenti! I did not expect you to come all the way out here to greet us."

Jordan sank deeper beneath the water. He wasn't body shy, but he wasn't ready to flash an unknown woman until he had a better idea of the customs of T'ukri's people.

"It is my job to protect you, my prince. You would not let me go with you when you left, but I will resume my post now that you are home."

"Of course you will." T'ukri rolled his eyes. "Stand guard if you must, but do not spend too much time staring at my mates. You would not want to make Cusi jealous."

Quenti retorted in their language, making T'ukri laugh again. "You do not have to see what I do in them. You have only to accept that they are what I have been searching for all my life."

Quenti inclined her head. "Then I wish you the goddess's blessing. I will guard their lives as I do yours."

Jordan might have bristled at that, but Quenti didn't know them yet. If she was T'ukri's guard, she had to be a damn good warrior herself based on the sparring he and T'ukri had done when they were waiting for dinner to be ready on their early nights. Since she seemed inclined to accept them, he'd ask if she wanted to spar with him sometime, see if she could teach him some moves.

She turned away, focused on the path leading to the pool rather than on them.

Jordan swam over to where T'ukri rested against a curve in the pool. "I don't remember you mentioning her. You talked about Cusi and Urpi, and your sister, of course. Did I miss it?"

"No," T'ukri said. "I could have mentioned her as Cusi's mate, but she is much more than that, and it would have required an explanation I was not ready to give. I suppose you would call Quenti a general. She sees to our defenses and leads our warriors if battle comes. She has also taken on the role of my personal guard, no matter how many times I tell her I am perfectly safe within our borders."

"We could try convincing her we're more than enough to keep you safe," Jordan offered.

T'ukri laughed softly. "You are welcome to try. She is more likely to believe we will pose too much of a distraction to one another and so will need protecting more than ever."

Jordan snorted. "Yeah, okay, I might see her point, but that's just when we know we're safe. If we were worried about any kind of danger, we wouldn't be distracted. Ask Victor. I've been watching his back for years without being distracted."

T'ukri frowned a little. "Is anthropology such a dangerous field?"

"When we're out in the field, it can be. You never know when someone'll decide to take exception to our presence. Hell, to our existence sometimes. We've pulled each other's asses out of the fire more than once."

"Then I continue to be glad you have had each other, for protection as well as for comfort and love," T'ukri replied.

"My prince, it will not win you any favor with the king and the elders if you keep them waiting too long," Quenti broke in. Jordan glanced her way, but her back was still turned respectfully. "You would not wish them to question your eagerness to present your mates to them."

Jordan didn't doubt T'ukri's eagerness to present them, but his own eagerness to be presented was getting smaller with each passing second. Before he could freak out any more than he already was, Victor joined them, freshly shaven, and squeezed Jordan's side. "Deep breath, Jordan. Whatever their titles, they're still the parents of the man we've fallen for, and that's what we're going to focus on. They want him to be happy just like we do. We're all on the same side here."

Easy for you to say, Jordan thought.

His thoughts must have shown on his face because Victor nudged his shoulder. "No putting yourself down, even in your head." He turned to look at T'ukri. "This is not a new problem. You have to help me break him of it. He's convinced he's worth less attention, respect, love, you name it, because of his past. I keep telling him the way other people have treated him says more about their worth than his. He still doesn't believe me."

"I believe I shall enjoy tackling this problem," T'ukri replied. "It will be no hardship to shower him with all the respect and affection I have to give."

Jordan wanted to sink beneath the surface of the water and disappear, but they wouldn't let him drown himself, which meant he was stuck. Then again, stuck between Victor and T'ukri wasn't a bad place to be. As long as he could stay there, he could deal with the rest. Like the fact that they'd fallen in love with a fucking prince.

VICTOR SMILED at T'ukri's reply and Jordan's reaction. It would be good to have an ally in his quest to overcome Jordan's insecurities. And if T'ukri approached Victor's own insecurities with the same determination, maybe he'd eventually come to believe they wouldn't grow tired of him. T'ukri had said he would rely on Victor to bring them home, and his tale of the guardian and the necessity of compassion underscored that idea, but that was small comfort when faced with the two gorgeous younger men next to him in the water.

He'd said for years that Jordan read him better than anyone else, and he proved it once again when he poked Victor in the side. "While we're working on insecurities, don't forget to tell Victor regularly that he's far sexier than he thinks he is. Otherwise he'll spend his time worrying we're going to throw him over for a younger model, which is bullshit. It's his experience that makes him so attractive."

T'ukri pushed off the wall where he'd been resting and swam close enough to brush against Victor, naked skin to naked skin. "That will be even easier than reassuring you. Our bonding day cannot come soon enough."

"My prince," Quenti called from above. "Remember your manners."

Victor winced at the thought of Quenti hearing everything they'd said since she arrived.

"Do not worry," T'ukri said in Victor's ear. "She is the epitome of discretion, and her loyalty to me is unassailable. She will tell no one of our conversation nor allude to it in any way. You need never fear speaking freely in her presence."

"I'll remember that," Victor said. "But she is right. We don't want to make things harder for ourselves when we meet your parents."

"That is true. Come, we should dress." He swam to shore and walked out, completely unconcerned by his nudity. Victor admired his confidence as much as his physique. He couldn't stop his glance toward where Quenti stood guard above them, but her back remained to them, so he followed T'ukri out of the water.

Two piles of cloth waited next to their dirty clothes. T'ukri picked up something from the first and tossed it to Victor. It took him a moment to realize it was a towel. Since leaving Ollantaytambo, he had mostly let his skin dry naturally, either because the chances to bathe had been rare or because he hadn't had a towel to use, but he didn't turn down the luxury now. Nor did he resist stealing surreptitious glances at both Jordan and T'ukri as they dried off and Jordan shaved quickly. The cloth alternately covering and revealing hard, muscled limbs was its own seduction.

When they were dry, T'ukri shook out the items from the other pile. He handed Jordan and Victor each a pair of dark trousers with drawstring waists. His own trousers were much more ornate, bright blue swirling through patches of yellow, and if Victor wasn't mistaken, that was gold thread at the hems and waist. Then T'ukri handed out long, straight tunics. Victor's was a solid dark green, simple but flattering. He handed Jordan a maroon one, so dark it was almost purple. Then he put on his own, the same yellow and blue as in his trousers. Unlike the ones Victor and Jordan wore, though, T'ukri's had ornate embroidery along the collar, the cuffs of the sleeves, and the hemline. It also fit more precisely along the line of his shoulders. This was clearly his outfit, not something brought out at random. And it was an ensemble fit for a prince.

He was starting to sympathize with Jordan's "just a kid from the country" routine. Victor had met heads of state before in the course of his field expeditions, as he sought permission from tribal leaders to explore their territory, but this was different. If T'ukri had his way, he'd soon be married to one, at least by the tribal customs of Machu Llaqta. Given that T'ukri was the prince of an isolated tribe and therefore unrecognized by any external authority only changed the way that union would be viewed by outsiders—and damn if Victor hadn't started thinking of the rest of the world in the same terms T'ukri did. It did nothing to change how Victor felt about it.

T'ukri slipped his feet into a pair of sandals. "I have no shoes to offer. We do not keep extras for wanderers returning home the way we do clothes."

"Our boots are fine unless that will be a problem," Victor said.

"They will be fine. I thought only of your comfort," T'ukri replied.

Jordan would be more comfortable in his boots until he got the lay of the land, Victor knew, and at the moment Victor was inclined to agree with him.

When they stepped back onto the trail they had taken to arrive at the pool, Cusi flanked them along with three other similarly dressed men—an honor guard for T'ukri or extra protection against outsiders. Victor didn't know which, but either explanation left him sympathizing with Jordan's reaction. They were dating a fucking prince.

When they reached the place where the path split, one back toward the jungle, away from T'ukri's home, and the other presumably toward the village, Quenti joined them as well, giving Victor his first good look at the warrior who was also T'ukri's personal guard. Tall and slender, she moved with the same deadly grace and harnessed power that he'd noticed when he met Jordan's friend Nandini. Not that he knew how to engineer it, but he'd love to see the two women spar.

"Who d'ya think would win?" Jordan asked him softly in English. "Nan or Quenti?"

"I'm not sure I could predict it," Victor replied just as softly. "Definitely not without seeing Quenti fight."

"That can be arranged," Quenti said from ahead of them without looking back. Though she had answered in Spanish, she had clearly understood. T'ukri had mentioned wanderers in his tribe often learned rudimentary English, but he hadn't realized Quenti was one of them.

"Actually, I'd really like that." Jordan switched back to Spanish as he took a step forward, but Cusi's spear blocked his path.

"Enough, Cusi," T'ukri said. "He was not threatening her. He was asking to spar with her. And who better to teach our ways than Quenti?"

"I meant no disrespect," Jordan added. "Sorry if it came across that way."

"It did not," Quenti said as Cusi grumbled. "My love is at times overly protective of me. While the warrior in me would remind him it is not necessary, the woman appreciates it too much to stop him."

And that was diplomacy if Victor had ever heard it. Both a reminder to Cusi to relax and permission to continue. Maybe she'd give Jordan lessons in that too.

The path turned sharply around a cliff face and opened out into another valley, far larger and deeper than the one where they'd bathed. Nestled in the valley was a… city. Not a village like Paucar's as he'd expected. Yes, the buildings had thatched roofs, but even the most basic couldn't be called huts. And the statue outside the most elaborate building gleamed golden in the sunlight. Whether it was gilded or solid was impossible to see from this distance, but either was more than he had seen outside of museums. This was… was…. This was Machu Picchu the way it might have looked before the Spanish conquest of Peru, only bigger. This was… a discovery that could make him a household name. He'd never have to worry about scrambling for grants again. He'd be offered tenure at any university in the world if he wanted it. Speaking engagements. Professional acclaim. Everything any academic could ever desire, right there in the valley below. All he had to do was reach out and take it. Publish the paper that would guarantee his future.

And if he did that, everything he'd started building with Jordan and T'ukri would come crashing down around him.

"I'm not sure the bath is going to make much difference by the time we hike all the way down there," Victor said to T'ukri.

"But that is the beauty of it. We do not have to hike." T'ukri led them the rest of the way around the bend to a structure of wood and stone with heavy ropes strung from it down into the valley. "All we have to do is activate the water wheel in the valley and this will bear us down to the city."

"That's ingenious," Victor said. Archaeological evidence suggested the Inca people had used similar technology, but in all of his time in South America, he'd never seen it still in use. More and less advanced technology, yes, but never this specific one. A part of him—the dreamer, not the anthropologist—had often imagined a last bastion of the Inca people who escaped both defeat and discovery by the Spanish, but with modern satellite imagery being what it was, he hadn't held out any actual hope. Uncontacted tribes, sure, but not a city of this magnitude. T'ukri could use whatever word he wanted for it. This was a city in the grand tradition of Machu Picchu and Pisac, with a temple in the middle that rivaled Qoricancha—what Qoricancha would have looked like *before* the Spanish sacked it. And if that was the case, then T'ukri really was a prince and his father more than just a chieftain. Anyone ruling over this city and any others like it was a king.

Oh *putain*, the papers he could get just from where he was standing now!

"It saves both time and labor. We use it for goods as well as for people," T'ukri explained.

Most inventions came from that exact desire, and T'ukri had mentioned wanderers multiple times, so one of them could have seen cable cars or something similar and brought it back. It didn't *have* to be left over from the Inca Empire—and if anyone believed it wasn't, he had a beach house in Arizona to sell them—but neither explanation accounted for the city being successfully hidden. He'd accepted T'ukri's assertions about the goddess as part of his beliefs, but now he wasn't so sure it was simply faith. Something was definitely going on here.

Quenti stepped into the first basket to reach the platform. She obviously expected T'ukri to join her, but there wasn't space for all three of them. "I will take the next one down," he told her. "I wish to arrive with my mates. Cusi, you should ride down with her. I would have you with me when I bring my mates before our people."

She scowled but didn't protest beyond that, and Cusi grumbled a little about guarding T'ukri's back even as he looked pleased to be included.

Victor braced himself mentally. If arriving with them was that important to T'ukri, they would probably have a welcoming committee at the bottom. He put on his best professional smile and posture. If he really was about to meet the lost descendants of the Inca kings, he wanted to make the best impression he could.

He forced that thought aside. He was about to meet T'ukri's parents, and that was far more important than any royal lineage.

The second basket arrived, and T'ukri gestured for Jordan and Victor to precede him into it. "Will this hold the weight of all three of us?" Jordan asked, his skepticism clear.

"It has held the weight of a full-grown deer and a hunter to steady the cargo. That is more than the three of us combined. I would not risk you if I had the slightest doubt about its safety," T'ukri replied.

Victor stepped in and braced himself against the side as Jordan, then T'ukri followed him. The contraption started to move, throwing

Victor off balance for a moment, but once in motion, it floated smoothly down into the valley. They reached the bottom in a matter of minutes. T'ukri stepped out first and turned back to offer a hand to both Jordan and Victor. Victor appreciated the help as much as he did the symbolism. He didn't know who was watching, but he was sure someone was.

When T'ukri moved enough for Victor to see beyond him, he was proven right. Quenti stood at attention to one side, spear held perfectly straight. When T'ukri stepped off the platform, she slammed the butt of her spear against the ground. Around her other warriors did the same. T'ukri nodded to them and turned to the group of people gathered beyond.

"Papãnin, Mama," he said with a deep bow.

One of the men stepped forward and embraced T'ukri. A woman stood directly behind them, and when the man—the king, Victor reminded himself—released T'ukri, the woman took his place. When she, too, stepped back, the king spoke to T'ukri in Quechua. No, Runasimi. T'ukri had said they called their language Runasimi.

Victor didn't understand what was said, but he could practically feel the cool disapproval radiating off the king in their direction. He kept his expression neutral because he could sense the tension in Jordan's body and could guess at the expression on his face without needing to look. At best he was frowning. At worst he looked halfway to murderous.

"I have heard your concerns, my king," T'ukri said formally, replying in Spanish, "but I would ask you weigh them against the blessing of the ancestors. Inti and Guaman both accepted Jordan and Victor as my mates. Chieftain Paucar holds them both in high esteem, and Kichka has promised to make a blanket for our bonding bed out of the hide from my ritual hunt. These things should not be set aside lightly. Give my mates a chance to prove themselves to you as they have to others."

"They may stay," the king said, "as long as they are worthy."

Deciding now was the time for boldness, Victor took a step forward to stand at T'ukri's side. He bowed as deeply as T'ukri had done. "Thank you for your welcome, Your Majesty. We will endeavor to be worthy of your approval and your son's affections in every way."

"You speak Spanish well," the king replied, surprise cutting through the coldness on his face. "That is unexpected."

Victor tried to reconcile the king in front of him with the father in T'ukri's stories and failed. Even taking into account the formality of the situation and the shock of T'ukri bringing home two outsiders as mates didn't help. Behind the king, the queen seemed carved from stone.

"Between us we speak many languages," Victor replied easily.

"What other skills do you bring to my people?" the king demanded.

"Papãnin," T'ukri protested, but Jordan ignored him. Victor hid a smile.

"My skill as a warrior or a hunter," Jordan said. "T'ukri can vouch for both, but I'd be happy to prove them again in any situation you choose."

"And you?" the king asked Victor.

Victor let his smile show. "The strength to stand beside T'ukri in battle and the compassion to guide him home."

CHAPTER 24

T'UKRI NEARLY burst with pride at Victor's reply. Victor might not understand the full significance of what he had said, but he could have chosen no better way of answering Huallpa.

"What did you tell them?" Huallpa asked harshly in Runasimi.

For once, T'ukri replied in the same tongue rather than in a language that would include his mates. "I told them the legend, nothing more. It was a way to explain our triad bonds. They are used to hearing the lore of different peoples as part of their studies. They took it as just that—another story. I would not endanger our secrets without your permission."

"Did you prompt him in what to say?" Llipya asked.

"No, Mama. I told them only to greet you both as they would other village chieftains. Anything beyond that, they have figured out on their own," T'ukri insisted.

"You said Inti and Guaman gave their approval, but there should have been a third ancestor," Huallpa said.

"Palta did not refuse the match but also declined to give her blessing." The guardian rumbled frustration at not having the ancestors' full support. T'ukri pushed down the reaction—he could not afford to show a lack of control now, when he was so close to fulfilling his deepest desire. "She looked at them and saw only outsiders, but when she challenged me to prove they could draw me back, I changed and returned to myself with no struggle at all. They *are* my mates, Papãnin. I will accept whatever test you propose, but when all is said and done, if they are still willing, I will bond with them."

"Palta outlived the guardian she mated and was killed by the guardian who brought home an unsuitable mate," Llipya reminded them. "She has reason to be wary."

"Wary, yes, but that does not change the challenge she put before me nor my success in completing it," T'ukri replied. "The thought of them was enough to bring me back to myself even before we bonded. How much more powerful then will our bond be when it is fully formed?"

"This is not the place for such a discussion," Huallpa said finally. "Settle them in lodgings and return home. We will discuss it more in private."

T'ukri had hoped for a warmer reception to his bonding announcement, at least after he shared the ancestors' approval, but they were in public. He missed Yuri more than ever. Tayta would have balanced Huallpa's and Llipya's stoicism. T'ukri refused to believe it was more than that. He would take Victor and Jordan as his mates even if it meant walking away. Having found them, no one else would do. The guardian roared its displeasure at the mere thought of considering other mates. He would not start with that when he talked to his parents, but if pushed to it, he would make his stance clear. It would unsettle the tribe even more if he left and they had to adjust to yet another Chapaqpuma in such a short time, but having T'ukri lose himself would be no better. Huallpa could argue all he wanted, but having made his choice, the guardian would not be easily denied.

Pushing his concerns aside for now, T'ukri turned to Jordan and Victor. "Come, let us get you settled."

Victor raised an eyebrow in a gesture T'ukri had seen him use with Jordan, a silent question requesting an equally silent answer. He shook his head, grateful Victor refrained from asking in public. He led them into the city to a small house set aside for the rare visitor. Occasionally a chieftain from another tribe would seek audience with Huallpa and would need a place to stay during their council. It would serve his mates until he could win his parents over and bring them into his bed.

"It is nothing fancy." He showed them around them the simple house. "A bedroom, a place to bathe, and a firepit should you wish to cook, although I hope you will eat with me instead of alone here."

"Your parents seemed less enthusiastic than I'd hoped they would be," Victor said with the gentle tact T'ukri had come to love.

"They didn't order us shot on sight, Victor," Jordan said before T'ukri could reply. "That's better than the reception we've gotten in some places."

T'ukri added that to his list of stories to ask about someday, even as the guardian protested the idea of his mates in danger. "They were among those who expected me to take Urpi and Cusi as my mates. Tayta—Yuri—was the only one who understood."

"They are still in mourning," Victor surmised, showing off his keen intelligence, his second-best trait in T'ukri's eyes. "How long has it been?"

"Two months." T'ukri's grief at losing Yuri warred with his contentment at having found his own mates. "We found him not far from the entrance to the valley. He had tried to cross a stream that was too deep and drowned. He never learned to swim. Papãnin and Mama have been disconsolate since."

"And here we come, barging in with the subtlety of a sledgehammer," Jordan said with a sigh. "No wonder they looked shocked."

"That is part of it," T'ukri said. "The rest is a sad story, but I do not believe it applies to us. I will do my best to convince my parents you are suitable mates, but it may take some time for them to come around."

"We have time," Victor replied. "No one is expecting to hear from us until December."

"I hope it will not take that long." T'ukri did not think he could wait that long without losing control of the guardian. Right now that would result in coming to find Victor and Jordan and completing the bond, approval or no approval, but the longer this dragged on, the less certain he was of how the guardian would react. Everyone knew cats were temperamental on a good day. When pushed, they could be unpredictable and downright deadly. Once he had his mates, it would not matter because they would be able to draw him back to his humanity and physically rein him in if necessary, but with them so close at hand but still denied, the guardian would be more volatile than ever.

"You and me both," Jordan said. "Are we allowed to kiss you before you go back to convincing them? I don't want to get you in any more trouble than we already have."

"I am not in trouble," T'ukri said. "Yes, it is the tradition of my people to seek the approval of the ancestors and the elders before bonding, but I am an adult, and the ancestors gave their approval. If the elders disapprove, it does not stop us from bonding. It only makes our lives more complicated. I prefer to avoid that if I can."

"That didn't answer my question," Jordan said, stepping into T'ukri's space. "Are we allowed to kiss you?"

T'ukri smiled and kissed Jordan as much because he wanted to as in reply. Jordan met him halfway, pouring all his fire into the kiss. Inside T'ukri, the guardian stretched and purred in delight.

T'ukri pulled Jordan closer, aligning their bodies. Jordan rubbed against him a little before wrapping one leg around T'ukri's thigh. The movement opened more space between them and let T'ukri thrust more directly against Jordan's groin. He ran his hands down Jordan's back and lower, intending to take Jordan's weight so he could feel both of Jordan's legs around his waist.

Victor cleared his throat. "As much as I'm enjoying the show, you both need to take a step back and a deep breath or you're going to end up bonded accidentally. And that *will* get us in trouble."

"Spoilsport," Jordan grumbled as he took the prescribed step back.

"Only because we promised T'ukri we wouldn't bond until we had his parents' approval," Victor said. "Otherwise I'd be right there with you, believe me."

"Not helping, Victor," Jordan said. "Now I'm picturing *you* climbing T'ukri like a tree, and that's too damn sexy an image."

Victor snorted. "I just watched you actually climb him like a tree, so don't even go there, *trésor*."

T'ukri was quite sure listening to them talk about bonding and all it entailed would set him off if they continued. He could imagine it far too easily, their bare bodies, eager hands, hard cocks, and all the time and freedom to explore and enjoy. He had never been so glad for the loose pants and long tunic that would allow him to go before his parents without embarrassing himself.

"When the time comes, I will gladly submit to being climbed or ridden or climbing or riding or any other variation of coming together that feels right in the moment, but for now, I should join my parents. The sooner I convince them, the sooner that time will come." He took an additional step away from the temptation embodied in his malku and caught Victor's hand. "As soon as I have a kiss from you as well."

Victor kept their kiss gentle despite T'ukri teasing him with the tip of his tongue. The guardian rumbled his dissatisfaction at Victor's ability to resist, but T'ukri admired him all the more for it. They needed one cool head among the three of them, and when it came time to pull himself back from the guardian, he would be glad of it.

No matter how frustrating it was now.

He took a backward step toward the door, half hoping Jordan would snap and take the choice away from him. It was selfish, he knew, but presenting his parents and his people with a fully functioning bond would have avoided all the discussion. Jordan's gaze stayed on him until he had to turn or trip on the steps, but he held himself immobile. No, if T'ukri wanted to break with his people's traditions, he would have to initiate it. And listen to his mother scold him for giving in to weakness.

"I will be back as soon as I can," he told them. "Think of me until then."

"Always," Jordan promised.

T'ukri sucked in a breath, poised on the balls of his feet. The guardian whined inside him, eager for the consummation that was so close at hand and yet so far away. He closed his eyes, struggling with himself, tensed slightly, and fled. It was that or take them both to bed.

AS SOON as T'ukri was out of sight, Jordan turned to Victor. "Are you as blown away by this as I am?"

Victor looked around him at the house T'ukri had brought them to. He might say it was nothing fancy, but the solid stone walls and thatched roof were as nice or nicer than most of the dwellings they'd seen since leaving Aguas Calientes. Even most of the buildings in Ollantaytambo had been mud brick rather than stone. Now here they were in the "village" of a tribe hundreds of miles from "civilization" in a stone house with multiple rooms and running water. "Knock me over with a feather," Victor confirmed. "Oh, the papers we could get out of this!"

"We can't do that," Jordan said immediately. "We can't betray him that way."

"I said 'could,'" Victor pointed out. "Not will. I know we can't publish them without destroying the very thing we'd be describing. But bon Dieu, Jordan, this is every anthropologist's dream come true. Something completely undiscovered to study."

"Yeah, you'd have heard about a city this size if anyone had stumbled on it before now, even if somehow that news didn't trickle down to me," Jordan said. "What do you think?"

"It's amazing. It's easily the size of Machu Picchu, probably larger, and that's assuming it's just the one city without additional tribal settlements or outposts. How have they managed to stay hidden?" Victor asked.

"I don't know," Jordan admitted. "It makes you wonder about that story T'ukri told. The goddess's protection, Pachamama, a guardian— it's the Philli-philli legend, only on crack. And then here we are in a valley that doesn't exist. I mean, I didn't keep exact track of where we hiked, but we've both studied maps of this area extensively. I would have remembered something this big, even if it didn't include *an entire Incan city.* So a valley that doesn't exist despite all the mapping technology and satellites now available. A tribe that has conveniences we didn't see in any of the other villages in the area without having any visible contact with the outside world. A more defined political structure."

"Distinctly Incan names," Victor added. "What do you suppose the chances are that we just met direct descendants of the Inca?"

"I thought most highlanders were considered their descendants," Jordan said.

Victor shook his head. "Not the people of the Incan Empire. The Inca themselves. The kings and queens who shaped the empire."

"Holy shit, doc," Jordan exclaimed. "I thought Túpac Amaru II was considered the last descendant of the Inca rulers, and that was in the 1780s. That's 250 years ago. They've been hanging out here all this time?"

Victor ran his hand over the smooth walls, the seams between stones so perfect he could barely feel them. "Somehow I don't think this city is that new. *Machu* means old. I think this is where they retreated when it became clear they weren't going to be able to drive off the Spanish. Or ma foi, for all I know, they came from here in the first place. The legend T'ukri told us sounded as much like a creation myth as anything else. The Lost Ones? A forgotten people? A land time passed by? Not to mention the goddess's protection and Chapaqpuma."

He scrubbed at his face, his professional curiosity warring with his heart. He wanted the life T'ukri was offering, and up until now, he hadn't considered that he was really leaving anything significant behind in accepting it, but oh, he was tempted now. Just one paper. One little paper to redeem his reputation. He wouldn't have to give a location. There were ways around that. They'd met T'ukri in Paucar's village and first heard the Chapaqpuma story there. Even just that was something previously unknown in anthropological literature on the area. It might bring more researchers to the general area, but that wouldn't expose Machu Llaqta. He could leave the city out of it entirely and just write the paper his grant had been designed for.

"If that's the case," Jordan said, breaking into Victor's spiraling thoughts, "it's all the more important to keep it to ourselves. He's brought us home to meet his parents. Fuck, Victor, that's like one step short of getting married. Nobody's ever taken me to meet their parents before."

No one had taken Victor home that way either, and he hadn't ever expected anyone would, given how gone he was for Jordan and that Jordan had no family left. "I know. I hate it, but I know."

"A paper means that much to you?" Jordan asked.

"It's not the paper, not really," Victor said. "It's everything the paper would represent. A great big 'fuck you' to everyone who ever sneered at me behind my back or refused to work with me on something completely unrelated because they didn't want to be associated with the crackpot who believed in Philli-philli, or passed me over for a grant or a promotion. I didn't realize how much all that bothered me until I have the chance to prove them all wrong."

"What does that mean for us?" Jordan asked. "You and me, but also you, me, and T'ukri?"

"I don't know," Victor admitted. "I love you. Nothing changes that. But the chance I'd be passing up…."

"What about the one you'd be passing up if you publish that paper?" Jordan pressed. "I mean, not just the chance to learn even more, but the chance at everything we've been building with T'ukri. Is giving the academic community the middle finger worth giving all that up?"

"Of course not," Victor replied automatically.

"Are you just saying that or do you really believe it?"

"I mean it," Victor insisted. "I just wish it didn't have to be an either-or situation."

"Maybe it is, maybe it isn't, but finding out means laying everything out for T'ukri and hoping it doesn't fuck everything up," Jordan said.

Victor shook his head. "It's not worth rocking the boat. I'm not going to publish the paper, no matter how tempting it is, so there's no reason to discuss it. We have more important things to focus on."

"Like convincing his parents to accept us so we can fuck his brains out until we're as bonded as we can get?"

Victor snorted. "Such a way with words."

Jordan rolled his eyes. "Dressing it up with pretty words doesn't change reality. I've wanted to get my hands on that ass since he flaunted it at me that first day in the jungle." He reached out and pulled Victor into the bedroom. "And when that's done, I can finally get my hands on yours too."

Victor grinned. "And if I want my hands on yours instead?"

"Time and place, babe," Jordan replied immediately. "Name them and my ass is yours."

Victor groaned. He should've known better than to hope his flirting would work on Jordan. Jordan was infamous for his banter, and Victor was more than a little rusty. Up until a few weeks ago, he'd always met Jordan's comments with complete deadpan, mostly because to respond in any other way might reveal his true feelings. Now that he could respond, he didn't know how.

"Hey," Jordan said. "That wasn't the look I was hoping for when I offered you my ass. You okay?"

"Of course. Just thinking how out of practice I am at flirting, that's all."

"Is that all? That's nothing to worry about. You don't have to flirt to get my attention. Just walk in a room and you have it."

"Even next to T'ukri?" The words slipped out without his conscious volition.

"Even next to T'ukri," Jordan said, as serious as Victor had ever heard him. "Yeah, I want him too. Yeah, I think the three of us will be amazing together, but that doesn't mean—will never mean—that I want you less."

"Sorry," Victor said. "Old insecurities die hard."

Jordan backed Victor toward the bed—a real bed with an actual feather mattress, not just a sleeping mat of woven reeds—and down to sitting. Then he climbed onto Victor's lap, straddling him. The position caused his tunic to ride up, leaving only the thin fabric of the loose pants between their groins. "We've both got old insecurities, and mine aren't going away any faster than yours, but don't ever doubt how much I want you." He rocked his hips against Victor's, letting Victor feel his erection.

Victor was tempted—bon Dieu, so tempted—to urge Jordan to keep going and find some reassurance in their mutual release. T'ukri had said it was fine since they were already "bonded," but it felt wrong when he couldn't find his own pleasure until his tribe agreed to their bonding as a triad.

It hit him all over again how crazy this was and at the same time how much he wanted it. Crazy or not, this was where he wanted and needed to be. In a hidden valley in the middle of Peru with two of the most incredible men he'd ever met, on the verge of bonding with both of them when he'd almost given up on having anyone to spend his life with.

"I'll try, and once we're bonded, you and T'ukri can remind me as often as you want, but right now we should figure out how to win his parents over. Otherwise that bonding is a long way off."

Jordan groaned and rolled to the side. He pulled Victor down next to him. "I already feel like Legolas, offering my bow, but that's all I got."

"Hey, remember that conversation about insecurities?" Victor pushed up onto his elbow and stared down at Jordan. "You're so much more than you know."

Jordan snorted. "Yeah, yeah, I pulled myself out of my shitty beginnings by my own fucking bootstraps. You know what? That's doesn't mean a damn thing when we're trying to convince Incan royalty I'm a good match for their only son."

"Okay, first of all, don't ever brush off the hardships you went through and the way you managed to retain your compassion and moral compass despite it all. You are a miracle, end of conversation. But even if we leave that out—which we shouldn't, but even if we do—how about the fact that you've turned your skills as a sniper into observational skills that match or outpace most full professors I know? Because you weren't ever put in the box, so to speak, you think outside of it easily, and that leads to conclusions and solutions other people wouldn't consider. You might think that's not important, but out here in an unknown situation and with people whose customs we don't have the slightest idea about, it's going to be crucial. Not to mention that gut instinct you talked about."

Jordan grumbled some more but didn't argue, so Victor leaned down to kiss him. "We're outsiders, and to some extent, we always will be. We're never going to blend in here, not physically anyway, so we have to make our status as outsiders something positive. What can we bring to them because we have a different perspective on things?"

"If nothing else, we think like outsiders, so we can look at things the way potential threats from outside would and help counter them, as much with my military background as with our anthropology background and everything you learned from your grandfather," Jordan said slowly.

Nkóko had been teaching Victor the shamanic traditions of his tribe before he insisted Victor go to Peru for the summer all those years ago. After his death, Victor had locked all that away on every level except academic. He would never be an Mbochi shaman, but he had drawn on those experiences.

"That's exactly what I mean. We could also sit in on negotiations of any kind to add a different perspective and, depending on who the negotiations are with, the perspective of the other party," Victor said. "And both of those are things you could do just as well as I could."

"Okay, so maybe I do have a few things to offer," Jordan said slowly. "Still doesn't mean I'm not totally out of my depth."

"Focus on the fact that T'ukri wants us here and believes we're who he needs in his life. Surely that carries weight with his parents."

"Yeah, I'm holding on to that like a lifeline."

"We'll get through it. I don't think they'll make it easy, but we'll measure up to any test they put us to. Together we can figure anything out, and if T'ukri is there to guide us, we'll have no trouble."

"I hope you're right," Jordan said with a deep sigh.

"Enough wallowing." Victor stood up and tugged on Jordan's arm. "We can do this."

CHAPTER 25

T'UKRI HAD barely crossed the threshold of his home when Ch'aska grabbed his hand. Every muscle in his body tensed at the assault, the guardian fighting his control to come to his defense. He took a deep breath and another, focusing all his will on keeping the guardian in check.

Ch'aska. Sister. Safe.

The mantra calmed the guardian enough that he could unclench his fists and focus on more than not lunging at the source of the attack. He took a deep breath and smiled at the smell of roast lamb that hung in the air.

Home. He was home and safe. He could let go of the watchfulness that protected him when he wandered.

"You should not grab me that way when I have just come home," T'ukri said as he followed her. "I have not had time to let down my guard."

"Pffft, you could not hurt me if you tried," she replied. "I heard Mama and Papãnin talking. You brought people home!"

"I brought my mates home," T'ukri corrected.

"Outsiders?" Ch'aska's tone betrayed her excitement as much as her curiosity. "When do I get to meet them?"

"As soon as I convince Papãnin to give them a chance to prove themselves. He is not as excited about outsiders as you are."

"What does he know?" Ch'aska asked with all the infallibility of youth. "They are your mates, not his. It is stupid that he gets to decide if they are right for you."

Privately T'ukri agreed, but having felt the guardian stir within him, he understood Huallpa's concern. It would be far too easy to lose control. "Because we are still feeling the repercussions of the last time a guardian chose an unsuitable mate."

"As if you would choose anyone unsuitable. You are the most responsible person I know," Ch'aska said.

"Then perhaps you do not know enough people," T'ukri retorted.

Ch'aska rolled her eyes. "Tell me about them?"

T'ukri grinned. He could not help it. Thoughts of his mates would always bring a smile to his face. "They are not young men, and they carry the weight of experience and maturity with grace."

Ch'aska smacked his arm. "You do not have to wax poetic for my sake. Save that for Mama and Papãnin."

T'ukri chuckled. "You say that as if I were exaggerating their traits for you, but I am not. That truly is how I see them."

"Where did you meet them?"

The memory of walking into Paucar's village and seeing them there swamped T'ukri. In the few short weeks since he had first laid eyes on them, they had become his everything. "I visited Paucar and Kichka as I often do when I go wandering. They were there and had been for several weeks. Long enough for Jordan to have impressed everyone with his ability as a hunter. They claimed he never missed."

Ch'aska scoffed.

"Do not be too quick to dismiss their claims," T'ukri said. "I traveled with him to come here, and I watched him spear the eye of a fish in moving water with an arrow that had a string attached. Not once, but three times in a row. That is no easy feat. And when I first expressed concern to Victor that he might have trouble because of the distortion from the water or the weight of the rope, he refrained from laughing at me, but I could tell he wanted to. He has absolute faith in Jordan's ability to shoot any target he says he can shoot, and I have yet to see Jordan do anything to shake that belief."

"What tribe are they from? Paucar gets almost as few visitors as we do."

"They are not from Peru," T'ukri said. "They are scholars here to learn more about our people and our ways. They came from America to study stories of the guardian."

"You brought colonizers home?" Ch'aska squealed. "Oh, this is going to be fun!"

"Really, Ch'aska," T'ukri scolded. "They are hardly colonizers. Outsiders, yes, and yes, Jordan is white, but they are not colonizers. They are academics, here to learn, not to conquer."

"As if the elders—the ancestors—will see it any differently," Ch'aska said.

"I cannot speak for the elders," T'ukri admitted, "but I sought and gained the approval of the ancestors before I ever began courting them, as is proper. They *are* my mates, no matter what anyone else says."

"I cannot *wait* to see you try to convince everyone of that," she said with a mischievous grin. T'ukri reminded himself she was both young and sheltered and that the arrival of Jordan and Victor was the most outrageous thing she had experienced. That it would mean the difference between a happy life and a constant struggle to control the guardian—if the gifts did not pass immediately on to someone else, perhaps Micay, should he be denied—would not register with her until she was older.

"I am glad to provide you with a source of amusement, but this is my future at stake. Had I never met them, I might have settled on others, but the guardian will not be dissuaded now. It will be them or no one."

Ch'aska sobered, and T'ukri knew she, too, had felt Yuri's loss and the changes his death had wrought on their family. "I am sorry, brother. I did not mean to make light. I do not count much next to the will of the elders, but you have my support."

And that was why he adored his little sister even when she drove him to his wits' end. "The most important thing you can do will be to help make them welcome. Papãnin and Mama will come around in time, and when they do, the elders will follow, however grudgingly, but Jordan and Victor must stay long enough for that to happen. They do not understand about Chapaqpuma yet. If they leave, it will destroy me, but they may do it thinking it will help."

"You have not told them?" Ch'aska exclaimed. "That is madness, even for you!"

"I will tell them," T'ukri said. He longed to tell them, to have their support and their strength at his side, not only symbolically but to the depths of his being. He had held his tongue for valid reasons, but it was becoming harder to keep silent. "I held back at first because I did not know them. Then I could find no easy way to bring it up. I dare not change to prove it to them before we have bonded, but how else are they to believe me? To them I am a matter of superstition and legend. It is to the goddess's credit that we have kept it to that, but it is not easy to bring up this late."

"Men!" she said, as if she would be any better in the same situation. "Always making things more complicated than they need to be. You act as if honest conversation would be worse than losing a limb. Really, brother, I thought Tayta had taught you better than that."

T'ukri flinched. Yuri *had* taught them that they lost nothing by expressing their emotions honestly, but at first it had not been about emotion but about the law. Until he had been certain Jordan and Victor were his mates, telling them would have been a crime. Since then the time had never been right, and a small part of T'ukri still feared their reaction.

"I will find the right time to tell them," T'ukri said. "Before we bond. I promise. But if I cannot convince Papãnin to give his blessing, it is better they leave not realizing the truth." He did not tell her he would leave with them. It would not matter because if he did, he would forfeit the gifts of the goddess, and in their eyes, the legend would remain a legend with no one to let the secret slip.

"Oh, you are insufferable!" She threw her hands up and shoved him out of the room. "Go talk to Papãnin and Mama. I am going to welcome your mates and show them around the city. I will make sure no one speaks out of turn, but if you do not tell them, I will. I am warning you now."

"Do not," T'ukri ground out. "I am serious, Ch'aska. This is not your secret to tell."

She glared at him. "And it is not yours to keep, but I will respect your wishes for now."

That did nothing to reassure him, but he could hardly forbid her from meeting Victor and Jordan. Even if he did, she would ignore him. Better to let her go with her agreement to respect his wishes than for her to decide to defy him not only in meeting them but also in keeping his secret.

"Show them all our favorite hideaways," he said instead. "They will appreciate them. Especially where we watch the sunrise. It is the wrong time of day, but it is always a spectacular view."

"No, I think I will leave that to you," she said. "You can take them there to celebrate your bonding."

T'ukri groaned at the thought, making her laugh in delight. But sweet goddess, the idea of leading them to the isolated cliff, of spending the night making love with them under the stars and then watching the sunrise together on their first morning as bondeds, was enough to shake the control he had recovered. "You are an evil, evil brat."

"And you are far too easy to rile," she retorted. "Go. The sooner you talk to our parents, the sooner you can live out whatever scenario just went through your mind."

He started out of the room, then turned back. "I love you, brat."

"I love you too, idiot."

He embraced her quickly, glad she had matured past the stage where she was too grown-up to say the words or accept the hug. He dropped a quick kiss on her braids and let her go. She smacked him as she walked toward the door of their dwelling. In the city the guards would let her pass without escort at first, although he fully expected to listen to a rant later about how they followed her the entire time she spent showing Jordan and Victor around. He would listen to it and agree with her about how unfair it was, because he had chafed beneath Quenti's presence more than once, even though she was one of his dearest friends. And then he would thank Ayar, Ch'aska's personal guard, for her diligence, if only because Ayar's presence would keep anyone who had not yet heard from overreacting to Victor's and Jordan's presence in the city.

Now he just had to convince his parents to be as supportive as Ch'aska.

Pachamama help him.

When Ch'aska was out of sight, T'ukri walked deeper into the house toward Huallpa's study, where he knew his parents would be waiting for him. All important family discussions took place there, the one place where they were assured of absolute privacy. No one other than family ever passed through those doors.

He knocked to let them know he was there but did not wait for a reply before entering. The first was polite. The second was the privilege of family. They were seated by the firepit as usual, though no fire burned within it.

Out of public view, his mother rose from her chair and embraced him warmly. "It is good to have you home, *churi*."

"It is good to be home, Mama," he replied as she pulled his head down so she could kiss his forehead. She was a tall woman, but he had outgrown her about the time he reached adulthood. She had never let that stop her when she felt the need to show him affection. "Papãnin," he added when his father did not rise. He did smile, though, so T'ukri left it at that and took his chair.

"You put quite a cat among the pigeons today," Huallpa said when he was seated.

"You do not know the half of it. Before we discuss my mates, I have other news—news that I did not wish to share in front of everyone," T'ukri said.

"What news?" Huallpa asked.

"Of men—outsiders—in the region."

"Outsiders besides those you brought home?" Llipya asked drolly.

"Yes, true outsiders, not my mates." T'ukri ignored his mother's gentle dig. "The morning we left Paucar's village, Peruvian men carrying guns arrived in the village. They made no open threats but made it clear they intended to accept no challenge to their presence. I found their camp that evening to warn them off, as a man, not as Chapaqpuma, under the circumstances. I killed three of the five in the scuffle. The other two were not in the camp when I found it. I did not see any additional sign of them during the rest of our journey back, but I did not want to draw attention to my activities, so I did not search as thoroughly as I might have had I been alone."

Huallpa frowned. "I have heard of instances of illegal mining along the great river. They could be thinking to exploit our isolation and that of communities like ours for their own ends. I will speak with Quenti and we will increase patrols along our borders. The chances of them finding their way into the valley are slim, but we should not rely only on the goddess's protection. Now, about your mates...."

"I could not think of a way to send word ahead. I was not completely sure until a few days ago that I would bring them home. I knew I wanted to, but I had to be sure they were the ones first. And by then we were so close that I just came home."

"You are Chapaqpuma now, not simply a wanderer. That changes more than just your need for your bonded. You will never be as happy outside our territory as you are in it," Huallpa said. "I wish I could have given you more time."

"That is *not* a worry for you to take on," T'ukri said hotly. "I know—better than most now—that if you had your way, Tayta would be sitting here today and for many years to come."

Huallpa flinched, but he smiled sadly nonetheless. "He would be so proud of you. He told me from the first time he laid eyes on you that you would be the best of us when your time came. I only wish he could have lived to see it, that age rather than loss had led to you taking on the mantle of Chapaqpuma."

"I know that, Papãnin. But I believe with everything I have that he is feasting among the ancestors at the news that I have found my mates."

"He always did love a feast," Llipya said, a waver in her voice that she would never have allowed in public. Quenti might be the greatest warrior of their generation, but woe to anyone who forgot that Llipya had once laid claim to that title. Huallpa and Yuri had been the envy of every man in the tribe when they won her favor to fulfill their triad.

"Have you completed the rituals?" Huallpa asked.

"I have. Paucar and Kichka bore witness in your absence. Kichka promised to prepare the hide from my hunt and send it for our bonding bed," T'ukri reminded them.

"Yes, you mentioned that. It is a generous offer," Llipya said. "She is as fierce as any warrior and as wise as any shaman we have. Your chosen must be impressive indeed to have won her approval."

"They are, Mama. If you would get to know Jordan, you would find the same warrior spirit in him as you carry within you—he was in the American Marines—and while it is hidden beneath intellectualism, Victor has the soul of a shaman within him as well," T'ukri said.

"So even in that, you have followed our laws."

"I have," T'ukri replied. "I could have been home a week ago or more, but I took a more meandering route so that I could be sure of my choices, so that I could choose based on more than just the initial reaction of the guardian, and in that time I have come to know them. Victor is capable in the rainforest, but while he can and will defend himself if necessary, it is not his calling the way it is Jordan's. Jordan would burn himself out in a fight if left to it, but Victor...." He paused, struggling to put what he sensed into words. "Victor would fight for as long as it took to protect those he loved, but it will never be his first instinct. He must be pushed to it. He will always try diplomacy first. He is the one who will always make sure everyone comes home. He will rescue them if he can and avenge them if he cannot, but he will bring them home and care for them once he does. He told you himself when you asked him what he had to offer us. The strength to stand beside me in battle and the compassion to bring me home."

"It was a daring answer," Llipya said.

"I did not prompt him, Mama. I told you that," T'ukri insisted. "I shared the guardian lore with them, but they still see it as a legend, not the truth. I will correct them when I have your approval. If we are not given permission to bond, it is better they leave believing it a story that colors our lives, not the one thing we hold above all others."

"You would accept it if we denied that permission?" Huallpa asked.

"I will continue to try to convince you for as long as it takes," T'ukri said, "but I cannot force you to accept my choice. I hope it will not come to that, though. We have lost too much already."

Llipya's gaze sharpened, but she let Huallpa continue his line of questioning. "Tell me more of your audience with the ancestors."

"What would you have me say?" T'ukri asked. "I have told you already that Inti and Guaman gave their blessing and that Palta declined to do so despite my success in facing the challenge she set before me. I know I am asking much of everyone by bringing home not only outsiders but foreigners as well. I know that my role as Chapaqpuma will bind Victor and Jordan here in a way it would not if I were anyone else. I recognize the challenges in my choice, but it *is* my choice. I do not know how else to make you see that I have made it, that the guardian inside me recognizes them as suitable. You must remember what it was like, Papānin. I have heard the tales of how hard Mama made you and Tayta work to win her agreement, yet you never wavered. You knew she was the right mate for you, and you did what it took to convince her of that fact. If she had continued to refuse, what would you have done?"

Huallpa gave Llipya a fond glance. "Lost my mind."

"Then you know what you would be asking of me if you refuse me the permission I need," T'ukri said.

Huallpa sighed. "Yuri said you would be the best of us. He did not say you would also be the most difficult."

T'ukri bowed his head, fighting back the emotions that threatened to swamp his control. He would not help his cause by losing himself in them.

"What would Tayta say if he were here now?" he asked without lifting his head. His voice broke, but he could do nothing to stop it.

Llipya barked a bitter laugh. "He would not be here now," she replied. "He would be sitting with your chosen already, getting to know them. He always did lead with his heart."

"He always said that anything else was folly and would lead to more pain than it avoided," Huallpa finished.

T'ukri looked up, knowing his eyes were wet, but his parents' cheeks glistened with their own tears, so he let his fall too. "We have lost our heart and our way without him here. I cannot bring him back, but I can bring a new stability to our family. Give them a chance. If they prove me wrong, then I will accept it, but do not judge them for the land of their birth. Let them show you who they are and how good they are for me. That is all I ask. The rest will come in time if you let it."

"Your heart is truly set on them," Llipya said slowly, as if she were only now coming to understand how deeply T'ukri felt.

"It is, and so is the guardian. If I cannot have them, I cannot be Chapaqpuma," T'ukri said. "There is no longer one without the other."

CHAPTER 26

"HELLO? ARE you here?" The woman's voice—girl's, really, from the sound of it—made Jordan jerk upright. He took a breath and focused on the fact that they were in T'ukri's city now and so among, if not friends, at least people who could be trusted not to stab them in the back. In the chest maybe, but they would do it honorably, face-to-face like warriors.

Reminding himself to be polite, he walked toward the entrance. Victor had gone into the bathroom and not come out yet, so Jordan would have to play diplomat. *Fuck.* He sucked at being diplomatic.

"Yes," Jordan replied, stepping into the area with the firepit. The girl—he'd been right, she wasn't more than fifteen or sixteen—wore elaborate braids and a brightly colored blouse and loose pants nearly as decorated as T'ukri's had been. "Ch'aska?"

She pouted, but her eyes twinkled. "How did you know?"

"Well, you aren't the queen because I met her already. You aren't one of the guards because you're not carrying weapons, and you came looking for us, so you know T'ukri well enough not to wait for an introduction," Jordan said.

Ch'aska's smile widened and she laughed delightedly. "Oh, I like you already, Jordan. You will make the elders crazy, which is perfect. If they are grumbling about you, they will pay less attention to me."

Jordan chuckled. "Unless they decide to give up on T'ukri and groom you to be the next ruler instead of him."

Her eyes widened comically for a moment before she narrowed them in a shrewd gaze that made him worry a little about what she might come up with next. "Where is Victor?"

"He'll be out in a minute."

"Good. Who knows how long T'ukri will be locked away with Mama and Papãnin? Since Tayta is not here to welcome you, I decided to volunteer."

"You don't think he'd be locked in there with them?" Jordan asked. T'ukri had mentioned his other father more than once, but rarely with enough detail to give Jordan more than a vague sense of the man.

"Great goddess, no! He hated that kind of thing," Ch'aska said. "He would leave them to argue tradition and the will of the ancestors, claiming it would tell him nothing he could not find out better by simply meeting you. We revere the ancestors, but they are not omniscient. Nor are they free from prejudice and other flaws. Tayta always said his own heart and an open mind were as good as any wisdom the ancestors might bestow."

"He sounds like a very wise man," Victor said from the doorway.

Jordan turned to smile at him. "Victor, come meet T'ukri's sister. Ch'aska, this is Victor."

"Your Highness," Victor said with a very correct nod of his head. *Fuck.* Jordan had forgotten to do that. Diplomacy fail. He'd be lucky if he didn't get them kicked out before dinner.

"Please, no," Ch'aska said with a shudder. "Save the formal manners for Mama and Papãnin. They appreciate that kind of thing. I can do it when I have to, but there is no one here to insist, not even my idiot brother."

Score! Jordan didn't pump his fist in the air at being the one to read the situation right. Victor was usually the one with better people skills.

"As you wish. I'm afraid we aren't set up to be good hosts."

She studied Victor with the same piercing stare he had seen from T'ukri early in their acquaintance. Jordan tried to see Victor through her eyes, but all he saw was the same warmth and kindness he had always seen beneath Victor's carefully cultivated façade.

"I am beginning to understand," she said after a moment.

Jordan opened his mouth to ask what she understood, but Victor shot him such a stern look that he shut his mouth fast enough to make his teeth click together.

"Come. I told T'ukri I would show you around the city while he convinces Mama and Papãnin that you belong here." She turned and winked at Jordan. "I know all the best stories. Not even Cusi can tell you as many embarrassing stories about T'ukri as I can."

Jordan whooped and started toward the door. "This I got to hear."

Victor just rolled his eyes and followed along.

Ch'aska laughed again, that same delighted sound Jordan could already tell he would love and hate in equal measure, depending on whether it was aimed at him or at someone else. Nobody would ever get a big head with her around.

He thought briefly of Nandini and wondered what it would take to get her here. Then again, he wasn't sure he wanted Nan and Ch'aska to compare notes. Nan had far too much dirt on Jordan that she would be thrilled to share so someone could burst Jordan's bubble when she wasn't around.

"Do you want the formal tour or the family one?" Ch'aska asked.

"The family one," Jordan said before Victor could reply. He'd probably ask for the formal one, and Jordan knew they'd need it, but they could learn as much or more by seeing things through Ch'aska's eyes. Especially since the family tour might give them some ideas on winning over T'ukri's parents.

"I was hoping you would say that. Come on. We will go out the back. Maybe that way we can slip away without Ayar noticing. She will not say anything, but I was not as lucky as T'ukri, to have my guard also be one of my friends."

"Is that wise?" Victor asked.

"Do I look like I care? Besides, T'ukri said Jordan was a warrior and a hunter. You will protect me if I need it, will you not?" Ch'aska batted her eyelashes at him in such an exaggerated fashion that he burst out laughing. He'd probably just given them away to Ch'aska's bodyguard, but Jordan didn't give a damn. Ch'aska was trouble with a capital T, and he loved it already.

"Anything for you, darling," he teased.

She laughed harder and led them out the back door. Jordan didn't need to look to know they hadn't evaded her guard, but since the woman hung back to give them the illusion of privacy, he didn't say anything. If he caught her eye later, he'd give her a nod to show he knew she was there, but for now he focused on Ch'aska.

She led them down a meandering path among the towering trees. The undergrowth had been cleared back enough to make for safe and easy passage, but the canopy above them was completely untouched. Someone flying over the valley wouldn't see anything except more trees.

"We are on the edge of the city here," Ch'aska said with a wave of her hand toward the temple Jordan had seen from the cliff above. "That is the formal tour. The informal tour is all out here. You saw the spring on the way in, I guess?"

"We did." Jordan fought to keep his voice even. If Ch'aska had been a little older, he might have given her a knowing wink, but he wasn't about to corrupt T'ukri's little sister. Not until he knew she was already corrupted.

"We learned to swim there," Ch'aska said. Her expression darkened for a moment. "I just wish we had made Tayta learn."

"I can see it being the perfect place to learn," Victor said gently while Jordan tried to find a way to lighten the mood.

Ch'aska's expression smoothed out at Victor's quiet words. "Do you swim?" she asked.

"We both do," Victor replied.

"Good." Jordan watched with growing admiration as she squared her shoulders and shook off the heavy mood. "Someone has to help me beat T'ukri the next time we go."

"Done." Jordan would always side with the underdog, and besides, if he helped Ch'aska win, he was sure T'ukri would make him pay for it later, and wouldn't that be fun?

"Behave," Victor muttered in English.

God, he loved that man. Even when Jordan didn't say anything, Victor could read his mind.

"The legends say the goddess herself warms the spring for us, you know," Ch'aska said. "Another of her many gifts. That is what Tayta always said. He would not come in the water with us, but he would sit on the edge and watch us as we played. He would never have drowned in the pool, even if he was there alone, but outside the valley, we lose much of the goddess's protection."

Jordan shared a pointed look with Victor. They'd already talked about the legend T'ukri had shared, but this was something else entirely. Maybe it was a child's simple faith, but something in Ch'aska's declaration shook him. They had considered T'ukri's talk of the goddess and her blessings as a sort of creation myth, but now Jordan wondered if that was true.

He could ask. She'd probably tell him, but they'd agreed to set aside anthropology in exchange for building a new life here. If the legends were true, they'd find out in time. "You promised us embarrassing stories. What's the dumbest thing T'ukri ever did in the water?" he asked instead.

The clouds in Ch'aska's expression disappeared and her smile broke out again, as bright as the sun. "He broke his leg when he was about ten," she said. "It happened before I was born, but Mama told me the story over and over so I would not do the same thing. He was showing off, you see. He had brought some friends with him, and he was being all puffed up and important since he knew how to swim. Cusi got tired of the bragging and dared him to jump into the water from the big rock on the far side of the spring. Only the water is not very deep there. T'ukri was not about to back down from a dare. Do not let him fool you. He still cannot. Anyway, he climbed up on the rock and jumped before anyone could stop him. He broke his leg when he hit the bottom and could not leave the house for months while it healed."

"I bet he hated that," Jordan said.

"He did, but Cusi got it even worse. His grandmother was so angry at him that she made him spend every day with T'ukri to help him with everything he could not do, so instead of getting to come in and taunt T'ukri with stories of all the things he had done while T'ukri was stuck inside, he was stuck there too, running to do T'ukri's bidding," Ch'aska said. "Tayta said he did not know whether they would end up brothers in all but blood or if they would never talk to each other again."

"It sounds like they ended up brothers," Jordan said.

"Yes," Ch'aska said with a huge sigh. "Unfortunately it means I ended up with *two* overprotective older brothers instead of just one."

Jordan smirked and leaned in close to whisper, "You're about to get a third. Victor's the biggest mother hen you'll ever meet."

"Just what I need," Ch'aska groaned.

"Don't worry. I know all the tricks for getting around him. We'll sneak out and see what kind of trouble we can get in together," Jordan replied.

"Or not," Victor replied dryly. Jordan shot him a leer over his shoulder. Victor could protest all he wanted. He hadn't tried to curb Jordan's mischievousness before. He wouldn't start now. It wasn't like

Jordan would do anything really dangerous with Ch'aska along anyway. He might be impulsive, but come on, he wasn't that irresponsible.

"Follow me. I want to show you the cave T'ukri was convinced would lead us to buried treasure."

Oh yeah, Jordan was definitely sneaking out with Ch'aska as often as he could get away with it.

JORDAN'S SIDES hurt from laughing so much when Ch'aska finally brought them back to the house T'ukri had offered them. If Ch'aska had an off switch, he had yet to find it, and she had no qualms about sharing all her brother's secrets. Jordan couldn't wait to tease T'ukri about his buried treasure.

"When I asked you to show my mates around the city, I did not expect you to disappear with them for hours." T'ukri glared at Ch'aska as soon as they walked into the house, which she gleefully ignored. Damn, but Jordan had to find a way to get Nandini here. She and Ch'aska would get on like a house afire.

"We went hunting for buried treasure," Jordan said with his best imitation of Victor's deadpan delivery.

Ch'aska giggled, and to Jordan's delight, T'ukri practically squirmed.

"I had hoped to spend some time with you before dinner," T'ukri said to Victor, ignoring Ch'aska's continued laughter and Jordan's smirk. That was okay. Jordan would make it up to him later. "My parents have invited us to eat with them tonight."

Jordan's stomach sank. *Fuck.* First a formal introduction he was only barely prepared for, and now a state dinner. They might not call it that, but Jordan knew it would be an interrogation either way.

He looked down at his slightly wet and rumpled outfit—they'd gotten caught in the afternoon shower before taking shelter in the treasure cave—and cursed his enthusiasm for climbing around in the cave with Ch'aska. Victor, of course, had managed to stay clean, if not dry.

"Do not worry," T'ukri said. "I have brought clothing befitting my mates rather than what we keep for wanderers coming home."

The knots in Jordan's belly tightened more. Not that he'd go to anybody's house but Nandini's looking like he'd been playing in the mud—what? He never got to play in caves when he was a kid. He was making up for it now—but "clothing befitting my mates" sounded awfully damn formal.

"Does this mean Mama will make me wear a dress?" Ch'aska asked, looking down at her own muddy clothing.

"You will have to ask her that," T'ukri said. "It matters not to us, but you know how she is about observing the formalities."

Ch'aska sighed and gave Jordan a halfhearted glare. "It is a good thing I like you. I *hate* wearing dresses."

T'ukri said something in Runasimi that made Ch'aska laugh and made T'ukri glare even harder. She waved at Jordan and Victor and left the house.

"She will be the death of me someday," T'ukri muttered when she was out of earshot.

"Better not be," Jordan said. "I'd have to kill her, and I like her too much for that."

T'ukri grimaced. "Having the two of you become friends might be even worse."

"Definitely worse," Victor said through a chuckle. "I'll help you keep them in line as much as I can. I've had a few years to practice on Jordan."

"How soon are your parents expecting us?" Jordan asked. "We really should clean up a bit."

"You have time enough for that." T'ukri handed them each a bundle of cloth. "Outfits for dinner. I will wait outside if you wish to wash quickly before you change."

"You don't have to run off," Jordan said. "It's not like you haven't seen us naked before."

"That was in the wild, where we had no real choice—or can justify it that way if anyone asks," T'ukri replied. "While I would stay gladly, I do not wish to give the elders any reason to question our courtship. Quenti will not speak of the time spent at the hot spring, but here, anyone could walk by and draw conclusions."

That didn't sound so good. It also didn't sound like what T'ukri had said on their way here. Had he misunderstood, or had something happened to make T'ukri draw back from them? He studied T'ukri's expression as carefully as he could without staring, but he couldn't interpret what he saw, as if T'ukri was struggling with something. All his self-doubt came clawing at his throat at the thought of what

T'ukri's parents might have said about their courtship, about Jordan's lack of anything more profound to offer than good aim, about all the reasons Jordan was no match for anyone, much less royalty. And it didn't matter if anyone outside this valley recognized T'ukri's parents as heads of state. Jordan knew royalty when he saw it.

Fuck, fuck, fuck. He should've quit while he was ahead and gone home with Victor without risking everything on the chance of adding T'ukri to their lives too.

"We'll get ready as quickly as we can," Victor said, interrupting Jordan's spiraling thoughts. "We want to make a good impression."

"Your answer to my father's question was a good start," T'ukri said. "I will wait for you outside."

Victor's answer. Not Jordan's because Jordan hadn't had an answer. *Fuck and double fuck.* Jordan looked down at the clothes in his hands and then over at Victor. "Am I the only one worried about this?" he asked.

Victor tipped his head toward the bathroom. Jordan followed him into the small space. Victor splashed some water on his face. "No," he said finally, "but delaying it won't help us any. Think of it as a mission. Keep your eye on the objective and roll with the punches as they come."

It never failed. When things got tense, Victor always knew what to say, in this case framing the upcoming dinner in the military terms that were familiar to Jordan even after being out of the service as long as he had. "I hope nobody starts throwing punches. I wouldn't put money on my chances against so many guards, especially since I won't have my bow."

"Figurative language is a thing," Victor reminded him.

Way to have a joke fall flat.

"Yeah. I'll be on my best behavior. I promise."

"That's not what I meant." Victor stepped aside to let Jordan wash up.

"Maybe not, but I promise anyway since we both know I'll be the one to fuck it up if one of us does," Jordan said glumly. He washed his hands, splashed water on his face, and scrubbed under his arms to get rid of the worst of the sweat. That would have to do since they didn't have a tub or a convenient hot spring in the house. He wondered if T'ukri had one or if bathing always involved going down to the spring.

"That's my partner you're insulting," Victor scolded. "I take it personally when people do that."

Jordan smiled as he knew Victor intended. His shithole of a brain ran in circles when something set it off, and nothing triggered him faster than feeling inadequate. Victor, though, always seemed to know what to say to break the vicious spiral. It was one of the first things Jordan had fallen for. Victor's faith had always settled him to the point that it might even be justified. He could do this. He just had to keep his wits about him and think before he opened his mouth.

They changed into the garments T'ukri had brought them, fancier versions of the outfits they'd worn earlier. Better fitting too. The first had been a bit tight around the shoulders for Jordan, but this one, while still snug, didn't leave him feeling like he might tear a seam if he moved the wrong way. Victor's fit him better too, showing off the breadth of his shoulders and his trim waist, and the sapphire blue practically shone against his dark skin. "Looking good there, babe."

"You clean up pretty good yourself, trésor," Victor replied. "Come on. Let's get this over with so we can get the king's and queen's approval. And then get on with the rest of our lives together."

That sounded pretty damn perfect to Jordan. He brushed his hands over the tunic one more time, making sure it lay smooth across his torso. Slipping his hand into Victor's, he walked toward the front of the house, T'ukri, and the future.

VICTOR TOOK a sip of the juice Ch'aska had offered them when they came into the sitting room a few minutes earlier and listened to her and T'ukri bicker. It reminded him of his siblings, a thought that made him smile around the pang in his chest. Even if his sexuality hadn't been an issue for his family, his decision to immigrate to the US to follow his career would have put a strain on their relationship, but he missed them sometimes, when he had a few quiet moments to himself. He didn't regret the choices he'd made in his life, but a part of him would always regret the rift.

Next to him, Jordan had the same grin that he'd sported the entire afternoon spent with Ch'aska. Victor was sure letting those two team up was a bad idea, but he'd never say that aloud, not when Ch'aska made Jordan smile in a lighthearted way Victor had rarely seen. Life had done its damnedest to grind Jordan down, so Victor would encourage anything that lifted him up again. Even if it meant more headaches for him.

The door swung open and the queen walked in, the king one step behind her. Victor rose immediately and offered them a half bow. Jordan scrambled to his feet, a far cry from his customary grace, and did the same. Victor hid his smile. If Jordan had let his guard down that far, then he would encourage Ch'aska to tease T'ukri every chance she got.

"Your courtesy is appreciated," the queen said, "but inside these walls, we are a family like any other."

"I didn't want to presume," Victor said.

"And that is to your credit. Sit. The meal will be ready shortly and we will eat. Until then, we can get acquainted," the queen said.

Victor waited until she sat before returning to his own seat. She might have said not to stand on formality, but he didn't see any harm in basic manners.

"T'ukri said you were once part of the American Marines," the king said to Jordan, speaking for the first time. "That is an impressive feat."

"It was the path open to me when I took it, but once I joined, the idea of protecting people who couldn't protect themselves appealed to me," Jordan replied.

"But that is no longer your calling?" the queen asked.

"I can and will still fight if necessary, but I didn't do so well with the military hierarchy," Jordan admitted. "When I left the Marines, I found anthropology, and that led me to Victor, and another way of protecting people."

"I have found that the best weapon of all is knowledge. The real war is the silent war, and that is won with fact and details and foresight. We strive to provide that through our research, thus protecting the people we have learned about and ultimately the world in a far more effective way," Victor added.

"A very diplomatic answer," Huallpa said with a small smile.

"And one Tayta would have agreed with," T'ukri added.

"You will have your hands full curbing that one's impulsiveness if you stay," Llipya warned with a fond glance for her son.

"I have years of practice," Victor replied.

"Hey," Jordan protested.

"Look me in the eye and tell me I'm wrong," Victor said.

Jordan blushed and ducked his head, rubbing at the back of his neck.

"As I was saying," Victor continued, turning back to Llipya.

She smiled as well, the expression changing her face from a mask of stone that not even Victor's CO could top to a kinder, more approachable one. There was the mother, not just the queen.

"Will you share your secret? I have yet to have any luck with either of my two cubs."

Victor chuckled as both T'ukri's and Ch'aska's hackles rose, much like the cubs Llipya compared them to. "I find bribery works quite well. Give them a sufficient reward for making the wiser choice."

That got a laugh from Huallpa. "Just as Yuri did with us, my love, even if he would not have put it that way," he said to Llipya. Then he turned back to Victor. "You have options open to you that a parent would not."

"Bribery is bribery. You just have to find the reward that works." Victor refused to let the heat curling in his gut show on his face. Yes, he had the implied options with Jordan now, but until a few weeks ago, that hadn't been true. And technically he didn't have those options with T'ukri yet, although he hoped it would not be long. Judging by T'ukri's expression, he felt the same.

"Do you agree with the value of diplomacy, Jordan?"

"It's taken a lot of years of Victor explaining things for me to learn," Jordan admitted. "Even then, my first inclination will always be to reach for my bow."

"As I reach for my spear," Llipya replied. "It will make it easier for you to be accepted among the warriors here."

Victor swallowed down the surge of hope at the comparisons T'ukri's parents were drawing. The more they could see on their own that the differences were on the surface, not at the heart, the more likely they would be to accept them.

"Mama, you should show Jordan how you use your spear. As talented as he is with a bow, he would learn it quickly, I am sure," T'ukri said.

Don't say it, Victor silently ordered Jordan.

"I would be honored," Jordan said. Victor let out a soft sigh of relief. He'd worried Jordan would either claim he could already use a spear—which might be true but was hardly diplomatic—or would insist he didn't need anyone to show him because the use of ranged weapons came naturally to him. Also true, but again not the impression they wanted to give.

He should have known better. Jordan might be brash when he felt comfortable, but he had some sense.

"Tomorrow, perhaps," Llipya said. An unknown man appeared in the doorway. "Now we should eat while the food is hot."

Everyone followed her into a different room with a table loaded with food.

"Mmm, lamb stew with yuca and purple potatoes and chirmuya for dessert," Ch'aska said as she rushed over to the table.

"Ch'aska loves lamb," T'ukri told Victor, "but we eat fish more, so she does not get it very often."

"Just for special occasions," Ch'aska said. "But this is a special occasion. It is not every day T'ukri brings outsiders home for us to meet."

"Not outsiders," T'ukri said. "My mates."

"Is that not what I said?" Ch'aska asked innocently.

"Ch'aska, stop baiting your brother." Llipya's tired tone suggested this was far too normal.

"Yes, Mama," Ch'aska said, but out of her mother's sight, she glared at T'ukri and made what was obviously their equivalent of the middle finger.

"Ch'aska," Llipya scolded without even looking.

"Sorry, Mama."

The words satisfied Llipya, but Victor saw Ch'aska's expression. She wasn't sorry at all.

To cover Jordan's chuckle, Victor said, "It all smells wonderful. We have discovered quite a few new flavors since we've been in Peru, but this will be another new one for us."

Huallpa took a seat at the head of the table and Llipya at the foot. Ch'aska sat on one side, but before Jordan could go to sit next to her, T'ukri caught his hand and Victor's and guided them to places on either side of him.

"It is good that you appreciate the different flavors of the region," Llipya said.

"We've found all kinds of things to appreciate since we got here," Jordan replied.

"Like T'ukri?" Ch'aska asked from across the table.

Victor leveled her a steady look. "Do you expect us to deny it when we've accepted his courtship?"

Ch'aska spluttered at his reply, making T'ukri laugh outright and his parents smile. "I am beginning to believe you will fit right in," Llipya said.

And that? That was the sweetest victory he had ever known.

CHAPTER 27

T'UKRI COULD have been walking on air, so thrilled was he with his parents' reaction to Victor and Jordan. He had known that would be the case if they gave his mates a chance, but he had expected it to take longer for them to warm up to the idea. Pachamama bless Ch'aska and her sometimes tactless ways. Or maybe he should say her manipulative ways, because he had no doubt she knew exactly what she was doing when she teased them during dinner.

Tonight he would talk more with Victor and Jordan about his people's beliefs and rituals. Before he could bond with them, he had to explain what it meant that he was Chapaqpuma.

If they took his revelation well—*please the goddess they will*— he would formally petition the elders to allow their bonding to take place within the week, and all would be right in his world again.

He followed them into the guest lodgings and reminded the guardian this was only temporary. Soon they would be back at his side again, in his bed this time rather than on bedrolls under the stars, and they would be bonded, with nothing to hold them back.

Not soon enough.

Nothing short of taking them to bed and bonding with them this instant would be soon enough, but T'ukri still had some control, and he had long known that the time of waiting as the elders considered Chapaqpuma's proposed mates was as much a test of the guardian's control as it was for the elders to make up their minds.

As soon as they were alone and away from prying eyes, he pulled Victor and Jordan to him, one with each hand. "You made my mother laugh. You have no idea how hard that is since Tayta died. For that alone, Papãnin will accept you."

He kissed them each thoroughly, starting with Victor because he had broken the ice and eased the underlying tension at dinner. When he pulled back to turn to Jordan, Victor looked decidedly glassy-eyed. *Good.* Let him feel a bit of what T'ukri was feeling.

The moment his attention turned to Jordan, Jordan pounced. T'ukri returned the kiss with equal fervor, nipping and biting at Jordan's lips as Jordan tried to devour him. *Gentle goddess, let the elders approve quickly.* He did not know how much longer he could wait.

"We should be careful or we'll get carried away," Victor said, ever the voice of reason.

Jordan groaned as he took a step back from T'ukri, looking as wild-eyed and desperate as T'ukri felt.

"Why don't we sit down?" Victor suggested. He took one of the seats and T'ukri sat in another, but Jordan remained standing. After a moment, he began to pace the space behind Victor's chair.

"Jordan?" T'ukri asked. "Is all well?"

"Of course," Jordan replied, even as he continued to pace. "But I think better when I'm moving."

T'ukri frowned. Had dinner not gone as well in Jordan's eyes as it had in his own? "Have you much to think about?"

"Nothing bad," Jordan said immediately, "but yeah. I mean, I wasn't exactly expecting a city when we got to your tribe. I was expecting something more like Paucar's village. Maybe a little bigger after you said it was the whole tribe, not just a settlement, but still, not"—he waved his hand to gesture at the room around them—"this."

"Not a permanent city with amenities half the villages on the map in the area don't even have," Victor continued. "We're not complaining about real beds and running water. We're just surprised."

"We allow so few outsiders into Machu Llaqta that I forget what it must look like to those who have never seen it before," T'ukri said.

"It's incredible." Jordan ran his fingers along the seam in the stones that formed the inner wall. "You don't see this kind of stonework outside Inca ruins most of the time."

"Except Machu Llaqta is no ruin," Victor added.

"No, my people have lived here as far back as our records go," T'ukri replied.

"What kind of records?" Victor asked, eyes bright with excitement and curiosity. "The Inca people didn't have any kind of written language that we're aware of."

"In the temple," T'ukri said. "The shaman continue to paint the lives of our kings on the walls as they add to the sagas of our history. I will show you when it is allowed."

"Any idea how long that is?" Jordan asked. "The records, not when we might be allowed to see the temple."

"It would be an estimate at best, for the life spans of those involved vary depending on circumstances, but easily a thousand years," T'ukri replied.

Victor's eyes widened. "That's almost two hundred years before the accepted date for the beginning of the Inca Empire. That's revolutionary."

T'ukri tensed, but Jordan laughed and said, "Not here, it isn't. We're the ones behind the times, not them."

"True," Victor said. "And since we're staying, we should get with the times. Did your people have any contact with the Inca people?"

"We are taught that Manco Cápac left Machu Llaqta with his family and followers because of… ideological differences with the king at the time," T'ukri replied. They had rejected the king's leadership because in that generation, Chapaqpuma had not been a member of the royal family, but that was more information than he was ready to share. "From there they created the Kingdom of Cusco, itself the foundation of what outsiders know as the Inca Empire."

Victor's jaw dropped. "And here I was thinking we'd be lucky if you were descendants of the Incas. I never even considered you might be their *predecessors*."

"Lucky?" T'ukri asked, wary again. Victor had said they were staying, but now T'ukri could not help but wonder.

"We came to Peru to research the Incan or Amazonian origins of a pop culture legend," Victor said. "And yes, all that is by the wayside now, but even so, this is our chance to learn about the culture that gave rise to the greatest empire in South America."

T'ukri was only marginally sure that was any better. "Even if that culture is simply our everyday lives?"

"Every culture is someone's everyday life," Jordan pointed out. "The curiosity that led us into anthropology hasn't gone away just because our lives suddenly took an unexpected left turn."

"Besides, the more we understand, the more easily we'll fit in," Victor added. "Obviously we've met your parents, but you mentioned a council a couple of times too. How does that work?"

T'ukri relaxed and settled in to share as much of their history and political structure as he could in the hours left to them that evening.

BY THE time the candles guttered, T'ukri had answered more questions than he had thought possible about minute details of life in Machu Llaqta, He should have returned home hours ago, but he could not make himself leave his mates, not when he could finally speak with them more freely than he had ever dared before. They had not brought back up the subject of Chapaqpuma and T'ukri had not searched hard for a way to introduce it into the conversation either. He still needed to tell them, but tomorrow was soon enough for that, or even the day after. The more support he had from his parents before he did, the less likely the elders would take exception to him having done so, since sharing those secrets with outsiders was the highest form of treason.

T'ukri would argue that by virtue of being his mates, Jordan and Victor were no longer outsiders, and once they were bonded, that would be irrefutably true, but until the goddess blessed their union, he walked a fine line, one that could result in exile or execution if he stepped wrong.

Jordan's huge yawn brought him back to the moment. "Sleepy, my malku?"

"A little," Jordan replied. "I don't sleep great under the best of circumstances. Add in all the excitement of the past few days, and I'm pretty wiped."

"I should go so you can rest." T'ukri rose to make good on his words.

"Or you could stay so I can rest," Jordan said with a lascivious wink. "I've slept better with you and Victor than I have in as long as I can remember, nightmares aside."

T'ukri wanted to throw caution to the wind and herd his mates into the sleeping area and onto the soft mattress there, but remaining in control had been hard enough in the rainforest. Here in the safety of the city with nothing to draw his attention away, he would surely never manage it. Even if he did stay in control, such actions, should they be discovered, would result in his mother insisting on constant chaperones, and that would complicate the conversations he still needed to have with his mates.

"As tempting as you both are, I cannot," T'ukri said. "Were my mother to learn of it, we would not have so much as a moment alone before our formal bonding, and that is not something I wish to contemplate."

Jordan pouted a bit, but T'ukri saw the understanding in his gaze. "Can you at least give us good night kisses before you go?"

Even that was not a good idea, yet T'ukri could not bring himself to refuse. He stretched out a hand in Jordan's direction. Jordan took it and stepped into his embrace in the blink of an eye. Had he been anyone else, T'ukri might have missed the movement, but he was Chapaqpuma no matter his form, and his human eyes saw more than most. For a moment Jordan peered up at him from beneath his lashes, almost coy, before abandoning all pretense and pressing the full length of his body against T'ukri. T'ukri took his weight easily, steadying them with one hand low on Jordan's hip and the other on his nape to angle his jaw for the requested kiss. Jordan twined around him, a vine climbing a jungle tree. T'ukri planted his feet more firmly to provide stable roots as he delved into Jordan's mouth and plundered.

The guardian rose in his chest in response to the savage heat, not to fight it, but to revel in it. To revel in Jordan's raw power and rough masculinity. He was a match for the guardian's physicality, muscle for muscle, sinew for sinew.

A cool touch on his arm drew T'ukri back from the brink.

"None of that," Victor told Jordan. "We promised T'ukri we wouldn't make him explain to his mother why we bonded without her blessing. You've met the queen. Do *you* want to explain it to her?"

Jordan grumbled but took a step back, leaving Victor in T'ukri's line of sight.

Not happy at having the kiss disrupted, the guardian rumbled in T'ukri's mind, but Victor was also his mate, a long, soothing drink of cool water to quench the flame of heat—not extinguish it, and indeed under the right circumstances… but now was not that time, and Victor was the control T'ukri lacked in this moment. Their kiss was no less deep, but Victor controlled it, not T'ukri or the guardian, teasing, yes, but tender at the same time, until T'ukri felt once again able to leash the primal beast inside him.

"Holy shit, you two are hot together."

T'ukri looked at Jordan.

At Jordan, who had stripped away his tunic and stood before them bare-chested. At Jordan, with his hand down the front of his pants. And all control deserted him.

For the second time in less than a day, he did the unthinkable and fled.

VICTOR STARED at Jordan as the cloth covering the doorway fluttered back into place behind T'ukri. He desperately wanted to lunge at Jordan, replace that hand with his own, and jerk Jordan off until he came with a shout, but they had agreed to wait until they could all be together, and he was a man of his word, no matter how tempting Jordan looked at the moment. He cast around for a distraction, any distraction, and his gaze landed on his notebook, sticking haphazardly out of his pack. Latching on to that as his salvation, he scrambled for it. In twenty-four hours—merde, in twelve—he'd learned enough to completely rewrite the history of the Incan Empire.

Bon, d'accord, he wasn't actually going to rewrite it. That would be a gross violation of T'ukri's trust, but he had to get it down. For the sake of the knowledge, even if he was the only one to see it. He had to make it fit with what he already knew. He had to understand!

"Victor?"

He looked up from his frantic scribbling to see Jordan's bemused expression.

"What are you doing?"

"Trying to get everything he told us on paper before I forget," Victor said. Wasn't that obvious?

"Why? I thought we decided not to publish anything about this place."

"We did, but that doesn't mean I want to forget any of it," Victor said. "It might be useful. Everyone here knows this already. We're going to be T'ukri's mates. People will expect us to know it too. And it's not like they have history books lying around for us to study."

"Are you sure it's a good idea, though? What if someone finds them? Someone outside the valley, I mean?" Jordan asked.

"Who?" Victor said. "Or more importantly, how? We wouldn't have found our way in without T'ukri. And even if someone stumbled in somehow—not that I see how that could happen, but let's pretend it did—they wouldn't know to look for notebooks of any kind, much less where. You're worrying over nothing."

Jordan didn't look convinced, but he stopped arguing, so Victor kept writing, trying to get as much down as he could while it was fresh in his head.

CHAPTER 28

JORDAN WOKE before Victor the next morning, not surprising given he'd fallen asleep to the sound of Victor's pen scratching across paper well into the night. He snuggled closer to Victor for a while, enjoying the warmth radiating from his body in the crisp morning air, but eventually his bladder demanded attention. He forced himself out of bed, took care of business, shaved, and started through a series of stretches. He didn't know what the day would bring, but it didn't hurt to be prepared. Either it would be physical and he'd be glad of the warmup or it wouldn't and the stretches would keep him from getting twitchy as quickly. Nandini had pounded that realization into his head—rather literally—within a few weeks of meeting him.

"Hello?" a woman's voice called from outside. "Prince T'ukri's mates?"

Jordan frowned. Yeah, he was going to be T'ukri's mate when they got all the approvals, but he hadn't planned on that being his identity or his title or whatever. He stuck his head out the entrance to see who was calling.

"Good morning, Prince T'ukri's mate," Quenti said with a sharp salute—the hand holding the spear snapping across her chest and back to her side.

"Good morning," Jordan replied. "Think you could call me Jordan? Or Harris if Jordan is too casual for you?"

"I had not wanted to presume," Quenti replied with a bow of her head. "But in a private setting, I will address you as you prefer."

"Jordan it is, then. I'm not quite ready to give up my identity yet."

"I did not mean to imply that you should," Quenti said hurriedly. "Only that I had no other title to give you. Once you are bonded, I will know how to address you formally, and since I had not asked what you would prefer in private, I chose to err on the side of caution."

"Makes sense," Jordan replied. "Want to come in?"

Quenti shook her head. "I came to see if you wished to join our warriors for breakfast and training this morning, as I imagine

Prince T'ukri will be busy with the elders and the council today as he endeavors to convince them of his choice."

"Sure. Let me just get Victor."

"I believe Urpi has plans for him in the temple, although if he would prefer to go with us, he would be welcome," Quenti replied.

Jordan laughed. "No, given the choice between training and the temple, he'll choose the temple for sure. I should still tell him where I'm going, though, so he doesn't worry. Should I bring anything with me?"

"Prince T'ukri tells me you are a wonder with your bow."

Jordan shot her a cocky grin and stepped back inside. He shook Victor awake enough to tell him the plans for the day and got a mumbled acknowledgment, then grabbed his bow and headed back outside. "Lead the way."

Quenti took Jordan past the palace—*a real motherfucking palace!*—where they'd had dinner with T'ukri's parents the night before and on toward the edge of the city, where they approached a series of terraces split by a long set of stairs that led even deeper into the valley. And seriously, how deep was this valley and how was it possible when they were already out of the mountains? He'd have to ask T'ukri about that next time they were alone.

"What are they going to plant?" he asked as they started down the steps.

"Corn, quinoa, potatoes, coffee, and all manner of other vegetables," Quenti replied. "The valley is self-sustaining where grains and produce are concerned. We harvest enough for ourselves and our livestock, although we hunt to supplement our meat supplies, but we must be careful not to draw attention to ourselves when we do. Not all outsiders are as harmless as you."

"Harmless?" Jordan squawked.

"Do you mean us harm?" Quenti asked. Her tone never changed, but Jordan caught the sudden tension in her shoulders.

"No, of course not, but that doesn't make me harmless."

"If you do us no harm, you are harmless, are you not?"

Jordan was sure there was a logical fallacy in there, but given they were both speaking a foreign language, he decided not to argue it. "If you say so. I'm happy to help with the hunting if it'll make it easier for you to stay hidden."

"It may. It may not. You are not exactly inconspicuous. Not many native Peruvians have blond hair and blue eyes, and of those who do, they do not hunt with a bow and arrow."

"I can hunt with a rifle too, although I wasn't allowed to bring one into Peru," Jordan said. "I just like the bow better. I can reuse the ammunition. Easier than going somewhere to buy more."

"That is certainly true."

When they reached the base of the stairs, Jordan looked around the cleared, open space that had been leveled to make a training area, including a building to one side that could be barracks. Quenti said something in Runasimi—Jordan would have to ask if or when he'd be allowed to learn. He was already over not being able to understand what people were saying—and one of the warriors gathered in loose groups brought them each a granola bar and a cup of coca tea.

"We had these on the Inca Trail and in some of the settlements," Jordan said.

"These are easy and portable trail snacks," Quenti replied. "We always have them at the training grounds for those who have stood watch or do not have the time or inclination to cook breakfast for themselves. Not all of us have mates or families who cook well. I am one of the fortunate ones."

Jordan bought himself a bit of time by taking another bite of the quinoa and honey bar and trying to figure out what else they'd included in it while also thinking about everything T'ukri had mentioned about Quenti, Cusi, and their families. When he swallowed, he smiled and said, "T'ukri mentioned Cusi's grandmother was a good cook. I take it the trait runs in his family."

Quenti smiled. "Cusi's grandmother still cooks for us at times, but his mother is also an excellent cook, a trait she has passed on to her son. And one I hope he will pass on to our children should the goddess bless us with any."

"Victor cooks," Jordan said, not about to touch the subject of children when he had no idea of cultural norms around birth control, infertility, inheritance, or any related topics. Obviously same-sex relationships as a part of triads were accepted, and T'ukri hadn't seemed concerned about bringing home two male mates—outsiders, sure, but not men—but Jordan still kept his mouth shut. He was nobody's fool, and Quenti looked like she could have his balls for breakfast.

"Then you are fortunate indeed. T'ukri does not cook well."

"It didn't seem that way when we were coming here," Jordan said.

"Perhaps I should say not well by our standards," Quenti amended. "I have never found the match for our cooking outside our borders. Not for our own style of cuisine."

"You were a wanderer, then?" Jordan asked.

"In my younger days, before I rose to my current role, I had that privilege. I could hardly lead my warriors if I knew nothing of those that would threaten us."

That made sense.

"I'm happy to help with that," Jordan said. "Any insight or other help I can offer, it's yours."

"Then let us see what kind of help you might give us," Quenti said with a much more formal nod. She took a step back, pounded the butt of her spear on the ground three times, which brought the gathered warriors to attention, and saluted Jordan as she had done that morning. The other warriors mirrored her immediately.

Feeling incredibly awkward, Jordan swung his bow off his shoulder and repeated the salute, hoping he wasn't stepping on all kinds of protocol or that he'd be forgiven if he was. For once, he seemed to have guessed right. A number of the warriors smiled or nodded approvingly as Quenti turned and started barking orders. Jordan relaxed back into the familiarity of military discipline the world over and prepared to learn whatever he could.

VICTOR WOKE slowly and frowned when he reached for his lovers, only to find empty space on either side of him. He shook his head. He'd only been sleeping beside them for a short period of time, but that was all he needed subconsciously to come to expect it, apparently. Hopefully it wouldn't be long before waking up alone would be completely a thing of the past. Then again, this morning was his own fault. If he hadn't stayed up so late, he would have gotten up when Jordan did rather than going back to sleep and waking up alone.

Rubbing the sleep from his eyes, he dragged himself out of bed and into the bathing area. He shivered a little in the cool air and braced himself for the same icy water they'd encountered in the highlands, but when he turned on the water, it was surprisingly warm. He hadn't noticed it the day before when the temperature was higher, but now he wondered if the water came directly from the hot spring. If so, it would make chilly winter mornings much less unpleasant. But that was a mystery for another day.

Jordan had said something about Urpi showing him the temple today, and that meant getting dressed and finding food. He'd spent so much time asking T'ukri questions about the city and their history that he hadn't asked about practical matters, and for once Jordan hadn't called him on it. If it came to it, he still had some rations in his pack he could pull out. It wouldn't be the most delicious meal he'd ever eaten, but it would hold him over until he could figure out a better option.

He had just pulled on the less formal tunic and pants, which had dried overnight, figuring it would be more appropriate for a day at the temple than Western attire, when he heard a voice calling out.

"Come in," he called back as he stepped into the central area of the house.

He didn't know the woman who stepped through the doorway. She wore an outfit similar to the one Ch'aska had worn the day before and had her long hair pulled away from her face in a simple braid down her back. She set a covered—and colorful—woven basket on the table and greeted Victor with a small bow. "I am Urpi. Prince T'ukri asked me to send his regrets that he cannot join you for breakfast this morning. The Council of Machu Llaqta has insisted on his presence. He hopes you will allow me to be your guide and that a day spent exploring the temple will make up for his absence."

"It's nice to meet you, Urpi. Prince T'ukri spoke of you often on our way here." Victor removed the cover on the basket to find a large bowl of porridge. He wasn't going to worry about what the council wanted with T'ukri. He couldn't do anything about it, so he was going to concentrate on the chance he was getting instead. If they got kicked out, he was going to have to turn what they'd learned into a paper that would save his career without exposing Machu Llaqta and its people to unwanted scrutiny, so the more he learned, the more he'd have to work with. "I hope you plan to join me for breakfast. This is far more than I can eat by myself, and Jordan has already left for the day."

Urpi smiled. "Quenti told me her plans to steal him away for a few hours, so yes, this is for us to share, Dr. Itoua." She drew two bowls, two spoons, and a ladle out of a cloth bag Victor had not noticed hanging on her back.

"Is there a rule that says you have to use my title?" Victor asked. "And if there is, what title should I use for you? T'ukri left a few details for the last minute, so I didn't get a chance to ask all the questions I should have before we got here."

"Only in formal or ceremonial circumstances," Urpi replied, "and I have no particular title. Unlike Quenti, who is a *kuraka*, or the council members, who are elders, I am simply a citizen. T'ukri's friend and sometime confidante, but not a formal advisor. Which is exactly the way I like it."

Victor suspected she was far more help to T'ukri without any formal title, but he kept that thought to himself. Until he knew for sure they'd been accepted and would be staying, he'd be keeping most of his thoughts to himself. "Then in that case, please call me Victor. We'll save the full titles for situations when they're necessary."

"They will be necessary at the temple," Urpi warned as she filled the bowls and sat down across from Victor to eat. "*Paya* Tamya will welcome you to the temple herself, and none of the others would dare to contradict her openly, but do not mistake Tamya's welcome for a universal one."

Called it in one. "Thank you for the warning and the advice. I will be on my best behavior."

Victor took a bite of the porridge, expecting something similar to what they'd had on the Inca Trail or in the settlements on the way to the city, but the flavor that exploded across his palate was much richer and more complex. He paused in his chewing to let it sit on his tongue for a moment before swallowing. "What is in this? Besides quinoa, I mean?"

"Each family has its own recipe," Urpi replied. "I prefer to add honey, cinnamon, and a hint of pepper to mine. Why do you ask?"

"Because it's both the same as and yet quite different from what we've had dozens of times since we got to Peru," Victor replied.

Urpi flashed him a grin. "Could the same not be said of everything you have experienced since arriving in Machu Llaqta?"

Victor's cheeks heated as he remembered kissing T'ukri the night before. He could hardly argue, so he focused on finishing his breakfast quickly. "Am I dressed appropriately, or should I change into the more formal outfit T'ukri gave me last night?"

"You are fine," Urpi assured him. "We may be going to the temple, but we are attending no formal rituals."

Victor ran his hand over his hair, took a deep breath to steady his nerves, and followed Urpi through the city. The temple was simpler than Qoricancha in Cusco or the temple of the sun in Machu Picchu, but it made sense, in a way. T'ukri had always referred to Pachamama or the goddess when he spoke of their beliefs. And yet, for all its simplicity compared to the "grander" buildings, this temple still had all the hallmarks of a place of worship. The stones beneath the thatched roof fit together so tightly not even a blade of grass could grow between them and were angled at the perfect slope to keep them stable during an earthquake. Victor thought they would have been far enough away here not to worry about that, but perhaps that hadn't always been the case. He was an anthropologist, not a geologist, after all. The grounds around the temple were carefully tended, herbs he could identify and some he couldn't, partitioned off into careful sections: alfalfa, sage, peppermint, raspberry, dormant for the winter, and more. Homage to the goddess, the mother who protected and fed them. And outside, in pride of place, stood the golden statue he had seen from the valley's edge. Up close finally he saw the familiar motif of the condor, the puma, and the serpent, although unlike in Aguas Calientes, this statue had no Inca at the center. No, the only focus here was the animals and all they represented.

"Paya Tamya?" Urpi called as they reached the arched entrance with a lattice bamboo door across it. No one answered right away, but Urpi didn't hesitate to push the door open and walk inside.

Victor followed more slowly. Where outside had been warmth and sunshine and sound and light, inside it was dim, light coming only through the few windows to land on the altar. The thick walls muffled the bustle of the city, leaving him alone with Urpi and the goddess, but when he glanced around, even Urpi had gone, and it was just him in the temple. He took another step toward the altar, gaze drawn to the image painted on the surface where the rays of light fell. He reached out as if to touch, but he stopped himself, fingers hovering reverently a hair's breadth above a sight he'd feared he would never see again. Philli-philli. Or Chapaqpuma.

His knees gave out and he caught himself on the side of the altar, hoping he wasn't committing all kinds of sacrilege. After over twenty-five years of doubting his own mind, he finally had some proof besides his own eyes.

He struggled back to his feet as Urpi reappeared with an elderly woman with a wide, toothless smile.

"Alli p'unlla, Paya Tamya," Victor said in his best Quechua, hoping it was the same in the Runasimi they spoke in Machu Llaqta.

CHAPTER 29

GIVEN THE spate of words that came at Victor in return, he'd probably miscalculated, but he'd had to try. He was going to be living here, and that meant learning as much Runasimi as he could. Immersion might not be the best teacher until he had a better base to build on, but he had to start somewhere.

"Help?" he said softly to Urpi.

"Tamya, slowly," Urpi said in Spanish, then in Runasimi.

Victor repeated the word, committing it to memory.

"I only speak a little Runasimi," Victor said carefully, "but I wish to learn all I can."

"I only speak a little Spanish," Tamya responded in Spanish, "but I will teach you what I can." She reached for his hand and he offered it, letting her grip his fist with both her gnarled hands. Her strength surprised him. She probably didn't even weigh half what he did, but that didn't stop her from digging her fingers into his until they seemed to reach into his very core.

"Come. Learn."

He followed her to the wall of the temple to the right of the doorway and what seemed to be the first of the murals around the room. As she began to talk, he only caught a few words—*Pachamama* and then a few moments later *Chapaqpuma*—but when Urpi started to translate, Victor stopped her. Between the images and T'ukri's stories, he knew this one. This was the creation story of their people, how the goddess had chosen them, or they her, and how she had granted them a protector to keep them safe from outsiders. A protector who, from the images in front of him, was the same creature who had saved his life when he was sixteen.

Tamya finished her tale and started to move on, but Victor stayed where he was, transfixed by the images. He didn't touch. He had too much respect for religious iconography to do that. This trip had been his last-ditch effort at finding his erstwhile savior. If he'd failed, he would've given up. Not his belief in what happened, but his attempts to prove it to anyone else. He would've faded into obscurity as just another anthropologist interested in the Incan Empire. And d'accord, that's all he'd be now, since he'd be staying in Machu Llaqta and wouldn't be sharing his discoveries with anyone but Jordan, but *he* knew now.

If T'ukri's estimates were correct, these were the oldest extant Incan images in the world, but more than that, they represented the religious beliefs of the people he was claiming as his own. He had never been a particularly religious person, but his experiences with Nkóko had nurtured a great respect for others' beliefs. The brightly colored figures called to him, and he leaned closer to study Chapaqpuma and his mates. Of all the images on the panel, this one called to him most. Though the artist had depicted them as three distinct figures, the aura that surrounded them unified them clearly, setting them apart from the others. Victor wanted that union for himself with Jordan and T'ukri.

Soon, he reminded himself.

Giving himself a mental shake, he turned to where Tamya and Urpi waited at the next image. Tamya began her explanation, more names and fewer words that seemed apocryphal to Victor. *Inca* this, *Inca* that, *Chapaqpuma* this, *Chapaqpuma* that. Interestingly the two were only the same about half the time, so however the Chapaqpuma role passed through the tribe, heredity was only one part of it. His curiosity burned through him, but he kept silent. He would ask T'ukri if he got the chance or save his questions for later, when he was more accepted. He had a lifetime to learn everything he wanted to know.

They continued around the room, spending more time in some sections than others. Even with Urpi helping, Victor could only guess at some of the meanings behind the drawings. Certain pictures were more tightly packed than others, which he presumed to show a faster turnover of kings or periods of time when the Inca and the Chapaqpuma were not the same. And to his delight, more than one depiction of Chapaqpuma was clearly female, just as he'd told Jordan before they met T'ukri. This was so much more than he'd ever imagined finding, and shared so openly.

Mon Dieu, what he'd give to rub it in Fowler's face! All his assertions proven in one series of murals. Whether it was legend or truth was irrelevant. It wasn't just pop culture. It was *real*.

"Excuse me, Urpi, you are needed."

Victor didn't know the person who summoned his guide, but he could read the displeasure on her face. "Go on. I'll be fine," he told her. "Tamya will use small words, yes? Like a child."

Tamya grinned again. "Go," she told Urpi.

Urpi glanced at Victor one more time, but he nodded. He didn't know who had sent for her or why, but he was sure it was important. He would learn what he could from Tamya and through looking at the murals. He could always ask T'ukri for clarification later, but this wasn't the first time he'd resorted to simple words and gestures to communicate with someone whose language he didn't speak.

At least Tamya *wanted* to talk with him.

When Urpi left, Victor started toward the next panel on the mural, but Tamya frowned and skipped that one. Victor took a second to study the images. The colors were much more somber and the story portrayed far more violent, and none of the figures bore the familiar triad aura of Chapaqpuma. A time in their history when they had been without their protector somehow? Given what he'd already gleaned, that thought chilled him to the bone.

Tamya waited patiently for him at the next panel in the mural, but she made no move to return to where he stood and explain the images in front of him. Victor didn't know if she was deliberately leaving it out or if she didn't think she had the words to help him understand it, but she clearly wasn't going to budge, so he let it go and moved to stand beside her. She patted his shoulder, pointed to the panel in front of her, and continued her history. He didn't recognize the first few names she said, but he knew the final set of figures: Huallpa, Yuri, and Llipya. And they had the same aura around them as the other kings who had also been identified as Chapaqpuma, so Victor pointed to Huallpa's icon. "Chapaqpuma?"

"Not now," Tamya replied.

"Who now?" Victor asked.

Tamya shrugged. Had Victor asked the question wrong, or did that mean she didn't know? Or wasn't telling? Or had the tribe once again entered a time without their protector?

Regardless, Huallpa or perhaps his father would have borne the title of Chapaqpuma when Victor was in Peru in his teens. Could that mean he owed his life to T'ukri's grandfather? To Huallpa himself? They weren't that far from Vitcos, but they weren't exactly close either.

It wasn't impossible, given what T'ukri had said about wanderers, but that assumed it was a real title, not a ceremonial thing, and that there was only one, not one per tribe or something.

He stifled a snort. An hour ago he'd wondered if he'd ever find proof, and now he was wondering if there was more than one. He was losing it for sure.

"Thank you, Tamya."

T'UKRI STRODE into the council chambers, fully aware not all the elders would be as understanding as his parents had been. Only one who had borne the title of Chapaqpuma or been mated to one could truly understand the bond that grew between a guardian and their mates. Even T'ukri, who felt the beginnings of the bond, could only understand in part, though he had seen it play out in his parents' lives. He did not *think* any of the others would attempt to gainsay Huallpa and Llipya once they made their approval clear, but the Council of Machu Llaqta had great influence and could not be discounted.

T'ukri bowed first to his parents and then to the gathered elders before taking his accustomed place, leaving the empty seat where Yuri once sat. Perhaps one day soon, Victor would occupy that seat, but until such time, it would remain empty in Yuri's honor.

"Honored elders, we welcome our prince home from his wandering," Huallpa said formally when everyone had taken their seats. T'ukri bowed his head again in acknowledgment.

"But he did not return alone," Raphi, Cusi's grandmother, observed.

"I did not, Elder Raphi," T'ukri agreed. "I brought my mates home with me."

"This is not our way," she said harshly.

"It is true that we rarely find love outside our own people, but it is not unheard of," Huallpa said calmly.

"Have you forgotten, all of you, what happened the last time the mantle of Chapaqpuma passed to one who had an outsider as a mate?" Raphi demanded, rising to her feet. "I have not, for I still bear the scars of that terrible day and night." She pulled the sleeve of her tunic up, revealing jagged scars, white with age, that ran the length of her arm. "They came in the night, the outsiders, and attacked the city. Chapaqpuma rose up to meet them, but when the attack ended, he could not find his way back to himself, his humanity lost beneath the great cat, and he turned on us as well. Hundreds died that night, with hundreds more wounded before he fled into the jungle. And now you return with two outsiders and ask us to accept them among us? You dare much, young prince."

T'ukri started to rise, but Huallpa gestured him to keep his seat. "You are right to point out certain similarities, Raphi, but do not be too quick to cast judgment, for the cases are not entirely similar. Remember our history. Túpac became Chapaqpuma when my grandfather was severely injured and lost his leg and my father, Inti, was only a child. Túpac had never imagined the role would pass out of the royal line, for the king was young and in his prime and the succession assured into the next generation, so when he wandered and found love, he did not hesitate to marry in the ways of her people. Why should he have? He was a citizen of Machu Llaqta like any other until Sunqu lost his leg and the guardian stirred within him."

T'ukri had heard the story as a child, but never the details, only enough to teach the perils of the outside world—not that it had done him any good.

"It is what he did then that condemned us all," Raphi declared. "Or rather what he did not do. If he had listened to the elders when he returned and found proper mates as they asked, the tragedy could have been avoided."

T'ukri could not let that pass unchallenged. "Who is to say what makes someone a proper mate for Chapaqpuma? Is not the guardian the best judge of that?"

"Clearly not when he would not give up his mate from the outside. She was the first to perish beneath his claws when he did not recognize her even though she was pregnant with his child," Raphi spat.

"Enough," Llipya roared as she slammed her hands against the table. "She refused to bond with him according to our rituals, claiming they were already married and that should suffice, and she refused a second mate on the grounds of her religion. As T'ukri has arrived with two mates, the latter does not apply in this situation, and T'ukri tells us his mates have agreed to bond with him according to our laws, so the former does not apply either. If the goddess blesses their union and the bond is true, I see no reason to oppose it."

"You were not there," Raphi replied coldly.

"And you were never mated to Chapaqpuma," Llipya replied, her tone just as icy. "You do not know the power of a true bond. Once it is forged, there is no breaking it. If these men are my son's true mates, no power in the universe will separate him from them."

Least of all you, T'ukri thought vindictively. He wanted to feel sorry for Raphi, knowing she had lost her entire family in the tragedy, but it had been just that—a tragedy. Certainly nothing to do with him and his mates.

"And if they are not, he too will run amok and doom us all," Raphi said.

"That risk would be just as great if we forced him to take mates from among our people but with whom he could not form a true bond," Huallpa said. "You have equated the danger as coming from the outside, but that is not so. Each time Chapaqpuma rises anew, we face that risk as a people because the chosen one must find their mates and those mates must accept the full burden of their roles as well. *Only* a true bond will ground T'ukri through the change and draw him back to his humanity."

"Jordan and Victor are my true mates," T'ukri insisted. "I have courted them according to our traditions and won the blessing of the ancestors. I beg you all to consider the repercussions of a guardian who does not bond with his true mates before you deny us your blessing."

"Honored elders," Llipya said, breaking the staring contest between Raphi and T'ukri, "I shared Elder Raphi's hesitations when Prince T'ukri first returned home, but after spending time with his mates last evening, I have come to see the wisdom in his choice. We are not under attack or the threat of attack, and our warriors are strong. We need not bless a union in any hurry. We can take days or even weeks for you to come to know his mates before we make any hasty decision that might result in more tragedy and heartbreak for us as a nation and for me as a mother. After all, they must both complete their trials to be accepted into the tribe as warrior and shaman before the bonding ritual can take place."

Around the table, the other elders nodded. Raphi still looked mutinous, but she did not speak out against Llipya's proposal, for which T'ukri was grateful. He rose and bowed respectfully to the council before excusing himself. The rest of their business for the day did not include him.

T'ukri walked outside and tipped his head up to the midday sun, wondering for a moment if Victor was still at the temple and if he should join him there or if he would have better luck joining Jordan with the warriors, when Umaq, one of the warriors who often spent time with Micay, T'ukri's older cousin, called his name.

"Welcome home, Prince T'ukri. Would you walk with me?" Umaq asked.

"Of course," T'ukri replied. "Have you news of Micay? Or of Sinchi?"

"None," Umaq said. "Neither has returned. I had hoped you would bring news, but I take it you did not see them in your wanderings."

"No, though I looked for them at every turn, I saw no sign of their passage," T'ukri replied. "It is the one sad spot on my otherwise joyous return."

"I fear I may have another pall to cast," Umaq said. "I went to the guest house in search of your mates. I did not find them, but I did find a book full of writing. Why would your mates have such a thing?"

"Why would you go through their things?" T'ukri asked.

"I did not," Umaq said. "It was sitting out on the table, open. I merely looked at it as I walked by."

"They are scholars," T'ukri said. "Academics who came to Peru to study the people and culture of the region. Of course they have notes. They had been here for months before I ever met them. You are looking for trouble where there is none."

"You have placed a great deal of trust in strangers," Umaq said.

"I have placed a great deal of trust in my mates," T'ukri corrected, pushing aside the niggling worry that arose again as he remembered Palta's concern that Jordan was more than he appeared. "They are good men. They will not betray that trust."

"I pray you are right," Umaq said. "To allow outsiders into the very heart of our city, to train one as a warrior and to share the secrets of our temple with another… these are our most sacred ways. I very much fear what may come of this."

"I understand your fear," T'ukri assured him, "but you must believe I would never do anything to bring harm to the city or anyone in it. It is my sacred duty as prince and as Chapaqpuma to protect the valley. If I thought for a moment Jordan and Victor were a threat, I would never have brought them here. Indeed I spent weeks with them when I could have been here in days so that I could be sure myself."

"Then I must believe that you made the right choice," Umaq said. "I bid you good day." He bowed sharply and left T'ukri alone.

T'ukri took a deep breath and tried to regain some of the pleasure he had taken moments ago in the clear sky and warm sun, but Umaq's words on the heels of Raphi's tirade left him unsettled.

He had known from the moment he met his mates that they were learned men, and not only that but men who had come to study the ways and cultures of the tribes who lived in the region. Even the smartest of men with the best of memories would take notes to help them remember details. That they had such notes and that their notes were out where Umaq might see them meant nothing. Even if they had added to those notes since their arrival in Machu Llaqta, it did not have to mean betrayal as Umaq had implied. The outside world viewed the Inca Empire—as they called the Runa—through a certain lens, one that did not include Machu Llaqta or Chapaqpuma, which was exactly the way they wanted it. Yesterday T'ukri had drawn back the veil for Victor and Jordan, giving them a glimpse of several hundred more years of history, even if he had not yet revealed the full truth about the valley's protector—about himself. It would not be remarkable that they would want to record those observations in order to make sense of everything. How else would they keep track of it all and know what else to ask? How else would they remember all the details of how to act and who played what role within society? Things that were second nature to T'ukri would be completely foreign to them, but they did not have a lifetime to learn as he had done. They had days, weeks at the most, before they would be expected to stand at his side and act, if not speak, as members of the tribe. They would be foolish *not* to take notes on everything he had shared.

And not one word of his increasingly hurried thoughts erased the unease growing in the pit of his stomach. Curse Raphi and Palta and Umaq as well for making him doubt himself and his mates. They would not betray him. They were good men with steadfast hearts who had promised to stay in the valley with him and be his mates. Why was he questioning that now?

Because he had spent the day defending their relationship without the comfort of having them near. But that was easily remedied. He knew where they were or would be. He could go to them and bask in the solace of their presence. He could even find a way to ask about the notes, discreetly of course, to get the reassurance he did not need so that the next time someone questioned his choices, he could defend them confidently.

He started at the training grounds, but even from the top of the terraces, he could see that Quenti had dismissed the warriors. Returning to the house where they were staying meant passing by the temple, which was empty, so T'ukri hoped he would find both his mates together without anyone to chaperone them. He would observe the proprieties enough to make sure they did not bond prematurely, but he needed the comfort of his mates' arms around him.

His step lightened as he approached the house, buoyed by the thought of his mates, but he faltered when their voices drifted out to him.

"Can you imagine the reactions, Jordan? This sets everything we thought we knew about the development of South America on its ear!"

T'ukri could not hear Jordan's reply. He crept closer, torn between barging in to confront them and waiting to hear more.

"I know," Victor replied to whatever Jordan had said. "I'll tell Dr. Fowler next time we go into town."

Suddenly the notes Umaq had mentioned took on a much more ominous significance. They had said from the beginning that they were searching for Incan ruins and Philli-philli, the outsider name for Chapaqpuma, but while their interest in him and the Runa had not waned, they had not brought up the legends recently, enough that he had assumed they had set aside their search in favor of being with him. More than that, as he had gotten to know them, he had come to believe his secret—his people's secrets—were safe with them. Everything they had said and done had shown them to be honorable men, but how well did he really know them? It had been less than a month since they met, even if they had spent an inordinate amount of time together since he had walked into Paucar's village. Had he so misjudged them and the situation that he had fallen in love with ephemera?

He should not fear the worst. He should give them a chance to explain what he had overheard, but could he believe their answer? If they truly planned to betray his trust by revealing the Runa's existence to the wider world, they would not be stupid enough to tell him. They would explain it away with pretty words and solemn reassurances but continue on their path behind his back as they had already done by not taking notes where he could see them. And if they suspected he was Chapaqpuma and had stayed to prove it, the betrayal went even deeper than he feared.

Pain lanced through him at the idea that their relationship had been one-sided. He wanted to curse but could not find a word strong enough in any of the languages he spoke for this betrayal.

From birth, all Runa learned one lesson above all others: Do not betray their secret to the outside world. And T'ukri had done just that. Oh, he had not known he was doing it, but that was no consolation now. He would be lucky indeed if he was simply exiled for his trespass. Others in the past had been executed for less.

He had to think, and he could not do that here, so near the presence of his mates, for even now, with turmoil and betrayal swirling inside him, the guardian whined for him to go to his beloveds. He could enter the house and confront them, demand an explanation and listen to whatever excuses they might make. He might even believe them, but he was too raw right now, too angry. He would say things out of fear and anger that he might later regret. No, this conversation needed a cool head and cooler heart. He would go to the grotto where he so often watched the sunrise. He would rest there and meditate, and when he could consider the matter without wanting to rage or cry, he would return and ask for an explanation. If his mates could give him one, he would accept it and they would move past it. If they could not, he would have to live with the consequences, as would they.

He sprang away and up the path toward the edge of the valley where the grotto awaited, a bitter laugh on his lips. *Live with the consequences.* There would be no living with them, not for him. Not in the valley. He would have no choice but to leave, if only so he did not hurt anyone in his grief. The guardian had chosen, for good or for ill, and without Jordan and Victor, T'ukri would be unable to control himself for long. Denied his mates, he would soon lose himself to the beast and rampage as Túpac had done. Ch'aska would carry on the royal line, taking her place on the throne when Huallpa died, perhaps even T'ukri's place as Chapaqpuma since he would be unfit to bear that title, although it might pass to Micay since she was older. He had only to ensure he did no harm to his tribe—or any other innocents—before he was put down like the rabid beast he would become.

He could seek out this Ramos who was encroaching on the area, whether for gold or some other nefarious purpose. He could do his best to root the man out, thus fulfilling his role as the valley's protector. If they killed him in the process, his title would pass more quickly to a more worthy member of the tribe, someone more likely to find suitable mates rather than outsiders who would betray them at the first opportunity.

No, no, no! He buried his head in his hands as he tried to stop his spiraling thoughts. He had to give Victor a chance to explain. He had to trust his mates. He just needed to calm down so he could go back and ask rather than jump to conclusions, but how could they explain what he had heard when Victor spoke of changing all they knew about the development of South America and telling Dr. Fowler the next time they went to town?

Crack!

The sound echoed off the walls of the valley, the loud report of gunfire where there should not be any. T'ukri tensed. It had come from the lip of the valley, not from within. Someone was invading his home, and he was without his mates and without weapons to defend it.

He glanced toward where the attackers would come from, then back toward the city, torn between letting the change take him and hoping his mates could draw him back even without a bond and despite the tension between them or going back for his usual weapons.

Pain flared across the back of his head and darkness overtook him.

CHAPTER 30

CRACK!

The dry snap of wood breaking, only with extra punch, echoed through the comfortable silence between them as Victor worked on his notes from his morning in the temple and Jordan stretched. It had been a while since he'd worked as hard as he had with Quenti's warriors. He'd mostly been a sniper, not doing hand-to-hand. A second later Jordan heard it again. Victor's head jerked up and their eyes met. That sound—the sound of gunfire—didn't belong in the valley. He didn't know who was attacking or if any of the nearby tribes even had access to guns, but it didn't matter. They'd come into *his* territory with hostile intent.

Jordan was already moving before Victor stood. This, he knew. He grabbed his weapons and raced out of the house into the shadows of the jungle. He hoped the entrance to the valley had a logical bottleneck where people with guns trying to invade would have to pass. As he ran, he heard the sounds of fighting. He didn't approach the valley's warriors, not wanting to interfere with their lines of defense. Instead he scaled one of the huge trees and settled in the vee of two thick branches. He grabbed an arrow, focused his senses outward, and fired at a gunman in the woods.

Training took over and he fired without conscious thought, picking off the invaders before he ever saw most of them, the sound of their guns and the movement of the underbrush all he needed to find them. Battle raged across the space beneath him. He couldn't look to see if T'ukri led the fight or if he was elsewhere, defending his home from a different vantage point. He couldn't allow any distraction. One unlucky enemy stuck his head up from cover, giving Jordan his first clear view of the attackers.

Fuck. Whoever they were, they were local types. He couldn't see what they were wearing, but that would make it harder to tell friend from foe. Were these the same men who they'd seen the morning they left Paucar's village or others in league with them? Had they been followed somehow? He'd like to think he would have noticed, but he'd been so wrapped up in T'ukri that he hadn't paid as much attention as he might have otherwise after the first few days with no sign of them. Jordan took the man out and moved on to the next. They'd deal with that later. First they had to stop the invading forces.

Shouts below him drew his attention to where Quenti and Cusi fought hand-to-hand with one of the outsiders. Not hearing more gunfire for the moment, Jordan took aim and waited for an opening.

Goddammit, the first thing they were doing when this was over was sparring together until he knew all their moves so he would be able to take out an attacker without hitting them in the process. Finally he got a break and shot the man right through the eye.

Quenti looked up and gave him a sharp nod before moving on to engage the next in the flood of outsiders. Feeling like he'd been given the highest of accolades, Jordan shadowed the Runa warriors from the trees, moving forward as they did and harrying their adversaries.

He wished wistfully for a comm unit so he could check in with Victor. If he had to guess, he'd bet Victor was in the city getting the noncombatants to safety and then doing anything he could to protect them, but he had no way of knowing what their status was or of apprising them of the progress of the battle. That made it all the more important that Jordan hold the line. If he failed, the city would have no warning.

This would be a really fucking good time for Philli-philli—or Chapaqpuma—to show up, but no animal roar split the air, just the shouts of the warriors below as they marshalled their forces.

That was the second thing Jordan was doing—learning enough of the language to follow their battle plans. He couldn't help by clearing a path if he didn't know where they were going. At least their enemies were just as clueless, falling to the attack-and-fade style of fighting.

The sounds of gunshots became more sporadic. Jordan hoped that meant they were winning rather than that the invaders had gotten what they came for and were leaving. If he had any idea who they were or why they were attacking, that would help.

"Try to take one alive," he shouted down to Quenti. She lifted a hand to show she'd heard him. With the aid of two other warriors, she brought one man to the ground.

"Pull back," the man she'd tackled shouted. "Tell Ramos we need more men."

Oh fuck, oh fuck, oh fuck! He had to find Victor and T'ukri and prepare the valley for a bigger invasion!

VICTOR SPARED a thought for all his notes, but now was not the time for that. He needed to focus on making sure the citizens of Machu Llaqta were safe. He grabbed his knife and stepped outside the house to see if he could find anyone he recognized to tell him where everyone should go. He hadn't gone more than a few feet when Ch'aska's guard—Ayar, he thought—ran up to him. "Come with me. I will get you to safety."

"I can take care of myself," Victor assured her. "Where are you sending people to stay out of the fight?"

"To the temple," she replied.

He considered for a moment. "They'll listen to you before they listen to me. I'll guard our retreat as we move people toward the temple."

She gave him an appraising look before relenting. He followed her from house to house as she urged people toward the heart of the valley. The very young and the very old were all who remained. Everyone else, it seemed, had gone to join the fight.

As the rapid *crack-crack-crack* of gunfire continued, he ached to be out there with them—with Jordan and T'ukri—but this came first. The valley had plenty of warriors. They needed someone to watch over those who couldn't protect themselves. Besides, his knife would be of limited use against guns.

He kept a sharp eye in the direction the sounds of battle came from as they gathered people ahead of them, but the noise didn't seem to get any closer, and he thought he heard fewer gunshots as time passed. Jordan taking out the shooters, he hoped, and not them shooting less because they had no one else to shoot at.

Jordan's the best there is, he reminded himself, but even Jordan could fall victim to a stray bullet or a lucky shot.

He pushed those thoughts aside. Jordan would do everything in his power to come back alive and unharmed.

They reached the center of the valley and the temple. Llipya and Huallpa stood on either side of the entrance, spears in hand.

"Shouldn't you be inside where it's safe?" Victor asked them.

"I may not be as young as Ayar these days, but I can still throw a spear hard enough and straight enough to kill a man," Llipya replied. "I will do my duty as I always have. Defending the temple is exactly where I belong."

"Apologies, Your Majesty," Victor said, because he was clearly speaking to the queen in that moment. "I forgot your history. If you will allow it, I will stand guard with you."

"You do not wish to join Jordan and T'ukri in the heart of the fight?" Huallpa asked.

He wished for nothing more, but Ayar had already abandoned them, and while Victor had no doubt both king and queen were formidable warriors, spears against guns was a recipe for destruction. "There's nothing I can do that they can't do as well or better," he replied. "Jordan will know I'm here to guard those who can't fight if someone gets past them. Do you have any idea who might be attacking? T'ukri gave us the impression the valley was usually peaceful."

"We are not without our enemies," Huallpa replied, "but few of them attack with guns. Those are the weapons of outsiders—guerilla groups who terrorize small communities such as Paucar's village, government forces who try to neutralize the guerillas, foreign hunters in our forests for sport, human traffickers thinking to take advantage of our apparent lack of protection, drug runners or gold miners who would turn the bounty of our lands into poison."

The choice of words caught Victor's attention. *Apparent* lack of protection. Now was not the time to ask, but when this was all over, Victor would come back to that.

In the short term, Huallpa's reply didn't give Victor any additional insight. He himself had run afoul of one of those guerilla groups years ago. And he had long attributed the widespread sightings of Philli-philli to political unrest and the kind of lawlessness that allowed drug lords to flourish. He didn't see how any of the threats Huallpa mentioned could have found the valley, though, unless they stumbled on it by sheer luck. If he and Jordan hadn't been with T'ukri, they wouldn't have found the path, and Jordan was trained in that kind of tracking. Then again, the attackers could be native to the region and possibly know about the valley from experience or hearsay.

Either that or someone had followed them in. Given how soon after their arrival the attack was taking place, he couldn't dismiss that possibility, no matter how much he wanted to. After the first few days with no sign of the men who had arrived in Paucar's village, he had trusted that the only threats would come from the jungle itself. That might have been hasty.

The sounds of gunfire had already become less frequent. Before long, Jordan would come swaggering up to the temple, sweaty and grinning, flushed with victory. Victor had spent years holding himself in check each time he saw Jordan returning from a hunt that way, but now he wouldn't have to. And if they were lucky, T'ukri would find the look as irresistible as Victor did, and they could find some time alone this evening.

Movement among the houses drew his attention, and he readied himself to fight, whether that meant throwing his knife or keeping it close to hand and engaging their attackers directly.

"Hold," Llipya ordered. "They are our warriors returning."

Victor lowered his knife, though not his guard, and waited. A warrior Victor didn't recognize approached the king and bowed before beginning to speak in Runasimi.

"He is telling Papānin about the attack."

Victor didn't jump at Ch'aska's words only by dint of years of Jordan appearing behind him out of nowhere. "What is he saying?"

"That the attackers were Peruvian—treasure hunters, terrorists, or possibly drug runners," she replied before falling silent to listen.

Language lessons. As soon as they had completed the courting rituals, he would insist on them, because the man spoke for far too long to just tell Huallpa they had been attacked by terrorists or drug runners.

"He is describing the attack," Ch'aska said after a moment, "and especially praising the archer in the trees who made every shot he took, even one to kill an attacker fighting Quenti and Cusi directly."

While completely unsurprising, the news settled something in Victor. Jordan had made it to the fighting and had helped turn the tide in their favor.

"He says they never saw him, but every time someone fired a gun, an arrow took the shooter out within seconds," Ch'aska went on.

If they never saw him, then Jordan had stayed hidden in the trees, out of reach of the attackers, and that meant he'd be making his way back with the last of the returning warriors once he knew they'd eliminated the threat. As the number of people in the area outside the temple grew, Victor expected Jordan to arrive with Quenti any second. He looked around for T'ukri, who surely would have come to the front to stand with his family if he had returned, but Victor didn't see him. He was probably with Jordan and the others. Or just with Jordan.

That thought did nothing for his concentration, and he couldn't let that wander right now. He needed to learn what had happened and anything he could about the reasons behind the attack so he would know if they needed to brace for more.

He heard muttering at the back of the throng of warriors. Then Jordan pushed his way through to the front. He was sweaty and flushed, just as Victor had predicted, but the victorious grin was nowhere to be seen. Victor frowned as Jordan came to stand beside him.

"Drug runners or terrorists probably," he said under his breath, barely loud enough for Victor to hear. "We captured one, but he ordered the others back to 'Ramos' to call for reinforcements."

Victor's stomach sank at the realization that they might well have been followed. They'd do whatever they could to be sure all the reinforcements were eliminated, or the valley would never know any peace again.

"Did you see T'ukri?" Victor asked in English just as softly. "We need to warn him. If you didn't get them all, they'll keep coming until they get what they want."

"No, I haven't seen T'ukri since last night," Jordan replied.

"What are you saying?" Ch'aska asked.

"Do you know where T'ukri is?" Victor said instead of answering her question.

"No. None of the warriors have mentioned him."

Jordan's frown deepened. "That doesn't strike you as odd?" he asked her.

"Very odd," Ch'aska replied. "He should have been the one leading the attack."

"I saw Quenti and Cusi, but no sign of T'ukri," Jordan said.

"Is there anywhere he might have gone that he wouldn't have heard the gunshots?" Victor asked, hoping against hope they could find a rational explanation for T'ukri's absence.

Ch'aska shook her head. "Unless he left the valley entirely, he would have heard. Sounds echo through the whole area so we always have warning of someone coming."

"I spoke with him after he left the council meeting, not long before the first shots rang out," a man Victor didn't know volunteered from the crowd. "I do not believe there would have been time for him to leave the valley."

"We've got to find him," Jordan said. "He could be hurt and need help."

"Wait," Ch'aska said as another warrior pushed her way to the front.

The woman's voice was sharp and breathless as she delivered her news. Next to them, Huallpa and Llipya froze and Ch'aska let out a gasped moan.

"They took T'ukri."

No. No, no, and fucking hell no.

"What do you mean, they took him?" Jordan demanded.

"They captured him," Ch'aska snapped. "Knocked him over the head and dragged him off unconscious. What else would I mean?"

"Fucking outsiders messing with shit that's none of their fucking business," Jordan spat. He spun around, intending to grab the rest of his gear and start tracking. He'd burn the fuckers to the ground for this.

"What do you know?" Huallpa said sharply, interrupting Jordan's cursing. "Who took my son?"

"Jordan heard one of them tell the others to come back with reinforcements," Victor said before Jordan could let loose any more of the curses on the tip of his tongue.

"What do they want with us?" Llipya asked.

"You would know that better than we would," Victor said as Jordan grew steadily more impatient. The longer they stood here talking, the farther away those bastards took T'ukri.

They may have followed us, Jordan thought bitterly.

"Did you bring them here?" Huallpa asked.

"No," Victor replied firmly. "We have no association with anyone who would wish harm upon the valley."

"Very well. Since you seem determined, go after them. Bring T'ukri back or do not come back," Huallpa said.

If they didn't find him, Jordan wouldn't want to come back.

"It will be done," Victor replied formally.

Fucking finally. Released from the king's presence, Jordan sprinted for the house they were staying in. He'd gathered most of his arrows after the battle as he searched the dead for clues. He hadn't found any, but he'd refilled his quiver, and that was far more important now.

He muttered nonstop under his breath as he dug through his pack for the rest of his weapons. He strapped a hunting knife to his thigh, grabbed his extra quiver, and filled it with every available arrow. He didn't know why the fuckers were here or what they wanted with T'ukri or the valley, but they'd pissed him off now. He'd make damn sure they understood what a mistake *that* was—before he ended them for good.

Behind him, Victor made his own preparations. Jordan didn't bother watching. Victor would make himself ready however he chose, and Jordan would rain hellfire and brimstone down on the motherfucking bastards who thought they could steal their mate.

The sound of footsteps outside broke his concentration. He spun and sent his knife flying through the air to land at the feet of whoever was approaching.

"It is Ch'aska," she called. "I need to talk to you. Please."

"Bring the knife back with you," Jordan replied, "and talk fast. The longer we wait, the harder it will be to find them."

"No, this is important. I need you to listen to me," Ch'aska insisted. "There is something you must know before you go after him."

"Ch'aska." Quenti came up behind her, a frown on her face. "That is not your story to share."

"No, but if I do not tell them, no one will."

"Tell us what?" Victor asked, all conciliation and gentleness.

Fuck that. They needed to get moving.

"The legend of Chapaqpuma," Ch'aska said. "It is not a legend. T'ukri is Chapaqpuma, but he cannot control those gifts without bonded mates to ground him."

"You're seriously telling me he can turn into a half-beast creature," Jordan said. After hearing the story of Victor's encounter with Philli-philli, Jordan had accepted—okay, mostly accepted—that Philli-philli was real, but he'd imagined a solitary creature who spent most of his life hiding out until his help was needed. He probably should have reconsidered that when T'ukri shared the lore of the Runa with them, but he'd taken that as a creation myth, both for the Runa and for Chapaqpuma, not as a literal man-becomes-beast situation. And now Ch'aska was telling them Chapaqpuma was real, and furthermore it was T'ukri. Sure, he'd compared T'ukri to a cat more than once, but he hadn't made that final mental jump.

And it was coming back to bite him in the ass.

He looked helplessly at Victor, at a loss how to make all the pieces fit in his brain again now that Ch'aska had rewritten his worldview in a few simple words, but Victor looked as dumbfounded as Jordan felt.

"Yes, but now that he has met you, he will not change again until you have bonded," Ch'aska repeated urgently, drawing Jordan out of his thoughts and back to the situation at hand. "If he does and he loses control, he might never return to himself. You must bond with him when you find him. Once you have, he will be nearly invincible, but until then, he is as vulnerable as any of the rest of us. And if he loses control and changes before you arrive, completing the bond will be even more important."

"Fucking hell," Jordan muttered. Rescuing T'ukri had just gotten that much more important… and that much more complicated. "How the hell are we supposed to do that?"

"Ch'aska will be staying here," Quenti said with a glare at the girl, "but Cusi, Urpi, and I will come with you to help you find him and protect you as you complete the bond."

"Does the king know about this?" Victor asked.

"He did not forbid us to go," Quenti replied.

Great. Not only did they have to rescue T'ukri, they had to complete the bond *and* do it all without the king's knowledge or blessing. This day couldn't get any worse.

"Fine, got it. Find him, bond with him, get the hell out of there, and destroy the entire camp on our way out," Jordan said. "Let's go. We're wasting time."

Quenti sent Ch'aska back into the heart of the valley. "You understand that in order to complete the bond—"

"Yeah, I got it," Jordan interrupted. "T'ukri didn't leave out that part." And they would be having words about keeping vital secrets when Jordan found him. If he'd just fucking told them, they could have bonded before the battle started and T'ukri could have defended himself better. Jordan had sparred with him enough during their trip through the jungle to know he was a good fighter even without his extra gifts, but to have the power of legends at his fingertips and not be able to use it? Yeah, they were having words.

"Do not be angry with him," Quenti said. "It is forbidden to share that lore with outsiders."

"Even the ones he's planning on bonding with?" Jordan said as he started back toward where they had fought the initial battle. "That seems like pretty important information for us to have."

"He would have told you before the bonding ceremony," Quenti replied as Cusi and another woman—Urpi, presumably—fell in beside them. "He is an honorable man."

"Yeah, yeah." Jordan was in no mood for platitudes. They had a job to do. "Tell me the goddess's protection or whatever you call it gives you a way to track him."

"Unfortunately not," Cusi said. "Once outside the valley, we must rely on our own skills. Only Chapaqpuma retains the goddess's gifts outside our borders."

"Fuck," Jordan said as they climbed out of the valley toward the place where they had come in. The sun was setting, giving them a limited amount of time to track the people who'd taken T'ukri before they'd have to wait until morning. "What's the plan?"

"Find their camp," Victor said. Jordan *knew* Victor had to be as thrown by the revelation of T'ukri's dual nature as Jordan was, but it didn't show on his face or in his voice. No, he was all business. Slick, sexy bastard. Not even having his professional dreams come true in front of him could shake his calm when the cards were down. "Once we do, Quenti, Cusi, Urpi, and I will provide a distraction while you get inside and locate T'ukri."

"And fuck him or get him to fuck me," Jordan said. "Gonna need something to ease the way for that."

"As long as you bring each other pleasure, the method does not matter," Quenti interjected.

Fine, so he'd suck T'ukri off instead of fucking him. Didn't make it any better.

"Once you've found him and gotten him free, preferably as Chapaqpuma, we finish off the camp and get the hell out of there," Victor continued. If Victor had any misgivings about Jordan bonding to T'ukri first or without him or even under such crazy circumstances, it didn't show on his face. Jordan wished they could have a moment alone so he could check in, but the situation was too urgent.

"And then we will stand guard while you complete the bond and bring him back to himself," Urpi said.

Now *that* was an idea Jordan could get behind. And once all that was done, the three of them were going somewhere private to hash out T'ukri keeping something so huge a secret from them.

They passed the stones that marked the entrance to the valley. Around him, everyone gripped their weapons tighter. Jordan set an arrow to the bowstring, ready to pull and fire at a moment's notice. They couldn't be too careful.

"About time you boys got here."

Jordan spun around, sure he was hallucinating, because Nandini's job with Interpol generally kept her in Europe, not in the jungle outside Machu Llaqta.

"What are you doing here, Rakkar?" he asked.

"Saving your ass." She tossed him a rifle. He didn't have to look at it to know it was the same kind he'd used in the Marines. Like she'd known she would find him here. "Again."

CHAPTER 31

JORDAN SPLUTTERED at Nandini's reply, still not sure what she was doing there. Her answer wasn't helpful.

"No, seriously, what are you doing here? Last time I talked to you, you were dealing with a human-trafficking case in eastern Europe," he said.

"That was in April. It's August. Now I'm dealing with an illegal mining case in Peru," Nandini replied. "Quenti."

"Nandini. It is good to see you again," Quenti said.

"Wait. You two know each other?" Jordan demanded. "How?"

"This isn't my first trip to Peru," Nandini replied.

"You know I was a wanderer," Quenti said at the same time. "Our paths have crossed before."

That was *so* not an answer. He opened his mouth to demand a better one, but Nandini smiled at Quenti, a soft, dare he say wistful smile Jordan wasn't sure he'd ever seen on her face before, and that was enough to shut him up.

"I only wish they were crossing again under better circumstances."

"I too. Outsiders have captured my prince," Quenti said.

"Well, fuck. That complicates things. The conglomerate I'm tracking got Interpol's attention when they hijacked a ship containing mining equipment in international waters off the coast of Brazil, but I've got a detachment of Peruvian soldiers with me too because they're encroaching on protected tribal territory. If the same group took T'ukri, this is going to get messy." She turned to Jordan. "I take it you found what you were looking for."

"You could say that," Jordan replied. "Stupid fucker neglected to tell us a few things, though, before he went and got himself captured."

Nandini raised one elegantly arched eyebrow at him. *Shit.* He'd have some explaining to do. "Not now," he told her, knowing she'd understand. "First we get him back. Then we talk."

She rolled her eyes at him and turned back to Quenti. "Introduce me?"

"Of course. Nandini Rakkar, this is Cusi, my mate and T'ukri's brother of the heart, and Urpi, our sister of the heart," Quenti said.

"Good to meet you both," Nandini said. "We located their camp a few hours ago, but it was mostly empty. I left my detachment to keep an eye on it while I did some scouting. I admit, I was hoping I'd stumble across you. I knew I was close to your city from what you told me the last time we met."

"Do you have a plan?" Victor asked.

"Yeah, burn the whole fucking camp to the ground," Jordan said. "They found the valley. We can't let any of them get away or our secret will be out."

"*Our* secret," Nandini said, an amused lilt to her voice. "We will definitely be talking after, *Annie*."

"We'll talk all you want," Jordan said, "but for now, we need to move. You said you know where they're located. Lead the way."

Nandini took off toward the east, beyond where they had gone as they came from Paucar's village. "What does mining equipment have to do with an Incan city?" Jordan asked as he ran to keep pace with her.

"There's a growing problem with illegal mining in the region," Nandini replied. "I'm not quite sure how that connects to the valley, but it's not my job to figure it out. It's just my job to stop them. The analysts can figure it out later. Or not."

"As long as they realize they can't have T'ukri," Jordan grumbled.

"But you can?" she teased.

"Hell yeah, I can." He glanced over his shoulder at Victor who was two steps behind him. "*We* can."

She laughed softly. "About time you manned up and got your head out of your ass."

"Yeah, yeah, you told me so. Tell me so later. After we rescue T'ukri."

She slowed suddenly and raised a hand for silence. The others gathered around her until they could see the dim lights of a small encampment, a mixture of tents and prefab buildings, carved out of the jungle. She led them around to where a small contingent of soldiers in Peruvian uniforms hid in the bush.

"Report."

"They returned about an hour ago, yelling about unexpected resistance, with an unconscious prisoner in tow, Agent," the ranking soldier reported.

"Where are they holding him?" Jordan demanded before Nandini could say anything else.

She glared at him but nodded for the soldier to answer.

"In that hut off to the side. There's been no sign of the stolen equipment or of Ramos, but there's been a lot of traffic in and out of the big hut in the center of the camp."

"Estimates on numbers?" Nandini asked.

"Fifty, I'd say."

"It will not be the first time we have faced impossible odds together," Quenti said. Jordan glanced between the two women again, at the soft look Nandini gave Quenti and the surprisingly affectionate smile Quenti gave her in return, and decided he really, really didn't want to know.

He studied the layout of the compound and the movement of the guards on rotation. "They're expecting an attack," he murmured. "They may not know who they captured, but they're still expecting retaliation."

"From what they think is an uncontacted tribe," Nandini replied. "They aren't expecting trained soldiers, much less two Marines. If they were, there would be more of them patrolling. We use that to our advantage."

"What's our play?"

"What was your plan before you found me?" Nandini asked.

"The four of us create a distraction while Jordan finds T'ukri and gets him free," Victor replied.

"It's as good as any and better than some of my plans," Nandini said. She held out a pistol to Victor. "Do you know how to use this?"

Victor took a minute to examine the weapon. "I've never fired this particular pistol, and I'll never match Jordan's aim, but I can definitely use it well enough to help create a diversion."

"Give me five minutes to get into position, then start the attack directly opposite." Jordan shook his head when Nandini offered him a comm unit as well. "Give it to someone who will need it more than I will."

"What if you need help?" Quenti asked.

Jordan snorted a bitter laugh. "If I need help for what I have to do, we'll be far beyond hope anyway. You know Nandini. You know what she's capable of. I'm just as capable."

Quenti nodded and tucked the comm unit into her ear.

"Good luck," Jordan said to the others.

Nandini nodded sharply and started in the direction of the planned attack. The others followed quickly, leaving him alone with Victor.

"Be careful," Victor said.

"I'm always careful," Jordan joked. "You know that."

Victor snorted. "I mean it. I expect you and T'ukri to be unharmed and bonded the next time I see you. I have a few promises to keep to both of you."

Heat curled in Jordan's gut, but he pushed it down. He couldn't drop his guard no matter how much he wanted the bonding that would occur before the night was over. They had too much to do between now and then to let it distract him.

"You do the same. I want you able to keep those promises."

Victor pulled him into a tight hug and kissed him hard and deep before releasing him just as abruptly and following Nandini and the others into the darkness of the jungle.

Okay, yeah. Mission. T'ukri. Rescue.

Jordan took a deep breath, checked the placement of his weapons one more time, and headed toward where T'ukri was being held.

He ghosted through the shadows toward the closest point to the building that was his target. The bad guys were smart enough to light the area too well for him to sneak in at ground level, but as always, they lacked the imagination to look up, and this was obviously a temporary camp, so they hadn't cleared the bigger trees, just the underbrush.

That was fine for the usual line of attack, but not for a Marine-trained sniper. With positively feral glee, he climbed a tree at the edge of the compound and made his way silently through the branches from tree to tree until he was directly over the building. Landing on the roof would give him the high ground for a few seconds longer.

As he waited for Nandini to start the battle, he tried to get a glimpse in the tiny window to see if the soldiers were right and T'ukri was inside, but the angle was wrong from his perch, and he could only see a small patch of bare dirt, not even a shoe or a piece of cloth. Although the fact that there was a light on in the building was encouraging. Someone was in there, either T'ukri or someone Jordan could make pay for taking T'ukri—and wring information out of in the process.

Dr. Fowler liked to think his department was full of upper-class academics, but that was all on the surface. Beneath the mask of TA Harris, he was still the ruthless bastard who would stop at nothing to fulfill his mission. And that was his mate in there. Mr. Harris had fucked off the moment Jordan realized someone had taken T'ukri.

Jordan held position, forcing himself into the same still place he went when he was in sniper mode. He cataloged everything within range of his eyesight, keeping track of guard movements, the guy smoking behind one of the tents, the one jerking off in another. That one he dismissed as unimportant. Caught with his pants down—literally. When the mission was over and they were all safe, he'd find that funny. Now it passed through his consciousness and out again, no threat, so not worth his attention.

He could hear the guards talking, mostly in Spanish, but their voices were too low for him to make out much of what they were saying.

He should have kept the comm unit so he'd know when Nandini gave the go signal, but then she'd be able to hear as he bonded with T'ukri, and the only person who should hear that was Victor.

A flaming spear flew out of the woods to land at the foundation of one of the tents.

Really? A flaming spear? Jordan appreciated a good entrance, but that was too corny even for him. Then again, it certainly announced their presence. Below him, shouts went up as everyone scrambled for cover while moving toward where the spear had come from.

He tensed, readying for the drop to the roof below. He wouldn't move until he was sure everyone who was going to head into the fight had moved that way, but he couldn't afford to delay any longer than necessary. When all but two guards had moved away and the two remaining had taken up defensive positions, he judged it was time and dropped onto—and through—the roof. He'd known it was a temporary building, but damn, this was ridiculous!

He rolled to his knees, rifle pointed at the door. In his peripheral vision, he could see T'ukri struggling against whatever held his hands behind his back, but he had to deal with the remaining guards first. At least no one else was in the room with them. That would make things a little easier.

The guards burst in a second later. Jordan shot them between the eyes—*pop, pop*—before they could even get off a shot. He stayed where he was, fully on guard, for a few moments longer to make sure no one else came to investigate, but the sound of gunfire and explosions appeared to have everyone else occupied.

Satisfied they were as safe as they were going to be for now, Jordan got to his feet, set his rifle aside but within reach, and turned to examine T'ukri. He was shirtless, his hands pulled tightly behind his back, his feet shackled to the chair legs with heavy chains, and a gag in his mouth.

No, his dick didn't twitch at the sight of the gag, thank you very much. He wasn't *that* much of a pervert.

"Hold still, you stupid bastard. Let me get rid of the gag, and then I'll see about the rest," Jordan said.

T'ukri glared at him, but he stopped struggling, so Jordan figured that was a good start. "I should be so angry with you," Jordan said as he untied the gag. "You spend weeks listening to us talk about our research and then we have to find out from Ch'aska that Chapaqpuma is real, and what's more, it's you. If I weren't so fucking glad to see you unhurt, I'd leave you here to stew for a few more days."

He released the gag and walked behind T'ukri to see metal handcuffs threaded through the metal bars on the back of the chair holding T'ukri's wrists.

Well, fuck. "I don't have the tools to pick these," Jordan told T'ukri. "I was really hoping to avoid this, but the only way I see out of them is for you to call up the guardian and break them. Ch'aska said you're pretty much invincible in that form."

"I cannot do that," T'ukri said. "It is not safe until we have bonded."

"Yeah, I know. Ch'aska told us that too." Jordan glared down at T'ukri. "How do you want me to do this? I can jerk you off or we can go for a quick and dirty blowjob."

"You mean to do this now?" T'ukri asked. "Here, like this? Without Victor?"

"Victor is out there distracting the bastards who dragged you in here so I *can* do this, so unless it won't work without him, yeah, here, like this," Jordan replied. "I know it's not hearts and flowers and declarations of undying love, but it wasn't ever going to be like that. Not with as worked up as we all are."

He cupped his hand around T'ukri's cheek, relieved when T'ukri leaned into the touch. "Victor, Nandini, Quenti, Cusi, and Urpi are out there fighting everyone left in the camp. We've got to get out there and help them, and the only way for you to do that is to unleash the guardian, or whatever you call it. And if that means we bond right now, quick and dirty, then we do it, and later, when it's all over and it's just the three of us, we add Victor in and do it right. But if we don't do it now, we may not have a later."

Another explosion rattled the walls of the building. "Like, right now."

"Use your hands," T'ukri said. "As much as I have dreamed about your mouth, you will be less vulnerable this way."

"We're coming back to that mouth thing," Jordan said as he reached for T'ukri's pants.

"I look forward to it," T'ukri replied in a gravelly voice that did *things* to Jordan's insides.

Jordan got his hand inside and wrapped around hard, hot flesh. He wanted to strip all the fabric away so he could see as well as feel, but with a battle raging outside, he didn't dare. They needed to keep their guard up as high as they could and still complete the bond.

T'ukri's head fell back as Jordan stroked up and down his shaft, thumbing across the sensitive spot just below the head every time. T'ukri bit his lip, making Jordan want to lean down and soothe the spot with his tongue. *Later*, he promised himself. When this was over and they were alone and safe, he'd do all the things he couldn't take the time to do now.

Like find every sensitive spot on T'ukri's body until he was out of his mind with pleasure.

"Kiss me," T'ukri said around a low, throaty moan. It was a bad idea without someone standing guard at the door, but Jordan couldn't refuse, not when T'ukri looked at him with blown pupils and an open, gasping mouth.

The moment their lips met, he felt it, this sudden sense of *other* and *partner* and *mate*. He'd never been one to believe in fated anything, much less fated lovers, but when he grasped the sensation, it felt right in a way few things in his life ever had. He sped up his strokes along

T'ukri's cock, his desire to draw this out warring with his awareness of the battle that raged outside. With his free hand, he unzipped his pants and straddled T'ukri's legs so he could get both of them in a grip. Hopefully that would count as mutual orgasms enough to cement the bond so T'ukri could break out of the cuffs.

"Yes," T'ukri gasped into Jordan's mouth. "Make it happen."

Jordan kissed the sound away and worked them over faster as he tongue-fucked T'ukri's mouth. *The strength to face calamity*, he chanted over and over in his mind. That was what he offered the guardian. His strength and cunning and skill, his aim and his years as a Marine, all the resources and knowledge they'd pounded into his head, sometimes despite his best efforts. All of that was T'ukri's for the taking now. Jordan didn't know what calamities they'd have to face later, but they were facing one now, and Jordan would face it at T'ukri's side, as his lover and his mate and a source of strength for the guardian. And when it was over, they would lay their battle-weary bodies in Victor's hands and let him guide them home.

His climax blindsided him, leaving him panting against T'ukri's mouth as hot liquid coated his fingers. He let his cock slip free of his grip and gave T'ukri a testing stroke, but some of the stickiness on his hand was from T'ukri. He wiped his hand on his pants leg, zipped himself back up, and met T'ukri's gaze. "Did it work?"

Jordan didn't hover as he waited for T'ukri's answer. Really, he didn't. He just stayed close enough to help if necessary. Except he'd done what Ch'aska said. He'd gotten them both off. If it didn't work, he'd blown their chance because recovery time was a thing, and even if it wasn't, Victor and Nandini were out there along with the others fighting these invaders, and he couldn't stay in here doing nothing in the hope he could get it back up again so they could try a second time.

Or maybe being Chapaqpuma gave T'ukri magical recovery powers. Jordan bit back the slightly hysterical laugh that wanted to escape. *Not the time, Harris.*

Except being Chapaqpuma meant having two mates, and Jordan had come alone. Would that fuck things up? It would be just his luck. The only good thing in life he'd ever managed to hold on to was Victor, and now he was out there fighting, and Jordan was in here, fucking around—

"It worked. Take a step back so I can release my hold on the guardian without worrying about hurting you as I change," T'ukri said softly.

"You won't hurt me," Jordan replied with an assurance he shouldn't have felt even as relief rushed through him. "The guardian picked me too, right?"

T'ukri nodded as he closed his eyes. Jordan waited, not sure what to expect. T'ukri shuddered from head to toe, and when he opened his lids again, the slit of cat eyes had replaced his rounded pupils. He took a deep breath and seemed to taste the air before bunching the muscles of his chest and shoulders and snapping the cuffs apart as if they were nothing. *Fuck*, that shouldn't be hot.

When T'ukri brought his hands around to the front, Jordan saw that dagger-like claws had replaced his fingernails. He stretched his hand out without hesitation, determined to step up to the plate and be the strength the guardian needed.

"You should not trust me so much," T'ukri said. Or maybe the guardian. The voice was the same, but something in the inflection was subtly different.

"I have no reason not to," Jordan replied, "and plenty of reasons to trust you." He stepped fully into T'ukri's space and kissed him quickly. "And I'll prove that to you as often as I need to, but for now we need to get out there and make sure none of these fuckers escape. If they do, the valley won't ever be safe again."

T'ukri growled deep in his chest, a sound that should have sent fear scurrying down Jordan's spine. He'd heard the shrieks of cougars and pumas sometimes when they were really in the middle of nowhere with the military, and he knew what those sounds meant, but coming from T'ukri, the sound meant only vengeance on their enemies, not danger to Jordan himself.

"Besides Victor and me, Quenti, Cusi, and Urpi came from Machu Llaqta. There's also Nandini—long black hair pulled back in a braid, darker skin than anyone from around here—and some Peruvian soldiers in uniform who showed up with her. They're here to help. Anyone else dies."

T'ukri nodded and sprang out the door, not quite on all fours, but definitely not human in his movements. Jordan grabbed his rifle and followed.

The fire from the flaming spear was spreading, but not fast enough for Jordan's liking. He took stock of the fighting in a split second and veered off to where Victor was grappling hand-to-hand with a goon twice his size.

Victor was kicking his ass.

"Victor," he shouted as he took aim with the rifle. Victor ducked automatically, leaving Jordan a direct line to the man's throat. The bullet pierced his jugular with a satisfying spurt of blood.

"Where's everyone?" Jordan asked when Victor straightened.

"Scattered around the camp."

Jordan nodded. "T'ukri is free. He recognized me after he changed, but I don't know for sure if he'll recognize you until you've bonded. Be careful, okay?"

"Always," Victor replied as an inhuman scream rent the air. They looked across the compound to see T'ukri slice a man's throat with his claws. When T'ukri tossed the limp body aside, they caught sight of Cusi pressing a hand to his bleeding shoulder.

"You're a better field medic than I am," Jordan said.

Victor nodded sharply. "How are you on ammunition?"

Jordan checked his clip. "I'm good. Besides this, I've still got my bow, and you're the one who's been doing most of the fighting. Go. I'll cover you." He covered Victor as he made his way to Cusi, then turned to find Nandini.

He found her a few seconds later as she took down an invader. She passed him a comm without even looking at him.

"We need to blow this place," Jordan said. "You got any explosives?"

"What do I look like? A walking armory?"

"Usually," Jordan replied.

She glared at him for a moment. "No, I don't have any explosives, but the buildings are burning like they're made of paper. We just have to spread the fire, something I'm sure our local friends can tell us how to do best."

"You're telling me about that before you leave," Jordan said.

"You know I don't kiss and tell," Nandini replied.

Shit. It was even worse than Jordan thought.

He pushed the thought of Quenti and Nandini and whatever mischief they'd gotten up to out of his mind. "Find them and spread the fire. I'll hold the perimeter."

"You want a boost?"

It never failed to amaze him just how strong she really was. He nodded and used her cupped hands as a vaulting point to reach the lowest of the branches overhead. He swung up until he was straddling one and drew back on his bow. From his perch he could see the entire camp and everyone still in it. The remaining criminals were starting to look frantically for escape routes, like they'd get far in the jungle with Chapaqpuma on the loose. Even so, Jordan wasn't taking any chances. Any time he had a clear shot, he took them down.

Before long he saw Nandini and Quenti with thick branches in their hands, spreading the fire from building to building and driving everyone ahead of them… right into the guardian's waiting claws and fangs. The smart few ran toward the soldiers and surrendered instead.

Watching the camp burn was really fucking satisfying.

When the flames started to gutter and the only movement below was from his team, Jordan slung his bow and rifle over his shoulder and swung down to the ground. "Everyone okay?" he called.

"Cusi got the worst of it, but the bullet missed anything vital and came out the other side. I stitched him up, so as long as it doesn't get infected, he'll be fine," Victor reported.

"I've got two wounded terrorists and no mining equipment," Nandini said. She turned to the Peruvian soldiers. "Take the wounded to the hospital in Cusco. I'll rendezvous with you there after I've secured the camp here and made sure there isn't anything else to learn from what's left behind."

"Agent." The officer saluted, took his prisoners and his men, and retreated the way they'd come.

"I need to secure the camp," Nandini began.

"There is no time," Quenti said. "Jordan and Victor must complete the bond before T'ukri loses control of the guardian, but this place is tainted now. We must return to the valley where we can guarantee their safety and their privacy."

Jordan looked over to where T'ukri stood apart from the rest of them, eyes wild and fangs still bared. "I don't know if we'll make it that far."

"Any distance from here is better than none," Quenti insisted. "You are his mate. If you lead, he will follow you."

That was probably true, up to a point, but while the quick hand job had been enough to create the bond, it hadn't really satisfied either of them, and it hadn't included Victor. T'ukri would follow, but Jordan didn't know how long his patience would last.

"There is a little grotto not far from here," Urpi said. "It would provide shelter and a defensible position the rest of us could guard. It is not ideal, but it is better than the middle of a battlefield if you do not think we can make it back to the valley."

Jordan weighed the options. Sooner was better in terms of keeping T'ukri from losing himself, but they'd be on the hard ground of this grotto with nothing between them and the rocks and dirt and whatever else was around. Plus they wouldn't have any of the plant T'ukri had used as lube.

"Or we can head back to my camp," Nandini said. "It's not exactly a safe house, but I have a tent and a bedroll. That's a step up, at least." She smirked at Jordan. "I might even have a few other necessities. And it will allow us easy access to this site as well."

That sounded like the best option they were likely to find.

"You're the best, Nandini. Let's go."

CHAPTER 32

THE GUARDIAN followed his mates and the others away from the place of blood and fire, glad to have it behind them. The smell of gunpowder lingered in the air around him, making his nose itch, but nothing would keep him from his mates, not even the stench of violence and outsiders.

He scented the air again. He recognized his mates and the members of his tribe, but the other woman... he did not know her. A growl rose in his throat as she bumped her shoulder against Jordan's, but his mate had said she was a friend. He struggled to pull the information from his memory—a sister?

"It's okay, T'ukri. She's safe," Jordan said, turning back to look at him. "I'll introduce you later. You'll like her. She reminds me of Ch'aska."

Ch'aska. Sister. Safe.

Later.

She led them to a camp that smelled like her with two shelters. She dug into one and handed something to Jordan. Then she looked T'ukri directly in the eye without flinching. "You can stand down. We have the watch."

He looked around the little clearing at Quenti, Cusi, and Urpi, who wore equally serious expressions. Quenti bowed deeply and saluted him with her spear, arm across her chest. He returned the gesture automatically. His other self wanted him to do that.

They disappeared into the fading night like mist, but when he cocked his head, he could hear them nearby, rustling the leaves as they took up position at the four points of the compass. Letting awareness of them fade, he focused all his senses on his mates, who stood together near the other tent. Jordan smelled like him beneath sweat and gunpowder, but Victor reeked only of the fight.

Not right. Not acceptable. His mate. He needed to claim his mate.

He leaped forward and landed right in front of Victor.

"Hello, *mon amour*." Victor lifted a hand, no fear in his gesture or in his scent, and laid it against his cheek. The guardian leaned into the gentle caress. Gentle. Victor wanted gentle. He could be gentle. "Come back to us now."

The guardian blinked. Back? He was right there.

"I know you're in there, T'ukri. The fight is over. Let go of Chapaqpuma and come back to us."

His other self stirred inside him, like waking up in the hot sun after a long nap. The guardian growled at him to go back to sleep. He wanted to play with his mates, but T'ukri did not listen. He grabbed hold of the guardian by his ruff and pulled him to the side. The guardian tussled, not ready to let go yet, but T'ukri did not force him down, just to the side. The guardian purred. He would get to play with their mates too.

"I am here," T'ukri said, the rumble of the guardian still in his voice. "Where are we?"

"Nandini's camp," Jordan said. "How much do you remember of the fight?"

T'ukri reviewed everything that had happened through the lens of the guardian's eyes: bonding with Jordan, the fight, the fire, a woman he did not know with long black hair. "Enough," he replied. "I remember you falling through the roof and shooting the guards and initiating the bond."

The guardian purred at the memory of Jordan's hand around them, hot and hard and strong, stroking them together until the bond snapped into place so he could break free, but it was not enough. He could feel Jordan on the edge of his consciousness, but the connection was fragile. He reached for them both, heedless of the claws that still protruded from his fingers. The moment he touched their skin, the claws shrunk back to the normal shape of his hands. The guardian would not risk hurting his mates with unsheathed claws. He wanted to play, not to hurt.

"I'm sorry I missed that," Victor said. "Both the falling and the bonding. I'm sure he made it look dashing."

Jordan made a face at Victor, like it was a joke between them. The guardian rumbled. He wanted that attention back on him. "You were not there."

"I'm here now," Victor said, stroking T'ukri's cheek. He pulled his T-shirt over his head and dropped it. "And I'm very much looking forward to bonding with you too."

T'ukri's mouth watered at the sight of Victor's bare skin. He had seen it before, but then it had been a forbidden pleasure. He had looked, but he had not allowed himself to touch the way he wanted. He buried his nose in the curve of Victor's neck and breathed deeply, saturating his senses in the scents of home and safety that emanated from Victor's skin. He felt more than heard Jordan move behind him, pressing along the line of his back and sandwiching him between them.

Yes, this was right. This was what he needed, his mates surrounding him with their strength and their love.

"How are we doing this?" Jordan's breath rushed over T'ukri's skin as he spoke and raised pebbles along his flesh.

T'ukri knew the answer. He had learned the lore at Tayta's knee. *The strength to support him and the compassion to rein him in.* Not the line from the legend, but the private lore, shared only from one guardian or guardian's mate to the next. He turned in their embrace so he was facing Jordan and thrust against him once before pushing his hips back into the cradle of Victor's thighs. "Like this," he said. "Your strength as our foundation and Victor's compassion as our guide."

"If I'm the guide, I'm going to guide us into the tent," Victor said. "With a whole lot less clothing on."

Yes, less clothing. Less clothing was good. T'ukri shed his without a thought, the guardian in full agreement. It hated the constriction around its limbs. It took Jordan a little longer to get undressed, and T'ukri had to resist the guardian's urge to shred the garments with his claws. Jordan would want them later, and if T'ukri destroyed them now, everyone would see his mate. The guardian bristled at the thought. Jordan and Victor were his, not anyone else's.

T'ukri took a deep breath and leaned back into Victor, seeking the tenderness that would soothe the guardian back beneath T'ukri's control. Yes, he wanted to shout his claim to the heavens as much as the guardian did, but he could be civilized about it. A few bites along their necks where they would show would be more than enough indication they had been well and truly claimed. He did not need to go feral to prove that.

Victor kissed the curve of his shoulder. "I'm here," he murmured in T'ukri's ear, the sound rubbing along his skin like silk with his senses still enhanced by the guardian. "We're both here."

T'ukri closed his eyes to enjoy the moment and the heat of Victor's body along his back until he heard the zipper on the tent. He opened his eyes to the scrumptious sight of Jordan's bare body disappearing inside. He fell to his knees and crawled in after him, free finally from the constraints that had held him back for so long.

Jordan rolled to his back and reached for T'ukri to pull him down until he lay flat along Jordan's body. He undulated against Jordan, craving the contact of skin against skin. They had too little of that when they started to bond.

"You do too much of that and this'll be over before Victor even gets in the tent," Jordan warned from beneath him. The guardian growled possessively at the thought and bent down to attach his teeth to Jordan's neck, right below his jaw, where the mark would be visible to anyone who looked. Jordan angled his head to give T'ukri better access. The noises he made drove T'ukri wild. He humped against Jordan's thigh with more determination even as he reached around to press his fingers into Jordan's crack, seeking the entrance to his body.

Victor's hand, cool and calming on his back, startled him into releasing the now-livid mark on Jordan's neck. "Gently, remember?" Victor said. "We don't have to rush now."

T'ukri shook his head to clear it of the fog of lust and need that poured from the guardian. And from himself, if he was honest. But Victor was right. They had no need to rush, and as satisfying as it would be to simply plunge into Jordan, drawing it out as they made love would be even better.

He rolled to his side and made space for Victor on Jordan's other side.

"I thought you were supposed to be in the middle," Jordan teased as he lifted his arms behind his head, putting every muscle in his chest and arms on display.

"Behave, Harris," Victor ordered.

"No, do not behave," T'ukri said. "I like you like that. And we are all here together. That is all that truly matters."

"You said something about my mouth earlier," Jordan drawled. "You gonna do something about those promises?"

"He is a mouthy bastard," Victor agreed. "In this case, though, he lives up to the hype."

"Just in this case?" Jordan asked, looking offended.

"Give him something to do with his mouth or we'll be here all day," Victor told T'ukri.

That sounded pretty much perfect. Actually, Jordan's mouth on him sounded pretty perfect too. "Come, my malku," he said as he stretched out next to Jordan. "Show me what your mouth can do."

Jordan sat up and pivoted so he faced T'ukri's feet.

"Slowly." Victor caught Jordan's head before he could dive for T'ukri's cock.

"C'mon, Victor, we've been waiting for weeks, and now you want me to go slow?" Jordan whined.

"Yes. We only get one first time, one bonding. I want to do it right."

"That is why he is the guide and you are the strength," T'ukri said, even though he agreed with Jordan. It was not about agreeing or disagreeing. It was about love and tenderness and giving the guardian a reason to let go and trust his mates.

"Fine," Jordan huffed. He bent so he could brush T'ukri's belly with his lips, playing his tongue around and into T'ukri's navel. That had never been an erogenous zone before, but with Jordan's attention, it was linked straight to his erection. He rested a hand on Jordan's shoulder, not trying to guide him, but needing some grounding in his strength. Jordan glanced up at him and winked, and T'ukri fell in love all over again.

"What will you do while Jordan proves his prowess?" T'ukri asked, looking at Victor, who so far had sat to the side, observing.

"I'm trying to decide where to start," Victor replied.

"Kiss me while you are thinking," T'ukri suggested breathlessly.

Victor chuckled. "Believe me, once I start kissing you, neither of us will be thinking."

The guardian purred at Jordan's attention and the thought of beginning to bond with Victor. "Even better." He stretched his free hand in Victor's direction, intending to pull him close. Victor caught it and lifted it to his lips to press a kiss to each finger in turn.

"Such strong hands, so careful with us."

"Always with you," T'ukri swore, the words catching in his throat as Victor sucked one of his fingers into his mouth. His hot, wet mouth that was just as alluring as Jordan's.

T'ukri closed his eyes to better absorb the sensations. The guardian lolled to the side, glutted on the surfeit of attention from his mates. T'ukri focused on the twin presences, strengthening the bond he had already begun with Jordan and searching for Victor's aura so he could complete that connection.

Where Jordan was hot as molten lava and as solid as granite, Victor flowed over and through him like summer rain, refreshing and renewing him and bringing him to life once more. He latched on to the growing connection between them until all he knew was the feeling of both of them inside his mind.

He arched into the wet heat of Jordan's mouth, as lush and generous as he had known it would be, but that pleasure was secondary to the rich emotion that bloomed between them as Jordan lavished attention on him. The physical was undeniable—and T'ukri had no desire to deny it—but their lovemaking went so far beyond that.

Then Victor bent to kiss him, and T'ukri fell into it, the sensation buoying him on wave after wave of desire.

"Close," he gasped, reaching for Jordan's hand. He could find release like this so easily, but he needed more than that. He needed them joined as intimately as possible so their touch, their presence, would be etched into him indelibly. The guardian would be satisfied with nothing less than giving his everything to them and taking everything from them in return.

"But I was just getting started," Jordan drawled, his breathing rushing over T'ukri's hot skin.

"We don't have to stop," Victor said, "just change things up a bit. Lie back, Jordan. You can put your mouth on me for a bit while T'ukri enjoys you. If that's enough of a switch?"

The guardian perked up. "As long as I get a taste of you before the day is done."

"You don't have to ask twice," Victor replied. "But Jordan first."

Jordan flipped onto his back and wrapped his hand around Victor. T'ukri took a moment to enjoy the perfection of his mates pleasing one another, but the guardian was not content to watch for long. He traced Jordan's lips where they were sealed around Victor's cock, savoring the contrast of textures, Jordan's slightly chapped lips and Victor's velvety skin. Then even that was not enough, so he leaned down to lick Jordan's brown nipples, one, then the other. He tasted of salt and sweat, of the fight and of their bond, a deeply heady combination T'ukri would never tire of. Jordan moaned, and Victor's breathy cursing made T'ukri wonder what the vibration was doing to Victor. He lifted his head to take in Victor's rapt expression in the pale light of dawn. Sweet goddess, he was a lucky man!

Jordan arched beneath T'ukri's lips, drawing his attention down again, to Jordan's erection, slick and dripping onto his skin. T'ukri licked his way down to the thin line of hair bisecting his belly and from there to where the head of his cock smeared fluid onto his skin. He licked and nuzzled until all he could taste was skin, and then he turned so he could tongue at the slit instead. Jordan was bitter and salty and absolutely delicious. T'ukri could drink from this fountain for the rest of his days and be content. He slipped one hand between Jordan's legs to cradle the soft pouch in his hand. It was drawn up heavy and tight against Jordan's body despite their earlier release.

"Here," Victor said. "Use this."

T'ukri looked up to see a small bottle in Victor's hand.

"Lube," Victor added. "To slick him up."

Comprehension dawned. If they had been in the valley, he would have used aloe as he had in the purification ritual, but he had not had time to gather any for this unplanned bonding. Fortunately for him, his mates were prepared. He coated his fingers in the slick fluid and sat back between Jordan's thighs. Jordan pulled his knees up and open with the amazing flexibility he had shown as they stretched and sparred in the jungle. Something else to explore in the future.

Feeling bold, T'ukri bent his head and licked across the little pucker of flesh. Jordan let out a hoarse shout and pulled away from Victor, panting. "Fuck! Warn a guy next time, T'ukri. I nearly bit Victor, and that would put a damper on the rest of our day."

"Apologies," T'ukri said. "You were too much for me to resist."

"Don't resist on my account," Jordan insisted. "Now that I know what you're planning, I'm good."

"Very good," Victor said with a smirk. "Go on, T'ukri. Get him wet and open so you can pound him later. He's been waiting for it for weeks now."

"Only if you prepare me as well," T'ukri said. "After we bond, your presence will steady the guardian even if you are not beside me, but today, now, he is still too close to the surface. I would lose myself in Jordan and then in the guardian without you to bring me back."

"Hands and knees, then. You can fold Jordan in half to get to him if you need to. I've seen him bend himself into tighter positions."

That seductive flexibility again. The thought hit him deep and hard, driving the air from his lungs and all thought from his head. The need to gorge his senses in them drove him to a frenzy.

T'ukri braced his elbows on the mat and lifted his hips into the air, offering himself to Victor as he lowered his mouth to Jordan's hole again. He licked and sucked and pressed as deeply inside as he could while before him, Jordan thrashed and cursed and begged for more and behind him, Victor worked cool, slick fingers into his passage.

The guardian roared in pleasure at the dual connection, taking and taken, holding and held. He would not need much more before he lost all control and gave himself into his mates' keeping. He lifted his head and reached blindly for the bottle Victor had held before. As swiftly as he dared, he pressed his fingers into Jordan's tight passage, stretching him until he could fit three fingers inside.

The snug heat would welcome him so easily and feel so good around him, as good as Victor would feel inside him. The guardian lunged against his control, no longer content with the pace Victor was setting. As satisfying as it would be in the moment to give in to that animalistic lust, their bonding was about more than that. They would be no less bonded if it happened, but he wanted—no, he *needed*—his mates to understand how deeply his feelings ran, and that meant consummating the bond before the guardian overwhelmed him.

"Now," he said, looking over his shoulder at Victor. "It must be now."

Victor reached around T'ukri to run a slick hand over his shaft. "Nice and easy, just slide in until you can't go any deeper."

"Fuck, yes," Jordan said. "I'm so open you don't even have to go slow."

The guardian pounced on that offer, ready to slam into Jordan, but Victor held him back, keeping his pace torturously slow.

"Victor!" Jordan begged.

"Lie back and enjoy, Jordan," Victor said. "There's no reason to hurry."

Jordan locked on to T'ukri's biceps with a steely grip as T'ukri slid deeper and deeper until he was fully seated inside Jordan. Victor held his hips in place and began his own slow glide into T'ukri's body.

T'ukri was no virgin, but the playful encounters of the past paled next to the overwhelming feeling of being surrounded by his mates. Victor pressed all the way home, holding both him and Jordan in place, his grip as inexorable as the rising and setting of the sun. Jordan might be the foundation that supported them all, but Victor's indomitable will would always keep the guardian on a leash.

Then, just as slowly, Victor began to pull back, drawing T'ukri with him until only the tip of Victor's cock remained inside. The guardian howled in protest, but Victor did not slip free. Instead he drove back into T'ukri, pushing him into Jordan again.

Jordan groaned and braced his feet more firmly on the ground. He reached overhead to brace his hands on the frame of the tent as well, wincing when the poles creaked beneath his grip. T'ukri leaned over him and latched on to the patch of skin across his collarbone, sucking and licking at it as he was buffeted between them.

Closing his eyes, he let himself fall fully into their hold, all control of himself and of the guardian entrusted in their hands.

They did not disappoint him.

Jordan arched beneath him, keeping him balanced and braced for Victor. And Victor guided him so they moved seamlessly together, their bodies joined as one, three spirits entwined for eternity.

Love and lust and need and passion swirled in him into one colorful blur, and he flew on the wings of his malku, tethered by Victor's hand until all thought was gone and only completion remained.

Completion of body, mind, and spirit, all wrapped up in the sweaty, sticky, perfect tangle of bliss.

CHAPTER 33

JORDAN BLINKED back to consciousness slowly, held immobile by the weight of two strong, hard bodies on top of him. He braced himself against the instinctive urge to struggle free, only to realize he didn't feel it.

Hot damn! He couldn't remember the last time he'd been confined in any way without having to hold back the urge to free himself. He didn't know what this was, but he could sure as hell get used to it.

He blinked a few times to make sure he wasn't dreaming, but the situation and his reaction to it held. When he felt a shift in the weight on him, he looked over the top of T'ukri's head to meet Victor's gaze. "Hey, babe, did you get the number of the bus that hit me?"

"Funny, Jordan," Victor replied.

Jordan jolted to realize he could almost feel Victor's amusement behind the deadpan reply.

"No, seriously. I've had sex before. Hell, I've had threesomes that ended with me in exactly this potion, but I've *never* felt like this. Not from sex, not from drugs, not falling-down drunk or stone-cold sober. When I'm sparring, if I can't break a pin, I tap out within seconds. There's no way I should be lying here beneath the two of you and not be freaking out, even if I tried to cover it, and I'm not."

T'ukri stirred atop—and inside—him. *Fuck.* Were they going for round two already? He wasn't sure his ass was up for another pounding, though if either of his lovers asked, he'd spread his legs, stick his ass in the air, or hold any position they asked him to, sore ass be damned. He'd do *anything* either of them asked, no matter what the cost.

He'd known for years how gone he was on Victor. He'd accepted he loved T'ukri just as much on the way to Machu Llaqta. Nothing in that willingness should be a surprise, because wasn't that what love meant? But the sheer depth of his determination was breathtaking.

"Hello, my bondeds," T'ukri purred. Damn, but he sounded more and more like the cat inside him with every sound out of his mouth.

"Is that what we are now?" Jordan asked.

T'ukri pressed his lips to Jordan's jaw. "Yes, my love, that is what we are. Close your eyes. Can you not feel the guardian's contentment resting next to your own? I can certainly feel yours."

Jordan was skeptical, but hell, after the events of the past twenty-four hours, he wouldn't rule anything out. He closed his eyes and focused inward, and suddenly the sense of *other* and *partner* and *mate* he'd briefly felt while jerking T'ukri off during the fight sprang into his mind fully formed. And there, next to his heartbeat, was the guardian's contented purr and Victor's tender devotion.

Well, fuck!

"Can you hear what we're thinking now?" he asked, not sure he was ready for that level of intimacy.

"No, nothing like that," T'ukri assured him. "That would be a recipe for madness all around. From what I understand from my parents, it is more a sense of each other. We would feel it if one of us were hurt or in danger. If one of us were captured again, we could use the bond to track the location. Papãnin and Mama knew the second Tayta died."

Jordan felt the wave of fear from T'ukri at the thought.

"Hey," Jordan said. "I'm a little harder to kill than the average person, okay?"

"Jordan's right," Victor said. "But this isn't a subject for our bonding day. We're supposed to be celebrating our bonding."

"Yeah," Jordan agreed. "Right now, it's time for round two."

The guardian roused to eager anticipation, making Jordan laugh even as his dick hardened at the wave of lust that accompanied it. From T'ukri and from Victor.

VICTOR HADN'T completely recovered from the aftershocks of his first orgasm, and Jordan expected him to go again? "Have pity on an old man."

In a move so fast he didn't see it coming, Jordan and T'ukri had him on his back between them like they'd practiced it a thousand times. "Who are you calling old?" they said in unison.

Victor couldn't help it. He burst out laughing, at their words, at the way they'd spoken as one, at the surge of indignation he could feel from both of them. And wasn't that a revelation? He'd be thinking about that later. Right now, he had ruffled feathers to soothe. "If you two stay that in sync, the world will never be safe again."

"Are you complaining?" Jordan asked as he ran his hand over Victor's chest.

"I don't know. It depends on what you plan to do with your newfound synchronicity."

"Seduce you," T'ukri replied. Even as sated as he was, Victor's cock tried valiantly to fill.

"You two are going to be the death of me," Victor told them.

"But what a way to go," Jordan replied before he licked one of Victor's nipples. T'ukri mirrored him, and Victor couldn't do anything but lie there and moan and wonder if anyone had ever actually made love to him before.

"I bet Nandini has some kind of wet wipes or something around here," Jordan said.

Victor blinked a couple of times at the non sequitur. They weren't done, were they? "What?"

"I really wanna suck you, but hygiene and all that jazz."

Victor's brain shorted out, but Jordan didn't wait for a reply. He was already rummaging through Nandini's things. Victor would be disavowing any involvement in that when they finally emerged from the tent.

If they emerged from the tent. The way T'ukri was sucking a bruise onto Victor's chest, Victor wasn't sure he'd be letting them up any time soon. He wondered in passing how long before their guards grew impatient with them, but surely the Runa had some idea of what a bonding would entail.

"Stop thinking so loud," Jordan said as he returned with a pack of unscented wipes and proceeded to clean Victor's belly and cock before handing the package to T'ukri. "It's distracting. Think about what T'ukri's doing to you instead."

If Victor thought too hard about that....

All coherency disappeared when Jordan tossed the cloth aside and nuzzled Victor's balls with cheeks covered in stubble. And when T'ukri blew across his damp skin, his eyes rolled back in his head as he gave up doing anything but writhing between them and forgetting everything but how damn good they made him feel.

Minutes or maybe hours later—he'd lost all sense of time beneath the onslaught of their attention—Jordan nuzzled his ear. "Your turn in the middle. You want T'ukri's ass again, or are you ready for mine?"

The question shorted out his two remaining brain cells. He'd been lusting after Jordan's ass for years, though, and the lure of finally being able to make love to him properly won.

"Yours, but you set the pace." He patted his thighs. "I don't want to hurt you."

"You won't," Jordan said, but Victor wasn't taking chances. He looked up at T'ukri. "You don't mind waiting, do you?"

"You say that as if watching you together is a hardship. I am sure I can find ways to involve myself while our malku rides you. The sight alone will be more than enough for me."

"Don't say that," Victor replied. "I expect one of you to fuck me before we leave this tent, and I don't know how long they'll leave us undisturbed."

"As long as it takes," T'ukri said. "Any bonding takes time, but fueled by fear and danger as ours has been? They will not be surprised if it takes days rather than hours."

Days… days of rolling around in the tent together, naked and horny and gorging on each other. It sounded like heaven on earth. "If that's the case, someone better tell your guards to start hunting. I'll need something to keep me going if I'm supposed to keep up with the two of you."

T'ukri laughed. "We will make sure you are fed. We should return to Machu Llaqta before nightfall. My parents will be worried."

"About that," Victor started.

"Later," Jordan interrupted, slamming himself down on Victor's cock.

Victor swore at the sudden heat surrounding him. He reached for T'ukri, needing the connection with him as well. T'ukri moved closer, putting his groin at the perfect level for Victor to turn his head and draw T'ukri into his mouth. It wasn't what they'd discussed, but it was too much temptation to resist.

T'ukri took the hint and straddled Victor facing Jordan, putting him at the perfect angle to kiss Jordan and giving Victor a magnificent view of his ass. His glorious, muscular, naked ass. Victor grabbed on with both hands, kneading the twin globes and teasing himself with glimpses of T'ukri's hole. Damn, he'd fallen into clover.

They worked him between them, Jordan's movements pushing him up into T'ukri, T'ukri's thrusts pushing him down toward Jordan until his dick throbbed and his throat ached and he needed to come like he needed to breathe. With a strangled shout, he swallowed hard around T'ukri, feeling the spurt of hot fluid down his throat as he spilled inside Jordan's clinging passage.

He ought to be embarrassed at coming so quickly after the first time, but he couldn't feel anything but blissed out as Jordan spurted all over his stomach and rubbed the stickiness into the hair around Victor's cock. He'd be making Jordan clean that up later.

"Sleep now," T'ukri instructed as he stretched out on one side of Victor. Jordan took the other side and rested his head on Victor's shoulder.

Victor let the comfort of being surrounded and still lull him into sleep. Everything else could wait for a few more hours.

T'UKRI WOKE some hours later, the new bond hanging quietly in the back of his mind and the guardian still in sated slumber. He stretched slowly, careful not to wake his mates.

His mates.

From his earliest memories, he had listened to the guardian lore and known his time would come. Not as it had, with grief from Tayta's death coloring the moment, but come nonetheless, and he had known almost as early that he would find his mates and that when he did, they would complete him as Mama and Tayta made Papãnin whole.

Now he was here, bonded to his mates, whole for the first time, fulfilled in ways he had not imagined possible. He let his gaze wander over their bodies entwined with his. He had seen their attractiveness from the beginning, and that had only increased as he had come to know and love them. To outsiders, indeed to his own people, it might seem as if he had rushed blindly into the relationship, but the guardian had instincts no one but another guardian could understand, and the guardian had seen in them worthy mates. T'ukri could have delayed by days, weeks, months even, getting to know them before performing the rituals to initiate a courtship, but those days would only have proven what he already knew. These were the men he wanted, the ones he needed.

They had proved it yesterday when they fought to defend the valley and again when they came after him. Then Jordan had initiated a bond, not just to free him, but because he wanted it. T'ukri had no illusions they would not expect an explanation for the secrets he had kept, just as he still wanted an explanation for the conversation he had overhead, though he knew their hearts now in a way that could not be questioned. Whatever he thought he had heard, leaving was not something they were considering. They were as committed to Machu Llaqta as he was. Once they had seen to the formalities and dealt with the issue of the possible threat, T'ukri would insist they be allowed a week of seclusion to settle into their bond and resolve the remaining issues. If the valley came under attack again, they would defend it, but beyond that, he would allow no disruptions.

"Why are you awake?" Jordan grumbled against Victor's shoulder.

His malku was not an easy riser, but T'ukri would not complain about cajoling him awake with kisses and caresses every morning if that was what it took.

"Because for all that our friends stand guard, we are not in the most secure location. Because my people—my parents—will be worried, and the longer we are gone, the more they will fret. Because delaying our explanation of how and when we bonded will only make my mother harder to appease. Shall I go on?"

Jordan grunted at him and buried his face deeper in Victor's neck as if he could block out reality if he blocked out the light.

"Come on, Jordan. Up you go," Victor said, his voice gentle.

Jordan grumbled a little more, but he rolled onto his back and scratched at his belly. "We stink."

"A battle—or two—followed by two rounds of athletic sex will do that," Victor replied. "We might want to schedule a bath in there before we explain ourselves to your mother. I doubt she'd appreciate our stench."

"She was a warrior. She will understand," T'ukri said. "There is no shame in wearing the marks of victory on our skin."

"One of these days I'm getting you naked in that spring when I can take advantage of it," Jordan said.

"The moment we are free of everyone," T'ukri promised. "You are not the only one who has dreamed of that."

"This is gonna mean more formal shit, isn't it?"

"I am afraid so. We skipped a few stages last night and this morning. One way or another, we must answer for that and satisfy the elders," T'ukri replied.

"You can coach us through it on the way back to the valley." Victor sat up and reached for his clothes. "And we'll need to clean up Nandini's gear. She still has to finish her investigation into the invaders."

"I will not hear of her staying here," T'ukri said. "She is welcome in the valley as the sister of your heart. She will have use of the house I had offered you. You will not need it now."

They would sleep in *his* bed from now on.

T'ukri looked down at himself as he contemplated all they needed to accomplish before that could happen. "My memories of last night and this morning are filtered through the eyes of the guardian, and we do not share the same priorities. Do you know what became of my clothes?"

"You were already shirtless when I found you, but your pants are probably outside with the rest of our clothes." Jordan sat up and softly kissed T'ukri's shoulder.

T'ukri hoped so. He had no desire to hike all the way back to the valley nude. The guardian cared little for such human concerns, but T'ukri had his pride, and it had taken enough of a beating when he was captured. He did not need to add to his humiliation.

"I'll check," Victor said, already wearing his pants. "Just in case the others hear us moving around and come to check on us."

"Thank you," T'ukri replied.

Victor unzipped and crawled out of the tent, letting fresh air in. It made T'ukri even more aware of the scent of their lovemaking in the small tent. He would owe Nandini more than just his gratitude for allowing them to use her space. Jordan would know if the bedding could be cleaned, and if not, how to replace it.

"Perhaps we should take care of this part of the camp ourselves," he said. "I fear your sister would not appreciate the state in which we have left her belongings."

"She knew what was going to happen when she offered it to us," Jordan said with a shrug. "And really, this isn't the worst state they've ever been in. We've bled all over each other's things more times than I care to count."

The guardian stirred at the thought of Jordan and Victor in danger, but T'ukri soothed it back to sleep. That was in the past. In the future, they would face what danger came together, where T'ukri could protect them if necessary.

"Here." Victor handed their clothes through the open flap of the tent. "I'll let the others know we're ready to head back to the valley as soon as we pack up camp."

VICTOR DIDN'T know exactly where he'd find Nandini and the others, but they had spread out evenly around the camp, so he headed due north, figuring someone would be there. He made no effort to hide his passage. He didn't want to surprise anyone and find himself at the wrong end of a gun or a spear, but he also hoped it would draw whoever was in that direction to him if he wasn't walking right toward them.

About two minutes outside of camp, he found Cusi standing at careful attention, though his spear rested against the tree next to him. When Cusi saw him, he immediately crossed his left arm across his chest and brought it sharply down to his sides. "Prince Consort."

Victor blinked, his one concession to his surprise. He and Jordan had talked about the fact that T'ukri was a prince, but they hadn't ever discussed what that would mean for them.

"Cusi," Victor replied with a slight bow of his head. He wouldn't return what was clearly a salute until he'd discussed protocol with T'ukri. He didn't want to overstep his bounds. "How is your shoulder this morning?"

"It is fine. Urpi packed it with a poultice to ward off infection while we waited."

"I'm glad to hear it," Victor said. "We're packing up to return to the valley."

"I will tell the others," Cusi said.

Victor nodded and turned back toward camp. He got there just in time to see Quenti give Jordan the same salute and the same title Cusi had given him. Victor hid his smile at the deer-in-the-headlights expression on Jordan's face. When T'ukri emerged from the tent behind Jordan, he received the same salute, which he returned easily.

Jordan escaped to Victor's side. "What was that?" he muttered.

"That was an acknowledgment of our new position in Machu Llaqta," Victor replied. "What did you think would happen when we bonded with T'ukri?"

"Not a royal title and people saluting me," Jordan said.

"Get used to it. This is our life now."

"Fuck."

Victor couldn't help the laughter that burst forth at Jordan's succinct response.

"What has made you laugh so delightfully?" T'ukri asked. "I would have you laugh like that as often as I can manage."

"Jordan was a little startled by Quenti's greeting," Victor explained. "It amused me."

"Is aught amiss?"

"Not at all. It will just take us a bit of time to get used to being saluted the way you are," Victor replied. "Things have happened rather quickly."

"I cannot delay the rest of today, but after that, we will have time to ourselves when we can adjust to everything that has happened," T'ukri promised.

"One more question, then," Victor said. "Would it be appropriate for us to return the salute they have given us?"

"Yes, as my mates you are one of us now," T'ukri said.

"Fucking hell," Jordan said. "All right. Show us how to do it correctly. If we're expected to do it, I don't want to fuck it up."

"It is simple," T'ukri said. "Left arm crossed in front of your chest, weapon in hand if you have one with you. Then snap your fist down to your side."

He demonstrated, and Jordan and Victor both imitated him. "Perfect," he said with a smile that suggested he referred to far more than just the salute. Victor wasn't sure about them being perfect, but he basked in the warmth he could feel through the bond. With that kind of constant affirmation coming from both Jordan and T'ukri, his old insecurities were bound for a quick death. Victor wouldn't be sorry to see the last of them.

CHAPTER 34

BY THE time they had Nandini's camp packed up and ready to move to Machu Llaqta—he'd be giving her the tent he and Victor had brought with them because the poles on the tent they'd used last night were too bent to fold—Jordan had almost talked himself out of his freak-out. *Prince Consort.* What a mind fuck, but damn, he wished his mother could see him now. She'd love the fact that he suddenly had a title, even if he'd been born trailer trash.

"I don't know what you're thinking, but whatever it is, stop," Victor said at his side. "No beating yourself up, remember?"

"I was just thinking Ma would get a kick out of the idea that I now have a title, even if it's one that would never be recognized outside Machu Llaqta," Jordan said.

"And?" Victor prompted.

Jordan sighed. Victor was too damn perceptive. "And that it was a damn big step up from trailer trash."

"I do not know that expression," T'ukri said from behind him. Fucking cat, so light on his feet Jordan didn't hear him coming. "But I do not like the sound of it. You are not trash, my malku, not of any kind."

"It means I grew up poor and with not a lot of education," Jordan explained.

"But there are ways to say that without insulting yourself," Victor insisted. He looked at T'ukri. "I told you we'd have to work on his insecurities."

The wave of love and admiration that hit Jordan from both directions nearly took him to his knees. "Fuck, that's not fighting fair," he gasped as his head spun from the onslaught.

"Am I mistaken? I thought you had the expression 'all is fair in love and war' too," T'ukri said. "There can be no doubt that we love you, so how can sharing that through our bond not be fair?"

Victor laughed again. "He's got you there, Jordan."

Jordan grumbled a little under his breath, but he couldn't hide his pleasure at their words. They loved him enough to fight for him, even if that meant fighting him.

Before he could decide what to say, Nan whapped him on the back of the head. "What was that for?" he complained.

"That was for being an idiot," she replied. "Do it again and I won't just slap you."

"That would be a sight to see," T'ukri said. "Jordan has spoken often of sparring with you. Perhaps before you leave Machu Llaqta, you will demonstrate for me and a few of my warriors. We could learn much from observing your methods."

"It would be my pleasure," Nandini said. Jordan groaned. He was in for a royal ass-kicking.

"My prince, my prince consorts, we should return to the valley," Quenti announced formally.

"Lead the way, Quenti," T'ukri said.

"You take point, I'll watch our backs," Nandini said.

Quenti inclined her head and strode in the direction of the valley. Jordan muttered a little more under his breath as he followed next to T'ukri and Victor. "Can we make her stop that when it's just us? It really freaks me out when she calls me that."

"For your sake, I will try, but she has a mind of her own and a will as sharp as any spear," T'ukri said. "She addresses me as she decides is most fitting, regardless of what I may say on the matter."

Great. Just what he needed. Another strong-willed woman running his life.

It took them less time than Jordan expected to get back to the valley. The night before and that morning were more of a blur than he wanted to admit, between his worry for T'ukri last night and his desire to finish their bonding this morning. He stopped when he reached the huge stone that marked the entrance to the valley, but Quenti, T'ukri, and Cusi kept walking. "Isn't that the way into the valley?"

"Not anymore," T'ukri replied. "The entrance moves as needed to protect us. Now that we are bonded, I will be permitted to teach you the way of finding it. But for now, trust me to lead you home."

Jordan was caught between loving the idea of having a real home for the first time and freaking out at yet another odd thing to add to the growing list. At some point they had to be done with surprises, right? *Right?*

He was having trouble believing it at the moment.

They walked for another ten minutes before turning the opposite direction from where Jordan thought they should and beginning their descent into the valley. *Okay, seriously? What the ever-loving fuck?* His sense of direction wasn't *that* bad.

"The goddess's ways are mysterious, but her protection is unfailing," T'ukri said by way of explanation. This whole sharing of emotions thing was going to take some getting used to.

They didn't meet anyone as they entered the valley this time, much to Jordan's surprise. After the attack, he would've expected them to be on high alert. "Where is everyone?"

"Urpi went ahead to tell everyone of our victory and our arrival," T'ukri said. "I am sure the whole tribe has gathered at the temple to witness our return."

"Are you sure we shouldn't bathe first?" Victor asked.

"Ask Quenti if you do not believe me," T'ukri said.

Quenti turned her head before Victor could say anything. "It would be a dishonor to both you and to our people for you to wash away the marks of your victory before we have celebrated it."

Jordan shrugged. Whatever worked for them. Yeah, he wanted a bath, but he'd been dirtier for longer and survived. He could wait until they were alone after all the formalities.

They rode down to the valley floor in the same baskets as before, but no one waited for them there either. When the second basket brought Nandini, Quenti, and Cusi down, T'ukri stepped out in front. Jordan hung back, intending to walk next to Nandini, but T'ukri gestured for him and Victor to stand beside him.

"We are as one now. You share my status as you share my life. Where I walk, you may walk. Where I stand, you may stand. And this victory belongs to all of us." He stretched out his hands and the claws from the night before reappeared, still stained with blood. "Bear your weapons proudly in hand so all may see how well we fought."

Jordan didn't know a whole lot about royalty and all that shit, but being allowed to keep a weapon in hand while approaching a head of state seemed like a damn big honor. He unhooked his bow from its place on his shoulder and cradled it comfortably in his hand. Next to him, Victor drew the pistol Nandini had given him and ejected the magazine with the remaining bullets in it. Those went in his pocket. Nandini followed his lead, and Quenti and Cusi hoisted their spears.

"The victorious warriors return," T'ukri intoned solemnly.

Jordan stood straighter, not quite at attention but close, shoulders back, head held high, as he fell into step with T'ukri, Victor on T'ukri's other side. Nandini, Quenti, and Cusi followed a few steps behind, and as they neared the city, Urpi joined them as well. As they passed the house they'd been offered until their bonding, children came running toward them with necklaces. T'ukri bent to let them place one over his head. The yellow and white beads and shells stood out against T'ukri's bronze skin. Then one young girl stopped in front of Jordan. Feeling distinctly out of place, Jordan bent to let her put a necklace on him too. As he straightened, the child gave the same salute that Quenti had given him at Nandini's camp. *Fuck. Even the kids?* He dutifully returned the gesture.

He glanced over to see Victor smiling as he returned another child's salute, a similar necklace around his neck. He was glad Victor was coping better than he was. They needed at least one rational head between the three of them.

Then they turned into the center of the city, where the temple with its golden statue was located, and Jordan had to stomp on the urge to turn around and march right back out again. The streets were lined with people, three and four thick, with not even enough space between them for the children to squeeze through. And everyone, from the oldest to the babes in arms, seemed to have put on their best clothes and jewelry for the occasion. Many of them had even found time to paint their faces with different markings.

One more thing for Jordan to learn.

As they passed, people started chanting in time with the pounding of hundreds of spears against the stone-lined walkways. Jordan didn't know what they were saying, but from the pride he could feel through the bond, T'ukri was pleased with the reaction. He stood a little straighter, let a hint of swagger into his stride, angled his chin a fraction higher, and let the sweet taste of victory wash through him.

As they approached the temple, Jordan caught sight of the king and queen, with Ch'aska standing beside them. T'ukri marched right up to the temple steps and crossed his left arm in front of his chest, claws on prominent display. Jordan hurried to imitate him. He couldn't see Victor without craning his head—and now didn't seem like the right time—but he was sure Victor had done the same.

When Huallpa and Llipya returned the salute, T'ukri snapped his arm down to his side, and silence fell over the entire valley.

"It would seem you have been busy during your absence," Huallpa said with an arched eyebrow.

Fuckity fucking fuck. They were in for it now.

T'UKRI KEPT his face impassive in the face of Huallpa's challenge and did not need to look to know his mates did the same. The guardian bristled at the tension he felt from Jordan, though. T'ukri tried to rein him in, but his fangs started to elongate. Then a wave of calm and confidence rushed through him.

Victor.

He had indeed chosen wisely when he picked Victor to be the one to guide him home.

"We did what needed to be done," T'ukri said simply. "The valley is safe, and those who would harm us have been eliminated."

Huallpa inclined his head in acknowledgment. "You have not returned alone."

T'ukri stepped to the side so Nandini was directly visible. "King Huallpa of Machu Llaqta, I present Nandini Rakkar, sister of the heart of my mate. Without her assistance, our victory would not have arrived as quickly or as smoothly."

Nandini bowed formally but did not speak.

"For your help in saving my son, you are welcome in Machu Llaqta," Huallpa said.

Again Nandini bowed silently.

"And the rest?" Llipya asked.

"We did what needed to be done," T'ukri repeated.

Anger clouded his mother's face, and he dreaded the storm to come, but she would not unleash her fury in public.

"See to your guests and join us."

"I have only one guest," T'ukri said.

"And I will see her settled comfortably, Your Majesty," Quenti interjected. "We are old friends."

T'ukri smothered a smile, knowing it would only invite more of his mother's ire, but it did not stop his amusement at Jordan's reaction to the sight of Nandini walking away between Quenti and Cusi, Quenti's hand low on her back. Cusi was a lucky man indeed.

"Come." Llipya swept Huallpa, T'ukri, Jordan, and Victor up in her wake.

JORDAN FOLLOWED the queen away from the temple, trying very hard not to think about Nandini going off with Quenti and Cusi. She was his sister, dammit. He didn't need to know that much about her sex life. He had no doubt she'd be burning off battle fever of her own now that she was safe and had someone to watch her back.

That was bad enough, but the waves of disapproval from T'ukri's mother were so strong he felt them like a fist in the gut.

"We're in trouble, aren't we?" he muttered.

"It will be fine, my own. She will rage, but what is done is done, and she will come around in time," T'ukri assured him.

Jordan wasn't reassured. His experience with raging parents hadn't ended well the last time around, and this time they had no reason at all to hold back, not that being related had ever kept his father in check either.

They followed Llipya in tense silence until they reached the palace. How the hell had it been less than forty-eight hours since they had first eaten there together? Waaaay too much had happened in that time.

As soon as the door closed behind them, Llipya dismissed the servants and turned on T'ukri. "Explain."

Jordan winced at her clipped tone.

"Mama," T'ukri said calmly. Jordan tried to bite back his reaction so he wouldn't mess with T'ukri's emotions, but while he was damn good at controlling his visible reactions, he'd always done that by letting them run loose in his head. He'd have to find another outlet.

"Do not 'Mama' me. Explain yourself."

Oh shit, they were in trouble. Even his fuzzy memories of his own mother were enough for him to recognize that tone. Behind the queen, Ch'aska rolled her eyes.

"Ch'aska, this conversation does not include you."

"I said nothing," she protested. Jordan could have kissed her for taking a little of Llipya's focus away from them, even if only for a second.

"See that it stays that way."

"The attack on the valley caught me by surprise. I had left my mates to reflect for a time and was lost in my thoughts," T'ukri began. Jordan had wondered what happened, but there hadn't been a good time to ask. Reassurance and love emanated through the bond with the promise that T'ukri was safe now. "Without a bond and without my mates nearby, I dared not release the guardian. I was outnumbered. I remember a blow to the head and then nothing until I woke in a small building, chained wrists and ankles to a metal chair. The ones who took me came in asking questions that I pretended not to understand. I spoke only Runasimi, and only to insist I did not understand and to ask to be set free."

"What did they want?" Huallpa asked.

"They sought the valley, in the hope of finding gold, and to see if the legends were true. They could hardly take control of the area if the mythical guardian of the Incas was real," Victor replied.

No, Victor. Bad idea. Let T'ukri tell it.

"And how do you know that?" Llipya demanded.

Told you.

"I heard some of what they were saying while we were getting in place to attack their compound and free T'ukri," Victor replied. *Damn,* Victor was a cool one. Jordan had always known he could project calm no matter the circumstances, but even with the bond letting him sense Victor's emotions, there was nothing but composed confidence.

"Go on," Llipya said, her voice still cold.

"We—Nandini, Quenti, Cusi, Urpi, and I—created a distraction to allow Jordan to sneak into the compound and free T'ukri," Victor continued.

She turned her glare on Jordan. Jordan did his best to project the same calm Victor did, but he was pretty sure he failed miserably.

"Mama," T'ukri said, drawing her attention back to him, "you gain nothing by trying to intimidate them. If you must be angry with someone, be angry with me."

"I am," she replied, "but I am waiting to hear the whole story first."

"I told you I was chained to the chair," T'ukri said. Jordan wouldn't blush at the memory of how good T'ukri had looked, shirtless and sexy as hell, or at what came after. He wasn't a child to be scolded for a perfectly normal human reaction. He wouldn't blush. He wouldn't blush.

He was blushing.

"Jordan tried to free me, but they used cuffs to hold me, not merely ropes he could untie. The only way to get free would be to get the keys from one of the people holding me or to let the guardian free."

"There was no other way?" she demanded of Jordan.

Jordan couldn't stop himself from standing straighter, as if he'd been called to attention. "Not if either of us was going to help with the fight outside," he replied as confidently as he could. "And with the odds already in the other side's favor, we had to help or some of them would have escaped, even if they didn't win. That would have been just as bad, because they were too close to the valley, and some had already found their way in."

"They will not find their way back so easily," Huallpa said.

"Yeah, I figured that out," Jordan said, still having trouble believing the valley seemed to have moved somewhere completely different, "but even so, they could make it impossible for anyone to come or go. I know you're self-sufficient, but I also know you send out wanderers. No one who is out would be able to come home if they set up a permanent camp in the area."

"With the guardian safely free, we won the fight, but the only way back for me was through my mates." T'ukri turned to look at his father. "You know what it is like, Papánin. This was no ceremonial change, nor proof to the ancestors that I could control the guardian. This was the bloodlust of battle. With no one left to fight, the guardian needed a different outlet. My mates were there and as eager to bond as I was."

That was the biggest understatement Jordan had ever heard.

"So you disregarded all of our traditions," Llipya finished.

They were digging themselves deeper and deeper, but Jordan didn't know what else they could say. They had done what they could in the situation they were in. He didn't know what else Llipya wanted to hear.

"Enough, my queen," Huallpa said gently. "T'ukri is hardly the first guardian to bond with his mates in the heat of the moment, and he is here before us, in control of himself and the guardian, so the bond is true. That cannot be denied."

It sounded like they'd managed to win the king over. That was a start, he hoped.

"I acknowledge you, bondeds of my son," Llipya said stiffly with a nod of her head to Jordan and Victor. Then she turned sharply on her heel and left them in the hallway.

Ouch. Okay, maybe not a start.

T'ukri grimaced. "That did not go as well as I had hoped."

Ya think?

"I do not know how you expected it to go differently when your bondeds have not even completed the rituals to be accepted as members of our tribe," Huallpa said. Then he turned to Jordan and Victor. Jordan braced himself for whatever Huallpa would say. He only hoped it wouldn't be an order to stay away from T'ukri, because that wasn't happening.

"Be welcome here, my sons. Llipya is a woman of many virtues, but even as her besotted mate, I cannot claim she does not also have her faults. Once the formalities are observed, she will come around."

Jordan jerked like he'd been shot. *Son.* He hadn't been anyone's son in over twenty-five years, and it hadn't been a very good experience the first time around.

"Breathe, Jordan," Victor said, slipping an arm around his waist. "We've got you."

And there, in the middle of the budding panic attack, was the bond and the love and support it offered. "Not sure I know how to be someone's son," he admitted to Victor and T'ukri.

"Then it is high time you have the chance to learn," Huallpa declared.

He must not have spoken as softly as he thought he had. *Fuck.* He was somebody's son again.

CHAPTER 35

"PAPÃNIN, I know we have more to discuss, but please, can you give us a few minutes? We have not eaten since yesterday, and it has been a challenging and emotional time," T'ukri said as Jordan's continued distress radiated through the bond.

"Ch'aska, will you see to juice and snacks for your brothers in my study?" Huallpa asked. "I will leave instructions that you are not to be disturbed. When you have refreshed yourselves, we must discuss Jordan's warrior trial and Victor's spirit quest. They must take place as soon as possible since your return left no doubt about your relationship."

"I know, Papãnin, and we will discuss them today. We just need a few minutes."

Huallpa rested one hand on T'ukri's shoulder. "I am proud of you. You have proved worthy of the title of Chapaqpuma and one day of the title of king."

T'ukri bowed his head in thanks for his father's blessing.

"Come, Ch'aska. We should leave them alone."

T'ukri almost defied Huallpa and led them to his rooms, but he had bucked tradition as far as he dared for one day. Instead he led them as Papãnin had said into his study.

Jordan was still in shock when they walked inside. T'ukri looked down at his torn and dirty pants as he sat on the couch and wished he had thought to ask for a change of clothes. He held out his arms and did his best to radiate calm as Victor pushed Jordan toward him. Victor sat down on Jordan's other side to wrap his arms around both of them.

Jordan lifted his haunted gaze to stare into T'ukri's eyes. "I told you about my parents and what happened after. I don't... I can't...."

His voice broke as he trailed off into silence and buried his face against T'ukri's shoulder. T'ukri looked helplessly over his head at Victor.

"That's the beauty of family," Victor said softly. "Real family, anyway. There's no right way to be. All it takes is acceptance and love. Just like with Nandini."

T'ukri's heart broke at Jordan's confusion and Victor's quiet words. "You will never be alone again, Jordan. Not as long as we live. And even then, you will have a place here. Nothing will ever take this home from you."

Jordan took a deep, shuddering breath and looked up with a tremulous smile. "Sorry. I got a little overwhelmed there."

"Nothing to be sorry for," Victor said.

"You have every right to feel overwhelmed," T'ukri agreed. "I have upended your life completely, and without telling you all of it ahead of time. We must get through the next few days. Then we will have time to ourselves to settle into our new relationship and our new lives. You both have much more to adjust to than I do, but I will also need time to grow used to our bond. Once it has settled fully into place between us, it will be a source of great strength and comfort, but right now it is disconcerting for me to sense your emotions as well as my own, and I am sure it is the same for you." They needed to talk about what he had overheard, but he would not bring it up now, with Jordan already so upset. He no longer doubted them, with all the devotion he could feel through their bond.

Jordan laughed a little, a watery sound but better than the choked gasps from before. "Just a little." He reached for T'ukri's hand and gripped it tight. "But I don't regret it. I'm sorry it happened the way it did because it's made things complicated now, but I'm not sorry it happened. Okay?"

"Okay," T'ukri said.

"Food is here," Ch'aska called from outside the door. "You better be decent."

"As if we would be anything else in Papãnin's study," T'ukri called back.

Ch'aska looked suspiciously at all three of them as she carried in a tray filled with juice and fruit.

"These trousers are torn beyond repair," T'ukri told her. "Can you find a new pair for me? I do not know what the rest of the day will bring, and it will go better if I do not look like a beggar. And perhaps you could send for Jordan's and Victor's things as well. They are still at the other house."

Ch'aska snorted and then gave Jordan and Victor a critical once-over. "I cannot do anything to help with Mama, but I can make sure your things are brought here."

"Just our clothes," Victor said. "We'll get the rest of our gear later."

"Bring the outfits they wore to dinner as well," T'ukri said. "They will need those for the bonding ceremony." It would probably be a day or two before they could complete the warrior trial and spirit quest, no matter how much he argued to have them expedited, but it did not hurt to be prepared.

"They will be the first things I get," Ch'aska said. "Though I imagine you will be more comfortable in your own clothes during your seclusion."

They would not need any clothes at all during that time, but T'ukri would not say that in front of Ch'aska.

"Is that like a honeymoon?" Jordan asked.

"Yes," T'ukri said.

"Then I'd think clothing of any kind would be optional."

Jordan had decided to say it for him.

Ch'aska blushed and hurried out of the room.

"You shouldn't tease her like that," Victor scolded.

"Yes, you should," T'ukri replied. "Otherwise she forgets which of us is the elder."

VICTOR GROANED at the thought of Jordan and T'ukri ganging up on Ch'aska if she got too full of herself. T'ukri really didn't know what he was unleashing. He shook his head and wrapped his arms more tightly around Jordan and T'ukri. Jordan might have been the most shocked at Huallpa's ultimate welcome, but Victor had felt an echo of it as well. It had been so long since family had meant anything but duty to him. It wouldn't be like that here. Even Llipya's anger, as disconcerting as it was, obviously came from a place of love for her son and concern for his future.

"Huallpa mentioned a warrior trial and spirit quest. Can you elaborate?" Victor requested. He'd always done better with a clear plan, even if it went sideways the moment they began.

"First we eat," T'ukri said. "I was coming to find you, before the valley was attacked and I was taken, to explain everything the council had decided would be required for you to become citizens of Machu Llaqta. I had hoped our bonding today, however precipitous, would make such things unnecessary, but it appears I was wrong."

"What does *everything* entail?" Victor asked.

"According to our tradition, Chapaqpuma takes one mate who is a warrior and one who is a shaman, so you must each be accepted into those guilds. All warriors undergo a test of skill, which Jordan will have no trouble completing, I am sure. As a shaman, you must undertake a spirit journey to prepare yourself for your new role within the tribe. Once those two things are done, we will go to the temple and declare our intention to bond before the elders, the ancestors, and the goddess. Then we will speak our vows to one another. And then we will feast until we can slip away for our time of seclusion," T'ukri elaborated.

Jordan pushed out of their embrace. "When can I start?"

"Your enthusiasm does you credit, churi, but you fought yesterday, through the night, and then bonded with Chapaqpuma. You are exhausted. You would do yourself no favor by beginning now, not when the trial must be completed in a single day," Huallpa said from the doorway. He looked at the untouched tray. "You have not eaten yet. The guava is sweet, or if you prefer something different, I can send for it."

"Guava is fine." Victor took a piece for himself and offered one to T'ukri. Jordan shook his head when Victor held one out in his direction, too anxious still to eat. Victor sent soothing thoughts tentatively in his direction, not sure it would work. Jordan looked at him in surprise, so something had gotten through. "Tell me about the spirit journey."

"A spirit journey is a rite of passage that we undergo before momentous occasions in our lives," T'ukri explained. "The transition from youth to adulthood, from apprentice to master, from tribe member to elder. To a lesser degree, my seeking the approval of the ancestors for our bonding could be considered one as well, though that was less about facing my own fears and more about demonstrating the strength of my commitment to our courtship."

Huallpa sighed. "If Yuri were here, he would guide you through this spirit journey, for becoming Chapaqpuma's mate is more complex than taking any other mate within the tribe, more so as you were not born into our traditions. I have asked Tamya to guide you instead. If anyone can help you, it will be her."

At least it would be someone Victor knew.

"But that too will wait for tomorrow. Like Jordan, you are tired, and while the danger of a spirit journey is not physical, it would not do to lose yourself on the metaphysical plane."

"So warrior trial and spirit journey tomorrow and bonding ceremony the day after?" Jordan asked.

"That would not be a good idea," Huallpa replied. "Your bond is too new for you to attempt both on the same day. Instead of strengthening each other, you would be a distraction to one another. No, while I understand your desire for haste, it is better to do one each day and complete each ritual successfully. Tomorrow at the earliest, Victor will undergo his spirit journey. Jordan will face his warrior trial the day after. And on the third day you will appear before the goddess and complete your bonding ceremony." He fixed them each with an implacable stare. "And in the meantime, you will remain in the house provided while T'ukri resides in the palace, as is proper."

Victor swallowed down the protest that rose in his throat at the edict. The echo of it in the bond assured him T'ukri and Jordan were just as unhappy about it as he was.

"Is that truly necessary, Papãnin?" T'ukri asked.

"You are not simply a citizen of Machu Llaqta," Huallpa reminded him. "You are Chapaqpuma and my heir, and you have brought back outsiders as mates. If you do not wish to risk a challenge to your position, you must observe tradition, and that means not bonding until your mates have been accepted into the tribe."

"It is too late for that."

"But the only ones who know without doubt that are unassailably loyal to you. Do not give fuel to those who would seek to fan the flames of dissent. I will give you some privacy to eat and discuss all you have learned. Do not make me regret my faith in you."

Victor frowned as Huallpa left. He hadn't realized the royal succession was in question. Something else to ask T'ukri about when they had a minute. Then again, the panel on the temple after Huallpa, Llipya, and Yuri had been blank.

"Wow, NOTHING like putting pressure on us," Jordan griped when Huallpa left. "I mean, sure, I said I'd do the warrior trial today, and I meant it—I mean it—but I didn't realize how much was at stake. Could someone really challenge your position as prince?"

"It is possible," T'ukri replied, "though I do not think it likely. Only two people have the standing to do so—Ch'aska and my cousin Micay—and Ch'aska adores you. Micay might do it with enough provocation, but she is not even in the city at the moment."

"Still, it means we need to get this done as fast as we can," Jordan said.

A knock on the door interrupted them. T'ukri opened it to allow a servant to enter with a larger meal, meat of some kind along with rolls. Jordan's stomach rumbled, making him realize just how hungry he was. Fine, he'd eat, but as soon as he was done, he was going to the training grounds, and someone was going to explain to him exactly what the warrior trial entailed so he could prepare for it. He'd ask T'ukri, but that would distract from the focus on Victor's spirit journey, and that wouldn't help any of them. "I don't like the idea of anyone being able to use us against you, no matter how remote a possibility it is."

"Agreed." Victor filled a plate from the tray and handed it to Jordan before making a second one for himself. "I will need to talk with Tamya if I'm to complete the spirit journey tomorrow, but my Runasimi isn't good enough to understand everything she tells me, so I can't do that alone."

"I can accompany you," T'ukri offered. "If Jordan does not mind going to the training grounds alone?"

"There'll be someone there who can talk to me, and if not, shooting doesn't require anything other than a target," Jordan replied. "You can fill me in on the details of the warrior trial after Victor's spirit journey. You did do one of your own, didn't you?"

"I did," T'ukri said. "And I have no doubt you will complete it with no trouble. It is a formality, nothing more, not for a warrior of your skills."

Jordan wasn't so sure, not because he doubted his abilities but because he still didn't know what would be required of him here.

As soon as he finished his meal, he kissed Victor and T'ukri, resisting the urge to linger, and headed for the training grounds. If he only had two days to prepare for the test that would determine whether he'd be accepted as T'ukri's mate, and if one of those days was going to be spent supporting Victor through his own test, he was damn well going to take advantage of what little daylight he had left today.

Most of the warriors ignored his arrival, but Llipya turned to face him, her spear in hand.

"Your Majesty," Jordan said, hoping he wasn't about to get stabbed.

Llipya twirled her spear and eyed him speculatively. "It has been a difficult day. I find practicing with my spear a good way to release tension."

Jordan nodded and held up his bow. "Do you mind if I join you?"

Llipya shrugged and gestured toward the piles of straw set up as targets. Jordan stepped up beside her but didn't immediately draw. She gave him the side-eye, but when he simply waited, she shrugged again and threw her spear with enough force to embed it deeply into the target. He whistled appreciatively. T'ukri had said she'd been quite a warrior when she was younger. Seeing her now, he believed it.

"You are as formidable as ever, my queen."

Jordan turned to see Quenti descending the final steps into the training grounds, a loose, satisfied smile on her face.

Nope, not thinking about what might have put that there. He half expected to see Nandini right behind her, but Quenti was alone. Actually, that might have been worse.

"You should ask her if she would be willing to teach you," Quenti said to Jordan.

"I'll take her up on it if she will. That was an impressive throw," Jordan said. "Although I'm also hoping someone will teach me Runasimi. During the fight yesterday, I couldn't understand what everyone was saying, which made it harder to know how I could help. I don't have to be fluent, but basic directions, formations, that kind of thing are a necessity if I'm going to fight alongside you."

"A reasonable request," Llipya replied, unbending a little at the compliment. "I have heard tales of your abilities with a bow, but I have not yet had a chance to see them. Impress me."

Jordan grinned, sure it had a maniacal edge to it. He never turned down a chance to show off.

Two hours later, Jordan was still grinning. He had shot and shot at progressively smaller and more distant targets until Llipya had admitted to being impressed. Then she and Quenti had demonstrated their abilities with their spears, both as a ranged weapon and as a staff to use in close quarters. Then they had proceeded to kick his ass and rap his knuckles until they were bruised as they made him practice with them. Short of sparring with Nan, he couldn't remember the last time he'd had so much fun while training. Only after they had left him feeling like a newbie all over again did Llipya offer him her spear. "Throw it. Let us see if your aim carries over when you must use a different weapon."

Jordan took the spear with due reverence, quite sure Llipya didn't give just anyone her personal weapon. He sure as hell didn't. He took a moment to appreciate its beauty and its balance before weighing it more carefully. When he had its measure, he turned to the nearest target and sank into the same heightened awareness that always accompanied his shooting. Then, mimicking their form, he took a step forward and hurled the spear toward the target. It hit dead center.

Oh yeah. He still had it.

"Most impressive," Llipya said as Quenti tossed him a waterskin and leaned against one of the towering tree trunks.

Jordan took a sip of water to cover his reaction to the praise. "I've always had good aim. I mean, I've worked my ass off to perfect it, but even the first time I picked up a bow, I hit the center ring, although not the bull's-eye."

Llipya nodded sagely as if his statement were completely expected. "The goddess's gifts are many."

Jordan tried not to bristle at that. He'd worked damn hard to perfect his aim. "Hard work had a little to do with it."

"Of course it did. Even the most powerful gifts must be nurtured to come to fruition."

Jordan had even less of an idea of how to deal with that, so instead he turned to Quenti. "Well? Do I pass?"

"Were it only a question of my approval—of our approval—I would give it and call you one of my warriors immediately," Quenti said, "but every warrior who wishes to lay claim to the title here must prove his or her worthiness through a series of challenges."

"What kind of challenges?" Jordan asked, serious now where he'd been joking before. He'd had to certify in all kinds of skills in the military, so he had some experience proving his abilities in a standardized way, but he wasn't sure that was what Quenti meant.

"Some are straightforward, like demonstrating your aim or sparring against another warrior to prove your skills, which you have amply demonstrated yesterday and today, but the final trial is more of a survival test. Your goal is to reach the temple while a group of warriors do their best to keep you from doing so. Spears and arrows all have blunted or covered tips so the candidate will not be hurt, but if they strike you with one, you are disqualified and have to continue training before you can try again. Likewise if they can pin you in combat, you are disqualified. If you make it to the temple, then you are accepted among our ranks," Quenti explained.

"A gauntlet of sorts," Jordan said. "Or an obstacle course with more than just physical obstructions. I can do that. Huallpa said the day after tomorrow."

"He is correct," Llipya said. "Support Victor through his spirit journey, and after that is done, you can undertake your trial. And in the meantime, you can work on protecting your legs with the staff. I should not land so many hits to your knees."

"That's what Nan always tells me," Jordan muttered.

"She is a skilled warrior," Quenti replied, and this time her smile gave no doubt to what she was thinking.

Jordan grabbed the spear they had let him borrow and pushed off the tree. He wasn't going there, no matter how big an opening Quenti gave him.

CHAPTER 36

VICTOR EXPECTED T'ukri to take him back to the temple when they left the palace, but instead T'ukri took him toward a small house that sat between the palace and the temple.

"Hatunmama?" he called as he neared it. "Are you home?"

Victor didn't hear an answer, but T'ukri must have heard something because he didn't hesitate to go inside. Victor followed more slowly, unsure of his welcome in a stranger's home.

"T'ukri!" Tamya exclaimed as she hobbled into the front room, leaning heavily on her cane. Victor didn't understand the spate of Runasimi that followed, but Tamya smiled and gestured for them to sit.

"Victor must complete a spirit journey," T'ukri explained when Tamya had finished fussing over him.

She nodded sagely and turned to him, saying something in Runasimi. "Have you entered the spirit world?" T'ukri translated.

"No, my grandfather was an Mbochi shaman, and he always intended to teach me, but he died before he initiated me in their ways," Victor replied.

"The process itself is simple," Tamya said through T'ukri. "When you are ready, you will drink a tea made with ayahuasca, a special herb that will help you reach the spirit plane. Once you are there, your journey will begin. The rest will be up to you."

"Up to me in what sense?" Victor asked.

"Every spirit journey is different," she explained. "For some—and in some situations—it is as simple as speaking with the ancestors and receiving their blessing on whatever step in life has brought you to the quest. For others, it is more complicated. If the step requires a significant change or effort, it could mean facing fears or demons from the past that have yet to be fully settled in that person's mind. Which it will be for you is something I cannot predict. Perhaps not even something you can predict, for we often do not know ourselves as well as we think we do. This is why we make these journeys—to help us know ourselves in ways that will help us in our future endeavors."

Victor frowned. What could he possibly need to know about himself that he hadn't already learned as he struggled to earn his degrees and to convince people of the validity of his research? He knew his abilities, his strengths and weaknesses, to the nth degree. He had to. Granted, being accepted as a shaman was a far cry from being an academic, but the different expectations didn't change who he was.

"How long does a spirit journey usually last?"

"There is no 'usual' duration. For some, it is minutes. For others, it lasts for days."

Days. They didn't have days. He was supposed to complete his spirit journey tomorrow so Jordan could do his warrior trial the following day and they could have their formal bonding ceremony the day after.

"Relax," T'ukri said, breaking into Victor's spiraling thoughts. "It will take the time it will take, but I do not think it will take days. Not for you."

"I hope not."

A flash of heat through the bond was T'ukri's reply. Victor did his best not to squirm and give them away. He didn't know if Tamya had been there to see them return earlier with T'ukri's fangs and claws on full display or if she would know what it meant if she had seen, but if she didn't know, he didn't want to be the one to give them away now.

"Is there anything else I need to know?" he asked Tamya. "If not, I will prepare tonight and begin in the morning. It is getting late in the day, and I am already tired and hungry. I doubt that's the right mindset to start a quest."

"You are wise," Tamya said. "I would have encouraged the same decision if you had asked my opinion."

"And if I had simply gone ahead and said now?" Victor asked, curious about how much guidance she could give.

"I would have asked if you were sure, if you had considered all aspects of the situation, but the journey is yours, not mine. If you had insisted, I would have prepared the ayahuasca while you summoned your mates," she replied. "My role is to guide, not to dictate, and wisdom comes from experience more easily than from the counsel of others."

Victor chuckled, thinking of all the times he'd tried to convince Jordan of the wisdom or lack thereof when, well, anything was concerned. It had taken a long time before he fully trusted Victor's assessment of situations when their opinions differed. "I have a bit of experience with that."

Tamya smiled in return. "I have no doubt. I *have* met your mate."

Victor groaned. "Is T'ukri as bad as Jordan?"

Through the bond, he felt T'ukri's protest, but T'ukri didn't say anything except to translate Victor's words into Runasimi.

"I do not know Jordan well enough to say for sure, but I know T'ukri quite well." Tamya's eyes twinkled as she smiled at T'ukri before continuing, "You will have a time tempering that impulsiveness. There is a reason Chapaqpuma needs someone to guide them home."

T'ukri did splutter at that, but Tamya soothed him gently.

"I won't fail them."

"I never thought you would. T'ukri would never have picked you otherwise," Tamya replied. "But the formalities must be observed, for not all are as confident as I am, and you would do yourself and your mates no favors by opening up your place to criticism or questions now or in the future."

"I knew we'd have to convince people to accept us even before I knew T'ukri was a prince," Victor said. "I wouldn't be here now if I wasn't willing to do what it takes."

"Which is why you are the right mates for T'ukri, no matter what some may say about outsiders. The goddess's ways are mysterious and not for us to understand. You will be a great boon to our people. You have only to give them time to realize it."

"As long as it takes."

"Then enjoy your evening with your mates and come to me in the morning, rested and well-fed, and we will begin your journey," Tamya said.

Victor thanked her and let T'ukri lead him out of the Tamya's house.

"Can we walk a little before we return?" he asked T'ukri. He needed to think some first. About what it would mean to go on this spirit quest and what he might have to face, at how he would explain… well, any of this later if he had to. He didn't question his commitment to Jordan and T'ukri, or even to Machu Llaqta, although that was newer. It was more a matter of how different it was compared to the life he had created for himself up until now.

"Of course, my own," T'ukri said. He led Victor to an out-of-the-way place and sat with him under a huge tree. Victor closed his eyes and let it all roll around in his head.

He'd been sitting there for several minutes without making any great breakthroughs when T'ukri took his hand. "You are troubled."

"Not troubled, exactly," Victor said. "Just thinking about the spirit quest and what that might mean. I understand the urgency, and delaying would not do anything to reassure me, but a part of me is… apprehensive."

"Understandably," T'ukri said. "Spirit quests are never easy. They are not meant to be. But the first is usually the hardest because you have no idea what to expect."

"What was yours like?" Victor asked.

"Which one?" T'ukri asked. "I completed one when I grew to adulthood, as do all Runa, another one when Tayta died and the mantle of Chapaqpuma passed to me, and a third when I sought the approval of the ancestors on our bonding."

Victor considered that. "The one when you became Chapaqpuma, I think. It seems most like what I'm going to do, since it's so I can become a shaman."

"It may well be a combination of all three," T'ukri warned. "Since you did not do one as a boy becoming a man."

"I haven't been a boy in a long time," Victor reminded him.

"And yet the children we were live inside us always," T'ukri replied. "But I will tell you of the quest for Chapaqpuma." He shifted a bit, getting comfortable. "I always knew I would be Chapaqpuma one day, although the gifts of the goddess pass to the one she chooses, not always through the royal line, so I did not go into the quest with doubts about my ability to fill the role. Instead I went in with perhaps too much confidence in my abilities as a warrior and in the strength of mind and spirit it would take to live with the guardian and control it until I found my mates. The ancestors took it upon themselves to teach me humility."

Victor flinched. "That doesn't sound pleasant."

"It was not. I was forced to face futures in which my arrogance destroyed both me and Machu Llaqta. Over and over until I accepted that I was a man like any other and that the goddess's gifts were gifts, not something I had or ever could deserve. Only then did I envision a future that I could accept. The faces of my mates were blurred in the vision, for I had not met you and Jordan, but it gave me hope that I would find you in time. While a spirit quest is meant to teach us, the goddess and the ancestors are not cruel. They will not promise a future that cannot be attained. Not easily attained, perhaps, but attained nonetheless."

"So that means I'll have to face scenarios where I fail, either as a shaman or as a mate?" Victor asked.

"I cannot imagine it would be so," T'ukri said. "My visions came from my weakness. I do not see your wisdom and compassion as weaknesses, because while you rely on them, you are not deaf to the considerations of others. I have listened to you and Jordan talk and plan. When we were coming here, you knew your strengths and weaknesses. You encouraged him to hunt rather than insisting on doing it yourself, though I have seen you shoot. You could have hunted for us."

"Not as well as he did."

"That is exactly my point. You knew he would be better, so you encouraged him to do it while you took care of other pieces of the journey. And both he and Quenti have told me it was your plan that resulted in my freedom. And my mother told me of your choice to guard the temple during the initial fight. You are confident in your skills but not blind to others' strengths, and you do not grab for glory but rather place yourself in a position that utilizes everyone's skills most effectively. That is far different from my own reaction when I became Chapaqpuma."

"If not that, what?" Victor asked.

"Sometimes even a quest that is undertaken for one reason ends up being about something else entirely," T'ukri said. "Once we enter the spirit realm, the reasons for being there are less important than the lessons we need to learn while we are there. Tayta always said that the reason we function as well as we do as a people is because we trust that our spirit journeys will teach us what we need to know about ourselves, and that learning those lessons makes us more honest. When you cannot hide from yourself, you have fewer reasons to hide from others. Of course, that is not infallible, but on the whole, it has served us well."

"Whatever the spirits think I need to learn about myself," Victor said with a sigh. "That isn't terribly reassuring."

"Just remember that you are not alone," T'ukri said. "Jordan and I cannot enter the spirit world directly to be at your side. We would end up on our own quests if we tried, but our bond, even as new as it is, is a powerful thing. Lean on us as you face your trials, and draw strength from our love and belief in you."

Victor nodded and stood. He offered T'ukri a hand and, when he took it, pulled him into a tight embrace. "Thank you. I needed that."

"Anything I have to give, it is yours," T'ukri replied. "That is what our bonding means."

"I know," Victor said. "I'm just still coming to understand exactly how deep that goes."

T'ukri kissed him, a combination of tenderness and passion that Victor was fast becoming addicted to. "Tonight, if I can sneak away, we will show you how deep our faith in you goes so that tomorrow you will go into your journey armed with all the strength we have to offer."

"I'll take it."

T'UKRI SAID good night to his parents and returned to his rooms to pace on silent feet until the palace grew still. He considered bathing again, if only to pass the time, but he had done so before dinner, and doing so again would increase his frustration at being denied his mates' presence. They should be sharing his rooms and his bath. He should be lavishing attention on them in the pool in his room, not prowling alone until he could sneak away like a thief in the night.

And yet, here he was, a caged animal waiting for his chance to escape. When he deemed enough time had passed, he pushed open the covering on his window and climbed out. It was a long drop to the ground, but not so much he could not manage.

He ghosted through the shadows until he reached the house where Jordan and Victor were staying. Lamplight flickered through the shutters. Good. They were still awake. He rapped lightly on the doorframe before pushing the cloth aside and slipping inside.

"About damn time you got here." Jordan pulled him into a kiss almost before the cloth fell back into place, a kiss T'ukri returned gladly. The guardian, restless after hours with little chance for intimacy with his mates, purred in contentment.

"Victor?" T'ukri asked when Jordan broke the kiss. As much as he desired Jordan, he had two mates, and it would not do to neglect either of them.

"Perhaps we should move away from the door first," Victor suggested. "And the windows, since I doubt your visit is an authorized one."

"It is not," T'ukri admitted. "I waited until my parents slept and jumped out the window."

Jordan snickered. "That was my trick when I was a kid. I didn't expect it to be useful as an adult."

"Not that I'm not glad to see you, but is this a good idea?" Victor asked. "Jordan and I are on thin ice here. I don't want us to get kicked out before we have a chance to complete the rituals. That might make it hard to be your mates."

T'ukri shook his head. "That will not happen. Yes, my mother is right that you must be accepted as members of the tribe before we can be bonded in the traditions of my people, but we *have* bonded in all the ways that matter. Nothing can undo that." He had not asked Llipya and Huallpa if they could still sense one another now that the gifts of Chapaqpuma had passed to him, nor would he, but they were as in tune with one another as they had ever been.

"You said earlier today you were coming to tell us about the spirit journey and the warrior trial when you were captured, but there's more to that story, isn't there?" Victor asked.

"There is," T'ukri admitted as he smothered a yawn.

"Here's an idea," Jordan interrupted. "Let's go in the other room and get comfortable while we talk. You are staying, right?"

"The goddess herself could not drag me away," T'ukri replied.

Victor raised an eyebrow.

"Although perhaps my mother could," T'ukri amended.

"Bedroom?" Jordan repeated.

It was the best idea T'ukri had heard all day. He picked up the rush lamp and led his mates to the bedroom. He set it carefully aside and stripped off the wrap that was all he had bothered to put on after dinner before reaching for Jordan and Victor. He had not had the luxury of undressing them before their bonding, too lost in the guardian to take the time for such niceties, but he reveled in the chance to do it now. He started with Jordan, lifting the T-shirt over his head. Victor started to remove his own T-shirt, but T'ukri caught his hand. "Let me. Please."

Passion flared in Victor's eyes, and T'ukri knew he had made the right call. The heat and rush of their initial bonding aside, it was care and tenderness his mates craved. He removed Victor's T-shirt next and ran his hands over both their broad chests. "I am a fortunate man, to have such strong and virile mates. I will be the envy of all Machu Llaqta when we leave the temple and go to our bonding bed."

"You said we bonded already," Jordan said.

"We started, certainly," T'ukri replied, "but surely we have not exhausted all the possibilities already. And each time we make love, whether with tenderness and love or fire and lust, we strengthen the bond anew. That is the secret, you know. We never reach the end of our bonding, just because the ceremony and the time of seclusion are complete. If I remember correctly, it is your turn to be in the middle, my malku."

Jordan shivered at T'ukri's words, and T'ukri resolved to make the next time the slowest, most pleasurable yet. Anything to make Jordan look at him like that again. He unbuckled Jordan's pants but did not push them down.

"I will let you take care of your boots while I take care of Victor."

Jordan had them off in a flash and went back to watching T'ukri with that hot, sharp gaze T'ukri could already feel like a caress. T'ukri pushed a burst of love and heat through the bond, hoping it would work in the sending as well as the receiving. His parents had reached that stage by the time he was old enough to ask about their bond, but he had never asked how quickly it developed. From the look on Jordan's face, some of it had gotten through. Later, when they had more time, they could test it and even practice to see if they could speed up the development, but they had other priorities now.

T'ukri bent to look at the bruise on Victor's collarbone. "Which of us left this little souvenir?"

"I don't know," Victor replied. "You both seemed to like that spot. Does it matter?"

"Not at all," T'ukri said. "I was curious, nothing more."

Victor dealt with his own shoes as T'ukri turned back to Jordan and slid his hands inside the heavy pants to pull Jordan flush against him. The fabric dropped to Jordan's knees and, with a little shimmy from Jordan, to the floor. "As soon as we reach our seclusion, this is how I will keep you until we must return to our duties. I cannot get enough of touching you. Either of you."

"It's mutual," Jordan said, rutting against T'ukri's thigh. Great goddess, T'ukri wanted to bear his mates onto the bed and take them now, one, then the other, until none of them could even think of moving.

He turned to Victor and stripped him as well. Victor pressed a biting kiss to T'ukri's collarbone, exactly where the bruise was on his own chest.

"How many rules are we breaking?" Victor asked when he lifted his head.

T'ukri laughed. "All of them, but the ceremony is a formality now. You are my bondeds as I am yours. It is only right that we should prepare together for the trials that will allow us to announce it to the world."

"To the world, huh?" Jordan asked breathlessly as T'ukri bore him down to the mattress.

"To my world." T'ukri reached for Victor and pulled him into bed as well. "If you wish to announce it to those in your world also, we would have to discuss when and how."

"Unfortunately, our old world wouldn't recognize our triad, but this is our world now," Victor replied.

"Damn straight," Jordan said. "Nandini is here, and no one else needs to know."

"No one? I...." T'ukri looked down, unable to meet their eyes. It would break the mood to bring up his doubts, but they were alone now, something he could not guarantee would happen again before their bonding ceremony. More importantly, if he was to support Victor through his spirit journey tomorrow, he needed to put his own doubts to rest first. "I told you I was coming to see you before the battle. I overheard you talking. Something about upending everything the world knew about South American development and telling Dr. Fowler? I am ashamed to admit I feared the worst."

"Machu Llaqta—the history in the temple here, everything about the city and the people in it—does upend our understanding of South America prior to the arrival of the Spanish," Victor said, his hands falling to his sides. "And the anthropologist or team of anthropologists who first broke the story would become legendary in academic circles and possibly beyond. Hiram Bingham is mentioned in classrooms the world over for his discovery of Machu Picchu." He reached out and took one of T'ukri's hands in his own. "Six months ago—merde, six weeks ago—I would've given anything for that kind of academic recognition. Then I met you and we came here. While I'd still love to rub my colleagues' noses in the fact that they were wrong about Philli-philli—or Chapaqpuma—being just a figment of overactive imaginations, I'm not going to do it because I would *never* endanger you or the valley that way."

"We're here to stay." Jordan bumped T'ukri with his shin. "We talked about it the night we got here and realized what this place was. I don't have any family except Nan. Victor's estranged from his family. As long as he sends them a postcard from time to time, they won't even know the difference. We'll have to go back into town to tell Fowler we quit—that's what we were talking about telling him—but beyond that, you're stuck with us. As far as anyone else is concerned, we just... fell off the face of the earth."

"Or into a valley in the Amazonian headwaters and never came out." Victor squeezed T'ukri's hand. "Are we okay now?"

T'ukri smiled at them, relief flooding through him at the realization that all his worry had been for nothing. He had told Palta, Umaq, and anyone else who would listen that Jordan and Victor were good men, worthy of being his mates. He should never have let them call that into question. "Better than okay. Will you let me explain why I reacted the way I did?"

VICTOR CURLED around T'ukri and felt Jordan do the same on his other side. "We were threatening your home, your friends, your very way of life, or so you thought. I'd say you were pretty justified," Jordan replied.

"Yes, we will listen if you want to explain, but Jordan's right. You don't need to," Victor said.

"I think perhaps I do. The Runa are taught two things from the time they are old enough to understand."

Victor nodded against T'ukri's shoulder. If nothing else, they would need to know this as adopted Runa. He could feel his brain switching over to fact-finding mode, the same as when he was on an expedition.

"The first is that we owe our safety, and indeed our very existence, to Pachamama. The second is that we are never to reveal our existence to outsiders."

Victor flinched a little as he remembered how many people had referred to them as outsiders since their arrival. T'ukri had broken some serious conditioning to bring them home.

"As we grow older and capable of more discernment, outsiders become divided into categories. Some, such as Paucar, are only partially outsiders. He is not part of our tribe, but he keeps to many of the old ways and so has some awareness of us. He knows I am prince of Machu Llaqta, for example, though he could not find the valley without help. He does not know I am Chapaqpuma. He does not even know for sure if the guardian is real or part of our lore. Others—even tribesmen from farther afield—are true outsiders and know nothing of our existence. To them, I am a wandering guide looking for work and willing to take people on excursions into the rainforest."

Exactly what they had taken T'ukri for up until the moment he told them he was a prince. Bon, d'accord, Jordan had mentioned some oddities, but nothing concrete enough to act on. "You do a good job with that cover," he told T'ukri.

"I have had much practice," T'ukri replied with a small smile. "When we finally reach the age where we can wander if we choose, we learn one final lesson: that betraying our secret is a punishable offense, one that will result in our banishment. You have seen the goddess's hand in action. Only those who know how to look can find the entrance unless someone leads them there. A banished Runa cannot find the entrance again. The goddess will not allow it unless the banishment is lifted. For most of us, it is the worst fate imaginable. I have always had wandering feet, but the idea of never being able to return.... I truly do not know if I could go on, were that to happen to me."

It made sense now, T'ukri's fear that they would publish a paper revealing the existence of the valley or worse. It would not only spell disaster for the valley itself but also the end of T'ukri's connection with his people.

"We won't tell anyone," Jordan said before Victor could. "We wouldn't do that to you, I swear. Even if for some reason we left—we aren't going to, but if we were forced to—we wouldn't tell anyone. Not about Machu Llaqta or about Chapaqpuma."

"I know that now," T'ukri said. Victor tested the bond a bit only to feel T'ukri's absolute confidence in them. Relief flooded through him. They might have things to answer for still, but they had put at least one set of fears to rest. "But can you see why I kept my secrets as long as I did? If you had rejected my suit before we arrived in Machu Llaqta, I could let you go. If you had known, I would have spent the rest of my life worrying you would let something slip and that I would lose my place in Machu Llaqta—and perhaps my life—because of it."

"I get not saying anything until you were sure of us, but why didn't you say anything about Chapaqpuma once we got to the valley?" Jordan asked. "By that point you knew we were here to stay."

"I thought I knew," T'ukri said. "I was coming to tell you when I overheard you talking about the paper—what I thought was the paper—and telling Dr. Fowler. All I could think was that I had shared my secrets with people who were now talking about betraying me. I needed time to compose myself, to talk myself out of the irrational spiral of thoughts that threatened to overtake my good sense, and then I was captured."

"I still wish we'd known," Jordan said. "Maybe the initial fight would have gone better and you wouldn't have been captured. At the very least, we wouldn't have had to suffer through Ch'aska trying to explain to us what bonding meant." Jordan's cheeks went pink at the memory.

"I wish I could have seen that," T'ukri said with a chuckle. "I was working up to telling you. I would never have bonded with you without telling you, but it was hard to find the right moment after saying nothing for so long."

Victor nodded in understanding, thoughts of his first encounter with Philli-philli—Chapaqpuma—coming to mind. He had kept that secret for twenty-five years. Not from T'ukri exactly, but that didn't make it easier to bring up now. "When did you know you were destined to be Chapaqpuma?"

"I always *believed* I was destined for the role," T'ukri replied with a chuckle, "but you have been to the temple. My grandmother showed you the murals.

"Wait. Tamya is your grandmother?" Victor asked.

"Yes. She is Tayta's mother," T'ukri said. "I thought you knew."

Victor shook his head. "No one mentioned it."

"Another thing for which I must apologize." T'ukri ran a hand over his face. Victor caught it and gave it a tender squeeze.

"No need to apologize. We've rather turned your world upside down in the past two days. We'll figure everything out with time. What about the murals?"

"The role of Inca—of king—is hereditary, but the role of Chapaqpuma is not," T'ukri said. "Or not necessarily. So while I believed I was destined to take the role after Papãnin, I did not know for sure until the guardian stirred within me after Tayta's death."

Victor nodded again, trying to do the calculations in his head, but Urpi had left by the time Tamya reached modern times, so while he had understood that Huallpa had been Chapaqpuma before T'ukri, he did not know when he had taken on that role. "How long was your father Chapaqpuma?"

"Close to thirty years," T'ukri said. "The gifts of the goddess make Chapaqpuma nearly impervious to attack, but they are no protection against sickness. Papãnin's mother died before I was born, and that robbed Inti, the previous Chapaqpuma, of the stability he needed to continue in the role."

And that answered the question Victor still did not know how to ask.

Jordan poked him in the ribs. "Tell him."

"Tell me what?"

"That Huallpa saved my life when I was sixteen and on a summer dig in Vitcos," Victor said. "It's what made me decide to go into anthropology, specifically into studying the tribes of Peru. Regardless of what people in professional circles say, I knew there was some truth to the legends, and I hoped one day I'd get the chance to say thank you. I never imagined the valley, you, and all the rest, but I'll certainly take it."

"How long ago was this?" T'ukri asked.

"Twenty-six years," Victor said.

"Soon after I was born but when he was not yet king." T'ukri pursed his lips, lost in thought. "I remember a time when he was often gone, but few of the details. Only that Mama and Tayta always seemed upset when he was not there. I was too young to ask or understand at the time, but now I can only imagine how it must have been for them, knowing he was out there alone, unable to go with him because they had to stay with me."

Victor shuddered at the thought and felt Jordan do the same. "It hasn't even been twenty-four hours and I can't begin to imagine. If something like that happens, you're taking us with you."

"Damn straight," Jordan said.

T'ukri smiled. "I would have it no other way."

"I owe Huallpa my life," Victor said. "When the time is right, I would very much like to thank him."

"Papãnin will tell you he was fulfilling his calling from the goddess in defending those who could not defend themselves, but I too owe him my thanks," T'ukri said. "If he had not been there, we would not be here now."

"In more ways than one," Victor replied. "Even if I had survived, I wouldn't have pursued Philli-philli with the same passion if I hadn't seen him. I probably would have viewed the stories with the same skepticism as most of my colleagues, and I certainly wouldn't have applied for a grant specifically to study the origins of those legends. And without that—"

Jordan rolled Victor onto his back and silenced him with a devouring kiss. Victor opened beneath it, letting Jordan take what he needed to calm the panic in the bond. The sense of his lovers might be new, but it was already most useful. He didn't have to guess at what Jordan was feeling anymore.

He reached blindly for T'ukri as well, more to include him than because T'ukri needed the same reassurance Jordan did in the moment. Finally Jordan lifted his head, panting as he stared down into Victor's eyes.

"I'm here and perfectly safe, and Huallpa did show up at just the right moment to save my life and set it on the course it followed so that we could all end up right here, right now."

"Where you belong," T'ukri added. "The goddess's ways are always mysterious, but this is one time when faith is easy."

Jordan barked a sharp laugh. "I'll say. I kinda like this goddess of yours."

T'ukri bumped his forehead against Jordan's. "She has claimed you both as surely as she has claimed me, or we would never have been able to bond. You might think about claiming her in return."

Jordan did his best stunned deer impression, much to Victor's amusement.

A yawn overtook T'ukri before Jordan managed to recover from his shock. He shook his head, as trying to push away the weariness. Then Jordan yawned as well.

Victor chuckled and rolled away long enough to extinguish the lamp. "Sleep," he ordered. "There will be time for sex in the morning."

CHAPTER 37

MUCH TO T'ukri's dismay, there was in fact not time for sex in the morning. He awoke to sunlight filtering through the shutters. He muffled a curse as he scrambled for his wrap, regretting now that he had not worn a tunic and pants. If he had, he could have claimed an early morning walk if anyone saw him, but in only a wrap....

"We still have the outfits we borrowed the day we arrived," Victor said sleepily. "They won't fool your mother, but they'll be less obvious than a wrap from a distance."

"As smart as you are handsome, my own," T'ukri said, dropping a quick kiss on Victor's lips. "But now I must return to the palace. I will meet you at the temple for your spirit journey if I do not see you sooner. Not even my mother can keep me from being at your side as you undertake that quest. I swear it."

"Go," Victor said, his voice gentle and his aura soothing through the bond. "We will see you in a few hours at the most."

T'ukri dressed quickly in the ill-fitting clothes. They would not fool anyone up close, so T'ukri would still have to be on his guard if he did not want his mother to learn of his midnight stroll.

He would not be able to pass through the city unseen in daylight as he had at night, so he left through the back, hoping to move through the forest surrounding the city instead. He had gone no more than ten meters when he heard Cusi's drawl. "Did you have as good a night as I did?"

T'ukri spun around to face his oldest friend, the brother he had never had. Cusi wore the smuggest smile T'ukri had ever seen on his face—and that was saying something after all the adventures they had undertaken together. "You would not believe me if I told you," he said after a moment. After all, they had only slept, and Cusi would never believe that when their bonding was less than a day old.

Cusi laughed. "Nor would you if I told you. Here. You will need these if you wish to get back inside without everyone else knowing."

T'ukri took the bundle of his clothes from Cusi. "Where did you get these?"

"Urpi got them from Ch'aska. She saw you leave last night and thought you might want them this morning. Sneaking out in just a wrap? Really, T'ukri? Has your bonding stolen all your common sense?"

T'ukri groaned. "Who else knows?"

"I do not keep secrets from my mate," Cusi said, "and Nandini was there as well when Urpi brought your clothes. If your mates are half as intriguing as she is, you are a lucky man indeed."

Cusi did not know the half of it. "The goddess has blessed me beyond my wildest dreams. You cannot tell anyone of this until the formal bonding ceremony has taken place. Mama is... not pleased as it is. I do not wish to anger her further."

"Nor does anyone with any sense," Cusi replied. "More than that, we are your friends. We will tell no one. Now, change your clothes quickly and let us finish our morning walk back to the palace together so that if anyone wonders where you have been, they will realize you came to take counsel from your oldest friend."

T'ukri laughed. "Or maybe they will think you needed counsel from me. Which of us has more experience with new and intriguing outsiders?"

Cusi shoved him lightly. "Which of us has more experience with women?"

JORDAN'S GRUMBLING woke Victor from the doze he'd drifted in and out of since T'ukri left. He rolled over and buried his face in the pillow, trying to block out the sound, but Jordan poked him until he opened his eyes.

"You promised me morning sex, but T'ukri left already."

Victor huffed and looked toward the window where the sunlight filtered through the slats in the shutters. "We were more worn out than any of us realized, I guess." He scrubbed his hands across his face. "We should get up and get ready. I don't know when we'll be expected at the temple to start the spirit journey, but I don't want to be late."

He sat up, groaning at the aches in his muscles. He was getting too old for this.

Jordan mumbled something behind him and tugged the pillow over his head. Victor ignored him and pulled on a pair of underwear before going into the other room to clean up. They didn't have a bathtub, but the water that ran into the basin was warm, and he could use that to wipe himself down and to shave so he was presentable.

When he was dressed, he went back into the bedroom to wake Jordan, only to find him up and dressed. "Give me five minutes to shave and we'll find breakfast and then get this thing done. The sooner we start, the sooner we finish, right?"

"Right." Victor caught his hand and pulled Jordan into his arms. "Thank you."

Jordan's brow wrinkled. "What for?"

"For everything. But mostly for being here with me."

Jordan kissed him, hard and fast. "Always."

And that? That was worth the spirit journey, his career, his immigration status, and everything else.

He let Jordan go because if he didn't, they'd end up back in bed, and that didn't feel right without T'ukri there, plus he didn't know when someone would come looking for them. Instead he went into the main area of the house to wait for Jordan to finish.

"Victor?" Urpi called from outside. "I brought breakfast again."

T'ukri really did have the best friends. "Come in. Jordan is just finishing up. He'll be out in a minute."

They ate quickly, Urpi regaling them with stories of T'ukri, Cusi, Quenti, and herself as children. It was exactly what Victor needed to distract him from the worry and tension of the upcoming spirit journey.

When they were done, Urpi gathered up the remains of their meal and said, "Come, I will take you to the temple. Tamya will be waiting for you there, and if I know him at all, T'ukri will as well."

The thought of T'ukri waiting for them sent a jolt of awareness through Victor in a way the stories of T'ukri's childhood hadn't, and the bond stirred to life in the back of his mind. It was an odd thing, dormant and nearly forgotten when T'ukri wasn't around. Somehow he didn't think it was supposed to be that way, but he couldn't do anything about it except to jump through the hoops laid out for him and hope delaying the formal bonding didn't cause irreparable damage.

"Alli p'unlla, Tamya," Urpi called when they reached the temple.

"Alli p'unlla," she replied with the kind smile Victor had already come to appreciate. As Urpi had predicted, T'ukri was there as well. When

Tamya continued speaking in Runasimi, he translated for her as he had done the day before. "Will you take tea with me before we begin?"

"That would be nice," Victor replied. "If nothing else, it will give us time to explain everything to Jordan. T'ukri knows what to expect, but Jordan would probably appreciate a rundown of what's going to happen."

"Of course," Tamya said as she set out four cups and poured a light amber liquid into each. "This is just an herbal tea I enjoy in the morning. Nothing to worry about."

"Is there something to worry about later?" Jordan asked sharply.

"No quest is without risks," Tamya replied. "It is rare on a spirit quest for the danger to be physical, but there are cautionary tales of taking too much of ayahuasca and not returning from the spirit realm. I have never seen it happen myself. And Victor has more reason than many to return to this plane when his journey is done. Not everyone is fortunate enough to have two devoted mates and the goddess's blessing on their bond."

Victor looked at T'ukri sharply. He hadn't realized Tamya knew they'd started to bond, but T'ukri's face was serene and no distress came through his mind, so whatever the situation, it wasn't something Victor was going to worry about now.

"All right," Jordan said, only slightly mollified. Victor squeezed his knee to reassure him. "So what's going to happen while he does this?"

"It will appear as if he is sleeping," Tamya said, "except perhaps for movement of his eyes. Physically there is no challenge. It is all inside his mind."

"You saw me on my quest for the ancestors' blessing," T'ukri said. "It will be much like that."

"The day I wondered if you'd stopped breathing," Jordan said.

"At least this time, you will be close enough to check," T'ukri said.

Jordan huffed a laugh. "That's some consolation." He looked back at Tamya. "So the challenges he faces internally won't affect his physical body at all. Like, if he gets hurt in a fight, the wounds don't carry over?"

"No, they would not. As long as his body is unharmed here during the quest, he will feel no effects other than some exhaustion when he awakes. And with you keeping guard, I have no fear harm will come to him here."

"Hell no, it won't," Jordan muttered.

"Do you have other questions before we start?"

"Just one. Are we allowed to touch him or talk to him during his quest? Like if we feel him struggling through the bond?"

"I do not know that any such intent will get through to him in the other realm, but it breaks no taboos for you to do so," Tamya replied. "If nothing else, it would provide some comfort to you, which can only help strengthen your bond. You must understand, child. We use the term *bonding* for all who wish to pledge their lives to one another, but the kind of bond you share is unique, and so we know much less about its effects than you might wish. Very rarely do Chapaqpuma or their mates undertake these quests, mostly because Chapaqpuma themselves are rare among our people—only one at any given time— and they do not always have a need for a spirit journey during their tenure."

"So Victor becoming a shaman isn't something all guardians' mates do?" Jordan asked.

"One of Chapaqpuma's mates is always a shaman, but rarely is that mate not yet a shaman when the bonding occurs," Tamya said.

Victor finished his tea. "I'm ready unless Jordan has more questions."

"Not that I can think of," Jordan said.

"You may ask them at any time during his quest," Tamya said. "I will not leave the temple grounds except to fetch more water if we need it. If the quest lasts into the night, someone will bring us food."

Days. She had said a quest could last for days. Victor *really* hoped his wouldn't be that long. Jordan was supposed to undertake his warrior trial tomorrow so they could have their bonding ceremony the day after, and Victor didn't want anything to delay that. Plus, Jordan would worry, and he'd have enough on his own without adding Jordan's fears, no matter how reasonable.

"I will ask one last time, Victor. Are you ready?"

"As ready as I'll ever be," he muttered. She smiled at him as T'ukri squeezed his shoulder.

After listening to Jordan's descriptions of how T'ukri had painted his face before his own quest, Victor had expected Tamya to do the same for him, but she only counted out six leaves into a fresh cup and crushed them with a pestle until they were almost powder. Then she poured boiling water from a kettle over them and swirled it around. Victor took the cup gingerly and sniffed.

"Give it a moment to finish steeping and to cool a little," she said. "You do not want to burn your tongue."

Victor blew across the steaming surface to help it cool faster. He didn't want to wait so long that his nerves got the better of him. After about a minute, Tamya said, "It should be ready. You can drink it whenever it is cool enough."

"All of it?" Victor asked.

"The more the better," Tamya replied. "The taste is not strong. It should not be hard to swallow."

Victor took a deep breath, looked at Jordan and T'ukri for reassurance, and drew a mouthful of the brew into his mouth. It tasted a little earthy, a little floral, but not strong or bitter. He swallowed and took more. He didn't know how fast it would work, and Tamya said he should drink as much of it as he could. By the third swallow, he could feel the beginnings of the effects, a little blurring around the edge of his vision, a slight buzzing in his ears, just enough to obscure the others' conversation without blocking their voices.

He took another quick swallow, then drained the rest of the cup and set it by his knee. As the blurriness in his vision increased, he reached blindly for Jordan and T'ukri, but if he managed to find them, he couldn't say because suddenly he wasn't in the temple but in a vague, misty landscape that resembled nowhere he could ever remember being.

Huh. So there was something to this spirit realm.

Bon, so he had to take a journey and find his way home. Home meant Jordan and T'ukri now. T'ukri had said as the bond developed, they would be able to use it to find each other. Focusing his mind, he searched until he could feel it, but it remained distant, like a staticky phone connection or the lag of an overseas call. Still, that was a place to start, so he walked in the direction their bond wanted him to go. He'd taken only a few steps when his father's voice sounded to his left.

"What *are* you doing, Victor? With your brains, you could do anything—be anything—you wanted, and instead you've chosen, what? A life of derision because you never gave up your delusions about that Philli-philli nonsense, and now a life of... nothing in the wilds of Peru? You're a disappointment and a disgrace to us, you know."

Victor hunched in on himself at his father's attack. He had never said any of these things to Victor's face, but Victor had learned to read people a long time ago, and his father's attitude had been clear. The words hurt. No, he didn't regret the choices he'd made, but that didn't make it any easier to know he'd disappointed his parents so completely.

Not real, he reminded himself, except this was his spirit quest, which meant these were his issues to face and overcome. He would've said if asked that he'd come to terms with his family's disapproval, but in truth, he was more resigned than anything else.

"I made the best choices I could at the times I made them," he said because he had to say something.

His father snorted in derision. "Total failure right up until you decide to go bushman and end up in a gay ménage with a country bumpkin who wouldn't know culture if it bit him and a tribal nobody who calls himself a prince. I thought we'd imparted some sense of taste, but I see I was wrong."

Victor could not let that pass. "You don't know the first thing about them if that's all you see. They are two of the most admirable men I know. Say what you want about me, but leave them out of it."

"How can I?" his father sneered. "They're the reason you're doing this. They're the ones who've brought you low."

"No," Victor insisted. "They're the ones who've lifted me up. They make me want to be a better man so I can be worthy of them."

"Better man? How about gayer man? You're such a fag that one wasn't enough for you. You had to play bottom boy for *two* men. What does that say about you that it takes two men to fuck you hard enough?"

Victor laughed. Bitterly, maybe, but he had to laugh. It was the one piece of himself he reveled in. "Attacking my sexuality isn't going to get you anywhere. I came to terms with that a long time ago. As for the rest, either one of them would be enough for me. I'm just lucky I get to be with both of them."

"And how long will that last? How long until they get bored with you and drop you like the pathetic old man you are?"

"Which of us is pathetic?" Victor retorted. "You're the one who's never done anything more exciting than work in an office. Respectable job, respectable wife, 2.5 kids since we all know I barely count in your eyes. Everything about you is respectable, but what did you ever accomplish? Whose lives have you changed with your respectable choices and caution? I've seen places you've only dreamed of, traveled to more countries than you could list, and I've done that in the service of humanity through my research, no matter what you think of it. The world is a *better* place because I'm in it. Can you say the same?"

"This isn't about me, though, is it? This is about you and all the things you know deep down you won't get to do if you follow this path." The mist cleared to show Victor his parents as he'd last seen them, his brother and sister there as well, all gathered around the dining table with the remains of a large family dinner waiting to be cleared away. "This is what you're walking away from. Can you live with that?"

"I've lived with it for years," Victor replied.

"Maybe, but there's always been a chance things might improve, that the next phone call might include an invitation to come home. That invitation will only ever be for you, though. If you stay, it will never come. There's no place for *them* at this table."

Victor gave the scene one last, longing look. His father was right. Jordan and T'ukri would never fit in that idyllic scene. Victor's mother had a pleading look on her face, like she was asking him to deny everything she'd heard, but he couldn't. To do that would be to deny himself. Even more, it would be to deny his mates. If he had still been alone, he might have gone back, tried to pretend he still fit in that picture, but he wasn't alone now. He had Jordan and T'ukri and a whole new kind of family.

"There hasn't been room for me at that table since I came out," he said slowly. "Maybe you could accept me if I pretended to be straight—or at least bi—but I'm not. I'm gay. I like cock. I like it in my mouth, I like it up my ass, and I like mine in another man's mouth or ass. If it weren't Jordan and T'ukri, it would be some other man, and you'd never accept that either. As much as I regret the way things ended between us, there is no going back that wouldn't be a lie, and I won't do that to myself. I'm not a child anymore, desperate for your approval. I earned the respect of my peers in the field, and now I have the love of two amazing men. And through T'ukri, I have a chance at a new family, one who will embrace me exactly as I am instead of insisting I conform to someone else's idea of who I should be and how I should live my life."

"Are you sure?" his father scoffed. "Then why are you wearing their clothes and participating in their rituals?"

"Because I have the choice," Victor said firmly. "And I have chosen this tribe and these lovers who will carry me to a future that's brighter than anything I ever imagined for myself. The fact that you can't imagine it for me is your problem, not mine."

"If you do this, there's no going back. Our bonds are broken for good."

Victor closed his eyes against the sadness that evoked. He'd never wanted to lose his family, but he had never found a way to keep it from happening. "I'm sorry you feel that way, but I have to follow my heart. If you can't be happy for me at finding my own happiness, then there are no ties to break anymore. I will always love you, but it's been a long time since you've acted like a father to me."

"On your head be it," his father said as the mist enveloped the family scene. His mother's sobs resonated, but when he took a step forward to comfort her, there was no one there.

He sank to his knees and let the tears flow for the relationships that ended. The fact that they had ended years before was of no consequence. He had said goodbye to them for good.

JORDAN FROWNED at the apprehension he felt through the bond. This was the first time he'd felt anything this strongly other than desire when they weren't touching. Victor wasn't supposed to be in any danger, so what could be making him react like that? He reached for Victor's hand and tried to push all the love and reassurance he could through the bond. He didn't know how it worked, but it couldn't hurt. Could it?

"Spirit quests have a tendency to drag up the worst of our fears and doubts to make us face them," T'ukri said. "But Victor is strong, and he has us to act as a beacon to show him the way home."

Victor's doubts and fears. *Fuck.* That could be any number of things, from the insecurity about his age (which was ridiculous, but Jordan had yet to get him to believe that) to feeling like he was letting down the university by leaving to… hell, for all Jordan knew it could go back further than that. Victor's childhood hadn't been as fucked-up as his own, but his relationship with his family was strained.

Or it could be something else entirely. Jordan didn't claim to know everything about Victor, even if he was pretty sure no one knew him better. "We can do that," he said to T'ukri. "Whatever he's facing in his head, we're stronger. Isn't that the point of the bond? To give all of us the things we need when we don't have them in ourselves?"

"That is one way to put it," T'ukri said. He scooted closer to Victor and bracketed him with his knees. "But it cannot hurt to provide a tangible reminder that we are here as well."

CHAPTER 38

VICTOR FINALLY pulled himself up and focused on Jordan and T'ukri again. His sense of them had grown stronger, which both saddened and delighted him. His confrontation with his family had cemented his relationship with his mates that much more, but it felt like an unfair choice to have to make. Except Jordan and T'ukri weren't the ones putting that choice on him. His family had forced that choice on him years ago, and he'd resigned himself to their distance. Or so he'd believed. Maybe he hadn't accepted it quite as much as he'd thought if they could still bother him in this realm.

That was a question for Tamya and for later. For now he had to focus on what mattered, and that was finding his way home. He followed the tug from his heart and let it guide him through the thick mist. He'd hoped it would clear a little as he went, but if anything, it thickened to the point he could find no distinguishing features to help orient himself. For all he knew, he could be going in circles.

Don't think like that. Focus on the goal. That's how you get yourself safely home.

The mist cleared again to reveal the valley this time, although Machu Llaqta was not visible. Jordan slunk forward from tree to tree, dressed in camouflage and armed with his bow. He even had his face painted to help his skin blend in to the surrounding foliage. As Victor watched, a spear flew out of nowhere and embedded itself in a tree trunk an inch above Jordan's head. Jordan flinched and shrank deeper into the undergrowth, barely visible even to Victor, who knew where he was.

Victor started to ask Jordan what was going on, but that would give away Jordan's position. If someone was hunting him, which seemed likely given Jordan's clothes and the spear quivering above his head, Victor didn't want to do anything to put him in more danger.

No, that wasn't right. This was just a trick of the spirit realm. Jordan wasn't here. He was safe in the real world. And Victor could say that a thousand times. It didn't stop him from flinching when Jordan let out a pained grunt from his hiding place.

Not real, Victor reminded himself as he crouched down and started to crawl toward Jordan's position. He had to face this and get through it, but it wasn't real.

Jordan didn't show any signs of noticing Victor as he burst from his hiding spot and sprinted for another group of bushes about fifty yards away. Shouts rang out from the trees, the cadence familiar enough for Victor to identify it as Runasimi without being able to understand the words, and a hail of spears and arrows followed immediately. Jordan dove for cover, but one of the arrows hit him in the thigh.

Not real, not real, Victor chanted silently as he tried to figure out how to get to Jordan without getting hit himself.

He wasn't a soldier, his obligatory military service aside. Furthermore he had never wanted to be one. He could shoot straight enough to hunt and to protect his expedition team if it came to that, but the fight to rescue T'ukri was more action than he'd seen in years, and he liked it that way. While he would never voluntarily leave Jordan—or anyone—to be hurt, he wasn't anyone's ideal for the perfect rescuer. Nor was that supposed to be his role in the valley and in their triad. He was the shaman, the advisor, the voice of reason, not the fighter. So why was he here now?

"Ready to give up, Malku?" someone called.

That wasn't right. No one called Jordan malku except T'ukri. Did that mean the attackers were from Machu Llaqta?

"Fuck you," Jordan shouted.

The insult resulted in another barrage of arrows into the copse of bushes where Jordan had taken shelter. Victor broke cover and raced in that direction, praying to whichever gods and goddesses might be listening that he wouldn't end up with an arrow in the back. He had to know if Jordan was still alive.

No, Jordan was alive. Victor could feel him in the bond, in the real world. This was a test, nothing more.

He scrambled through the bushes until he found Jordan, an arrow sticking out of his chest. "No," he gasped, searching for something to stabilize it. "Hold still. Let me see."

"Too late," Jordan said, blood bubbling on his lips as he struggled to speak. "Beware the traitor pr…."

Not real, not real, not real.

Which would have been more effective if Jordan didn't feel so heavy in his arms. "I'm sorry," he whispered.

In the distance he heard an inhuman roar and flinched at the pain and desperation in the sound. That was Chapaqpuma, only he had lost one of his mates and he was alone. Torn, Victor looked between Jordan's body and the forest surrounding him. He could do nothing for Jordan now, but he might offer T'ukri some consolation.

The compassion to bring him home. That was Victor's role in their relationship, if he could find T'ukri in time. He rose from his hiding place and started into the forest, only to have T'ukri drop down in front of him.

He had seen Chapaqpuma as a boy when it was Huallpa who bore the title and again when T'ukri had bonded with them. Even at the height of transformation, Victor had been able to see the human in the animal, but as he looked at T'ukri now, bent forward onto all fours, claws and fangs fully visible, the humanity in his face was gone, leaving Victor face-to-face with a puma. "No," he said. "No, not you too, T'ukri."

The puma roared at him in reply. He could be forgiven for not saving Jordan—not that he would forgive himself, but others would say it was not his job—but bringing T'ukri back from the brink was his job. He stretched out his hands and focused on how much he loved and needed T'ukri, now more than ever, but the puma flinched away from him with another low rumble. "It's just me, mon amour," he said softly. "I won't hurt you."

The puma snarled and sprang away into the mists. Victor took a step to follow him, but it was hopeless. Not even the best tracker would be able to follow T'ukri under these conditions.

Not real, he told himself again as he sank to his knees in despair.

Jordan wasn't dead. T'ukri hadn't lost himself in the guardian. They were safe in the temple, waiting for Victor to return from this gods-bedamned spirit journey. This was a test, not reality.

Jordan and T'ukri. He had to focus on Jordan and T'ukri. If he could find them through the bond, he'd know they were safe and that this was just a waking nightmare. He'd had those before—flashbacks and panic attacks. Not in years, granted, but he knew how to deal with them. Focus on the tangible, the here and now.

Except he wasn't in the here and now. He was in the spirit realm.

No, that didn't matter. No matter what realm he was in, he knew what was real. He focused on his feelings for Jordan and T'ukri, on their newly formed bond, opening himself to it as fully as he could. It wasn't as strong as he'd hoped, but he could feel Jordan and T'ukri, separately as well as a blend of both. He clung to that feeling, drawing strength from the fact that while he felt their concern, he didn't feel any pain or distress. Jordan wasn't *really* lying dead in the forest. T'ukri wasn't *really* lost to grief and the guardian, somewhere in the mists. They were in Machu Llaqta, in the temple, waiting for Victor to come home.

He could still feel the blood on his hands and still hear T'ukri's feral cry, but he blocked them out in place of the bond. He wished it allowed him to hear words instead of just feel emotions. He could have used a few positive voices in his head at the moment, but the bond didn't work that way. He would be satisfied with the bedrock of love and trust and the memory of just how thoroughly they had made love when they had bonded the day before. If it had only been that long.

Time didn't work right in the spirit realm, but he couldn't worry about that. He had to think about completing his quest. Whether hours or days had passed in the mortal world, it wouldn't matter if he couldn't find his way back.

No, he couldn't think like that. He had Jordan and T'ukri to bring him home. And with the bond wide open, he knew exactly where to go. He just had to get there.

T'UKRI BENT nearly double under the onslaught of fear and anger from Victor.

"The fuck was that?" Jordan asked.

"I wish I knew." T'ukri probed the bond as deeply as he knew how. "Something he saw or heard hit him painfully hard."

"Yeah," Jordan muttered. "Let me tell you. This fucking sucks. No way of knowing what's going on, no way of helping. Nothing to do but sit here and wait. It's been four hours already. How long is he going to have to suffer?"

"As long as it takes," T'ukri replied, though he was not nearly as sanguine as he sounded. "And it does not have to be all suffering. Often a spirit quest will show what we desire most as well as forcing us to face our fears."

"He sure as hell is facing fears," Jordan said. "He could use a few good dreams at the moment."

"Then we must do what we can to help him find them," T'ukri said.

"How? I thought we couldn't influence the quest."

"We cannot directly, but even now, the bond works both ways. Just as we can feel his fear and anger, he can feel us. We must share our strength with him when his begins to fail."

"Yeah, okay. It would help if we knew what he was afraid of."

"Even not knowing the details, we can assure him of our faith in him and our love for him that is stronger than any challenge he might face in the spirit realm," T'ukri said.

"You sure about that? We've both got some pretty nasty demons in our pasts."

"Do any of these demons, as you put them, change the way you feel about Victor?" T'ukri asked.

"Not one fucking bit," Jordan swore.

"Then your faith and love are stronger," T'ukri said. "And while I may not know the face of all his demons, I know the core of him. Of both of you. Whatever pieces of your past haunt you, they do not change that you are good men. And that is all I need to know. Everything else is superfluous."

"Okay," Jordan said. "Then let's bring him home."

T'ukri reached for Jordan's hand, completing the circle of the three of them and digging as deep as he could, focusing all his love and faith and desire into the bond. When Jordan did the same, the emotions were so strong T'ukri could almost see them in his mind. He squeezed Jordan's hand, and as one, they *pushed* until the ball of emotion moved from between them to surrounding Victor.

Enough, T'ukri hoped, to bring him back to them.

"MY MATES are capable in many ways, but it would seem preparing you for this quest and especially to be the rock on which our son will rely is not one of them."

The unknown voice startled Victor out of his spiraling thoughts. "Excuse me?"

"Ah, but I forget. You do not recognize me. I am Yuri, Huallpa's and Llipya's mate," the man said. Victor studied him. In his eyes he saw both the kindness and the mischief from T'ukri's and Ch'aska's stories. Except, of course, this was a projection, his own imaginings, not the real Yuri.

"Am I not real?" Yuri asked. "Of course nothing I could say now will convince you, but when you return to the physical plane, ask T'ukri how old he was when I caught him kissing Atoc behind the temple. He will splutter and claim he did not know what they were doing, that they were just children playing at being their parents. And then when you ask him again how old he was, he will admit that he was five."

Victor blinked. He didn't even recognize the name Yuri mentioned, much less the rest of the story. Perhaps he had been hasty in judging the reality of this realm. "What is it I need to know?"

"There are many answers to that question," Yuri replied, "but the first is that you may be the rock on which T'ukri relies, but he is still the author of his own choices. The second, from the vision you just had of failing to bring him back to himself, is that you need do nothing. Your very existence is all he needs to reclaim himself from the guardian, but his success or failure in doing so is up to him. If he is determined to lose himself to the guardian, nothing you can do will stop him."

"I'm not sure if that makes things better or worse."

"Neither," Yuri replied. "It simply makes them as they are. You fear failing T'ukri—both of them, really—to have had the vision you just did, and while there are many ways in which you might fail them, the one you focused on is not among them. Your touch, even your voice, *will* settle the guardian. If T'ukri ignores that and retreats into the cat within him, it will be because he chose it."

"Is there nothing I can do to avoid that tragedy? I have heard the stories," Victor asked.

"Perhaps, but you will need more training as a shaman first," Yuri replied.

"More training? I haven't had any training," Victor said.

"Have you not?" Victor spun at the sound of his grandfather's voice. "Did you learn nothing from the summers at my side, Mayangi?"

"I wondered when you would arrive, Elombe," Yuri said. Victor had not heard anyone use his grandfather's given name since his grandmother died. "It seemed odd that I should be the one guiding your grandson rather than you."

"You know each other?" Victor blurted out.

Nkóko sighed. "I had hoped you continued your studies after my death, but it seems you did not. The place we are in goes by many names and serves many functions, but just as we all live on the same plane in life, we inhabit the same plane in death. Yuri and I have become fast friends over the past few weeks."

"Give him some credit, Elombe. He has studied many things that have led him here as the goddess intended," Yuri said. "And he can still learn what he will need to know for his new life. Our people have many able shaman to guide him when he returns to the mortal plane."

"I don't understand," Victor said. The goddess had intended him to be here?

"No, I don't suppose you do," Nkóko replied. "Each of us has a path laid out before us, one we can choose to walk or not, but one that, if we accept it, will lead to a life of fulfillment and grace. Your path has led you here."

"Even the chosen path is not without its challenges," Yuri continued. "But the goddess blesses those she has chosen for greatness. T'ukri has the guardian. Jordan has his aim. You, mate of my son, are the descendant of shaman with all the power and responsibility that entails, but it is up to you to learn to harness that potential. We— Elombe, my mother, the other shaman of the Runa, me—we can guide you, but as in all things, the decision must be yours."

"But—"

"We have said all we can and perhaps more than we should have," Yuri interrupted. "Cleave to your mates and your bond. The rest will come in time."

Victor opened his mouth to insist, to ask the thousand questions that assailed him at their revelations, but only the mist remained.

Cleave to your mates, they said. Victor could do that. He *would* do that. He closed his eyes, not that he could see anything with them open, but Nkóko had talked about seeing with an inner eye when Victor had visited him as a child. He focused inward, seeking a different kind of vision, until he found the bond. It pulsed gently at his core, a soft, golden presence that strengthened him. He took a deep breath, letting the awareness of his mates suffuse his soul until he felt ready to face whatever challenges lay ahead.

CHAPTER 39

VICTOR STRODE forward confidently, basking in the warmth of the bond. He could hear shuffling sounds on either side of him, but he didn't let them distract him. He had more important things on his mind and two mates to reach.

As if summoned by the thought, T'ukri and Jordan appeared in front of him. Relieved, he took another step forward, only to hit a wall. He couldn't see it, but it wasn't letting him through to his lovers.

Damn the spirit realm and this stupid quest. Victor wanted his mates, and he wanted them now. He pounded on the wall, hoping to get their attention, but they didn't turn his way.

Bon, he'd find some other way to get in. He ran his hands up the wall as high as he could reach, looking for a seam, a crack, even a chip. Anything that would indicate a weakness or an end he could get over or under or through. Even reaching all the way up onto his toes, he couldn't feel a top, though, so he worked down to the bottom, but the surface was infuriatingly smooth.

On the other side of the glass—it probably wasn't glass, but it felt that way to Victor—Jordan pulled T'ukri into his arms and kissed him so deeply, so thoroughly that Victor felt himself react to the sight of it. He'd been on the receiving end of a few of those kisses himself. Actually, he could use one of them now. He edged to the left. The wall had to end somewhere, and when it did, he was going around it so he could join them.

To his frustration, it curved instead of stretching out straight, letting him circle Jordan and T'ukri as they slowly stripped each other bare without letting him get any closer.

Eh bien. If he couldn't join them in this realm, he'd just keep going the way he had been toward the tug of their emotions until he got home to the physical plane and could join them for real. The spirits weren't going to stymie him this easily.

He turned away and focused on the bond, basking in the love and reassurance he felt. Whatever the spirits had thought to torture him with by showing him Jordan and T'ukri together, his faith in them was stronger.

It had to be.

He took three steps forward before he hit another wall. Letting out a sigh of frustration, he set his hands against it and followed it, but it only forced him back around to look at Jordan and T'ukri, completely naked and stretched out on T'ukri's bed. They were still kissing, but they'd started petting each other while he'd had his back turned. For all their surface differences, they were so much alike it almost hurt to look at them together.

They were so goddamn beautiful, both of them. He didn't doubt that they loved him and wanted him, but looking at them together, he couldn't help wondering what they saw in him.

Jordan kissed his way down T'ukri's broad chest to suck on his cock. T'ukri threw his head back and grabbed at Jordan's shoulders as he thrust into Jordan's mouth. Victor pressed a hand to his groin, willing down his erection. He wasn't going to jerk off in the spirit realm to a hallucination of his lovers. That was one step too far.

"Hurry," T'ukri said to Jordan. "Victor will be home soon."

Victor frowned. That wasn't right. T'ukri wouldn't say something like that. He wanted them all to be together. He had said so from the beginning.

Jordan didn't reply, and Victor couldn't see his face at that angle, but he pushed down, taking more of T'ukri into his mouth, deep-throating him like a champ. That could mean he agreed with T'ukri, but it could also mean he was simply horny and wanted more of T'ukri's dick. Victor chose to believe it was the latter.

T'ukri came seconds later and pulled Jordan up to kiss him deeply. He'd started to reach for Jordan's cock when something drew their attention. Victor watched in growing horror as an older version of himself tottered into the room, feeble and stooped over a cane—a beautiful, no doubt handmade cane, but a cane nonetheless. He was wearing glasses, larger and thicker than the ones he only needed for reading, and behind them, his eyes were clouded and rheumy. He'd lost all but a few embarrassing tufts of hair across the back of his head, and what little he still had was a dull, steely gray, not even an elegant white or silver.

Jordan sprang from the bed to take his elbow and help him over to it. Older Victor didn't seem to take any notice of Jordan's nudity or even his erection. Instead he hobbled with Jordan's support to take a seat on the edge of the mattress. Jordan knelt and helped him slide off his sandals—sandals! Like he couldn't simply slip them off himself— and propped him up against the headboard like an invalid.

"Just rest," Jordan said as he tucked a blanket over older Victor's legs. "I'll get you something to eat."

T'ukri patted his knee before reaching down for his discarded clothes and pulling them on. He didn't give older Victor another glance as he left the room. Jordan came back a few moments later with a tray, which he set across older Victor's knees. He pulled a chair from somewhere and sat down to cut older Victor's meal into small bites, which he proceeded to feed him.

Victor grimaced. He might be nine years older than Jordan and an unknown amount older than T'ukri, but he wasn't infirm yet.

No, his traitor mind replied, *but you will be. They'll still be young and beautiful, and you'll be ancient and of no use to them. How are you supposed to keep T'ukri grounded when you're like that? You'll be lucky if he doesn't lose control and go rogue.*

"Stop," he said with a shake of his head. "I'm not that much older than they are."

Old enough, the voice sneered as Jordan wiped older Victor's chin. *Useless. That's what you'll be to them. A burden they'll have to see to on top of all their responsibilities to the throne.*

Victor covered his ears, trying to block out the voice, but it did no good against his inner fears. They loved him and wanted him now, and Jordan obviously still cared about him if he was taking care of him so tenderly, but the older version of himself hadn't even spoken. Could he still function as a shaman in the state he was in? He'd been somewhere other than their room at the beginning of the scene, so he was doing something, however slowly. Then again, it could have been the Runa equivalent of a doctor's appointment rather than anything helpful.

"FUCK THIS," Jordan said when Victor's fear and anger changed to despair. "He's coming back to us now."

"We cannot affect the spirit realm except through our bond," T'ukri said.

"Whatever," Jordan replied. "We have to try." He released his hold on Victor's hand to grasp his shoulder instead and gave it a gentle shake, glad Tamya had stepped outside a few minutes earlier. "Come on, Victor. Wake up. This is just another nightmare, whatever you're seeing. It's no different than any of the others we've woken each other with over the years. You just need to snap out of it."

Victor's eyes shifted behind his closed lids, but he gave no other indication of having heard Jordan.

Fuck.

He shook Victor a little harder. "Come on, doc. You're scaring me here. You need to open those beautiful brown eyes I love so much and let us see you're all right."

Whatever Victor was seeing in the spirit realm at the moment, he sure as hell wasn't all right. Jordan had never known him to be as defeated as he now felt through the bond. Frowning, Jordan moved from Victor's shoulder to his cheek, tapping it lightly.

That got a flutter of lashes, but no other reaction.

Logic dictated he should slap a little harder since that had gotten the most reaction so far, but Jordan couldn't bring himself to do it. Instead, he leaned forward and kissed Victor with all the desperation and longing and worry and, yes, fear currently roiling around in his chest, a mixture of Victor's emotions and Jordan's own with a healthy dash of T'ukri's thrown in for good measure. Victor *had* to come back to them.

VICTOR FROWNED at the sudden surge of anger and worry through the bond. He was torn for a moment between the scene of Jordan caring so tenderly for his failing self and the sense of his mates, but this vision, like the ones before it, was a lie. The feelings through the bond were real. If one of his mates—Jordan, he thought—was that angry and worried, he needed to get back to them. Now. Whatever they were facing, they shouldn't have to do it without him. He closed his eyes, shutting out the depressing scene still playing out in front of him—he was done with the traps and tests of the spirit realm—and centered all his concentration on the bond. He felt the ghost of a kiss, grabbed hold of the sensation, and *pulled*. Hard.

Immediately he felt an answering tug. With his eyes still closed, he stood and followed. He hit the wall, but he ignored it and kept walking. It resisted, trying to hold him within the spirit realm, but he was done with this *maudit* quest, with anything that would keep him from his mates. He dug deep within himself to the core of power Yuri and Nkóko insisted he possessed and answered the ever-more-frustrated pull with a hard push of his own until the wall simply disappeared.

When he opened his eyes again, it was to the sight of Jordan's and T'ukri's worried faces.

"Are you all right?" Jordan asked immediately.

"I was about to ask you that," Victor replied. "What's wrong?"

Jordan rolled his eyes and looked at T'ukri. "What's wrong, he asks. Seriously, Victor? You were…. God, I don't even know how to describe it. You were angry and scared and hurting and we couldn't do anything to help. We couldn't even figure out what was causing those feelings. Of course we were upset. Now answer my question."

Victor looked down at his hands—*his* hands, not the gnarled useless imitations from the spirit realm—then back up at Jordan. He really needed to remember that the bond went both ways and that his mates loved him just as much as he loved them. "Not sure yet, but I will be fine now."

"Can you tell us what you saw?" T'ukri asked. "I do not mean to pry, but we felt your distress and would ease it if we can."

Victor smiled. *This* was what he had come to expect from T'ukri, not the almost indifference of the last vision from his quest. *Not real*, he reminded himself one last time. The spirit quest might force him to face his fears, but it did not make those fears reality. Now or in the future. It just highlighted where he struggled. "It started with my family," he told them. "The conversation was… disappointing but expected. My father had no patience for any of my choices, least of all for being with the two of you. He found it beneath me to have two lovers, but that is his problem. I knew a long time ago that they wouldn't ever be able to accept me as I am, and while it hurts to be reminded of it, I've come to terms with it. I am building a new life here with, I hope, a new family now, one that will embrace me rather than just accept me."

"Damn straight," Jordan said.

T'ukri chuckled. "Those are not the words I would have chosen, but Jordan is correct that you will have a family here in Machu Llaqta that will not turn its back on you for preferring the company of men or for having two mates. And if the time comes that you wish to attempt a reconciliation with the family of your birth, we will stand beside you as you do so."

"I couldn't put you through that." Victor shuddered as his father's cruel words echoed through his mind. Yes, they were words from the spirit realm, but he didn't expect a real-life conversation to go any better.

"Just so long as that's your decision for you, not for us," Jordan said. "I mean, it's not like he could say anything to me I haven't heard a hundred times or more."

"You are both better off here," T'ukri agreed.

Victor laughed, the pall from the spirit realm lifting a little more at the familiar back-and-forth. "So after I told my father his prejudices weren't my problem, I walked on for a while until it morphed into a vision of you being hunted, Jordan."

Jordan jerked his head around to look at Victor. "Hunted? By who?"

"By warriors speaking Runasimi," Victor said, pushing down bile at the memory. "They surrounded your hiding spot and shot it full of arrows. You died in my arms."

"Nuh-uh." Jordan grabbed Victor's shoulders and gave him a little shake. "Look at me, Victor."

Victor blinked a couple of times and focused on Jordan's face. His very alive, not bloody or in pain face.

"I know." Victor rested his hands on top of Jordan's and let the contact seep into him. T'ukri squeezed his knee in silent support as well. "Even as I was dealing with it, I knew it wasn't real, but it's going to be a long time before I stop seeing the life fade from your eyes as blood seeped from the hole in your chest and you tried to gasp out a warning with your dying breath."

"Okay, I really coulda done without that image," Jordan said, but he only tightened his grip.

T'ukri scooted closer until he could wrap an arm around Victor's waist. "What warning?"

"Beware the traitor, and there was a final word, but he didn't finish it," Victor said.

"That sounds more like precognition than a fear from within," T'ukri said slowly. "If that is the case, you are more powerful than any of us realized. I would not delay our bonding to do it, but we must speak with Tamya to understand what this means."

Victor wasn't sure if that made him feel better or worse. On the one hand, it was nice to know he didn't have a buried fear of failing Jordan and T'ukri in a way that caused Jordan to be killed and T'ukri to go mad. On the other hand, the thought that he'd predicted a future in his spirit quest where someone was hunting Jordan in the hopes of sending T'ukri feral wasn't exactly encouraging.

"Is there more?" T'ukri asked.

"Like that isn't enough?" Jordan interjected.

"It is more than enough, but that does not mean it is all," T'ukri replied evenly.

"No, it's not all," Victor said. "Losing you, Jordan, sent T'ukri mad. He disappeared into the mist with the guardian completely in control. Although before I could dwell too much on that, my grandfather and Yuri appeared in my vision. Tell me, T'ukri, how old were you when you kissed Atoc behind the temple?"

"I did not kiss him," T'ukri spluttered exactly as Yuri had predicted. "We were playing at being adults, as children do."

"Yes, but how old were you?" Victor pressed.

T'ukri glanced to one side, embarrassment visible in every line of his body. "Five."

So that part had been real.

"Did Ch'aska tell you about Atoc? I did not realize she knew that story," T'ukri added.

"Yuri told me," Victor replied. "He and Nkóko told me a number of interesting things that I must think about more before I decide how I feel about them."

"It is not unheard of for the spirits of the ancestors to appear during spirit quests, although I do not think it is common unless we seek their blessing," T'ukri said. "What did they say to upset you so?"

"It was not them," Victor said. "I had a final vision after I left them, one I don't even want to think about it, much less talk about it."

"Then do not," T'ukri said. "Spirit quests are intensely personal. No one, not even we, have the right to force you to share yours."

Victor considered leaving the last scene out. Jordan wouldn't like it, but he'd leave it alone for now, even if he asked about it again later. T'ukri would accept it and move on. But Victor wasn't sure he could. He knew it was a nightmare vision like all the others, but the others had a grain of truth to them beneath the lies. He had fully repudiated the first one and Yuri and Nkóko had drawn him out of the second one, but the final one felt incomplete somehow. He had walked away from it because Jordan and T'ukri needed him, not because he had overcome it. If he didn't face it now, the fears that drove it would continue to fester, and his mates deserved better than that.

"I saw a future version of myself," Victor said slowly. "Old and feeble, barely able to function on my own, while you were both still fit and strong. Jordan had to take care of me like an invalid. I couldn't even take my sandals off by myself. I had become nothing but a burden to you."

"You took care of me that time I got dysentery the summer we were in Mexico. You really think I wouldn't return the favor?" Jordan snarled.

Victor closed his eyes. "No, I know you would return the favor, and you did."

"But I did not," T'ukri surmised.

Victor flinched. "I'm sorry."

"Victor," T'ukri said softly, "look at me. Please?"

Victor took a bracing breath and opened his eyes.

"You have had years to learn to trust Jordan. The weeks we spent traveling here and the day since our bonding cannot begin to compare to everything you have shared. Of course you know he would not abandon you, but you are still learning to believe that about me," T'ukri said. Love pulsed through the bond, so bright Victor could almost touch it. "But your fears are, I believe, a product of the society you grew up in, where elders are pushed aside into impersonal facilities and forgotten. Look at Tamya. She is old and frail, dependent on her children and grandchildren for more tasks than not these days, yet she remains a pillar of our community. We value her for her age and experience rather than dismiss her. No one, from the youngest child to the elders only a few years younger, would think twice about doing for her anything she requires. On the contrary, they would go out of their way to do it as a sign of respect. It will be the same for you when you reach her age."

"And it's not like we aren't going to get old right beside you," Jordan said. "I know you, and I'd bet my bow that we hadn't aged a bit in that vision."

Victor sighed. Jordan really did know him well. "No, you hadn't." He focused back on T'ukri. "It really doesn't bother you that my vision played out that way?"

"It saddens me that your experiences have taught you that your only value comes from being useful and that your usefulness will diminish as you age," T'ukri said, "but spirit quests are designed to make us face ourselves—our doubts, our fears, the cracks that, if not addressed, could cause our relationships to crumble like a house built on sand rather than on stone. Now that you have acknowledged the fear, we can face it and defeat it. If you take any lesson from the quest, let it be this: even when you crossed to the spirit realm, you were not alone. You will not be alone ever again, even if death takes one or both of us before it takes you. We three are one spirit now, and not even death can sever that bond."

CHAPTER 40

VICTOR HAD no answer to T'ukri's declaration, only a profound sense of gratitude that rose from T'ukri's understanding. Their conversation could have gone very differently—very badly—if T'ukri had been a different man.

T'ukri didn't wait for an answer from either of them. He simply stood and offered each of them a hand. Jordan flowed to his feet with the same easy grace he did everything. Victor let himself lean on T'ukri's support a little more than necessary so T'ukri would know how much he appreciated the gesture. Plus he'd been sitting, unmoving, for some number of hours, and his muscles had stiffened up more than he cared to admit.

"Here," Tamya said, appearing from somewhere and taking Victor off guard, a testament to how out of sorts the spirit quest had left him. "Drink. It help," she said in Spanish.

Victor could feel both Jordan's and T'ukri's impatience at the interruption, but neither said anything, so Victor took the cup Tamya offered. He sipped the sweet juice slowly, his whole body feeling unsettled still from the spirit quest or the ayahuasca that had taken him into that realm or even the lack of food while he was there. The juice helped almost immediately, calming his queasy stomach and easing the feeling of ants crawling beneath his skin.

"When did you come back in?" Victor asked after a few sips. He hoped she had only just gotten there. If she had been there long, he would be more than a little embarrassed at everything she'd overheard, although she might not have understood most of it.

"I waited outside until I heard you beginning to move around," she replied through T'ukri. "I wanted to be near in case you needed help, but not so near that I would impose on your private time with your mates. The first spirit quest is always a challenge, and for one not born to our traditions, I feared it would be worse."

Thank God—or Pachamama—for small mercies. Victor drank more juice to cover his reaction. "What happens now?"

"Now you recover," Tamya said. "And when Jordan has been accepted into the warriors, you return to the temple for your bonding ceremony. Then after your time of seclusion, you take your place as a shaman."

Just like that. Bon, d'accord, so maybe it hadn't been *that* simple because nothing about the past few hours and the painful images he'd faced were simple, but unless Tamya had heard more than she let on—and understood it even if she heard it—he wouldn't have to provide any explanation or anything else to justify his presence. He had completed the spirit quest, so he was one of them.

"I look forward to it," he said because Tamya's comment seemed to need some acknowledgment.

She smiled in return.

"Let us get you home," T'ukri said.

That sounded like the best thing Victor had heard all day. And it had been all day, Victor realized as they left the temple. They had arrived in the temple shortly after breakfast, and the sun was now nearing the valley walls.

They walked across the city hand in hand until they reached the house. Ch'aska was waiting outside for them as they approached, but T'ukri waved her off with a shake of his head, for which Victor was grateful. They'd see her later, but right now, he needed his mates and the comfort only they could provide. The juice had helped his body, but his mind and emotions still felt rubbed raw. A meal waited on the table inside.

"Will you be able to eat?" T'ukri asked.

"Not yet, I don't think," Victor said. "I need...."

"You need us," Jordan replied, crowding into Victor's space. Victor leaned against him, taking comfort in his solid presence, as he had always done, but that was part of the problem, wasn't it? He had relied on Jordan for so long, and he didn't know how to rely on T'ukri.

"You need not have a large meal, but you should have something. Try the passion fruit, *yanaymi*," T'ukri said, drawing Victor's attention back to him and the piece of fruit he held out. Suddenly ravenous, Victor reached out to take the offering, but T'ukri pulled his hand back. "I did not take care of you in your spirit vision. Let me take care of you now"

"That was a product of my own fears, not any fault of yours," Victor protested.

T'ukri chuckled warmly. "You say that as if it is a hardship to care for you. Come, Jordan. Our mate is tired. Bring him to bed. You can hold him while I feed him, and he will know that he is loved."

Victor wanted to renew his protest, but the thought of his lovers pampering him after the harrowing day was too tempting to resist. He followed Jordan into the bedroom and let them strip him down to his underwear again before climbing into bed to lean back against Jordan's hard chest. T'ukri perched on the bed next to them and brushed a piece of fruit across his lips. It was as sweet and juicy as T'ukri had promised, but it was the brush of T'ukri's fingers over his lips and tongue that made him moan.

A piece at a time, T'ukri plied him with fruit until the tray was empty and all three of them were vibrating with barely restrained desire.

T'ukri set the tray aside and pulled Victor into his arms. "I very much want to make love with you right now."

Like Victor was going to say no to that.

"I'll just sit over here and watch," Jordan said with a grin as he slid out from behind Victor.

Victor started to shake his head, but Jordan kissed him soundly. "Let him make love to you," Jordan insisted. "I won't feel excluded, I promise. And when he's left you a puddle of goo on the bed, I'll join you. You need to be the sole focus of his attention for a while. You *deserve* to be the sole focus of his attention."

The "deserve" part of that statement was pushing it, but Jordan had his stubborn face on, and arguing with him in that mood was like arguing with a brick wall. Besides, it wouldn't be any hardship to bask in T'ukri's undivided attention for the next little while. And he had years of experience with the feeling of Jordan's gaze on him, even before it had turned from professional to personal. Jordan could pack more of a punch with just his eyes than most of Victor's previous lovers could with their entire bodies.

Which probably said something about how crazy in love with Jordan he was and had been for years.

"What does my mate desire?" T'ukri asked formally.

Victor looked deep into his eyes as he considered the question, but really there was only one answer. "You."

"Then you shall have me," T'ukri replied.

Victor smiled up at him gratefully. "You have me in return."

"And I could not ask for a greater gift."

Victor must have done something truly spectacular in a previous life to deserve the devotion in T'ukri's voice. He leaned in for a kiss, which T'ukri gave him immediately, drawing him into a tight embrace and covering Victor's lips with his own.

Victor returned the kiss eagerly, desperate for the love and desire he could feel through the bond. T'ukri swept him into his arms, hovering over Victor like he was the most precious thing T'ukri had ever seen. Victor wanted to look away or close his eyes against the emotion—how could he possibly deserve it—but he silenced that voice. It came from his fears, not from reality, and while only time would dispel that voice completely, Victor had faced it and had chosen to come back to Jordan and T'ukri rather than give in to it. He tugged on T'ukri's shoulders, wanting to feel his weight grounding him in the present.

T'ukri settled atop him and kissed him again, delving deep into Victor's mouth as if he could climb inside him and make them one in body as he had declared them one in spirit.

"My prince, your mother bids you return to the palace."

Victor muttered a curse under his breath. Jordan didn't bother muffling his outburst. T'ukri rolled to the side, panting harshly as he tried to bring himself back under control.

"Tell her I will return shortly, Urpi," T'ukri called when he could speak normally.

"We covered for you last night. We may not be able to do so again, especially as you have yet to return," Urpi warned.

T'ukri groaned and buried his face in Victor's shoulder. "I will find a way to return. I have promises to keep."

Promises Victor yearned for him to keep, but he shook his head. "Do not take the risk tonight. Tomorrow Jordan will start his warrior trial at dawn. He needs to be well rested, which won't happen if you sneak back in and we stay up half the night. Especially if there's any truth to *that* vision. Our bonding ceremony is two days away, and after that, no one will ever separate us again. We've waited this long. We can wait two more days."

T'ukri rose from the bed with a frustrated growl. "Then I must leave now before I forget myself. I would wish you luck tomorrow, Malku, but I know you do not need it. Instead I will say that I will be waiting for you at the temple."

"I'll be there in time for lunch," Jordan replied cockily.

"And when we are finally alone together," T'ukri said, looking back at Victor, "I *will* keep those promises I made and show you exactly how deep my desire for you runs, my own. I would not have you doubt me ever again."

"I look forward to it," Victor replied.

"T'ukri," Ch'aska called from outside. "You have about five minutes before Mama comes looking for you herself."

"Go," Victor said. "We will see you tomorrow."

T'ukri kissed them each swiftly, though the kiss he gave Victor was hot and hard and claiming, full of tongue and desperation. Victor could only imagine he kissed Jordan the same way, and then he was gone.

Victor slumped back on the bed and looked at Jordan. "Sometimes being the voice of reason sucks."

Jordan snorted. "That's why it's your job, not mine." He crossed the room and climbed into bed next to Victor. "Don't worry about tomorrow, okay? I'll be careful and I'll be fine."

"You damn well better be," Victor said. "I just got you. I'm not losing you now."

"You won't," Jordan said as he ran his hand down Victor's side to hover over his erection. "You want me to take care of that for you?"

"I meant what I told T'ukri. We've waited this long. Just think how much sweeter it will be when we finally get through all the formalities and can just be together."

"Okay, but don't blame me if I keep you up half the night tossing and turning," Jordan replied.

Victor rolled him onto his side and spooned up behind him. "Go to sleep, trésor."

CHAPTER 41

JORDAN TRIED to do as Victor said. He really did, but he couldn't get his mind to settle. Part of that was blue balls, but he could mostly ignore that. Okay, it was a little harder now that he had the feedback loop of desire from T'ukri and Victor bubbling along in the back of his head, but even that he could still mostly deal with. No, it was everything else that was keeping him awake, Victor's premonition most of all.

He'd come to terms with his mortality and the risks he took when he was in the Marines, but things were different now. He had Victor and T'ukri, which gave him a hell of a good reason to stay alive, and if that weren't enough, if he died, it could be enough to send T'ukri mad. Only maybe, because Yuri had died and Huallpa hadn't lost control of himself. Sure, he'd stopped being Chapaqpuma, but he hadn't gone feral and killed anyone or abdicated or anything irrational like that.

That might mean Victor's vision was just fear, not an actual premonition. Quenti had said the warriors only used blunted weapons—although whether that meant covered in something or with the edges dulled, he didn't know. It wasn't impossible to kill someone with blunted weapons, of course, but it was a whole lot more difficult. In the scenario Victor had described, Jordan could have gotten away if they were only using blunted spears and arrows. He'd have been bruised and battered at the end of it, but alive. And the thought of anyone going mad because he died was a little too over-the-top for him to believe, even on his best day.

Fuck it. He wasn't going to get any sleep like this. Instead of lying there tossing and turning and possibly keeping Victor awake, he'd just get up and see if he could scrounge up some bits of cloth or leather to blunt the tips of his arrows for his warrior trial the next day. No way in hell was he using unfamiliar weapons when succeeding meant being accepted to the tribe and getting to complete the bonding ceremony with Victor and T'ukri. He was tired of getting cockblocked at every turn.

He grabbed his bow and quiver and went out onto the steps that led into the house. The moon was full, giving him enough light to see by, so he set his bow down and started sorting through his arrows.

"Should you not be sleeping?" the queen's voice came from the shadows.

Jordan hadn't heard her approaching, but he managed to quash the urge to draw his bow or throw one of his knives in self-defense.

"I tried that. It didn't work," he said. "Um, Your Majesty." *Fuck.* Victor would kick his ass for forgetting to use her title or stand up when she arrived or show some other sign of respect when their positions were still precarious and she was pissed as hell at them.

"That seems to be a common problem tonight." She stepped into the splash of moonlight in front of the house. "I left T'ukri pacing the confines of the palace. He spoke to me of Victor's vision. As the queen, I cannot let him dispense with protocol, no matter how much he desires to be with you. As a mother, as one who was mated to Chapaqpuma before that mantle passed on, I understand what drives him as few others can, so I promised him the next best protection in the valley."

Jordan waited, but she didn't say anything else.

"Yours?" he ventured.

"Mine," she agreed. "Few are those who would dare raise a hand against me, and of those who might dare, fewer still are they who could beat me. And in the time it would take them to do so, you would have killed them."

"Pull up a rock," Jordan offered. "It's the best I've got to offer."

"It is more than sufficient," Llipya replied. She set a bag on the stoop between them. "I brought leather to blunt your arrows May I help you prepare your weapons?"

Jordan's first reaction was to say no. He didn't let anyone handle his gear before a mission—and Llipya was enough of a warrior to accept that if he refused—but he could always check the balance of the arrows in private to make sure they were all the same.

"I would be honored."

They worked in silence for a time. "The warrior challenge is not simply a test of martial skill," Llipya said eventually. "It is a test of cunning, of woodcraft, and of strategy as much as it is of your ability to fight. Rarely will we have more advanced weapons than those who would attack us, so we must use stealth and the goddess's gifts to our advantage. Remember that there is no limit to the number of times you can try again, and few are the warriors who succeed on their first try. There is no shame or dishonor in failing the trial, only a chance to learn and improve your skills."

Jordan almost said *fuck that*, but his mostly forgotten sense of propriety held him back. "Yeah, sorry, but no. I was a soldier for years. I'm not a kid trying to earn his first set of stripes."

"Do not underestimate the damage even a blunted spear can cause when thrown with force," Llipya said. "I knew a warrior who ended his first attempt with a broken arm because he was too prideful to carry a shield."

"I'm taking it seriously because I'm seasoned, not stupid," Jordan said, "but I gotta say, it doesn't feel like the same level of test as what Victor had to go through today."

"Does every test have to be equal to the one before in order for it to be valid?" Llipya asked. "Life demands different things of us at different moments. At times it may demand more of Victor or of T'ukri than it demands of you. Would you deny them your support at those times?"

"Of course not," Jordan said.

"And at times it may demand more of you. Would you be angry at them for not being under the same stress you were experiencing in that moment?"

"No," Jordan replied.

"Then why must your challenge to be accepted into the tribe be the same—or even of the same apparent difficulty—as Victor's?" Llipya asked.

"Because that's not fair to Victor," Jordan said. "I know everyone is still pretending we haven't bonded fully because we haven't had the bonding ceremony or whatever, but I sat in the temple and *felt* what he was going through today. He faced every nightmare you could imagine."

"But is this not your worst nightmare?" Llipya asked. "You see yourself as a marksman, rightly so, and thus this task should be an easy one. If you complete it, then it will be an easy one, but our tribe will see you completing the same trial as every other warrior who serves our people, just as Victor completed the same trial to become a shaman as every other shaman, as is fitting for you both. That you are already a warrior and have already fought with us is not the issue. It is not a question of whether your skills are enough. It is a question of how the tribe sees you, just as it was for Victor."

Jordan didn't see how it was the same thing at all, but he also wasn't going to get anywhere arguing with T'ukri's mother, and they'd finished with the last of the arrows. "I should try to get some sleep," he said, although he knew it wouldn't work. Dawn was only a few hours off, and he'd be too on edge waiting for the knock that signaled Quenti's arrival to sleep now, but it would end the conversation without offending anyone. "If you see T'ukri when you get back to the palace, tell him I'll see him at the temple tomorrow."

"I wish you good rest. I will leave you with one final piece of advice. Your bond is new, and you have not had your time of seclusion to solidify it, but let it sustain you through your trial. It can do more than let you sense one another's emotions. Tomorrow, we must be the king and queen of Machu Llaqta as we watch your trial, but Huallpa and I were both warriors once. We know the challenges you will face, and though we cannot show it, in our hearts, we will be cheering you on."

"Thanks," Jordan said for lack of knowing what else to say. He gathered his arrows and went back inside, only to find Victor sitting in the dark. "Were you awake the whole time?"

"Long enough," Victor replied. "She's got you pegged, you know. For as long as I've known you, the fastest way to provoke you has always been to question your abilities in the field. And you continue to believe at some level that your aim is all you have to offer."

"So you're saying I need to fail so I'll know the people here won't judge me for it? How about no?"

Victor sighed, and when Jordan turned to look at him, he was wearing his Harris-you're-an-idiot expression. "No, that's not what I'm saying. I'm saying you define yourself by your marksmanship and your skill as a soldier and resent anything that seems to call that into question, but the warrior trial isn't calling a damn thing into question. It's a hoop to jump through, like military recertifications. *You* never thought twice about them because you knew you could do them, but when you were still in the Reserves, I remember you telling me that every year there were people who had to redo training courses in areas outside their usual fields because they were out of practice. They did the course, they took the test again, and they moved on. And nobody cared because once they passed the test, it went in their file and nobody looked at it again. This is the same thing, but you've turned it into something far more than it should be."

It wasn't the same thing at all, but Victor wouldn't ever be able to see it from his perspective. "You know what? It's late and Quenti said they'd be here at dawn. I'm going to get some sleep."

He stalked into the bedroom and laid down. He could hear Victor milling around in the other room. Pretending to sleep wouldn't do any good with the bond, but hopefully his closed eyes would let Victor know he wasn't interested in more talking. Even as he settled, he felt a dual wave of love, fainter from T'ukri with the physical distance between them but still undeniably there. Tomorrow might be an epic disaster, but they loved him.

He didn't know what he'd done to deserve them him, but he sure as fuck hoped he'd keep doing it.

A WET rag landed on his chest. "On your feet, Harris. It's time to get moving."

Jordan blinked awake. He hadn't actually expected to fall asleep, but apparently exhaustion had finally caught up with him. He pulled himself out of bed and wiped his face, under his arms, and around his groin so he wouldn't stink, not that he expected to be in close enough quarters with anyone else for that to matter.

When that was done, he pulled on camo pants and a black T-shirt, the better to pass unnoticed in the jungle. He didn't expect to elude all of Quenti's warriors, but he preferred stealth to combat where possible. Even so, he slipped his knife into his boot sheath and looked around for the one he carried along his inner thigh, only to see Victor holding it out to him with a familiar half smile. "Thanks, babe," he said.

"You treat everything like a mission. I've seen you 'suit up' more times than I can count," Victor replied. "Just remember to use nonlethal force today."

"I know," Jordan said with a roll of his eyes. "When have I ever made that mistake?"

"Never to my knowledge," Victor said, "but we don't want today to be the first time."

Jordan sobered as he strapped his quiver around his waist. "It'll be strange, running a mission entirely on my own. Even in the Marines, I always had someone in my ear."

"We have something better now." Victor tapped Jordan's chest.

"Well, yeah, but the bond can't exactly guide me through a fucked-up mission," Jordan retorted.

"Maybe not, but it can guide us back to each other. It's how I found my way out of the spirit realm."

Jordan looked into Victor's earnest face and reminded himself that Victor had triumphed because he had trusted Jordan and T'ukri and the strength they all brought to their new relationship. *Okay.* He could do that.

He *would* do that.

A knock on the door broke the moment. Jordan grabbed his bow, squared his shoulders, and summoned a smile for Victor. "See you at the temple in a few hours."

"We'll be waiting," Victor promised.

And, well, everyone knew Victor Itoua always kept his promises.

JORDAN HAD expected Quenti, and she'd told him she would have two warriors with her to escort him somewhere in the valley where they would leave him to find his way back, but he hadn't expected Nandini to come with them. Then again, given that Quenti was there, that Cusi was one of the two warriors with her, and that Nandini was spending her nights with the two of them—no, not thinking about it—he shouldn't have been surprised.

"Their familiarity with the terrain will give them an advantage," Nandini said before Jordan could even say hello.

Jordan smirked. "I still have a few surprises up my sleeve."

She gave a pointed look at his bare arms. "If you say so."

He threw his head back and laughed. She punched him in the upper arm, hard enough it would bruise. When he sobered and looked back at her, she raised her arm for him to bump. "Oorah."

Quenti approached then with the blindfold. "Do try to leave my warriors *some* pride?"

He grinned. "No promises."

Then the world went black.

JORDAN RESISTED the urge to fight off the hands guiding him through the jungle and to tear the blindfold off his face. He clung to the bond like a lifeline, using it to push down the panic clawing at his throat over his blocked vision.

He could do this. They weren't leading him to some torture cell. This was just part of the trial. Not just whether he could get to the temple without being stopped, but whether he could find his way there if he didn't know where he was starting from. Quenti had explained that detail several times, and Jordan got it. Really, he did. Part of defending their home was knowing the lay of the land and being able to use it to their advantage, especially since any outside attackers wouldn't have a fucking clue what to expect. How could they, when the valley didn't show up on any maps or satellite feeds?

T'ukri's explanation for that—*the goddess protects her own*—had been unsatisfactory at best, but Jordan was learning to live with it. The unexplained, even inexplicable, was fast becoming part of his daily life.

He tried to keep track of the twists and turns, of the number of steps, but they were in the jungle where straight lines weren't a thing, even when the people leading him weren't trying to confuse him. Instead he focused on the steadiness of the bond and how, even as they kept going, it never faltered or weakened or changed. Their bodies might be in different places, but their emotions were linked.

He could work with that.

After a few minutes or a couple of hours—time was meaningless without his vision—they stopped. "The trial begins now," Quenti said. "You have until sunset to reach the temple."

Jordan ripped the blindfold off as soon as she spoke, but he was already alone in the small clearing. He had to give them credit. They moved fast.

He took a moment to survey the terrain. Three faint paths led away from the clearing—two more or less ahead of him and one off to his left. He would have expected one slightly behind and to the right given the way they had come in, but either they hadn't followed an established path or having his eyes covered had messed with his spatial awareness more than he thought. He would have sworn they were on a regular path. He hadn't felt the brush of leaves or branches to suggest they were walking through undergrowth.

He shrugged the thought aside. It didn't matter how he'd gotten into the clearing. He needed to focus on how he was getting to the temple. He examined the three visible paths more closely, but none of them showed sign of recent use, which meant Quenti and her warriors were even better than he'd thought, because there should have been *some* sign—a broken twig, a fallen leaf, disturbed ground cover, a footprint in the dirt, something.

Fuck this. He was wasting daylight. Falling back on his training, he scaled the tallest tree in the vicinity to get the lay of the land. He didn't expect to see the city or the temple, between the canopy and whatever magic protected them from outsiders, but it would give him a place to start.

The one constant since they'd arrived in the valley was that it stretched east to west. Not when they were outside—and he still wanted an explanation for that—but within the valley, the cardinal directions stayed the same. When he reached a high enough branch that he could see above the canopy, the sun was just cresting the horizon behind him, and the valley—somehow he knew where it began and ended with a quick glance—lay spread out in front of him. Good, west it was.

He made his way back to the forest floor, checked his orientation one more time, and forged into the bush parallel to the trail that led due west. He wasn't stupid enough to take the trail itself. Quenti's warriors would have it watched. They'd probably be watching the rest as well, but he'd have more cover away from the trail.

Five hundred yards or so into the forest, he startled a bird.

"Shit!" He dropped to the ground and belly crawled into the brush. He'd barely made it under cover when a spear thudded exactly where he'd been standing. *Damn.* How many warriors did Quenti have out, or had this one been tracking him from the start? He thought only Quenti and the two warriors with her were supposed to know where he would be coming from, and the three of them weren't supposed to participate, so either someone was cheating or the guard was more numerous than he'd counted on.

Out of habit, he started to turn and relay the intel to his team, but he didn't have a team this time. So what would Nandini tell Jordan to do if she were with Jordan right now?

That was easy. *Neutralize the attacker.* Usually that would mean an arrow or bullet to the eye, but even blunted, he'd do some serious damage if he did that, and the warrior who'd thrown the spear was just doing their job. He eyed the spear again, automatically calculating trajectory. If the warrior hadn't moved, it would put him in the trees about fifty yards farther into the valley, a little to the right of his current position.

Working with that point as a target, Jordan backed deeper into the brush until he was on the far side of a large tree that would provide cover. He climbed it quickly until he was higher than where the spear had been thrown from. After the fight against the miners, word might have gotten around that he was a sniper who preferred the high ground, but he hadn't practiced enough with anyone for them to know his exact moves. He carefully made his way forward, drawing on all his skills to hide his passage until he caught sight of the warrior who had thrown the spear.

Gotcha!

Jordan fired an arrow at the man's calf. He'd have a bruise, but if the arrow hadn't been blunted, it would have been a flesh wound, so he wouldn't have a broken bone.

"Well played," the man called with a salute in Jordan's direction before dropping his remaining weapons to the ground. "Good luck."

Jordan grinned, even knowing the man couldn't see him. *One down. Unknown number to go.*

He debated for a moment between staying in the canopy or dropping back to the ground. On the one hand, the canopy was less stable, so he'd have a greater risk of movement in the branches as he went. On the other, would the warriors really be looking up? Damn, he missed having a team at his back. Nandini would weigh the risks and benefits in a split second and tell Jordan what to do.

Fuck that. He was an experienced soldier. He could make the decision. Wasn't that the point of this? For him to see himself as more than just a good shot?

With all the wildlife in the valley, the warriors might dismiss movement in the canopy as another monkey or bird, but they'd also be on high alert. He'd stick with the ground where he'd be less likely to be seen in the first place unless circumstances changed.

Adapt as you go, Nandini always said. Jordan could take her advice even if she wasn't right there to give it.

Decision made, he dropped back to the ground and continued toward the center of the valley. He spied a second warrior before the man had caught sight of him and snuck up behind him to tap him on the back of the head with his sheathed knife. When the man turned, he was little more than a kid.

"New recruit?" Jordan asked.

"Yes," he replied, embarrassment clear on his face.

"Don't sweat it, kid. No matter how good you are, there's always someone out there who's better. You gotta learn from every encounter so you don't make the same mistakes again, but don't let it get to you. I may be new here, but I've been fighting longer than you've been alive."

That probably wasn't strictly true, but it was close enough, and from the look on the kid's face, it was exactly what he needed to hear.

"Thank you, Your Highness."

"Aw, kid, no," Jordan said. "Out here I'm a warrior, just like you. Nothing more, nothing less. Got it?"

The kid smiled shyly, although Jordan wasn't convinced he understood half of what Jordan had said. "Yes."

Jordan grinned back and gave the kid a two-fingered salute as he left. The kid waved back. When this was over, Jordan would have to get the kid's name and see what he could do to help him out. First, though, he had to finish running this gauntlet. Not that it had been much of a gauntlet so far.

He couldn't help the bit of swagger in his gait as he strode forward, sure now that he'd have no trouble making it to the temple in record time.

A rustle overhead alerted him, and he froze for a second before diving for cover.

Thud!

When he looked up, the spear quivered in the bark of the tree, the metal point gleaming in the filtered sunlight.

Someone had thrown a live spear.

OH HELL no! It's on now.

Jordan's focus sharpened as he scoured the surrounding area for the source of the spear. At that angle, it hadn't come from above, which meant his adversary was at ground level.

Jordan felt the surge of worry from Victor and T'ukri, but he couldn't take the time to reassure them. He had a target to neutralize.

Nonlethal force because *he* hadn't broken the rules of engagement, but beyond that, all bets were off. He forced back the fear that the rest of Victor's premonition might come to pass. He didn't have time for fear or doubt. What had started as a hoop to jump through had just become a fight for his life.

It took a moment as he sought his target to realize he could hear rustling to his left, farther away than he could usually pinpoint sound.

What the hell? His vision was fucking awesome, sure, but the rest of his senses were normally not as reliable in the best of circumstances. He wasn't about to look a gift horse in the mouth, though. He tracked the warrior's movements in deadly stillness, every muscle poised but unmoving. This was familiar, a sniper's trance, but it took on an extra dimension as he tracked his prey with more than just his eyes. He knew where the man was long before he saw him, knew from the weight of his footsteps that it *was* a man, a large man. Jordan lay in wait as the man crept closer, looking for signs of Jordan but not finding any.

When he had taken two steps past Jordan's hiding spot, Jordan pounced, forcing him to the ground with an arm behind his back as he landed face-first in the dirt.

The man struggled, but Jordan just jerked his wrist higher, hyperextending his shoulder until the struggling stopped. Jordan pulled a zip tie from one of his pockets and secured the man's arms. "If I remember, I'll tell them where to find you before dark. If I remember...."

The man said something in Runasimi that Jordan didn't bother trying to decipher. If he was asking for mercy, tough shit. Jordan had been as merciful as he was going to be, and if it was anything else, it would just make him angrier. He didn't have time for that now. He had something to prove, now more than ever.

Leaving his attacker hog-tied, Jordan stalked through the jungle, every sense on high alert, including some he'd never noticed before. He'd always prided himself on seeing better than average, but even that felt sharper than ever before. His hearing had let him bring down this attacker, but that wasn't all. The breeze prickled over his skin in a way he'd never felt before despite always keeping track of it when he was shooting. Now it pressed against him until he could almost see it. And on that breeze came more smells than he had ever noticed. He sniffed experimentally, taking in the scent of loam and leaf mold overlaid with animal musk—T'ukri could probably tell him what animal, but Jordan wasn't familiar enough with the local fauna to guess. It took a moment before the oddness of being able to identify even that much struck him. He was all too familiar with dirt and mold, and even the stench of animal shit, but he'd never been able to pick the different odors apart and extrapolate from them the way he could now. He took another deep breath, tasting it as much as smelling it, letting it seep into him until it called up instincts he knew he hadn't possessed this morning—the guardian's instincts.

Sweat. Human sweat. And human fear.

Like they knew they were being hunted.

Good. Let them stew in that fear. They deserved it. His attacker had at least one accomplice for him to still smell their fear, but instincts driven to new heights by the bond told him it was more than that. He might or might not catch them, but there wouldn't be anywhere safe for them once T'ukri found out about their plans. Assuming they survived whatever Quenti would do to them first.

His mates couldn't come for Jordan physically, not without nullifying Jordan's trial, but Victor's cool head infused the bond, giving Jordan the patience to take a step back mentally and plan rather than forge ahead as he would have done unchecked.

He heard a rustle to his left and faded back into the underbrush. His years as a sniper had given him plenty of practice blending into the shadows, but this felt different somehow.

He doesn't move through the forest so much as he becomes the forest.

His description of T'ukri hunting filtered through his memories. That was what it felt like. Like he was so much a part of the forest that no one would notice his passage unless he chose to show himself. Forget his earlier plan to take out everyone between him and the temple to make sure none of them were hunting him. He could do better than that.

And wouldn't that just burn whoever was trying to sabotage or even kill him, if he showed up at the temple without anyone else even realizing he'd gotten past them, proving once and for all how much stronger the bond made all three of them?

CHAPTER 42

"MY PRINCE."

At the sound of Quenti's voice, T'ukri looked away from the place he expected Jordan to emerge any moment now.

"What is it, Quenti? Jordan will be here soon, and I would not wish to miss his entrance."

"Arkaryu has returned from the warrior trial with disturbing news," Quenti replied.

T'ukri frowned as Victor turned too.

"What news?" Victor asked sharply before T'ukri could.

Quenti hesitated, never a good sign.

"What is it, Quenti?" T'ukri prompted.

"As Arkaryu was making his way back, having been bested by your mate, he found Umaq with his hands bound and this spear embedded in a tree nearby."

"Embedded?" T'ukri repeated. "They were to use blunted weapons."

"I am aware," she replied. "Ayar checked every weapon the warriors took with them into the woods to make sure they were properly prepared, yet here this is."

T'ukri took the spear from Quenti and examined it carefully, but it was a standard spear, the kind they kept in the training yards for anyone to use, with no personalized markings at all. "Has Umaq offered any explanation?"

"None," Quenti replied. "He sits in silence, not even acknowledging the questions I ask."

"Let Nandini talk to him," Victor muttered. T'ukri opened his mouth to ask before deciding he had no wish to know what Nandini would do.

"We will wait for Jordan," T'ukri said finally. "If Umaq will not speak, to defend himself or otherwise, then we must learn what occurred from Jordan. Perhaps hearing Jordan's side of the story will loosen Umaq's tongue."

Quenti saluted sharply and withdrew.

"It is the vision from my spirit journey coming true," Victor said when they were alone again. His anger burned through the bond, white-hot and deadly, making T'ukri hope Victor never had reason to turn that anger on him. "He's not wearing any body armor. If that spear had hit him...."

"He is well," T'ukri soothed. "We would both know if he were not."

"That doesn't change the fact that it happened and could happen again," Victor ground out. "It was one thing for him to risk his life when he was in the military. He knew what he was getting into when he suited up. Even in the fight against the miners, we knew the score. This is different. It was supposed to be a training exercise, not a fight for his life!"

The guardian stirred at the thought of Jordan in such a fight without anyone to watch his back, but T'ukri pushed him down ruthlessly. With Victor already angry, T'ukri could not afford even the slightest waver in his control or the guardian would take over and Umaq would not get the opportunity to explain himself. When Jordan returned safely and the formalities had all been observed, then T'ukri could let the guardian out to assure them both that all was well with their mate. Although he might have to wait in line behind Victor for that privilege.

"And if what we fear is indeed what happened, Umaq will pay for violating the warrior code," T'ukri promised, already imagining all the ways he could take retribution. If Jordan was unharmed—and despite everything that had happened, T'ukri felt nothing through the bond to suggest Jordan was injured—Huallpa would most likely decree banishment, and that would be the end of it. That knowledge did nothing to change the twisted pleasure T'ukri took in picturing Umaq begging for mercy beneath the guardian's claws.

"He may not be working alone," Victor replied. "In my vision...." Despite the even tone of voice, T'ukri heard what Victor did not say— that he did not believe for a moment that Umaq had done this without help. The thought turned T'ukri's stomach.

"Then we will face that reality as well," T'ukri said with a sigh. "Though it saddens me to think any of our warriors would be so disaffected."

Beneath the anger that still roiled the surface of their bond lay a sour smear of guilt. That would not do! He took Victor's face in his hands. "Look at me, my own," he commanded gently. Victor lifted his chin so their gazes met. "You are the mates the goddess chose for me. Our union has been blessed with our bond. It is not a burden for you to take on."

"You say that like it's easy," Victor replied, his voice dry. "I've always believed there's no problem that can't be resolved, but this...."

"We will find a resolution," T'ukri promised. "But first we must wait for Jordan."

"That's the hard part," Victor admitted. "I know he's not hurt. We'd be able to tell if he was, and I know he's more than capable of completing the trial without any assistance, but the temptation to go look for him is strong."

T'ukri rested his forehead against Victor's. "We felt the same when you were on your spirit quest. Did we not have the assurance of our bond, I would order Quenti to call off the trial and begin an immediate search, but we do have that assurance, and to call it off now would mean starting the trial over another day and delaying our bonding ceremony even more."

"He'd strangle us both in our sleep." The small chuckle that bubbled up from Victor's chest broke the tension that had gripped them both since Quenti's announcement.

"We shall await his victorious arrival. Then we will deal with the rest."

Victor took a deep breath and smiled, both the anger and the guilt receding as he did. "Sounds like a plan."

VICTOR RESISTED the urge to pace with a veneer of implacable calm. He *knew* Jordan was safe, could feel it in the cocky pride that was beginning to build back up under the anger and determination he could sense through the bond, but until he saw Jordan with his own eyes, he wouldn't be able to relax completely. He'd had too much experience of how Jordan saw what he was feeling as weakness—physical or emotional—and too few days of trusting their bond.

As Jordan drew nearer the temple, it became easier to pinpoint his location until Victor could tell exactly where Jordan would emerge from the forest. Even with all his field experience on expeditions, he didn't see any indication of Jordan's presence, though, until he stepped into the sunlight.

"What the hell?" he muttered. Jordan was good, but Victor had never had trouble before spotting him when he knew Jordan's location.

"The blessings of our bond run deep," T'ukri said.

"All the more so because your mates were not born to our tribe and your bond is so new," Llipya added. "I should not have doubted the goddess's guiding hand."

"Thank you, Mama," T'ukri's words might have been simple, but Victor felt the deep gratitude at her acceptance.

Victor offered her a smile as well and leaned a little more deeply into the bond as Jordan strutted through the village toward the temple. Bon Dieu, Victor loved every cocky inch of him. Best of all, though, was the confidence that radiated through Jordan, all the way to his core. Jordan could fake it so well no one would ever guess at the insecurities that lay hidden beneath the surface, but in this moment, those insecurities were absent. Only time would tell if they would stay banished, but Victor would take what he could get.

He did his best to keep his expression neutral, but all his years of practice failed him as Jordan came nearer with every step. He couldn't help it. The mixture of pride and love and pure, base lust was stronger than his composure. He glanced at T'ukri to see if he was any more successful, only to stifle a groan at the animal hunger in T'ukri's eyes.

Getting through the investigation into what had happened with Umaq was going to be torture.

Jordan strode up to the temple steps, shoulders back, chin lifted in defiance, attitude radiating from every pore, and Victor had never wanted him more. "Your Majesties," he said with a slight bow to Huallpa and Llipya. Then he turned to Quenti. "*Kuraka.*"

Quenti didn't smile, although the light in her eyes might have been amusement. Instead she saluted him smartly. All the gathered warriors followed her lead. "Prince Consort. Be welcome in the ranks of Machu Llaqta's warriors."

"It is an honor I will always strive to deserve," Jordan replied, and the truth in his words resonated so clearly Victor didn't need the bond to know this was an oath that would bind Jordan for the rest of his life.

Ch'aska broke ranks with the rest of the royal family and rushed down the steps to hug Jordan. "I am so glad you are back safe."

Which brought them right back to the elephant in the room.

Or whatever the appropriate Runasimi idiom would be.

Jordan was back safe, but someone had tried to keep him from returning at all.

Jordan just laughed, though, and hugged Ch'aska back. "So am I. What's next? Do I get a feast to celebrate?"

"You do, but first we must deal with the traitor who would have kept you from returning at all," Huallpa said.

THE MOMENT Cusi dragged Umaq into the room where Huallpa held court, the guardian surged to the fore, determined to eliminate the threat to his mates. T'ukri squashed the impulse as best he could but let the guardian's fangs and claws appear. It could not hurt to remind Umaq exactly who he had attacked in the forest. He had been unwilling to answer Quenti's questions. Maybe the sight of the guardian would loosen his tongue.

Cusi deposited Umaq on a stool, his hands still tied behind his back, and saluted sharply. "Your Majesty, Your Highnesses."

Jordan's discomfort at the title radiated through the bond, but he did not protest it as he returned the salute. The guardian rumbled with satisfaction at seeing his malku accepting all the accolades of his new role.

"May I proceed, Your Majesty?" Quenti asked.

"The floor is yours, kuraka," Huallpa replied.

"Prince Consort, will you tell us what happened during your warrior trial?" she requested, turning to Jordan.

"Kuraka," Jordan said with a salute.

The guardian strained against T'ukri's control, impatient with any delay, but T'ukri approved of the bit of theatrics. Jordan was a Runa warrior now. He had completed the trial despite Umaq's attempt. T'ukri grabbed the guardian by its ruff and wrestled it back beneath his will.

"The trial began pretty much the way you told me it would. I ran into two warriors. They both had blunted weapons, and although they put up a good fight, they tapped out when I got the clear upper hand.

They both wished me well, and I continued on. A few minutes later—more than five but not ten—I heard a rustle in the brush and found cover, expecting an encounter like the first two. Instead a spear landed in the tree where my head would have been if I hadn't moved in time."

"Not bounced off the tree," Quenti verified.

"No, embedded in the tree," Jordan said.

"This spear?" Quenti asked when Cusi offered it.

Jordan examined it and shrugged. "That one or one like it. I didn't take the time to study it."

T'ukri made no attempt to silence the guardian's displeased rumble at hearing about his mate in danger and took great pleasure in watching Umaq pale at the sound. Sensing weakness in its prey, the guardian lunged against T'ukri's control hard enough to drag him two steps forward. Victor caught his arm before he could go any farther, his presence through the bond a cool wash of calm over a will of iron that not even the guardian could shake off. T'ukri grabbed on to Victor with all his might. If he lost control of the guardian in open court, no matter the provocation, Huallpa would expel him.

"Easy," Victor murmured. "We'll get our turn, and Umaq knows it."

T'ukri took a deep breath and another, until the guardian settled again beneath his control.

"What happened then?" Quenti asked.

Then Jordan kicked the bastard's ass, T'ukri thought with no small amount of pride in his mate's prowess.

"I figured out where the spear came from and got the drop on the warrior who threw it," Jordan replied, his tone even despite the anger radiating off him. "I took him down, tied him up, and kept going. I had my warrior trial to complete."

"Is this the man who attacked you?" Quenti indicated Umaq with a sharp nod of her head.

"Yep, that's the fucker." Jordan flushed. "Um, apologies, Your Majesty."

Huallpa tried—and failed—to bite back a smile. "You described him most aptly."

"Did he say anything?" Quenti asked. She masked her amusement better than Huallpa had, but T'ukri had a lifetime's experience reading her expressions. "Offer any explanation or excuse?"

"He said something in Runasimi," Jordan replied, "but I haven't learned enough to figure out what."

"Thank you, Your Highness," Quenti said with another salute that Jordan returned. She moved to loom over Umaq with all the weight of her height and rank. "You stand accused of attempting to assassinate a warrior of our tribe, the prince consort and mate of Chapaqpuma. What do you have to say for yourself?"

Umaq cowered but remained silent.

"You would do well to remember what you are accused of and the range of punishments you could be facing," Huallpa said from his seat.

Umaq's gaze flickered between Huallpa and T'ukri. Huallpa's expression remained impassive, but T'ukri bared his fangs. If Huallpa did not banish him, Umaq would have to face the guardian's justice, and while it would be final, it would be neither swift nor merciful.

Victor squeezed his arm, reining him in again. T'ukri would have resented his cool demeanor if he had not felt the same roiling anger beneath Victor's façade.

"Who else went into the jungle without blunting their weapons?" T'ukri demanded. "Give me names and perhaps the guardian will be merciful."

Umaq fixed his gaze on a point above T'ukri's head and said nothing.

"May I, Your Majesty?" Victor asked.

Huallpa looked surprised. "Go ahead, churi."

"Kuraka, will you translate for me so I can be sure the accused understands me?" Victor asked.

"It would be my honor, Your Highness," Quenti replied.

Victor walked forward until he stood directly in front of Umaq. The guardian tensed, even knowing Umaq was bound and helpless. If he were to escape and get his hands on a weapon…. T'ukri cut off that train of thought. Victor was no less dangerous because he was not a warrior.

"It must be hard," Victor said sympathetically. "All your life, you've been taught to be wary of outsiders, and suddenly there are two in your midst, and not just here, but mated to your prince and participating in your sacred rituals."

Umaq did not reply, but he did focus on Victor when Quenti translated his words.

"Change is always hard," Victor continued. "I mean, look at Jordan and me. Everything about the situation is a change for us. The language, the food, the clothes, the traditions, our roles within society, even our relationship to each other...."

Umaq's expression shuttered again, making T'ukri wonder if Victor had misstepped, but Jordan did not seem worried. If anything, he was amused, like he knew exactly what Victor was doing and was just waiting for Umaq to fall into the trap.

"And I know what you're thinking. Everything might have changed for us, but it's change for the better. We haven't lost anything. We've gained status, family, a whole tribe of people. And you're right about what we've gained, but we've lost too. We had jobs that we've given up. We have friends we won't see often now, or maybe ever again, since Prince T'ukri won't want to travel far and we don't want to bring outsiders into Machu Llaqta without reason."

Victor paused to let Quenti translate. T'ukri took the opportunity to flood the bond with as much love and gratitude as he could. Victor might be leading up to something with Umaq, but the words he spoke were truth regardless of his reasons, and T'ukri needed Victor to know he was aware of the sacrifice they had made to stay with him.

"But this is where the difference between us becomes clear," Victor said, his voice and face hardening. "It is the measure of a man how he deals with change. Does he embrace it? Does he work to accept it? Does he resign himself to it? Or does he reject it? And if he does reject it, how does he show that? Through avoidance? Through passive resistance? Or through violence?"

"It is sacrilege to bring outsiders into Machu Llaqta!" Umaq said, finally breaking his silence.

T'ukri opened his mouth to argue in defense of his decision, but Victor beat him to it. "But that is where you've misjudged."

T'ukri frowned. He had not expected that any more than Umaq had.

"You look at us and see men who were not born in the city, so therefore we must be outsiders, and you reject us without looking any deeper, to the point that you tried to kill Jordan," Victor said. "But we are the mates of Chapaqpuma, a bond blessed by Pachamama herself. A *true* bond. How can we be outsiders, regardless of our place of birth, if Pachamama has accepted us? And not just accepted us, but given us gifts of our own that have prepared us for our roles as Chapaqpuma's mates? We have passed every test and trial put before us to prove ourselves worthy of our new roles. We have risked our lives for Machu Llaqta and its people."

He paused again to let Quenti translate before finishing. "What have *you* done besides attack the chosen mate of Chapaqpuma?"

"Machu Llaqta ñawpa!" Umaq spat.

The isolationist slogan broke T'ukri's control. He lunged at Umaq, claws fully extended. Victor caught his wrist just before he tore Umaq's throat out. Umaq reared back in fear, and Victor leaned down until he was at eye level with Umaq. "You fear Chapaqpuma, and with good reason, but he is not the one you should be most worried about. No matter what your fate today, no matter what punishment Inca Huallpa hands down, you would be wise to spend the rest of your days looking over your shoulder, because I will not forget what you tried to do."

"Tell us who you conspired with and I will spare your life," Huallpa said from the throne. "Otherwise I will leave your fate in the hands of my sons."

Umaq's eyes rolled back until only the whites showed, and he began babbling names.

CHAPTER 43

VICTOR WAITED patiently while Huallpa issued orders. Quenti, T'ukri, and warriors loyal to the throne sprung into action the moment Umaq finished naming names. Victor was pleased to see Jordan included in their number. Cusi dragged Umaq out with them to execute his banishment along with the other traitors'. The rest of the council left until only Victor and Huallpa remained in the chamber. Huallpa sighed deeply and slumped back into his seat.

Since he had seen the murals in the temple, Victor had been looking for a chance to speak to Huallpa alone, but the opportunity had never arisen. Now, though, Huallpa looked like he could use some cheering up, and Victor hoped this might do it. He *had* told Umaq he would leave his fate in the hands of his sons, after all. And he had welcomed them when they'd returned after bonding with T'ukri.

"Your Majesty. Huallpa."

Huallpa looked up.

"There is something I've been meaning to tell you, but the time has never been right," Victor said. "Would you have a moment now before we join everyone for Jordan's feast?"

"Of course," Huallpa said, straightening in his seat. "What would you have me hear?"

"I know from what T'ukri and Tamya both have said that you were Chapaqpuma for many years, and I'm sure you must have protected many people in that time, but do you remember saving a boy from the Shining Path in Vitcos twenty-five or so years ago?" Victor asked.

Huallpa pursed his lips. "I do remember that. It was farther afield than I wished to go, with T'ukri so young, but I felt compelled to do so. Each morning when I awoke, alone and missing my mates, I questioned my sanity, but each time I took a step toward home, it seemed as if I walked through the thickest mud, yet when I turned to continue on, I had never moved so quickly, even when fully in the form of Chapaqpuma. But how do you know of it?"

Victor blinked back tears. "I was the boy you saved that day. I swore then I'd find you again so I could say thank you. Pretty much every choice I made after that, from studying anthropology to applying for the grant that paid for Jordan and me to come on this expedition, has been motivated by that promise. So first, thank you for saving my life. And then, thank you for what my life has become because of that moment. I never imagined it would lead here, but now that it has…."

He couldn't get the rest of the words out around the lump in his throat, but when he looked up, Huallpa had tears in his eyes as well.

"You spoke truly at Umaq's trial. The goddess protects her own, even when they were born outside her borders," Huallpa said finally. "I cannot welcome you more than I have already done nor claim you more fully as my son than I will tomorrow when you bond with T'ukri, but if I needed more proof that I made the right decision in either of those acts, I have it now. Welcome home, churi."

Victor accepted Huallpa's embrace, the tears he had been fighting falling freely.

Victor had spent years telling himself he was a grown man long past the need for a father's approval. He had resigned himself to stilted conversations and empty platitudes on his birthday and Christmas cards after his coming out strained his relationship with his family almost to the breaking point. To have parental approval and affection so freely on offer now nearly broke him in a way the lack had never done, except that Huallpa didn't want to break him. Huallpa wanted to build him up, to support and encourage him as he supported and encouraged T'ukri and Ch'aska. Huallpa offered a new family, not one with the sometimes weak fault lines of in-laws, but a fully integrated one.

Victor was no fool. He was grabbing on with both hands and never letting go. "Thank you, Papãnin."

JORDAN LEANED back in his chair, stuffed to the gills on everything the village chefs had prepared for the feast. He hadn't managed to eat breakfast before Quenti showed up for the warrior trial and then they'd had to deal with Umaq and the other traitors, so he'd been starving, even more than usual.

"Happy, my malku?" T'ukri asked from next to him.

"Very," Jordan replied.

"T'ukri," Cusi called, interrupting their conversation, "you have competition, my friend."

"Competition?" T'ukri asked. Jordan sat up straighter, alert for any threat, but Cusi was smiling, so Jordan hoped it was a joke, not something serious.

"For the fastest time through the warrior trial and for the fewest number of warriors who spotted the initiate," Cusi replied.

Jordan relaxed again, hoping he hadn't broken any unspoken taboos by beating T'ukri's records. Not that he could do anything about it now.

"I am not surprised," T'ukri replied, pride in his voice and in the bond. "He is an able warrior and a worthy addition to our ranks." He looked beyond Cusi and raised his voice slightly. "And it would behoove everyone to remember that, unlike most who celebrate this victory, Jordan is no novice, but rather an experienced warrior with much more to teach us than he still has to learn."

Jordan leaned a little farther back in his chair and clasped his hands behind his head, stretching and letting his pride and—*yes, Victor*—his cockiness show. He'd earned his place among the warriors, even if he hadn't learned his skills in Machu Llaqta, and he'd be damned if he'd apologize for it.

Cusi bowed to them both and, loud enough to be heard, replied, "I, for one, look forward to any lesson our prince consort is willing to share."

"As do all warriors loyal to the throne," Quenti added from her place at T'ukri's shoulder.

Suck on that, bastards, Jordan thought with a feral grin that matched the one T'ukri wore.

Cusi's announcement—or Quenti's not-at-all subtle support, Jordan wasn't stupid—acted as a signal for the other warriors, because as soon as he stepped away, others lined up to offer their congratulations. Jordan knew some of them. Others he recognized from the fight against the miners or from sneaking past them in the woods. And a few were completely unfamiliar to him. He'd have to fix that. He needed to recognize everyone so he'd know who was on their side if it came to a fight against people who weren't conveniently wearing Western attire.

Jordan smiled when the kid he'd encountered in the woods approached the table. The kid looked like he couldn't decide whether to congratulate Jordan or run away screaming.

"Hey, kid," Jordan said, determined to set him at ease. "I didn't get your name out there."

The kid blushed, either at being singled out now or at Jordan letting everyone know he'd been bested, but he stopped looking like he was going to run at any second, so Jordan counted that as a win. "It is Manqu, Your Highness."

Jordan started to correct him again, but he couldn't get away with his *I'm just a warrior* shtick when he was sitting next to T'ukri with Llipya and Huallpa farther down the table after Huallpa had claimed both Victor and himself as his sons at the end of the trial. "Good job out there today, Manqu. We'll have to spar sometime."

The blush deepened, almost indigo, but Manqu held Jordan's gaze. "I would be honored."

That wasn't quite what Jordan was going for, but he'd take it.

"You will have your own acolytes if you continue like this," T'ukri observed with a smile. "Not unlike Victor's Jedi Knights, I think?"

Jordan couldn't help it. He burst out laughing at the thought of anyone looking up to him that way. "I've spent *way* too much time in the shadows to be compared to a Jedi," he said when he got his laughter under control.

"You know it's not that cut-and-dried," Victor started.

"I know," Jordan said, cutting off the impending lecture, "I still don't measure up."

Victor looked like he was going to argue, so Jordan turned back to greet the rest of his well-wishers. They could discuss the rest later— or never, as far as Jordan was concerned. He'd played the hand life had dealt him, and he was making his peace with the way it had turned out. After all, it had led him to the Marines, to Victor, and finally to T'ukri. He'd take that over any other outcome.

WHEN THE feast ended, Victor expected to be shunted back to the house again, to spend a final night alone before the bonding ceremony, but Ch'aska looped her arm through Jordan's and Huallpa rested a warm hand on Victor's shoulder, and before he knew it, they'd been swept into the palace with the rest of the family.

T'ukri must have felt his surprise, because he drifted to Victor's side when they reached the private area of the palace. "You have done what was required of you to become members of our tribe. You have proven yourselves to my parents each in your own ways. My mother may always gripe about the way our bonding came about, but she no longer questions the validity of my choice. She will insist you return to the guest house one last night, but you are welcome here now. And the bonding ceremony is tomorrow. We have much to discuss."

"Like what?" Jordan asked as he joined them.

"Like the particulars of the ceremony," Victor replied. "How the day will go. What will be expected of us."

"Nothing complicated. We will go to the temple and declare our intention to bond before the elders, the ancestors, and the goddess. Then we will speak our vows to one another. And then we will feast until we can slip away for our time of seclusion," T'ukri elaborated.

"What are the vows supposed to say?" Jordan asked before Victor could.

"There are no specific words," T'ukri said. "It is not like wedding vows in Europe or America. The words should come from the heart, although usually they include the promise to love one another and, for Chapaqpuma and his or her mates, to protect Machu Llaqta for as long as that mantle rests on their shoulders."

"Bonding isn't limited to Chapaqpuma?" Victor asked, his interest caught by that little detail.

"We use the same rituals regardless of who is bonding, but in most cases, the word is more symbolic than in our case," T'ukri explained. "And not everyone has two mates. Cusi and Quenti, for example."

Jordan groaned. "Don't remind me. Nandini is still with them. I don't need that image in my head."

"Then don't think about it," Victor said, amused at Jordan's antics.

"It has also happened that what starts as two later becomes three. My fathers were mated for several years before they persuaded my mother to join them," T'ukri continued. "As long as all partners are willing, the bond can expand. Cusi is nearly as lucky as I am."

Jordan shook his head. "No, no, no. Not listening."

Victor gave up trying to hold in his laughter. It felt good after the tension of the day.

T'ukri chuckled as well.

"My prince," Quenti said from the doorway, "we have come to celebrate the impending bonding ceremony with our fellow warrior."

"Come, Jordan," T'ukri said. "A night of revelry awaits us."

"Forgive me, my prince, but you will have to celebrate on your own. Tonight is for Jordan."

Victor watched, surprised and a little envious as Jordan strutted out the door with Quenti.

"She won't let him do anything stupid, will she?" Victor asked.

"Before a bonding ceremony, the friends of those who will bond celebrate with them. Chicha, dancing, the telling of tales. At the most they will drag him to the spring and throw him in so he will be freshly bathed. Someone—probably Quenti if I know her at all—will stay sober to make sure everyone is safe."

"Good. He deserves to make a few new friends," Victor said.

"Do not despair. A shaman will be here to collect you soon, I am sure." As if summoned by T'ukri's words, a man Victor didn't know appeared in the doorway.

"Prince T'ukri, if you would excuse us?"

"Of course, Poma," T'ukri said. "Victor, this is Poma, a shaman Tayta mentored."

"Yuri was a wonderful mentor and also a good friend," Poma said. "I look forward to telling you about him, but tonight is a night for celebration. Come, the others are waiting. With the rush to induct you both into the tribe, we have not had the chance to welcome you properly. I am only sorry that your welcome and the celebration of your impending bonding will be combined rather than two separate celebrations. The warriors claim to have the best parties, but do not believe them. They have never been to one of our parties."

"DID THEY leave you here alone?" Huallpa asked when he came into the sitting room a few minutes later.

"Quenti claimed Jordan for a celebration of his becoming a warrior, and Poma whisked Victor off to a shaman party," T'ukri replied. "I was invited to neither."

Huallpa took a seat across from T'ukri and offered him a glass of chicha. "Let them have this night, churi. They are new to the tribe and to their roles within it. While being your mates will define much of their future within the tribe, they are still individuals and deserve to have friends of their own. The days and years ahead will be long for them. I am not questioning their commitment to you or to us, but think about what Victor said today at the traitor's trial. They have left *everything* behind to be with you. You should be thanking the goddess Quenti and Poma and others have taken it upon themselves to step into the spaces that will be left empty by that choice. A new bond feels all-consuming, but as much as we love our mates, we cannot be all things to each other. Your mother still goes to the training grounds to practice when I am busy with other things. You know how much time Tayta spent in the temple. Jordan and Victor will need those same outlets, and they do not have the years of their childhood spent here to have gained the same connections."

T'ukri probed lightly at the bond and felt the happiness that radiated back from both Jordan and Victor. Not the same joy and bone-deep contentment that came from being together, but a different kind of satisfaction.

"You are wise, Papãnin. Thank you."

"Come, let us see that all is prepared for tomorrow. Your mates will need outfits for your bonding ceremony, and I have the perfect thing."

T'ukri picked up his mug of chicha and followed Huallpa deeper into the palace.

CHAPTER 44

BY DAWN, the patience T'ukri had found the night before had evaporated with the morning mist. He wanted his mates and he wanted them now. And if he did not get them soon, he would not be responsible for his actions.

He marched out of the palace and across the city, uncaring of who saw him or what they thought when they did until he reached the house where Jordan and Victor had slept for the last time. Tonight they would sleep with him in the grotto he had ordered prepared for their time of seclusion, and when that had ended, they would sleep with him in his bed in his rooms in the palace.

Where they belonged.

He found them still in bed, awake but bleary-eyed in the way he associated with too much chicha. "There will be coffee in my rooms by the time we get back."

"Is that allowed?" Victor asked, though he perked up at the mention of coffee.

"I no longer care," T'ukri replied. "You have been fully accepted into the tribe, and our bonding ceremony is in a matter of hours. You have no family to help you prepare, and Papãnin has already adopted you. We will prepare together." He held out his hand. "Please. I need my mates."

Within seconds, they flanked him, wrapping him in the embrace that had been missing since he returned to palace after Victor's spirit journey. All the tension that had built up at the base of his skull eased with the contact. He rested his head against theirs and breathed in their presence until he no longer felt like he was trying to climb out of his skin.

"When did it get this bad?" Jordan asked. "You should have said something."

"I did not realize it had until your touch eased it," T'ukri admitted. "So much about our bonding has been outside the way things are usually done that I am finding unexpected effects at every turn. To have started to bond and then be forced to wait to complete it, to find my mates only after I ascended to the role of Chapaqpuma, to have my mates come from outside Machu Llaqta in the first place…. We have no path to follow for any of these circumstances, much less for all of them together."

"After the bonding ceremony, that's it, though, right?" Jordan said. "I mean, no more formalities, no more hoops to jump through? After that, we'll be together, no matter what comes?"

"Yes, the bonding ceremony is the final step," T'ukri said.

"Then let's go." He released T'ukri and started toward the door.

"Clothes, Jordan," Victor said. "Unless you were planning on flashing the whole city?"

The guardian rumbled its displeasure at the thought of anyone else seeing Jordan's bare skin, although given his mate's predilection for sleeveless shirts, he would not be able to keep the sight entirely to himself.

Jordan grumbled and pulled on pants and a T-shirt before continuing on his path toward the door. Victor dressed quickly and followed, T'ukri a step behind him.

Ch'aska met them at the door to the palace. "I will delay Mama as long as I can, but I do not know how long that will be. Do not get *too* distracted."

T'ukri waved his thanks as he ushered Jordan and Victor through the palace and into his private space. The moment they were alone, he stripped his T-shirt over his head and dropped the loose wrap from around his waist. Jordan whistled—teasing and appreciative in one sharp, sexy sound, making Victor laugh and T'ukri grin.

"Come," T'ukri said. "I will prepare the tub so we can bathe before the bonding ceremony."

He walked into the bathing area, certain they would follow him, and set the tub to filling. The guardian purred in his chest as he turned back to his mates. The wait was almost over. In a matter of hours, the formalities would be complete, and they would be alone together for a week—a full, long, blessed week of seclusion with nothing to do but glut their senses in one another and strengthen their bond into the bedrock that had supported his parents since their bonding.

He turned back to Jordan and Victor to see them peeling off the last of their clothes. "I had thought to do that," he said.

"Tonight," Victor said. "We don't know how long we have this morning, so we shouldn't linger too long, but tonight, when we know we won't be interrupted, we can take our time and do all the things we haven't yet had time to do."

"Tonight," T'ukri echoed. He might have been denied undressing them, but he would not be denied washing them. He took a handful of saqta and worked it into a lather as he stepped into the waist-deep tub. Jordan and Victor followed.

T'ukri slid his hands over the expanse of Jordan's chest, the suds from the saqta easing the friction between their skin. Jordan arched eagerly into his touch, encouraging T'ukri to linger, but Victor's warning—and Ch'aska's—hovered on the edge of his consciousness. His mother would be there soon, and while she might accept finding them together, finding them bathing together would only set off another flood of lectures that he could do without on the precipice of their bonding ceremony. Instead T'ukri rubbed cleansing foam into the hair at Jordan's groin, forcing himself not to stroke Jordan to full hardness—not that it would have taken much.

"Sit," he urged when he was done.

Jordan sank into the water, looking perfect in T'ukri's rooms. He would look even better in T'ukri's bed, but he pushed that thought aside.

Soon, he promised the guardian, who did not understand the delay.

"Your turn," he said to Victor.

Victor stretched his arms wide, offering himself to T'ukri, and T'ukri smothered a curse. Surely not even his mother could expect him to resist such a sight.

Except that she would never see it, and even if she did, she had eyes only for Papãnin—and Tayta before his death. And while she might understand, she was too much the queen to approve.

He groaned as he rinsed his hands and reached for more of the saqta to wash Victor. Victor stood perfectly still as T'ukri bathed him, but his obvious erection and the throbbing beat of his heart through the bond belied his exterior calm. Still, to have a mate who could appear calm even under these circumstances would be a great boon.

When he had finished with Victor as well, he sank into the water himself, intending to bathe quickly, but Jordan and Victor had other ideas. They pulled him between them and cleaned him as thoroughly and as carefully as he had cleaned them.

Then Jordan brushed his fingers over T'ukri's entrance. "I've been waiting to do this since I watched you outside Paucar's village."

T'ukri spread his legs. "It is important to be clean before any ceremony."

"Then I had better make sure you're as clean as possible."

Jordan's fingers were thick and perfect inside him. He did not press deeply, instead stretching and teasing the entrance, but even that was enough to have T'ukri hard and aching for more.

"Think about that during the ceremony," Jordan purred in his ear. "When we're alone, I'll finish what I started and more. Is that enough motivation to get us out of there quickly?"

"More than enough," T'ukri said. He stifled a groan of protest when Jordan pulled his hand away, but they still had to dress before his mother came looking for them, and he did not know how much time had passed.

"Good." Jordan kissed him, all fire and heat and lust and need. T'ukri tried to soften it, but Jordan broke the contact and pulled himself out of the pool, water sluicing down the muscles of his back and over the honey-gold skin of his buttocks—another sight T'ukri would never grow tired of.

"I just want to bite him," Victor said next to T'ukri. "Right there on the smooth curve of his ass."

Jordan looked over his shoulder. "What's stopping you?"

"The fact that we have an appointment with a queen, a council of elders, and a hopefully benevolent goddess," Victor replied dryly. "But once that's over, I'm going to cover you in so many bruises you won't be able to sit down for a month."

"I will help," T'ukri said, letting his fangs show the slightest bit. He would never break the skin or do anything to hurt his mates, but the idea of Jordan's perfect flesh covered in bruises from his teeth was too enticing to resist.

Jordan's eyes went dark with lust. "Do it. One each, right now. Let me feel it while we bond, knowing I've got your marks on me already."

T'ukri did not need to be asked twice. He lunged forward, catching Jordan's hips in his hands, so he could apply his teeth to the tender skin where buttocks curved into thigh. Jordan howled above him, already begging for more. The guardian stirred at the idea, but T'ukri held back. *Soon*, he reminded the guardian. Soon they would be alone and bonded in the eyes of his people as well as in the eyes of the goddess, and they could revel in each other's bodies for hours on end.

When he pulled away, the red mark was already deepening to purple. A quick glance showed a similar mark from Victor's teeth on the other cheek. "Perfect. But now we must dress."

T'ukri offered Jordan and Victor the clothes Huallpa had helped him pick out the night before while his mates celebrated their impending bonding ceremony with their respective guilds, but T'ukri had not needed to search for an outfit for himself. Tayta had helped him make it when he reached adulthood in preparation for this very day. Now that it had arrived, he would wear it proudly, even if Tayta was not with them in this plane to see it. He would be watching from the ancestral plane and celebrating alongside them.

CHAPTER 45

JORDAN TOOK the outfit T'ukri offered and looked around for his underwear, only to see T'ukri pull his own pants on without anything underneath.

Okay. Jordan could freeball it. Between the loose pants and long tunic, no one would be able to see anything he didn't want them to. He caught the flash of heat in Victor's eyes as he pulled the trousers over his bruised ass. He'd be feeling the twin bites every time he took a step, exactly the reminder he needed of how much Victor and T'ukri wanted him.

That was easier to accept than the rest of the emotions he felt through the bond—had been feeling for the past three days. He was used to people wanting to fuck him. He had a hot ass and knew it. The idea of someone loving him—much less two people—was still new and scary and too big to take in. He'd get used to it eventually. If he knew one thing about himself, it was that he could adapt to new circumstances, but it wouldn't happen overnight.

He smoothed the tunic over his chest, appreciating the fine material and detailing. He might prefer ratty jeans and a soft T-shirt in his off hours, but he'd spent enough time with Victor and Nandini to recognize quality when he wore it.

They had only a sharp knock as warning before the door swung open and Llipya sailed in, wearing an elaborate dress with a huge headdress covering her hair. A servant hovered in the doorway behind her.

"Good, you are ready." She gestured for Jordan to come toward her. He glanced at T'ukri, but he looked as confused as Jordan felt. *Great. No help there.*

He approached silently and gave her a respectful nod when he reached her side.

"Bonded of my son, strength to support him, warrior in your own right, who has proved his valor already, defending Machu Llaqta and rescuing its prince." She took a bowl of something from the servant and dipped her finger in it. He almost pulled away when she reached toward his face, but he remembered their entrance to the city and all the different patterns on people's faces as well as the ways T'ukri had painted his face during the precourtship rituals.

She drew a single line between his eyes down the bridge of his nose, then put dots carefully around his eyes. "Your aim is perfect and your eyesight even better. I claim you for the Condor, in recognition of your gifts, and welcome you among the warriors of Machu Llaqta."

Jordan bit back his gasp and bowed deeply before stepping aside.

She turned to Victor. "Yuri is not here to welcome you, bonded of my son, guide of his soul, keeper of his humanity, so it falls to me instead. You protected the temple, guarding those who could not guard themselves. You protected our prince at the risk of your own life though you have the soul of a shaman, not a warrior."

She painted a line across Victor's cheeks, almost one ear to the other. Instead of dots around his eyes, she placed them in a circle around his forehead. "In recognition of your words of wisdom and your gentle soul, I claim you for the Serpent and welcome you to the Council of Machu Llaqta."

Jordan's eyes bugged out at that. Warrior of Machu Llaqta was honor enough, and they'd talked about Victor becoming a shaman, but he suspected this was the first time an outsider had ever sat on the council, much less someone as much of an outsider as they were.

Victor bowed deeply after Llipya's pronouncement.

Finally she turned to T'ukri. "My son, my pride and joy, you have confounded me from the moment you were born. You have become a man to make our people—and your fathers—proud, the best of both of them." Slowly she traced the same marks on his face that he had put there during his rituals in Paucar's village. "The goddess has blessed you with other gifts beyond this world. In times of need, you bear the strength and senses of the great goddess Pachamama herself—speed, stealth, vision and hearing, claws and fangs—to defend yourself and defeat our foes. Those gifts come at a price. You have chosen mates to help you bear the weight of her command. Bind yourself to them with the blessing of the ancestors, the goddess, and the throne."

Jordan's breath caught in his throat. He knew Llipya had thawed toward him after the warrior trial, but this was far more than that. She had given her formal blessing. Hopefully in time, this would be a funny family story rather than a point of contention.

Families—real families—had those, right? It wasn't just something portrayed on TV and in the movies?

T'ukri bowed formally to his mother and reached for Jordan and Victor. Llipya swanned back out of the room, giving them a moment alone.

"Did she mean that?" Jordan asked. "Or was that something she had to do whether she liked it or not?"

"Nothing requires her to do it, though it is often the queen who does when Chapaqpuma is part of the royal family," T'ukri replied. "She could have sent Papãnin if she did not want to do it."

Jordan relaxed slightly. It wasn't Huallpa's warm welcome yet, but it was better than the cold anger from earlier.

"Are you ready?" T'ukri asked.

Jordan wasn't sure anything could make him completely ready, but they had already delayed too long, as far as he was concerned. Radiating as much confidence as he could, he nodded.

Holding tightly to their hands, T'ukri led them out of the room and the palace and toward the temple. All along the route, people gathered, even more colorfully dressed and tightly packed than when they had returned from saving T'ukri, driving home to Jordan how big a deal this was for them. The next few minutes wouldn't just change Jordan's life. They would change the lives of every person in the valley.

Shit. He wasn't ready for that kind of responsibility. He could barely keep his own life together. How was he supposed to be in any way responsible for an entire tribe?

"Breathe," T'ukri said softly. "And smile. They are happy to see us."

Jordan did his best to smile, but he suspected it was more of a grimace.

As they approached the temple, Jordan saw that Huallpa and Llipya were now joined by half a dozen others, men and women in full formal dress, although the headpieces were less elaborate than the ones Huallpa and Llipya wore.

"The elders?" Victor asked.

"One from each major line of the tribe," T'ukri replied. "I will introduce you to them properly another time."

More to learn. Just what Jordan needed. Then he caught sight of Nandini standing with Quenti, Cusi, and the other warriors. She wore a traditional outfit similar to Quenti's and as wide and genuine a smile as he had ever seen on her face. As they neared, the warriors saluted as one, their faces stern beneath painted marks similar to the ones Llipya had put on Jordan. Then Quenti caught his eye and winked, and Jordan relaxed. They might have their game faces on for the ceremony, but these were the same men and women who'd done their best to get him falling-down drunk last night while telling him more wild stories than he was willing to believe.

T'ukri inclined his head in response to their salute but did not let go of Jordan's and Victor's hands, so Jordan figured it was okay if he just nodded and smiled too.

Finally they stood at the foot the temple steps. Jordan glanced at the statue of the Incan trilogy. With the marks on his face still fresh and Llipya's words ringing in his ears, the imagery took on a whole new level of meaning.

"We come to petition the goddess's blessing on our bond," T'ukri said in Spanish before saying something in Runasimi. Jordan hoped it was simply a repeat of the words, not something he was missing.

One of the elders replied in Runasimi. Llipya shot him a fierce look and spoke in Spanish, "All who seek her blessing are welcome in the temple."

She stepped to one side and Huallpa to the other, clearing a path for them to enter.

Jordan clung to T'ukri's hand and to the steadiness of the bond as they walked into a dim space lit only by a few oil lamps. At the far end was a large gold statue of an earth goddess.

T'ukri led them across the open space until they stood directly in front of the statue. Behind them, people crowded into the temple until they could barely move. Jordan took a deep breath and tried not to search for alternate exits or think about how vulnerable they were to an arrow or spear if someone wanted to take them out right now.

Then Tamya stepped to the side of the statue. "Who comes before the goddess?" she asked in broken Spanish.

"T'ukri, son of Huallpa, Llipya, and Yuri, prince of Machu Llaqta, chosen by the goddess as Chapaqpuma, the guardian of her people," T'ukri said formally.

"And who do you bring with you?" she asked.

"My chosen mates to whom I wish to bind myself, body and spirit, for the rest of our days. The Condor, Jordan Harris, warrior, marksman, source of my strength, adopted son of Huallpa; and the Serpent, Victor Itoua, diplomat and wise man, source of my humanity, adopted son of Huallpa."

Jordan blinked, fighting back the emotions that threatened to overwhelm him at T'ukri's introduction and the reminder of Huallpa's acceptance.

Tamya turned to Jordan. "Child of the Condor, are you here freely to enter this bond?"

"Yes," he choked out, hoping that was enough of an answer.

"Child of the Serpent, are you here freely to enter this bond?" she asked Victor.

"I am."

She gestured for them to continue.

T'ukri lifted both their hands to his lips and kissed their knuckles. "Long has my spirit sought its mates, but I found them not among my own people. I searched for many years, hoping to encounter them as I learned of the outside world and brought news back to my people, but that hope, too, was denied. When the mantle of Chapaqpuma passed to me, I feared I would soon have no choice but to settle on less than my heart's desire for fear of otherwise losing all control. Then I walked into Paucar's village and I saw you. Everything about you called to me even as I wondered how you could possibly accept my courtship. But the goddess blessed me, and you did. You followed me here, accepted my suit, braved my family, and fought alongside my people. You opened your hearts to the guardian as you did to me, and even when you learned that I was tied to this land, you did not turn away. My Condor, my Serpent, my strength and my humanity, I pledge my life and my love to you for as long as the goddess sees fit for me to walk this realm, and I claim you now in front of the ancestors so that even when I pass into that plane, I can find you again."

Victor raised an eyebrow at Jordan, but he shook his head. He couldn't get words out around the lump in his throat at the moment.

Victor repeated T'ukri's gesture, kissing T'ukri's knuckles, then reached for Jordan's hand and kissed it too.

"Jordan," he began, "I have known you and loved you for years, but I never thought I stood a chance. When I look at you, I see everything I'm not, but somehow you looked back and saw someone you could love in return." He squeezed Jordan's hand and held tight as he turned to T'ukri. "Your arrival in Paucar's village was what started it all. It brought my feelings for Jordan into the open even before we realized your intentions. When we decided to accept your suit, we didn't know everything that meant, but we knew we wanted to be with you. The rest—the prince, Chapaqpuma, the titles, and everything they represent—are not why we're here. We're here because you looked at us and didn't see outsiders. You looked at us and saw your mates. As a young man, I pledged myself to knowledge and its pursuit to the benefit of all. Today I pledge myself to a different cause, one that will see me through to the end of my days. I pledge myself to you, T'ukri, and to you, Jordan. To Machu Llaqta and its people in whatever capacity I can best serve them."

They both turned to look expectantly at Jordan. To buy himself a second more, he kissed each of their knuckles. "I'm not good with words," he said, "but I know this. I know I love you both and can't imagine my life without you now. This is where I choose to be. I'll fight for you and for Machu Llaqta for as long as I have strength to draw my bow, and when that fails, I'll find another way to keep on fighting. I...." He tried to remember T'ukri's exact words, but they wouldn't come. "I love you," he said again, "and I'm yours."

The lamps guttered as a sudden breeze swept through the temple. When it passed, the light returned, even brighter than before. Behind them, people started cheering and stomping their feet. The cheers resolved into a musical chant Jordan couldn't understand, but he could feel T'ukri's joy, so he figured it was a good reaction.

T'ukri released their hands and turned around. As soon as they turned as well, he wrapped his arms around their waists. "It is done," he told them. "We are one."

Huallpa's voice rang out over the chant, and silence fell immediately.

"People of Machu Llaqta, I give you the prince and his consorts, Chapaqpuma and his mates."

T'ukri released his hold long enough to cross one arm over his chest. Jordan hurried to imitate him, holding the pose until everyone in sight had joined them.

"Kushikilpayuk Pachamama, amachana Machu Llaqta." T'ukri's voice rang out clearly as he snapped his arm down to his side.

Jordan repeated the words with the crowd as he finished the salute.

He was home.

VICTOR STAYED where he was, next to T'ukri and in front of the statue of Pachamama, as people milled around in the temple. He recognized a few faces outside of the royal family from the party the night before, but not many, although they all knew him now.

Eventually the crowd in the temple thinned out, leaving only the royal family, the elders, and the few others Victor had already met. He'd have to learn everyone else's names, but that could wait until a little later.

"We should enjoy the feast before we leave," T'ukri said. "We will need our energy."

Victor hoped the heat in his gut didn't show on his face, although the way Nandini was smirking at them, he had given himself away somehow.

"I could eat," Jordan said from T'ukri's other side.

Jordan could always eat if food was available. He never complained if they were short on supplies and had to ration, unlike some interns Victor had worked with, but Victor almost wished he would. Oh well, another thing time would remedy, now that they had a permanent home.

They walked together back out into the sunshine, where a feast had been assembled, table after table, all piled high with different dishes.

"We aren't putting the tribe at risk of starving later, are we? Two feasts in as many days?" Victor asked. He'd seen how carefully Paucar's people used their stored food.

"We will be fine," T'ukri said. "The growing season has already started here in the valley, and the goddess will reward our labor with her bounty. No one will go hungry because we feast today."

That reassured Victor, and he let T'ukri fill their plates with tidbits from dish after dish. Victor didn't know how he was supposed to eat everything on his plate, but he'd do his best. T'ukri had mentioned seclusion several times, and Victor didn't know what that meant in terms of food. If they were back to his cooking, he'd take his time appreciating the variety offered now.

T'ukri led them to a table slightly apart from the others. Quenti took up position behind them. "Will you get to eat?" Victor asked her.

"Cusi will save all my favorites for me. I will eat when you have left."

"Didn't we take care of the traitors yesterday?" Jordan asked.

"Hopefully, but my role comes with a ceremonial side as well as a practical one," she replied.

Victor wasn't entirely comfortable eating knowing she was standing there at attention while they relaxed, but she seemed unbothered, as did T'ukri.

They had only a few minutes of peace before Tamya approached, with a younger woman at her side. Victor had been pleased to see her presiding over their bonding.

"Hatunmama, it is good to see you." T'ukri rose from his seat and embraced his grandmother tenderly.

"I am Jaylli," the younger woman said in Spanish. "I speak for Elder Tamya."

"The goddess blessed me with health so I could witness your bonding as the shaman foresaw at my birth," Tamya said when T'ukri returned to his seat. "When I join the ancestors, I will do so having fulfilled my calling." She patted Jordan's hand and then Victor's. "You are welcome here, for your arrival was foretold before any of you first drew breath. Long life and many blessings on you all."

Victor had even less idea what to make of that, but Jordan thanked her gravely.

"What?" Jordan asked when she left. "If I've learned one thing, it's not to dismiss old women with the Sight. Sure, most of them are fakes, but every once in a while, someone has a real gift. It's always better to assume they know what they're talking about, just in case."

Victor still wanted to know more about this foretelling she referred to, but he added it to his list of things to talk about later.

"Honored grandmother," T'ukri said as another woman approached, a scowl on her face, "do not judge the present by the past. My mates may have been born outside our borders, but the guardian and the goddess have both recognized them."

The woman's expression didn't change. T'ukri sighed. "Victor, Jordan, this is Raphi, Cusi's grandmother, another of our elders. Her family was killed the last time a guardian brought a mate from the outside. Please forgive her distrust."

"Ask no forgiveness on my behalf," Raphi replied. "I will not speak against them until they give me a reason to do so, but do not expect me to be happy either."

"We will do everything in our power to ensure you never have a reason," Victor promised.

She huffed and moved away. He marked her firmly in the column of people likely to oppose his suggestions purely because they came from him. She and Tamya would cancel each other out if it came to a vote. Assuming Tamya's health allowed her to participate actively in the council. And assuming it was a question of voting, not of raising issues for discussion and then bowing to Huallpa's decision. That would be easier for Victor, in a way. He wouldn't have to worry about the displeasure others might feel at having him there. He'd only have to worry about explaining his thoughts to the king.

"Please," T'ukri repeated.

"There's nothing to forgive," Victor assured him.

"That's a hell of a thing to put behind her," Jordan added. "Don't worry about it. We won't take it personally."

"She is not the only one who remembers that terrible time," T'ukri said. "Her family paid the highest price, but others will also be slow to welcome you."

"Outside of the Marines, I've been welcome exactly one place in my entire life," Jordan said, "and that was in Victor's office at the university. I can deal with it while people decide if I'm trustworthy."

Victor had counted six people standing with Huallpa and Llipya before the ceremony, but no one else approached their table until Ch'aska came running up to them, Urpi in tow.

"Welcome to the family," she said with a bright grin that wiped away any lingering worries Victor might have had. Ch'aska was the face of the future, not elders who were nearing the end of their lives. She leaned across the table to kiss Jordan's cheek and then Victor's.

"Welcome to Machu Llaqta officially," Urpi said when Ch'aska was done. "And thank you again for helping us save T'ukri. He is annoying at times, but we would be poorer without him."

"So would we," Victor replied. "Thank you for your help too. I don't know if Jordan and I would have done as well alone."

"That is the beauty of this place," Urpi said. "You never have to face anything alone except by choice."

After years of holding himself aloof to avoid his colleagues' disdain, that thought was especially appealing.

"That's something I'm looking forward to," he admitted. "I've been alone—we've both been alone for a long time."

"No longer," T'ukri said, and the depth of his promise grounded Victor as nothing else had ever done.

He met Jordan's eyes and smiled.

They were home.

CHAPTER 46

JORDAN HAD hoped they could slip away for their honeymoon without a lot of fanfare. He should have known better.

The moment T'ukri pushed his chair back to stand, the people closest to them began clapping and chanting, probably something suggestive if not flat-out dirty, based on the embarrassment he could feel from T'ukri.

"Do I want to know?" Victor asked on T'ukri's other side.

"Blessings on our bond," T'ukri explained. "Very... detailed blessings."

Jordan snorted. "Long-lasting erections and the stamina to fuck each other silly?"

"Something like that," T'ukri said.

"See, now I want to know exactly what they're saying that's making you squirm like that," Jordan said. "So I can make sure to follow through. I wouldn't want to disappoint them my first night as your official mate."

"Warning a target ahead of time?" Victor joked. "I thought you knew better than that."

"Yeah, but if he's worried about me, he'll never see you coming."

"He's already seen us both coming—more than once," Victor replied.

Jordan nearly choked on his tongue in surprise. "I didn't think you had it in you, babe."

"I haven't yet," Victor said. "I expect you to fix that tonight. Both of you."

The image shook a groan from Jordan's chest as he shifted to accommodate his erection. They made their way through the chanting crowd until they reached the edge of the city. Only then did Quenti halt and plant her spear, stopping the others from going any farther. "Enjoy your time of seclusion," she said. "The goddess's blessings on your union."

"Where to now?" Jordan asked.

"My favorite place in the valley," T'ukri replied.

Jordan smirked. "The treasure cave?"

T'ukri laughed. "That was my favorite place when I was a child, but I have matured since then. Come, I will show you."

At this point, Jordan would follow pretty much anywhere T'ukri led, so he fell into step next to him, Victor on his other side. As much as Jordan understood the ritual significance of T'ukri standing between them, he was ready to reaffirm his connection to Victor too. Without that, he wouldn't be here in the first place.

T'ukri led them on a narrow path that snaked up the hill overlooking the spring-fed pool. Jordan didn't know how strict the seclusion part of the time of seclusion was, but he hoped they'd make it down to bathe, swim, and fuck at some point. Not now. They'd bathed right before the ceremony, and the arousal that was always on simmer around Victor and T'ukri was working its way up to full boil. But sometime this week.

When they reached a flat section of the trail overlooking the valley, T'ukri squeezed through a narrow crevice in the rock and gestured for them to follow. Jordan shrugged and went with it. When he came out the other side, they were in a large... *cave* wasn't really the right word, given how open and airy it was. Grotto, maybe? That was a question for Victor. Either way, they were in a large space open on the far end with nothing to obscure their view of the horizon.

When T'ukri struck flint to steel and lit the oil lamps around the area, Jordan saw the space had been outfitted with a large bed, king-size easily, possibly even bigger, and a pile of clean sheets. Someone had been here and set it up for them.

"If you have no objections, we will spend our time of seclusion here," T'ukri said. "Usually we would have picked the place and prepared it together, but with all we had to accomplish before our bonding ceremony, it seemed simpler to make these arrangements myself."

"It looks perfect," Victor said. "A bed, privacy, and a beautiful view. The only thing missing is somewhere for me to cook."

"You need not worry about that," T'ukri said. "Mama will see to it that we are sent food each day. Unless you wish to cook, of course."

"No, I'm happy to let someone else do it," Victor said with a rueful smile. "I enjoy cooking, but I'd rather spend my time making love with both of you."

Making love. Jordan wasn't used to thinking about sex in those terms. Fucking, sure, but that was pretty much all he'd ever known. It would take him a while to wrap his head around anything else, but even in Nandini's tent, lost in the desperate need of bonding, Jordan had felt the difference. Sure, it had been fast and sweaty and physical and all the things he loved about fucking, but beneath all that had been the bond, and that changed everything. Yeah, he could get used to making love.

"About that." He grabbed Victor's hand and yanked hard enough to bring Victor flush up against his chest before running his hands down over Victor's ass. "You're overdressed."

"Do something about it," Victor said, a teasing challenge in his eyes.

Jordan bunched the tunic up so he could get to Victor's pants, untied the drawstring holding them up, and pushed them down. "I've waited for years to get my hands on your ass. Now that I have the chance, I'm going to take my time until you're begging for me to fuck you already."

"Big words." Victor stepped out of the pants and pulled his tunic over his head. "Are you going to follow through?"

Oh, it was *on.* Jordan bent and picked Victor up bridal-style. T'ukri's surprised gasp made him grin, and Victor's breathy moan sent what little blood remained in Jordan's head rushing south. He thought about tossing Victor onto the mattress, but that wasn't the mood he wanted to set. No, he wanted to give Victor all the love and tenderness he could, because Victor deserved nothing less. Probably more, but definitely nothing less. Instead he laid Victor down gently on his back and simply stared at him for a minute. By some miracle or goddess's blessing or twist of fate or other divine intervention, he had Victor in his life and his—well, T'ukri's—bed, and he would never stop being grateful for that. He pulled his own clothes off quickly and knelt on the bed at Victor's side. A moment later, T'ukri pressed up behind him. Jordan hadn't even seen him get undressed, but all he could feel was smooth, hot skin.

"I did tell you it was your turn to be in the middle," T'ukri purred in his ear.

That hadn't been Jordan's plan, but he could work with it. Hell, he would take anything either of them gave him and say thank you.

He rocked his hips back against T'ukri, shifting until the hard line of T'ukri's cock fitted neatly between his cheeks. When the tip bumped his entrance, he groaned deep and low in his chest. If T'ukri kept that up, Jordan would bend over and beg for it without a thought.

"Take care of Victor." T'ukri nipped Jordan's shoulder, drawing another moan from him, but he focused back on Victor, who was watching them with greedy eyes.

"See something you like?"

"I see someone—two someones—I love," Victor replied.

What was Jordan supposed to do with that except bend down and kiss Victor as deeply as he could? He could taste the lingering tang of the chicha on Victor's tongue as he licked his way into Victor's mouth. He took his time with the kiss, savoring every bump and hollow, until he knew every inch of Victor's mouth the way he knew his own. Victor clung to him as they kissed, sliding his hands restlessly over Jordan's arms and chest. Jordan was tempted to flex a little, but he didn't need to show off. Victor had watched him shoot, in the field and during training. He'd seen Jordan at his best and at his worst. And he still loved him. How the fuck was that possible? He didn't have an answer, but he sure as hell wasn't complaining.

He raised his head to stare down at Victor for a moment, just taking in the sight, lips swollen from kissing, cheeks a little flushed, his hair a mess. Victor gazed right back, not hiding anything. He reached up and traced a line between Jordan's eyebrows. "I think this is the first time I've ever seen you without a little furrow of tension right there."

"You've seen me happy before," Jordan protested.

"Yes, but the lines never went away completely. Now they're gone."

"I guess that's what a new home and a bonding ceremony will do to you," Jordan replied, trying to deflect the wonder in Victor's eyes. He didn't deserve that kind of adoration.

In response he got a blast of love from both sides of the bond, so strong it left him dizzy for a moment.

Got it. No thinking bad about himself.

He'd think about proving how much he loved Victor and T'ukri instead. Victor first, though, because he'd started and because he needed that connection. He stroked Victor's cheek and the line of his jaw, slightly rough with stubble. Neither of them ever got much more than scruffy, so it didn't matter that they hadn't shaved before the bonding ceremony. Victor leaned into the caress with a soft smile.

"I've always loved your hands," Victor said. "They're so gentle with the things that are important to you."

Jordan looked at his hands with their odd calluses, beat-up nails, and faded scars. *Gentle* was not a word he associated with that, but he could be gentle for Victor. He traced down the tendons in Victor's neck to his shoulder and the bruise there. They'd promised to cover him in similar bruises before the week was up, and he planned to leave a few of his own, but for now, he kissed the mark instead.

When he straightened again to run his hand across Victor's chest, T'ukri caught him and sucked gently at the spot where his neck and shoulder met. Not hard enough to leave a mark or anything. Just a reminder of his presence and that Jordan was in the middle this time. He tilted his head to invite more kisses as he circled Victor's nipples with his fingers.

T'ukri leaned against his back, a wall of pure heat, and slid his fingers over Victor's chest next to Jordan's. "He is a delight, is he not?"

"An absolute fucking delight," Jordan agreed.

"This delight would like it if you got on with the fucking part," Victor said dryly.

"All in good time," T'ukri said before Jordan could. "Everything happened in a rush when we first bonded, even with you trying to slow things down. Now it is time for the slow, tender caresses we missed then."

"Slow and tender," Jordan repeated before stretching out beside Victor so he could lick and nuzzle at his chest. He'd never had slow and tender in his life, but if anyone could bring it out of him, it would be Victor and T'ukri.

VICTOR HAD dedicated the past eight years to studying Jordan's every expression until he could predict Jordan's mood, so he didn't need the bond to tell him when Jordan floundered at the idea of slow and tender. He had such an easy, rough masculinity that promised an awesome roll in the hay but automatically kept people at a distance. Jordan had shared enough of his life on the streets for Victor to understand why, but Jordan's walls were always up. Now, though, they'd stripped all that away, leaving nothing but raw emotion matched by physical need. Of course Jordan was floundering.

And as he had done every time since they met, Victor reached out to help.

He ran his hand through Jordan's hair as Jordan nuzzled near his armpit. Jordan lifted his head enough to meet Victor's gaze. Victor imbued his expression with all the love he could and hoped that steadied him. "Everything you do feels so good. I bet you could make me come a dozen times before you ever got inside me if you set your mind to it."

"A dozen, huh?" Jordan said. "You sure you're up for that?"

Victor chuckled. "Bon, d'accord, so it wouldn't be all in one go, but you make me feel so good without even trying. Just the fact that you want me here with you is enough to have me ready to go off. There's no right or wrong way to do this, as long as we all enjoy ourselves."

Jordan's face softened. "You always know the right thing to say."

"To you, I do," Victor said. "I've made a career of it."

"I'm sure Fowler would disagree."

"Can we not talk about him in our bonding bed?" Victor retorted.

"Should I be jealous?" T'ukri asked, sounding amused. Victor felt out the bond carefully to make sure he was reading the situation correctly, pleased when he found only amusement coloring T'ukri's mind.

"No," Victor replied. "He's definitely not relevant to us right now."

"Then I suppose I will let him live… for now. As long as thoughts of him do not continue to distract my mates," T'ukri replied.

Jordan snickered against Victor's chest. "Very understanding of you."

Victor smiled at the image of T'ukri and Fowler meeting. Fowler would shit himself if he realized T'ukri was Chapaqpuma. That would never happen now. Victor found he didn't regret it at all, not when he got Jordan and T'ukri instead. But that was a thought for another time.

Right now he needed to coax—or coach—Jordan into the right mood for the next few minutes or hours or days. T'ukri had said Jordan needed to be in the middle to cement the last step of the bond. Maybe if they…. He met T'ukri's gaze.

Yes, that would work. "We're going to play a game," Victor told Jordan.

"A game?" Jordan asked skeptically.

"Yes. We're going to play Follow the Leader. T'ukri is the leader, and you're going to do to me whatever he does to you."

"And what are you going to do?" Jordan asked.

"Besides lie here and enjoy? I'm going to do my damnedest to show you both how much I appreciate you," Victor replied.

HOW DID Victor know him so well? Jordan would never figure it out, just like he'd never stop being grateful for it. He could play Victor's game and never have to admit he didn't know how to do slow and tender because whether they managed it or not, he'd just be following T'ukri's lead. And if they did manage it, he'd know for next time.

T'ukri stroked Jordan's arm from wrist to shoulder, a light, almost teasing touch that made the fine hairs stand to attention—a little like his cock, except it wasn't getting any attention at the moment. He pushed that awareness aside and focused on what T'ukri was doing and on touching Victor the same way. Victor shivered beneath the caress and curled his hand around Jordan's other bicep, just holding instead of stroking, but the dual contact went through him like a lightning bolt. *Oh fuck.* They were going to kill him.

He rested his head against Victor's shoulder again, trying to catch his breath. The simple touch of their hands on his arms shouldn't affect him the way it was, but he couldn't bite back the half moan, half sob that escaped him. The way they touched him, the way they loved him—God, the bond *sang* with it—cut him off at the knees. He'd dealt with torture better than he was dealing with them touching his arms. Not even his ass or his dick or his nipples. His fucking *arms*.

Then T'ukri kissed the side of his neck, no hint of teeth and barely any tongue, and Victor leaned up as Jordan leaned down, mirroring the caress until Jordan was surrounded by them, by heat and hard bodies, yes, but also by tenderness and devotion and a love so deep it deserved a better name, and he choked on a sob against Victor's neck.

He held on to his composure by the skin of his teeth as T'ukri licked and kissed and caressed his way up and down Jordan's upper body. When Jordan could, he repeated the contact with Victor. When he couldn't—T'ukri's lips on his shoulder blade felt amazing, but Victor was facing Jordan, not looking away—he improvised, kissing along the curve of Victor's chest muscles instead. And with each touch, something inside him broke a little more, all the past hurts and fears crumbling to dust in the wake of their caring. He couldn't even cling to the past as he usually did, using it as a reminder that everyone left or betrayed him or hurt him or used him. Not when he could feel them through the bond, feel the absolute, bone-deep, unquestioning determination to never leave, never hurt, never use or betray what they had somehow built among them. This was it. There was no turning back now. They'd done the impossible and somehow joined minds, hearts—hell, *souls*—until they were one entity with three bodies.

"I need...," he gasped, unable to finish the thought.

"We know," T'ukri whispered in his ear and ran a slick hand over his cock before guiding him into Victor's body. Had he slicked and stretched Victor? Had T'ukri? He didn't even know. All he knew was how right it felt to finally be joined with Victor so intimately. T'ukri slid slick fingers between Jordan's cheeks and into him. It probably should have stung, but Jordan only felt a sense of rightness as T'ukri stretched him and then filled him so that Jordan was completely surrounded by their bodies and their love.

He buried his face in Victor's shoulder again and gave himself over to their care and their passion.

For good.

T'UKRI HAD never doubted either of his mates' commitment to their bond. From the moment Jordan had crashed through the ceiling of the hut where he was being held and had stalked toward him, all heat and predatory intent even as he cursed at T'ukri for being a fool, he had known Jordan would follow through and their bond would be a glorious thing that would transform his life. He had not realized then how much it would also transform Jordan's and Victor's lives. His parents had spoken of the all-encompassing nature of the bond, of course, but they had come to theirs with far more shared experiences than separate ones, whereas Jordan and Victor brought a lifetime of experiences T'ukri had not shared. They had spoken of some of those times as they hiked toward Machu Llaqta, so T'ukri had known some of the pain and betrayal in their pasts, especially in Jordan's.

The emotional outpouring from Jordan over the past hour, however, took him off guard. He wanted to rage at a world so callous and cruel that it had left his beloved adrift at the first sign of tenderness. And he wanted to wrap Jordan up in the finest wool and cotton and never let any hardship or heartbreak near him again. That was a fool's errand when he had bound himself to a warrior of such depth and determination, but the sentiment remained. Looking over Jordan's shoulder at Victor's expression, torn between repletion and sadness, T'ukri knew he was not alone in his feelings. As he had done when they were joined in body as well as in spirit, he covered Jordan in as much love and tenderness as he could push through the bond, wanting him in no doubt that the connection between them went far beyond physical acts, no matter how tender and loving, into a plane that would support them all no matter where their bodies were or what state they were in. When they were all as old and frail as Tamya and years beyond the memory of physical passion, they would still have this connection. Even death would not sever it completely, only delay it until they could be reunited. Jordan was *his* now as he was Victor's as Victor was his and Jordan's, and around and around until they made a circle with no beginning and no ending, only a unity too deep for any power to break.

"I love you, my own," he said firmly. He kissed Jordan's cheek, then leaned forward to kiss Victor as well. Jordan stirred between them, but Victor hushed him back to sleep. T'ukri smiled and settled down to rest as well. Tomorrow they would bathe and talk and make love again and talk some more and learn to live with this new, incontestable reality of oneness as they renewed and reaffirmed the bond in everything they did. Now and for the rest of their lives.

CHAPTER 47

THE TRILLING of songbirds roused T'ukri the next morning as the first hints of pink and blue shone along the eastern horizon. *Good.* It was early enough today to see the sunrise, but they had a few minutes yet. Time enough to wake his mates leisurely and in the most pleasant way possible. He stroked his hand down Jordan's arm, appreciating the strength inherent there even when he was completely relaxed. When Jordan stirred against him, not truly awake, but aware, T'ukri kissed the back of his neck and flicked the tip of his tongue along Jordan's hairline.

That got a more definite reaction, although when T'ukri pushed up on one elbow to look down at Jordan, his eyes remained closed and his expression peaceful. Exactly the way T'ukri wanted him to feel. He ran an experimental hand down Jordan's side to his hip, watching to see how Jordan responded, and when Jordan rocked back against him, T'ukri reached around to find his growing erection.

Yes, he could definitely work with this. He gave Jordan one lazy stroke and waited. Jordan shifted, making space between his legs for T'ukri to slip his thigh snug up against Jordan's sac. Jordan rocked a little more firmly, but T'ukri soothed him back to rest. They had no reason to rush this morning. If they missed the sunrise today, they would have other chances. The rest of their lives, if necessary. He glanced at Victor to see him awake and smiling softly at T'ukri and Jordan. T'ukri pursed his lips in approximation of a kiss, not quite at the right angle to lean down and give him a proper one. Victor's smile widened before he returned the gesture and scooted a little closer to Jordan, so that his cock brushed the back of T'ukri's hand.

The memory of Jordan bringing the two of them to climax in the miners' hut flashed across T'ukri's mind, so he relaxed his grip on Jordan until he could hold both Victor and Jordan in his hand. He did not press hard, wanting to keep the mood light and relaxed, choosing instead to tease along the shafts with the tips of his fingers and play with the heads, one circumcised, one not. He wondered at the difference. His own people did not practice the custom, but he had encountered it in his wanderings and had been given to understand it was common among outsiders. Perhaps he would ask another time, but this morning, he simply wanted to enjoy.

With Jordan all but purring in his arms and Victor looking at him with tender adoration, T'ukri stroked and teased and played until both his mates were rutting into his hand and against each other. He bent to nibble at Jordan's neck again. Another time, perhaps, he would bite harder and leave a bruise, but not now, not when everything was soft and quiet in the slowly growing predawn twilight. They could save that for a day when they were in a rough-and-tumble mood. Instead he licked along the line of tendon standing out beneath Jordan's skin, tasting the saltiness of sweat to go along with the scent of sex that covered all three of them.

He rubbed against Jordan's cheeks, seeking friction for his own cock as he drew his lovers toward release with tender, teasing caresses. Using their spiraling need, as strong as his own through the bond, to guide his actions, he brought them to the brink twice, then backed away, before finally tipping all three of them over the edge.

"I could get used to waking up like that," Jordan murmured when their breathing had finally returned to normal. He snuggled deeper into T'ukri's embrace and pulled Victor along with him, both of which suited T'ukri perfectly. He tucked the furs on the bed a little more tightly around them.

"Watch," he told them. "The sunrise here is the most beautiful I have ever seen."

As if to prove him right, the sky brightened with a mix of red and orange, black giving way to shades of blue until the first hint of sun peeked over the horizon, washing them in morning light.

"Beautiful," Victor agreed, but when T'ukri glanced over at him, he was looking not at the sunrise but at Jordan and T'ukri himself. T'ukri squirmed under the steady gaze and unexpected compliment, but he could not deny the burst of pleasure at being desirable to his mates. Needing such affirmation after everything that had transpired in the past days seemed silly to him, but Victor just smiled more widely and stroked T'ukri's arm until he found his hand and twined their fingers together, resting them against Jordan's hip.

When Inti, the sun god, had finished putting on his morning light show, Jordan shifted between T'ukri and Victor and scratched at his belly. "I need a bath. I've got dried spunk all over me, and it itches."

"Way to ruin the mood, Harris," Victor teased, but he rolled to his back and sat up.

"That's Harris-Itoua, um, son of Huallpa to you," Jordan replied with a grin. "I mean, we did get married, in case you forgot."

A rush of pride swamped T'ukri at the memory of Jordan and Victor standing proudly at his sides, first as returning warriors flush with victory, then as his mates, seeking the blessing of the goddess. And now Jordan had claimed their names as his own. "That is who we shall all be," T'ukri declared. "Our names shall match as our hearts do, so that all will know we are one."

"Only if it doesn't complicate things," Jordan said in a rush. "I was mostly joking."

"I know, but as you said, only mostly, and I find that I like the idea of proclaiming our bond in ways that outsiders as well as my people will recognize," T'ukri replied. "They may not understand the full depth of what we share, but I doubt any but another guardian or guardian's mates could truly understand. It will be enough to have our bond acknowledged."

"I like it," Victor agreed. "It's a bit unconventional, but then, so are we. And really, how often will we need to introduce ourselves formally?"

"We do not have frequent visitors, it is true," T'ukri said, "and now that I am Chapaqpuma, I will wander less than I once did. My place is here, protecting my people."

"Our people," Jordan said, a stubborn look on his face. "We completed our trials and your dad adopted us, so that makes us part of Machu Llaqta too."

"You are correct, my own," T'ukri said. "Our people."

"So, about that bath?" Jordan said, bringing them back to the subject that had started the conversation. "Any chance we can go down to the spring and clean up without being disturbed?"

"At this hour of day, it should be deserted," T'ukri said, "and if it is not, people will not linger when we arrive, knowing it is our time of seclusion."

"We don't want to run anyone off," Victor said quickly. "If we go down quietly and see people there, we can wait until they leave to show ourselves. We might not have quite your skill blending in with the jungle, but we've both had some practice at staying hidden when we don't want to be seen."

"Indeed," T'ukri said. "Had I not possessed the senses of the guardian, I would never have known Jordan was following me during the preparation rituals. As it was, I felt safe completing them outside Machu Llaqta because I knew he would let no harm come to me, even if you did not accept my courtship."

Jordan blushed and rubbed at the back of his neck. "I'd apologize, but without my spying, I'm not sure we would have figured out what you were doing as quickly as we did."

T'ukri smiled warmly and rolled to his feet, unconcerned with his nudity in the privacy of the grotto, not that he would have been overly concerned anywhere else either, and gathered three wraps from the pile of necessities against the wall. He tied one around his waist and offered the other two to Jordan and Victor. "These will provide enough covering for us to go down to the spring without having to dress completely."

Victor wrapped and tied his with the ease of someone who had done so before, but Jordan looked at the piece of cloth like it was a snake about to bite him.

"Um, a little help?" he asked.

"Gladly." T'ukri wrapped the rectangle of fabric around Jordan's waist and knotted it securely before pulling the back between his legs to tuck in over the knot. "All done."

Jordan twisted back and forth a bit before smiling at T'ukri. "I could get used to wearing this instead of pants. It's comfortable."

"Especially when it is hot outside," T'ukri said. "Or when you want a simple covering to provide a modicum of privacy. Something that will be easy to remove later."

Heat flashed in Jordan's eyes. "I'm holding you to that."

T'ukri leaned in to kiss him as he reached for Victor. "Anytime, anywhere."

JORDAN FOLLOWED Victor and T'ukri back through the narrow passage to their honeymoon suite. Okay, fine, it was a glorified cave, but he'd slept in bivouacs and hotel rooms that weren't as nice, so he could call it a honeymoon suite if he wanted to. Besides, he'd finally gotten Victor and T'ukri naked in the spring without anyone around or any reason not to take advantage of all that bare skin. He was in a good mood. Sue him.

The minute they were back in the grotto, Victor dropped the wrap he was wearing, leaving himself bare-assed again. *Fuck.* Jordan could get used to this new nudist tendency. He undid the knot on his own wrap, pleased when he saw T'ukri undoing his as well.

T'ukri had said they would eat after they bathed. They'd taken care of the bathing part, and food and fresh linens—he'd have to find out who to thank later—sat in a basket hanging from a rope on the pulley system near the open end of the grotto. A honeymoon suite with room service. If this kept up, he was never leaving.

"Come, let us eat," T'ukri said as he lifted down the basket. Jordan took a moment to admire the flex of muscle beneath T'ukri's skin.

"What did they send us?" Jordan asked as T'ukri pulled out two covered dishes.

"Quinoa porridge and spicy eggs," T'ukri replied. "My mother knows me too well. This was my favorite breakfast growing up."

"Were you a picky eater?" Victor asked.

"Not especially, but I was very definite in what I liked best, and I had no shame about telling anyone who would listen," T'ukri said.

Jordan chuckled. "I can just see you as a kid, a stubborn pout on your face when someone brought you something you didn't want."

T'ukri smiled and served three plates. Jordan took his and settled in the nest of furs and pillows opposite the bed that constituted the only sitting area. Sure, they had clean sheets for the bed, but he wasn't raised in a barn, just in a trailer park. He had some manners. Victor and T'ukri joined him immediately.

Jordan took a bite of the dish, hoping for something good since it was T'ukri's favorite. The eggs had a spicy sauce on them, something that gave them a nice bite. He could see why T'ukri liked it. "This is good," he said when he'd swallowed the first bite. "Victor, you can learn how to make this, right?"

"I'm sure I can if someone will show me how," Victor replied.

"You are welcome to learn, but we usually eat as a family," T'ukri said. "Although I suppose we could eat by ourselves if that would be your preference."

"Not at all," Victor said before Jordan could reply. "Don't feel like you have to change things for us. We're part of your family now. We should act like it."

"What he said." Jordan emphasized his words with a sharp nod of his head. He hadn't had a family of any kind since he left the military, and he'd never had a real family. He wasn't about to lose the one he'd just gained by trying to change things. Especially not when those things sounded perfect to him.

T'ukri rewarded their comments with a kiss for each of them, then settled back on the furs to finish his meal. Silence stretched between them, comfortable at first while they were still eating, but as they set down their dishes, tension started growing in the silence until Jordan couldn't stand it anymore.

"What?" he demanded, looking at T'ukri. "I can't tell what you're thinking, but you have something on your mind, and it's driving me batshit."

"Jordan, you can't just demand an explanation like that. T'ukri is still allowed his thoughts and emotions," Victor said.

Jordan glared at him, feeling like a scolded child. "Fuck that. I know the bond is new, and maybe I'll get used to it eventually, but right now it's like there's this itch under my skin. I know it's because T'ukri's got something stuck in his craw and won't spit it out. So just tell me what it is so we can deal with it and move on."

"It is nothing." As T'ukri spoke, he radiated calm, but Jordan wasn't having it.

"It's not nothing if it has you that worked up. You can try to hide it, but it'll just come back and bite me in the ass later, so just say it, whatever it is."

T'ukri opened his mouth to say something—Jordan didn't know what—but before he could, Victor moved between them, and Jordan went down like a puppet whose strings had been cut.

"What the fuck was that?" He winced at the rough croak. It didn't even sound like his own voice.

"Feedback loop would be my guess," Victor replied. "You picked up on whatever T'ukri was feeling and it magnified your feelings until you set each other off."

"Why weren't you affected?" As much as Jordan hated being managed, he was man enough to realize that without Victor there, he wouldn't have stopped until T'ukri gave in—if he gave in. And even if he did, that might not have been enough. As hard as he tried, he still hadn't completely gotten past the belligerence that had sometimes been his only protection.

"There is a reason Chapaqpuma does better with two mates," T'ukri said from Victor's other side. "You are strong enough to fight me if it came to that, though I pray it never will, but neither of us knows when or how to back down from that fight. Without Victor to remind us there are other ways, we would tear each other to shreds. Even knowing the risks, for I cannot tell you how many times I watched Tayta step between Mama and Papãnin, I could not stop it once it started."

"Is this gonna happen every time one of us gets in a bad mood?" Talk about fucked-up, not to mention unfair to Victor. Jordan had enough trouble managing his own bad moods.

"I believe not. Our bond is new, so an adjustment is necessary for all of us." T'ukri reached around Victor and took Jordan's hand. "As we grow more accustomed to it, we will all learn the warning signs and how to react more appropriately, but also, I think we will learn how to… differentiate, I suppose is the word. To separate what we are feeling from what each other are feeling and so to lessen the drag of negative emotions. Not always, especially if we have reason to be annoyed or angry with one another, but enough that irritation at the council, for example, will not result in a fight at home."

"That's a relief," Victor said with a wry smile. "While I can think of all kinds of good reasons to get between you, breaking up an argument over nothing really isn't one of them."

Jordan could think of a few himself. With the hand that still held T'ukri's, he tipped Victor back into their nest and stretched out nearly on top of him.

Victor laughed and wrapped one arm around Jordan's shoulders and the other around T'ukri's. "I'm an old man, Jordan. I'm not going to be able to get it up three times in one morning, no matter how tempting you two are."

"You're not old," Jordan said, making Victor laugh again.

"Maybe not, but I'm older than either of you."

"How old are you?" T'ukri asked.

"Forty-two," Victor replied. "And Jordan's thirty-three. What about you?"

"Thirty," T'ukri replied. "My parents bonded young, but they were not ready for children then. After I was born, nearly ten years later, it took many years before they conceived another child. My mother says it was because I was all the three of them could handle at one time and they had to wait until I had matured before they could consider giving a second child the attention it would deserve."

"I bet you were a terror," Jordan said, content with the lighter mood. He snuggled in closer to Victor and let his calm soothe the rough edges of his soul. Maybe in time, those edges would be smoothed enough that they wouldn't keep catching on things unexpectedly, but for now, he'd take what he could get.

CHAPTER 48

THOUGH T'UKRI tried to keep his thoughts better under control after the outburst of the morning, they kept wandering back to the question that had occurred to him earlier. Jordan might not be receptive to the question, but worrying about it and not asking had only led to an argument. When they had napped and eaten again and were once more curled up together in their bonding bed, he did as Jordan had demanded that morning and simply asked. "What made you decide to go into the Marines?"

Jordan squirmed, reluctance radiating through the bond, but before T'ukri could take back the question, Jordan took a deep breath and answered. "It was better than life on the streets."

The answer itself was simple—and understandable—but the emotions running through Jordan were anything but. "You said you left the group home as soon as you could. What did you do once you had?"

"Anything people would pay me to do. I looked for odd jobs—mowing yards, basic construction, that sort of thing when I could get it—but that kind of work is in short supply in most places." He shifted behind T'ukri again, so clearly ill at ease that T'ukri tipped his chin up to look at Jordan. Jordan would not meet his eyes, sending tendrils of unease down T'ukri's spine. He had known Jordan's childhood and adolescence had been full of neglect and abuse, but this was something else. When Victor wrapped his arm more tightly around Jordan, T'ukri made up his mind.

Using some of the guardian's strength, he lifted Jordan into his lap and pulled Victor against his side so Jordan was surrounded. "Whatever it was, my own, it is in the past. I will not judge you for what you did to survive," T'ukri promised.

"You say that now," Jordan muttered.

"Did Victor judge you?" T'ukri asked.

"No," Jordan said as Victor replied, "Never."

"Then have the same faith in me."

Jordan nodded and rubbed the back of his neck as he tucked his face against T'ukri's chest. "I stole food, I rummaged in dumpsters outside restaurants or begged for what they were about to throw away, and if that failed, I… um…." He mumbled something against T'ukri's skin. Victor clearly knew what he'd said, because he tipped Jordan's chin up and kissed him.

"You did what you had to in order to survive," Victor said in what was clearly a well-worn refrain. "Any fault is on them, not on you."

Jordan took a deep breath, and T'ukri could feel him bracing himself for what came next. T'ukri tried to push his love through the bond to give Jordan some reassurance, but it was Victor on whom Jordan focused when he finally spoke. "Sometimes it was a choice between giving some guy a blowjob and starving."

T'ukri's heart broke for Jordan, eighteen, alone, and at the mercy of a cold, cruel world where odd jobs and prostitution were his only means of survival. He could not help but wonder if blowjobs were all Jordan had been forced to barter in exchange for enough to survive, but he did not ask. He was not sure he wished to know. Once again, he wished to have those who had harmed his mate beneath his claws. He would show them exactly as much mercy when they begged for it as they had shown Jordan. With that denied him, he focused on Jordan instead. He had shrunk in on himself as if awaiting a blow or worse, and that would not do. "That is a poor reflection on them, not on you. You were a child left to fend for yourself when you should still have been safe with your family. I wish I had found you then. I would have spared you that if I could."

Never mind that he had been a child as well and in no position to help.

"I got tired of being told I was only good for one thing," Jordan said, his tone so bitter T'ukri nearly lost control of the guardian. "I was looking for a place for the night and ended up huddled in the doorway of a recruiting office. The guy who worked there found me the next morning, brought me inside and gave me coffee and a hot meal, and when that was done, told me if I got tired of life on the streets, he could help me. He didn't promise me the moon or anything. He didn't even try giving me the usual speech about patriotism and serving my country and all that shit. He just told me I'd always have a roof over my head, a meal in my belly, and someone to watch my back. After a lifetime alone, it sounded like heaven on earth. I enlisted the next day—Marines, because if I was going to prove the fuckers wrong, I was going to prove them totally wrong—and met Nandini my first day of basic training. She was the first real family I ever had. Not a traditional one, for sure, but a real one."

"Family has many definitions, depending on where in the world you live," T'ukri said. "The family you built with Nandini, the one you have with Victor, the one we are building now, is worth far more than one of blood who would abuse you. I am glad someone was there when I could not be. I am fortunate never to have been hungry beyond the need to forage for my next meal in the rainforest nor without shelter beyond sleeping under the stars by choice when I wandered. Who can say what I might have done if I had found myself in your position? But I know this. What you did to survive changes neither who you are nor how I feel about you. Despite the hardships you have faced, you have remained a good man, and that is all that matters to me now. Beyond seeing to it that you are never hungry or alone again."

Then a thought struck him, cold and terrible. He tipped Jordan's chin so their gazes met. "If ever I do something to remind you of that time, some act you cannot enjoy because of it, you must tell me. I would never want you to feel pressured."

"No, it's not like that," Jordan said, though Victor was no more convinced than T'ukri was, to judge from the frown on his face. "This is why I don't like to talk about it. People look at me differently when they know. Even if they don't judge, they start treating me like I'm made of glass or like I'm somehow not gonna want to blow them anymore or whatever. Or else they decide it'll be a turn-on to call me a slut or a whore."

The self-loathing in Jordan's tone suggested those words hurt because he believed them too.

"Checking to make sure we aren't pressuring you into anything is basic respect, not treating you like you're fragile," Victor said. "Consent is sexy, you know."

That startled a snort of laughter from Jordan. "Yeah, okay. But don't treat me different because you know."

"Jordan," Victor said with a voice full of patience and tenderness, "I've known for years. It never mattered to me, and it doesn't matter now."

"Nor does it matter to me," T'ukri said. He scooted down so he was reclining on the furs and pillows more than sitting and pulled Jordan down between himself and Victor. "But I think it matters to you, more than you wish us to know."

Jordan shrugged. "It's over, and it has been for years."

T'ukri wanted to believe him, but the bond said otherwise. He let it go for the moment. Pressing Jordan would only make him tense up more. Even in the short time of their acquaintance, T'ukri had learned that much. Instead, he curled more tightly against Jordan's side and stroked tenderly over his skin, offering comfort rather than passion. Jordan stirred a little but mostly lay where he was and let T'ukri and Victor snuggle him between them.

That was enough for now. Later, when their emotions were less raw, they would have to talk about it again, to see if they could somehow lance this wound on Jordan's soul, lest it fester and continue to haunt him.

VICTOR STIRRED from the light doze he'd fallen into when T'ukri had snuggled Jordan between them. Victor had known what Jordan had done to survive before he joined the Marines, but hearing Jordan talk about it didn't make it less of a shock. Not that Jordan had resorted to prostitution to survive. Victor had heard stories like that far too many times to count. No, what shocked him was the self-loathing in Jordan's voice when he said it. Of all the things he'd done to be proud or ashamed of, that was the one he couldn't seem to get past. He wished he could convince Jordan to let go of that guilt and shame, but he didn't know how. At least now, with their new bond, Jordan would know he was telling the truth when he said Jordan's past didn't matter to him.

"You are restless," T'ukri said quietly over Jordan's sleeping form. "Are you well?"

Victor smiled at T'ukri. He still hadn't quite gotten used to suddenly having two lovers when he'd never believed he'd even have one, but he wasn't about to complain. "Just thinking about Jordan and his past. Nothing I say ever seems to get through to him."

T'ukri fell silent for a moment. "I had the same thought earlier and an idea that might help, but I am not sure how Jordan will react."

"What idea?" Victor asked.

"We have a purification ritual that we perform for a variety of reasons. I completed it before I began courting you, for example."

Victor chuckled. "Jordan told me about it. In great detail."

T'ukri laughed lightly in return. "It is not truly about physical cleansing, though it does involve washing the body. It is as much or more about emotional and spiritual purification. About letting go of those things that weigh us down so that we can move forward without negativity that should be left in the past. Jordan would not have seen that part of it, as I performed the ritual alone with no one to guide my thoughts from outside. If we helped Jordan complete it, we could perhaps convince him to let go of the guilt and shame that colors his thoughts whenever he thinks of his past."

Victor considered T'ukri's suggestion. It sounded like exactly what Jordan needed, but he'd spent years trying to get Jordan to ask for help dealing with his issues, with no success. Though, this wouldn't be relative strangers trying to make him talk about his past or his triggers or to analyze him. This would be Victor and T'ukri with him. "It's worth a try."

"When he wakes up, then," T'ukri said.

Victor shook his head. "Not right away. He only wakes up fast in the field or if something brings him up fighting. He'll be restless, though, so we could go back to the spring to swim. After he's had some exercise, then we'll bring it up. He'll be more receptive then."

VICTOR FLOATED lazily in the water and admired the continued flex and release of Jordan's muscles as he powered through another lap across the spring. He'd been right about Jordan needing exercise—he'd spent enough time on expeditions to know how Jordan got when he sat still too long—but even he hadn't expected Jordan to still be working off adrenaline or extra energy or something two hours into his workout.

He closed his eyes and focused on the bond, trying to tease out Jordan's emotions so he could understand what was going on in his head. At first he found only the bone-deep contentment of a good workout, highlighted by the pulse of tired muscles. Victor knew that feeling well enough, but when he concentrated a little harder, he could feel the oily smear of something beneath it, pushing Jordan to keep going rather than relaxing. So he *was* obsessing over something.

Victor moved from floating to idly treading water, just enough to keep from sinking. When T'ukri turned his way, Victor tipped his head in Jordan's direction, hoping T'ukri would understand. T'ukri nodded slowly and swam toward the far side of the spring where the water butted up against a sheer plane of rock. He hoisted himself the few inches up to the bank and plucked saqta leaves from where they grew on the ground above.

"Jordan," Victor called when Jordan showed no sign of stopping to see what T'ukri was doing. When Jordan didn't reply, Victor rolled his eyes and dove beneath the water until he was directly behind Jordan. He reached up and grabbed Jordan by the waist to pull him into an underwater hug.

Jordan spluttered and coughed as they broke the surface of the water. "What the hell, Victor?" Victor might have worried except Jordan was smiling as he spoke.

"You didn't answer when I called you. I had to get your attention somehow."

"Uh-huh. And you couldn't think of a better way than trying to drown us both?"

"We weren't in any danger of drowning. We both swim better than that, and you know it," Victor replied, conscious of T'ukri listening to their conversation.

"Okay, fine, so that was an exaggeration. What did you want, anyway?" Jordan asked.

"T'ukri and I want to try something, if you're willing," Victor said.

Jordan's grin turned cocky. "Ooh, is it kinky?"

"No, we saved that for later," T'ukri replied with perfect seriousness, making Victor raise an eyebrow in curiosity. He would be asking about that when they went back to the grotto.

"What is it, then?" Jordan asked.

"You still carry the guilt and shame of your life before the Marines," T'ukri said. "Where Victor and I see only the strength in you that allowed you to survive, you see weakness, even a flaw in your character. We would help you wash away those emotions if you will let us."

"I don't understand," Jordan said. "Wash them away?"

"You watched as I purified myself before beginning our courtship," T'ukri said.

Victor hid a smirk at the memory of Jordan describing how thoroughly T'ukri had cleaned himself—inside and out. To judge by the slightly glazed expression on Jordan's face, he was remembering it too.

"It would be similar. What you could not see as you watched me meditate after washing was all the negative emotions I left behind in the pool there. All the disappointment that it took me so long to find potential mates, all the fear I would spend my life alone, the grief at Tayta's death that might have kept me from opening my heart to new love. While it was important to bathe, it was more important to free myself from those things that might hold me back. That is what we would offer you—a chance to free yourself from the shame and guilt you still carry with you."

"I don't—" Jordan started to say.

"Don't deny it," Victor interrupted. "We can feel your emotions now, just like you can feel ours. Unless you're hiding some other secret you think is shameful?"

Jordan shook his head. "I keep thinking it's behind me, and then something will bring it back up again. It sucks donkey balls."

"Such a way with words," Victor teased before sobering. "Will you let us help?"

"I guess it can't hurt," Jordan said with a shrug. "Although I think you're making too much out of this."

Victor almost argued with him, but it hadn't worked in the past eight years, so it probably wouldn't work now. Better to show him.

"Come over here," T'ukri said as he swam toward the shallows. When he reached a point where he could stand, he waded toward shore until the water was only up to midthigh. Victor waited for Jordan to start in that direction before following them. When Jordan put his feet down and stood as well, Victor couldn't help the jolt of possessive pride at the sight of them.

Bon sang, he was one lucky son of a bitch.

CHAPTER 49

VICTOR JOINED them and looked to T'ukri for guidance. T'ukri handed him some of the leaves in his hand and crushed the remaining ones to bring out the slippery liquid inside. Victor followed his lead until his hands were coated in the stuff.

T'ukri moved to stand behind Jordan. Victor watched to see how Jordan reacted, but he didn't tense more than he already was, so Victor shifted to stand in front of him. He tipped Jordan's chin up so their eyes met and leaned in for a quick kiss. Jordan responded, which Victor took as a good sign.

"The past is done," T'ukri said, a more formal, almost ritualistic tone to his voice. "It cannot be undone, but it can be overcome."

He ran his hands over Jordan's shoulders, washing and massaging at the same time. Victor mirrored his actions along Jordan's collarbones, feeling more of the tension leave Jordan as the contact steadied him.

"What was done to you, what you were forced to do, is a reflection on the people who abused you, not on you," T'ukri continued, working his way down Jordan's back. Victor hesitated for a moment. Working down Jordan's front would put him in sexual territory almost immediately, but T'ukri gave him a pointed look, so Victor mimicked his actions again.

Jordan closed his eyes when Victor moved his hands down across Jordan's chest, but the tension that had invested his body finally eased completely, reassuring Victor they were on the right track.

"We are washing away their touch," T'ukri intoned, "and with it, the shame and guilt you associate with it. Touch, intimacy, affection, and desire come from us now, not from those who would use you for their own ends."

Hoping he was reading T'ukri's cues right, Victor focused on Jordan's nipples, not trying to arouse him specifically—although he could feel the stirrings of interest through the bond—but more trying to emphasize T'ukri's words with his actions. He desperately wanted this to work, because if it didn't, he was out of ideas for how to help

Jordan let go of his past. While he was willing to spend the rest of his life helping Jordan battle his demons, he'd much rather see them put to rest.

T'ukri slid his hands down to the globes of Jordan's ass, so Victor moved his to Jordan's lower belly. The temptation to close his hand around Jordan's cock was high, but he reminded himself of their goals and kept his touch focused on washing, not on jerking Jordan off. "They can no longer reach you. You are here now, with us, long past the situation that left you vulnerable to their abuse. Even the memory of them cannot touch you, surrounded as you are by our devotion. The guilt and shame you have carried with you are washing away, as fleeting as dirt on your skin—a temporary blemish at most, and as easily cleansed."

Jordan arched and moaned breathily. When Victor angled his head to look, he caught sight of T'ukri circling Jordan's entrance. "Let go of the past, of the negativity, and focus on today, on our bond and the love we bear for you. You are free of those days. Let yourself be free of those emotions. They are washing away with the liquid on your skin."

T'ukri matched actions to his words, sluicing water over Jordan's skin with his hands. Victor did the same, washing away all traces of the cleansing liquid from the saqta. T'ukri caught Victor's eye and gestured for him to continue pouring water over Jordan as he moved toward the nearby shore. He returned a moment later with aloe this time. He slicked his hands again before passing the rest of the leaves to Victor. Victor crushed them and coated his hands also, waiting to see what came next.

Jordan opened his eyes at the sudden lack of contact, but he made no move to escape or to pull them closer, just watched Victor with hooded eyes. Victor wondered for a moment how to interpret it when he remembered he didn't have to guess anymore. Concentrating on the bond, he smiled to feel a lightening in Jordan's emotions. T'ukri's idea was working.

Then Jordan moaned again and desire started to color his thoughts.

"The past is gone," T'ukri repeated as he fingered Jordan open. "You are refreshed and renewed. All that remains is the future and the joy it will bring to all of us. No part of you carries their taint, only our touch."

Victor got with the program and ran one hand over the growing curve of Jordan's cock like he'd wanted to do moments ago while he reached the other between Jordan's legs to cradle his balls. He didn't know if any of the men Jordan had been with at that stage in his life had ever bothered with getting Jordan off too, so maybe it was a moot point, but this was more symbolic than literal anyway, and he refused to be left out.

Jordan's breath caught as Victor and T'ukri continued their mix of purification and lovemaking until he was trembling between them and only upright because they each had a grip on one of his hips. "Fuck me," he finally begged.

"No," T'ukri said. "That was what *they* did. But we will take you back to bed and make love to you."

"Exactly the way you deserve," Victor added.

IF ASKED later, Jordan couldn't have said how they got from the spring back up to the grotto. He assumed they walked because there wasn't another option, really, but it was all a blur to him. He went from Victor and T'ukri washing and making love to him in the spring to them on either side of him in bed, their hands on him as tender as they always had been.

He shifted between T'ukri, still gently fingering him, and Victor, who had gotten his mouth on Jordan's dick and was slowly—*fuck, so slowly!*—sucking Jordan's brains out. T'ukri said something in Jordan's ear about Victor and blowjobs and Jordan's past, but he was too far gone to follow the words.

All he knew—all he cared about—was the dual connection of body and bond.

"Need you," he gasped. "In me."

"Soon," T'ukri crooned in his ear. "Let me get you ready."

Jordan levered his eyes open when Victor pulled away. Victor sat on his knees, reaching behind himself to stretch his own ass, but that wasn't what Jordan wanted. "In me," he said again. "Both of you."

Victor and T'ukri both froze for a moment, just long enough for Jordan to open his mouth to insist. Then Victor was on him again, kissing him deep and wet and so passionately Jordan lost what was left of his breath. It didn't matter. He didn't need oxygen. He just needed Victor and T'ukri, and they flooded his mind to the exclusion of all else.

"How?" he heard T'ukri ask, but he didn't answer. Couldn't, really. That much thought was beyond him. He just knew what he wanted.

"Lie back," Victor said, then positioned Jordan on T'ukri's chest, looking down into his dark, soft eyes with their blown pupils, so full of love that Jordan wished he could look away. He didn't deserve—

He hadn't even finished the thought before Victor and T'ukri hit him with another surge of love and devotion.

T'ukri claimed his mouth again as Victor pressed his fingers inside, stretching Jordan more aggressively than they had done in the spring. Jordan pulled his knees under him so he could arch his back and lift his ass into the contact. He wanted Victor to crack him open and just crawl inside.

He added another finger and pumped them slowly in and out until Jordan was whining with the sensation—the slight burn of the stretch, the occasional brush of Victor's knuckles across his prostate, the fullness that came with more fingers than he usually needed. "More," he begged.

"I'm getting there," Victor said with a light tap on Jordan's ass. "I don't want to hurt you."

They couldn't hurt him if they tried. Not in any way that mattered. They didn't have it in them.

He didn't get a chance to say that, though. T'ukri captured his mouth again, drawing Jordan's attention back to him. Jordan threw himself into the kiss with all the frantic need the purification ritual had inspired, made even stronger by the thought of what was coming.

Jordan hissed when Victor stretched him even wider. He had to be up to four fingers now. But he pushed back against the intrusion in encouragement. Yeah, it stung, but he wanted it. He wanted it all. And he wanted it now.

He felt the brush of their minds against his, checking on him, and the care in the gesture nearly undid him. He did his best to project back his need—and his impatience—although if either got through, it didn't make Victor speed up any.

When he was finally satisfied, he pulled his fingers free, much to Jordan's dismay.

"Scoot up a bit so you can ride T'ukri." Victor patted Jordan's hip to get him moving, not that Jordan needed any encouragement. He pushed up on his arms and moved until he was directly over T'ukri's cock. With Victor guiding him, he sank down onto the hard shaft, sighing as it slid easily inside. He posted up and down a few times before Victor pushed gently between his shoulder blades. "If you want us both, you're going to have to lean forward so I can stretch you some more."

Jordan lowered himself onto his elbows, which had the added advantage of letting him rub against T'ukri's broad, smooth chest.

"Hold still," Victor said.

Yeah, right. Like he could hold still with T'ukri inside him. Victor was implacable, though, one big hand holding him in place. A moment later, T'ukri added his hands so Jordan was immobile. Oh, he could have gotten loose if he'd tried. Hell, all he'd have to do was think about being uncomfortable and they'd probably let him go, but for all the desire to move, to keep fucking himself on T'ukri's cock, he wanted Victor inside him too with a desperation that bordered on manic, and if that meant holding still, he'd do it.

Somehow.

Victor probed along the rim of Jordan's hole, and Jordan did his best to relax and project his need and desire in both his body language and the bond. The thing was, he knew it was going to hurt a little, but he didn't care. It would feel too good in the end. Victor worked the tip of one finger in alongside T'ukri's cock, making Jordan moan at the stretch and the feeling of fullness. They were breaking him open and filling in the empty places.

"Easy, trésor," Victor soothed, stroking Jordan's lower back as he spoke, and damn, hearing Victor call him his treasure soothed all the tender spots in his soul. "You look so good like this, all stretched around T'ukri and still making room for me."

"Yes," Jordan begged. "All of you."

Victor pushed the finger deeper. Jordan cried out as Victor pegged his prostate dead-on. "Don't make me come yet," he gasped.

"Just making sure it's good for you too," Victor said, but he moved his finger away.

Beneath him, T'ukri shifted a little, spreading his legs, which forced Jordan's even wider. That was fine. Jordan was flexible. The extra inch of space let him sink deeper onto T'ukri's cock and Victor's finger. Fuck, it felt good. He started to tell Victor he was ready for another finger, but Victor beat him to the punch.

Jordan sobbed out a moan against T'ukri's shoulder, unable to stop the sounds now that Victor had two fingers in him, nearly as deep as T'ukri was. He expected Victor to make him wait, but he added another finger almost immediately. Damn, that was hot, thinking Victor wanted it so badly he stopped being so fucking careful.

He thrashed between them, completely wrung out on sensation but still needing more. He could still think, could still feel beyond their lovemaking, and he needed to let go completely, until there was nothing left but Victor and T'ukri taking him apart and putting him back together again with them at his center.

Victor pulled his fingers free. "Easy now," he said. "T'ukri, pull out almost all the way."

Jordan whined at the loss of fullness, but Victor steadied him with a kiss to his spine. Then the pressure doubled—fuck, tripled—and he whined for a different reason. They checked on him mentally, which was a good thing. He couldn't have gotten words out to tell them how good it felt as his hole stretched and stretched and burned and stretched until they were both inside him, tunneling deeper and deeper, hollowing him out until all he could do was cling to T'ukri as they moved inside him as one.

He hung there, suspended between them, as they fucked him—made love to him—into oblivion. Jordan couldn't say if the idea scared him or excited him more, but as the last of his internal walls came down, it didn't matter. He was so full of them that nothing else mattered. His cheeks were wet, but he let the tears come, let all the pain and abandonment of his past flow out in healing absolution until he had nothing left to grieve or regret. And when T'ukri kissed one side of his mouth and Victor licked at the opposite corner, he was remade anew into the warrior who would defend Machu Llaqta and lay down his life for his people if it came to that, who would stand between his loved ones and any enemy that tried to put them in its sights, into the man who would stand proudly at Victor's and T'ukri's sides as they led Machu Llaqta into the future, into the mate the guardian *and* the prince needed, with the strength to bear whatever burdens came their way until the goddess called them home and beyond.

They flooded his ass, coming at almost the same time, and that was all it took. Jordan's heart clenched along with his ass, and he collapsed onto T'ukri's chest, his vision whiting out as he shook in the throes of an orgasm like he'd never known.

T'UKRI HELD back a grunt as Jordan collapsed on top of him. He probed gently at the bond, checking in as he had more than once over the past few hours, but all he felt on the edges of Jordan's consciousness was pure contentment. Reassured as to Jordan's state, T'ukri focused back on his own feelings. He and Victor were still lodged inside Jordan's body, pressed together so tightly he could feel Victor's pulse beating in time with his own, all surrounded by the tight, wet heat of Jordan's passage.

Of all the ways he had imagined making love with his mates over the years, this had not been one of them, but sweet goddess, it had been amazing. The connection he had felt to them from the very beginning, that had deepened into a life-giving bond, had exploded within him as they shared the purification ritual and joined together inside Jordan. He could almost imagine he could hear flickers of thought alongside their emotions, though he did not pursue them.

Jordan stirred against him, dislodging their softening lengths from inside him. Victor rolled to one side, easing his weight off T'ukri, although T'ukri would not have complained. For all that Jordan's strength was their foundation, T'ukri was more than capable of bearing that weight as needed. When Jordan opened his eyes, T'ukri studied his expression. The usually sharp gaze was unfocused still, a little lost as if he could not quite believe the recent experience was real. Determined to ground Jordan in the present, T'ukri ran his hands down Jordan's arms, stroking tenderly but with enough pressure to draw Jordan's attention.

"How are you feeling, my malku?" he asked.

Jordan mumbled something unintelligible, but the contentment T'ukri had felt on the edges earlier burst into full bloom at the question.

The pulley mechanism that would bring another basket of provisions rattled to life. Jordan tensed, but T'ukri soothed him immediately. "It is just Mama sending us food."

"I'll get it," Victor offered. "You two stay there and relax. You've worked hard today."

Jordan grumbled a little at that assertion as well, but he made no move to rise, not even to watch as Victor retrieved the basket. "Guava, mango, and banana," Victor said as he pulled fruit from the basket. "A perfect afternoon snack."

Just what Jordan needed to rebalance his body as they had hopefully rebalanced his mind. Victor cut the guava into pieces and handed one to T'ukri before offering one to Jordan. Jordan stirred to reach for it, but Victor shook his head and held it to Jordan's lips. Jordan took the bite and chewed it slowly, his eyes drifting closed as he did. For such a simple gesture, it was incredibly erotic, and T'ukri wanted in on the fun. He held his hand out for the next piece and brushed it against Jordan's lips.

Without even opening his eyes, Jordan parted his lips and let T'ukri slide the guava between them. Victor let out a smothered gasp, but T'ukri did not need his stunned expression to know what an incredible show of trust Jordan's action had been. He swore silently to be always worthy of that trust.

Victor cut the next slice, but instead of handing it to T'ukri, he held it to T'ukri's lips. So that was the way Victor wished to play the game. T'ukri could work with that. He let Victor place the fruit on his tongue, but before Victor could draw away, T'ukri closed his lips to suck a hint of juice off the tips of Victor's fingers.

As often as they had made love since coming to the grotto, T'ukri doubted any of them would be ready again soon, but the tease, the anticipation, was half the fun, and from the way Victor's eyes widened and heat flared across the bond, Victor agreed.

Jordan must have felt it too, because he opened his eyes, clearer now than earlier. "I don't think my ass is up for another round."

T'ukri reached down and slid his hands over the globes of Jordan's buttocks, heedless of the juice leaving sticky trails behind.

"You have been on the receiving end rather more than your share of times since we bonded. We can switch things around for the rest of our time of seclusion."

"I don't need that long," Jordan replied quickly, making T'ukri smile and Victor chuckle.

"Greedy bottom," Victor teased.

Jordan shrugged. "Your point?"

"No point," Victor said, "but T'ukri's right. We can switch things up to give you a break. It's no fun for us either if it hurts you."

"I know that," Jordan said softly, though he sounded like the thought was a new one. At T'ukri's skepticism, he added, "Really, I do. It'll take some getting used to, but I do know it."

Once again T'ukri wished for the chance to go back and kill those who had hurt his mate, but it was in the past now, washed away by time and the purification ritual. Letting go of his anger at those who had used or abused Jordan would never be easy, but he took a deep breath and did his best. It was time now to focus on the future.

CHAPTER 50

"MICAY, YOU are back!" T'ukri shouted as they made their way down from the grotto on the morning of their seventh day as fully bonded mates. Victor tensed automatically at the presence of an unknown entity in an area he had come to think of as their own, but the happiness in T'ukri's voice—and in the bond—countered the instinctual reaction. Instead Victor focused on the woman bathing in the spring. To Victor's practiced eye, she appeared near T'ukri's age, perhaps five years older.

T'ukri sprang down the last few feet from the path to the bank of the spring and waded into the water, heedless of the wrap around his waist, to embrace the woman.

"Is that his cousin?" Jordan murmured.

"Maybe. I just know T'ukri is glad to see her," Victor replied as softly.

Jordan made a little humming noise Victor had long since learned acknowledged the receipt of information without giving any opinion on it. After he'd had time to mull it over, Jordan usually had more to share, but he always took the long view.

"Jordan, Victor, come meet my cousin," T'ukri called as the woman waded onto the bank, heedless of her nudity, and tied a wrap around her body.

"That answers that question," Jordan said.

Jordan vaulted down the bank the same way T'ukri had done, but Victor walked down more circumspectly. He could have recreated the feat, but he had nothing to prove to his mates, and physical prowess was not what the Runa would look for from him.

"Micay, daughter of Sinchi, I present my mates, Jordan and Victor Harris-Itoua, sons-of-Huallpa," T'ukri said formally. Then he turned to Jordan and Victor. "Micay is the daughter of Papãnin's younger brother."

"Nice to meet you," Victor said, offering his hand. Micay eyed it warily and said something to T'ukri in Runasimi. T'ukri had begun teaching them some basic words and phrases during their time of seclusion, but not enough to follow the rapid-fire conversation. Whatever Micay said, though, T'ukri wasn't happy to hear it.

Victor stepped closer, Jordan right on his heels, offering T'ukri their silent support. Whether it was bad news or something else, they would deal with it together.

After another terse exchange, T'ukri gave Micay a sharp nod and turned toward the city. Victor and Jordan followed silently. Victor could feel Jordan's curiosity bubbling up, but he didn't ask. Victor caught Jordan's eye and smiled approvingly. They could ask T'ukri about it when they were somewhere private.

T'ukri did not slow until he entered the house where Victor and Jordan had stayed until their bonding.

"Is everything okay?" Victor asked when they were alone. "Your cousin seemed upset."

"That is a kind way of putting it," T'ukri replied. "My uncle, her father, disappeared over a year ago after my aunt died of an illness we could not cure. Micay went searching for him after a few months. I had hoped her return would mean good news, but she found no trace of Sinchi anywhere she looked."

"We could ask Nandini to keep her ear to the ground," Jordan said. "No guarantees, obviously, but she's got connections in more places than God. That won't help if a wild animal got him or if he's just holed up in Cusco or somewhere, but it would rule out one set of possibilities anyway."

"You would do that?" T'ukri asked.

Jordan would do anything for the people he cared about, even if it hurt him in the process. Victor knew that all too well. Fortunately this one didn't seem likely to hurt anyone except maybe the people who had Sinchi, if that turned out to be the case.

"Of course," Jordan said. "I'd do more if I could think of any other ways to help. We may still turn up empty-handed, but we might find a lead or two, even if we don't find him right away."

T'ukri reached out for both Jordan and Victor. "Each time I think I have discovered the full joy of having you as my mates, you surprise me again with some new gesture. It means the world to me that you would use your contacts and resources to help find my uncle. Even if nothing comes of the search, your willingness to help is appreciated."

"Anything for family," Jordan said immediately.

"Does your cousin speak Spanish?" Victor asked. T'ukri had told them everyone in the royal family learned it, but Micay had only spoken Runasimi, making Victor wonder if he had misunderstood. "If she tells us where she searched and how, that might speed things up."

T'ukri sighed. "That is the rest of the problem. Micay and I have different opinions on the world outside our borders. While I believe in the wisdom of remaining hidden and preserving our way of life, I do not assume all those outside our borders are a threat to our existence. Micay says I am too trusting. She was displeased to see I have brought you home with me."

"She's hardly the only one," Jordan muttered.

"We'll win her over as we win everyone else over," Victor promised.

T'ukri kissed Victor swiftly. "I do not doubt that for a moment." He took a deep breath and squared his shoulders. "Come, we should return to the palace and let my parents know we are here."

T'UKRI STRODE into the audience chamber where Huallpa heard petitions from his people, Jordan and Victor on either side of him. They had returned to his rooms to change into more formal attire, but they had not lingered beyond that. He greeted his parents with a bow of his head and the traditional salute, which they returned. He did not know if they had not yet begun the audience for the day or if they were in the midst of a recess, but either way, they were alone.

"You look well," Llipya observed as she came to embrace him.

"Better than I have ever been," T'ukri replied honestly. The only thing that could have made this moment more perfect would be to have Yuri sitting in the empty chair to Huallpa's right.

"Be welcome to the Council of Machu Llaqta," Huallpa said to Jordan and Victor. He rose from his seat and hugged all three of them. "Today is the day of open court. We will hear petitions and grievances of any who come before us."

"This will be only the third open council since we lost Yuri. We have felt the absence of his wisdom. We will look forward to any thoughts you might share with us," Llipya said.

Victor's unease resonated through the bond, though none of it showed on his face.

"Relax, my own," T'ukri murmured. "You have earned your place here."

Before Victor could answer, Huallpa returned to his seat. Llipya followed, sitting in her usual place on his left, and T'ukri took up his position at attention behind his parents.

"Sit here, churi," Huallpa pushed back the chair to his right and looked up at Victor. T'ukri's chest swelled with pride as Victor took the seat hesitantly. Victor might question his place on the council, but T'ukri's parents did not. He flooded the bond with love, determined to bolster Victor in his new role.

"Jordan, stand with me." Jordan joined him behind the throne, as puffed with pride as T'ukri was.

Quenti opened the door as the other elders of the council filed in and took their seats in a horseshoe on either side of his parents. They all bowed to Huallpa and Llipya and acknowledged T'ukri. Most also nodded to Jordan and Victor, although Raphi ignored them completely. T'ukri bristled on their behalf, but he said nothing. Only time would change her opinion, and perhaps not even that. Tamya, however, gave all three of them a blindingly bright smile. T'ukri returned it, but unease stirred at her presence. She had long since ceded her seat on the council, claiming age and uncertain health. That she would choose to return today of all days worried him.

The first few petitioners in court brought news as much as anything else, requesting aid where animals had gone missing or crops had been damaged in the attack a week earlier. Poma took note of each request as Huallpa promised help or compensation and translated quietly for Victor, T'ukri noticed. By tomorrow people would be in the terraces helping to replant the damaged crops. Replacing the animals would take longer, perhaps even a trip to one of the nearby villages, but Huallpa would see it remedied.

"Micay, daughter of Sinchi," Quenti announced when the crowd had dwindled to nothing.

T'ukri frowned as Micay stalked into the court, a scowl on her face. "*Yayanki, Ipa,*" she said with a bow and salute.

"Welcome home, Micay. You did not need to come before the court to tell us of your search," Huallpa said.

"I am not here because of my search," Micay replied, her voice cold and brittle. "I come with a grievance."

"And what grievance would that be?" Huallpa asked.

"From childhood we are taught the dangers of outsiders," Micay began. T'ukri tensed. He had known Micay was not happy about his bonding, but to bring a formal grievance to the council.... "Yet even now, our prince, heir to the throne, has brought outsiders into our lands. Not the technology of outsiders that might aid us. No, he has brought the outsiders themselves. This is no behavior fit for the heir to the throne."

"Chapaqpuma must choose the mates who can ground him or her," Huallpa reminded the council before T'ukri could protest. "Even I cannot challenge the goddess's blessing on that."

"I do not speak of Chapaqpuma," Micay retorted. "I speak of your heir, your choice of who will sit next upon the throne of Machu Llaqta, and I say T'ukri has violated our most basic law and is not fit to wear the crown."

The council exploded in an uproar of voices, Llipya's "You would dare?" the loudest among them, but T'ukri did not pay attention to any of the protests, his gaze fixed on his cousin. Next to him, Jordan and Victor demanded answers because the entire exchange had been in Runasimi, but T'ukri ignored them too.

When the furor died down a little, Micay's voice rang out over the remaining noise. "I, Micay, daughter of Sinchi, challenge T'ukri, traitor to Machu Llaqta, for the throne."

Anger blazed inside T'ukri, so strong not even Victor's cool hand on his arm could stop him. He took a step forward so he stood clear of the throne with nothing between him and Micay.

"I accept."

JORDAN DIDN'T have to understand Runasimi to know the shit had hit the fan when T'ukri stepped forward and said something to his cousin, but that didn't make it any easier to stand to the side as the shouting continued. Finally Huallpa barked something that silenced everyone. Micay gave a sharp nod and walked back out, cocky as hell. Jordan's fingers itched for his bow. He'd put a dart in the woman's ass to teach her a little humility.

When the rest of the council rose and left too, Jordan turned to T'ukri. "What just happened?"

"Not here," T'ukri replied tersely. "Come with me."

Jordan scowled but followed T'ukri out of the council chamber and back to his rooms in the palace.

"What was that all about?" Victor asked when they were alone.

T'ukri sighed deeply and scrubbed at his face with his hands. "Papãnin is the older brother, but Sinchi had children first. It took Papãnin and Tayta time to convince Mama to accept their courtship, and even then I was not born right away. Micay is seven years older than I am, old enough to have been treated as heir to the throne until I was born and to remember that. I had hoped we had grown past the animosity, but it would appear not to be the case."

"What did she do?" Jordan ground out.

"She challenged my position as Papãnin's heir on the basis that because you were born outside our borders, our bonding violates the most basic tenet of our laws," T'ukri replied. "We will meet at the sun's zenith tomorrow, and we will settle the matter once and for all."

Yeah, no, Jordan didn't like the sound of that at all. "How exactly are you going to settle the matter?"

"Ritual combat," T'ukri said. "I will spare her life if I can, but I do not know if she will yield."

Fuck no. "She sure as hell won't spare yours if she gets the upper hand."

"No, she will kill me if she can because as long as I am alive with you at my side, I am Chapaqpuma, and so she could not banish me, even if I yielded."

"Which you won't," Victor said with a shake of his head. "What are the rules of this combat?"

"A single weapon and a shield for each of us, and no outside assistance," T'ukri said. "And I cannot fight as Chapaqpuma, only as myself."

"Fuck that," Jordan spat. "Why shouldn't you use all the resources available to you?"

"Because Micay has not challenged Chapaqpuma. She has challenged the prince, so it is the prince who must fight her tomorrow."

"Meaning we have to stand there and watch helplessly as you fight," Victor summarized.

"Ritual combat or not, I'm not going to do nothing and let you get killed. If that means forfeiting, then we'll fucking forfeit, but I'm not letting her kill you. I can't." Jordan ran his hand through his hair because the other option was pacing, and that would just add to the tension in the room.

"Not unless it is to stop a killing blow," T'ukri said. "I will not cede my birthright for anything less."

Jordan almost challenged that assertion, but he wasn't a prince, was barely even a prince's consort, so what did he know about it? Still, he'd make sure to have several throwing knives hidden on him tomorrow in case the first one didn't take Micay down fast enough. He'd love to take his bow with him too, but he figured that was a no-go. Maybe he'd drop a word in Nandini's ear if he had the chance. She'd help them out.

THE AFTERNOON had been a constant parade of people through their rooms—Quenti came to remind T'ukri of his weaknesses and how to compensate for them, Cusi to remind him of Micay's weaknesses and how to exploit them, Ch'aska to yell at him for being a fool and validating Micay's ridiculous claim by accepting the challenge—but he did not expect Tamya to visit.

"Hatunmama," T'ukri said with a bow when she walked in, "to what do we owe the pleasure of your visit?"

As he spoke, Jordan and Victor both rose as well, and Victor offered her his chair.

"Sit, sit," Tamya told all of them. Victor perched on the arm of Jordan's chair so she would have a seat of her own.

"When I was born, the shaman who welcomed me to this plane foresaw that I would live to see a time of great upheaval for our people, a fork in the road of our destiny. At the head of one path stood a shining figure, a scion of our line to lead us into a time of prosperity, and at the head of the other path stood a tainted figure, an imposter set to lead us into ruin," she explained gravely.

T'ukri had heard her speak of a prophesy even before their bonding a week earlier, but this was the first time he had ever heard the details. He quickly translated what she had said and gestured for her to continue.

"Some would argue that you are the imposter with your outsider mates and your openness to the world beyond our borders, but I do not believe that is true. You will face the greatest challenge of your reign tomorrow, before you ever take the throne, because you face the one person who can call your birthright into question, the only child of the royal line older than you, though her father was the younger one. You must hold to your convictions and to the strength your mates can offer you, T'ukri. If you fail, our future will be bleak indeed."

"Did the shaman give any indication which of us would triumph?" T'ukri asked hoarsely.

Tamya smiled sadly. "Prophesies do not work that way, my child, for it will always be our actions that determine the course of our future. I pray the goddess will guide us to the path that is best for us all." She turned her steely gaze to Jordan and Victor. "I trust you will not let him falter."

"Not while there is breath or strength in our bodies," Victor promised.

She gave a decisive nod. "You will do very nicely indeed."

Before any of them could decide how to reply, she swept out of the room, leaving them alone with her pronouncements and their thoughts.

"I don't know if that makes it better or worse," Jordan said after a moment of silence.

"Better," Victor replied. "Not easier, necessarily, but better. If there were no hope, the shaman wouldn't have foreseen it at all. He might have foreseen a coming ruin, but not the fork in the road. For there to be a fork, there has to be the option of it going either way."

"But that means there's still a chance it could go the wrong way," Jordan pointed out.

"Any chance is better than no chance," T'ukri said, though his stomach roiled at the thought of facing—and possibly killing—his cousin tomorrow. He closed his eyes and focused on the bond with his mates, the pulsing, vibrant connection that had sprung to life in the miners' hut and had only grown in power since. "Tamya is right about one thing. I have you on my side, and that is something Micay cannot easily match. She may be older, but that does not make her stronger now that we are both adults, and while she perhaps has fewer hesitations about using any trick to best me, I have a reserve of strength and a reason to fight that she does not. All the greed in the world cannot compare to fighting for my future at your side."

CHAPTER 51

AFTER TAMYA'S departure, Jordan tried to settle into the same stillness he relied on as a sniper to calm his thoughts and to project the strength and confidence T'ukri needed right now, but his mind raced despite his best efforts. Finally he gave up. "Do you need me here? I mean, is there some rule or ritual or tradition that says I should be here while you prepare for tomorrow?"

"Not specifically," T'ukri said. "Why?"

"Because I'm going out of my fucking mind sitting here. I thought I'd roust Nan from wherever she's hiding and go a round or two with her. That usually clears my head. And I can talk to her about your uncle while I'm at it."

And all the other things he needed to ask and explain that he hadn't had time to tell her before the battle and bonding and honeymoon.

"But only if that won't cause problems because I'm at the training grounds rather than here."

"It will not. Talk with your sister. Much has changed since last you were together. And when you have settled your body and spirit, we will be here. Unless you intend to go with him?" T'ukri finished, turning to Victor.

"As much a sight as it is to behold when they get going, I'll stay with you. That way they can talk without an audience."

"I don't have anything to hide," Jordan said. "Not anymore. You know all my secrets now."

"That doesn't mean you want a witness to your conversation," Victor said. "Go talk to Nandini. We'll be here when you get back. Or if not, we'll leave a note so you can find us."

Jordan gave them each a quick, if filthy, kiss and sent a burst of gratitude through their bond. Before the expedition took them out of cell range, he and Nan had texted every few days, but they hadn't been in the same room to really talk for several months, and he'd missed her. Besides, he'd learned a couple of moves from Quenti that he wanted to try out. Then again, Nandini had probably learned them from her already.

He wondered what Cusi made of Nandini and her strap-on. She'd had quite a reputation in the Marine Corps. He'd watched guy after guy—macho, alpha, hetero guys—fall for her come-hither looks and drop-dead body, sure they'd be different, only to leave her quarters walking funny the next day. Then again, with the number of triads in the city, maybe Cusi didn't have those same hang-ups and assumptions.

On second thought, Jordan didn't want to know. It had been almost a joke between him and Nan at the time because they'd known it didn't matter. It was stress relief, nothing more, but Jordan suspected things were different now. They certainly were for him.

He walked by Quenti and Cusi's house, but no one answered his call. That left the training grounds. He started down the steps only to hear a cheer ring out from below. When he looked more closely, he saw Nandini and Quenti circling each other in the center of the training grounds. Neither woman had any weapons, just their fists, feet, and wits.

Jordan took the rest of the steps two at a time and found Cusi to one side, watching the women with a mixture of awe and adoration.

"What are the odds?" he asked.

Cusi blinked a couple of times and tore his gaze away. "What?"

"The odds. Don't tell me no one is betting on this. The greatest warrior of your generation against an outsider. Someone is running a book."

"Quenti would have my balls if I allowed such a thing," Cusi said.

Jordan smirked. "You mean she and Nandini didn't already do that?"

Cusi shifted a little, making Jordan grin even wider. "They are still attached."

"When they're done—and if you can spare her—I'm going to steal Nan for an hour or two. I need to talk to her."

"Now that you are here, she will have more reason to visit," Cusi said. "That will make Quenti happy."

"And you?" Jordan asked.

"What man would not be happy to find himself at the mercy of two such powerful and charismatic women? I will be sorry to see her leave and most happy when she returns."

That was Nan settled. Now Jordan just had to get used to his new titles and all would be right in his world—well, after T'ukri kicked Micay's ass tomorrow and put an end to this pretender fuckery.

Quenti and Nandini finished their round to the applause of all the gathered warriors. As far as Jordan could tell, neither had "won," but that was probably by design to put an end to the bets.

"Hey, Annie," Nandini said when she caught sight of him. "Back from your honeymoon?"

"Yeah. You want to take a walk?"

"I need a bath. I stink."

"I can take you to the hot springs. I even promise not to peek."

Nandini snorted. "Like I give a damn about that. Nothing you haven't seen before, and you're too gay—and too in love with your mates—to be interested. Show me where these springs are. I wasn't kidding about the bath."

Jordan led her up the stairs and through the valley toward the springs. "I'm surprised your... friends haven't shown it to you yet."

Nandini elbowed him in the ribs, not hard enough to make him double over, so he figured she was in a good mood. He owed Quenti and Cusi some serious thanks for that. "If you have something to say, Harris, say it."

Jordan considered it, considered Nandini and their history and the life he was building here with T'ukri, and decided that he agreed with Cusi. He liked his balls right where they were, thank you very much.

"Tell me about the mining conglomerate." She wouldn't be able to tell him everything, but she'd tell him what she could. More importantly, she'd tell him what he needed to know, security clearances be damned.

"What about them?" she asked.

"What do they want with the valley?" Of all the unknowns in the situation, that bothered him the most. He couldn't see what they thought to gain from attacking the valley.

"What could criminals possibly want with a valley completely hidden from outsiders? Illegal gold mining is rampant in the Amazon basin. There's every reason to believe this is yet another attempt to get in on the action." A week, give or take, of good sex hadn't blunted her sarcasm, not that he'd really expected it to.

"You knew the valley was in the area," Jordan pointed out as they reached the springs. He took a seat on a rock near the shore, fully expecting her to strip down and take advantage of the water, but she sat next to him instead, face as serious as he knew his own had to be. *Well, fuck.* Did that make things better or worse? Hell if he knew, but they'd rarely met a problem they couldn't solve between the two of them, so he put his mind to solving this one.

"In the area, yes. Where it was or how to find it, no," Nandini said. "From things Quenti said, I was hoping I'd get lucky and trigger some sort of periphery alert, something that would bring someone out to me—her, preferably, but someone I could talk to, and possibly you if my guess was right and Philli-philli was the same as Chapaqpuma, and if it was real and you had found it. My luck held, at least as far as that was concerned."

Her luck had always been exceptional. It had saved his life more than once, not that he was counting. Things had gone far beyond that between them. Even so, she was here on a job, not to see him, no matter what she'd hoped to find when she came looking. "I wasn't sure you'd stay. You have to wrap up your case."

"I'm not the only agent on the case. I dealt with the cell assigned to me, even if we didn't find the mining equipment, and now I'm smoothing things over with the locals. My superiors will be satisfied. And we got all of them. They're either dead or headed for long prison terms. They won't be coming back, if that's what you're worried about."

"Maybe not, but someone else might. That's not it, though. I'm worried about how they found us in the first place. I couldn't find the valley without help. You couldn't. So how the hell did they get inside and kidnap T'ukri?"

"Inside job?" Nandini suggested.

Fuck, fuck, and fucking hell. Jordan didn't want to think about that. Machu Llaqta seemed like such a peaceful place, the people who'd tried to kill him notwithstanding. The idea of that kind of underlying conspiracy left him feeling tainted., but he had to consider the possibility. Nandini's suggestion made more sense than anything he'd come up with on his own. "Maybe, but who? I mean, I don't know everyone, and yeah, there was the group that tried to take me out, but there's a big difference between trying to eliminate outsiders and leading some into the valley. T'ukri doesn't seem worried about it. Has Quenti said anything to you?"

"No. She shrugged it off as a fluke. She seems to think they stumbled through just right. It has happened before, apparently, although with less disastrous consequences."

"I don't buy it." Unless they knew the city was in the area and had fanned out search-party style so they could cover large areas at once, the chances of anyone stumbling onto the right path without meaning to seemed ludicrous.

"If not an inside job, then what?"

"Could they have followed us? Victor, T'ukri, and me, I mean?" That thought was even worse, but it was one he couldn't get rid of. They hadn't been careless. He was still a trained soldier, and T'ukri was Chapaqpuma. But they also hadn't made any concerted effort to hide their trail. A determined tracker could have followed them.

"To what end? You're anthropologists talking to outlying villagers."

God, he loved Nandini. She always knew exactly what to say, even if he wasn't sure she was right this time. "Asking about a legendary—well, not so legendary, but they don't know that—creature and Incan ruins. Maybe they thought we were onto something and if they followed us, they'd find lost treasure. Stealing Incan gold would be easier than mining for it."

"Watching *Romancing the Stone* again?"

So he liked cheesy adventure romances. Sue him. When he was a kid and his own happy ending seemed impossible, books and movies had been his only escape. "Fuck you."

"No, thank you. I'd much rather fuck someone else, and I doubt either of your mates would take kindly to my presence."

Jordan nearly choked on his tongue. No, Victor and T'ukri wouldn't, not that Jordan wanted her there either. Quenti and Cusi were welcome to her.

"It's just all too coincidental, you know? We get here, they attack, T'ukri's captured, and then we come down from our honeymoon to T'ukri's cousin ranting about outsiders and challenging him for the throne. Something just doesn't sit right."

"You think she had something to do with it?"

"Fuck, I hope not, but T'ukri said she's resented losing her place as heir ever since T'ukri was born, and that she's definitely isolationist. If she could pin the attack on us and use that to bolster her claim, it could be possible. I mean, I just met the woman, and for all I know she's a really nice gal when she's not challenging my mate to a fight to the death."

"We didn't leave a lot behind when we torched the camp, but I'll see who Quenti trusts and can spare, and we'll go back over the remains. Maybe we'll find something to shed some light on it. And if we don't, I'll still have that part of my job done when I report back in."

"Thanks, Nan. T'ukri's uncle—the cousin's dad—is missing too. Probably completely unrelated, but if you'd keep an ear open for any rumors, we'd appreciate it. I know it's a long shot, but I told T'ukri I'd ask."

"Anything for you, Annie. Now, if I'm going back into the jungle, the bath can wait."

"Nan. The fight is at noon tomorrow. Be back by then. If things go badly…."

"The goddess herself couldn't keep me away."

CHAPTER 52

T'UKRI DRESSED carefully the morning of the duel. When the time came for the actual fight, they would strip down to little more than loincloths, but he would arrive at the arena in full regalia. Micay could say whatever she wanted, T'ukri was heir to the throne, and he was determined to show it.

He took careful stock of his body as he finished his preparations, but their lovemaking the night before had been as tender as it was urgent and had left him energized in all the best ways. He was as fit for the fight as he would ever be, however much it hurt to think about. He did not want to kill Micay, but the fight could not end any other way.

Victor joined him in the sitting area of his rooms, dressed in the same outfit he had worn for their bonding ceremony, and pressed a tender kiss to his nape. "Are you ready for this?"

"No," T'ukri admitted, "but no amount of time or preparation would change that. As a young child, I idolized Micay. She was everything I wanted to be. Once I grew older, I began to sense her resentment without understanding why and wanted to please her so she would like me. I outgrew that in time as well and hoped age and maturity would smooth things out between us. Over the past few years, I thought we had reached that stage, but then her father went missing. I blamed her worry for the return of her temper, but I no longer know what to think."

"We'll just have to hope you can get her to yield," Victor said.

"Even if she does, Papānin will still be expected to banish her. Whatever hope I had for a reconciliation between us is gone now," T'ukri said sadly.

"Sometimes you just have to let it go," Victor replied. T'ukri sensed the sadness behind Victor's words and remembered Victor's estrangement from his own family. He had promised himself he would offer both Jordan and Victor a new, better family, but he had not done a very good job so far.

Before T'ukri could think of a reply, Jordan came into the room, dressed as he had been when he dropped through the ceiling to rescue T'ukri. Victor frowned and started to say something, probably about Jordan's choice of clothes, but T'ukri stopped him. He never wanted either of them to feel obliged to wear tribal dress, and in this circumstance, reminding any onlookers—and Micay herself—that Jordan was a warrior would not go amiss.

"Thank you," he said to both of them. "Whatever happens today, however this fight ends, remember that I love you."

"Do us all a favor and don't talk like that," Jordan said. "Victor yells when I get fatalistic, and we're all under enough stress as it is. You're going to go out there, and you're going to kick that fucking pretender's ass and show her that you're Chapaqpuma *and* the heir to your father's throne and that she can just slink right on out of Machu Llaqta and back to whatever hole she crawled out of. She isn't fit to kiss your feet."

"You know I cannot let the guardian loose during the fight," T'ukri said.

"Changing form isn't what makes you Chapaqpuma," Jordan said. "And keeping that under control only makes you more powerful, not less. Just because you don't give the guardian free rein doesn't mean you can't still channel those instincts. I watched you hunt that deer—and carry the damn thing all the way back to Paucar's village by yourself. You don't need to change at all to be the deadliest fucking thing in the jungle. It's time you remembered that."

T'ukri took a deep breath and tried to draw Jordan's words deep into his soul. For all his bravado in accepting Micay's challenge, being taken captive and only able to escape after he shifted had shaken his confidence in ways he had yet to accept or explore, but Jordan did not seem to see the weakness in those events. T'ukri wanted desperately to believe him, but even a malku's eyes could be tricked with the right camouflage.

"I know you don't believe me right now," Jordan went on, reminding T'ukri of just how deeply their bond ran. "You don't have to believe me. I have enough faith for both of us."

"As do I," Victor said.

A knock interrupted them. T'ukri wanted to snarl at the interloper to leave them alone, but time marched on, whether he was ready to face his cousin or not. "Come."

To his surprise, Huallpa came in, dressed in his ceremonial robes. "My sons," he said, opening his arms to the three of them. T'ukri went easily into the embrace, wishing he were once again young enough to hide behind his father's cloak. Victor and Jordan followed more slowly, but Huallpa waited them out until he had embraced all three of them.

"Sit," Huallpa said. "We have very little time, and I have things to share that you will need to know before you face your challenger."

T'ukri closed his eyes briefly. Micay was no longer his cousin. Live or die, she was only a challenger now. "Yes, Papãnin?"

"First, your mother says to watch your left side. You always forget and leave it vulnerable."

T'ukri wished he could smile at the familiar reminder, but it only drove home more what he was about to do. "I will remember."

"I wish we had more time for you to learn the many ways in which your new bond will enrich your lives, but that has been taken from us," Huallpa said. "Only you can face Micay physically, but from the moment you bonded with one another, you will never face anything truly alone again. Lean on each other, not only in the moments of love that you share, but always. The deeper you let the bond take root, the stronger you all become, not only in your hearts and in your convictions, but in your bodies." He turned to Jordan and Victor. "Your strength, my sons, is T'ukri's strength when his own is gone. Your faith is T'ukri's faith when his own falters." He leaned forward, pinning them with the most intense stare T'ukri had ever seen on his father's face. "If the need is great enough and the bond strong enough, your skills may even become his skills." He sat back, though his expression did not falter, and pinned T'ukri with his gaze. "Micay must not win this fight."

"I will do my best, Papãnin," T'ukri promised.

"No," Jordan said, reaching for T'ukri's hand. Victor closed his around their joined fingers. "We will do it. *We* will make sure Micay does not win."

Huallpa laid one hand on Victor's shoulder and the other on Jordan's. "I made the right choice when I recognized you as my sons in your own right, not merely as my son's mates. You are a credit to your families, though they be too blind to see it. Their loss is my gain—and Machu Llaqta's as well. When next I see you, I must be the king, not the father, but my heart will be with you."

The depth of longing from Jordan at his father's words nearly choked T'ukri, but when Jordan lifted his head, his gaze was clear and his voice strong. "Thank you, Papãnin."

T'UKRI STOOD at the mouth of the tunnel that was one entrance to the ritual combat arena, spear in one hand, shield in the other. He would have to be careful not to let Micay break the shaft or T'ukri would lose the tip of his spear and, with it, his weapon. Micay would probably have a sword of one kind or another, if experience was any guide.

He could hear people gathering on the tiers of the rocks around the arena, chants of his name resonating across the valley, but he could hear his cousin's name almost as strongly as his own. He would have much to do in healing the rift Micay had caused if he won.

No, *when* he won. He would not give doubt power over him. He had promised that much to Victor and Jordan.

Papãnin would look out for them as best he could if this went badly, but it would not be safe for them with Micay as heir, much less as queen. He hoped they realized that and would leave if worst came to worst. He would do everything his power—in *their* power, if Papãnin was right—to keep that from happening, but he fought this battle as a human, not as Chapaqpuma, and his recent capture had shown how vulnerable his human side was.

"It is time," Tamya said from outside the tunnel.

T'ukri took a deep breath, raised his spear and shield, and strode into the light to cheers from all around and chants of his name. He took a moment to find those dearest to him in the crowd. Cusi and Quenti, each wearing traditional garb with approving smiles on their faces. Urpi, standing one step behind Ch'aska like she was determined to keep her from interfering. His parents, regal as ever with stern expressions, but his mother met his gaze and lifted her left hand slightly—*keep your guard up.* He nodded in return—*message received.* And finally, Jordan and Victor, tight-lipped but determined, Nandini at their side in the same uniform she had worn when she first arrived, each of them a force to be reckoned with, even more so as a unit. She also caught his gaze and nodded. She would get Jordan and Victor to safety if it came to that.

T'ukri lifted his spear across his chest and snapped it to his side. All of Machu Llaqta saluted in reply.

"Micay, daughter of Sinchi," Tamya intoned.

Micay came from the other side of the arena, not one but two short swords in hand. T'ukri frowned at the unexpected gear. He looked at Huallpa, but the king made no protest. Whatever loophole Micay had found, it must be legitimate.

Micay also saluted Huallpa and Llipya. They responded, though it lacked the snap of the salute to T'ukri. Then Micay turned to face T'ukri.

"Well, cousin?"

T'ukri said nothing as he removed his formal robes, but he could almost hear Jordan's *Fuck you.* It was probably just as well the bond did not extend to actual thoughts because T'ukri could not have kept himself from laughing.

Micay took his silence as an invitation to attack. T'ukri caught the first blow on his shield and blocked the second with the long blade of his spear. He pushed back as hard as he could, hoping to unbalance Micay enough to get in a blow of his own. The movement let him draw his spear free and land a glancing blow across Micay's shoulder, first blood, but not a winning attack.

"Is that all you have?" Micay goaded. "I should have known you were nothing without Chapaqpuma."

T'ukri did his best to block out the taunting words as the guardian stirred in response to his anger. He took a deep breath and leaned into Victor's calm presence in his mind. He could do this, and he could do it without the guardian.

They fell into a rhythm, block, thrust, parry, round and round the arena, neither of them able to gain the upper hand. Not surprising really when they had the same teachers. Blood trickled down Micay's arm, but it had no visible effect on her ability to hold her swords.

T'ukri wanted to disarm her in the hope of forcing her to yield, but that would be an even harder fight than killing her.

Pain sliced across his ribs as Micay took advantage of his distraction. He hissed and jerked his arm up, covering his vulnerable side with his shield. Quenti and his mother had both warned him, but he had let his worries draw his focus away from the fight. Most of the crowd booed, but T'ukri heard too many cheers for his peace of mind. He blocked them out as well as he could. The last thing he needed was another distraction. He had to focus on the fight to the exclusion of all else.

He took a deep breath, kept his shield high, and renewed his attack. Micay met the flurry of blows with parries of her own but left her legs unprotected, the opening T'ukri had been looking for. He swept out with his spear, knocking Micay's legs out from beneath her. She tumbled to the ground, and T'ukri followed with a knock to her head with the butt of his spear, hoping to stun her enough to get the upper hand.

The maneuver served only to enrage Micay. She sprang back to her feet and slashed at T'ukri again, leaving another gash behind, on T'ukri's thigh this time.

"Where is your fabled strength? Should you not have beaten me already? Or have your outsider mates made you weak?"

T'ukri glared but did not reply. Victor and Jordan did not make him weak. If anything, they gave him more strength than ever. And yet, without them, he had not been able to fight off the men who captured him. He pushed the thought away. Now was not the time for doubt. Now was the time to prove himself worthy of his name and position. He struck at Micay again, knocking one sword from her hand. That evened the fight somewhat, but if anything, it only enraged Micay further.

"Nothing but a boy," Micay spat. "Hiding behind your Papãnin's robes instead of going out and proving yourself like a man. Where is your fabled prowess now?"

T'ukri sprang back to escape a vicious swipe at his belly, but as he landed, the rock beneath his feet shifted, and he fell to one knee. Micay was on him in a heartbeat. He raised his shield to block the blows, but he could not get out from under them long enough to regain his footing or his advantage. Then a particularly well-aimed blow knocked his shield from his hand. He blocked Micay's sword on his spear and grabbed Micay's wrist to try to force it away, but Micay had the advantage of gravity, pressing down with her full weight as well as her strength. T'ukri sank backward, trying to evade the killing blow. He managed to change the angle enough that the sword sank into his shoulder rather than his heart, but he would not be so lucky a second time.

The guardian fought his control, and for a moment T'ukri considered it. With the help of the great cat, he could overpower Micay, twist free of the blow, and win the fight, but if he did, he would lose the war. Perhaps his cousin was right, and without the guardian, he was nothing.

"Show her who you are!"

Llipya's voice resonated across the crowd and through the depths of T'ukri's being. Who he was... who he was. He was T'ukri, son of Huallpa and Yuri, son of Llipya, prince of Machu Llaqta, Chapaqpuma, the guardian of his people, mated to Jordan Harris and Victor Itoua. He was the rightful heir to the throne, destined to lead his people into a bountiful future with his mates at his side. His mates who loved and strengthened him.

He closed his eyes momentarily, blocking out Micay's shout of victory, so he could draw on the bond. Strength surged through him, Jordan's and Victor's both, and he rolled, taking Micay down with him. The sword went flying, leaving them both unarmed but for their fists. And that... that Jordan knew how to exploit. T'ukri leaned as heavily on his mates as he could. His fists and feet flew without his conscious volition, bloodying Micay's nose first, then her lips where her teeth cut into them. T'ukri took no pleasure in the sight of his cousin's blood, but neither did he let up. He needed to defeat Micay so completely that no doubt could remain.

A swift kick took Micay's knees out from under her. T'ukri followed up with another kick to her jaw that knocked her backward. Her head hit the ground with a resounding thud, and she lay there limply. T'ukri approached warily, not willing to let his guard down until Micay had yielded. She struggled to rise, but T'ukri pinned her with a knee to her chest, careful to keep the pressure light enough not to cut off her air entirely.

"Do not make me kill you," he demanded, not sure if Micay would—or even could—listen.

Micay batted ineffectively at T'ukri's side. T'ukri grabbed her wrist and pinned it as well. "Yield. You have fought with honor. You do not need to die for it."

Micay tried to jerk her wrist out of T'ukri's grip, but T'ukri pressed harder, keeping her in place. "If you die today, we cannot help you find your father. Yield."

It was, perhaps, a low blow, but T'ukri had to try. Finally, Micay tapped the ground twice, indicating her surrender. T'ukri heaved a sigh of relief as he released his grip and stood. Lifting his arms in victory, he turned to face the assembled crowd.

"I give you T'ukri Harris-Itoua, son of Huallpa, heir to the throne of Machu Llaqta," Tamya declared.

Cheers broke out from the crowd, Ch'aska's loudest among them, as Quenti and Cusi gave him sharp nods of approval and his parents beamed down at him. T'ukri took two steps forward, basking in the moment of approval, when the cheers changed suddenly, and a burst of sheer panic fired through the bond.

The flash of light on metal startled him, and he spun to see Micay falling backward, her sword in hand and a knife embedded deeply in her eye socket.

He spun back around to find Jordan poised with a second knife in hand, ready to throw. Next to him, Victor looked as furious as T'ukri had ever seen him. He gave Micay one last look, but she lay unmoving. He bowed his head, but he could not grieve the woman on the ground. His cousin, yes, he would mourn his cousin, but the woman Jordan had killed had ceased to be T'ukri's cousin a long time ago.

He could feel Jordan's stubborn defiance through the bond, the insistence that he had made the right decision. Later, T'ukri would assure him that with the ritual combat ended, Micay had cheated in coming at T'ukri's back and that Jordan's actions were justified in protecting his mate. For now, though, he simply pushed as much gratitude and love toward his mates as he could. Without Victor's control and Jordan's sharp reflexes, he would be the one lying dead, and he did not intend to forget that.

CHAPTER 53

JORDAN HAD taken two steps toward T'ukri when one of the elders—Cusi's grandmother, maybe?—shouted a challenge to T'ukri's victory because Jordan had thrown the knife that had killed Micay.

Jordan winced and stopped, determined to face the music here with a responsibility he had not always shown in the Marines.

"Go," Llipya said, waving him and Victor off. "We will handle matters here. T'ukri is wounded and will need his mates."

Next to him, Victor gave her a swift salute, and then they were running toward T'ukri and the entrance to the arena through which he'd entered at the beginning of the fight. T'ukri was still upright only from adrenaline and borrowed strength, and Jordan intended for him to be far away from prying eyes before he collapsed.

The moment they were completely concealed by the rock, T'ukri grabbed Jordan and pushed him against the wall, kissing him wildly.

"Not here," Victor said, though he sounded as wrecked as Jordan felt after the fight and the knife throw and the kiss. "You're bleeding, and this isn't private, and when I finally get you both alone, I'm not going to want any interruptions."

"It is nothing," T'ukri insisted. "A scratch."

Jordan could tell from the pain through the bond that it was more than just a scratch, but he left it to Victor to worry about. Jordan could dress a wound if it came to that, but Victor was faster and had a better idea of what was serious and what wasn't.

"This still isn't private," Victor said. He tugged on T'ukri's hand and gave Jordan a pointed look, so Jordan pushed off the wall, grabbed T'ukri's other hand, and moved with Victor in the general direction of the palace. He figured once they got going, T'ukri would take charge and make sure they found their way back.

T'ukri got the message and prowled into the lead, a confidence—hell, a swagger—in his step that had been missing since the fight against the mining conglomerate. When T'ukri looked back to urge them to walk faster, Jordan caught a glimpse of his eyes. Chapaqpuma's eyes.

Oh, this was going to be fun.

VICTOR IGNORED the desire pulsing through the bond from both T'ukri and Jordan as he examined the wound on T'ukri's thigh. He still had to treat the one on his shoulder as well, but the bleeding there had mostly stopped, making Victor hope it was more of a scratch than anything else. The one on his thigh was more troubling. It wasn't deep enough to have hit the artery, but it really needed stitches, and he didn't know where his field kit had ended up.

"Jordan," he said, drawing Jordan's attention. "See if you can find my gear."

"Look in the baskets by the door to the bathing room," T'ukri said. "They were not there before our time of seclusion."

Jordan went to the baskets and lifted the lids to look through them while Victor poked gently at the gash on T'ukri's thigh. He ignored the current of desire running through the bond and the effect T'ukri's deeper-than-usual voice had on him. They could fuck one another silly after he was sure T'ukri wouldn't do himself more damage.

"Found it," Jordan said, coming back with Victor's pack. He tore into it and found antiseptic wipes, sterile gauze, and a suture kit.

"You may have to hold him," Victor warned Jordan as he knelt at T'ukri's feet so he was at eye level with the worst of his injuries.

T'ukri ran a hand over the back of Victor's head, trying to guide him toward his groin. As much as Victor would enjoy blowing him, tending his injuries came first. T'ukri—Victor looked up and saw the slits of cat eyes rather than round pupils—no, the guardian was about as easily swayed as Jordan when it came to medical treatment, though, and tried again.

"Or else distract him," Victor added to Jordan.

Jordan snorted and moved from behind to beside T'ukri so he could kiss him. That worked well enough as a distraction that Victor could tear open the wipes and clean the area around the thigh wound. When the alcohol hit the open wound, though, T'ukri hissed and turned his attention back to Victor.

"More distraction," he said as he worked on making sure the wound was as clean as he could get it in the current circumstances. Now that they were staying, he'd have to see about getting supplies for more than just field dressing, since they wouldn't have easy access to medical care. Of course he also hoped they'd need those supplies less frequently.

T'ukri moaned again. Victor looked up to apologize for hurting him, only to see Jordan sticking his hand beneath T'ukri's loincloth. Victor leaned forward a bit and nuzzled the back of Jordan's hand and T'ukri's erection. He still had to stitch up the wound, but he could let his lovers know he was game for more once that was done.

"Now who's getting distracted?" Jordan teased.

"T'ukri," Victor said firmly. "I'll be distracted after I get him stitched up."

"Stitch fast, babe," Jordan replied as he worked his hand around T'ukri's cock.

Victor forced himself to focus back on closing the wound. The sooner he finished with the first aid, the sooner he could join Jordan and T'ukri.

He used another antiseptic wipe to sterilize his hands and opened the suture kit. He would deny until his last breath that his hands shook a bit as he started to stitch up the gash. He had done this multiple times on field expeditions, had even done it for Jordan once, so he couldn't use the excuse of having to do it to someone he loved. None of that changed his having to take an extra breath to steady himself before he pressed the needle through already inflamed flesh. He glanced up to gauge T'ukri's reaction to the first stitch, but he didn't even seem to notice. Not surprising, Victor decided, given how worked up he could feel both Jordan and T'ukri getting. Reassured, he finished stitching up the wound quickly, applied the antibiotic cream, and wrapped it in gauze.

"Let me check your shoulder," he told T'ukri, but the guardian was done waiting. T'ukri grabbed Victor's hands and pulled him to his feet. Victor went along with it because the wound had already stopped bleeding, so it could wait if T'ukri insisted.

T'ukri shifted the grip on Victor's hand to spin him around and press him against the wall. *Bon, d'accord.* The wound could wait. He pushed his hips back against T'ukri's groin, reveling in the deep groan that tore from T'ukri's throat. With the adrenaline of the fight still pulsing through them all and the guardian so close to the surface, he was bound to get ravished.

He couldn't wait.

T'ukri had him out of his clothes in the blink of an eye. He braced himself more solidly against the wall and spread his legs in anticipation of slick fingers and the weight of T'ukri's body as he fucked Victor into oblivion.

After watching T'ukri fight—and nearly die—Victor needed it as much as T'ukri did. The expected weight didn't come, though. Instead T'ukri pulled away, leaving Victor's back cold in contrast. He started to turn to see what had drawn T'ukri's attention, although he felt nothing out of place in the bond. Before he could twist around, T'ukri grabbed him again, one hand on his hip holding him steady, the other on Victor's ass, pulling his cheeks apart.

His knees tried to buckle at the thought of what that meant, but he locked them in place.

"You like that, don't you?" Jordan purred in Victor's ear. He nipped at the tender skin of Victor's neck before sucking on his earlobe. "I bet it feels amazing, T'ukri eating you out like you're the best thing he's ever tasted."

"Merde, oui," Victor rasped. "Feels like heaven."

"You know what would feel even better?" Jordan asked.

Victor shook his head. He couldn't imagine much of anything feeling better than T'ukri licking him open.

Jordan didn't answer in words. He just dropped to his knees, squeezed between Victor and the wall, and sucked him deep.

Victor threw his head back with a hoarse shout. His knees buckled, but Jordan caught him.

Without blinking an eye or easing up on the blowjob.

Victor might not have the sheer muscle mass of Jordan or T'ukri, but he wasn't a small man. And Jordan was holding him up like he weighed nothing at all. Bon Dieu, that was sexy.

T'ukri speared him from behind as Jordan swallowed him deep into his throat, and Victor lost it, jerking back and forth between their mouths, fucked by T'ukri's tongue and fucking Jordan's throat. Sweat dripped into his eyes, blurring his vision. Then his climax hit and his vision whited out completely.

And Jordan and T'ukri kept right on licking and sucking and draining him dry.

His eyes rolled back in his head as he collapsed, letting them take his full weight and use him as they pleased.

WITH THE taste of Victor still in his mouth and Jordan's desire adding to the animalistic need from the guardian, T'ukri surged to his feet and swept Victor into his arms. He placed Victor gently on the bed and turned back to Jordan, who had risen as well and looked as primal as T'ukri felt as he tore his shirt off over his head.

Flight never crossed his mind, and fighting his mate would never be an option.

"There's a third option in that equation, you know," Jordan drawled.

T'ukri frowned, not understanding.

"Fight or flight?" Jordan said. "That's what they teach in school, but there's a third option. Fucking."

The guardian roared at the thought, and T'ukri pounced. Jordan took his weight and spun him around, wrestling him against the wall, his legs wrapped around Jordan's hips. He latched on to the curve of Jordan's shoulder as they rutted against each other, both still partially dressed. He could stop, pull away, undress them the rest of the way… but that would mean giving up the delicious frottage—and his hold on Jordan's shoulder.

A puma never released his mate once he had his teeth in.

"Do it," Jordan said as he pressed T'ukri harder against the wall. "Bite me. Give me a scar with a good memory for once in my life. Let the whole world see I've been claimed."

T'ukri dropped his feet to the ground and flipped them so Jordan was facing the wall with T'ukri behind him. He pushed his loincloth and Jordan's pants out of the way and slotted his erection between the globes of Jordan's buttocks.

"Come on," Jordan goaded. "I'm still loose from this morning. Spit in your hand, fuck me like you mean it, and *bite me*."

All thought flew from T'ukri's head, leaving only Jordan's words and a desperation he had no hope of denying. He lifted his head enough to do as Jordan had said and to line himself up with Jordan's entrance. He had enough awareness to push in slowly so he would not hurt Jordan, but Jordan took even that from him, thrusting back to impale himself the moment T'ukri breached him.

The scream that escaped him was pure cat. He pistoned into Jordan with all his strength and sank his fangs into the meat of his shoulder. Jordan howled and writhed beneath the onslaught, the sound driving T'ukri to madness. He slammed home one more time with blood on his tongue and Jordan's climax subsuming him through the bond.

T'UKRI WOKE slowly to the feel of soft sheets beneath his skin and pain everywhere else. He opened his eyes to the sight of the stone ceiling and woven tapestries of his own bedroom and the soft sounds of his mates' voices, too low to pick out words.

How had he gotten back here?

He shifted through his memories, but the last clear thought was of Jordan's knife saving him from Micay's final attack. He took careful stock of himself, finding a bandage around his thigh and one over his shoulder. He rolled onto his uninjured side to find Victor and Jordan. They came into focus in time for him to see Victor finish putting a bandage on Jordan's right shoulder.

That was not right. Jordan had not been injured in the duel. Micay's treachery had not run that deep.

"What happened?" He winced at the rasp of his own voice and the pain in his throat as he spoke.

"You fucked me so hard you passed out," Jordan replied with a grin.

That would explain the lassitude he felt, and even some of the pain if he had done that on top of the strain of the fight, but that was not what he wanted to know. "To your shoulder."

"You bit him," Victor replied.

"It was awesome," Jordan added. "I bet the scar is gonna be a perfect imprint of your fangs."

Scar. Fangs.

Great goddess, what had he done?

"At least it was his right shoulder, not his left," Victor said. "He can shoot with either hand, but he prefers to draw with his left."

T'ukri blinked again. None of what they were saying made any sense. He would never hurt his mates.

He pushed up onto one elbow, fighting down the bile that rose in his throat at the conclusion he was rapidly drawing. Somehow he had lost all control of the guardian and had bitten Jordan badly enough that it could impede his shooting and would leave a scar.

"Oh no," Jordan said as he pushed T'ukri back down onto the bed and straddled his waist. "Get whatever you're thinking out of your head right now. First of all, I *asked* you to bite me. You didn't bring it up. Secondly, I loved every fucking second of it. I've got dozens of scars, and I can tell you where every damn one of them came from. Everything from my father's cigarettes to a foster mother's belt to knife and bullet wounds from my time in the Marines. The only one I've ever wanted to show off is the one you just gave me, and I will show that one off like a fucking gold medal because it's the one that proves I'm your mate. The world can take everything else from me, but they can't take your bite from my skin."

"How bad is it?" T'ukri asked Victor.

Victor patted T'ukri's thigh and squeezed his hand. "It'll scar, but he's been hurt worse and shrugged it off. At most it'll mean using the rifle Nandini gave him instead of his bow until the muscle heals, but unless we end up in another firefight before then, it won't matter."

"There will be no fighting at all until it heals," T'ukri declared.

Jordan thumped him lightly in reply.

"I don't think this has sunk in yet. I. Asked. You. To. Bite. Me." He punctuated each word with a jab to T'ukri's sternum. "So stop kicking yourself for something I damn well loved. If anyone needs to be focused on healing, it's you. I'm not the one who just went ten rounds with a fucker carrying two swords."

Victor rolled his eyes. "Spare me your alpha tendencies. Both of you. It was a stupid thing to ask for, *especially* when I was too out of it to make sure it didn't go too far. Next time you have a harebrained scheme, wait until we're all fully in control to bring it up." He nudged Jordan's shoulder, then fixed his glare on T'ukri. "As for you, stop beating yourself up. You were in pain, high on adrenaline and fear, horny as hell from eating me out like a champ, and he asked. It's a wonder he's only got one bite on him instead of dozens. Now, are we done, or do I need to get Nandini and Quenti to kick some sense into both your asses?"

Quenti would take one look at him in his current state and laugh until she cried. T'ukri probed the bond, seeking the truth of Victor's and Jordan's assertions. Jordan remained mulishly stubborn in the face of Victor's scolding, but T'ukri could detect not even a hint of regret. "You do not need to call Quenti."

"Jordan?" Victor prompted.

Jordan huffed. "Fine. Next time I get that turned on, I'll ask permission before I get T'ukri to fuck me."

"Rakkar it is," Victor said.

Jordan yelped and grabbed for Victor as he stood. "Don't do that. I'll think things through better next time. Seriously. I don't regret the bite or the scar, but I didn't think about how it would make T'ukri feel later." He stroked T'ukri's cheek. "I didn't mean to upset you. I asked for something I wanted, and you gave it to me. It didn't occur to me it would be a problem. I'm sorry."

"You should always ask for what you want. Just make sure I am myself before you do?" T'ukri requested.

"Deal," Jordan said, "although the guardian wouldn't hurt me any more than you would. We're your mates no matter which side of you is in charge, remember?"

"That is easier said than done when the result is something I would not have done in my right mind," T'ukri admitted.

Jordan reached up and loosened the bandage on his shoulder. "Look. Victor covered it so it wouldn't get infected while it healed, but it didn't even need stitches."

T'ukri angled his head to peer at Jordan's shoulder. Rather than the mauled tear of muscle he had imagined, he found four neat holes, two in front and two in back. While they would definitely leave scars, they were precise and nowhere near any major blood vessels, nothing like the mangled, unrecognizable carcasses left by hungry pumas.

He took a deep breath and focused on the guardian inside him, somnolent, replete, and more than a little self-satisfied. When he poked at that feeling, he realized the satisfaction came from giving Jordan what he had asked for *without* hurting him. T'ukri sank back against the mattress, the last of the fear and tension leaving him. Jordan was right. The guardian would never hurt Jordan or Victor, even in full control.

CHAPTER 54

A KNOCK on the door woke Jordan from the light doze he'd fallen into after they finally convinced T'ukri not to freak out. He slipped from Victor's and T'ukri's embrace, pulled on a pair of underwear, and went to see who was there.

"Nandini," he said when he peeked out.

"You look better," she said as she gave him a thorough once-over. "How are Victor and T'ukri?"

Jordan gave her his best shit-eating grin. "Do you really want the answer to that question?"

"Depends on how much you want to know about Quenti… and Cusi?" Nandini shot back.

Jordan slapped his hands over his ears, more because she'd expect it than because he had any doubts now about their relationship. "No. No, no, no. I'll be good."

"Jordan?" Victor called blearily from the other room.

"It's just Nandini," Jordan called back. "Go back to sleep."

"I have news," she said. "They'll probably want to hear it as well, but I'll tell you first and let you break it to them, if that's how you want to handle it."

Jordan thought about it for all of a second, but they'd already paid a price for keeping secrets once. He didn't want to pay it again. "No, let me get them. You can tell us all at once. That way they can ask any questions they have too."

Jordan walked back into the bedroom and shook Victor and T'ukri awake gently. T'ukri reached for him to pull him back between them, but Jordan resisted. "As much as I want to, Nandini is in the other room and has news. She went back to the mining camp yesterday to see if she could learn anything else. I thought you'd want to hear what she has to say directly."

That got them both moving, although T'ukri still needed help to get the wrap secured around his waist. He wouldn't let them help him into the sitting area, but he did sit down immediately.

"What did you find?" Jordan asked when T'ukri was settled.

"A body we missed." Nandini crossed to squat in front of T'ukri. "I'm very sorry to have to tell you this, but they had your uncle. Urpi identified him."

"And you think he led them here?" Through the bond, Jordan could feel T'ukri's denial and the pain of his loss. He took a step closer and rested a hand on T'ukri's shoulder, trying to offer silent support.

"I think they forced it out of him," Nandini replied. "He had been tortured—expertly, repeatedly, and over a prolonged period of time, judging by the marks on his body. No matter how strong, everyone has a breaking point. I think they finally found his."

Jordan winced, but it was nothing compared to what he felt from T'ukri. Jordan caught Victor's eye. When Victor nodded and took his place at T'ukri's side, Jordan drew Nandini to the other side of the room. "Anything else? We'll tell him, whatever it is, but he was already feeling betrayed, he's wounded, and now this. I don't want to spring any more surprises on him."

"Nothing from the camp. We left the body at Urpi's house until the fight was over and we could break the news. She said she would sit vigil as long as necessary. And now it's time for me to say goodbye. I stayed as long as I did to make sure you were well and truly settled, which I can see that you are, but now that I have proof this wasn't just coincidence, I need to report in."

"Just about the miners," Jordan said quickly.

"Of course, Annie," Nandini assured him. "I've been keeping this secret—or part of it—even longer than you have. Besides, I have a few reasons of my own to come back. I'm not going to jeopardize that."

"Sorry, I know that. Their caution is rubbing off on me."

She gave a dismissive sniff. "That's not the only thing rubbing off on you. Although I do see the appeal."

"My mates," Jordan growled.

Nandini laughed, a low, husky sound that had lured men and women alike to her bed. "I meant in general. You keep your mates. I'll keep... mine."

Jordan almost asked, but the flash in Nandini's eyes warned him off. She'd tell him what she wanted him to know when she wanted him to know it.

T'UKRI COULD not block out the entirety of Nandini's goodbyes to Jordan—the guardian remained too close to the surface after the fight with Micay for his senses to have returned to their usual human levels—and the thought of her returning Quenti's and Cusi's affections made him smile through the pain in his body and his mind.

His beloved, laughing uncle, tortured to the point of revealing their most closely guarded secret and then killed when he had outlived his usefulness to his captors. T'ukri's stomach churned, and he had to swallow down the bile that rose in his throat.

As soon as the door closed behind Nandini, Victor pressed a bowl into his hands. "Let it out. You'll feel better."

T'ukri shook his head, but the next surge of nausea was too strong to resist. When he had finished heaving, Victor moved the bowl away and Jordan offered him a cloth to wipe his mouth.

What had he done to deserve such mates?

"Thank you." He cleared his throat, trying to get rid of the lump that had settled there, but it did nothing to help. "I must tell my parents."

"I'll get them." Jordan started toward the door.

"Jordan," Victor called. When Jordan turned back, Victor looked him up and down pointedly. "Put some clothes on first."

T'ukri snorted a laugh despite himself at the thought of Jordan searching for his parents in nothing but his underwear. They covered as much as any loincloth, if a bit more snugly. Still, T'ukri had only just claimed his mates. He was not ready to share the sight of them with the palace.

Jordan flushed an intriguing shade of pink, a sight T'ukri intended to revisit another time, as he returned to the bedroom to pull on his pants,. After he broke his father's heart again and they saw to Sinchi's funeral rites. Had they not suffered enough? First Yuri, now Micay *and* Sinchi? Almost half the royal line gone in a matter of months. Was Tamya wrong about which heir was the tainted one and which promised a brighter future?

"Whatever you're thinking, you can stop now," Victor said from his side. "You are not responsible for Sinchi's fate."

"And yet I cannot help but wonder how the miners became interested in Machu Llaqta in the first place," T'ukri said. "Did I draw their interest, wandering as widely and as visibly as I did?"

"Nandini never gave us a name for the conglomeration, much less any associations they might have. For all we know, their interest dates much further back. Perhaps as far back as twenty-six years, when Chapaqpuma kept the Shining Path from kidnapping or killing a French teenager. Perhaps it's even further than that," Victor replied. "Or maybe it was nothing more than a crime of opportunity. The more Sinchi resisted, the more convinced they became he had something to hide, and so they kept going until he broke and they found out they were right. Nandini may get some answers for us as the investigation continues, but we may never know, and beating yourself up for something that might not have been your fault—probably wasn't *anyone's* fault—isn't going to help."

"What is not T'ukri's fault?" Llipya asked as she walked into the room, Huallpa and Jordan right behind her.

"Mama, Papānin." T'ukri struggled to his feet, shrugging off Victor's helping hand, and reached for his parents. "Uncle Sinchi is dead."

Llipya took the news with her usual stoicism, but Huallpa sagged in their embrace. "I feared as much when he did not return after so long. How?"

"Let's sit down," Victor interrupted. "T'ukri is hurt, and this isn't going to be an easy conversation."

Huallpa sighed even as he took the offered seat without ever releasing his hold on Llipya's hand. "The outsiders."

"Yes," Victor said. "Jordan probably knows the most detail."

"It just didn't sit right with me," Jordan explained as he sat on the arm of T'ukri's chair. T'ukri squeezed Jordan's thigh and held on, grounding himself in Jordan's strong, solid presence. "I asked Nandini to go back to the camp before the fight. I wanted to make sure there wasn't any indication they'd somehow followed us in. Micay hadn't outright accused Victor and me of bringing them here, but I figured that was her next gambit if challenging T'ukri didn't work, and I wanted to be prepared if it was. Nandini made it back just in time to witness the fight but not in time to tell me what she found. Turns out, she found Sinchi."

"How would she know it was him?" Llipya asked.

"Urpi went with her," T'ukri said. "She sits vigil with him now. But that is not all. Nandini believes they forced Sinchi to lead them to us."

"She didn't give details," Victor said, "but she did say he was heavily tortured before he was killed."

"She didn't say it outright, but I think she was impressed he held out as long as he did," Jordan added. "He may have led them here eventually, but he didn't do it willingly or easily."

"Thank you for bringing the news in person and in private," Huallpa said, "but now I must see to my brother. We must honor his memory and the pain he endured to keep our secret safe for as long as he did."

"Do you need help?" Jordan asked, half rising from his perch. "T'ukri needs to rest, but you don't have to do this alone."

Llipya smiled at Jordan, though the expression did nothing to lift the sadness from her eyes. "Your offer does you credit, but he will not be alone. Stay and tend to your mate. I will tend to mine."

When they left, T'ukri sagged back in the chair and buried his face in his hands. "It is all too much. Everything has happened so quickly. I cannot make sense of it."

"That's exactly what I said to Nandini yesterday," Jordan said. "Finding your uncle's body doesn't change the timing, but it does provide an explanation for the events. This isn't on you or us, no matter what Micay might have said."

"Or implied," Victor added. "Let's get you back to bed so you can rest and heal. We can keep talking as much as you need to, but we can do it where you'll be most comfortable."

T'ukri submitted to their help, now that no one was around to see, because his injuries throbbed with every step. "I only wish we had discovered the truth in time for Micay to learn her father's fate."

"Would it have changed anything?" Jordan asked as he curled up against T'ukri's side.

"Probably not," T'ukri replied, "but I am sure the pain of not knowing is part of what drove her. Even if discovering that her worst fears had been realized and outsiders had indeed caused her father's death in their quest to discover—and decimate—our city had only hardened her resolve, at least she would have known."

A loud noise from the other room had both his mates jumping to attention and reaching for weapons, but T'ukri recognized the footsteps.

"It is just Ch'aska come to torment me."

"I heard that," Ch'aska said as she barged into the bedroom. "I am not coming to torment you. I have come to see to your injuries."

"Victor did that already," T'ukri said as he carefully ignored her red-rimmed eyes. She had heard the news, then.

"And I am sure he did an admirable job, but I am going to check them anyway." She pushed the wrap around T'ukri's waist out of the way so she could reach the bandage on his thigh, completely heedless of his mates or his modesty. He sighed and shifted to give her easier access. He had long since learned some arguments were not worth having.

He yelped when she prodded none too gently at the stitches on his thigh. "I am in enough pain already. You do not have to add to it."

"I am checking for infection," Ch'aska replied tartly. "And that cannot be done by sight alone, as you would know if you paid attention to Tayta's lessons."

"I paid attention," T'ukri insisted as he resisted the urge to pull away from her probing hands. Victor took one hand in a firm grip and Jordan latched on to the other, supporting him, yes, but also keeping him firmly in place.

Traitors.

"Oh, do not scowl at your mates, either. They know I am right." Ch'aska slathered some foul-smelling poultice on his thigh and rewrapped it in the bandage Victor had used. "That will help stave off any infection."

T'ukri caught her hand when she reached for the wound on his shoulder. "Tell me the truth, sister. How many others feel as Micay did?"

Ch'aska shook off his grip and pulled aside the second bandage. "This needs stitches too. I should have brought my needle and thread."

"I have more," Victor offered. "I did not have a chance to take care of it before we were interrupted."

"I asked you a question," T'ukri said when it became clear Ch'aska was not going to answer.

"I heard you, but since it was a stupid question, I elected not to answer. Now, are you going to stay still or do I have to ask your mates to hold you down while I close the wound?"

T'ukri's pride demanded he tell her he could stay still, but the fight with Micay, the injuries, and learning of Sinchi's fate had sapped his willpower. "They should hold me down."

Ch'aska frowned as she gestured for him to recline on the bed. "You are our prince, even if you are also my idiot brother. A few may feel as Micay did, but not many. And even some of those were swayed to your side by her treachery after the fight. If she had accepted her defeat with honor, she might have kept their loyalty, but by attacking you from behind, she undermined the legitimacy of her claim. Even Raphi, who protested Jordan's interference, admits that Micay forsook her honor when she attacked after the fight had ended."

"So I didn't make things more complicated by stopping Micay?" Jordan asked. They had talked about this, but apparently Jordan still needed reassurance.

"Of course not, q'atat," Ch'aska said. "If she had not yielded, it would have been a problem, but once she yielded, the challenge was over—her attack was on your mate and her prince. That is treason. You did what any warrior of Machu Llaqta should have done, only you were faster. It is not our way to act without honor, and they trusted her word when she yielded. You saved T'ukri's life, and I for one am grateful, as any *true* citizen of Machu Llaqta should be."

Ch'aska turned to Jordan and Victor. "Hold him tightly now."

T'ukri bit his lip and did his best not to whimper each time the needle bit into his flesh. She finished eventually and set aside the instrument of torture.

"You should be celebrating, you know," she said. "You have faced and defeated the only possible challenge to your reign."

"Thank fuck," Jordan muttered in English.

"At the cost of our cousin's life," T'ukri replied.

"No." Ch'aska grabbed his good shoulder and shook him gently. "You did not cost Micay her life. You *spared* her life. You defeated her without killing her."

Before Jordan could say anything, she turned her glare on him. "And you do not get to blame yourself either. You did not cost Micay her life. You saved T'ukri's life when Micay attacked T'ukri from behind, forsaking all honor. You would not have acted thus had she not forced your hand."

"And yet she did force our hands," T'ukri said. "I find it hard to set that aside."

"Oh, you are insufferable!" Ch'aska threw up her hands. "I am not suggesting you celebrate Micay's death, but do not diminish your victory either. I know you need your rest, but if you can, come outside long enough to see the celebration. It would do you good, and it would make our people happy to see you as well."

T'ukri nodded, which assuaged her enough that she left him alone with Jordan and Victor. "Do you think she is right?"

"I don't think she's wrong," Victor said. "You did your best to spare Micay's life, and you certainly didn't have anything to do with Sinchi's death. They're both unfortunate, but they aren't your fault, and they aren't anything you could have stopped. Micay was looking for a fight. If it hadn't been Jordan and me, it would have been something else, and if it hadn't been today, it would have been another day. Let's go outside. I do think Ch'aska is right about one thing. I think the celebration will do you good."

"Can you walk?" Jordan asked. "I can carry you. To the door, if not outside."

"Just to the door," T'ukri said. "They need to see me strong."

Jordan hefted T'ukri into his arms and started toward the entrance to the palace. When they reached the front, he lowered T'ukri's feet carefully to the floor. "Lean on me as much as you can. I know they need to see you strong, but don't set back your recovery just for your pride."

"Pot, kettle," Victor muttered behind them. T'ukri would ask about that another time. For now, he took a deep breath, gritted his teeth, and walked as steadily as he could onto the terrace. Almost immediately a cheer went up from the crowd in the plaza below.

Perhaps Ch'aska had been right after all.

CHAPTER 55

DEAR DR. Fowler:

Please accept this notification of my resignation as Associate Professor of Anthropology. The research for the grant is going far better than expected, and I will have a paper to submit that should fulfill both the terms of the grant and your requirements by the end of December. I intend to remain in Peru indefinitely to continue to my research.

Thank you for your support over the years. I wish you and the department as a whole all the best.

Sincerely,
Victor Itoua, PhD

DEAR DR. Fowler,

This is my official resignation as Teaching Assistant and as a doctoral degree candidate in the Department of Anthropology.

Jordan Harris

YOU COULD at least have put a *sincerely* in there before your name," Victor said as he looked over Jordan's shoulder at the email he'd just sent.

"He'd know it was bullshit," Jordan replied with a shrug.

"He'll know my closing line is bullshit too, but that didn't stop me from writing it," Victor replied. "There is such a thing as professional courtesy."

"Like I need that now. I just quit my job and my degree program," Jordan reminded him.

"Your name will still be on the paper when we get it finished and submitted," Victor said.

Jordan flashed a grin at T'ukri. "If we can write one T'ukri approves of."

"You can," T'ukri replied. "Many tribes like Paucar's have tales of a guardian on a level that endangers neither me nor Machu Llaqta. As long as we keep the paper to those tales, you will have what you need to fulfill your grant while keeping our people safe and hidden. And given that Nandini's capture of Ramos and the breakup of the mining conglomerate convinced the government to increase patrols and strengthen penalties for people caught inside protected tribal lands, it will be harder than ever for the simply curious to find us by accident."

"Next you're going to tell us the valley has mysteriously moved inside the borders of the preserve when before it was in a gray area," Jordan said with a shake of his head.

"There is no mystery about it," T'ukri replied. "But you know the way of it now. Unlike the warriors Papãnin banished, you will always be able to find your way home."

Home. Six weeks was nowhere near enough for Jordan to get used to the idea that he had a real home now. Addicted to it, hell yes, but not used to it. Then again, he wasn't sure he wanted to get used to it because that implied appreciating it less, and he didn't think he ever would.

"We have a few other things to take care of before we have to worry about whether I can do that," Jordan replied. "Like get Nandini to empty out our apartments so we don't have to fly back to the States."

"What have you decided to keep?" T'ukri asked.

They'd spent a fair amount of time discussing it. For Jordan, it was easy. "My Lord of the Rings T-shirts, the copy of the books Pam gave me after Scott died, and the hunting bow Scott bought for me. Everything else either came with the apartment or won't do me any good in the valley."

"The first Luke Skywalker figure I bought with my own money, although I'll ask her to store the rest of my collection. At some point

I'd like to go back and sort through it properly, give some pieces to fellow collectors I met over the years, sell the good ones, that sort of thing. But there's no rush on that. They can sit in storage for a while. Maybe when it's time to do edits on the paper. Other than that, I have most of my field clothes and gear with me, and the suits won't do me any good. Those can all be donated. Same with the furniture. I'll have her pack up my books because there are some of those I'd like to keep, without being able to give her a comprehensive list via email."

"Let's get that email written, then," Jordan said. "After all these months in the rainforest, even Cusco is too big and noisy for me. I'm ready to start back home."

T'ukri lifted his mug of chicha. "To going home." Jordan clinked his mug against T'ukri's and Victor's.

"And to the dead," Victor added.

T'ukri bowed his head as he sipped the drink. "We mark el Día de los Santos Difuntos at the beginning of November because it makes us less conspicuous, but while the *tantawawas* and *achahis*—and the horses to transmit the deceased from Pachamama to Alaxpacha—are traditions that date all the way back to the days when our people ruled all these lands, the timing of the celebration is of colonial origin, and it is colored by their religion and traditions. Given that we laid Micay and Sinchi to rest a mere six weeks ago and that I spent time in the company of the ancestors before I began courting you, I feel less obligation than usual to mark this particular day this year. Next year, when we are home, we will mark the day as it is meant to be celebrated."

"I look forward to it," Victor said.

Jordan did too, although he hoped he wouldn't know very many people to honor. Death was a part of life, and with the spirit quests and everything that was part of Runa culture in Machu Llaqta, it was less final than elsewhere, but that didn't make him eager to lose people he had grown close to.

Jordan logged out of his university email and into his personal email. "Let's do this. I'm ready to head back out."

"As soon as we pick up the supplies we ordered," Victor said.

"Yeah, yeah," Jordan replied. "That's part of heading out."

"I do miss our bed," T'ukri said. "The one at the hotel is not designed for three."

"Exactly," Jordan said as he started typing the email to Nandini. "In fact, why don't you two pick up the supplies while I email Nandini? That will speed things up even more. The sooner we get done here, the sooner we can get on the road. Even if we just make it to Ollantaytambo tonight and have to wait 'til tomorrow to catch a ride to Quellouno, we'll still have that much more daylight to start the hike to Paucar's village to pick up the deer hide Kichka prepared for us."

T'ukri laughed. "Fine, yanaymi. I will get the supplies, but Victor should stay with you to make sure your instructions to Nandini include everything he wants her to do. Neither you nor I would be happy if that ended up handled wrong."

Jordan shuddered at the thought. "Meet us back here when you're done?"

T'ukri downed the last of his chicha and gave Jordan and Victor each a quick kiss. "I will be as fast as I can."

Jordan didn't know how much of Chapaqpuma's gifts would carry over to moving through a crowded city instead of the rainforest. With the heightened senses he retained even with the guardian fully under control, the noise and crowds were weighing even more heavily on T'ukri than they were on Jordan, so he figured "as fast as I can" wouldn't be long. With that in mind, he finished typing his part of the email that would sever the last of his ties with his old life. When he was done, he turned the computer for Victor to add what he needed to.

"One last email," Victor said when he'd sent the one to Nandini. "I may have a new family, but I still don't want my old one to worry."

Jordan squeezed Victor's hand and sent a burst of love and support through the bond. "We'll have to come to Cusco to submit the paper, and at least as far as Ollantaytambo a couple of times a year for supplies, so it's not like you're cutting all ties with them. Just changing the parameters."

"I know. It's just hard. Anything involving them is hard."

"So send the email, log off, and have another chicha to forget about it. Like ripping off a Band-Aid."

"I love you, trésor," Victor said as he started typing quickly. A couple of minutes later, he pushed away from the computer and grabbed his mug. "Done. Let's go home."

Jordan leaned across the table and kissed him—with far too much tongue for a public place, but who the fuck cared? Not him, that's for damn sure. "As soon as T'ukri gets here."

AS THEY neared the entrance to Machu Llaqta, Jordan fell back a step, letting T'ukri take the lead.

"Come, my malku," T'ukri urged. "You no longer need to wait on me. You are one of the Runa as surely as I am. Use your sharp eyes to guide us home."

Jordan hesitated. He'd bonded with T'ukri and been accepted by the majority of the people, but he hadn't done a spirit quest like Victor.

"Maybe Victor should—"

"Victor shouldn't anything," Victor interrupted. "Until you do this, you're going to keep pulling this merde where you put yourself in second place or question whether you belong or whatever other *bordel* is going through your head. As you're so fond of saying, fuck that. You're as much a part of Machu Llaqta and our triad as I am. You're as valuable a member of the tribe and as contributing and necessary a member of our bond as I am. Just like you and T'ukri need me to calm the waters when things get turbulent, we both need your strength to support us when times are hard. The council may want to hear my 'wisdom,' but there's a time for talking and a time for action, and we both know I err on the side of caution sometimes and sometimes you act without thinking. So in the interest of not having the same fucking argument for the rest of our lives, please, for the love of the goddess and all that's holy, guide us home."

Jordan couldn't stop the surprised laugh that escaped him at Victor's diatribe. "Tell me how you really feel, babe," he joked, but the words warmed him through.

Okay, he could do this. T'ukri had shown him the secret, one that lay in his heart as much as in his eyes, which was why it didn't work for anyone who'd been banished. Once their hearts had been declared untrue, the secret simply didn't work.

He closed his eyes and took a deep breath, then another, letting the doubts fall away in the face of T'ukri's and Victor's faith in him. When he opened his eyes, the rainforest hadn't magically changed, but the path that meandered off to the left was no longer the only path visible. A fainter trail led to the right, and when Jordan took two steps down that path, a familiar rock face came into view. He reached up reverently and brushed aside the moss that covered the stone, revealing the carved head of the great cat.

"This way," he said.

Victor and T'ukri followed him down the path. Moments later, Cusi stepped from the undergrowth and saluted them sharply. "My prince, my prince consorts. Welcome home."

DEEP IN *the rainforest, in a land time passed by, dwell a chosen people known as the Runa. We live as we always have, simply and in harmony with the land. From time to time, one of us wanders the wider world to see what has been learned in our absence and, if we deem it worthy of the goddess, brings it back to aid the Runa. The goddess has blessed us for our faithfulness, bestowing on us Chapaqpuma, a guardian who makes sure no harm comes to us.*

The role and gifts of the guardian pass down from generation to generation, parent to child to grandchild and beyond, for the need of the goddess's protection never wanes. The gifts of the goddess are bountiful, but the price is high, and Chapaqpuma cannot walk that path alone. Instinct pushes the guardian to find mates in whom to balance the senses so that the guardian can always return to the valley in proper form, for few are they who can meet all of a guardian's needs. Thus it has become our way for the guardian to take not one but two mates, a balance to each other as much as to the guardian, so that when calamity comes, Chapaqpuma has the strength to ward it off and the humanity to return home after.

Thus is our way.

Exclusive Excerpt

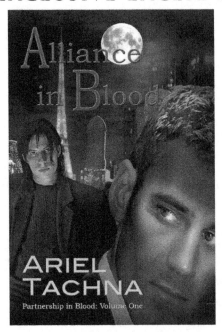

Partnership in Blood: Volume 1

Can a desperate wizard and a bitter, disillusioned vampire find a way to build the partnership that could save their world?

In a world rocked by magical war, vampires are seen by many as less than human, as the stereotypical creatures of the night who prey on others. But as the war intensifies, the wizards know they need an advantage to turn the tide in their favor: the strength and edge the vampires can give them in the battle against the dark wizards who seek to destroy life as they know it.

In a dangerous move and show of good will, the wizards ask the leader of the vampires to meet with them, so that they might plead their cause. One desperate man, Alain Magnier, and one bitter, disillusioned vampire, Orlando St. Clair, meet in Paris, and the fate of the world hangs in the balance of their decision: Will the vampires join the cause and form a partnership with the wizards to win the war?

Now Available at
www.dreamspinnerpress.com

PARIS SPREAD out at his feet, the lights of the city sparkling like diamonds on black velvet. If he squinted, he could make out the individual monuments: Notre-Dame with her twin bell towers, Sacré-Cœur gleaming white on the top of Montmartre, la Tour Eiffel, towering over the city. With a sigh, the white-haired wizard turned away from the arched window with its carved stone flourishes. His eyes scanned the office, taking in its familiar dark paneling broken only by a flickering map and inset shelves lined with the marks of his rank and power: the medallion that signified his position as the commanding general of the Milice de Sorcellerie; the plaque with the names of all the previous heads of l'Association Nationale de Sorcellerie; photos of him with the President, the Premier Ministre, and various heads of state.

He focused on the map, watching the orderly progression of lights that indicated a patrol's progress through the fifth arrondissement. A snap of his fingers changed the parameters, pulling back so he could keep watch over the entire city. He could pull back to show the whole country if he chose, but Pascal Serrier's interest lay in overthrowing the national government in Paris, and that was where he focused his guerilla-style attacks.

He frowned at the sight of a patrol not moving near l'Arc de Triomphe—hopefully they hadn't been ambushed by Serrier's rebel wizards—but before he could call down to the soldier on watch at the full-sized map, a knock sounded at his door. He opened it with a gesture and waited for his captains to join him.

"Bellaiche has agreed to meet with us," General Marcel Chavinier told them when they were seated, picking up the letter he had received from the chef de la Cour of the Parisian vampires. It had taken him weeks to locate any vampire, even longer to find a name and location for their leader, but Marcel hoped it would pay off. If Serrier took his attacks beyond Île-de-France to the countryside, Marcel might need different allies, but as long as the focus stayed on the capital, Bellaiche and his vampires were their last, best hope. "Tomorrow night at midnight, in the Père Lachaise cemetery. One of us and one of them. More than that, and they see it as a declaration of war." He dropped his bombshell and waited. He knew the two men in front of him on the other side of the desk. Had known them since they were little more than children, when first Alain, then Thierry, had arrived at l'ANS to learn the wizarding craft.

"No way in hell," Thierry Dumont exploded. Marcel almost smiled. Thierry's reaction was completely predictable. Now if Alain Magnier's was as predictable, they would be able to make some plans. "We are not sending a lone wizard to meet with a vampire. What if the vampire isn't alone? What if he attacks? What if…?" The old diplomat turned general listened to Thierry's ravings and waited for the other man to stop him.

"I'll do it," Alain interrupted his best friend and fellow soldier. "It's a gesture of good faith. They're offering to make one by sending just one vampire. We have to make one in return by sending just one wizard. Besides Marcel and you, I'm probably the most powerful of anyone we would trust to send. It would take more than one vampire to overwhelm me. You know they're our best hope, Thierry. Let me do this. We'll agree to a length of time, and if I'm not back by the agreed-upon time, you can bring in the cavalry and rescue me. It's a chance we have to take."

There was one other reason for him to go rather than Thierry, but given Thierry's reaction any time it was mentioned, it was a reason best left unspoken. Thierry still had a chance at happiness. Alain had lost that chance two years ago. If one of them was going to this meeting with the vampires, better that it was him, not his friend.

Alain knew the risk Marcel had taken even contacting the leader of the vampires. To admit that they were not strong enough to defeat Pascal Serrier, the powerful dark wizard who had started this war, took a lot of courage. It also left them incredibly vulnerable if Jean Bellaiche decided against them. Not only would this fight determine the future complexion of their society, but it was also upsetting the balance of the world. Not just the balance between natural and supernatural, but the balance of elemental powers that stabilized everything. Unfortunately, public opinion was divided on the issue of what contributed to the magical imbalance, with wizards and governing bodies worldwide debating the cause of the problem as well as possible solutions. As far as Alain was concerned, the evidence was incontrovertible, but not everyone shared his opinion. Even those who did couldn't agree on what to do about it. Still, one thing was clear. Without wizards to keep that energy in check, everyone and everything would succumb to chaos in time. Alain knew it. Marcel knew it. Thierry knew it. Alain hoped, for their sake, that the vampires knew it as well. They hadn't been able to get an edge in the war, and casualties were mounting swiftly on both sides. They needed reinforcements before there was no one left to save. They'd tried reaching out to wizards in the surrounding countries, but the response had been clear. This was an internal problem that needed to be solved internally. Unless the effects of the disequilibrium spread beyond the borders of France, they were on their own.

Thierry muttered curses under his breath, the air around him sparking with the power called up by his emotions.

"Calm down, Thierry," Marcel ordered. He knew the wards surrounding his office would hold if Thierry's magic got away from him, but the younger man needed to learn better self-control. "I agree with Alain, so unless you're offering to go in his place, you need to help me figure out how to keep him safe."

"Bad idea," Alain said before Thierry could reply. "Your temper is too unpredictable. You'd fly off the handle at some imagined slight and we'd be in the same situation or worse. Trust me to handle this."

"I trust you. It's Bellaiche and his kind I don't trust," Thierry retorted. "If you haven't checked in within half an hour after the meet, I'm coming after you, guns blazing."

Alain agreed to Thierry's condition. It made sense to have a backup plan. The vampires had never shown any sign of getting involved in this conflict between wizards, but that was no reason to take unnecessary chances. After all, they were about to ask the vampires to get involved. Serrier was racist, not stupid. If he hadn't already had the idea of approaching some of the other magical races, he would soon, assuming he could overcome his ingrained disdain for those he considered inferior. They couldn't afford to assume he wouldn't.

ALAIN THOUGHT carefully about every aspect of his preparations. He was willing to give the vampires a chance to prove their good will, but he had seen too much since this war began to trust naively. If he had to go to this meet alone, he was going to be as prepared as magic and modernity could make him. He dressed simply in dark wool pants and a black turtleneck sweater. If it had occurred to him to look, he would have seen as well that the dark colors were the perfect foil for his sandy-blond hair and lightly tanned skin. He had stopped caring about the impact of his appearance, though, two years ago. Only practicalities remained. The long cloak he used for winter would keep him warm in the cool October night and was easy to discard if it came to a fight. His pants and sweater were loose enough that they wouldn't hinder his movements, but not so loose that they would provide a handhold for a foe. His cell phone fit into a holder on his belt. It would be no use in a fight, but if he didn't call in, Thierry would know there was a problem. He had long ago mastered the art of wandless magic, one of only a few wizards who had expended the time and energy it took, but he carried a wand anyway. Giving it up or putting it out in the open might help convince the vampire that his intentions were honorable. Outside l'ANS, few people knew any wizards could do wandless magic.

He was about ready to leave when someone knocked on his door. Reaching out with his magic, he felt Thierry's aura outside. With a flick of his wrist, he released the wards on his door to let his friend inside. "What are you doing here?" Alain asked as he swirled his cloak around his shoulders.

"Going with you," Thierry answered.

"You'll get us both killed that way," Alain retorted.

"Not to the meet," Thierry elaborated. "Just in the Métro. I'll find a bar still open nearby and that way, if there's trouble, I can be there fast.

Alain agreed and the two friends set out for Anvers, the nearest subway stop, resetting the wards that protected Alain's apartment as they left. It was an easy ride down line number two to the Père Lachaise stop. Alain and Thierry made it in plenty of time, giving them the chance to find a bar for Thierry. "I'll call in half an hour," Alain promised as he left Thierry sitting in the little café just down the street from the entrance to the cemetery.

Arriving at the cemetery, Alain stretched his senses, magical and physical, to check out the situation. His magic detected no aura, no presence, but he knew better than to believe he was alone. For all he knew, vampires had a way of masking their presence from those who were hunting them. The wind whistled around him, blocking any subtle sounds he might have heard to indicate if the vampire had yet arrived, and the shadows from the monuments and trees kept his eyes from piercing the darkness. Deciding not to take any risks, Alain drew his wand to open the gate. If the vampire had arrived, he didn't want to give away his knack for wandless magic. It was his ace in the hole if he needed to get out of there in a hurry. The gate opened soundlessly, an added benefit of the spell he used. He slipped inside and shut the gate behind him, leaving it unlocked, one less barrier for Thierry if he had to arrive in a hurry or for Alain himself if he had to leave quickly.

"Throw your wand down," a disembodied voice said from the darkness. Alain spun around, seeking the speaker. The voice was velvety soft, with a distinct British accent.

Alain did as the voice directed, dropping his wand and taking a step back. "I'm unarmed now," Alain said. "Step out where I can see you."

Movement in the shadows drew his eye, and he turned to face the vampire. Alain knew that members of the various magical races came in all shapes and sizes, so he had no preconceived notion of what the vampire would look like, or even if he would meet a male or a female, but he hadn't expected the vision before him. Dark hair surrounded a face the color of honey, with dark eyes and hairless skin. The vampire was about Alain's height, and likewise dressed in black. The vampire, however, wore no cloak or coat against the chill air, a stark reminder to Alain of the nature of his counterpart. He knew vampires didn't age physically once they were made, so the creature could have been anywhere from the twenty years he appeared to be to hundreds of years old. He had been captured on the cusp of manhood, old enough to be an adult, yet young enough to appear innocent still. Alain reminded himself that this was a vampire, and that, as such, he hadn't been innocent since he was made.

ARIEL TACHNA is a polyglot linguaphile with a passion for travel, yarn, orchids, and romance. She has explored 45 states and 13 countries. The rich history and culture of France, the flavors and scents of India, and the sunrise over Machu Picchu in particular have left indelible impressions and show up regularly in her writing. Her passion for yarn has resulted in an overflowing stash and more projects than she'll probably finish in a lifetime, but that has yet to stop her from buying more. Her orchid collection has outgrown her office and spilled over into the rest of her house (much to her children's dismay), but that hasn't stopped her from adding to her collection or from resuscitating any unhappy ones she finds.

When she isn't writing, knitting, or poking at her orchids, she spends her time marveling at her two teenagers, who never cease to amaze her with their capacity for love and acceptance and sports—they certainly didn't get that from her!—and their refusal to accept injustice of any kind—she hopes they got that from her.

Visit Ariel:
Website: www.arieltachna.com
Facebook: www.facebook.com/ArielTachna
Email: arieltachna@gmail.com

TALKING
C(IN)DE

ARIEL TACHNA

Some things crumble under pressure. Others are tempered by it instead. For three former soldiers, a tragedy might be the catalyst that binds them together—stronger than ever.

Richard Horn and Timothy Davenport met in the SEALs twenty years ago and have been lovers ever since. Now running their own paramilitary organization, Strike Force Omega, they work in the shadows to protect their country and its people. When Tim falls for Eric Newton, a deadly sniper and strategist on their team, Richard accepts that Tim's heart is big enough for two men. He respects, admires, and even desires Eric enough to accept him into their relationship—and their bed—but he's never been fully a part of what Eric and Tim share.

Then Eric is captured by terrorists and Tim is gravely injured in an op gone wrong, bringing Richard's world crashing down around his ears. Even if he gets his men out alive, Eric must face the aftermath of months of physical and psychological torture—and without Tim to lean on, Eric's PTSD is tearing him apart. Richard has to figure out the third leg of their triangle fast, or Tim won't have a life to come back to.

www.dreamspinnerpress.com

FOR **MORE** OF THE **BEST GAY ROMANCE**

DREAMSPINNER PRESS

dreamspinnerpress.com